Praise for the Novels of Jussi Adler-Olsen

★ ★ ★ ★ ★

The Washington Decree

"Adler-Olsen writes as if he's lived in the United States his entire life, and the novel reads as if it were written recently, not years ago. This thought-provoking and timely political thriller shows the author can craft more than compelling crime scenarios." —Associated Press

"A tantalizing and timely premise makes this political thriller one of those all-too-real scenarios that leave you thinking once you're done. Spicy, smart, and entertaining." —Steve Berry, *New York Times* bestselling author

"Adler-Olsen weaves a thought-provoking dystopia. . . . A hauntingly timely political thriller." —*Booklist*

"Scarily relevant." —*Library Journal*

"Absolutely terrifying." —The Real Book Spy

The Scarred Woman

"Scandinavian crime novels don't get much darker than Jussi Adler-Olsen's Department Q police procedurals." —Marilyn Stasio, *The New York Times Book Review*

"Satisfyingly dark, both in tone and content . . . an undeniable page-turner." —*Publishers Weekly*

The Hanging Girl

"Adler-Olsen wields a one-two punch of psychological suspense, as his trademark parallel plot follows the remorseless killer's manipulations while the humorous, sometimes touching rapport between Mørck and Assad threatens to steal the show. A must for procedural devotees and fans of Scandinavian mysteries." —*Booklist* (starred review)

"Jussi Adler-Olsen is a name to know. . . . In a crowded genre, Adler-Olsen is an outlier." —GQ.com

The Alphabet House

"Adler-Olsen meticulously constructs the Alphabet House . . . and the stomach-turning evils of Nazi culture to create a pitch-perfect thriller atmosphere." —*Booklist*

"This is a suspense/thriller to beat them all. Not only does it offer action, but readers will start waiting for the rabbit to jump out of the hat and change everything." —*Suspense Magazine*

The Marco Effect

"If you like the dark humor, wisecracking, and layered betrayals of Raymond Chandler, then read Adler-Olsen's Department Q series." —*Men's Journal*

"A tense, pleasurable read." —*USA Today*

The Purity of Vengeance

"A sordid tale . . . inspired by actual events during a dark period of Danish history. Ah, but there is more, so much more in this frenzied thriller." —*The New York Times Book Review*

"Adler-Olsen merges story lines . . . with ingenious aplomb, effortlessly mixing hilarities with horrors. . . . This crime fiction tour de force could only have been devised by an author who can even turn stomach flu into a belly laugh." —*Publishers Weekly* (starred review)

A Conspiracy of Faith

"A shattering parable of honest individuals caught up in the corruption of our times." —*Publishers Weekly* (starred review)

"This series has enough twists to captivate contemporary mystery readers and enough substance and background to entertain readers with historical and literary tastes." —*Library Journal* (starred review)

The Absent One

"Adler-Olsen, Denmark's leading crime fiction author, outdoes his outstanding debut, *The Keeper of Lost Causes*, with his second Department Q novel." —*Publishers Weekly* (starred review)

"Adler-Olsen has created a wonderful addition to the detective fiction genre in his sleuth. . . . While the book can be read as a stand-alone novel, readers will be unable to resist seeking out and devouring the first and subsequent series titles." —*Library Journal* (starred review)

The Keeper of Lost Causes

"Comparisons [to Stieg Larsson] are inevitable. . . . Adler-Olsen's prose is superior to Larsson's, his tortures are less discomfiting, and he has a sense of humor." —*Booklist* (starred review)

THE WASHINGTON DECREE

A Novel

★ ★ ★

Jussi Adler-Olsen

Translated by Steve Schein

DUTTON

DUTTON

An imprint of Penguin Random House LLC

penguinrandomhouse.com

Previously published as a Dutton hardcover, 2018
First paperback printing: August 2019

THE LIBRARY OF CONGRESS HAS CATALOGED THE
HARDCOVER EDITION OF THIS BOOK AS FOLLOWS:
Names: Adler-Olsen, Jussi, author. | Schein, Steve, translator.
Title: The Washington decree : a novel / Jussi Adler-Olsen ; translated by Steve Schein.
Other titles: Washington Dekretet. English
Description: New York : Penguin Random House, 2018. | Description based on print version record and CIP data provided by publisher; resource not viewed.
Identifiers: LCCN 2017045636 (print) | LCCN 2017047896 (ebook) | ISBN 9781524742546 (ebook) | ISBN 9781524742522 (hc)
Subjects: LCSH: United States—Politics and government—Fiction. | Political fiction lcgft
Classification: LCC PT8176.1.D54 (ebook) | LCC PT8176.1.D54 W3713 2018 (print) | DDC 839.813/74—dc23
LC record available at https://lccn.loc.gov/2017045636

Printed in the United States of America
10 9 8 7 6 5 4 3 2 1

Dutton trade paperback ISBN: 9781524742539

Set in Apollo MT Std
Designed by Cassandra Garruzzo

Dedicated to Elisabeth and Lennart Sane
for their great contribution and indispensable confidence

The legislative developments in *The Washington Decree* are based on already existing presidential decrees as well as existing federal agencies and institutions whose purpose, among other things, is to assure the implementation of these decrees in critical situations. The list of decrees and institutions can be found at the back of the book.

"All over the world, particularly in the newer nations, young men are coming to power—men who are not bound by the traditions of the past—men who are not blinded by the old fears and hates and rivalries—young men who can cast off the old slogans and delusions and suspicions."

—John F. Kennedy, speech upon being nominated as candidate for president at the Democratic National Convention in Los Angeles, July 15, 1960

"Let work in public administration be a proud and interesting career. And let every man and woman who works in any area of our national government, in any branch, at any level, be able to say with pride and with honor in future years: 'I served the United States government in that hour of our nation's need.'"

—John F. Kennedy, State of the Union speech to Congress, January 29, 1961

FOREWORD

IF THERE'S ONE THING ABOUT WORLD HISTORY THAT IS CERTAIN, IT'S THAT nothing is certain. Nothing is eternal and nothing's imperishable. Today's hero is tomorrow's bad guy; mighty empires come and go. Everything is a series of epochs: the Phoenician Empire, the Roman Empire, the Pharaoh's Egypt, the French Empire, the Ottoman and Byzantine Empires, the Grecian cradle of democracy—all world powers that disappeared.

Sometimes it takes hundreds of years; other times it's from one day to the next.

Who could have imagined that a single shot in Sarajevo would provoke a world war that resulted in millions of deaths? That Adolf Hitler could get away with murdering the entire leadership of his SA Corps in a single night? That a superpower like the Soviet Union and the entire Eastern Bloc could collapse so quickly? Who would have thought that a single event on the eleventh of September 2001 could totally change the world's stability? And who, with knowledge of the Hundred Years' War, the Inquisition, and the Crusades, could have been able to predict that the main cause of war and unrest in the twenty-first century, fed by a widening gap between the world's rich and poor, would once again be religion—Christianity versus Islam—where twelve drawings of the Prophet Muhammad, published in a tiny Western country with five million inhabitants, could unite the entire Muslim world in its rage?

In 1975, Pol Pot's Khmer Rouge emptied all of Cambodia's cities from one week to the next, and an unprecedented reign of terror became reality. Since then, similar radical upheavals have taken place all over the world—in Indonesia, Khomeini's Iran, Milošević and Karadžić's Yugoslavia, Rwanda, and Idi Amin's Uganda. People have been persecuted, deported, and purged; laws and the judicial system have been disregarded. At the same time, so-called civilized states have attempted to guard themselves against such situations with all the means at a democracy's disposal: legislation, legal principle, rules, and regulations.

In Europe—despite the British wish for a Brexit—we seek peace through our cooperation in the European Union, which is why new states, after careful consideration, keep being invited to join. Our politicians say this is the surest way towards stability in our part of the world. The question is whether one forgets that we're creating a superpower in the wake of all these peaceful intentions, a superpower that must eventually challenge other superpowers culturally, economically, and even militarily. It's difficult to see how Russia, China, or a prospective future confederation of Arab or Muslim states would benefit from an expansionist EU policy.

George Washington, the first president of the world's current sole superpower, once stated that one can trust a nation no further than its own interests dictate, and that no responsible statesman would deviate from this rule—that national interests are stronger than ideology. In spite of these words—and in spite of the fact that history shows that long-term stability in the world is an illusion—Washington's successors to the presidency have attempted to assure such stability time and again, and today many oppressed people and nations have the United States to thank for a better life, at least in part. But at the same time, in recent years, the United States has undergone a series of constitutional "adjustments" that the White House itself has called "the biggest restructuring of the federal government since 1947." A restructuring of constitutional mechanisms that, in the wrong hands and under the wrong conditions, could have unpredictable consequences—consequences that could easily result in situations very reminiscent of those that the US military has felt itself obliged to rectify around the world in the past.

With the creation of the Department of Homeland Security (DHS), President George W. Bush saw to it that all security agencies in the United States were brought together and coordinated under one administration. The crucial difference between this setup and similar security systems in Stalin's Soviet Union and Hitler's Third Reich lies in how the DHS is intended to be used in regard to its country's own citizens. Although the department was created in the wake of 9/11 to secure the United States against terrorists from abroad, it can also handily be used to monitor and control its own people.

In *The Washington Decree,* unfortunate circumstances cause the president of the United States to lose his good judgment and, despite his best intentions, unwittingly set a chain of events in motion that rapidly lead to a situation where the DHS, the Federal Emergency Management Agency (FEMA), and the military are vulnerable to misuse, and all constitutional guarantees are revoked.

We've seen this kind of situation arise before, and it will arise again. And it can happen suddenly, before you know it.

—Jussi Adler-Olsen, 2007

THE
WASHINGTON
DECREE

CHAPTER 1

★ ★ ★ ★ ★

EVEN THOUGH SHE WAS STILL ONLY FOURTEEN YEARS OLD, DOGGIE KNEW: JUST as every adventure has a beginning, it also has an ending. In Doggie's case the ending couldn't have been worse.

It all began with Governor Jansen's office sending Virginia's biggest local television station a suggestion for a new quiz show, plus the capital to get it off the ground.

It was to be a geographical quiz where everyone who could correctly name China's most populous city was invited to participate. The TV station went for the idea.

After the initial elimination round, only forty-eight participants were left, and among them—quite sensationally—was a fourteen-year-old girl. The excitement rose for four weeks: Both the sponsor, Leatherman Auto Tires, and Governor Jansen's campaign office wanted to get their money's worth.

The first programs were broadcast in the afternoon, but the show quickly found its way into prime time. A good three-quarters of Virginians followed the event on their TV screens. This was a new viewer record.

Throughout the Commonwealth of Virginia, people bet on the outcome. Each had his or her favorite. But most, by far, backed the girl with the dimples, who was also the youngest contestant: Dorothy Curtis, also known as Doggie.

Three weeks and three episodes later, Virginia's TV audience finally got their three winners—and what winners they were! Governor Jansen beamed like a Hollywood star, the host had his wages doubled, and the newspapers went crazy. With the exception of a blonde with silicone breasts and full hips who lost out in the last round (but instead got her own talk show on which to display her attributes), the winners couldn't have been more popular.

First prize went to Rosalie Lee, a big African American woman from New York who happened to be in Virginia for the first time, visiting her sister Josefine. Rosalie was a showpiece of a woman, with pearly teeth, roaring laughter, and winks to the audience, and few could match her talent of using so much time to answer a question that the audience was about to go crazy.

Only one point behind her came T. Perkins, a pale-faced, practically albino sheriff who came from one of the smallest counties in the northwestern part of the state. A man who, in his youth, had been one of the nation's best dart players. And finally, in an impressive third place came Doggie Curtis, the girl with the dimples. What a triumph! The winners couldn't have been more different, and everyone involved with the show was pleased. How could any part of the population feel overlooked with those three? It simply wasn't possible.

The lucky winners couldn't believe it when they heard their prize being announced live on the show. Along with the graduated cash jackpots came nothing less than a trip to the other side of the world for the three of them.

For Doggie especially, it was all unreal and incredible. They were to travel to China with Governor Bruce Jansen, his staff, and an official Chinese delegation. They'd be entering a closed world, and everything would be paid for.

It sounded like a fairy tale.

Doggie's father was proud about his daughter being so bright, but not about her prize. He was a right-wing Republican and hated Bruce Jansen, who was "old money" and a Democrat besides.

"Jansen? That swine?" he yelled at her. "You don't plan to participate in a PR stunt like that, advancing the ambitions of that fucking untrustworthy Democrat, do you?!" He forbid her going, and Doggie's mother was forced to use all her powers of persuasion to make him change his mind.

As fate would have it, this was the last time Doggie heard them quarrel. Her parents were divorced just five months later, a divorce that descended into a fight over money and custody of their child. Doggie ended up being installed in her mother's house with her mother's maiden name.

In a way her father was right. It *was* all a PR stunt, but so what? Governor Jansen was a clever man. He'd taken three ordinary people and made them everybody's darlings, and via them, invited Virginia's entire population of seven million souls along to a far-off, enigmatic land. It was practically the only thing folks talked and read about. School newspapers, ladies' magazines, and even Doggie's father's boring hotel business newsletter wrote about it. And everyone wanted to talk with Doggie. She'd been approached by twenty-one of Virginia's thirty-four newspapers, either for interviews or to publish the last month's entries in her diary.

It was quite an achievement: Bruce Jansen had embraced the entire population all at once, and vice versa. He may have been calculating, but a swine he was not. He was quite fantastic, actually.

Doggie's heart was pounding as she bid her mother farewell and ascended the portable stairway to the huge airplane, glittering in the sunshine. She'd flown at least twenty times within the States, plus to Mexico and Puerto Rico, but never in a plane that size. It was a little frightening.

When she reached her seat, Sheriff T. Perkins was already in the next seat by the window, looking sleepy and absentmindedly cleaning his fingernails with the point of a gilded dart. Governor Jansen's wife, Caroll Jansen, came over and patted her on the cheek. "You're a clever girl, Doggie," she said. "It was wonderful, you winning third place. Just magnificent. I think we're going to have a fine time together, we two." She nodded graciously to a few of the passengers and sat down a couple of rows forward, between her husband and his indispensable right hand, Thomas Sunderland.

Then Rosalie Lee came blustering down the aisle. She gave everyone a hearty greeting and planted herself next to Doggie, her bulk flowing over onto Doggie's seat. She immediately emptied a giant paper bag of Coca-Cola cans, crackers, chips, and a great variety of candy bars and began offering goodies to all her neighbors. It had been like that in the TV studio, too. No one in Rosalie Lee's company was going to go hungry if she had anything to say about it.

Chewing away on her portable feast, she entertained Doggie with talk of New York, her little apartment in the Bronx, and her three wonderful sons, finishing with peals of laughter as she described how she'd kicked her loser of a husband out of her home, ass first.

Rosalie's unrestrained laughter woke Sheriff T. Perkins up a bit, and he looked around in bewilderment. He was pretty easygoing—slept now and then and didn't say much. He'd clearly been the most knowledgeable of the three quiz winners, but even though Rosalie Lee had sometimes seemed slow-witted, appearances were deceptive. Her brain was capable of changing gears suddenly and leaving everyone in the dust, and that was how she wound up winning the contest.

A couple of hours later, a young man who'd been sleeping since takeoff leaned his head towards the row of prizewinners in front of him. "Wesley Barefoot." He presented himself with luminous teeth. "Well, looks like we're going to be together the next couple of weeks. Maybe you know my mother—she's Governor Jansen's secretary." The three shook their heads politely.

"Congratulations, by the way," he continued. "I watched all the episodes, just like everybody else. You were all brilliant!"

They smiled obligingly—just the cue the man needed to launch into his life story. He was studying law and loved politics and British rock bands. Et cetera, et cetera, et cetera.

Doggie thought he was nice and smelled good.

Bruce Jansen took one female prizewinner under each arm as they walked towards the welcoming deputation of photographers, cameramen, and journalists in Beijing's airport. The weather was cold and gray, and everyone was talking at once. After the obligatory questions from the Chinese press, the governor turned to face the international press that was standing behind a row of blue-clad Chinese soldiers.

Doggie quickly noticed one of the journalists, a very little man with intense, dark eyes and a receding hairline. A man who was obviously receiving more attention than the others and got all his questions answered, one after the other. When the interview was over, the governor and his wife disappeared in a black limousine, along with two Chinese officials. The rest of his staff followed in another official car, and the crowd of journalists began breaking up. Apparently, the diminutive, dark-eyed journalist was the only one who seemed interested in the rest of Jansen's party. He waved to his photographer and made straight for the little group.

"Hey, my name's John Bugatti," he said with a hoarse voice, and cleared his throat. "I work for NBC. I'm supposed to follow along with you and Jansen on the whole tour, so I thought I'd say hello." Close up, Doggie could see he had more freckles than she'd ever seen. An irresistible little guy. She was really enjoying this trip—her father's objections had been completely unfounded.

Doggie Curtis's last day in Beijing began like a fairy tale, just like all the others. As usual, the little group of Americans had begun by eating breakfast in the hotel's dining room, surrounded by smiling waiters. Aside from Rosalie Lee and Caroll Jansen, whose finer motor functions seemed to be on the level of a stranded jellyfish, everyone was eating with chopsticks.

Doggie gazed through the large windows at the city's skyline, with its scalelike tiled roofs on clusters of hutongs. They had wandered through the Summer Palace's enchanting, long corridors, breathed the air at Beihai Lake, and silently contemplated the calm that enveloped the Hall of Prayer for Good Harvests. The days had flown by, and now they were going to take a bus ride to the silk market, followed by a walk along the market's narrow streets to the nearby American consulate. That evening they were going to the circus, and the next day they would begin a trip around the Chinese countryside—Xi'an, the Yellow River, Hangzhou, Shanghai, and back again. It was a question of getting as much out of these remaining days as possible.

The market seemed remarkably quiet. Even the few curious people who were following along after the group were silent. None called out to them; no one was pushy.

"They sure do business in an orderly fashion here," whispered John Bugatti at Doggie's side. "You should see how they assault you in Hong Kong or Taipei. It'll probably be like that here in a couple of years, just wait and see."

She nodded and let her eyes wander over counters overflowing with bolts of material and multicolored silk dresses and scarves. One she saw would look perfect on her mother.

"What do you think that one costs? What's that say?" she asked Bugatti, pointing at a sign written in Chinese.

Suddenly, Caroll Jansen came out of nowhere and put her arm around Doggie's shoulder. "That one would look perfect on you!" She smiled, took out her wallet, gave the seller some money, and chose to ignore the fact that he didn't smile back as he folded up the scarf and handed it over the counter's rough planks.

"Come over here, Doggie!" called out Governor Jansen, who was standing before a large population of small Chinese figurines of an indeterminable material. "Look! This one brings good luck. May I have permission to give you one?"

The shopping took only a few more minutes, and they were on their way towards the consulate, Doggie with a new scarf over her shoulder and a little, hollow Buddha figurine under her arm. She was proud and happy. Governor Jansen had looked her deep in the eyes and assured her that the little icon symbolized an eternal bond of friendship between them. "You just come to me if you ever need help," he said. It was amazing.

She hunched her shoulders and took a deep breath of the sharp morning air. Everything was perfect: her traveling companions, the exotic trees, and all the people going about their business. She smiled at the workers sitting on the edge of the sidewalk with chopsticks and small bowls, eating warm food from the stalls lined up behind them.

Wesley Barefoot was walking in front of her with a smile so broad, she could see it from behind.

He was pointing in all directions with one eye glued to a cheap, newly acquired camera. T. Perkins was walking along beside him, eyes alert, a plastic bag in each hand filled with all kinds of toys for nieces and nephews. At the head of the procession strode Governor Bruce Jansen in the best of moods with his wife under his arm. As they approached the consulate, he waved to one of the officials who was on his way across the street to greet them. Doggie looked up at the building. As she expected, it was smaller than the embassy on Xiushui Bei'jie where they'd eaten a delicious welcoming dinner two days before, but it still made a vivid, pompous impression in the sunshine, with the Stars and Stripes flapping in the breeze and an erect Chinese sentry standing on a low platform before the entry gate.

Doggie glanced over her shoulder, back down the crowded, narrow street of tradesmen and their stalls. There was a world of difference between the Western-style, official opulence of the consulate and the flimsy, thrown-together stalls of the silk market. It revealed a huge gulf in wealth and customs.

A little street seller was casting one of his many colorful dragon kites up into the breeze, and the group paused to watch it wriggle towards the sky.

Then it happened.

Caroll Jansen suddenly screamed and struck out with both arms, her purse clutched in one hand. Doggie whirled around as her cry ended abruptly and she sank to the ground, blood squirting from her neck, while Governor Jansen's advisor, Thomas Sunderland, lunged after the young Chinese attacker. Sheriff T. Perkins flung away his plastic bags, so the sidewalk in front of the consulate came to life with bouncing rubber balls and small, plastic animals of every description, and in one leap he succeeded in cutting off the man's escape route back into the teaming silk market. Doggie would always remember the assailant's bloody knife, still gleaming as he tried to ward off the charging sheriff.

Next she saw Governor Jansen falling to his knees, the figure in his arms already lifeless. Her lips moved silently as people rushed from all directions to help. She saw everything: Rosalie Lee shredding her best blouse into strips to try and stem Caroll Jansen's bleeding, the soldiers racing over to T. Perkins, who, with blood running down his arm, had pinned the kicking, howling killer to the ground. And she saw Wesley Barefoot, standing still as a statue in the middle of everything, his face white as a corpse.

She was also witnessing the moment when Wesley Barefoot became a man. The toothpaste smile would never be the same.

There was a crowd growing and a tumult of cries and confusion as John Bugatti and the governor's advisor, Thomas Sunderland, struggled to carry Caroll Jansen into the consulate building. People were left standing in shock with their heads in their hands, in stark contrast to the quiet whimpering of the captured assassin.

Doggie sank down on the sentries' platform, her back against a pillar bearing a gigantic brass plate identifying the US consulate. And there she remained.

"Come here, my girl!" T. Perkins was calling to Doggie. By now it was ten minutes since the fatal attack. He kneeled down, put his arm around her, and held her close. "Did you see it happen?" he asked.

She nodded.

"I'm afraid she died, Doggie." He kept still a moment as though to see her reaction, but Doggie said nothing. She already knew.

He got her into a large, white room in the consulate where a couple of employees had been assigned to try and help them. The atmosphere was hectic and crackling with tension. Most of the officials were wearing grim expressions as they pecked at their computers or talked on the phone. This was clearly a serious crisis. A great number of authorities in China and the United States had to be contacted and consulted. Secretary of State James Baker's name was mentioned several times.

Outside, one could hear the hurried steps of people running back and forth on the street. The young Chinese attacker was now standing under guard, pressed up against a wall, shaking. His wild eyes suggested he had no idea what was happening.

"I don't think he's normal, Doggie," said Rosalie Lee, who then squeezed her arm.

They watched as men in uniform screamed their rage and contempt in his face. Then a flatbed truck came with more men in uniform, and they tossed him in the back. The young man's eyes were terrified.

"A shot in the back of his head within two days, wanna bet?" grunted one of the consulate employees.

Doggie stood up, trying not to lose sight of the doomed assailant. Nothing was making sense; all she knew was that she wanted to go home. Then she sat down quietly again and stared into space until John Bugatti stuck a cup of steaming tea in her hand.

"It's a terrible thing that's happened, Doggie," he said, attempting a smile. "We're all so sorry you had to witness this, but you mustn't let it shatter your soul, do you hear me?"

She nodded. It was a strange way of putting it, but she understood him.

"It's just by chance you were here, that's all. I can understand if right now you're feeling small and afraid and very, very sad, but it's over now. In a couple of days we'll be home again."

Doggie took a deep breath. "Yes, but we were supposed to go see all kinds of things. . . ." She was just beginning to realize that the great adventure was over. "The mountains and the Ming graves and the terra-cotta soldiers . . . We were supposed to see all that, weren't we?" Now she could feel that pain in her soul.

Bugatti laid his arm on her shoulder. "Listen, Doggie, what happened will bind us all closer together," he said, as Rosalie Lee nodded her agreement. "Because of what we've experienced today, we belong together from now on. All of us: you and me and T. Perkins and Rosalie Lee and Wesley. Do you understand?"

Doggie looked at them. Each was sitting there with his or her own version of confirmation of Bugatti's statement painted on their face. Wesley tried to nod his agreement, but he couldn't. It was like his body was paralyzed.

Bugatti cleared his throat. "I think from now on we'll belong together in a special way, and we'll always be able to seek each other out if we need comforting. Remember that, Doggie. From now on you'll always be able to call me if you need my help. I'm sure the others feel the same way."

Rosalie and T. Perkins both nodded.

Doggie gave them a dejected look. That was just something people said. "How would I ever be able to get hold of you?" she asked. "You're probably always in China or New York or Camp David or somewhere." She shook her head. "You're a famous journalist, and I'm only me! Don't you think I know that?"

Bugatti nodded. Then, with permission, he took the Buddha figurine that Bruce Jansen had given her only a half hour ago and put it in his lap. Again asking permission, he borrowed T's gilded dart and scratched a little paint off the Buddha's parted lips, thus making a small opening into its hollow insides. Then he pulled a notebook out of his breast pocket. "Look, Doggie," he said. "I'm going to give you the phone number of my dear uncle Danny. You can always call Danny, because if there's one person who knows where I am, he's the man." He rolled the slip of paper tightly together and forced it into the figurine's mouth. "There! Now you can always get hold of me if you need me."

At that moment Governor Jansen stepped into the room, closely followed by Thomas Sunderland. Neither of them looked well.

Jansen stood still for a moment, shoulders sagging, with sad, empty eyes staring straight ahead. Next he straightened up in a way that made everyone avert his gaze, and then came the part Doggie would never forget:

"My dear friends," he said. "You did what you could. May God bless you for . . . for . . ." Then no more words would come.

CHAPTER 2

Fall 2008

★ ★ ★ ★ ★

THIS WAS THE THIRD TEAM OF JOURNALISTS DOGGIE HAD LET ONTO THE CAM-
paign bus. By now she knew many of them well, and she tried to
smile, but she was tired and irritable. The first half of their campaign
tour through the United States had been a piece of cake. The Democratic frontrunner in the 2008 presidential election, Senator Bruce
Jansen, and his beautiful wife, Mimi Todd Jansen, had campaigned in
twenty states, conquering one after another. It had been nothing less
than a triumphal procession, and Doggie ought to have been in high
spirits. The problem was that she hadn't caught much sleep the past
forty-eight hours, and her batteries were low.

Cary Simmons, a hard-bitten journalist from *The Washington Post*,
noticed her shaky state immediately and took her aside. "Come on, let
someone else take over, Doggie. Get some sleep, else you'll just begin
snapping at us, and who the hell needs that? Happy birthday, by
the way."

Doggie smiled and nodded. He was right.

She called over one of the latest arrivals on Bruce Jansen's campaign
team, a live wire by the name of Donald Beglaubter, and had him fill in
for her. Then she threw herself down on the bus's back seat. No, it didn't
pay to be snapping at people, but that was the kind of day she'd had.

Early that morning her father had called to congratulate her on her
thirtieth birthday. Thirty! This was the age where one found out
whether one's choices in life had led to dead ends or not. It was the
moment where one had to evaluate whether one was doing the right
thing. She'd discussed this with other women, as though that would
help. Now she was thirty, and half of her girlfriends were already
decorating the bedroom for child number three. She might have felt
better if some of them envied her a little, but they didn't. Why work
so hard when her father was wealthy? Why put off what women were
put on earth to do? She knew what they thought, which is why she
didn't feel like seeing them anymore.

At first her father had been sweet enough, but then came the inevitable needling over the fact that his only child worked for a Democratic presidential candidate. She'd asked him to stop, but that had
made him come down even harder on Jansen and use language that
she hated. So she'd answered him in kind, which only made her angry
with herself, because he loved it when she fought back.

"You think Jansen's an angel?" he'd said with a laugh. "Why do
you defend that bastard, Doggie? Are you trying to get your hooks in
him? Are you trying to oust that dirty communist bitch Mimi Todd?"

At that point she'd flown into a full-blown rage. Then she just sat
there, sneering at him long after she'd hung up on him. Everyone on
the bus had been able to figure out why she was in a lousy mood—
even Thomas Sunderland and Wesley Barefoot up by the driver's seat.
Bud Curtis's political views and temperament were well known and so
were his daughter's.

There were only a couple of people left on Bruce Jansen's staff from
the fateful trip to Beijing sixteen years earlier. They were the ones
who had followed Jansen through the course of his successful career,
first as governor, then as spokesman for a series of key issues in the
House of Representatives, then his period as senator, and now through

one of the most outstanding presidential campaigns the country had ever experienced.

People were crazy about Jansen, which gave the Republican candidate—brother to the departing president—something to think about. Every single opinion poll was condemning the present government's politics to the trash bin of history, and people close to the president said he seemed severely shook up, which was understandable.

Day by day, Jansen's charm offensive gave his Republican opponent's campaign leaders new gray hairs, not to mention his own Democratic rivals. Thanks to Jansen's easily understood, logical arguments, unofficial estimates were already giving the senator 61 percent of the delegates' votes at the coming Democratic Convention. It was looking like a landslide.

Jansen's staff hadn't been sleeping on the job, either. They'd all been working hard for months under Thomas Sunderland, Jansen's hard-nosed campaign manager, and therefore it was understandable that Sunderland's star was rising fastest among the staff workers. Sunderland was lean and unsmiling, a decorated military officer who'd always stood at Bruce Jansen's side—and in his shadow—through thick and thin, and now his reward, in the form of a powerful position in government, was within reach. Different possibilities were being mentioned, particularly White House chief of staff.

Doggie had joined Jansen's team just after receiving her law degree and, after a few months' loyal assistance, was promised an office job in the White House if they won the election. This scenario suited her fine.

Wesley Barefoot had been Jansen's man since the fateful trip to Beijing. Like Doggie, he'd attended Harvard Law School, passing his bar exam four years before she did, and would likely become her boss in the West Wing. He was very bright and an exceptionally adroit communicator—not to mention manipulator. He was popular, and sooner or later a majority of the prettiest and smartest females attending Harvard had surrendered to the combined firepower of his charm, good looks, and gift of verbal persuasion.

He may have had a reputation as a "pussy thief" and Don Juan, but, so far, his obvious assets and conversational talents hadn't brought him as close to Doggie as he would have liked. Of course she wasn't impervious to his charms and enjoyed his company, but there was still a ways to go before he could expect to get her into bed.

When she'd started running into him again at Harvard, she decided that at some point they'd get serious, and that's how she still felt. In the meantime, a pretty girl like her had no problem finding guys to have sex with. She was saving Wesley for later.

She rubbed her eyes and looked at her watch. The twenty minutes she'd been sleeping seemed like days. She looked towards the front of the bus and was pleased to see how well Wesley was handling the journalists' different versions of the same five questions they'd been asking for weeks.

She enjoyed watching him in action, just seeing his lips move.

Yes, he was saying to them, he could confirm that Bruce Jansen was more than satisfied with his opponents' and the incumbent president's falling popularity and that his nomination as Democratic presidential candidate now seemed a sure thing, and that, by the way, he could also confirm that Mimi Todd Jansen was pregnant.

Doggie sat up so abruptly, she almost banged her head on the ceiling of the bus. All the reporters started babbling at once. What was it Wesley had just said? Was Mimi Jansen pregnant?! This was the news flash of the year! One could almost hear all the pens scratching frantically away on notepads. When was the blessed event? Was it 100 percent certain? How long had it been known? What did Senator Jansen have to say about the prospect of becoming a father at the age of fifty-five? Wasn't it a rather frightening proposition? Had the child's sex been determined?

All questions about lobbyism and subsidies for agriculture and why certain states in the Southwest hadn't embraced Jansen's campaign were immediately forgotten. Mimi Todd Jansen was pregnant! This meant that if Jansen won—and this latest news bombshell would doubtlessly increase his chances even more—there would once again be the patter of tiny feet in the White House, for the first time since JFK. The entire assembled news media was enraptured.

John Bugatti pushed his way to the back of the bus with a strange smile spread over his face. Sleepily, Doggie smiled back.

"Doggie, goddammit! Why haven't you told me?"

She shook her head and he understood. This was news to her as well, it really was.

The next day it was on the front page of all the newspapers. *The Washington Post* printed an in-depth analysis of what the big event would mean for the new administration's social and family-related policies, and *USA Today* even printed a manipulated photo of Mimi Jansen with a baby already in her arms. Now everyone was assuming Bruce Jansen would win; his ratings were rising in even the most belligerent states, including the incumbent president's own home state of Texas.

In short, Mimi Todd Jansen's pregnancy was the biggest PR scoop one could ask for, both for Bruce Jansen's campaign and the media. She was the personification of the perfect first lady, and she'd taken Caroll Jansen's place not only with humility, but also with an authority one usually saw only from seasoned politicians.

People could sense something special about Mimi Todd from the moment she and Jansen announced their love for each other publicly. She looked everyone in the eye and gave straight answers to all questions—including those relating to her past as a peace activist during the first Gulf War—and the journalists loved her for it. Mimi Todd was a true American, a pioneer who wasn't afraid of anything. Countless columns were written about her. Thanks to the media, the entire country knew she'd completed her graduate studies in economics at NYU at the top of her class and had wept in public on a visit to a hospice in Salem, Massachusetts. And who didn't remember her spectacular national TV debut where, as the new wife of a very wealthy senator, she'd been asked about her many pronounced social and political views? She'd personally chosen the interview to be held on the front steps of a shelter for the homeless in Anacostia, DC's number one hell on earth, a decision that seemed doomed to failure. Mimi Todd had looked totally out of place in her expensive clothes, and a bunch of young men had lost no time heckling her for trying to capitalize on their poverty. This had upset her, it was clear to see, but instead of calling off or postponing the interview—and in spite of warnings from the camera crews—she'd descended the stairs and mingled with the crowd, talking with them until they'd settled down. Then she'd climbed the steps again and gave a speech about how people should live together and respect one another, and the way she did it was breathtaking. The silence was so complete afterwards that even the journalists were quiet—as the cameras kept rolling. No doubt about it: This was one high-caliber lady.

And now she was pregnant besides. Beautiful, neither too young nor too old, and with nothing about her present or past that might discredit her or her husband.

No wonder the media was going wild.

Doggie's father called the following morning, sorry and embarrassed about their last phone conversation, and willing to do anything to repair their relationship.

Doggie was skeptical as to his true motives. Bruce Jansen had just won overwhelmingly in the Pennsylvania Democratic primaries, and now it was Virginia's turn. This was where Doggie had lived most of her life and also where her father's classy hotel chain had gradually become well established, so it was far from unthinkable that he was cooking something up for the occasion.

Hesitantly she accepted his peace offerings and agreed to meet him at the Splendor Resort and Conference Center, the largest of his establishments on the Virginia coast and the absolute most beautifully renovated hotel in Virginia Beach. They were to meet the following day, which suited Doggie perfectly, since it was her day off and she could stand being spoiled a bit by her daddy. Months of countless nights in random hotels and numerous attempts to sleep on the campaign bus had taken a toll on her. Now it would be radically different: When you were Bud Curtis's daughter, you slept in a five-star hotel in a luxury suite with salmon-colored furniture of Scandinavian design. She could already feel the delicious sensation of being immersed in a nice, steaming bubble bath.

So what if her father had some hidden agenda? He always had one, anyway, and besides, in the end, she *did* love her old man.

He wasn't at the hotel when she arrived. Instead, Toby O'Neill was waiting out in front like some kind of weird watchdog. Doggie had never really been able to understand why her father had this oddball working for him. His behavior was repellent, and his ill-fitting, worn-out, tasteless clothes made him look like a bum, especially in these luxurious surroundings.

He scuttled up the marble stairs with her suitcase and shoved the doorman aside so he could hold the door for her himself—an act more pathetic than touching.

"Nice to have you home again, Miss Curtis," he said.

"Rogers, dammit! My name's been Rogers ever since my parents got divorced. Remember that, Toby!"

"Beg pardon, Miss Rogers. It's nice you're home again."

She noticed how he struggled and sweated, getting her suitcase over to the elevator. He was a simple soul who'd been at the mercy of life's ups and especially its downs—ending as a prisoner of his own short-comings. She shook her head. Yes, it was nice that there were people in the world who looked after people like him; that was one good thing she'd always been able to say about her father. But, his streak of kindness aside, she didn't much appreciate her father's welcoming committee. She'd expected to be greeted by her father himself, or no one.

She turned away from O'Neill to take a look around. A lot had happened since she'd last been there. The lobby had undergone an impressive renovation. Cozy nooks of fine hardwood furniture, marble floors and columns, plenty of brass and flower arrangements, and sub-dued lighting, even in daytime. Discreet signs clearly pointed the way to the conference and meeting rooms, the restaurants, restrooms, and other facilities, as well as the fitness center. There were smiling, smartly uniformed personnel everywhere, ready to serve at a glance.

Pretty amazing, she thought, and she noticed the feeling of pride growing inside her until she spied a twelve-foot-high fiberglass copy of the Statue of Liberty, flanked by a gigantic gilded vase full of severed branches of blooming cherry blossoms, the size of the tree itself. These huge, gaudy ornaments were so out of place that it seemed to be a deliberate sabotaging of the architect's intentions. She shook her head again. How typical of her father. He'd grown up in a puritanical home where the only decoration had been a set of old buffalo horns and a picture of J. Edgar Hoover. He'd been overcompensating ever since.

She read the sign leaning against the vase: PRESIDENT OF THE UNITED STATES OF AMERICA, 2009–2013——MAY THE BEST MAN WIN!

How tasteless could one get?

After a couple of hours' sleep, she stepped onto the balcony and looked out over the Atlantic Ocean before heading back downstairs—fresh, well rested, and in good shape for whatever her father might have in store.

It was easy to tell Bud Curtis was a man who demanded attention, the way he strode towards her across the lobby.

"My lovely young lady," he trumpeted, still ten yards away. He pulled Doggie close, and she let him. She loved these fleeting moments: the security, the warmth, and an authentic sense of love. In spite of everything, he'd always been good at that.

They sat down and talked about the renovation of the hotel, about how beautiful the restaurant looked without the faded lilac carpets, and about how much it all had cost. Her father was clearly proud, and for good reason: fifteen hotels and they all turned a good profit. Now he wanted to expand his chain of Splendor hotels to include the West Coast, he said, and nodded to himself as he thought for a moment. Yes, the investors were going to sit up and take notice.

Here it comes, thought Doggie. So he was looking for investors, was he?

"So that's it!" she said. "Is that what I'm here for?"

Her father ignored the question and nodded greetings to random guests.

His plan was becoming clear to her. "You want to have Bruce Jansen stay here when he kicks off the state primary the day after tomorrow, am I right?"

"No."

"Okay. Then what?"

"Then nothing."

"What?! Come on, say it!"

"I'd like you to help me get him to come to celebrate his election victory in November and stay here. Wouldn't that be great, Doggie?" He tilted his head coyly to the side, but it didn't work on his daughter. Not anymore.

"You're out of your mind!" she gasped. "And why are you talking like he's already won? He has to be nominated at the convention first, doesn't he? And then he has to beat a pretty popular president's little brother, remember? And you—the most far-right, reactionary Republican in the country—how can you suggest something like this? You'd rather break an arm than see Jansen become president, I know you would."

Her father smiled. "Is it possible you haven't noticed that your hero's popularity is spreading across the country like wildfire? Him and his pretty wife and that work of the devil, brewing in her belly? No, my dear," he cooed, "even if he's a Democrat, he's my man from now on!"

She pushed back her chair, about to get up. "Keep your opportunism to yourself, do you mind?"

"Hold on a second, Dorothy, and listen to me."

Here came the hard sell. He was even calling her Dorothy now.

He leaned over the table and took her arm. "Jansen's okay, Doggie. Yes, it's true I don't like his attitude, his politics, his looks, or his sickening method of reasoning, and see nothing but deception in his eyes. I don't believe he's a man you can trust. He's a dormant volcano, but his wife's enchanting and he'll win because of her and because of fantastic campaign workers like you, my girl." He patted her hand. "So he's okay with me. If you say he's your man, then he's my man, too. The hell with all the rest."

This about-face was one for the books. "You must be crazy!" she exclaimed. "Do you really need publicity that bad? You've already piled up more money than you could ever use in a lifetime."

He laughed. "There's also supposed to be something for you and your mother, isn't there?"

"Oh, come on, give me a break. You're cooking up some kind of plan right now, and I don't like it. And you shouldn't get Mom involved in this, either. She'd be angry." She pulled her hand away.

"Take a look. Don't I have a beautiful hotel here?" He flung out his arm and let it pan slowly across the room with its sumptuous crystal candelabras and exclusive clientele. He was still avoiding the issue, and she hated it.

"Right here, in Senator Jansen's own little commonwealth-by-the-sea. Can you think of a better or more relevant place to celebrate the fruition of all your great efforts? I'm simply saying I'm offering Jansen and his staff lodging for a week. Everything free of charge. It's up to him. And the Secret Service, or whoever the hell protects him, can have free rein of the hotel. Can't you see how it would be, Dorothy? The president-elect standing in the lobby on his own home turf, with the Statue of Liberty in the background, speaking to the whole world. What setting could be more fitting?"

"Dad, you're insane." She looked at his funny smile and shook her head, but she couldn't stop herself from smiling back. This was business and politics in a nutshell, and Doggie's father cracked these kinds of nuts with his bare hands.

Then he changed the subject—another of his specialties. "How's your love life, dear? Anything happening?"

She shrugged her shoulders. It was none of his business.

"How's it going with that guy Wesley you always used to talk about? Something going to happen soon with you two?"

This time it was her turn to pat *his* hand. Aside from an over-developed business sense and questionable political views, her old man was okay.

After their dinner together she swam a couple of lengths of the swimming pool and then sat on her balcony to let the breeze dry her hair. The stars were blinking in gentle, pulsing waves, and she'd drifted far away when the telephone rang. She reached for it lazily, sure that it was her father wanting her approval of his proposal. No, thanks, she'd say, no drinks at the bar for her. She'd promised to pass the invitation on to Thomas Sunderland—that should be enough. Right now she just wanted to be left in peace and go to bed.

But, even though it was a voice she knew well, it wasn't her father's. Speak of the devil, it was Wesley Barefoot's, and it definitely wasn't routine procedure for him to contact her outside working hours.

"Hello, Doggie. Am I interrupting something?"

To her irritation, she noticed she was holding her breath.

"Have you checked the poll figures today?" he continued.

That wasn't a very creative way to start the conversation. Of course she'd checked them. "No, I'm not going to Richmond this evening, if that's what you're fishing after," she said. "I'm off work. I need some sleep. It can keep till tomorrow, can't it? For once I'd like to—"

A "whoa, now" cut her off. "I was in St. Luke's Church in Smithfield today," he said. "Isn't that where sweet little Dorothy was baptized?"

She frowned. *Where in the world was he going with this?*

"Pretty impressive, seeing the oldest existing church in the United States. Gothic style, I believe."

She shook her head. "Wesley, you were in St. Luke's because Bruce and Mimi Jansen were married there. I heard they held a special evening mass to make the local TV stations happy, so don't try and tell me you're into Gothic architecture or care about where I was baptized. What do you take me for?"

"But it made me think of you."

"*Okay* . . ." She put emphasis on the second syllable and fastened her eyes on one of the brightest stars. There was the sound of police sirens, growing slowly in the distance. In a weak moment like this, something was romantic about that, too.

"I just wanted to let you know."

"Yes . . . ?" She waited a moment. "And . . . ?"

She didn't succeed in drawing him more out in the open, but it was enough for Doggie. They'd carry on for now, business as usual, working hard for the next half year on the primaries, the nomination, and the national election, and then it would be time to let him get a little more intimate. At least now she knew he was interested.

She slept late the next day, letting the chambermaid knock in vain a couple of times before she was ready to face the world. Although it was a raw, cold day, she was planning to spend the rest of the morning sitting out on her mother's veranda in Chesapeake with her boots up on the railing. She was planning on the two of them wrapping themselves up in old blankets and having a good laugh or two at her father's expense, but Wesley called again before she got out of the hotel. He explained that Bruce Jansen and his entourage would be in Richmond before noon, and Doggie should be ready and waiting when they all met in the governor's office in the state capitol building at one o'clock. Apparently, some kind of threat had been made against Jansen, and Sunderland wanted to gather the troops.

"What kind of threat?" she asked, but that was all Wesley knew. She understood: Jansen and Sunderland had chosen to brief all of them at once.

She packed her little valise and took the service elevator down to the parking basement. She had a nice, old MG with spoke wheels that she'd saved up for out of her modest wages. No way was she having a valet fetch it, fooling with those sensitive manual gears.

When the elevator door rolled open in the parking garage, she found herself standing face-to-face with a grinning Toby O'Neill. He was unshaven and wearing a gray smock, apparently on his way to compress some paper in the wastepaper baling machine. "Well, well, Miss Curtis, on your way again, I see," he muttered.

Doggie was about to give him her correct name again but then just nodded. What was the use?

"On your way back to your big asshole of a boss?" She tried to ignore him and walk past.

"Back to that asshole Jansen and his whore of a wife who are duping the whole country and the whole world, those two cheating assholes."

She stopped. "What was that again, Toby?"

"He's an asshole, and his stinking wife's exactly like all the other whores!"

She felt like slapping him across his grubby face. "Listen here,

Toby O'Neill, you don't use that language with me! Where do you get that filth?"

O'Neill rubbed his chin. It was hard to tell how handicapped his brain actually was. Sometimes he acted normal, sometimes like a six-year-old. He was indefinable and unpredictable. He could shrink into himself one minute and flare up the next.

She regretted her question and continued walking towards her car.

"That big asshole has eyes like a reptile and a gross, forked tongue!" came his voice. "Him, we don't trust in these parts. Nope, we don't trust him or his whore, so now you know. We sure don't."

She turned, walked back towards him, and put her hand on his shoulder. "Who are 'we,' Toby?"

"Not you, that's for sure," he said with a laugh.

"Is it my father who's said these things to you, Toby?"

He smiled for a second, then stiffened. "Your father?" He suddenly looked serious. "Your father doesn't say anything at all about stuff like that. Nope."

She noticed he was looking over her shoulder and turned around. A couple of yards behind them stood her father, studying them with a disturbing expression. What on earth was he doing down here? She looked around. Had he just come in his car? She hadn't heard anything. She turned back to look at Toby again. He looked very frightened.

"You talk too much, Toby," said her father, giving the skinny little man an angry look. "We don't want to hear that kind of talk about Doggie's employer, you got that?"

She drove north on the highway, her head swarming with thoughts, and stepped into the governor's conference room a minute past one.

The entire staff was already seated for the briefing around an enormous oval table in the high-ceilinged room. They looked like they'd already been waiting a long time. She plopped down in a chair next to Wesley.

Sunderland was just entering the room. He nodded briefly to the assembly and sat down.

"At 10:05 A.M. the police gave us a tip about threats having been made against Senator Jansen," he said, and gave everyone in the room a hard look, as though they had something to hide.

Doggie felt the presence of a ghost from the Beijing trip tragedy and looked at Wesley, but apparently he didn't sense it.

"We're still not sure what it's about," Sunderland continued, "so therefore I've been compelled to inform Senator Jansen that security measures have been tightened. It looks like we've entered phase two of the campaign, where we all must behave as though we were representatives of a coming government, which will make us targets for all kinds of deranged people's hatred and wickedness. Naturally, this is regrettable, but that's the way it is."

Sunderland nodded towards the door that one of the governor's office's security guards had just opened, and six severe-looking men in black suits filed in, one after another.

"From now on, Jansen won't be showing himself anywhere in public before the site has been searched and analyzed. But now you have an opportunity to meet our new security people, so let's welcome them!" He clapped a couple of times. "This corps is under the command of special agent Ben Kane, who is presently being introduced to his new employer. From now on, these men will be in charge of Senator Jansen's personal security and will coordinate their work with the Secret Service and its standard security procedure for presidential candidates that begins in July, a hundred and twenty days before election day. As of today you are to do whatever these men tell you, is that understood? Take a good look at these men because they may make a vital difference in all our futures."

Doggie studied them, one by one. It would take a mother to tell them apart. They were all clones of identical height and bulk, with the same dead eyes. She was about to mention this to Wesley, but the door opened again and Jansen came in, accompanied by another man in a black suit—presumably the new security chief, Ben Kane.

"Good afternoon, ladies and gentlemen!" Jansen seemed completely unperturbed by the situation.

"Are we ready to congratulate ourselves, folks? Because I can inform you that we already have an exit poll for Virginia. Do you want to hear it?" There was a loud, positive response. "We're going to take Virginia with almost eighty percent!"

"Yes!" cried Wesley, and they all sprang out of their seats, arms waving in the air. It was early in the day for an exit poll, but . . . 80 percent! That was simply amazing.

A great wave of relief swept over Doggie. Now it looked like they were headed straight for the White House.

Thomas Sunderland raised his hand as the excitement died down. "Just a moment, ladies and gentlemen. This is wonderful—it really is. Let's give our next president and each other a hand." He began clapping and everyone joined in, adding yells of enthusiasm. Then Sunderland raised his hand again. "Yes, now it looks like we're right on course for election day in November, and therefore it's even more important that we finish discussing security. There are bound to be more threatening situations along the way." He turned towards Bruce Jansen. "Excuse me, Senator. I know it's become a tradition to let ourselves be received and applauded under open skies, and I know how much you're looking forward to meeting the press out here on the front lawn of your old domicile, but unfortunately, I must tell you we can't permit it today."

Jansen was undaunted. Smiling, he pounded Sunderland so hard on the back that it disheveled his hair. Doggie noticed how quickly he tried to smooth it down again.

"Everybody should be allowed to see how happy I am today, Thomas. We don't know who made the threat yet, or what kind it was. It's probably a false alarm and I believe we should treat it as such. I think the occasion calls for a big celebration and no one should be allowed to deny us it, should they, people?" He lifted both arms in the air. "Today is *our day*, friends!" he cried.

Most of the assembly stood up and cheered, but this time Doggie and Wesley didn't join them. If Sunderland thought they should be vigilant, then why not do it?

Sunderland straightened up in his chair. "I don't think that's a wise idea. We're winning the election on our strong viewpoints, but strong viewpoints make enemies. This is America, Senator Jansen. Presidents aren't a protected species, and that definitely includes presidential candidates as well. The world's a dangerous place. You should know that better than anyone, Senator."

Doggie saw Jansen's face darken. Allusions to the murder of Jansen's first wife were not welcome. Sunderland knew this, just like everyone else present.

Jansen stood silently by the window for a moment. Then he said, "I'm going down to meet them anyway. I'm going to stand in front of the fountain, dammit. Can't you just see it?"

Sunderland gave him an irritated look. "Not if I have anything to say about it!"

Jansen patted him on the back again. "Thomas, you can't build anything on distrust, can you? We'll take our precautions, okay, and go outside on the lawn, how about that?" Then he abruptly left for the chamber next door where the governor was waiting for him. Everyone looked at Sunderland, who was sitting still with a dark expression that said he was really fed up. "Okay!" he finally barked after a few seconds. He clapped his hands together. "You all know the routine, so let's get going!" Then he pushed back his chair and went over to talk quietly with his dark-clad men.

The room began to empty, but Doggie and Wesley remained seated. There was still at least an hour until they were "on."

Wesley saw her yawn and tilted his head. "Are you sure you got enough sleep?" he asked. She nodded. Was he studying her, wondering whether perhaps her sleep had been disturbed by an unknown rival? *So ask me, then,* she thought. But then Wesley blinked, and her fantasies evaporated. So much for that. Suddenly it was just good old Wesley again, asking how her day off had gone and what she'd had to eat. This was why he was a master at dispensing with journalists' impertinent questions.

He was both ice-cold and nice, attentive, and interesting.

Slowly he softened her up as they began chatting and got her to tell about her early days in Richmond, about the years after her parents' divorce, about her father's peculiar ways, and finally about her father's wish to have Jansen spend election night in November at the

Splendor Hotel in Virginia Beach. Wesley didn't seem particularly surprised to hear it, but he didn't comment, either. Then she told him she
wasn't sure whether she should pass the offer on, and how, for a long
time, she'd been upset by her father's vacillating attitude towards her
working for the senator. Wesley nodded as she spoke, as though it
were impossible to tell him something he didn't already know. It gave
her a strange feeling, one that somehow felt good.

"My father has this handyman at the hotel in Virginia Beach," she
continued. "His name is Toby O'Neill, and I can't stand him. He's obviously not too bright, so I guess you have to forgive him that, but sometimes he's just too much. Today he said some nasty things about Jansen
that made my skin crawl, so I don't think I want to tell Sunderland
about my father's proposal, and I don't think you should, either. Maybe
it's my father who's been slandering Jansen in front of O'Neill, and
maybe it's nothing, but after what we've heard today we know there are
people who hate our candidate like the plague. I know my dad's capable
of a lot. He's good at saying one thing and meaning something else;
otherwise he probably never would have gotten to where he is today."

Suddenly a voice came from behind them. "What was it this O'Neill
said about Jansen, Doggie?" She turned around to face a dead-serious
Sunderland. *How long had* he *been there,* she wondered. "Oh, nothing
in particular," she replied. "The man's an idiot."

Sunderland kept his eyes locked on her.

She sighed. "Okay, he called Mimi Jansen a whore and said that
Jansen was duping everyone. That he was a big asshole with the eyes
of a reptile and a forked tongue."

"I see. And . . . ?"

"He said that folks didn't trust him down here in the South, but it
looks like we proved him wrong today, didn't we?" She put on a big
grin. "Eighty percent! That's a figure that speaks for itself. You almost
feel sorry for his opponents." She laughed, making it sound as real as
she could, and noticed faint smile wrinkles forming around Sunderland's eyes. "Forget that idiot, Mr. Sunderland, he's not worth it."

Sunderland's smile withered as quickly as it had appeared. "Did
you say that your father offered us the Splendor Hotel in Virginia

Beach for our headquarters on election night? That's a quality hotel, isn't it?"

"Yes, it's just gotten its fifth star." Doggie shrugged her shoulders. "It's embarrassing, but my father'll do anything for publicity. I promised him I'd present you with his offer, and now I have. That's the only thing I promised him."

One of the black-suited men approached, catlike and silent. It was Ben Kane, a conspicuously attractive man with glistening black hair, the overall effect marred only by two grotesque, massive gold bracelets that dangled from his wrist. He laid one hand on Sunderland's upper arm and held the other up to his earpiece. Sunderland listened while Kane spoke in his ear, then nodded.

Threats or not, security preparations for the open-air press conference were apparently well under way.

It looked like the folksy Jansen tradition was going to be upheld.

CHAPTER 3

ELECTION DAY CAME, BUT IT DIDN'T COME ALONE.

The snowstorm hit without warning, icing the telephone poles along the county roads so they snapped like matches. A swath of the East Coast from South Carolina to Massachusetts exploded in whiteness, with such extreme low temperatures that the Potomac's current began slowing down as its surface congealed. There hadn't been a November this cold since 1980, and so much snow hadn't been seen since February 2002. People were afraid to leave their homes, threatening the voter turnout. Cars were stuck everywhere, whole neighborhoods were without electricity, and remote polling stations were largely understaffed.

But nothing was going to rob Bruce Jansen of his victory—this much was certain.

John Bugatti and his NBC television crew had arrived the day before at the Splendor Hotel in Virginia Beach, where Jansen's team and a group of dark-clad security people were already checked in, awaiting Jansen's arrival.

It was showtime. Bugatti turned to face the camera on a cue from his assistant. All of America was watching.

He peered into the camera lens, feeling in good form. "All indications point to an historical evening. In spite of a snowstorm of a magnitude that helped topple Jimmy Carter in 1980, nothing can challenge the fact that Senator Bruce Jansen is on his way to the White House. Exit polls point unanimously to Jansen's victory. Jansen does everything with a cool head, humor, and intelligence, and we love him for it. In spite of some fair results and solid support by the people of

Florida during his governorship, it looks like the incumbent president's brother hasn't a chance against the great popularity that Jansen and his beautiful wife have gained throughout the land. Jansen has taken the country by storm, and there's enormous sympathy for this man who lost his first wife so tragically in China some years ago, and who will be the first president in a generation whose White House will once again resound with the patter of tiny feet."

Next to him stood Wesley Barefoot, smiling and impeccably dressed as always, and smelling so damn nice that Bugatti's senses nearly sidetracked him. "Wesley Barefoot, you've followed Bruce Jansen for more than fifteen years, ever since his tragic visit to Beijing. Have you personally seen Jansen as presidential material all this time, and, if so, has this presidential candidate been evolving in the meantime?"

"In Bruce Jansen's case, you're never in doubt about what you're seeing. He was born to be president. I've never met a man who was so committed to the welfare of his country, and I can say without hesitation that he's always been interested in the job. Of course one evolves over the course of time, but, basically, none of all the fuss stirred up by the campaign and the media has changed Bruce Jansen's fundamental attitude towards life or politics. Not in the least!"

"And the murder of his wife in Beijing didn't change him?"

Barefoot was quiet for a moment. Bugatti had warned him that he was going to ask the question. As Bugatti expected, Wesley had his eyes on the floor as he answered. "Caroll Jansen meant everything to him, and one never gets over something like that. It was horrendous, what happened. You were there; you know!" He looked up and Bugatti nodded his agreement.

"But mourning matures the soul," Barefoot continued, "so maybe we have Caroll Jansen's tragic fate to thank for the senator's deep engagement in the battle against injustice, violence, and adversity. Actually, I believe the entire nation was changed by that sad event." He looked steadily into the camera. "But Bruce Jansen is the kind of man who maintains his balance in any situation. He's a symbol of stability and the essence of credibility upon which one can build in the years to come." Barefoot pointed straight at the camera. "Count on it."

Bugatti smiled. The polling places weren't closed yet, and nor, apparently, was Bruce Jansen's handsome chief agitator's mouth. That interview could probably bring home an extra vote or two.

He thanked Barefoot and continued, facing the camera.

"Here on the East Coast, the polling places close in half an hour, and in an hour we can begin speculating about what the future has in store for us the next four years. Right now we have a couple of hours' wait until Bruce Jansen's helicopter is due to land here on the beach by the Splendor Hotel, in spite of the snowstorm and poor visibility." He smiled and pointed towards the entrance of the hotel.

"He won't feel alone, in any case, because we and about two hundred other newspeople are ready to receive him and his beautiful, very pregnant wife. But I have a feeling he'll be ready for us."

Bugatti turned to his next interviewee, a local meteorologist who rapturously reported about practically catastrophic conditions, with two to three feet of snow in many places, icy roads, and several fatal road accidents. Finally, before giving the microphone to his assistant for the next news feature about an abominable sniper in New York City, Bugatti urged everyone who hadn't voted yet to do so, but to be careful outdoors.

Senator Jansen's arrival was not unproblematic. The bad weather had worsened. Now the snow was falling in thick blankets, visibility was close to zero, and Secret Service was worried about sudden gusts of wind that hammered in from the ocean. Meanwhile, the brass band warmed up their instruments with steaming breath, and the torches placed around them burned into the darkness. A few minutes before landing, Bruce Jansen's distorted voice came over the loudspeaker system from the helicopter's radio. "Take it easy, folks!" he said. "We're almost there. Our pilot says he's flown at least a hundred and fifty missions over Da Nang, so this should be no problem."

Bugatti didn't see the helicopter until its propeller swept away the snow on the beach beneath it. A series of floodlights were trained on the blue-and-white machine, giving it a silvery glimmer. It had the makings of a big event. In a few seconds the man who was likely the country's next president would step out and receive this sea of humanity. At least a thousand local inhabitants had braved the weather and were standing in their overcoats, flailing their arms. Something like this had never happened before in these parts.

Bruce Jansen stood in the helicopter's hatchway with both arms in the air. He was the personification of a confident winner, and the people loved it. He practically danced down the little stairway, followed by a smiling Mimi Jansen with flushed cheeks and wearing a large faux fur coat that couldn't conceal her highly advanced condition. She was enchanting.

The reporters shoved their way forward, and Bugatti's cameraman, Marvin Gallegos, was pushed aside two times. They all seemed determined to be the first to catch a comment by Jansen. Bugatti knew all about it.

He gave his camera crew the sign to run around behind the mob and up the stairs into the hotel. The second camera team would have to handle the shots from outdoors. Bugatti knew Jansen wouldn't linger out here in the darkness and cold. Why should he, when the lobby was floodlit like it was noontime? He'd photograph better inside.

The welcoming committee was ready and waiting in the middle of the lounge. Besides the gray-and-black-clad security people, it consisted primarily of the incumbent governor of Virginia, the hotel's owner, Bud Curtis, and behind them a cluster of delegates and their spouses. They all wore large badges bearing Jansen's likeness.

When the prominent guest had made his way into the lobby and brushed the snow out of his hair, he was welcomed by the hotel owner as heartily as if Jansen had been his long-lost brother. Curtis immediately ushered him towards the orchid arrangement and the copper-green Statue of Liberty, before which stood a podium draped with enormous gladioli.

Jansen gave his wife a kiss and his campaign manager, Sunderland, a pat on the back, then jumped onto the podium with the agility of a high school kid. "Ladies and gentlemen!" he cried, and looked out over his audience as though he recognized each of them individually.

"I have just this moment received the first state returns and can say with certainty that my worthy opponent, the governor of Florida, doesn't have a chance of catching up. The fantastic American people have defied the weather gods. The turnout is estimated to be sixty percent in the west and almost the same in the east." He raised his arms heavenward once more, and the crowd roared with enthusiasm. "The people's verdict concerning the country's future is crystal clear. At least sixty-five percent of those who voted have bestowed a sacred responsibility on me and my loyal team. I think it's safe to say . . . *victory is ours!*"

At this point the audience went wild. They threw whatever was at hand into the air and then, as if by magic, a blizzard of confetti descended from the ceiling like a ticker-tape parade on Broadway. Aside from being multicolored, it didn't look much different from the snowstorm outside.

"Sixty-five percent!" Bugatti muttered to himself. Here was a statistic that spoke for itself. This would give the Republican Party and the present government something to think about, by God! It was an unprecedented landslide victory, and he lifted his arms and howled as loud as he could, like everyone else in the room.

Jansen was his man, too.

Senator Bruce Jansen used the next couple of minutes to thank his opponent for a good and fair campaign and spread warm greetings around to his staff. Then he drew his wife up to him on the podium, waved to everybody, thanked God and the American people, said more kind words about his fallen opponent, and grinned for the glowing TV cameras.

Then he made room for his spokesman, Wesley Barefoot, and stepped down into the flock of security people. "Ladies and gentlemen, you've just heard the next president of the United States of America," Wesley proclaimed, and gave a sign to John Bugatti. Now was the time, if he wanted an interview with Jansen. Bugatti, in turn, gave a sign to his cameraman.

"We'll say good-bye to Senator Jansen for the moment," continued Barefoot. "Needless to say, his wife needs some rest, and the remaining election results have yet to come in. But we'll be seeing more of our presidential-couple-to-be later tonight—that's a promise. In the meantime, enjoy these lovely surroundings . . ."—he nodded his thanks to the hotel's owner, Bud Curtis—". . . and eat and drink and dance! The party's just begun!"

Bugatti and Marvin forced their way behind the mass of victory dancers and reached Jansen and his entourage just as Bud Curtis was ushering them through a side door, presumably a shortcut to the pressroom.

Jansen saw Bugatti right away and reached to shake his hand. "Hey, John. Welcome!"

"Congratulations, Mr. President," answered Bugatti. "This is magnificent!"

"You can call me *president* in a couple of months, John. Till then, we have to follow protocol."

Bugatti nodded to Jansen's wife. She looked very tired close up. There was a nurse in uniform at her side, followed by a frigid-looking female doctor whose job it was to accompany Mrs. Jansen to the hospital if she went into labor, or assist the birth if there wasn't time. Beside her walked Thomas Sunderland, who for once allowed himself a lavish smile, and behind them two huge bodyguards, one in gray and one in black, followed by all the VIP guests. Spearheading the prominent group was Bud Curtis in his tuxedo. All the extra security precautions seemed largely unnecessary, since Jansen's personal security team and a couple of Secret Service agents had been booked into the hotel for days and by now must have known every nook and cranny of the enormous building.

"Hey!" whispered a voice behind Bugatti. He turned around and saw Doggie edging her way towards him in her evening dress. She was looking radiant. "Nice evening, don't you think?" She took his arm and squeezed it.

They turned a corner and found themselves standing by a passageway that connected the narrow corridor they'd just left with the next section of the hotel. At least a hundred flags were hanging from the ceiling, and everyone raised their eyes. What an imposing setting for the president-elect. It was like an awe-inspiring archway. Bugatti glanced back at his cameraman and ascertained that the camera's red light was already on. This was a unique scoop, and he could already hear the champagne corks popping in NBC's boardroom.

Curtis brought the group to a halt for a moment. "Ladies and gentlemen! As a small gesture to Bruce Jansen's fantastic campaign and to his beautiful wife, we have arranged a modest unveiling!" Then he nodded to a slouched-over, skinny man in a red jacket who had been waiting with one of the gray-clad Secret Service men in front of a curtain of hanging banners.

Bugatti felt Doggie flinch. She seemed a bit edgy. A pair of well-dressed security men was approaching the little man in the red jacket from different directions. One was short and blond-haired and wearing a gray suit; the other was a husky hunk in a black Armani suit and heavy gold bracelets. The man in gray stepped forward and searched the little man with lightning-quick movements. *If only it were* me *they were frisking like that,* thought Bugatti, forgetting all about Doggie's sudden state of agitation.

When the security agent was finished groping the man, Bud Curtis bid the guests step closer, gave a sign, and the little man pulled a cord so the banners fell away to reveal a painting that measured at least fifteen by fifteen feet. It depicted Senator Jansen and his beautiful wife standing before the White House. A beaming couple in front of a crass backdrop of sunshine, blossoming trees, and flittering birds, like out of a Disney movie. It was the worst "art" of this kind Bugatti had ever seen, outdoing a thousand lousy Norman Rockwell look-alikes.

Still, everyone clapped and crowded closer, so the little man had to retreat to the side and back into the masses to avoid being crushed against the wall. Bugatti followed him with his eyes. He was so distinctly different and seemed out of place in these surroundings.

At that moment Mimi Todd Jansen stepped forward to get a better look at the painting. In spite of her well-trained sense of propriety, it was clear from her expression that she'd seen art that was better. She gave a forced smile and exchanged a few words with Curtis, who nodded and smiled and then immediately worked his way through the crowd, disappearing through a side door. Senator Jansen was leading his pale wife by the arm towards the conference room where the interview was to take place, when a cry was heard.

Bugatti's eyes flew to the spot where it had come from and saw a mixture of hands and bodies, some trying to flee, some trying to get closer. Thomas Sunderland was one of those who Bugatti could see most clearly in the midst of the confusion. He looked horrified, standing stiffly as if someone had hit him, his tie out of place and one of his suit pockets inside out. The biggest of the black-suited security guards shoved past him. Then the little man who'd unveiled the painting took two steps towards Jansen and his wife and there was the unmistakable sound of a gunshot. It was then that Bugatti noticed the revolver in the man's hand. The smell of gunpowder filled the air, and people began screaming and throwing themselves to the floor. More shots were heard, and the assailant's brain matter splattered over the painting. Then Bugatti felt a stabbing pain in his side. The man next to him was clutching his midriff. They'd apparently both been hit by ricocheting bullets. The blinking TV camera lay on the floor next to him where his photographer had dropped it in the midst of the chaos. Bugatti watched fearfully as a bloodstain spread over his shirt below his arm. Doggie had let go of him and was screaming along with the others. Clutching his wound to stop the bleeding, he finally realized what had just happened.

Security had pulled Senator Jansen to the floor, but nothing could conceal his horrified expression. Before him on the carpet lay his wife, gasping for breath with eyes open and wild, as a pool of blood formed around her. Her body was completely still.

Then Bugatti felt the sharp pain again and sank to his knees.

The hotel lobby was totally deserted except for security people, Bugatti, and his dazed cameraman. Bugatti was going on the air for the fourth time since Mimi Todd Jansen had been shot two hours previously. Both she and Senator Jansen had been brought quickly out of the fray, and in the meantime dozens of investigators from the FBI and Richmond's homicide squad had been questioning everyone who'd been present in the corridor at the time of the attack. A specially trained team was thoroughly analyzing the hotel's video surveillance tapes and the tape Bugatti gave them from the NBC transmission truck. At the same time, an army of technicians repeatedly scoured the narrow corridor for clues and photographed the brains on the wall plus every other detail in the festively decorated corridors and rooms.

As it turned out, several people had been wounded by the ricocheting shots fired by security, but luckily, none of them seriously. Bugatti had already received stitches for the flesh wound in his lower back, and they'd given him more painkillers than he cared to think about.

He listened to his producer over his earpiece. Although the voice was calm, the news was serious. For a moment he froze. Then, after several deep breaths, he nodded gravely to his cameraman, and the red light went on.

"A few seconds ago the doctors at CJW Medical Center informed us that Mimi Todd Jansen has passed away." He paused as he tried to look straight into the camera. "A great and prominent person has been robbed of her life in the most outrageous manner, and America is in shock. Two hours have passed since the attack, and at this moment, doctors at CJW Medical Center in Richmond are still fighting hard to save her child's life. Due to the severity of the storm in the Virginia Beach area, the helicopter had to land south of Lanexa, and the rest of the trip was made by car via the I-64 to Chippenham Campus." Now he was looking directly into the TV camera. "Let us hold a minute of silence to honor a great person who we never got the chance to know."

The minute felt like an eternity. People rushing through the lobby stopped when they saw the motionless, silent group around Bugatti.

Finally, Bugatti's producer told him to continue.

He turned towards his monitor. "Is there any update from the hospital on the child's condition, Erica?"

An indistinct picture of his colleague Erica Nelson appeared on the screen. She was standing in front of the hospital, her breath steaming. "No, John, I'm afraid there's no news. We know there's hectic activity here on the third floor just now. The baby was delivered by caesarean in a ground-floor operating room, but I've been told the child's been brought up to the intensive care unit."

"This could mean the baby is alive. Has there been a statement from any of the doctors, Erica?" Now there was a close-up of Erica Nelson. She looked numb with cold, and it was hard to see her face in detail for all the falling snow. Behind her loomed the blurred yet impressive buildings that housed Chippenham Campus, one of the country's best hospitals. "Just a second, John . . ." For a moment she stared vacantly into the camera. "Okay, we've just been told that the chances of the baby surviving are very small. Even though the child wasn't hit in the shooting, Mimi Todd Jansen lost a lot of blood, and it's unfortunately quite probable that the baby won't survive this trauma."

"What were the doctors doing with Mrs. Jansen on the way to Richmond, Erica? I assume they did everything they could."

She nodded. "Yes, John, there's no doubt Mrs. Jansen received the proper emergency treatment. The question is whether the child did, too. We know they gave Mimi Jansen blood transfusions, but I haven't received all the details yet." She tilted her head a bit and adjusted her earpiece. Then she nodded a couple of times as her expression became still graver and, clearly moved, looked into the camera.

"I regret having to say . . ." She stopped a moment to swallow. "I've just been told the child's life couldn't be saved. The delivery went well, but the baby was so weakened that death came after a few minutes."

Bugatti let her pull herself together for a moment. It was all incredibly sad, but it was also hair-raisingly good television.

"I know it's difficult, Erica, but I must ask you, anyway: Do we know the baby's gender?"

"Yes, it was . . . He was a boy. He was . . . He was . . ." She looked down and tried to continue but couldn't.

Over the earpiece, Bugatti's producer told him to take over, but it was very, very hard.

He took a deep breath. "We've just been faced with one of the most tragic incidents in our country's history. At precisely the moment when Bruce Jansen has reached the greatest pinnacle of his career, he loses his wife and unborn child. A man's life comes crashing down from one second to the next. A tragedy of unfathomable dimension has occurred."

The national election prognosis came a half hour later. Senator Jansen was the United States' next president with an overwhelming majority, exactly as expected. This was supposed to be the moment of his life's triumph, but no one knew where he was. Some guessed Chippenham Campus, others, his country home in Onancock. Some even said the White House.

In any case, he was gone.

Thomas Sunderland didn't come on TV until 2:00 A.M., when he reported to the public that their new president was safe and in good health. That he hadn't been hit by the gunman, but he'd hold off on a statement until he'd gotten over the first great shock. Then Sunderland thanked the American people for their support and bowed his head for Mimi Todd Jansen and her dead child.

Despite the late hour, it was the most-watched television program in the country's history. Bugatti was dead on his feet and could have done without making the final, concluding transmission, as his producer ordered him to do. But he gave a friendly nod to the camera lens, as always.

"Our thoughts are with President-Elect Bruce Jansen and Mimi Todd Jansen's family. May God bless them all. The question is, what will happen now? The Constitution demands we have a president, but since there are two months until the swearing-in on January twentieth, a lot can happen in the meantime. Bruce Jansen has a decision to make. Can he take over the presidency under these circumstances, or will he hand over the reins to his vice president and former Democratic opponent, Michael K. Lerner? We know Mr. Lerner as a rather dry but reasonable and honorable lawyer who in many ways stood in the shadow of the party's main candidate, and who the American public has seen as a serious person, if not particularly charismatic. Time will tell. There hasn't been a president who has lived alone in the White House since the divorcé Woodrow Wilson in 1915. If Bruce Jansen accepts his calling, he'll be the fifth widower-president, and the first in one hundred twenty years." Bugatti held his breath a moment before he continued. "Besides these five presidents and Wilson, only the unmarried James Buchanan has lived alone in the White House. Buchanan was met by a land in grave conflict, on the verge of civil war. The inner conflicts Bruce Jansen is being confronted with at the present time must be just as brutal and dreadful to deal with. Therefore we all must send him our best wishes from the bottom of our hearts. May God give him strength!"

He waited until the red light on the TV camera went off. He knew he hadn't rounded off his news spot very well, but his brain could hardly function anymore. He'd been up twenty hours by now. Twenty hectic, insane, and very dark hours that had affected him deeply. He made a sign to the security men that he was ready to take the elevator up to his room, but they shook their heads and asked him to stay put in one of the lobby's easy chairs. Obeying orders, he sat down and absently watched the floor numbers light up on the panel above the elevator.

All the elevators had been standing still on the twelfth floor for at least ten minutes when suddenly and simultaneously several security people tilted their heads and listened intensely to their earpieces. A couple of them checked out the hotel's entrance as if to make sure there was free passage. Then one of the elevators began to descend. First the one, then the others, all on their way down as though in a race.

Bugatti made to stand up but was asked to sit down again. Security was waiting for the first elevator to arrive. Its doors opened and a phalanx of men with intense expressions stepped out with someone tightly wedged between them. Bugatti stood up but couldn't get a glimpse of the man's face as he was rushed towards the entrance and met by more men in dark suits. Outside, floodlights lit up at least a couple of hundred press people and local citizens, all waiting to hear more news.

The next elevator brought Thomas Sunderland and his closest assistants down to the lobby. Then came Wesley Barefoot, Doggie Rogers, and other members of Jansen's staff. Doggie's face was white as chalk, and everyone looked very worried.

With no one to stop him this time, Bugatti rose and joined the others on their way towards the hotel's well-guarded entrance.

"Stay here while we get the arrestee out." The command from the big bodyguard with the golden bracelets rose above the tumult. Other gray-and-black-clad security men opened the front doors and led the apprehended man out to the snowstorm and questions from the flock of reporters.

Bugatti could hear Doggie shouting something through the swell of voices, but he couldn't hear what. Grabbing the arm of a man who had come down on one of the elevators, he yelled, "What's happened?"

"They've caught someone who they think is behind the assassination!" the man yelled back. Bugatti swore. His state of exhaustion had to be put on standby once more. If only this had happened ten minutes earlier, he could have gotten it onto his last nationwide broadcast. He'd be hearing from his boss for this.

By now the first group of security had made it through the flashbulbs and floodlights with their valuable cargo. The hotel doors were closed, and suddenly it was possible to hear oneself think again.

"Do you know who they took into custody?" he asked the man next to him.

"Yeah, it's the hotel owner, Bud Curtis!" The man nodded when he saw Bugatti's expression.

"That's right, Doggie's father."

CHAPTER 4

February 2009

★ ★ ★ ★ ★

WESLEY BAREFOOT CLUTCHED HIS LEATHER BRIEFCASE CLOSE TO HIS BODY AS he passed the FBI building. All in all, he was pretty satisfied with his life. The president had made him his press secretary. One couldn't do much better than that at such a young age.

It was two weeks since Bruce Jansen had taken over the office of president, and Wesley was already used to Washington's bustle and noisy streets. His apartment in Residences on Market Square was pure luxury and only a fifteen-minute stroll from the White House. He had no particular expenses, was one of the most desirable bachelors in town, had a private chauffeur at his bidding, and so far the press adored the White House's new, young spokesman. He loved all of it. He led a truly privileged life—almost the life he'd always dreamed of.

Almost.

Because, if he put his ear to the ground, something didn't sound right. There was a serpent hissing somewhere in paradise. A disquieting atmosphere was spreading, growing day by day from behind closed doors in the White House.

President-Elect Jansen hadn't appeared in public the first weeks after his wife's murder three months previously. Some said he worked day and night; others said he was about to drown in grief. Needless to say, there was enormous speculation about his state of mind, but the vice president–elect, Michael K. Lerner, had calmed people down, even though he wasn't particularly known for having the warmest relationship with Jansen. He reported that the president was fine, all things considered.

Jansen had finally gone on television and explained how he battled every day with his grief and shock but managed to maintain an even keel. He did so with composure but also very sadly, and when he said he intended to be the best president in history, no one doubted that he wasn't only a fantastic person but that his intention would become reality. Here was a real man, worthy of being a leader—exactly as a president ought to be. He was of the kind of stuff reserved for the very few.

Barefoot became all the more devoted to his chief as he watched Jansen dealing with his grief and the enormous burden he'd accepted with the presidency. Wesley would work his ass off for that man and see to it that nothing ever tarnished his reputation. He'd do everything in his power to shield and protect him, as was his duty as press secretary.

Then New Year's Eve came, along with plenty of snow, and Wesley and the rest of the staff-to-be were invited to Jansen's country home in Onancock to give their next four years together a festive send-off.

Many of them were surprised to see the opulent setting that greeted them, Wesley included. While most of them knew that the Jansen clan's nationwide drugstore chain was one of the country's twenty-five biggest businesses in terms of turnover, not many had speculated over how so much wealth actually manifested itself. When the pine grove parted to reveal fifteen gigantic, mahogany-beamed pagodas, Wesley stopped in his tracks. It was a sight that spoke of endless riches, and he thanked his maker for his foresight in having hand-picked serious journalists to attend the evening's event. Was there any point in making folks more envious than necessary? No, the gossip journalists would have to find other juicy stories, and the poor voters who eked out an existence in Maryland or Georgia's "wagon towns" could easily do without seeing this kind of wealth.

Jansen received them with dark circles under his eyes, yet he embraced each one of them and said he hoped it would be a good evening. Wesley surveyed the scene. The setting was both festive and touching. Here they were, those of them who'd stood shoulder to shoulder during the long campaign and who, more than anyone, believed in Jansen's visionary ideas. Here were the local campaign whips, the fund-raisers, lobbyists, and office workers. There was Lance Burton, Thomas Sunderland, and all the others who'd sat on the tour bus through most of 2008, sweating away in the standard belief of campaign workers that, with their help, America could be a better place. They were all there except Doggie. Wesley hadn't seen her since the murder, but people had told him she felt like hell. Donald Beglaubter, who was to be Lance's assistant, had told her there was a job for her at the White House because the president felt he owed her for all her campaign work, but she wasn't going to be invited to the New Year's party. Jansen was a nice guy, but that would be a hug too many for one evening.

Jansen himself spent most of the evening in the corner of a rococo-inspired parlor that had long purple drapes and enough crystal chandeliers to light up Madison Square Garden. There were plenty of women during the course of the evening who would have liked to console him, but there were also those who kept away. There was talk of a kind of "Kennedy curse" that hung over the women Jansen attached himself to, and no one wanted to be the third victim. Not the bright ones, in any case.

In spite of everything, Jansen managed all the intense attention that was directed towards him. Even though Wesley could see he still suffered, a family instinct automatically kicked in, built up over generations of his relatives holding dinner parties for members of America's elite. Shortly after midnight he brought a toast for the New Year and the coming administration, promising the gathering that under his leadership the country was to experience great and radical changes. Wesley noticed how several of Jansen's closest staff raised their eyebrows at the word *radical*, but it didn't bother him. There were influential press people present, so why not give them the impression that

Jansen was fit for fight? No, the word was just fine, no matter how one interpreted it.

After the toast, Jansen encouraged people to enjoy themselves, even though he himself was going to retire for the evening. Most of the guests understood.

Jansen kissed a couple of the women standing nearest and walked past Wesley without seeing him. Close up, there was no doubt. Here was a man who needed to be watched over if he was ever to become his old self again.

They'd been working hard up to the twentieth of January when Jansen was to be sworn in as the United States' forty-fourth president. Many things still had to fall in place, like Cabinet post candidates who had yet to find favor in staff chief Sunderland's impassive eyes. Wesley had heard the two of them arguing many times behind closed doors. Sunderland's face was often completely drained of color when he left these meetings, but he never let a word slip as to what had gone on.

It wasn't until the president's acceptance speech that Wesley began sensing something was wrong. He had written the text, but Jansen wound up improvising, and what he said gave the speech an indefinable sense of foreboding. It made Wesley feel strange, as though he no longer knew where Jansen stood.

He assumed he was the only one who felt like this, since the rest of the world had listened enthusiastically to the new president's speech, and most of the newspapers' front pages had proclaimed their approval of, and respect for, the calmness and composure Jansen exhibited at his inauguration ceremony. And even though he'd aged since the death of his wife and unborn child, Wesley had to admit there was no doubt that the man standing there, taking an oath before God, looked like a man with a firm grip on the situation. This, in spite of the fact that he'd just heard Jansen say words he'd never heard before. Words like *false security, vigilance, rule of law, day of reckoning,* and *uncompromising.* Underneath it all lay an undertone of bitterness and unpredictability that Wesley couldn't define, even after listening to the speech many times. Later it turned out that others *had* noticed— some of the regular White House reporters as well as members of the staff—but it apparently hadn't made them uneasy, so Wesley forced himself to cool down.

It had been only during the past couple of days that most people could finally see it. Bruce Jansen was changing.

Wesley had tried speaking a couple of times with staff chief Sunderland about Jansen's mood changes and his increasing number of savage attacks on the country's federal authorities and legal system, but Sunderland had played it down. What was so strange about it, considering the violent events the president had been through?

So Wesley let it ride. Bud Curtis's trial had just begun, another great source of pressure on the president, as it would have been for anyone so closely involved in a murder case. Jansen had suffered severe wounds to his psyche, Sunderland had said, but time would heal them. What else could Barefoot do but relax and see what happened?

Bud Curtis was to be arraigned in a couple of days, and the president wasn't the only one who was affected by it. Quite understandably, it was a particularly rough time for Doggie Rogers, too. It had been impossible to coax a smile out of her since her first day at the White House. She just sat in her little office, day after day, hurt and silent. And in the course of the trial it could get worse, Wesley reckoned. He'd decided he had better keep an eye on her, the thought of which didn't bother him at all. Besides being a good companion and colleague, Doggie was by far the finest and most interesting female employee in the West Wing, and at one point he'd considered making serious advances. He was thirty-four, and it was getting to be time for a wife and kids. Doggie was the perfect match for any man; she was intelligent, beautiful, and rich as well. But at this point he didn't know. If her father were convicted of incitement to commit murder, Doggie would clearly be too big a liability to his career. Wesley knew Washington: Nothing was sacred. When Bruce Jansen's term was over, Wesley would be replaced, simple as that. But if he did an outstanding job as presidential press secretary, his future would be very, very bright. The offers would roll in, and he could pick and choose. So it was better to wait and see, and in the meantime help Doggie when he could. And even though her hair was like silk and her lips were disturbingly tempting, it should never blind him to the fact that there were other fish in the sea, and Wesley loved fishing.

He passed the busy Willard Hotel on his right and then the White House appeared, as if out of nowhere. He looked at his watch. The morning briefing was in twenty minutes in the Oval Office, and he was late. He nodded to the guards at the entrance, the same two uncouth jerks as the day before, and just managed to read his e-mails and skim the front page of *The Washington Post* with the latest news on the New York sniper, before stepping into the inner sanctum.

Besides Barefoot, there were four men in the Oval Office, as usual, and every morning it struck him how politically correct the little gathering was, ethnically. Communications Chief Lance Burton was compact and black as night. He could trace his roots back to the first slaves who were shipped to America, way back at the beginning of the 1600s. Donald Beglaubter was Polish of Jewish extraction, President Jansen was Scandinavian with a little Irish blood thrown in, and Barefoot himself had an Italian mother and a Scottish father. He had no idea where Sunderland's family was from, but he was surely another ingredient in the great American melting pot.

Chief of Staff Thomas Sunderland and Communications Chief Lance Burton had plopped down, each on his own sofa, while Burton's assistant, Donald Beglaubter, sat down rigidly in a newly upholstered easy chair next to one of the sofas. The president sat at his desk, back to the window, with both elbows planted on his blotting pad as usual, ready to make running notations of their meeting directly on his laptop. Two busy weeks had already gone by without him once calling in his secretary to take notes. This was how Jansen preferred it. These were new times, even in the Oval Office.

Wesley sat down in an easy chair next to Beglaubter and waited. The plan was to discuss a congressional proposal to change the tax laws, plus the coming debate on educational reforms. It wasn't much to get steamed up about, so he stretched and smiled in anticipation of the nice cup of coffee Jansen's secretary would soon be offering them.

President Jansen removed his reading glasses and nodded to all of them. "Good morning, gentlemen! Let me begin by saying some small changes have been made to today's agenda." He gave a brief, strained smile. "As you know, Bud Curtis's trial starts for real in four days, and we have to expect this will put an unusual amount of pressure on all of us. Among other things, the prosecutor has subpoenaed the three of us here who were present when the crime was committed—that is, Wesley, Thomas, and myself. We've been called in to give evidence the first day of the trial, and we can expect the trial to run for several weeks. Apparently, the evidence against Bud Curtis is massive, but you never know in cases like this. The prosecutor promised us a transcript of the indictment this morning, but I don't think it's come yet. Has it, Thomas?"

Sunderland sat up on the sofa and removed some papers from a plastic folder. "Yes, we received this fax half an hour ago. I'm not a lawyer, but as far as I can see, the circumstantial evidence is overwhelming. Everything points to Bud Curtis having manipulated Toby O'Neill into committing the murder, and they've also found evidence of a large money transfer from Curtis to O'Neill." He rummaged through the papers. "Here it is. . . . Only ten days before the assassination, twenty thousand dollars was transferred from an account in Liechtenstein belonging to one of Bud Curtis's companies, to Toby O'Neill's account in the Community Bank on Nevan Road in Virginia Beach." He handed the paper to Jansen. "A transaction like this has never taken place between the two of them before. Toby O'Neill's wages were always paid in cash on payday, just like the rest of the personnel. Besides that, the police technicians have confirmed that the murder weapon was registered in Curtis's name." He ran his hand through his thinning hair. He looked worn-out, as though he'd been working all night. Wesley didn't doubt this could be the case. Few people needed as little sleep as Sunderland, and few people were so unappealing, with or without sleep.

Sunderland found another memorandum he was looking for. "Here it says that a number of witnesses have concurred with the prosecution's claim that on several occasions Bud Curtis had worked up a hatred in Toby O'Neill for the president and his wife."

Donald Beglaubter shook his head. "Something sounds strange here. Why did Curtis transfer money like that? He could easily have done it more discreetly. Why didn't he give him cash? That's what I would have done if I were as loaded as he is."

Communications Chief Burton sent him a stern look and cleared his throat. That meant a question was on its way that nobody could answer. "Do we know if there's a chance Curtis will confess?" Yes, Lance Burton was the guy who always asked the impossible questions, but someone had to do it.

Sunderland laid his papers down. "No, we don't, but why should he? He's been in pretrial detention for two months, he's been denied bail, and he still rejects all charges to anyone who'll listen. He knows the law and his rights, so we've got to expect he's going to proclaim his innocence to the bitter end."

Wesley Barefoot looked at his president. Jansen's expression was calm and attentive, but the old glint in his eye was gone, the fervor extinguished.

"Then we'll let that matter rest a while." Jansen pressed a button to call in his secretary. "As I oriented you on a week ago, for quite some time I've been working on a draft to revise case law in this country, and now it's ready." He nodded towards the door where his secretary had appeared with copies of his draft. "Read this through very carefully, then we'll meet here again in two hours."

They watched as the secretary handed out the material.

"Then we're waiting on school reform and the tax debate?" asked communications assistant Beglaubter as he accepted the few sheets of paper with CONFIDENTIAL stamped diagonally in red across each page.

Bruce Jansen nodded. "Yes, this matter takes precedence."

After reading five minutes of the president's draft, Wesley got up and locked the door to his office. He felt himself permeated by a strange unpleasantness and noticed how his pulse and body temperature were rising. He loosened his collar and took off his jacket. Then he sat down at his desk again.

Before him lay a proposal for implementing a new form of law and order in American society. He'd never seen anything like it. *Was Attorney General Lovell really involved in this?* he wondered. It was very hard to imagine.

He took a couple of deep breaths. When the president had promised "radical changes" in his New Year's toast, Wesley had noticed the reaction these words caused in some of the guests. Now the words seemed like an understatement.

Like everything else from his hand, Jansen's proposal was both direct and well formulated, written in the classic, intelligent Jansen style. The first sentence was devoted to a short, precise description of how American society was degenerating. It highlighted the increasingly violent, anarchistic behavior displayed by criminal gangs and paramilitary organizations. Next he focused on the weapon lobbyists, the courts, and elected politicians. At first glance they appeared to be quite normal, sober observations, but then came the conclusion that filled four of the five pages, and this is where it got scary. Here was a frontal attack on practically the entire Bill of Rights, with suggested changes that were capable of precipitating the downfall of both the president and his entire administration if they ever slipped out to the general public.

This was hair-raising stuff. The proposed doctrine would restrict citizens' freedoms in a way that lawmakers had fought vigorously to avoid for the past couple of centuries. There would be quicker executions of condemned criminals, huge restrictions on the sale of ammunition, and a radical revision of voting laws—just for starters. It was a redistribution of power that strengthened the executive branch so much as to be in direct conflict with the Constitution, so much so that it was bound to cause a massive, angry reaction.

It also contained a step-by-step timetable for implementing the drastic plan, kept just within the bounds of the country's legislative system.

He glanced at his wastebasket. That's where shit like this belonged. The proposal was undemocratic, un-American, and truly harrowing. How the hell could the country's president publicize something like that? Before the murder of his second wife, Jansen had always been an extremely sensitive politician and tactician who almost never surrendered to the temptation of responding impulsively or emotionally to political questions. But his wife's murder had really done a number on the man's head. Did Jansen really believe he could transform the United States so totally, just like that?

Wesley put both hands behind his neck, leaned back in his chair, and thought hard. How should the staff respond? There was no way they could recommend that Jansen present his plan to the attorney general, let alone Congress.

My God, he thought. *If Vice President Lerner has got wind of this, there's already a power struggle in the White House.* No American president could ever get away with this kind of thing—that's what they'd have to tell Jansen—no matter how grieved he was over his loss and no matter how justified many of his worries were.

Then the phone rang and the president's secretary informed him that the meeting had been postponed. Some guy had gone on a rampage at a school just outside DC. Four children had been killed and several wounded, and the president had decided to address the nation in person from the schoolyard. The perpetrator had gotten away without leaving a clue as to his identity.

The president's proposal was turning into reality even as it sat on his desk. Now there'd really be hell to pay.

CHAPTER 5

IT WAS AS WESLEY THOUGHT. THERE *WAS* HELL TO PAY.

One of the children killed in the schoolyard was the son of the House majority whip, Peter Halliwell. Two of the others were from the city's wealthiest families. Even Wesley knew someone who knew someone who knew these kids. Spontaneous processions of mourners appeared around Washington, DC, and the nation's flags were at half-mast. Even New York's "killer on the roof" took a couple of days' break.

It was the number one topic of conversation, a case upon which everyone had an opinion.

For a few weeks after the attack, Jansen's staff didn't discuss the president's law-and-order program. Everyone had plenty to see to, especially in the Oval Office. Not a day went by without the pro- and anti-weapon lobbyists trying to present their case, but discussions with these people were not brought up at the daily morning meetings.

Bud Curtis's trial was progressing without new, gruesome revelations, and Wesley began breathing easier. *Jansen must be having second thoughts, thank God,* he said to himself. *He's chosen to take the legislative path.* This was as it should be.

But Donald Beglaubter's grave expression didn't disappear upon hearing Wesley's thoughts on the matter. "I'm afraid I don't believe it," he said. "Just wait!"

The wait wasn't long. A couple of days after the Curtis trial had been completed in record time and the man had been transferred to the state prison in Waverly, Virginia, President Jansen's secretary asked the staff to meet in the Cabinet Room with their memorandums regarding the law-and-order proposals. It was precisely a month since the subject had last been discussed. *Jesus,* thought Wesley, *have members of the government been oriented without the staff's knowledge?* Were they really supposed to begin implementing Jansen's plan?

This was a frightening thought.

The light beaming through the windows of the Cabinet Room signaled the coming of spring, but the mood was more like that at a funeral. Secretary of Defense Henderson, Attorney General Lovell, and Secretary of the Department of Homeland Security Billy Johnson were sitting at their assigned positions around the long boardroom table, each with a copy of Jansen's program in front of him. None of them looked well.

Wesley nodded to each of them and found his seat by the window, next to Communications Chief Burton and his assistant, Beglaubter. He looked around. The vice president's chair stood empty, of course. This was nothing new, but where were the rest of the Cabinet members, and where was the president? Had he been delayed?

Thomas Sunderland stood up. "Welcome to this informal meeting, gentlemen," he began, nodding at the faces around the table and attempting a smile, his eyes cold as ever. "Now we've all read the president's proposal, and in a moment it will be open for discussion. Since we'll be dealing with extremely sensitive issues, normal etiquette and procedure will be suspended, and you'll be able to speak freely, without fear of the consequences. Having said that, I would naturally like to impress on you that nothing said here—absolutely nothing—is to leave this room." He put up his hand to ward off any reactions. "I would like to begin by adding my own comments to the president's proposal, as he has asked me to do. When I read this paper a couple of weeks ago—and I read it several times—I had the night to think it through before presenting it to the staff. You, on the other hand— honored Cabinet members—have not seen this proposal until now. Therefore I can imagine you'll react pretty much as I did. It is not what one would call easy reading."

At this point Secretary of Defense Wayne Henderson muttered something, but otherwise there was total silence. Attorney General

Lovell especially seemed to have withdrawn completely into himself. Wesley had no trouble understanding why. It had to be a terrible blow—in his capacity as the supreme law officer of the land—to first hear about all this now, and in front of this group of people besides.

"I can tell you are all reacting just as I did," Sunderland continued, "which is what I expected. Therefore I have advised the president that we meet again tomorrow morning so you can have time to consolidate your impressions after this discussion, just as I've had a chance to." He tried in particular to make eye contact with Communications Chief Lance Burton, but the hefty black man refused to oblige. "Naturally, there are many details that need polishing, and of course we must discuss how best to move forward legislatively, but most of all we ought to regard this proposal as highly courageous and brilliantly visionary."

Wesley glanced over at the coffee table. In a minute he'd get up, find the biggest cup he could, and fill it to the brim. Then he'd down the brew in one gulp and fill the cup again. Damn, damn, *damn*! What wouldn't he give to be anywhere else right now?

Sunderland paused again until he caught Wesley's attention. The look he gave Barefoot made his skin crawl. It was the look of a reptile that ate only once a year but never took its eyes off potential prey. No matter how well respected he was or good at his job, Thomas Sunderland made a point of being sure that absolutely *no one* could ever be certain what kind of mood he'd be in or when he'd suddenly lash out.

"The United States of America is a mighty nation, and our laws and Constitution are the best in the world," he proclaimed, "yet this country isn't as healthy a place to live in as we would like. This much, I believe, we all can agree on."

Wesley looked at Lance Burton and Donald Beglaubter. They never commented on anything unless asked, and their present grave expressions told him that doing so now would be a bad idea. He felt his face tightening into a mask.

"I propose that this be the moment when you tell us this is all a joke, Thomas!" It was Attorney General Lovell who finally broke the ice. His facial expression could best be described as that of someone who was getting over the initial shock of having just been kicked in the balls. It was pain personified. At his fifty-fifth birthday party the week before, he'd been cavorting about, frisky as a colt. Now he looked like someone headed for the grave.

"A joke? No, Stephen, I wouldn't say so." Sunderland looked at him. "When our president presents such a controversial plan, I think all of us realize that it emanates from his own personal suffering. But we mustn't forget that this is also a president who won an overwhelming victory by always going straight to the heart of every problem. Let's stop and ask ourselves if anything has been accomplished the last hundred years that has really made our streets safe. We all know the answer: No, there hasn't!"

"Hasn't there, if you look closely?" There was no mistaking the shock and bitterness in Lance Burton's voice. It was as though the communications chief had stopped just short of crying out: "The president has really lost it!"

Sunderland ignored the comment. "Well, who wants to start? How about you, Wesley? You're the youngest one here. You're the one who represents the future as well as the majority of the voters, so the rest of us old warriors ought to hear what you have to say." Once more Sunderland's attempt at a smile came off like a pained grimace.

Wesley clenched his fists in his lap. He'd strayed into a trap: Now he'd have to pay for not having spoken up on the issue during the past four weeks. He had an overwhelming urge to take the papers, crumple them into a ball in front of everyone, throw them on the floor, and stamp on them, then haul ass for good. Better to leave a sinking ship before it was too late. He unclenched his fists and studied the faces around the table. With the exception of Sunderland, they all looked like family men, honorable fellows who had worked hard their whole lives to support the wife and kids. Suddenly their loyalty was being put to the supreme test, and their bright futures hung in the balance. It was now they had to choose: Either agree to initiate a chain of events that would probably end with the impeachment of the president and the firing of his administration, or create a basis for speculation, insecurity, and scandal by resigning. No wonder they all looked depressed.

Finally, Wesley shook his head. "Honestly, when it comes to this proposal, it's impossible for me to imagine seeing things differently tomorrow or ever, for that matter. I've had weeks to think it over, and although I can see the good intentions, I still haven't changed my mind. Even if I liked the plan, too much of it would be impossible to implement. It would be political suicide. There would be too many hopeless battles to fight and unjustifiable standpoints to defend, and too much dirty backroom wheeling and dealing. As the president's press secretary, I would never be able to justify presenting this proposal to the American public."

"Then you probably ought to start looking for another job, Wesley!" snapped Sunderland.

So this is what Sunderland had meant when he said they'd "be able to speak freely, without fear of the consequences."

Sunderland caught his slip of the tongue and immediately began rummaging around in the pile of papers before him. It was a trick he'd learned from Jansen, only Jansen was much better at it. In Sunderland's case, even the slightest smoothing-over caused more suspicion than the Watergate break-in.

"Don't misunderstand me, Wesley," he finally said. "True, it's difficult presenting a manifesto like this, but try and see it as a challenge. What other press secretary in history has had such an important case to present—and present properly, mind you? You tell me that."

Wesley didn't go for the bait. "Goebbels was given the job of making the Germans love Nazism, long for war, and exterminate the Jews. That must have been quite a challenge, too."

Thomas Sunderland shook his head. He was enraged by the comparison, but he didn't show it. "We're not talking about using propaganda. We're not out to make life a living hell for our country's citizens, you know that. Everyone who knows the president knows that. He just wants to do what's best for his nation and his people."

"Just like Goebbels?" This time it was Donald Beglaubter who spoke up, his usual fearless self. "I agree with Wesley. We can't justify this program before Congress or to ourselves. It's undemocratic and impossible to implement from end to end. It would give us so many enemies, we'd always have to be watching our backs. People get killed for stuff liké this, which I suppose the president realizes."

Sunderland was busy with his papers again. If he didn't stop soon, Wesley would have a hard time restraining himself from walking over and flinging them out of the room.

"It's possible," Sunderland finally answered. "It's possible there are security risks involved, but I'm not so sure. What does our attorney general have to say? Stephen?"

Lovell scratched the dark blue stubble that was forming on his chin. It was getting to be time for the second shave of the day. "I must ask whether the vice president has been informed about all this," he stated.

"God help us, no!" This time Sunderland's smile looked almost real. "You know the man, Stephen. He wouldn't be able to keep it to himself for five minutes!"

"Isn't it more likely you haven't told him because he'd be opposed to this garbage?" Lovell patted his pile of paper. "He'd fight it so hard, it would be too big a mouthful for you and the president."

Sunderland's smile was gone again. "That, too, yes. But right now we're talking about what you think, Stephen, not the vice president. You're not prepared to reread the proposal with an open mind, either, are you?"

"Pardon me, but what in the world would make me want to do that?" The attorney general stood up, threw his suit jacket over the head of a bust of George Washington, and leaned over the table. "You listen to me! These are unlawful methods we're talking about here. Strict restrictions for lawfully operated weapon factories, compulsory surrendering of ammunition, compulsory conscription of the work-force, curfew for those not bearing ID, strict censorship of the media, the banning of gun clubs, and the criminalization of militia groups allowed by the Constitution. We're talking about surveillance, encouraging informants, and wiretapping on such a scale as to make the good old Soviet Union look like a kindergarten. We're talking about harder punishment for misdemeanors . . ." He paused and shook his head. "I can just see it: A perfectly normal schoolkid who finds a couple of joints in his big brother's drawer and takes them along to a party would risk having his life completely ruined."

"He'd be ruining his life just by smoking that crap. Don't be so naive, Stephen. You'd do better to notice there's no talk about punishment in the proposal, only criminalization. You'll find many interesting suggestions dealing with criminality that don't have to do with imprisonment." It was impossible to see whether Sunderland's eyes reflected anger as he continued. "Of course both you and Jansen realize all this can't happen at once. The president is quite familiar with the realities of your Justice Department and Congress. We're talking about a goal that can take years to reach. We've only just begun, haven't we? Who knows? Maybe we'll have eight years to implement it, or at least pave the way. Why don't we stick to the text of the document and see which elements we can use here and now, and which ones we can't?"

"What goal? Not mine! I know the president has a heavy burden to deal with. I was present when Mimi was murdered. But this proposition is a mess; it doesn't come anywhere near my own personal goal, as the president would have known if he'd bothered to consult me first!" It sounded like an ultimatum, an ominous one.

"We for sure won't get eight years to carry out this program, no matter what we do," said Wesley. He stood up and stepped over to the mahogany sideboard, under a portrait of John F. Kennedy that Jansen had hung up next to the American flag, and poured himself yet another cup of coffee—the fifth since he'd gotten up that morning. His hands had begun trembling slightly. "Jesus Fucking Christ!" he exploded, regretting the outburst the moment it passed his lips. "Politics is about pursuing your goal with cunning. This proposal is like pulling everyone's pants down in broad daylight. It's shabby and it's devoid of political flair, which doesn't resemble the president as I know him. What the hell has happened? The right wing of our own party will feel they'd been grossly maltreated, not to mention all the Republicans in the Senate and the House who are our real opponents. We won't last a month after publicizing this paper, if you ask me. The Republicans won't believe their luck."

"I couldn't agree more!" Now it was the government's oldest member who spoke up. Secretary of Defense Wayne Henderson frowned. When Henderson said something, one could be sure that millions of Americans thought the same way, and this was priceless knowledge.

"The president has gone way too far. If the government tries to put this plan into practice it'll cost the taxpayers billions of dollars. It'll put the country back thirty years economically," he rumbled. "These are practically dictatorial methods we're talking about that entail spending more money than the country can ever afford. And people will be sore as hell. This is America, not some goddamn oil sheikdom. Whatever is put forth must be approved by Congress, dammit, and ultimately by the American public, too!"

"Thinking about your defense budget now, Wayne?"

"What nonsense! Not at all. I'm thinking about what it will cost in lost earnings for industry and additional expenditure for the correctional system and social services. And I'm thinking about all the lobbies that fight with tooth and nail for more freedoms for the individual and how damn nasty they can get if you rub them the wrong way. But this isn't a case of rubbing, Thomas, it's mauling them to bits and then tossing them on the bonfire, for Christ's sake. I can't go along with it. Shall we take a vote?"

"Okay, Wayne, okay!" Sunderland said it calmly, Wesley had to admit, but his face was white with rage. This wasn't the chief of staff speaking, but the petty bureaucrat lurking in the wings. The one waiting to kiss Jansen's ass every chance he got, so long as it served his own ends. "I think you ought to read the proposal a little more thoroughly until next time, because your assessment of the costs is the exact opposite of mine. As far as putting it to a vote, I think it's more than a bit early for that, but, okay, everyone's free to express an opinion. Just as long as you remember that, regardless of the result, we're meeting again tomorrow and discussing the proposal with the president."

Then Attorney General Lovell broke in. "Why are these propositions being put forth right now? How can it be so important that all our other work must be put aside? Could the Bud Curtis trial have anything to do with it? Could it be the president wants to launch this before Curtis begins his appeal and there's a lot of media focus on him again?"

Sunderland took a deep breath. "Stephen, people will see a connection no matter what. That fucking murderer will be hovering there like a ghost even if we wait three years to present our proposal."

Lovell shook his head. "Of course people will see a connection between the murder trial and Jansen's plan. But maybe the president *thinks* they won't, if he just submits his proposal openly like this. Perhaps he's lost both his sense of occasion and his powers of judgment."

"People will start thinking he's completely lost his mind!" put in Donald Beglaubter.

Wesley would never have been so direct, but that was the deputy communications chief's role. All issues had to be pushed to the limit.

"Like the secretary of defense says, we ought to put this to a vote, whether the president has lost his mind or not," said Lance Burton, and looked around at the others. Everyone except Sunderland nodded his agreement. "Who is against proceeding with the president's proposal?"

Thomas Sunderland was the only one who didn't raise his arm. He turned towards Billy Johnson. "You've got your arm raised, too, Billy, and we still haven't heard what you have to say."

The secretary of the Department of Homeland Security thought for a moment. He was a big and foreboding man who'd seen plenty of unpleasant things in his time, yet he was probably the most sober-minded member of Jansen's Cabinet. Wesley had the greatest respect for him.

Finally he spoke quietly. "I think we have to face the fact that the time will come when we must do something that resembles these proposals. But at the same time, I must say with all my heart that I hope never to have to live in the kind of society the president envisions. My department was created in the wake of 9/11 as a safeguard against totalitarian regimes, and therefore I can't imagine allowing my department to use the same uncompromising methods as our enemies."

"Pardon me for saying it," said Sunderland, "but you yourself have lost close family members as a result of mindless violence. If we'd had these laws, your son might be alive today."

The big man sat for a long time, looking at the floor. "Don't you think I've thought about that, Thomas? Don't you?"

CHAPTER 6

WHEN WESLEY BAREFOOT REACHED HIS OFFICE THE NEXT MORNING, THERE WAS a message on his computer that their meeting would be held in the Cabinet Room again. He glanced through his mail, sorted the day's newspaper clippings, dictated two short press releases to his secretary, and adjusted his tie. Then he forced himself to walk down to the Cabinet Room, ready to resign if it became necessary.

The president rose from his seat and patted him on the shoulder when Wesley came in. Even though Jansen gave him a friendly smile, it was pretty clear he was reading Wesley's thoughts like an open book. Barefoot lowered his eyes.

"It's going to be all right, pal," the president said, and squeezed his arm. Then he went to greet the next arrival in the same fashion.

Five minutes later the men in black closed the door. The only person missing was Attorney General Stephen Lovell. *In a minute we're going to find out he's resigned,* thought Wesley. He probably wouldn't be the only one by the time this meeting was over.

Wesley looked around. Everyone was dead serious but also calm, as though they were privy to a hidden agenda. Could it be a threatened mass resignation? Would they do something like this without having consulted him? Didn't they trust him?

He looked around again. They were being forced to choose between two impossible alternatives. If they voted against the president, they were out of a job, and if they'd changed their minds during the night, they'd have the entire nation against them. Either way, they had reason to fear for their future.

The president stood up and leaned over the enormous conference table. He seemed quite serene, actually looking better than he had in a long time. Like a man who had things under control.

"We've been informed that the attorney general has been delayed," he began. "We don't know why yet, but it was his wife who called in and she seemed very upset, according to my secretary. We expect to hear more a bit later, but in the meantime I think we ought to get started."

He smiled and straightened up. "Well, I can tell you're not your normal selves today. You haven't even partaken of the canteen's bakery delicacies. Look, Danish pastry. What could be better?" He took a bite. "Okay, I guess we better get down to it," he said through the flaky crumbs, and brushed some sugar out of the corner of his mouth.

"It is my deepest conviction that, as guardians of this land, we don't use the funds that are entrusted to us properly. You know the statistics yourselves. Never before have there been so many inmates in our prisons, never have our schools been so run-down, never have we been so overweight or gotten so little exercise. We misuse money and resources, which has a great deal to do with why this country is languishing today. And indirectly, my proposal will put an end to this misuse." He walked around the table, grazing the back of each chair as he went. Wesley could identify his aftershave.

"You are the ones who are going to help me bring this land's true ideals back in focus," he continued. "Before I ask each of you where you stand, I'm going to tell you what I believe these ideals do *not* include." He paused by the fireplace at the end of the table. "You know this, but it must be mentioned anyway: In the United States, the likelihood of a child being murdered on the day it is born is higher than at any other point in the child's life. I'm not talking about abortion or things like what happened to my own unborn son, but about children born to people who ought to love and protect them but who take their life instead. Does this indicate our country has succeeded in teaching these innocent children's mothers and fathers to love life above all else? No, it doesn't." He looked at Billy Johnson, whose dark circles under his eyes told of a sleepless night.

"Billy! Naturally, at the time our communications chief, Lance Burton, recommended you to me as head of Homeland Security, I was informed that you—just as I—have experienced great sorrow, in that your only son was killed on the street in broad daylight. I remember hearing what a heavy cross you and your wife had to bear."

Billy Johnson sent Burton an appreciative glance and nodded silently.

"As I recall, all your son Andrew did was to put on a popular brand-name jacket. He was walking into town, and some young hoodlums killed him because he wouldn't give it to them. He was murdered for a jacket."

Johnson and Jansen made eye contact again while Billy Johnson heaved a sigh that no one could avoid hearing.

"Billy, in spite of the psychological effect of this terrible deed, I had no reservations in entrusting you with one of the most important and difficult jobs in our federal government. After a tragedy of the magnitude you've endured, it's essential to get back on one's feet again if anything is ever going to change. Because I'm convinced that you— like myself—would say your son was the victim of dark developments in this country, and that they must cease." Billy Johnson nodded again. "We're not going to stand by passively and watch material goods become more important than honor or another person's life, are we? In a country where we no longer fear God and look out for our neighbor, but fear our neighbor instead, and have the weapons to kill him? We chose you for this job because we know you have higher ideals than most, and now we have to put these ideals to the test. You must promise me to be loyal to them, and—in spite of your great sorrow—that you are capable of differentiating the past from the present, and of fighting for those who are still alive, like those boys and girls who'd like to go outdoors in their new jackets tomorrow and the day after."

This time it was Johnson and the president who gave each other an intense, portentous look.

"For years now Congress has been demanding stronger and stronger punishment for criminals. And it grants huge sums to the enforcement of this punishment, as you know. You also know that state aid is often granted on the condition that the states enforce federal laws and carry out this heavier punishment. But I ask you: Does this practice actually work?" He shook his head along with most of the others. That's how Jansen was. One not only listened, one participated with every fiber in one's body.

"No, crime and punishment are not entities which are easy to deal with properly. For example, is it wise and proper to incarcerate people for misdemeanors like prostitution, possession of pot, and petty larceny? Ought we chain people up for that? No, I say. No, no, no! Better to remove the chains, the prostitution, the narcotics, and the thievery. Okay, this may be easier said than done and it will take a robust effort to accomplish, but it should be our goal, do you understand?"

Jansen looked around. A few nodded, but most of those present seemed to be studying the beautiful grain in the tabletop. Wesley managed a brief nod.

The president swallowed and took a deep breath. "There are grotesque examples of how law and order are carried out in this land. Like, in some states today you can end up in jail for not having your dog on a leash or for driving without your license. That's sick, I say." He paused and took a drink of water.

Wesley had heard it all before—they all had. But no one said anything.

Bruce Jansen dried his lips. "I can easily mention many crimes that are much worse, that plenty of average citizens commit and go unpunished for every single day. Crimes you'd be beheaded for in Saudi Arabia." He permitted himself a smile, then his expression darkened.

"It costs us fifty-five dollars per day to feed a death-row prisoner, while the chemicals to execute him are a one-time expense of less than a hundred dollars. In the past twenty-five years we've spent almost two billion dollars on sending people to death row and keeping them there for years until maybe they're executed. Our prison population has just passed the three million mark; back in 1970 that figure was a mere two hundred thousand. The United States accounts for five percent of the world's population but has over twenty-five percent of the world's prison population. Makes you stop and think, doesn't it?

"We also know that in California more money is spent on the prison system than on education, so funds are lacking to give children a good start in life—exactly the kind of start that would minimize the risk of them landing in jail! It's gotten to the point where we don't even find it disturbing that children are body-searched on their way into school."

He turned abruptly to Donald Beglaubter, who was busy counting the arms on the chandeliers. "Hello? Donald? Don't worry, you'll have your chance in a minute, but first tell me what Paducah, Kentucky, means to you. Can you do that?"

Beglaubter apparently thought the question was irrelevant. The assistant communications chief's brain was sharp enough; he just didn't enjoy getting personally involved. "What Paducah means to me . . . ?" he echoed. "It's a pretty little town on the Ohio River. I'm not ashamed to say it's the town where I grew up."

The president took over from him. "Yes, Paducah is a beautiful town. A cozy little community where practically everybody knows each other. So therefore I'm sure you know at least one parent of one of the children who was killed a few years ago by their classmate."

Donald Beglaubter nodded. "Yes, I know one."

"And do you know how old the killer was?"

Beglaubter looked straight at the president. "I think he was fourteen, Mr. President, but excuse me for saying that I don't consider this unfortunate incident as being typical. Of course monstrous crimes are committed in a land the size of the United States, but these are only examples. If you ask me, the measures you're proposing are much worse than isolated tragedies like Paducah."

Everyone's attention was trained on Jansen.

"Thank you for being so candid, Donald, but for me the Paducah massacre is not an example—it's a symptom. It's only two weeks ago that Congressman Peter Halliwell had to bury his son. Apparently, he wasn't killed by a fellow student, but there are plenty of cases of kids killing their schoolmates. Fort Gibson, Oklahoma; Littleton, Colorado; Springfield, Oregon; Jonesboro, Arkansas—to name a few. How about Jeff Weise at Red Lake Senior High School up in Minnesota, or Seung-Hui

Cho at Virginia Tech, just two years ago? How many times has it happened? Or things similar? Like the Washington sniper seven or eight years ago, and the one terrorizing New York now. How many victims is he up to, Donald? If anyone here would know, you would."

Jansen looked as Donald Beglaubter held up nine fingers. "Yes," Jansen said. "Nine, that's right. Can we Americans say we feel safe? Do we feel like taking a stroll down 42nd Street or Madison Avenue right now with that monster around? Then why don't we do something about it?! Aren't *we* the ones who can—and must—do something? Who on earth else should it be?"

He looked around at the somber faces, nodding to the Cabinet members, one by one, as they returned his gaze.

"Yes, of course you get my point. Only we who are assembled in this room are able to. We, and no one else."

A few of them sighed profoundly while others kept studying the tabletop. Strangely enough, Thomas Sunderland hadn't spoken up once; he just stared blankly out the window. Apparently, Jansen's tactic was to bombard them with brutal facts and figures until they were softened up.

Then the president's secretary came gliding into the room, placed a message in front of her boss, and glided out again.

Jansen took a long look at the piece of paper.

Wesley was willing to bet it was the attorney general's letter of resignation. He looked at Donald Beglaubter, who was obviously thinking the same thing.

Finally the president put down his reading glasses. "It's a message from the attorney general. He informs the Cabinet that he couldn't be present today but that he gives the proposal his full support."

Good God! Wesley sat up straight in his chair like everyone else. He stole a glance at the paper as though it possessed some supernatural power. He could see the message was considerably longer than what they'd just been told.

Apparently, Secretary of Defense Henderson saw it, too. "Does Stephen give any reason for his absence or for this odd method of expressing his support?" he asked.

"Yes." The president nodded. "Yes, he does—both at once, in a way. He says that last night his poor old mother and sixteen-year-old daughter were attacked in his mother's home. They're both in a hospital in Baltimore, and the secretary is with them."

Thomas Sunderland finally spoke. "Good Lord, is it serious?"

"I don't know how the old dear is doing, but Stephen's daughter is doing all right, under the circumstances."

"'The circumstances'? What circumstances?" It was Sunderland again.

"They were both raped. Several men broke into the house in the middle of the night and after they were done wrecking it, they raped them. Then they set the house on fire before they took off, but the fire was put out in time."

The room fell completely silent. Clearly most of them were struck by the same thought. Wesley caught a look between Donald Beglaubter and his boss, Lance Burton. It was loaded with disbelief. For someone who knew them as well as Wesley, it was clear the two men were on guard.

Communications Chief Burton squinted and looked at the president. "Have the culprits been apprehended?"

"I don't know. It's not mentioned here, but we can find out after the meeting." The president and Burton were old friends—or rather, they'd known each other a long time—but the look they gave each other was anything but friendly. "What's this, Lance?" he continued. "Are you accusing me of something?"

Billy Johnson's labored breathing was the only sound in the room.

"Accusing . . . ?" This made Burton stop and consider his next words. "No, I'm just thinking that if *I* happened to be in the attorney general's place right now, there's no doubt I'd be the world's biggest supporter of the president's plan."

"Listen, Lance." Now Thomas Sunderland was on his feet. "I think that's how we all feel, okay? It's a terrible coincidence. We have to think clearly and objectively. What the attorney general is going through at the moment is his own affair. Each of the rest of us must fulfill our responsibility regarding this discussion."

The communications chief ignored Sunderland and looked straight at his president. "Just one more thing. If I'd been the one calling this meeting, I'd have assembled the entire Cabinet. Why isn't the secretary of the interior here today? If we're to make any progress, at least she and the vice president should be here. They *all* should! It would have been more logical than having me and Donald and Wesley present, doesn't the president agree?"

"The secretary of the interior sanctioned the proposal long ago," the president replied.

"I see . . ." What else could Lance Burton say?

None of them, including Wesley, knew the secretary of the interior very well. Betty Tucker had been on the move the whole time since the new government had come into power. Even though they didn't know much about what she was like as a person, they knew there was no one in the House of Representatives who was as effective a lobbyist as she. Nobody had as many personal friends in both parties, and no one was as young, attractive, and eloquent.

Jansen must have sent her out around the country to prime the local party organizations, unions, and other groups for what was to come. It was so obvious. One had to prepare the soil properly in order to reap a good harvest.

In the course of the day a large-scale manhunt was put in motion in and around Baltimore, but no leads emerged as to who had attacked Attorney General Lovell's mother and daughter. The incident was constantly in the news, and the public was outraged. Raping an eighty-two-year-old woman and her sixteen-year-old granddaughter was going much too far, and there was enormous pressure on the police to solve the case. Almost all precincts in the area were put on overtime, and the slightest clue was analyzed in minute detail, no matter how many man-hours it took.

Later that day the attorney general arrived by helicopter at the White House in a blaze of media floodlights. He was received on the lawn by the president and two bodyguards and led to the Oval Office to talk in private.

After they'd spoken together a few hours, Wesley and the rest of the staff were told to prepare for the next meeting. A few minutes later the vice president and the remaining Cabinet members arrived while Wesley stood outside the Roosevelt Room, receiving directives from Chief of Staff Sunderland. Most of the Cabinet seemed to be in a good mood, completely unaware of what awaited them.

Sunderland asked the vice president to come with him into his office while the others went into the Oval Office. That was worrying in itself.

Wesley tried to make himself picture his bed at home with the remote control lying ready on the nightstand. Sometimes this consoled him in stressful situations, but not now.

It seemed like the seventh of March had already been endless, yet it had only begun. It was going to be a long, long night.

CHAPTER 7

DOGGIE HAD BEEN KEEPING TO HERSELF THE PAST FEW WEEKS, AS SHE'D DONE pretty much since her first day at the White House. She went to work, did her job to everyone's apparent satisfaction, and twelve hours later left the office, took the metro from Metro Center to Dupont Circle station, and walked the few yards to her apartment. She went shopping once a week, stuffing a taxi with necessities, and that was about it.

Her apartment clearly reflected the extent of her despair; everything stood exactly as it had been left by the movers. Her bedclothes were bunched up in a pile on the futon in the middle of the room, and the moving boxes were stacked on top of one another, half-open. The only signs of life came from the traffic noise outside on Connecticut Avenue and the coffee maker that snuffled all night long on the kitchen counter. She couldn't even be bothered to have the TV running in the background. Three weeks had passed in this fashion, and even though her father's trial was finally about to begin, her state of gloom, disappointment, and burning animosity remained unchanged.

She was powerless to break out of this troubled mood.

Only days after the murder, Doggie's father's lawyers had filed a request as to where the trial would be held. Naturally, they wanted to have something to say about which court would handle the case, and they informed the prosecution that, due to the nature of the case and the celebrity witnesses that would be called to testify, they were asking that the trial be held in Washington, DC, rather than Richmond or Norfolk, which would have been the natural choices.

Then all hell broke loose. Of course Bud Curtis's lawyers could not care less how much time it took the president to get to and from the courthouse; what was important was escaping Virginia's all-too-well-known and very consistent method of dealing with murder cases. In other words, they wanted to make sure Curtis wasn't automatically going to end his days with a syringe in his arm in Sussex or Greensville State Prison's execution chamber.

Needless to say, the hard-boiled chief prosecutor wanted the opposite. With more than seventy murder trials under his belt, Mortimer Deloitte was looking for a death sentence. Time after time he'd claimed that "no punishment could be too severe for a traitor and conspiracy mastermind like Curtis." The problem for Deloitte was that he would never get his death sentence if the trial were held as a civil case in the District of Columbia. No one had been executed there since a certain Robert E. Carter, in April of 1957. So, if the trial had to be held in DC, he demanded that it be conducted as a federal case, and then if Curtis lost, there was little doubt he'd end up being executed at the federal prison in Indiana.

As Deloitte said: What was good enough for Timothy McVeigh, the Oklahoma City bomber, was good enough for Bud Curtis.

And the defense was back where it started.

Curtis took this unpromising news relatively well when they visited him in his eight-by-ten-foot pretrial detention cell in the Richmond jail. He weighed the situation and considered what should be done next, then asked his defense lawyers to tell the prosecution that he still wished to be tried in Richmond. Better here, he said, where all his friends and relatives lived, than in Washington, the headquarters of everything he despised.

Then two of Curtis's lawyers began listing the judges who might preside over the trial in Virginia. None of them sounded very encouraging, so they picked out the judge who looked most likely to get the case if it were tried in Washington. It was a certain Marsha W. Tanner, who had shown astuteness in complicated federal cases built solely on circumstantial evidence. She was known for being stringent and merciless but fair—someone who didn't allow bullshit in her courtroom. It wasn't a hard choice if one cherished one's life.

Afterwards, Bud Curtis asked for an hour to formulate a statement. In it he still proclaimed his innocence, but for a number of reasons he no longer opposed being tried in federal court in Washington. He stated that, in the impossible, unjust, and unreasonable event of his being sentenced to death, he would demand being imprisoned and executed in Virginia. This was the deal his lawyers had to promise to make with the prosecution.

As he put it, there was no way in hell he was going to die in Indiana.

Curtis's lawyers counseled him strongly against this kind of trade-off, but he was adamant. If there was to be a miscarriage of justice, it was damn well going to have to happen on his home turf. The lawyers' continued attempts at dissuasion resulted in Curtis yelling to the guards to be taken back to his cell.

This was the chain of events that Bud Curtis's lawyers conveyed to Doggie. It was the first time she was directly confronted with her father's case.

Since her father's arrest, Doggie had had neither the desire nor the energy to initiate any form of contact with him, and now his lawyers were calling with information she had no wish to know about. They also told her that dispensation had been granted for her to visit her father any day she wanted. This was so that her job wouldn't stand in the way of her seeing him and trying to persuade him to consider what they were saying. That is, to impress upon him the importance of having the case tried in federal court in one of the many states that didn't allow capital punishment, even though a brawl with the prosecution was unavoidable.

This countermove would draw out the case—that was the point. They said that, as the burden of proof stood at the moment, the greater the time interval since the crime was committed, the better. They could always settle for Washington, DC, if they had to.

No one asked her how all this made her feel, and even if someone had, she wouldn't know what to say. There was much too much at stake, and she felt taken advantage of. One moment she was cursing her father straight to the hottest regions of hell, and the next moment she was sitting impotently, staring into space. At times like these, she wasn't on her father's side. The evidence against him was strong, and he'd always been capable of doing what was necessary to achieve his goals, so why not this time, too?

Only at night—when sleep was finally overpowering her and she'd wrapped her blanket tight around her to protect herself from the world—could she see things differently. It was that murky moment where reason surrendered to feelings, where she realized that this person was her father, in spite of everything. Suddenly nothing was proven, nothing was predetermined, and her anger towards him vanished. But it only lasted a second.

Finally, on an ice-cold Friday afternoon a few days before her job in the White House was to begin, and after much soul-searching, Doggie arranged a visit to her father. She would tell him what the lawyers had asked her to, and the rest was up to him. That was all anyone could demand of her.

Her father had lost some weight and was very pale and quiet, but he was smiling, well-groomed, his orange prison uniform was freshly ironed, and he had the old devil-may-care glint in his eye. He actually looked better than he had in years, but she was still about to break down at the mere sight of him in the freezing, neon-lit visitation room. No matter how much anger she had inside, she still hated seeing her father like this: helpless and godforsaken, with chains on his legs and his arms handcuffed behind his back. No normal human being would enjoy seeing her father like this, she told herself.

The guards asked her to sit down at the table across from him, then retreated a few steps. They pretended to be unconcerned, but aside from the horrible sniper killings in New York, Curtis's case was the talk of the town. How could the guards ignore their conversation? Of course that was precisely why her father was sitting in this room and not in one of the glass stalls twenty yards away. Here nothing went unnoticed.

She nodded to her father and tried to reciprocate his smile.

After a moment's silence she explained the purpose of her visit, and he replied that the purpose didn't matter, after which he gave her such a gentle look that it felt like an accusation.

She shook her head. No, her father had lured her into suggesting to Bruce Jansen that he use her father's Splendor Hotel on election night, and then his fucking handyman had repaid her by murdering Jansen's wife. She hated her father for having used her, whether he was guilty or not, so he could quit eyeing her like that, as though she were a little girl.

She swallowed a lump in her throat and looked at her watch. They'd have to get going if they were to deal with the issues she'd come to discuss. She presented the defense attorneys' conclusion that it would be best to hold the trial in West Virginia, where capital punishment wasn't practiced. This would delay the trial, giving them time to fight the prosecution's demand of the death sentence. There were many angles from which one could approach the situation, they'd told her.

Her heart was beating hard as she finally prepared to say what, for her, was the most important thing of all:

"If you're guilty, now's the time to say it," she whispered. "Do you hear me? Then your attorneys will be able to negotiate a life sentence, just like what happened with the guy who assassinated Robert Kennedy, Sirhan Sirhan. Wouldn't that be better, in spite of everything?"

"I am innocent and I intend to prove it, so why should I plea-bargain? I'm paying lawyers a fortune to be exonerated, not to be locked up for life for a crime I haven't committed."

"And what if you're found guilty? Are you certain you have such a strong case? 'Cause I'm not."

Bud Curtis studied his daughter for a moment before replying. "Dorothy, you're my angel. I'm prepared to take things as they come, just as long as you're with me."

Doggie's temples began to throb. She didn't believe him; he never took things as they came. He was either lying or hopelessly naive, and she didn't believe the latter. And then he'd asked her to be with him. What the hell could ever make him ask such a thing?

"Dad, listen to me, and listen well," she said, ignoring how he was looking at her. "You say you're not guilty, but if you are, I want you to say it! I won't promise to visit you that often, but if you say you're innocent now and it turns out that you're proven guilty, don't expect to ever see me again. I mean it: never, ever! So I'm asking you again: Are you guilty in the murder of Mimi Todd Jansen?"

She closed her eyes, then raised her hand. "No, wait, I want to re-phrase that: Are you guilty of having prompted Toby O'Neill to commit murder? Did you pay him or in some other way lure him into doing it? Now's the time to say it, dammit!"

She finally looked straight at him.

Her father's eyes didn't waver in the least. He looked straight back and once again declared his innocence, adding that he had never agreed to move the trial to West Virginia.

But she wasn't fooled. It was obvious he was suppressing his feelings. There was despair hidden behind his calm expression—she just wasn't supposed to see it. He didn't want her getting involved too deeply. He was trying to spare her, and this hit her hard. There was always this air of doubt: She thought he was guilty, but she couldn't be certain—not the way he was making her feel now. That was the trouble.

She left the jailhouse, her eyes red and with an awful lump in her throat. She hadn't walked far before she bumped shoulders with an old schoolmate coming towards her the other way, someone whom she'd helped to graduate with top grades and now was a lawyer in town. He stopped in his tracks and quickly looked down before she caught his eye, then he began rummaging around in his briefcase. He only looked up again when she was half a block down the street.

That hurt, too.

Anyway, this was what she'd report to the defense lawyers: No, her father was not interested in changing his wishes as to where the trial should be held, and no, he couldn't plead guilty because he'd had nothing to do with the murder.

When the prosecution lawyers received a copy of Curtis's state-ment, they were said to have had a hard time concealing their glee. Of course there were juridical matters yet to deal with—plenty of them—but the demands Bud Curtis's lawyers presented looked like they could be worked out.

This meant the case would be tried in DC as a federal case, and if Curtis eventually received the death sentence, he would be executed in Virginia.

BUD CURTIS WANTS DEATH PENALTY CARRIED OUT IN WAVERLY, VIRGINIA was the front-page headline in *USA Today*. The New York sniper became second-page news.

This was far better than a Hollywood movie. The accused had demanded the right to choose where he'd be executed, and damned if they hadn't let him. There was a sharp rise in letters to the editor, and while the majority of people were offended by the mere notion that an accomplice in a crime of such a dastardly nature should have the right to say anything at all, a fair number praised Bud Curtis for his determination and courage, even calling him "the Real McCoy" or saying he was "taking it like a man." At the same time the usual zealous opponents of capital punishment demonstrated outside various state courthouses, and even more were picketing the 1,100 Jansen's drugstores across the country. Everyone had an opinion on this case.

Doggie followed developments with apprehension, telling no one she'd spoken with her father. She concentrated on preparing for her new job and avoided burdening anyone with her company.

The trying of case number 1:2008, cr.1312—*the United States of America vs. Bud Curtis*—was given February 9, 2009, as a starting date. As expected, the presiding judge would be Marsha W. Tanner.

Judge Marsha W. Tanner was an attractive white woman in her early fifties. She began by lecturing both sets of attorneys as to the difficult nature of the case, stressing that, since the prosecution's charges were built entirely on circumstantial evidence, its burden of proof must be incontestable and unequivocal.

After that, it took three days to pick a jury. Twelve citizens had to be found who, among other things, had neither a strange attitude towards shopping in a Jansen's Drugstore nor had spent the night in a Splendor Hotel. In the end, four black and eight white jurors were chosen—half men and half women— and the trial was under way.

Both sides' procedure regarding the prosecution's charges was brief.

The prosecution presented transcriptions of e-mails—sent from a number of Bud Curtis's confiscated computers to Doggie during the election campaign—where he lambasted Senator Jansen in no uncertain terms. For Doggie it was extremely unpleasant having these old private quarrels with her father spotlighted in this manner. On top of these were numerous other e-mails, even more vicious, that had been sent to a wide range of people.

Next the prosecution gave an account of Bud Curtis's past connections with the Republican Party's right wing, including his great engagement in lobbying for the rights of gun owners and working for Barry Goldwater's presidential campaign in the midsixties.

From her seat in the sixth row Doggie had a hard time recognizing the one-sided picture the prosecution was presenting of her father as an aggressive right-wing extremist.

Then the prosecution announced its ability to bring forth witnesses who would swear that Bud Curtis had goaded the simpleminded Toby O'Neill into loathing Jansen and his wife, and that there was evidence of a money transfer from one of Curtis's many bank accounts to O'Neill just before the killing. They could also produce the murder weapon in whose chamber all remaining cartridge casings bore the defendant's fingerprints. Next, the court was provided with tape recordings the Secret Service had made during a meeting just before election day between Bud Curtis and both the Secret Service and Jansen's bodyguards, where Curtis gave precise instructions as to which of them was to accompany Jansen's entourage into the hotel corridor and be present during the unveiling of the painting. The recordings also contained Curtis's specific request that Toby O'Neill perform the actual unveiling.

All this and much more indicated that Curtis was behind the

assassination, Mortimer Deloitte concluded, and for this the prosecution was asking that he receive the law's severest punishment.

Naturally, the defense lawyers had countermoves for—and ways of explaining away—each of the damning charges. An angry Bud Curtis denied emphatically ever having requested the Secret Service allow Toby O'Neill to unveil the picture. On the contrary: *They* were the ones who'd suggested it, he said, and demanded the tape be analyzed by impartial experts. Furthermore, anyone could have gotten hold of Curtis's gun, which always lay in his desk drawer, and any half-intelligent person could figure out how to phone-transfer money to O'Neill's bank account. But, he wondered out loud, if it *had* been him, why the hell would he do it in such a damn-fool, clumsy fashion? Besides, he didn't believe the bank account number from which the money was transferred was one of his. Next, the defense lawyers claimed that the proven fact—that as a very young man Curtis had played a completely unimportant, passive role in certain election campaigns—couldn't be held against him now, adding that Chief Prosecutor Deloitte had similar skeletons in the closet. Had he not once supported a certain Sheriff Brown's election campaign in his hometown, even though said Brown went to prison shortly afterwards when several cases of brutal torturing of prisoners surfaced that had taken place during his previous term in office? Could one at all be made responsible for the dirty deeds of others?

After the defense mentioned Deloitte's past political tastes and questioned the relevance of ancient political affiliations, Judge Tanner had to bang her gavel on the desktop to restore order in the court.

In the opening round of witnesses, each was questioned about the killing itself: Who happened to be where, and who witnessed what?

First questioned were all those who had been present during the murder of Mimi Todd Jansen in the passageway at the Splendor Hotel in Virginia Beach—twenty-five witnesses in all. This included security people, delegates and their spouses, the governor of Virginia, Attorney General Lovell, presidential staff members Thomas Sunderland

and Wesley Barefoot, John Bugatti and his cameraman, and—after the doors were closed to the public—the president himself.

None of them could shed any new light on the murder. They only described where they'd been standing and what they'd seen during the time the painting was being unveiled and the moments after, and how the killer struck. Each one said that, just before she was shot, Mimi Jansen had whispered something to Bud Curtis and that he'd then left the room. In other words, he wasn't in the room when the shot was fired.

Then it was Doggie's turn. Her story coincided with all the others, only for her the witness stand felt like the gallows. It was as if everybody was looking at her as the woman who was pulling the strings behind those who were pulling the strings. A heavy sense of guilt was pressing her down into her seat. Every word from both the prosecutor and the defense attorney felt like little stabs.

At no point during the questioning was she able to look at her father. It was only after she'd sat down again behind the prosecution bench that she dared steal a glance at his slumped figure. He'd lost even more weight since she'd seen him last; his favorite Armani suit looked three sizes too large.

A really depressing sight.

It was packed with journalists, photographers, and TV cameramen outside the courthouse. The scene was grotesque, and everyone was screaming at Doggie. Was it she who'd had the idea of holding election night at her father's hotel? Would she still have her job in the White House if her father were found guilty? What had the president said to her when his unborn child died? Et cetera, et cetera.

They pushed and shoved her savagely, and no courthouse guards came to her aid. She reached the base of the courthouse stairs only to be assaulted by a new wave of the merciless media. Someone grabbed her arm, and she turned angrily to fight the assailant off.

"Let go of me, I'll hit you!" she yelled, and looked directly into the sleepy brown eyes of her fellow quiz show contest winner, Sheriff T.

Perkins. She stopped struggling and relaxed. Suddenly his grip was like a mother's protective embrace. Now she felt safe.

In no time he spirited her past the notepads, flashbulbs, and floodlights and into his battered Chrysler. T. Perkins had had plenty of experience with situations like this.

"I had a feeling it would be good to wait for you here, Doggie," he said as they took off. He didn't slow down until they reached Scott Circle. "I'm staying at a hotel up behind the zoo," he told her. "I've taken a couple of days off, and if you want me to be around until you're finished on the witness stand, I'll be glad to."

It was a fact that Doggie's evenings at home would have been unbearable had it not been for Sheriff Perkins's solicitude. He sat across from her, calming her down with his soothing voice, allowing her to manifest her feelings. He put his arm around her shoulders as he spoke to her about normal, everyday things and occasionally flung his everpresent favorite dart into a well-punctured black spot he'd drawn on one of her moving boxes.

When it came to the law and the people who dealt it out, there wasn't much T didn't know. It even turned out that he knew the prosecution lawyer Mortimer Deloitte quite well. They were the same age and had both grown up in Floyd County, Virginia.

After spending fourteen months in the jungle hell of the Vietnam War, Perkins resolved never to obey an order he didn't like. He was currently serving his thirtieth year, first as deputy sheriff, then as sheriff, of Highland County, Virginia's smallest county.

He picked Doggie up every morning in front of her apartment over the Starbuck's on 19th Street, sat by her side during the trial, delivered her to the West Wing of the White House at 1:00 P.M., then picked her up again at seven and brought her back home. He was also in charge of the shopping, which meant the same dinner every night: T-bone steaks à la T. Perkins, with mountains of anemic french fries.

The first couple of days, they didn't discuss the trial at all.

A mere two weeks into the trial, the press was already as good as unanimous in its prediction that it would be all over in a hurry and Bud Curtis would be found guilty.

And how could anyone think otherwise? According to the prosecution, ever since Bud Curtis had taken O'Neill under his wing, pleasing his master was what had given the dim-witted future killer's life meaning. Horrible anecdotes about Doggie's father were mentioned, too, like how he'd bet his poker-playing buddies he could get O'Neill to lick his spit up from the floor, and how O'Neill repeatedly got into quarrels with the hotel personnel if he overheard them complaining about their employer.

Bud Curtis had had an uncanny hold on O'Neill, the prosecution concluded, and could have made him do anything. If Curtis had been able to get his simpleminded servant to lick up his mentor's spit, why couldn't he have him commit murder?

Despite all his anger, Doggie's father didn't seem sincere during his cross-examination, and she knew many of the things he said were directly untrue. How, for example, could he claim he'd supported Jansen's candidacy and that he'd had no other reason for offering Jansen his hotel on election night than to support his campaign? And how could he deny having actively partaken in George Wallace's racist gubernatorial campaigns when his name was on every list of Wallace's supporters? Why did he try to give a false impression of himself when everyone could tell he was lying?

Worst of all was when he was asked why he wasn't present when the murder was committed. What had Mimi Jansen whispered to him just prior to the painting's unveiling? When Curtis replied that she wasn't feeling well and had asked him for a glass of water, Mortimer Deloitte lay his trump on the table: Why, then, had he no glass in his hand when he returned a couple of minutes later?

To this he replied that he *had* had a glass of water in his hand, but he'd dropped it in shock as the dreadful shooting and chaos erupted. And he hadn't thought about the glass of water since.

The problem was that the glass, or shards of it, were never found, and the video surveillance camera in the corridor showed Curtis's hands being empty when he returned. A clear sign of a man who

couldn't be trusted to tell the truth, Deloitte remarked, suggesting
that Curtis had left the area so as not to be present when the killing
took place and even claiming that the video clearly depicted Bud Curtis looking over at his daughter to make sure she was out of the line
of fire before leaving.

The judge upheld the defense's protest over this far-fetched line of
speculation, but it did little to offset what the jury could see with its
own eyes on the video. Bud Curtis left the passageway just before the
murder, and he wasn't holding any glass when he returned. Ergo, the
man was a liar.

Last to be questioned was Ben Kane, head of Jansen's corps of personal bodyguards. Like the accused, he was also decked out in an
Armani suit, only this one fit snugly. And he was wearing his trademark heavy gold bracelets. Trained to interpret situations and imprint
them on his memory, his cold and tight-lipped presence impressed the
court. He naturally had no explanation as to why his now-suspended
Secret Service colleague had failed to find the gun when he searched
Toby O'Neill, but otherwise his testimony was like out of a movie
script where all the actors had specific roles and everyone performed
on cue. So and so much time had passed from the moment O'Neill shot
Mimi Jansen to the moment when O'Neill himself was shot. Mimi
Jansen had just stepped forward as O'Neill fired, so the bullet could
easily have been meant for the president. He also clearly remembered
hearing Bud Curtis speaking to Toby O'Neill over the hotel intercom
shortly before the incident. "Don't say anything, Toby," he'd warned,
"just do as I told you!" To top it off, when Ben Kane arrested Curtis
shortly afterwards, the latter had spit in his face and screamed that
the Democratic sow had gotten what she deserved.

At this point Doggie's father sprang from his seat, calling Kane a
liar, but to little avail. It was easy to see the jury was becoming more
and more thick-skinned.

Mortimer Deloitte was really in his element as he delivered his closing statement, and the jury needed merely four hours to reach its
verdict. They didn't doubt that the accused had planned the murder;
they just weren't certain as to whether the president was to be killed

along with his pregnant wife. Apparently, one juror had had a problem with the fact that Bud Curtis had done nothing to remove his fingerprints from the cartridges and that he'd made such an easily traceable money transfer to O'Neill instead of handing him cash.

But that's how it is with murder cases: At some point the killer always screws up.

T. Perkins stopped right in front of the White House West Wing and escorted Doggie past a row of rowdy journalists. Inside she was greeted by averted eyes and pained expressions. It was clear to her that no one knew quite how to react.

Wesley Barefoot came along and gave her a brief hug, but that was it. Being at work didn't feel good at all, and it didn't help that the entire West Wing was stretched to the breaking point by the suspenseful tension emerging from the Oval Office the past few days. She asked Wesley what was going on and could tell from his vague answer that it had to do with her father's trial. She was sure the court case had put a stopper to what she'd felt was a growing intimacy between the two of them.

She sat in her office and looked around. The room she'd been given to occupy was less than thirty feet square, there were no windows, the furnishings had seen better days, and the old shelves were stuffed to overflowing. On her shabby desk stood a computer with a nicotine-yellowed keyboard surrounded by piles of papers. None of her work was of much importance. Her position was next-to-lowest in the White House staff hierarchy, just above the young man assigned to shred the contents of their wastebaskets. If it weren't such a high-profile murder case, hardly anyone would have known her name. The only solace she found was in the Buddha figurine Jansen had given her in Beijing. It was perched like a paperweight in a corner of her desk atop a stack of departmental circulars about emergency water depots and fire inspection laws for public buildings. The little Buddha belonged to a previous life.

She sat for a moment with a lump in her throat, remembering the expression in his eyes as Jansen had handed her the figurine. This was the look that had later made her join his presidential campaign. If he'd never bought her the Buddha and looked at her the way he did, her father would be a free man today, and Mimi Todd Jansen and her child would be alive. How could such a tender, authoritative glance lead to such a disastrous quirk of fate?

She picked up the figurine and hugged it close. The president had promised her happiness and a lifelong friendship, but where were the happiness and friendship now? Had he devoted a second to keeping his promise during her father's trial? No, not a single word of consolation or even a sympathetic glance.

She considered tossing the little Buddha in the wastebasket but thought better of it when two secretaries walked past her open door with unconcealed looks of contempt. They turned their heads away quickly when she looked back, as though their merely looking at her could be harmful.

For the next half hour she considered just walking away from it all. Calling T. Perkins and have him fetch her and take her home with him to Virginia. This was obviously what her fellow employees wanted— that she left of her own accord.

She was actually about to pick up the telephone when Thomas Sunderland strode into her office. He was thinner and paler than she was used to seeing him. He'd been one of the most incriminating witnesses at her father's trial, and now it was apparently her turn.

"What are your plans now, Doggie?" he asked, the desired reply painted on his face. He wanted her gone, nice and easy—and voluntarily. Until then, the situation would be unstable. At the moment his ex–military man's sense of order and propriety was weighing on him heavier than if he were counseling the president on the ways of the world.

She didn't answer him.

"President Jansen hasn't formally asked me to say this, but I think he'd prefer not to have to run into you."

Doggie placed the Buddha back on top of the pile of circulars.

"I assume you can manage without having to work," he added.

"Yes."

"Then do you agree?" he asked.

"About what? That I should quit my job and just disappear, or that I shouldn't roam the halls so the president doesn't have to see me?"

"How can you keep working here when everybody knows it was you who arranged for the president to hold his election party at your father's goddamn hotel?"

Fucking arrogant, lying cocksucker! Was he actually trying to make her doubt her own memory? *Me?* As I recall, I was the one who was totally against even mentioning the idea. Was it not *you,* Mr. Sunderland, who kept pestering me to do it and then went on with the matter yourself?"

He didn't answer her question. He was weighing his options. Finally he just said, "Well . . . what do you say?"

She nodded, mostly to herself. This heartless ghoul wasn't going to get the better of her. "Well . . . I say I'll bet the president has more important things to think about!"

CHAPTER 8

BUD CURTIS WAS MOVED TO SUSSEX STATE PRISON IN WAVERLY FOUR DAYS after Judge Marsha W. Tanner sentenced him to death. His defense lawyers made their customary immediate appeal, and no one expected the appellate courts and board of appeals could reach their final decision in less than six years. That's how long the death chamber would have to wait.

But Bud could tell that "the people" had already pronounced judgment. There'd been none of his family present during the concluding legal procedures. No one asked him what he thought about the charges anymore, only if he regretted what he'd done, and that's what took the fight out of him. The newspapers were mostly occupied with negative coverage, boring deeply into his successful—but questionable—business methods as hotel owner. Not a word about the many lean and laborious years when he sweated blood for every dollar he could set aside. They weren't looking for a success story. Not anymore.

A lot of other things changed after the sentencing, too. The prison guards began treating him more roughly, they no longer listened to what he had to say, and from one day to the next, permission to have visitors was restricted to the minimum.

He'd been convicted of conspiring to murder the president's wife—or rather, the wife of a government official on duty—and a pregnant woman besides. He was to wait on the death row of one of Virginia's security-level-five prisons.

Ironically, if one ignored the chains and the circumstances—which of course was difficult—it was almost like returning home. He'd driven that same route to Richmond a couple of times a week for more than two years: through Virginia Beach, Norfolk, Isle of Wight, Wakefield, and Waverly. In Waverly he'd eat lunch at Marco's Italian Restaurant on Main Street, always the same pizza and ice cream in the same booth with its faded bullfight poster. Then he'd take a couple of turns on the pinball machine with the locals, maybe the same ones who now would fasten him to the execution pad one day. Finally he'd make the customary trip past his old aunt's dilapidated house that stank of cats and cheap perfume. It stood on Musselwhite Drive, just four miles from the quadrangular prison block. Who else had there been to look after her?

Now his aunt was dead, and here he sat.

They drove him out to the prison in an armored car. Through a little shutter in the side he could just make out the landscape passing by: the long straight stretch of road through swamp and forest, the eagles circling above the treetops, and the enormous spiderwebs that hung down over the branches and undergrowth like protective coats of mail.

All colors disappeared as the first gray buildings of Sussex State Prison began to appear. An anemic panorama of asphalt and concrete and gray silos whose only function was storing society's offal. A couple of orange prison suits behind the barbed wire provided the only dabs of color.

It was hell on earth. A hell devoid of nuance. Completely unreal and light-years away from Marco's.

Three days went by where Bud attempted to accustom himself to his new reality, such as making the steel toilet flush, lying properly on his flat mattress, getting used to the metallic slamming of doors, and insulating himself from the chorus of complaints from the surrounding cages where the animals they called "the condemned" were supposed to wait until their time came.

And then the true state of reality dawned on Bud.

He'd been collecting his thoughts until his head hurt, attempting to find a way out of this nightmare, to find something that would convince the proper authorities that his case had to be retried. Now he gave up.

The reality was that it was too late. He'd missed his chance. During the massive court case, hadn't not only the state prosecutor, but also his defense lawyers—and even he, himself—thoroughly accustomed themselves to the concept of his guilt? Who'd ever seriously take up his cause now? Doggie? He doubted it. Why should she? He and his lawyers had conducted the case dismally.

It was all over. That was the reality. The case was closed; conclusions had been drawn. He'd been convicted of something he didn't do, but he was going to die anyway. And no matter how many lawyers he had and how clever they were, and no matter how many reasons there were for a retrial, it was all going to end in the execution chamber a few yards from where he presently sat.

It was a nightmare. Blinking neon lights and a five-yard square box that wouldn't be approved even for the caging of wild animals. Cold colors, a steel sink, and smooth cement surfaces.

Inmates were yelling to one another all the time, and the big, black man in the adjoining cell—with huge hands that hung limply through the bars most of the time—was the worst. Although his mouth wasn't quiet for a second, things were okay as long as someone answered him. It wasn't until no one answered that he went out of control and all hell broke loose.

His name was Daryl Reid. He'd obviously seen and experienced too much in his lifetime and—what was worse—he felt it necessary to tell everyone about it.

"When my time comes, I want it all: cheeseburgers, two enchiladas, two tacos, and two Cokes—two giant Cokes. How big do they come these days? Really big? Half gallon? Yeah, two of them!" Then he beat his fists on the bars. "Hey, you, new man! Hey, you, Bud Curtis! What are you gonna have when they come for you?"

Bud had given the same answer a hundred times: He didn't know.

"Come on, man, you can get everything! Tell me!"

And while the poor guy chanted his life story next door, Bud suddenly understood. One day he'd have to choose. Tacos or pâté de foie gras. Of course it could take ten years and countless appeals, but he'd have to choose.

This was one thought among many that he was having a hard time dealing with.

Way back from the time of his pretrial detention he could see that powerful forces wanted to do away with him. During the nighttime interrogation after the murder, he'd told the police time and again that it hadn't been him but one of the president's security people—one Blake W. Wunderlich—who had suggested having Toby O'Neill unveil the painting in the corridor. "It wasn't me," Bud had repeated the whole night through, but no one believed him. The cop leading the interrogation had asked if he'd met this Wunderlich in person, and Bud had to explain that, aside from a single phone conversation, all contact between them had been written, but that he'd saved all their fax communications.

Sure enough, the next morning investigators found four faxes in Bud's office in Virginia Beach, all sent on the same day and signed by one Blake W. Wunderlich. During the next few days they apparently made a persistent attempt to locate the man but without luck. Neither the Secret Service, the FBI, the bodyguard corps, nor the CIA had had an employee by that name. They said the man didn't exist and that the faxes had been sent from one of Bud's hotels in Chicago. They showed him the faxes and pointed at the fax number. Yes, they were authentic— he recognized them. Did he also recognize the sender's fax number? No, of course, how could he? All in all, his various hotels must have hundreds of fax numbers.

Then they showed him a note he'd written in his appointment diary that indicated he'd been at the hotel from which the faxes were sent on the given day. Didn't he remember? Was he so often in Chicago that he couldn't remember what he did there?

Bud understood nothing. They'd said the man with the fax didn't exist, yet he'd spoken with him on the telephone, and he distinctly remembered the name.

The state prosecutor could also easily remember the name when the trial began. "Wunderlich, with his convenient activities but strangely imaginary being," as he described him. The prosecutor concluded that the faxes were sent from a man who didn't exist, from one of Bud Curtis's own hotels in Chicago. When a detective was able to confirm that Bud had been in that hotel office the same day the fax was sent, it looked like Bud was guilty as hell. He could see that himself. It was hard to refute the allegation that he'd constructed the events and the faxes himself, and that Blake W. Wunderlich had never existed other than in his own sick mind. Bud had to ask himself who would want the murder blamed on him?

But that was far from the only situation that was making Bud's future look dark. The series of similar ugly surprises in this case were endless. Among other things, two of the black-clad security men claimed to have seen his pistol lying on his desk at the hotel in Virginia Beach just two days before the murder, even though he hadn't had it out of the desk drawer in at least three years. Analysis of the cartridge cases had even revealed his fingerprints. But how could they, since he'd never loaded the gun himself? They also had a video of him at the moment when he claimed to have reentered the hotel corridor with a glass of water, but there was no glass to be seen in his hand. All this— even though he knew that none of it was true. Not to mention the mysterious money transfer they claimed he made to Toby O'Neill.

And no one came to his defense. None of his employees took the opportunity to tell the court about how much he'd looked forward to finally making peace with his daughter and how thrilled he was at the PR scoop it would be to have the next US president as his hotel guest on election night. And even though everyone knew it, no one bothered to soften his now infamous criticism of the president and Mimi Jansen by mentioning that he'd always criticized everyone and complained about everything—with a smile on his lips. Nor did anyone bother to draw attention to how little he'd actually participated in Barry Goldwater's and George Wallace's election campaigns as a sixteen-year-old kid. Or how much he'd done for his community after he came home from Vietnam. If one thought it over, the reason was probably that no one had noticed, and it was wishful thinking that people should dwell on the soft, humane side of a man as powerful as he was. It was as though it were his own fault that people had been made insensitive by his characteristic bossy tirades.

This was probably true, unfortunately, and it hit him hard.

He'd been expecting a fair trial, and that it wouldn't be hard to prove his innocence. But telling details—like the suspicion and doubt on Doggie's face when she visited him in prison, the way the jury foreman looked him straight in the eye, or when the police officer testified that the fax came from an imaginary person—made Bud Curtis realize that the fateful die was cast and the rest would fall in place.

No one is innocent until proven guilty.

There were twenty-seven men on death row. The oldest was sixty-two; the youngest was just a kid. Ten blacks, a couple of Latinos, the rest white. They were all condemned to die, and practically all were fighting like mad with the authorities and lawyers to drag time out.

The men's hands told the whole story, because they were all their fellow prisoners could see. These hands were their faces. They reflected despair and apathy and hung limply through the bars all day long.

The inmates on either side of Bud were out of their minds, a fact about which the prison guards apparently couldn't care less. Except for the newest guard, a guy named Pete. Pete Bukowski was the only prison guard who seemed to possess the vestiges of humanity. His eyes were almost kind, and sometimes he nodded to the inmates or smiled sadly, as though he were capable of putting himself in their place, of mourning man's fate.

The other guards were cold as ice. They performed their job of chaining the inmates and leading them out to the yard for their hour's exercise as though they were airing the neighbor's dog. It was a case of groveling like a dog, too, as he'd been warned by the man in the adjoining cell. Especially with the big, red-haired guard they called Lassie. Otherwise one's rations would come up short.

"Yo, Curtis, you lis'nin'?" His neighbor Daryl Reid was pounding on the bars again. He'd murdered twice, a couple of days apart, and he didn't give a shit. He was guilty and had never pretended otherwise. The only thing he cared about was getting it over with. Daryl had been sitting in his cell since 1999, and, aside from Bud's other neighbor, Reamur Duke, none of the men presently on death row had survived that long. By now, possibilities to appeal had been more or less exhausted. It wouldn't be long before Daryl would be enjoying his last, magnificent meal.

"You listening, I said?" He banged the bars again.

"What now, Daryl?"

"You're rich, man, aren't you?"

"Shut up, Daryl! How many times do I have to say it?"

"Then get hold of some cigarettes for Reamur Duke. Buy him some, and buy me some, too, okay?"

"What about buying us all some pot? Enough to blast our minds out of this fucking place!" someone else yelled. Several of them were shaking their bars.

"Not for Robert, that fucking child killer. Give him a shot of uncut heroin, right in the neck!" came another voice. Bud judged that the man was in cell number six or seven.

"Fuck that shit, Clive, and you, too, Dave! If Bud's gonna use his millions on something, it should be to get us some decent lawyers. Ain't that right, Buddy Boy? Whaddaya say? Half of us have only had shitty lawyers that couldn't tie their own shoelaces!" This time the voice was accompanied by a pair of big, white hands, gesticulating through the bars a couple of cells away.

Bud didn't answer. For a moment everyone was banging on his cell bars like a madman. Then suddenly everything got quiet.

In the end, they all got on one another's nerves.

"Hey, man, fuck them," whispered Daryl. "Just as long as you buy cigarettes for me and Reamur, okay?"

It was the fifth time at least that this conversation had taken place, and it was still only 10:00 A.M. It had happened about twenty-five times in the course of the previous day and the day before that. Tomorrow it would be the same. And the day after.

The thin steel walls on death row provided no insulation from this kind of grinding, everyday trivia. Only dreams could do that.

Reamur Duke cried at night and would never say why. Afterwards he'd recite the same nonsense again and again—words and numbers, all at once. "Get hold of eight comma six and the one, two, three, four signatures." Then he'd go on for a while about cigarettes and then back to the endless word-number combinations that were clogging his head. He was even crazier than Daryl but apparently not crazy enough not to be laid on the pad with a shot of deadly poison in his veins.

Bud hated to think about it, but it was merely a matter of time before they all lost their minds. Daryl Reid knew plenty of stories about how bad it got for inmates on various death rows, and one rarely heard him laugh as hard as when he told the one about the man who wanted to save his dessert until after his execution.

Bud never laughed. He'd been on death row for six days, and he was already about to crack up. Something had to happen.

CHAPTER 9

IT WAS TEN O'CLOCK IN THE EVENING ON THE SIXTH OF MARCH, AND BY NOW the night sky above the West Wing was pitch-black. Several hours had passed since the meeting between the president and his vice president had begun, and Wesley had done plenty of thinking in the meantime.

He had to shake his head at the thought of how hard he'd fought to get where he was today and how this wonderful period in his life was about to come to a close.

Wesley and the others heard Vice President Lerner's agitated voice well before he showed up in the doorway of the Oval Office. His face was not a pretty sight, red and swollen like he was having some kind of strong allergic reaction. He nodded curtly around the table, sat down on the only sofa, and crossed his legs. The president arrived a minute later, flanked by the attorney general and Secretary of the Interior Betty Tucker. Secretary Tucker looked harried, as though she'd just arrived from endless inspections of various public institutions around the country. Wesley scanned the faces of those present, letting his gaze fall to the floor and then rise again along Betty Tucker's shapely legs. He'd been there once, between those legs. Ms. Tucker felt—and ignored—Wesley's glance. For her, it was ancient history.

"Okay, Bruce . . ." The vice president was absolutely the only person who allowed himself to address the country's leader in this manner, and although Jansen didn't show it, Wesley knew he didn't appreciate it. All in all, Jansen had become a master at not manifesting what he was feeling inside.

"Now I'm asking you," he rumbled, "and it's up to you if you'll answer or have one of your coolies do it for you!"

Jansen looked at him steadily. "Fire away, Michael," he said, unaffected by his second-in-command's informality and aggressive tone of voice.

"I'm assuming those present already know everything we've been talking about in Sunderland's office," said the vice president.

"Yes, they do."

Michael K. Lerner turned to the others. "Did you know that everything you say in this building is recorded on tape?"

No one answered, and how could they? They were shocked. *Come on, Jansen, deny it. Don't let it be true*, said Wesley Barefoot to himself, but the president remained expressionless.

Wesley was on the verge of getting up and leaving, but he couldn't.

A few feet away the vice president was sitting with his jaw clenched. As rival presidential candidates, he and Jansen had courted the same voters, and Lerner had lost badly. Thus their present alliance was strictly one of convenience that no one expected would last. On the other hand, nobody could have predicted it would be ending almost before it began. "Yes, gentlemen," Lerner said, "I can see the cat's got your tongue for once, which is something you may want to learn to do more often, because what I'm telling you is true: Everything we say in the White House is taped and can be used against us if it becomes expedient. But this is only the first step. Just wait. This law-and-order package will eventually have the whole country under surveillance; isn't that correct, Mr. President?"

"For a limited time, yes."

Wesley looked over at Betty Tucker, whose rapid career advancement was the envy of Washington, but she seemed unperturbed by what she was hearing. Did he have the guts to speak up? He shook his head. No, he didn't.

"And the purpose being . . . ?" continued Lerner.

"The purpose is control," answered Jansen.

"So this is about control."

"If we seriously want to change things—yes!"

Lerner nodded as though he'd heard it all before. "The law-and-order proposal states that it can become necessary to override democratic principles. Are you willing to do this, Mr. President?"

"If necessary."

"Censor the media?"

"Yes."

"Forbid people to bear arms?"

"No. That goes against the Second Amendment," came Jansen's measured reply.

"But forbid them to buy ammunition, am I right?"

"Yes. The Second Amendment doesn't forbid that."

"And you'd go against the courts and grant amnesty to thousands of convicted criminals?"

"Yes, that, too. We must give the out-of-prison resocialization program very high priority."

"But you'd execute the inmates, even though they haven't exhausted their possibilities of appeal?"

"Yes."

The vice president shook his head. "And those who oppose the plan will just have to comply?"

"That's correct."

This brought on a few moments' silence—some of the most significant, unforgettable seconds in Wesley's life.

Here he sat, paralyzed but for his shaking hands, in fear of losing everything he'd believed in. He was caught in the net because he hadn't had the courage to get up and leave when he could have. But his legs were useless, and all he could manage was to raise his head and take a good look at his president—this all-powerful figure—and try and understand why all this was happening so suddenly. The more he thought about it, the more Lerner's sharp critique sounded like an understatement.

No one present in the Oval Office spoke.

Then President Jansen got up slowly. He wore a dark expression as he finally stood erect, towering over them.

"Michael . . ." he said, and paused until the vice president returned his look. "Our duty is to make the United States a better place to live. We've always had to fight threats from abroad—battles that have cost us dearly—but we've kept our country free. If things are to remain this way, then it's *now* we must act, only this time the enemy threatens us from within." The words made the vice president's expression even more hostile, but Jansen was unfazed. "You know the enemy I mean, don't you, Michael? It's an enemy with many names. I'm talking about the mafia, the militias, the crime rate, the ignoring of weapon laws and misuse of freedom of speech, violence of all kinds, injustice, and misuse of power. An enemy with many names and many faces, and all too many people are in their power—willingly or unwittingly—so obviously not everyone will be fighting this battle that must be fought."

"It sounds so noble, the way you put it, Mr. President," said Lerner, barely able to control his voice. "But we still need to follow the legislative process!"

"We're going to try."

This reply was finally too much for the vice president. He sprang out of his chair. "This isn't a goddamn case of trying! Don't you get it, Bruce? You follow the rules set down by Congress and the Constitution, understand? Else I swear we're going to have you removed from office, whatever the cost!"

Vice President Lerner's face was bright copper-red. Rumor had it that he'd had heart problems, and Wesley expected him to collapse any second.

The president stepped towards him. He was at least a half head taller than his vice president and twenty pounds heavier. *Here it comes . . .* thought Wesley, but it was just a kind of posturing, like a male lion ready to shake an unruly member of its brood by the nape of its neck until it did as it was told. He was letting everyone know who was king of the jungle. Lerner kept out of his way as Jansen strode past him to his desk. He looked at everyone in turn and sat down.

"Tomorrow I'm going to address the nation and present this country's citizens with the program which from now on I'm calling 'A Secure Future.' Anyone who has a problem with that should say so now."

A long silence followed. Wesley couldn't believe his ears. Did he actually dare expose his plan to the American public tomorrow? No lobbying, no negotiating with Congress on compromises, no backroom deals or handshakes to help him towards his goal? It was pure insanity. Then a thought struck him that was even more unbearable since it applied to him personally: Jansen was going to give this speech tomorrow and maybe he was expecting *him* to formulate all this bullshit in a press release.

Betty Tucker broke the silence. "I'm in."

Then Sunderland nodded his agreement.

Next was Lance Burton. "Me, too," he said, and looked at Wesley. "We're not going to have much time to get that speech ready, but both Donald and I are in." This was the only answer one could expect from a president's chief of communications.

Attorney General Lovell nodded. "I'll inform Chief Supreme Court Justice Manning as soon as this meeting is over and hold a Justice Department meeting this evening."

Wesley was speechless. Was that it? What tempting prospects were being held out to Lance Burton and Donald Beglaubter since they had no more to say on the matter? Were they by any chance maneuvering themselves into position for two of the Cabinet jobs that were bound to be vacated as a result of the inevitable showdown that was approaching?

Wesley kept quiet, and no one asked him what he thought. What could he do—just one man? If he said nothing, the others would assume he agreed with them. This notion set his knees bouncing nervously under the table.

"Mr. President, who will be your interim appointee when I notify the press of my resignation in a couple of hours?"

It was Lerner who spoke the words. His red-faced rage had turned to an icy, measured calmness. Clearly his fast-working, calculating brain was trying to figure out ways to turn the situation to his advantage. He was going to be a tough opponent of Jansen's "secure future."

"Oh, I think we'll be able to sort that out, Michael" was all he said.

He felt guilty as hell, peering apprehensively into the shadows as he crept home to write the president's speech. *Why didn't you get up and protest immediately?* he admonished himself. *You dumb, fucking coward!*

He spent the next three hours forcing his fingers to punch computer keys. He'd exchanged e-mails with Donald Beglaubter and spoken on the phone with Lance Burton about crucial details of the text. Now he was just about finished. Three empty soft drink cans sat next to the computer, and two TV screens were flickering behind him. Every few seconds he readjusted the position of his work chair.

There was an air of despondency in the room that was hard to ignore.

The first interviews with Vice President Lerner came on the news at five minutes past midnight. Full of self-confidence, he stated that he'd expressed to the country's new president his strong lack of confidence in him and had been forced to step down. That was how he worded it—nothing about it being his own initiative. No, he was "forced to step down." It was a clever way of putting it, and the commentator immediately implied that Lerner had been fired. Lerner was merciless in his criticism but knew how far to go without compromising his oath of confidentiality. So instead of naming concrete details of his disaffection, he dwelt on the president's mental instability since he'd taken office and the dangerous effect the tragic deaths of his two wives was having on his powers of judgment.

It was tailor-made for implying that the president was showing increasing signs of mental derangement that would soon manifest themselves in drastic, misguided decisions.

Within ten minutes, Wesley had John Bugatti on the line.

"Hey, Lerner's resigned. What's going on?" asked Bugatti.

"I don't have time right now, John. I'm in the middle of writing a press release that has to be ready in half an hour."

"Wesley, I'm sitting in some godforsaken hole in Montana, dammit. Media access here is terrible. Come on, buddy, give us a clue."

"The president's gone mad!" Wesley regretted his choice of words immediately, but it was too late.

"Mad? What's he done?"

"No, nonsense!" Wesley tried swallowing, but his mouth was too dry. "Naw, I didn't mean it, John. Jansen's presented a new, extremely controversial law-and-order plan that Lerner won't go along with. I can't give you any concrete details right now, but it will be brought up in Congress tomorrow in some shape or form."

"Controversial? How? Come on, Wesley, just one word!"

"Press censorship."

"You're joking, aren't you?"

"Yes."

"Come on, give me an example. I'll say I got it from the veep himself, if anyone asks. Jesus, I'm sitting here watching a tiny TV screen in this shitty little town, and there isn't even a DSL connection in the hotel, so please—make my day."

"Okay, here's your example: All TV programs that glorify violence will be taken off the air."

"Oh, yeah? That'll piss off Tom Jumper, ha-ha!" This was something Wesley knew Bugatti would love hearing. John Bugatti truly hated Tom Jumper's "reality show" featuring society's most pathetic losers. Stuffing their faces, balling left and right, and beating each other up—that's what the show's contestants were good at. Who'd ever miss a program like that? Not Wesley, that was for sure.

He paused with his mouth open, but the next sentence came out anyway. "And the cessation of the sale of ammunition to civilians."

"Okay . . ."

Wesley could clearly hear Bugatti take a deep breath. He was beginning to realize the gravity of the situation, and his mind must be racing to figure out what other sources could confirm this amazing bit of news, knowing he had to make sure to keep Barefoot's name out of it.

So Wesley dropped the next bomb. "All prison inmates will be granted amnesty, except for those on death row."

"Jesus Christ!"

Then Wesley hung up and began reading through his statement to the press. Why the hell hadn't he stood up to Jansen and handed in his resignation? Instead he'd written his best speech ever.

CHAPTER 10

JOHN BUGATTI HAD BEEN HANGING OUT ALL NIGHT IN THE PORTION OF JOHN-
son's Quality Hotel that a cracked enamel sign euphemistically called
THE RESTAURANT. In reality it was a dilapidated appendix to the hotel
that served as a truck stop café for long-haul truckers. Otherwise,
restaurants seemed to be an unknown concept in this town.

Like the cafeteria, the hotel itself was unusually unappealing, a
quickly erected prefab job, full of impressive examples of slovenly
workmanship and nonexistent maintenance. The carpeting and furniture had definitely seen better days, and crooked, yellowed tourist
posters shamelessly depicted scenes of breathtaking beauty awaiting
lucky lodgers just beyond the hotel's crumbling walls. Everything
about the place awoke disquieting memories of the early days when
Bugatti's status at the bottom of the journalistic hierarchy meant he
had to pay for his own hotel rooms.

But it was the only joint they called a hotel in Taver's Cliff, Montana, and it was this territory his current interviewee had chosen as
the setting for reaping his share of media limelight.

It had taken him and his television team three weeks to locate
Moonie Quale, founder of the Montana militia called the White-
Headed Eagles, and the interview was to take place the following
morning.

Wanted by the police, Moonie Quale was a headline maker, a big
guy with black hair like Rock Hudson, charming in his own way, and
he had many admirers. Most important, he was the country's biggest
proponent of merging all the paramilitary organizations in the United

States, with himself as leader. In that respect he was an extremely dangerous person who'd used his considerable rhetorical talents to threaten all kinds of people with fates worse than death. Getting a one-on-one interview with someone like him was every journalist's dream. It was Quale who decided if, when, and where such an interview took place. There were no second chances.

Instead of being thrilled with his news scoop and waiting to hear from Quale about the exact time and place they'd be meeting, Bugatti was hoping that when his cell phone rang, it would be his boss calling him home to cover the incredible events that were unfolding in Washington.

Earlier in the evening he'd briefed his office about the information Wesley Barefoot and a couple of other reliable sources had entrusted him with, and then had watched NBC to see what use they'd made of this information. Now he was practically in a state of shock as he followed the intense furor that had erupted in the aftermath of the vice president's resignation. Watching these events unfold on an ancient, nearly colorless television set in this dingy cafeteria made everything seem unreal. Never before had NBC's newscaster or the vice president looked so lousy as on that screen.

At 6:00 A.M. the hotel manager unlocked the glass door to the parking lot to let the first guests into the cafeteria. Then, without bothering to ask Bugatti, he changed the TV channel to Tom Jumper's reality show, where overweight airheads were hurling insults at one another. With Wesley's tip about Jansen's plans for the nation's media still fresh in his mind, John regarded the show from a new perspective. It wouldn't be long before this kind of entertainment would be history. Still, in this case maybe media censorship wasn't such a bad idea.

Bugatti changed the channel back to NBC the moment the hotel manager went out to the lobby. The waitress was oblivious, busy racing around, serving plates of eggs and toast. It was hard to say which was less appealing—the food or the waitress.

Judging from the truckers' accents, the majority of them were from the South. Their noisy commentary regarding what they were seeing on the TV screen was predictably, depressingly unintelligent.

It's good I don't have to listen to shit like this every day, thought Bugatti, as he tried to follow what the newscaster was saying.

There'd been yet another sniper killing on the streets of New York, and people were scared as hell. This time the victim was an old man; he'd died from the shock to his aged body, not his bullet wound. Although sad and sickening, it still wasn't quite as horrible as the previous week's shooting of two children.

The parking lot was getting crowded with huge, flashy sixteen-wheelers, and the café was filling up with red plaid shirts and baseball caps that promoted everything but sports teams. "Why the hell don't that New York police catch the sonabitch?" growled a long-haul driver as he sloshed a bottle of ketchup over his scrambled eggs.

"To keep themselves working, so they'll wind up with fat pensions!" came a voice over the clatter of forks and coffee cups. Most of those present laughed.

"They should catch him quick and toast him in the chair," came the final judgment from the corner, and everyone concurred.

Cameraman Marvin Gallegos, one of Bugatti's regular team, came down the stairs and sat down heavily across from him. "It's coming on now," he said in a tired voice and looked up at the screen, where yet another breaking-news program was being announced.

Two breaking-news shows in a row, and there they were, stuck in Nowheresville! Bugatti cursed his fate for the hundredth time.

The washed-out TV image of the news anchorman switched the scene to the White House pressroom.

Wesley Barefoot strode up to the podium, exuding calm and self-confidence, impeccably clad as always. He nodded to the journalists, but they didn't get the trademark flash of his perfect white teeth because his smile was absent.

Then Wesley introduced the president, and Bugatti sat up in his chair. For a moment the drone of voices behind him subsided.

"Good morning, ladies and gentlemen," began President Jansen, nodding to the press. "I hope you're sitting comfortably and that you're in a good, patient mood today because this is going to take a little more of your time than usual."

Jansen slicked down his hair and put on his reading glasses. "I know you all would like me to make a statement regarding Michael Lerner's resignation, but I'm afraid you're not getting one today, and no, no one has been chosen to take Lerner's place, either. What I wish to speak about today has to do with fear."

From that moment, the United States of America was never itself again.

"It has to do with fear, and removing it permanently. It has to do with you and me and the country we live in and love. It's about becoming free people, freed from the fear of being different and from fearing life itself. A free people, exactly as prescribed by the Constitution. And it's about the United States again being respected and admired by the whole world."

"Fuck him!" someone snorted.

Bugatti leaned over to his cameraman. "Turn on the camera, Marvin. Get these folks' reactions. This is where it's happening." If he couldn't be in DC, at least he'd capture the mood of some of these red-blooded fellow Americans.

"Rolling" was all Marvin whispered back.

Jansen's next words came without hesitation. "But, before we can get rid of a person's fear, we have to remove its cause." The president's eyes, trained on his audience, were glowing and intense, like a young man in love. "Today I will be calling for an immediate emergency convening of Congress, where the government will present a draft of some extensive law reforms to secure better social services for every citizen in the land. And now listen, fellow Americans, so you know what the future will have in store."

He paused. Except for one masticating glutton, the cafeteria scene froze.

"The days are over where our society is caught in a vise that's slowly squeezing the life out of us. From today, your government will work day and night until we have a fairer justice system, free medical care, a disarmed population, a healthier media, a more responsible approach to our children's education and daily life, and jobs for all. In short: a radically changed United States, where life will be worth living and we will no longer have to lock our doors at night. From now on, America will begin living up to its ideals."

The mouths atop the red plaid shirts were gaping now, except for one that cried out, "Fucker's out of his mind!" The man stood up and threw some dollar bills on the table. "Keep the change, Maggie!" he grumbled as he left. A few moments later his high-powered truck motor was grumbling, too.

Bugatti looked uneasily at the TV screen. Wesley sure hadn't exaggerated when they'd spoken on the phone.

The camera angle in the pressroom changed to give a glimpse of the journalists' faces, chiseled in stone and apprehensive all at once. He would give anything to be sitting there now.

"Have you caught that guy over in the corner?" whispered Bugatti, pointing to a trembling meat loaf that was screaming at the TV screen.

Marvin turned his camera discreetly as the press conference cameraman swung back to a close-up of the president. "We must all do our part—and we can," Jansen was declaring. "We're Americans; we can do anything!"

Now President Jansen was looking directly at the TV camera. "I envision a football game where the far right and the far left are sidelined, while the rest of us—and I mean the vast majority—move into the fray against violence, injustice, and moral decay. And in a year's time we'll be victorious. This country will have won its most crucial battle ever, and America will be a peaceful place where everyone has a job and the prisons are empty."

The president spoke for forty minutes while the truckers wandered in and out through the glass door of Johnson Quality Hotel's eating facility. His speech was interrupted several times by agitated questions and heckling from the journalists, but the security people's high-profile presence assured that things didn't get out of hand.

Chief of Staff Thomas Sunderland stood behind the president

during the entire affair, totally expressionless, while at his side Wesley Barefoot's face was getting whiter and whiter.

Bugatti knew how he was feeling. It was a bitch of a role to have to play.

"What the hell's going on?" boomed the voice of the latest café arrival.

Bugatti turned around. Flanked by two shaved-headed characters, there stood his interviewee, the paramilitary leader Moonie Quale, glowering at the television set. He couldn't have been less anonymous, wearing a complete military camouflage uniform decorated with white-headed eagles and a cartridge belt diagonally across his chest. Pure Che Guevara.

Marvin Gallegos nudged Bugatti. "There's your man."

"I see him. Pretty brazen, showing up here like this. Doesn't the man know he's one of the country's most-wanted fugitives?"

Gallegos looked at the specimens of humanity around them. "What place could be safer than here?" he replied.

Three minutes later the militiamen led them out to the parking lot to a windowless van that was devoid of any markings except for the mud-caked license plates. It had taken Moonie Quale only a split second to get the mob inside good and worked up, and angry yelling could still be heard from the cafeteria. "This is the end of our glorious empire!" he'd cried. "That fucking communist bastard Bruce Jansen isn't taking our weapons from us. He ain't gonna make life easier for the niggers and the beaners and the Arabs—I'll see to *that*!" he'd sworn, before punching his chest in the White-Headed Eagles salute.

They'd applauded him like he was some kind of pop superstar, these completely ordinary truck drivers from all over the country, screaming a fresh round of insults at the TV screen for good measure. It was an extremely disquieting spectacle. If President Jansen had been there, he might have had second thoughts. The question was whether he had any idea what he'd set in motion, and if Vice President Lerner might have been right in suggesting he had a screw loose.

Marvin Gallegos and Bugatti were shown into the closed-off back portion of the van, and there they sat in silence, listening as the asphalt under them was replaced by a bumpy, gravel road. The scent of crops grew stronger, and more and more dust was finding its way into the back of the van, indicating that they were way out in the country. Gallegos tried unsuccessfully to keep his equipment in place between his legs, and Bugatti looked at his watch for the fifth time. It was ten past ten in the morning. They must be at least fifteen miles away from Taver's Cliff by now. He assumed they were driving north, since the tiny crack of light that came through the double rear doors shone in towards the left. He also heard a freight train close by, hauling its way through the countryside.

Then the van reduced its speed and turned sharply. They could feel the van find two even wheel ruts in the road, so the ride became smoother.

"This is a hell of a situation. Why couldn't it have been yesterday, before Jansen went on television?" the cameraman wondered out loud, shaking his head.

"Take it easy, Marvin. The *timing's* not good, I'd be the first to admit, but the *interview* will be—you can be sure of it."

"But they're crazy, these people. Just listen to them. Jansen's really stoked some inferno that's raging in their sick brains."

Bugatti frowned and listened to the shouting coming from the other side of the van's partition. It had definitely grown louder, so that now the words could be heard clearly. It was a chorus of hatred. They were going to poke Jansen's eyes out, the men up in the cab. Slit the throats of the entire administration. Submerge the country in a sea of blood.

Bugatti didn't doubt for a moment that they meant every word they said. Just as long as they didn't start with journalists.

A half hour later they were led into a room with a high, oak-beamed ceiling. Enormous windows were divided into small panes, offering a great panorama of the surrounding farmhouse-dotted landscape. Everything in the room was tidy and completely restored. Driving by this farm, one would never suspect it housed the country's supreme violence-preaching militia leader.

Bugatti began counting the semiautomatic weapons that were deployed in locked racks along the walls. There were at least fifty, and above them hung huge photostats of the corpses of Martin Luther King, Robert Kennedy, John F. Kennedy, and Malcolm X. The far wall was practically covered by a tapestry with the white-headed eagle woven into a thicket of thorns and heathen symbols. There were no swastikas to be seen anywhere, but gold-framed portraits of Hitler and Milošević had their place of honor above the fireplace.

There they sat another half hour, staring at each other and the satanic wall decorations, while angry outbursts grew in volume in the room next door.

"I think Quale's on the phone, talking with some of the other militia leaders," said Bugatti's cameraman.

Bugatti began to sweat. Just as long as the cretins in there didn't suddenly suspect they were being overheard. He looked at Marvin. "I don't doubt it. You saw Quale's face when the president announced he was going to forbid people possessing ammunition without special permission, that you'd have to apply in writing for something that's always been a constitutionally guaranteed right."

The cameraman shook his head. "He doesn't give a damn, just like all the rest of the militias. Who's going to disarm them? The local sheriff?" He began laughing. It was a laugh Bugatti was glad he'd never heard before—and hoped he'd never hear again.

The laughter stopped abruptly. "No, John, what bothers Moonie the most is skin color. Jansen's law proposal will mean that tons of black and brown criminals will be back on the streets. *That's* what really pisses him off. Shit, it pisses me off, too!"

"The amnesty will include everybody, as I understand. Also criminal white folks."

"Yeah, but that's not what's bothering Quale, is it?"

Bugatti shook his head. He didn't believe for a second that Jansen's plan had a chance in hell. The speaker of the House was a Republican, an archconservative. There was an overwhelming majority in both chambers of Congress for a tightening of legal procedure, and no one had ever before proposed such extensive legislation without both parties and all the lobbies first having been thoroughly acquainted with it. The proposals were doomed. Jansen knew the legislative rules of the game, for Christ's sake, so why even try? It was incredible. He'd barely stated his agenda and the vice president had resigned, even publicly suggesting the president was mentally unstable. Jansen would face a massive barrage of criticism in the days to come. He'd be forced to resign or be removed from office within a week.

"Shh, they're coming now," whispered Gallegos, and positioned himself behind his camera. Moonie Quale had taken off his military uniform and replaced it with an impeccable coal-gray suit.

Here was a man who knew how he wanted to appear to a television audience.

Marvin lifted his camera, and Moonie Quale waved his shaved-headed bodyguards to the side of the room. Bugatti nodded to his cameraman. They were rolling.

"I thank the gentlemen of the press for making the long journey," Quale began. "We've been looking forward for a long time to explaining on national TV what our organization stands for, so that all Americans will understand that we only want what's best for the USA. But unfortunately events make it necessary to cancel this interview. The situation has changed—suddenly we're at war!" He looked straight into the camera. "I want America to know that Moonie Quale is going to prevent our mad leader's crusade! God bless America!"

He gave the cameraman a sign to stop filming and turned to his bald-headed cronies to bask in their approval. He was as theatrical as Mussolini but no doubt also as murderous as Saddam. Bugatti dried the sweat from his brow. It looked like they were going to let him and Marvin go. Moonie Quale's only demand was that the brief recorded sequence be broadcast on all the nation's TV networks.

He didn't have to worry. Bugatti could guarantee it.

"As a security precaution, I'm afraid I'm going to have to ask you to put these on," he said courteously, handing them two black scarves that he instructed them to affix tightly over their eyes.

Before doing as he was told, Bugatti had a final question: "So what's going to happen now?"

Moonie smiled. "If you can't figure it out for yourself, then there's not much to do about it."

They were pushed out into the back of the van again, only this time it was quiet up front. All Bugatti could hear was a faint car radio being changed from station to station, all of them discussing the same topic. The president of the United States had grossly overstepped his authority.

After ten minutes a voice broke in on all the networks, cutting off the babbling commentators, the skeptical local politicians, and the ecstatic analysts. The New York sniper had struck again. This time it was in two different locations at almost the same time.

CHAPTER 11

WESLEY'S DREAD OF THE MEDIA'S FIRST REACTION THE NEXT MORNING MEANT he didn't sleep that night.

But the White House press secretary received help from the most undesirable quarter imaginable: a despicable, merciless murderer who lay in waiting where normal people were supposed to be safe. If it hadn't been for the New York sniper, the attacks on President Jansen would have completely dominated every TV station's prime-time news program. It was hardly a coincidence to rejoice over.

The sniper struck, killing three people, less than two hours after the president presented the first stage of his controversial law-and-order bill. Two of them—a couple in their forties—were felled on 14th Street, just outside a shop that sold secondhand DVDs, and a mere forty minutes later a seven-year-old girl was killed with a single shot at a playground in Liberty State Park. Same caliber, same weapon.

Now the threat had crept outside the boundaries of Manhattan.

The same evening, a letter was found lying on a counter in the arrivals hall of John F. Kennedy International Airport. It was addressed to Mayor Springfield and consisted of just five words: "Bronx, Brooklyn, Queens—who cares?"

The city came to a complete standstill.

He'd been sitting in his office from the moment the press conference ended. How many hours ago that was, Wesley didn't know. He was dead tired and had no more to say, and the whole world wanted to talk with him. The president's law proposal was going to be debated in Congress in three-quarters of an hour, and then things would get even worse.

Wesley's mother had called a while ago and told him with a tearful voice that his father had taken all his boxes of cartridges out of the pantry and hidden them somewhere he wouldn't tell her. He sure as hell wasn't going to be disarmed, he'd said. The incident had frightened her and made her wonder whether something nasty might happen to Wesley, considering how bad the situation was getting.

She didn't define what "something nasty" might be, but Wesley took the words seriously because he was feeling the same way himself. He'd have to keep his distance when he was with President Jansen outside the White House. He didn't want to die or end up in a wheelchair like Reagan's press secretary James Brady. A would-be assassin could appear out of nowhere; NBC's alarming interview with Moonie Quale had just been aired and helped fan the flames. In any case, all right- and left-wing fanatics could agree on one thing from now on: Jansen and his lackeys had to go.

Open season had been declared on them.

He closed his eyes and tried to forget everything; his body felt heavier and heavier. Silent images slid by of his brother and himself standing on the veranda, using Budweiser bottles for shooting practice. And images of his father cheering when they scored a direct hit.

"Are you there, Wesley?" The voice was far away, and Wesley almost couldn't open his eyes. The figure stood before him, leaning over his desk. "Have you a moment?"

He opened his eyes grudgingly to find himself staring straight into his president's serious face.

"Take it easy!" he said, when Wesley flew out of his seat, attempting to adjust his clothing. The president sat down on the edge of the desk and asked Wesley to sit down again.

"Lance Burton and Donald Beglaubter will be here shortly to confer with you. I have to tell you there's been an assassination attempt on Attorney General Stephen Lovell and the chief justice of the Supreme Court."

Wesley felt his shirt sticking to his body. "An assassination attempt? Where? What happened?"

"They were on their way to Congress in the attorney general's car when it was hit by an explosion. We believe it was a bazooka, but we'll know in due time."

"Oh, God." Now Wesley remembered. "They were on their way to present the bill. What happened to them? Are they alive?"

"The chief justice was killed instantly, but the latest reports say that Lovell will survive."

Wesley shook his head. He simply couldn't comprehend it.

"We'll be postponing the congressional debate for security reasons," Jansen continued, "but we have to make a statement to the press before long. Do you think you can handle it, Wesley? I've briefed Lance Burton about what is to be said."

"Yes, yes, of course!" Wesley nodded, but he didn't mean it. He wasn't at all sure he could. What the hell were they going to want him to say?

The president stood up. "I value your loyalty greatly. You've already been fantastic. Your speech this morning was intelligent and very clear. We've already received positive reactions from Handgun Control, Inc., and several other gun control groups. They're very satisfied with our initiative. I'm sure you'll have a plaque under Jim Brady's in the pressroom one day. Maybe they'll even name the room after you. Who knows?"

Wesley's lips were dry. He attempted a smile, but discouragement seeped through his brain like acid rain. "So I suppose you've also heard from the gun lobbies. For sure the National Rifle Association's reaction was the opposite, wasn't it?"

"Don't you worry about the NRA or other organizations like that, Wesley. Just worry about telling the world an assassination has taken place and that it emphasizes the need for our proposals. That we must therefore do something drastic *now*!"

"Something drastic?"

"Speak with Lance Burton and Donald Beglaubter and meet me in a half hour in the Oval Office."

In the course of three hours the entire country was turned upside down. The news of Supreme Court Chief Justice Theodore Manning's violent death and the attorney general's injury sent all decent people into a state of shock.

At the same time, bomb threats were phoned into several liberal newspapers, Congress, two independent movie studios, countless pacifist organizations, and a major San Francisco art gallery that had just opened an exhibition entitled *Artists against Violence*.

Despite an intense manhunt, Moonie Quale succeeded in going underground and giving telephone interviews to several national radio stations with a deafeningly clear message: The White-Headed Eagles, Indiana's Partisans, the Rushmore Defenders, and all other related militia groups in the country were going into battle against the government's plans. They weren't behind the attack on the attorney general and the Supreme Court chief justice, and they had nothing to do with the bomb threats, but they'd soon take action in their own way. They didn't intend to let themselves be disarmed.

It was at this point that Jansen held a meeting with security chief Billy Johnson and the head of FEMA, the country's emergency management agency. The volatile situation sent shock waves throughout the West Wing. This led to a marked increase in White House activity that was matched by the increased presence of star-studded, medal-festooned uniforms.

Spokespeople for the NRA poured forth in the media, screaming to high heaven about violations of the Constitution and the Second Amendment's incontestable assurance of United States citizens' right to defend themselves with their own weapons. How were they supposed to do so without ammunition? This was a breach of the Constitution, and the president must resign.

Naturally, they were supported by the ammunition manufacturers' lawyers. And in the meantime, there were more shootings on the street than ever. People argued about nothing and everything and about the right to hit back, when justified. They stormed all the supermarkets and shops that sold ammunition. Weapon manufacturers' stocks shot up, and especially down, until the stock market had to close trading.

Everything seemed to be completely out of control. People in the streets and in housing projects were in a rage, and the representatives of law and order powerless. It was reminiscent of the race riots after the beating of Rodney King.

This was just what Michael K. Lerner needed. The just-resigned vice president was gladly giving interviews to anyone who asked. He was ready to try to depose the president by applying section 4 of the Constitution's Twenty-Fifth Amendment. And, even though everyone knew this would be more than difficult since thus far the president had shown no signs of lacking the ability to act, the vice president's allusions to the president's mental derangement were discussed far and wide.

All in all, there were plenty of problems to deal with.

Prayers were said for the attorney general in the churches and on prime-time TV shows, and even though the television was blaring constantly in Wesley's office, he no longer heard what was happening. He retreated into his mental inner sanctum, a quiet little world where he imagined everything was under control, where he felt alone but not impotent.

He often sat here dreaming about the feel of a woman's skin, particularly Doggie Rogers's. When all this was over with, he knew what he'd spend his time doing.

He opened his eyes and looked down at the papers before him. Back to reality.

He'd just written a reasonably good speech for Jansen about the profound state of mourning throughout the land after the loss of its highest court's chief justice, Theodore Manning, "the most ruthlessly just human being this nation has ever seen."

Next, he'd sent a strong warning to Moonie Quale and the other militia leaders regarding their plans and threats. No one should be in any doubt that anyone threatening the country's security would be dealt with harshly. Under no condition would the risk of a new Oklahoma City bombing arise.

Later in the day, after a record-breaking number of shooting fatalities, a temporary total ban on the sale of weapons and ammunition was decreed throughout the land.

The president himself went on television to tell the nation. There was no alternative, he stated, in spite of strong protests all the way down to the smallest sheriff's department. All law enforcement agencies had to brace themselves for an extra-heavy workload for a long time to come. From this day on, no one who broke the law was to feel safe. This was Day Zero, as he put it.

By nightfall it was apparent that the police had too much to handle, so FEMA was mobilized in accordance with Executive Order 13010. Two hours later the military proclaimed its full support for the president and its readiness to go into action. The national security level was set up a notch, and suddenly the country, in effect, was in a state of emergency.

The following day Wesley's office was overwhelmed by phone calls from the press. At four in the afternoon, when his secretary had broken down in tears and been sent home, he'd tried to find Doggie to replace her, but she was busy elsewhere. All the offices in the West Wing were strained to the breaking point. There were reports of more bomb threats, this time against waterworks, dams, and Disneyland, and the national security alert went up to orange.

At 2:00 A.M. Wesley finally called it quits and left his office. Accompanied by a team of bodyguards, he went out into the Washington night. Hundreds of people were staring up at the White House as though it housed the devil himself. A wall of journalists screamed out their accusations and frustrations, forcing him to retreat into an official vehicle. A familiar face squeezed its way towards the car and was stopped by the bodyguards. It was John Bugatti in a wrinkled shirt that appeared not to have been changed for months.

Wesley rolled down the window.

"You can't do this, Wesley! You have to give me an interview."

"What about all the other journalists?"

"Wesley, there are rumors that the president's going to appoint Sunderland vice president. Do you have any comment on this?"

"Where'd you hear that?"

"Let's go to your office for fifteen minutes, and I'll tell you."

Wesley looked around. The crush of reporters and their cameramen was about to break through the barrier of security personnel.

"Tomorrow, John. You'll get your interview tomorrow!"

The next morning they were assembled in the Oval Office, and Jansen's appointment of Sunderland as interim vice president was confirmed. None of the staff commented on this, including Sunderland, but naturally he wasn't unhappy about the development. He'd always had a good relationship with politicians from both parties, in both chambers of Congress. There wasn't much chance of any objections from that quarter.

"You're on in twenty minutes, Wesley," said Jansen. "Tell the journalists like it is, and tell them that Congress's hearing regarding Sunderland's appointment will have to wait. The situation at hand makes this necessary; we need peace in the White House so we can work."

Wesley avoided Sunderland's self-satisfied gaze. He found he had to force his legs to convey him to the pressroom.

The press conference was over in less than five minutes, even though the journalists had enough questions for five days. They drowned one another out with words like *unconstitutional, fascism,* and *insanity,* as well as terms such as *state of panic, vague decree,* and *new election.* It was too much at once, but patience and endurance came with Barefoot's job.

Afterwards, Wesley waved his friend John Bugatti out of the crowd and led him down to the Green Room. A couple of French Empire chairs had been placed in front of the fireplace, and President Jansen was standing at the window, looking out over a forest of signboards bobbing above a mass of demonstrators behind the White House.

He asked Bugatti to take a seat.

Bugatti wanted to know if he could use his cell phone camera as they talked, and Jansen consented by righting his hair.

They spoke quietly for a few minutes, and Jansen's expression darkened slightly when Bugatti warned his president that the situation was slipping out of control.

"We'll have martial law in this country before we know it. Is that what the president wants?" asked Bugatti.

"The only thing I want is for all Americans to live peacefully with each other. The means that will be used to achieve this will be decided by all of us. You have to be positive about this, John. You represent one of our most powerful media. You're an important player in this game."

Bugatti sat still for a moment, allowing the yelling of the crowd outside to become clearly audible. "Mr. President, I'm just trying to say that this is all moving too fast. Let Congress work with the problems so we have a proper legal basis."

"Gladly! But will it ever happen? Think of all the times it's been tried."

Wesley looked at Jansen. Did he really say that to a journalist who was seen by millions of people every day?

"I know, but the parliamentary process is the only way. One simply has to follow the beaten track. I think you know this better than anyone!"

They were interrupted by a knock on the door, and Communications Chief Lance Burton slipped into the room. He stopped when he saw Bugatti, but Jansen asked him to say what was on his mind, adding that he had nothing to hide from his old traveling companion.

Lance Burton's face usually bore a somber expression that could be difficult to read. Still, his demeanor seemed far graver than normal. "Sir," he said, and had to swallow. "A bomb has gone off in the Democratic headquarters in Madison, Wisconsin. Many were killed. We think everyone who was there because the building was leveled."

Wesley's head fell to his chest. It was a catastrophe.

President Jansen looked at Lance Burton for a long while before he again turned to face Bugatti.

"Be careful about what you write and say on television the next couple of days, John. You'll be doing us all a favor."

Wesley could clearly sense the threat behind the words. He felt like he was going to be sick.

CHAPTER 12

SHERIFF T. PERKINS'S DEPUTY HAD WOKEN HIM UP AT THREE IN THE MORNING.
A bunch of youths had just driven down the main street, emptying
the magazines of their semiautomatic rifles up into the air along
the way.

The officers on the scene had reason to suspect who'd done it, and
now they wanted a search warrant. As if that were possible at this
time of night.

He hadn't gone back to bed after that. Instead he'd driven to his
office, where he'd plopped down into a chair with his hat pulled down
over his eyes. But his thoughts wouldn't leave him in peace.

For as long as T. Perkins had been sheriff, nothing abominable had
occurred in his jurisdiction. Nothing really abominable, that is. Of
course there'd been murders. Things like that happened when people
had sex with someone else's partner or set each other's barn on fire,
but the acts had never been incomprehensible. No, for the most part
they were occasional incidents involving a few wild kids or girls who
complained about men making rude passes at them or minor brawls
after a few drinks Friday night. The last serious robbery-murder was
ten years ago now, the last consummated rape three years ago. He
remembered all his cases clearly.

His first case as deputy sheriff of Highland County was probably
still the one he remembered best. Leo Mulligan murdered his wife
with a baseball bat and was hospitalized indefinitely for safekeeping
at the mental hospital that came to be called the Marion Correctional

Treatment Center. It was a case that had become current again, in a way, since Leo had recently been declared well and released a few months short of thirty-two years in the mental ward. Once again he was living in his old shack east of town, and there was no cause for alarm as long as he stayed inconspicuous.

The marriage had produced one son, Leo Mulligan Jr., and it was he who was the main focus of attention in the newspapers. Tragically, the boy had witnessed his father beating his mother to death and shortly after questioning had vanished into thin air. Leo Jr. was still underage, and an intense manhunt was launched but without result. It was only some months later he was found by chance a few counties to the east, and not in a disheveled, pathetic state, as one might expect, but as a well-groomed, well-dressed, attractive young man who was at least as good-looking as the most successful boys from the great mansions around Middleburg. For a while no one seemed able to solve the mystery of what the boy had been up to in the meantime. It took an eau de cologne–scented letter to a local newspaper from a very frustrated woman to finally reveal how Leo Jr. had been transformed from ugly duckling to handsome swan. Since fleeing home, Leo Jr. had prospered by blackmailing married women he'd slept with, and the newspaper printed a big photograph of the boy along with a detailed reference to the letter they'd purchased from one of the women. It developed into a huge scandal, since plenty of wives had fallen for his youthful charms, and many domestic conflicts began erupting in the area around Highway 50, from Upperville to Gilbert's Corner. The boy himself was dragged through an embarrassing custody case and finally adopted. The net result was at least fifteen divorces and a few cuckolds who'd hanged themselves in the course of the dark winter months, their honor defamed. It was the kind of case no one forgot.

But since T. Perkins had been made sheriff, there hadn't been much to get worked up over, which folks mistakenly attributed to his performance in office rather than the record-low unemployment that a series of new businesses had brought to the region. And now this, too, was history.

T. Perkins had been furious every single day since Washington had lost its head. T had a difficult time understanding how his old traveling buddy from the trip to China could shake up this quiet little Appalachian Mountain community to such a degree. How their quiet existences could be given such radically new ground rules.

What the hell had happened to the cozy, neighborly evenings with the locals? Where were the invitations to the corn-on-the-cob barbecues and coffee parties leading up to the annual festivities? Now, of course, he didn't have time for anything, anyway, and people didn't want to see him, either. He was the tool of the enemy, when it came down to it.

The bombing of Democratic headquarters in Madison, Wisconsin, had sent the good old days down the toilet.

After four days the White-Headed Eagles took responsibility for the Madison bombing. They described the attack down to the smallest detail. How they'd placed the bomb on the second floor in the statistical analysis center of the Wisconsin Office of Justice Assistance, how the devilish instrument had been constructed and where they'd gotten the explosives. There wasn't much to investigate. The bomb had caused the building to collapse, and all that Moonie Quale and his insane disciples hated had been crushed beneath tons of concrete and twisted steel: the Democratic headquarters, the AIDS center, the statistical analysis center. The debris had ravaged the pedestrian street that lay in front of the building like a tropical storm, injuring hundreds of people. Chunks of concrete landed in Landon Street, yard-long beams wound up in Lake Mandota, and all the windows had been sucked out of their frames, from Henry Street to the state capitol. Sheets of colored paper from Art Mart in the building next door blew around the city for days. More than two hundred people died. It was a sickness of epidemic proportion, evident wherever you looked, to which President Jansen and his people had reacted amazingly harshly and uncompromisingly.

There had been a state of emergency for five days, and militia groups around the country had assembled. T dared not try to imagine what would happen if they struck again as devastatingly as they had in Wisconsin.

But the fact was that it could happen anytime, anywhere. FEMA—the Federal Emergency Management Agency—and the National Security Council, as well as the Department of Homeland Security, suddenly had plenty of work to do.

Differences of opinion flared up over trivialities, and people were furious about the new restrictions. Shooting incidents were on the rise in T. Perkins's own district, with two killed and several hospitalized. People hoarding ammunition cleaned out the country's stocks within hours. Selling it was now illegal, but there was none left to sell, anyway. People had stockpiled so much, they were equipped for this war and the next one, too.

A few days previously the nation's sheriff's offices had been ordered to check all credit card transactions during the past four days and confiscate all this ammunition. The Second Amendment allowed people to own guns but not necessarily bullets. The emergency laws that were created by executive decree took advantage of this fact, despite an overwhelming rage of opposition.

Confiscating the ammunition was easier said than done. For example, how the hell were they supposed to find two boxes of nine-millimeter shells on a farm half the size of downtown Washington, DC? Or how did the government imagine they were supposed to take Joe Fiske's shotgun shells from him when no one knew where he was? He knew the surrounding mountains better than any of them. And even if they found him, how could they make themselves do it, knowing Joe lived off the game he shot in his own forest? This wasn't Moonie Quale, for Christ's sake.

But what confused T. Perkins the most were the statements coming out of the White House pressroom every day. Apparently, the people in the White House did as they pleased. Of course there was massive resistance in both chambers of Congress, but now the country was in the highest state of alert, and FEMA was all-powerful. There were plenty of executive orders to choose from. *The Constitution was doing time in the doghouse,* thought T. And the implications were far-reaching.

The president had declared he was going to disarm America and empty the prisons at the same time. All sentences were to be converted to community service and the prisons used for other purposes.

Big, tough prison guards would become babysitters; they were to serve as pedagogues for habitual criminals and sick bastards who flipped out over a pair of bare tits or a nose that curved the wrong way. How were prison officers who'd made their living by giving orders and commanding respect with a bristling key ring and nightstick at their belt supposed to suddenly sit down and figure out a work plan for a brain-dead convict? And how was one supposed to punish the multitude of idiots who were running around now, using one another for target practice with banned ammunition? How was one to punish them, when they'd be released so quicky again, anyway? T didn't understand it, and he wasn't alone. There were all the Republicans, plus NRA lovers, members of Congress, and the lobbyists, to name a few. But what the hell difference did it make whether they understood or not? No one had any say in the matter as long as the president, the National Security Council, Homeland Security—and thereby also FEMA—agreed and had control over the generals so the National Guard and military could keep the country in a vise of emergency laws. There were already convoys of combat-ready troops patrolling the roads and highways every couple of hours.

He'd called Doggie Rogers to try and find out what to expect, but she knew nothing. She worked every single day, all day long, just fifty yards from the president of the United States, yet she knew nothing.

And now they were in the process of filling their jail like never before. The mere six cells he had at his disposal were loaded to the brim long ago. This, too, led to problems. Big, black Benni had ended up in the same cell with big, white Les Tanner, and they'd knocked each other's teeth out and bloodied up the floor so much that the eccentric, old cleaning lady was sure to have a fit. And as if that weren't enough, they'd forgotten a drunk in the shack behind the jail, and now he'd gone and shit and thrown up all over the place. The local volunteer fire department that used the room to store some of their equipment would lynch him.

This was fucking getting out of hand. Now they also had to find room for three more unruly kids who'd felt they needed to prove they still had ammunition and dared to use it.

Pretty soon only the broom closet would be left.

The telephone rang on T. Perkins's desk, and he shoved his hat back. "Yeah?"

"Chief, you've gotta come out here. I'm at Jim Wahlers's place. You're not gonna believe your own eyes!"

Jim Wahlers was an inoffensive guy who most people didn't have much to say about other than he was the town's undertaker and had three first-rate daughters and a wife who didn't mind telling them if the vegetables weren't fresh in Walmart. A sociable guy who looked after his job and had never bothered anyone.

His house was enormous—death being good, constant business—and it had been home to three generations of undertakers, so far. There was a vegetable garden, a two-car garage, and a two-hundred-square-yard cellar with a pool table and dartboard. T. Perkins had often been down there in his younger days when he was the town's dart champ, and Jim had been almost as good. It had been a nice cellar to practice in.

And here he stood again, as he did then, with his set of darts in his shirt pocket. He recognized the brown-painted stairs, the paneling they'd so often leaned up against with beers in their hands, the fine network of water pipes that branched off along the ceiling.

But then came everything he didn't recognize.

His men nodded and shrugged their shoulders when they saw his jaw drop. They'd just been through that same reaction.

All the walls' surfaces had been redecorated since the time when they were covered with movie posters and the Virginia state flag. There were still posters, but they were new ones, not from horror movies with rubber masks and screaming teenagers. No more sensual lip contact with Ingrid Bergman and Veronica Lake. No, this was clearly something else. T had never known that there were so many militia groups in the country that engaged in activities such as printing up posters like the ones stuck up on Jim Wahlers's cellar walls. He'd actually had no idea there were so many militia groups, period. The White-Headed Eagles,

the Bunker Group from Texas, Ohio's First National Pioneers, and dozens of others like them. Hanging side by side, these recruitment posters
were a fashion show of unintentionally comical uniforms, camouflage
makeup smeared across bare skin, displays of huge hand weapons, and
big, confident smiles inspired by the ardor of self-righteousness and the
need to demonstrate who wore the pants in the family.

"And look back here!" called his deputy.

T. Perkins went into the room where they'd once planted their
manhood in a pair of older redheaded sisters. He stood looking at
forty to fifty cartons. Each carton contained thirty-six boxes of two
hundred cartridges each. A little quick figuring, and that made more
than three hundred thousand rounds of ammunition.

"What have you done with Jim?"

"He's sitting in his bedroom, holding his wife's hand. He won't
move. He says we have to leave, that we have no business here. That
he hasn't done anything."

T. Perkins looked at the three weapon cabinets. "He hasn't, strictly
speaking, has he?"

"He bought the ammunition yesterday. It must have cost a fortune."

"Did you get the keys from him?" He nodded towards the cabinets.

"Here they are!" Dody Hall attempted to crowd into the room.
She'd been the latest addition to the sheriff's department.

He unlocked the cabinets and threw the doors open. Either Jim
Wahlers's funeral business was more profitable than he'd imagined, or
else he had some like-minded associates.

"Wow!" said Dody Hall.

There were enough semiautomatic guns and rifles to arm at least
three hundred men. But that wasn't the worst thing. What was worse
were the hand grenades. T had seen what they could do during a
training session for some soldiers in Richmond. If one of them were
used against a human being, Jim Wahlers could forget all about traditional funerals.

CHAPTER 13

NEW YORK CITY WAS IN A NASTY MOOD, AND ROSALIE LEE WAS SCARED.

Down in the subways, there were only two topics of conversation. One was President Jansen's law-and-order program that was coming to be known as the Washington Decree; the other was the sniper killings. But as soon as people were aboveground, they forgot all about President Jansen and his decree. The risk of their own sudden, random death took precedence, and it was only "The Killer on the Roof" that mattered. A bullet had taken the life of a little boy the day before as he walked along the street, holding his mother's hand, and the day before it had been a lady just like Rosalie. The woman's little stroll down 14th Street had proved fatal, but it sold newspapers. From the front-page pictures it was obvious she'd been in the process of buying fruit from a street market. Bananas and oranges littered the sidewalk, and her white T-shirt was splattered with blood as she lay there, her brown grocery bag crushed under her heavy body.

Rosalie hated the trip to her office downtown. She hated creeping along, as close to the walls of buildings as possible, and she hated glancing involuntarily at the rooftops all the time. She was frightened to death at the thought of the pain, the thought of the bullet boring its way into her body and knocking her to the ground.

By now the killer had twenty-one people's lives on his conscience, at least one a day. By now everyone knew someone who knew someone who knew one of the victims. She herself had met a man whose wife's nephew had been shot right in the temple and left half his cranium at the corner of East 59th Street and First Avenue. On the news, they said the killer had been sitting on the aerial cable car to Roosevelt Island, but it wasn't true. There was no lack of theories and speculation, but in the meantime he kept holding all the cards.

Each night Rosalie prayed they'd find him, that he wasn't black, and that her three sons would come home safe and sound. She feared what else could befall her boys on the streets of New York these days. And it wasn't only New York that had its hands full. Demonstrations in Chicago had been met with water cannons, and at night the National Guard were shooting rubber bullets at people who gathered on street corners. Roadblocks had been set up across the country, train and air traffic was being minutely monitored, and some bus routes had been temporarily shut down.

The country had been turned upside down.

Moonie Quale had raised the stakes ten days previously when he called together the leaders of the country's most rabid militias, continuously spreading his poisonous propaganda through a much-too-eager media at the same time. People in camouflage uniforms from every corner of the country had expressed their support for the perpetrators of the Madison bombing, after which they declared war on the government. They'd all reached the same conclusion: It was time to respond to the Jansen administration's abuse of power. The murdering of congressmen and local federal officials began immediately. The first night elicited a series of bombings and assassinations, and the next morning the nation's streets were full of police. The bombings continued throughout the day, and all levels of the judicial and defense systems were put on high alert.

Rosalie was sitting in her comfy green easy chair when President Jansen broke into a TV program to decree that the country was in a state of emergency. His face was so dark with anger that his voice trembled as he spoke. After that, things moved fast. In the course of twenty-four hours Congress was effectively emasculated, and emergency executive powers and presidential decrees became the order of the day. On the first evening more than half the land's newspapers and TV channels were temporarily shut down in accordance with Executive Order 10995.

The journalists' union could protest all it liked, and political groups on all levels, too, for that matter. Jansen's Washington Decree and FEMA's control of the situation were real life now, whether people liked it or not.

After that, life was tougher for everyone, not least of all in New York. Rosalie lived with her three small-time delinquent sons—plus five thousand other people—all within the radius of a couple of hundred yards, for whom justice depended on keeping a sharp blade or loaded piece in your back pocket. Here the illusion of law and order had evaporated ages ago; one had to survive as best one could. It was hard being a "law-abiding citizen" in the South Bronx, with or without a state of emergency. There was no doubt about that.

Rosalie's boys—James, Frank, and Dennis—had a lot in common: two-and-a-half-years age difference between the oldest and the youngest, each one physically fit and irresistible to the opposite sex, and all quick to talk back with their mouths as well as their fists. The others called them Huey, Louie, and Dewey—but not within earshot. These were three dudes who demanded respect and wasted no time in seeing to it they got it. She had tried to instill in them God's words about turning the other cheek and loving one's neighbor, but they weren't fast learners in this respect, which worried their mother. They were pretty touchy and slapped people around on the slightest pretense. None of them had been in jail yet, but now it seemed just a matter of time—if they lived that long.

Rosalie dared not follow this train of thought to its conclusion. Several of her girlfriends had lost sons; one had lost two. She loved her sons dearly, in spite of their glaring shortcomings. She tried to picture them, graying at the temples, her anchor and protectors when she reached old age. Rosalie's most fervent wish was for them to get out of the ghetto, and therefore she wasn't one of those who immediately condemned Jansen and his decree. Her sons did, of course, but not she.

The way things had gotten in the United States, there was a chance the decree might help. Help make it possible to walk the streets unafraid, without having to step around society's human discards, without having to see people with no hope of redemption. Without having to watch drugs course through families' lives and their children's veins.

Rosalie wanted so very much for her boys to listen to her, for them to avoid the consequences of the president's law-and-order campaign. That they avoid getting picked up bearing loaded weapons and stop taking dumb risks.

The Washington Decree had pulled American society up by the roots. People were returning from the prisons, most of them with money in their pockets and a brand-new job that consisted of keeping the neighborhood's youth out of trouble. Skeptical liberal elements had analyzed the situation from every possible angle, while the Republicans in Congress—and by now also a large portion of the Democrats—were screaming themselves blue in the face over what they saw as a case of letting foxes guard the chicken coop. But Rosalie Lee saw it altogether differently. These adolescent ex-cons weren't interested in landing back behind bars, and now they had something useful to do with their lives. Their parole officers were no longer their judges but their peers. They had the same goals, more or less the same pay, and they spoke the same language. Their job basically consisted of making the best out of practically nothing. Like getting the boys from the Latino gangs and the black brotherhoods to give up their weapons, getting them out of the alleys and into detox clinics.

Each of those released from prison was given five boys from different street gangs to supervise. Kids who had previously been enemies were forced to behave together, else they could expect a whupping. They did things where they had fun and laughed together, and occasionally learned something. They checked out Wall Street and got free tickets to the movies—stuff like that.

Gang members still dissed other gang members when they were back on their home turf, but now violence rarely escalated beyond the stage of rhetoric. Somehow it didn't feel right, beating someone up who you'd spent the afternoon having a good time with. There were still ugly episodes, but they were fewer and fewer. In some strange way it was like there was a new kind of solidarity in the neighborhoods, and the streets brought people together instead of dividing them.

In any case, Rosalie Lee was beginning to feel more secure in Throgs Neck than around Manhattan, the favorite haunt of the sniper.

Then her second-born son, Frank, came home one evening, wide-eyed, on crack, and in a vindictive rage after having been shot in the calf. The scene changed instantly. James, Frank, and Dennis quickly collected all the ammunition they had hidden around the apartment that their mother hadn't succeeded in searching out herself. Then they loaded their weapons and took off on a punishment expedition. Rosalie never found out what happened later, but three black kids were killed in the Bronx in the course of that night. She didn't really want to know more.

She was sick with dread, however, and confiscated the boys' guns while they slept. She took them down to Eastchester Bay and threw them as far out into the water as her heavy arms would allow. She listened to the boys' police radio for a couple of hours, and when no mention was made of any suspects in the Bronx killings, she decided to keep her fears and suspicions to herself.

That night she didn't sleep a wink. She repeatedly climbed out of bed, got down on her knees, and prayed. "Dear God," she whispered, "please spare my boys!"

Since Rosalie was born—three blocks away, forty-eight years ago—she'd been out of New York City only two times in her life. Once when she visited her sister in Virginia and was on the quiz show, the other the trip to China. Both occasions had been like gifts from heaven, but both times she'd thanked the Lord for being able to come back to the streets of the Bronx—these obscure clefts that crisscrossed mile after mile of dismal apartment blocks. Here her soul found respite; here was her world. In any case that's how it had been till the night her boys went out on their mission of vengeance. Now she wished they were all somewhere else, far away in the countryside.

She crossed herself and called out Jesus's name. Now her boys had possibly taken a life. Did that mean they were on their way into the abyss, just like thousands of souls before them who lived in the South Bronx? The consequences would be fatal if they were caught and found guilty. According to Jansen's decree, clemency was to be shown only for old offenses, not new ones, and definitely not ones involving homicide. A petty criminal could get off with a rehabilitation program and some months' community service, but not murderers—of course not. Short work was made of this kind of human garbage. It was the death sentence for them—end of story.

Eleven people had already been executed in Texas alone since the state of emergency had been declared. The condemned were executed around the country wherever there were proper facilities, and the process was sped up as well. Vice President Sunderland had declared that all death rows would be empty by autumn. That was one a day, he figured—at least. This now often entailed taking prisoners straight from death row to the execution chamber without a last visit from loved ones, without a last phone call, and without a last couple of hours' chance for quiet reflection—all of which used to be considered a condemned prisoner's unalienable right. But this was how it was now, no matter how loud the angry chorus of protest from countless organizations, citizens, politicians, the media, and even foreign governments. If you killed someone after March 12, 2009, you were executed. Simple as that. There was no provision for a pardon. *Habeas Corpus*—indeed, the Bill of Rights—had been invalidated.

Rosalie Lee asked her sons if they'd done something that night they oughtn't. They laughed at her. They laughed when she begged them to stay home at night, and they laughed as they flashed their new weapons, oiled and loaded.

Rosalie had voted for Jansen for president and, as recently as a week ago, was fiercely defending his emergency edicts. Now she was no longer so certain. She had three sons, and, although far from perfect, they were still hers. They were all she had. She'd regret it bitterly for the rest of her days if one of them should end up paying with his life for that vote she'd cast.

CHAPTER 14

THERE WERE TWENTY-SIX MEN ON DEATH ROW IN SUSSEX STATE PRISON IN Waverly. Five had been executed, and four new ones had arrived. It was a place where good news was a thing of the past.

The prison guards had spitefully informed the inmates about what was happening in Washington. That fucking amateur "Dumbocrat" of a president was in the midst of an act of political suicide that threatened the future of the entire nation. They laughed like madmen when they spoke about the state of emergency, perhaps due to the general bloodlust that was pulsing through the country. Or maybe it was just their apprehension about what they were supposed to do now. In any case, it was clear they had no idea what the repercussions would be for them.

The redheaded guard they called Lassie laughed hysterically, as though to hide his uncertainty. "In four weeks we'll all be out of work!" he joked. Later the personnel were told something else, that their job was to get all the executions over with and then change to more "proper" work. Namely, working with young criminals who were not as hard-boiled as the condemned, and trying to get them back into society.

Bud's reaction was like that of most of the guards. He didn't believe the plan would work, but there was nothing to do about it. The prison was already busy with the executions. They were all to be exterminated like disease-bearing rats, end of story.

And he wasn't guilty.

He was hearing plenty of rumors, and most of them were confirmed. Bud's lawyers came with their black briefcases and regretted that there was nothing they could do. They regretted that all their appeals had been shelved in spite of their great efforts and protests. Bud wondered how these high-paid vultures would survive if all their clients were killed off. It wasn't that he sympathized with them, but he'd prefer other conditions for the demise of their profession. They'd already begun executions in Maryland after years of moratorium, the lawyers said. In Texas they were now up to two a day, sometimes three. As though this were something Bud wanted to know. As if he hadn't already stood witness to more than enough. Here in Virginia they were methodically taking them one at a time—this he'd verified with his own eyes. Five condemned men had already been towed past his cell, heads bowed and clenched fists bound behind their backs, straight from a last meal in their death-row cell to the execution chamber. Apparently, they were starting up at the end of the gangway with the man in cell one, then cell two, then cell three, and so on, until they started over with cell one. One per day until it was over. The cells were reoccupied as quickly as they were emptied. People were flipping out on the streets, he'd heard. Apparently, a couple of the new prisoners had tried to defend their right to keep their ammunition, and the ensuing gun battle had gotten out of hand. They hadn't really been aiming, they whined from their cells, but folks had a habit of dying if you hit them right.

A couple of days ago they'd been average American family men who'd flirted a bit with the militias.

Now they were already history.

Bud sat exactly in the middle in cell number fourteen. The original prisoners in cells one to five had already been dispatched to the next world, and every evening at six o'clock they'd fetched a new one and led him past the other inmates down to the execution chamber. When it was

Dave the pothead's turn in cell two, he screamed so shrilly that the echoes could still be heard the following day. He was a much smaller man than Bud had imagined, and his eyes had been livid with fear.

"The angels grow pot in heaven, Davey Boy!" Bud's neighbor Daryl laughed, and he rattled his bars with glee as the condemned man was hauled by. Bud could still hear them echoing, too.

Bud couldn't imagine being as jolly when it was Daryl's turn, and there were only seven and a half days left. March 29: the day before his own death.

Prison guard Pete was one of the few who didn't complain about what was happening in the outer world. He adapted, resigning himself for the time being in the belief that he'd soon find another job. He followed orders and stayed quiet. Which is why the chief prison guard put him on the night shift, meaning he was kept awake night after night by the oaths and whimpers of the man who was to give his life the following day. This was what he got for being passive and never protesting.

He used to sit way up at the exit door by cell number one on a rickety wooden chair, until the day it was pulverized when inmate number six tore himself loose from his executioners and lunged for the only defensive weapon in the vicinity. The chair's back broke the arm of the first guard, but that's as far as he got. They overpowered him and refused to let him speak with the priest before they stuck the needle in and pumped death into him.

After that, there were no more loose objects on death row. If Pete didn't want to use the metal folding seat attached to the wall, he'd have to stand up.

The first night, Pete stood leaning against the wall for three hours before boredom and numbness in his hamstring muscles drove him on a walk past the cells.

Bud had said his prayers and was now waiting, up against the bars of his cell. "Come on, come on!" he whispered. He was hoping that the child killer Robert and motormouth Daryl would let Pete pass without making a scene and waking up everyone else, because he needed a couple of minutes alone with the guard. Just a few moments of undivided attention from a young man whose life he was capable of transforming.

"Pete!" he whispered, but Pete went past him and stayed for a long, long time at the other end of the hallway. It seemed like hours to Bud. Maybe he needed all that time to realize that his return trip past Bud's cell could be of unforeseen importance.

Bud called out once more when Pete finally walked by again, and this time he stopped, as though he'd already reached the end of the gangway or as if his feet wouldn't take him any farther. In any case, he'd reached his destination.

"I'll give you and your family a million dollars if you'll give me a cell phone," Bud whispered. "You just give it to me, and I'll call and have the money transferred to your account. Or your mother's account, or anyone else you want. You can also have it in cash. I'm sure I can arrange that, too." Pete looked at Bud as though Bud were already in the past tense. Like it was a dead body speaking to him to which he'd already answered no. Bud began sweating. He wanted to reach out and grab Pete but immediately realized it was a bad idea. If the guy retreated a step, he might be gone the next second.

"Pete, believe me when I say I'm innocent. I haven't done what they accused me of. I killed in Vietnam, it's true, but that was for my country. I was only twenty-three years old. It was over there I learned that life is sacred, believe me."

Pete tipped forward on his toes. He looked as though he were about to pass out. Maybe it was just because he'd been standing up so long, but Bud knew an offer like his could shake up a man like Pete. A million dollars would completely change his life; this was the kind of thing guys like him dreamed about. Win the lottery and your troubles are over. Just stick your coin in the right slot machine at the right moment and . . .

Thoughts like this were buzzing through Pete's mind—it was obvious. Should he put the coin in the slot? Should he take the chance?

Clearly he wanted to, but the odds weren't good, because Bud Curtis was no average death-row inhabitant. He'd ordered the assassination of the president's wife, people said. Should Pete take risks for a man like that? That was the question. And Bud knew it, too.

"He won't do it, Buddy Boy. He's not giving you the cell phone." Pete's body jerked when he heard Daryl Reid's voice from the cell next door. It was like a knife thrust through the semidarkness. Bud tried to quiet Daryl down, but Pete was already gone.

The next morning, Bud was told he had a visitor. Doggie was sitting in the visitor's room with downcast eyes, looking as if she'd lost her will to live. She turned her face towards him when they led him in and chained him to the chair opposite her. Her eyes were clouded and sad; the wrinkles on her brow reminded him of her mother.

He took a deep breath. "Thank you for coming, my . . . my sweetheart." Such simple words had never been harder to say.

She shrugged her shoulders. Maybe, like her father, she noticed the looks the prison guards were giving her. Doggie Rogers: Who in the entire United States didn't know her? Wasn't she the president's aide who began this mess? Without her there'd be no state of emergency, no roadblocks, no sporadic raids by the police and military. Yes, they were watching her, and she clearly wasn't enjoying it.

"It's Monday. Did you get the day off?" Bud asked.

"I worked all weekend."

He nodded. "This is probably one of the last times you'll be coming here, Doggie, if not *the* last. Things are really moving fast now."

She looked at him. "When?"

He counted on his fingers and gave her a smile. "Well, it might be as much as eight days. But you can never know what'll happen tomorrow. Maybe they'll speed things up some more."

The wrinkles on her forehead deepened. "Do you have any idea what's happening to the country right now?"

He nodded again. He didn't know much, but it was enough. Everybody was blaming him for what was going on.

"It all seems out of control, but it's worse than that because President Jansen knows precisely what he's doing." She was looking straight at him now, her voice low. "I think he's insane, in a way. The White House is like a fortress. They just sit there all the time, pulling strings. I'm just ten offices away from the oval one, and I know nothing." She put her face in her hands. "It's terrible, what you started, Dad. Do you know that?"

He let her sit like that until she was finished, let her dry her eyes and look up again.

"Listen to me, Doggie, because we only have a little time. Listen closely: I'm not guilty." He noticed the guard looking at the clock on the wall, but he wasn't about to let himself be stopped. "Someone's been conspiring against me. I don't know why, but I had nothing to do with Mimi Jansen's death. You've got to believe me. It's true that once I got Toby O'Neill to lick my spit off the floor, Doggie, but I was drunk and it was a bet!"

She looked at him with disgust.

"Yes, I know, but what's done is done! You have to believe me. Blake Wunderlich is the man who contacted me and suggested that Toby O'Neill be in charge of unveiling the painting, and, whether he exists or not, he was real enough at the time." He leaned towards her, as much as the chains would allow. "Listen. Someone must be able to check all the phone calls that went through my office. They're bound to find something. My lawyers have already thrown their towel in the ring, but maybe you can get hold of a private detective or something. I don't have much time. Can't you do that, my darling?"

The tenderness of his words made her squirm. "But how can that help? The way things are, no competent person will touch your case." She looked at the floor. "Plus, who'd want to help me? I've become a pariah, too, don't you understand?"

He would have given anything to squeeze her hand. "What about your friend from the China trip, the sheriff who was with you at your father's trial? He must know the case in and out. Can't you ask him to try and see if there's anything he can do? He must know the routine for things like this."

"T. Perkins? What can he do?"

"Go through it all one more time. The prosecutor's material and my lawyers', my testimony and all the others'. I know I can't appeal, but goddammit, there must be proof somewhere that I didn't do it. Tell T. Perkins the glass of water disappeared. That I'd brought it into the corridor, but it wasn't on the video. That there must be someone who was able to digitally remove that glass from the video, someone who had access. And say that I had enough of firearms in Vietnam and have never, ever, loaded my pistol or any other weapon since. And that, therefore, I don't understand how my fingerprints could have gotten on those cartridges. Tell him I think someone like the Secret Service is involved, that they've twisted what I said on purpose. Yes, I know I told Toby not to say anything when he unveiled the painting, but I just wanted him to keep his mouth shut and do what he was told! I know him. He was capable of saying the rudest things to people. You know that."

"Then why'd you pick him?"

"But I didn't, Doggie! How many times do I have to say it? It was Blake Wunderlich who chose him." He looked up at the approaching guard. "Oh, no you don't! There's still two minutes," he said, pointing at the clock. "See for yourself! You have to let me finish speaking with my daughter." The guard stopped, but it was clear he wasn't going to wait the full two minutes.

Bud turned towards Doggie. "And the money transfer to Toby. Would I do something that stupid, Doggie? Honestly, would I? It's so easy to check up on."

She bit her lip and looked up at the clock.

"Yes, I took part in the Wallace and Goldwater campaigns," he continued. "I've never tried to hide the fact. But I was still practically a kid, wasn't I? It was because I was in love with your mother, and that's where she was. Ask her yourself."

Doggie shut her eyes tight. She knew if she made any objections, it would take time that they didn't have.

Bud looked at her. Suddenly he was conscious of the chair beneath him and of how the walls' barren surfaces brought desolation to his soul. Of how his daughter seemed worlds away and that he was holding hands with death. "Oh, God," he whispered. "I wish your mother was with me now."

He put up his hand in protest when she began to stand up. "Don't go. Let me say it all. It may be my last chance."

She was close to tears. He'd seen it before, but it was long ago.

"I'll say it again, Doggie: I wasn't the one who suggested that Toby unveil the painting. It was Blake Wunderlich, one of the security people. I would have unveiled the damn picture myself, but this Secret Service agent thought an employee should do it. He said it was more proper! Yes, that was his expression, believe it or not. 'Proper,' like I was some kind of devious, ultrarevolutionary bastard! That's how it happened. If you believe that, can't you believe the rest, too? And ask T. Perkins to look at the case, won't you, please?" He tried to smile at her but felt how impossible it was. She was looking rigidly at his orange jumpsuit, so he had to bend over to catch her eye.

"Doggie, try asking yourself these questions: Who gave the assassin the gun? Where'd they get it from? Why didn't Toby hit the president at such close range? Could it be the president was never the intended target? And if that's true, why? What had Mimi Jansen done, and how come no one heard what Toby shouted before the first shot? There are so many questions that might help me here if I get some fast, correct answers, but I don't have much time. So think about it quick. Please?"

She hesitated a moment but nodded reluctantly when the guards stepped forward and unlocked her father's chains from the chair.

"Can't I give my daughter a last hug, for God's sake?!"

The smaller of the guards regarded him coldly. "Sorry. No bodily contact between the inmates and guests. You know the rules. Come along now, Curtis, don't cause any trouble. Your time's up." They heaved him out of the chair and shoved him towards the door to the cellblock.

"Doggie!" he shouted, as they opened the bulletproof glass door. "Offer Perkins however much money he wants, if that'll help. If he can't take the money because of his job, then offer him enough so he'll never have to work again. Or find someone else like him. But hurry, you're my last hope."

He managed to twist himself around to give her one last smile, but she was gone.

That night Bud tried keeping himself awake so he could keep an eye out for Pete, who was leaning against the wall at the entrance to death row, as usual. Maybe tonight he'd give in, but who knew when, or what it would take? Bud listened to the sighing of the ventilation system. Could that be a possibility? Could one crawl on all fours through the mile-long steel shaft and somehow wind up out behind the buildings? Was it possible to find one's way through the massive network of cameras and electrified barbed wire, get the hell out of there southwards through North Carolina, hire a hydrofoil, and make it to the Gulf of Mexico? Just toss his life overboard and make a new one in South America. He knew enough about survival and getting ahead and how one could disappear down there. Peru and Chile had lots of beautiful women, their regimes could be bribed, and there was plenty of cheap manpower. Life was simpler down there, as long as you knew what you were doing. And Bud did.

"Pssst, Buddy Boy," came Daryl's whisper. "Wake up, man, Pete's coming."

Bud flew to the bars of his cell and wedged his face halfway through. Pete was only two cells away, and everything was peaceful. He gave Daryl a piercing look as he passed his cell. Then he squatted down in front of the bars of Bud's cell and looked him straight in the eyes. "I want the money before you get the cell phone, understand?" he whispered. "I'm not here the next couple of days, so you get it ready in the meantime."

Bud shook his head. "Jesus Christ," he whispered. "How do you expect me to get the money without the phone? Dammit, Pete, don't you see? I need that cell phone first."

Pete was pale. Here he was in the killing zone, confused, with everything at stake. He was in a no-man's-land between death and rebirth. He knew, right there, that he now had a chance to soar high above Waverly and the state prison and never look back. The choice wasn't so difficult in itself, but the chance of getting caught was a big consideration.

Helping Bud Curtis wasn't like helping just anyone, as Bud well knew. No one in the country wanted anyone dispatched to hell faster than him, not even the worst serial killer or child rapist. Whoever got caught trying to help him escape would be in deep shit, and there was a sewerful of possibilities of that happening.

"A million dollars in three days, on March twenty-sixth. Then you get the cell phone, but not before."

"I'll give you five million if I get the phone first, all right?"

Pete got up and left. Bud tried unsuccessfully to stick his head farther through the bars, his heart hammering, but Pete never looked back.

CHAPTER 15

DOGGIE HEARD THEY'D ARRESTED TOM JUMPER—THE COUNTRY'S MOST POPU-
lar TV host—early on Tuesday afternoon.

The authorities would have preferred arresting him the previous
Saturday evening in the middle of his prime-time show, just to prove
to the nation they were serious about shutting down TV programs
that exalted violence, but the man was wily and disappeared. Afterwards his personal assistant spent the next two days standing on a
beer crate in Times Square, raging at the government over their trash-
ing of the Bill of Rights in general and freedom of expression in particular, until the authorities picked him up, too. Too many people
were agreeing with him.

On Monday, Jumper popped up on a pirate radio station that half
of Harlem had been listening to since the shutting down of the legal
stations. He encouraged people in the White House to remove the
president by force, which turned the search for Jumper into the biggest dragnet anyone had ever seen. Even though Doggie was unable to
see how it could be their role, two thousand soldiers and National
Guard volunteers joined the local police and security forces in their
hunt for the tiniest clue as to the TV host's whereabouts. This resulted
in several shoot-outs with a number of fatal casualties, as people with
bad consciences abruptly began fleeing town. The police were prepared with roadblocks, creating endless lines of stopped traffic. Some
of the "guilty" even abandoned their vehicles and tried to escape into
nearby fields and neighborhoods, but few succeeded. Triborough and
Queensboro Bridges and Macombs Dam to the east were closed

permanently, and lookout posts on the rest of the bridges and tunnels coming out of Manhattan were heavily reinforced. Tom Jumper was the symbol of a time that no longer existed—a symbol that had to be removed.

An anonymous tip blew his cover, and he was arrested on Tuesday in Alphabet City on the corner of 4th Street and Avenue B, in a little café called Kate's Joint. Jumper had resisted bravely, but he was seriously outmanned. The ensuing beating he suffered caused the regulars in the café to lose it, which in turn caused the nervous soldiers to begin shooting. A very short time later the whole city knew. More than ten people had been killed, and Jumper was said to have been badly wounded. What the public didn't know was that he'd been brought to the Downtown Family Care Center, patched up within an hour, and then had managed to escape down Essex towards Seward Park, in the company of a nurse and an orderly.

Doggie heard about it in the lobby of the White House, the place where White House employees went to hear gossip and unofficial news stories. Some people were infuriated by Jumper's cat-and-mouse act, but not everyone, as Doggie could clearly see behind their worried expressions and careful choice of words.

For the last couple of days, offices in the White House were manned by increasingly overburdened employees who answered calls, zombie-like, from government officials who hadn't a clue to what was happening and were seeking answers and solutions that didn't exist. Given the present situation, customs officers wanted to know about the legality of the mushrooming export of weapons and ammunition over the border to Mexico, and dairy producers were wondering how the hell they were supposed to deliver milk while it was still fresh, with all the time-consuming roadblocks.

Everyone was suffering a collective meltdown caused by Jansen's decrees and state of emergency. The penal system had problems finding qualified personnel to handle the massive job of emptying the prisons of inmates, which corresponded to the massive job the social services faced in assigning community duties to these same ex-cons. And new problems that had never been dealt with before kept arising every day.

It was depressing and frustrating, having to turn away this deluge of questions, but what it came down to was that all those who were qualified to make decisions were constantly busy elsewhere. White House staff began hiding in conference rooms and dumping problems in one another's laps. Doggie could hear them arguing through the walls, screaming at one another. The Situation Room was constantly booked by the National Security Council, and suddenly, there were more people in uniforms in the hallways than in civilian clothes.

It was like this all over the country, she was told. Uniforms everywhere, from the forests of the Northwest to the beaches of Florida. She'd seen it herself when she went to see her father. Normally the trip from Washington down to the prison in Waverly took two hours, but yesterday it had taken five. There were roadblocks all over, lines of cars stretching for miles with horns honking, poncho-clad National Guardsmen and civilians losing their tempers, screaming at one another. Suspicion, car searches, and hard looks were the order of the day.

Doggie had recently heard about two farmers who had flipped out in Madison County. An argument in a cafeteria had developed into a shooting episode, after which the two men had taken off with twenty sticks of dynamite in their trunk. A half hour later they blew up the city hall in Charlottesville. At least four hundred lawmen were quickly reassigned to give chase, and the two farmers eventually met their bloody demise on the road to Barboursville. Local folks had no idea what had happened, but dramas like this were unfolding all the time, all over the country.

A few streets away from her apartment, a minor fire on L Street grew into a conflagration because all available police had been ordered to control a half million angry demonstrators in front of the Capitol building and therefore couldn't be on hand to prevent the curious spectators in their cars from driving so close to the fire that the fire hoses were squeezed shut by their tires.

There were scenes of chaos almost everywhere one looked, and out of the general hysteria and anarchy a selfish, defensive attitude was emerging among the populace. Because, even though people were united in their horror at what was taking place in their beloved country, things were moving so fast that notions of solidarity quickly yielded to the primal instinct of self-preservation. Who knew what tomorrow might bring? Would there be any food to buy, any electricity, any water in the faucets? Spontaneous hoarding spread like wildfire, even though Executive Order 10998 specifically forbade it, and suddenly scenes of housewives staggering home with a year's supply of potatoes and rice were commonplace everywhere, from the biggest cities to the smallest rural towns.

Analysts were predicting that rationing would soon have to be implemented, as people kept stockpiling goods whether they needed them or not. In the unusual event that a business was hiring, people trampled one another underfoot to get to the head of the line, no matter what job it was or what it paid. At least this way, one avoided Executive Order 11000, and thus wasn't impressed into community work alongside released convicts, washing down streets and hauling away the mountains of garbage that had been growing in the alleys and along the train tracks. And all of those whose lifestyle revolved around never planning anything suddenly had to get their shit together to avoid getting in trouble, not only with the authorities, but with their neighbors as well. Street justice was spreading, growing in swiftness and impunity, because if one individual committed a crime, the entire neighborhood could suffer the consequences. The police were unusually short-tempered, and whereas they used to threaten to take people into custody who were suspected of withholding information, they now simply instructed the authorities to hold back welfare payments until the crime was solved. In this way, people were brought to heel and began informing on one another. The FBI's website— where Americans could send tips or report suspicious people—was swamped with mail.

Each day brought a chain reaction of new situations. Doggie was having a hard time discerning between good and bad—just like everybody else, as far as she could tell. Kids who used to cut school now trudged obediently to class each day because there was nothing else to do. There were fewer and fewer TV channels to watch, and hanging out on the street was no fun anymore. There were ex-cons everywhere in their shrieking-green overalls, admonishing and lecturing the neighborhood youth about all kinds of potential dangers. Throwing a chewing gum wrapper on the sidewalk could result in a slap upside the head. Unruly behavior unleashed corporal reprisals of a magnitude that discouraged any repetition in the near future. Suddenly, rough justice was being meted out left and right, and those youths who usually preferred the pleasant anarchy of the street were beginning to feel uncomfortable and homeless in the asphalt jungle. They, too, had to get used to a situation where not much could be taken for granted, and learn to deal with a new kind of constant dread.

Doggie's workday at the White House was changing character more and more, too. Where she used to spend her time making in-depth studies and analyses and projections into the future, she now merely dispatched tasks methodically for all the secretariats, doing so with such superficiality that her desktop was clean at the end of the day, regardless of the works' importance or complexity. The tasks she didn't get around to—well, that was just too bad. People were going to have to realize that the White House couldn't assist them much with their problems. Maybe this would help reduce her workload to fit the sixteen-hour day she spent slaving away in her little office. One could always hope.

Everyone who worked in the White House was more or less in the same boat as Doggie, but not all of them could handle the pressure. Yesterday one of Communications Chief Donald Beglaubter's older secretaries had said she wasn't feeling well after the morning meeting and sat slumped over her desk for most of the day until someone discovered she was dead. The shock her colleagues felt was intense but brief, and today everyone was back in high gear. Otherwise, there were many who broke down in tears from fatigue and confusion by noontime. The cafeteria stood empty most of the day; getting the workload cleared off one's desk by evening took precedence over eating.

Wesley had looked in on her a couple of times the previous week. He, too, was showing the effects of the overwhelming state of affairs.

His eyes wandered, and his trademark smile had withered. He looked ready to give up, like he'd lost interest in everything and everyone. Well, maybe everything except her.

He came into her office the day after she'd been with her father. Doggie barely managed to turn her back, moisten her lips, and pinch a bit of color into her cheeks. She didn't want him seeing how she was feeling, or discuss it with him, either. Because what could he do, anyway? How could the president's press secretary help her save a man convicted of killing the president's wife? He couldn't, so what was the point of talking about it? He sat down heavily on the chair upon which Doggie had laid the day's mail, compressing a considerable pile of desperate inquiries and complaints as he stared listlessly into space. Then his expression changed suddenly, became personal rather than collegial. "Hey, Doggie, let's get far, far away from here and have us a couple of chubby little babies and bathe all day in the Bungo Canal— whaddaya say?" He smiled, but a moment later he shook his head and withdrew into himself once more. This sad, neon-lit excuse for an office was so obviously his personal refuge that she didn't take his touching outburst for more than it was. She didn't answer, even though there was nothing she'd rather see than the two of them make their exit to never-never land together. It was too late. She was branded, the mark of Cain on her forehead. The moment for Wesley to initiate a serious relationship with her had definitely passed. Even if he couldn't get such foolish thoughts out of his head, there was no way he could just leave, anyway, not with his ever-present bodyguards. And nor could Doggie, for that matter. Not that the opportunity wasn't there; they'd surely heave a sigh of relief if she disappeared, and as heir to Bud Curtis's bulging bank accounts and enormous hotel empire, she could easily go live wherever she wanted. But she had to stay at the White House—this was essential. President Jansen could fire her, but in the meantime she had a mission: to vindicate herself, no matter how long it took. *Then* she could get out.

Wesley sat a moment longer, apparently lost in thought, then got up suddenly and removed both his and her identification badge-chips. Then he placed them, along with her telephone receiver, on top of a couple of circulars Doggie had been reading, carefully wrapped all three among the pages, laid them in her desk drawer, and closed it. Next he took his chair over to the door, tipped it back beneath the door handle, and squatted down before her. "Give me your hand, Doggie, would you, please?"

She looked at him doubtfully. "What are you doing, Wesley?" She made a sad attempt at a laugh. "Why'd you put this stuff in my drawer?"

He took her hand. "I don't want anybody but you to hear what I have to say," he said very quietly. She frowned. Had she and her office been bugged? Was there a microphone in her ID badge? Had it really come to this? Were they figuring her father would call her and confess everything? That she'd take over where Toby O'Neill left off and finish the hired assassin's job?

"Yeah, they're spying on all of us."

She felt her jaw drop. Did he say "all of us"?

He squeezed her hand. "If this situation ever gets better, Doggie, then remember what I'm going to tell you now. You're the only one here who I can trust." She nodded.

"There's going to be a showdown one day when all this is over with, I'm sure of it. There'll be hearings and trials, and those implicated will be punished, believe me. That's why it's important for me that there's someone left who can tell the world I didn't go along with this voluntarily, okay?"

"But no one believes you did, Wesley!"

"I'm the one who passes information on to the public and the whole world; I'm the one who writes all that shit. Do you think anyone's going to consider me innocent?"

"So get out."

"How?"

"Sneak out and disappear."

"The chip, sweetheart, the chip. None of the staff can leave this place without it. Alarm bells would be ringing all over. Don't you think I've thought about just dumping the thing into a glass of water and short-circuiting it?"

She knew he was right.

He loosened the grip on her hand. "Just remember, when the time comes, that I wanted to quit this job, but I couldn't."

They heard a muffled sound on the other side of the door, and Wesley shot to his feet. The legs of the chair wedged against the door teetered for a moment as he grabbed Doggie and held her close. The next bang from outside succeeded in toppling the chair, but by then he was hugging her tighter and giving her a passionate kiss. She glanced at the door before closing her eyes to accept the embrace.

Then his lips left hers, and he looked deep into her eyes. For a split second this brief intimacy seemed to have taken them both unawares. He held his breath, sighed deeply, then turned to stand face-to-face with their acting chief of staff, Lance Burton.

"Jesus, Wesley," said Burton, looking at him with disapproval, "I can't let you out of my sight for a minute, can I?" The staff chief shook his head, and Doggie was pretty sure she knew what he was thinking. Burton thought it was okay for Wesley to have sex with whomever he liked. Just not her.

He let go of her slowly. She followed Wesley's eyes down to the telephone and telephone cord that disappeared into her desk drawer. She moved a bit to the side to hide the sight.

His shallow breathing and the pulse pounding in his neck told her he was afraid, but his even, professional voice was calm as ever.

"Two seconds and I'll be with you, Lance," he improvised. "We have to discuss the Internet, right?"

Burton gave him a sharp look and a brief nod. "Okay. Two minutes. In my office." At no point did he look at Doggie. He closed the door after him.

"The Internet?" she whispered, while he took his chip out of the drawer and closed his hand around it. "What can you do about that?"

"We can shut it down in twenty-four hours. We're virus experts, didn't you know? We can crash the large servers and the satellite connections, too. The question is: When? Maybe in a couple of weeks, maybe not at all. It depends on how things develop and if they can find an alternative way to keep the defense and surveillance systems working without certain satellites. If you need to use the Internet, you better do it now." He stroked a few strands of hair out of her face and looked at her very gravely. Then he sighed again and left.

She sat for a moment with the phone receiver in her hand, trying to remember Wesley's eyes while they were embracing, but all she could see was the gray concrete of Sussex State Prison, all she could smell was a sterile prison odor, and all she could hear was the metallic clanging of barred doors. The prison's invisible aura hung over her like a melancholic fog. How was she going to make it go away? How could it, as long as her doubts about her father's innocence kept gnawing in the back of her mind?

Their meeting the day before had made a strong impression on Doggie. Earlier, during the trial, he'd just been part of the cast, a small gear in a relentless doomsday machine, merely the final piece of a puzzle. He'd looked small, defenseless—and guilty. In these surroundings she'd been unable to recognize this man who'd been like a god to her, and she'd hated him for it. But yesterday at the prison had been another story. His gaze had been unwavering and sincere, and he'd spoken his mind to her. His warmth and intensity had been there, too. Now her doubts were driving her crazy. It was like a nightmare.

Today was Tuesday. The following Tuesday her father would be dead.

She dialed the number to the sheriff's office in Highland County, and for the first time noticed a slight click on the line. So Wesley had been right. Tapping the phones was now part of everyday life at the White House.

After a moment a woman's grumpy voice came on the line and explained to her that Sheriff Perkins wasn't in his office. Doggie called his cell phone number and heard the faint click again, but otherwise there was silence. "Come on, T . . ." She sighed and finally hung up. "Why in the world haven't you activated your voice mail, you old fool?" she muttered, then called her mother.

She had one, specific question. "Mom, I'm calling to ask where you and Dad met each other. I don't think you ever told me."

"Why are you asking me this now, Dorothy?" came the quiet voice.

"Dad says you met during a political campaign. Is it true? Were you involved in Goldwater's and Wallace's campaigns?"

"No!"

Doggie shook her head. So it *had* been a lie, just as she'd feared. She felt her skin getting clammy.

What was worse now, the pain or the embarrassment?

"No, I wasn't directly involved, but your grandfather was . . ." she added, then paused before the crucial words finally came: ". . . and I went along with him."

The blood started pumping through Doggie's veins again. "You're saying that Grandpa participated in the Goldwater and Wallace election campaigns?" Doggie remembered her mother's father as mild-mannered, with soft hands and the kindest eyes. A nice person, full of love and warmth—at least where his family was concerned. "Did he really support *them*? That's not how I remember him at all."

Now there was an edge in the voice on the other end of the line. "Your grandfather was very active, politically. There's nothing wrong with that, Dorothy."

Did her mother really say that? Didn't she have a picture of President Jansen hanging above her cluttered shelves? Apparently, nothing was as it seemed. "So you met Dad at one of those meetings?"

"I've told you before, haven't I? Your father followed me around for months, at a distance!" There was a moment of laughter. "Yes, I knew he was interested, but I couldn't do much about it, could I? I was with someone else at the time, you know."

"And this guy was involved in the campaigns, too?"

"I'll say he was! He was very active."

"So Dad joined the campaigns just to get next to you?"

More laughter. There was no need for her mother to say more.

A virginal sheet of paper lay before her now, white and frightening. She had to document the facts and possibilities that could help Sheriff Perkins find out the truth—if she could locate the sheriff and he could be bothered to help her, that is.

Doggie thought it all through. She wrote about the glass of water that had disappeared; the security agent, Wunderlich, who appeared not to exist; and all the inconsistencies surrounding the assassination itself. She had to have it all written down before she spoke to T. Perkins so she'd have a chance of convincing him. Her father was scheduled to die in seven days, and she was the only one pleading his case.

CHAPTER 16

ONE DAY WHEN HE WAS IN LATE PUBERTY, JOHN BUGATTI WAS TAKEN ASIDE BY his father, a rural doctor who'd made it his specialty to examine women's lower abdominal regions, and asked what he wanted to do with his life. This question contained a veiled threat as well as an implied answer. His father wanted his only son to take over his practice, but John didn't share his father's obsession with human physical maladies—especially not women's. A couple of weeks previously he'd impulsively fondled one of the boys on the football team, and from then on he'd known. If there was one thing he wanted to do with his life, it was get in the pants of as many boys as possible, especially some rock star with long hair and plenty of mascara. So he'd looked at his father that day and made up his mind. He wanted to be a journalist and nothing else. Not surprisingly, his father was shocked. From his conservative point of view, this meant a huge plunge in his son's local social standing, but upon reflection he realized this disastrous choice could one day make his son editor of the local rag—and that was something else. That meant status.

John was content with the idea of becoming a freelance writer for *Rolling Stone,* where he could come in close proximity with all the rock stars he wanted, but here his father put his foot down. If John wanted the family's moral and financial support, he'd have to pursue a traditional journalistic career.

Thus followed several boring years of studying and working for local and regional newspapers until he landed a job in New York and finally reached the top as NBC's Washington correspondent. By then the scene had changed, the rock stars and their makeup had faded, and John's career was leading him in new directions. Now he was interviewing one intriguing, handsome man after another. No, he had no regrets as to his choice of employment. It had turned out to be the perfect blend of business and pleasure.

Thus was his life's motif until he met "Uncle Danny," as friends called his lover. Danny was completely different from the New York queers he used to throw himself at in the sauna clubs, and he was different from the more stable—yet just as noncommittal—safe-sex relationships that ensued. Danny was fantastic and beautiful and just as sincerely interested in life's deeper meaning as John was disinterested. And it was Danny's influence, along with the inevitable process of maturity, that slowly shaped him into the person—and especially the journalist—he'd now become: dedicated to his profession's principles of free expression and pursuit of the truth. If he hadn't met Danny, John Bugatti would scarcely have been bothered by the media censorship and other calamities unleashed by President Jansen's state of emergency. But Danny had made him see things in a new light—and he was angry. He was angry about Homeland Security's directives that dictated the behavior of what was left of the news media, angry about the daily closing down of newspapers and TV and radio stations, and particularly angry about his inability to do anything about it.

Conditions had become ugly and unbearable. It was the rule of the ironclad fist; Stalin couldn't have done better. Anyone who still dared speak out critically could be sure of being monitored by forces capable of silencing him. So people kept their mouths shut, and the very few TV stations that the government still allowed on the air were forced to attend daily self-censorship meetings in the name of self-preservation. And each day Bugatti got more and more pissed off.

That morning he'd checked out the mood of the nation over a cup of steaming coffee in the Cosi café at Washington DC's Metro Center, a place where everybody came and everyone knew one another. Even the Capitol Hill messenger boys were there, with plenty of time on their hands since their employers in Congress had been protectively interned as a security precaution resulting from the recent militia disturbances. It was here that John received his tips in the days before Jansen's regime came to power, subtle comments from the guy sitting next to him that were clarified and elaborated upon by the guy sitting behind him. Knowledge that others wanted him to have, that he could subsequently do with as he wished. But those days were over. Now everyone stared into their coffee cups and tried to keep the conversation going without saying too much. People nowadays were equally afraid of what they knew and what they didn't know. Among many other things, no one even mentioned Tom Jumper's spectacular escape from the police the day before. The tempo out on the streets had slowed down, too; people no longer hurried determinedly from place to place. There were fewer trucks and less traffic; only the police and the military were busier than ever, to everyone's dismay—even John's. For him, the attraction of a man in uniform was long gone.

The mood up in NBC4's editorial offices on Nebraska Avenue was funereal, the same routine, day after day. John began each morning by looking through his day's assignments. That morning he really hoped his eyes were deceiving him. If he—the station's premier Washington expert—was expected to spend several hours interviewing women, they'd damn well better be the wives of important politicians, not the intended flock of innocuous, discarded, middle-aged bags who ran the catering at the 7th Street Convention Center. What the hell did he or his viewers care, even though the point of his assignment was to show a workplace going to pieces as a result of the current chaos? He crossed it off his list. "One less waste of energy," he mumbled, then raised his head to see his boss's pale face hovering above him. Once she'd been a delectable goddess on the New York media scene. But now, like most top reporters, she'd been restationed in Washington, had developed dark circles under her eyes, no longer cared how she dressed, and had the charisma of an empty mayonnaise jar.

"We've all got a meeting with Hopkins," she said, attempting a smile. This didn't sound good. Like the rest of NBC's journalistic and editorial elite, he turned up at the editor in chief's office fearing the worst. The legendary Alastair Hopkins was at his desk, gazing distractedly out his tinted panorama window, tight-lipped. He was obviously affected by something he'd just been told by the two black-clad men standing on either side of him.

As always, Hopkins got straight to the point. "From now on, all your interviews will be recorded. There will be no more direct transmissions. I've been informed that, in accordance with Executive Order 10995, all our work must be approved by these two gentlemen"— there was a trace of irony in this last word—"before we broadcast anything." He raised his hand in an attempt to maintain order, but the assembled journalists hadn't gotten this far in their profession by keeping quiet. In the ensuing vocal mayhem, the two security agents instinctively edged away from the windows, some of which could be opened. They were outnumbered, and it was a hell of a fall to the pavement if these reporters got seriously aggressive.

Hopkins stood up. "Jesus Fucking Christ, people, take it easy! Do you want to get us closed down already? Don't you get it? If you don't do as you're told, you'll be out of a job in ten minutes—so just relax!"

By the time Bugatti slipped out of the meeting, the atmosphere had become positively odious.

He got hold of Wesley Barefoot as the latter was eating lunch. He heard a couple of faint clicks on the line, but by now he'd grown accustomed to eavesdropping being the order of the day. One just had to be careful about what one said.

Bugatti cleared his throat. "What the hell's happening over there at the White House, Wesley? I hear a couple of the leaders of the militia coalition have been caught in Ohio, and people are saying they've been killed. Is there anything to the story and, if so, who'd they catch? Who do I talk to? How am I supposed to do my job?" He waited a moment; Barefoot was apparently thinking. Then he continued. "Listen: You're the White House press secretary and you clam up just like all the others, but it can't go on like this, Wesley. If you want to help yourself and Jansen and that administration you stand for, then you know that we . . . I mean, the whole country needs an interview with the president so we can find out how long these measures are going to remain in effect. Won't you see to it that I get some time with him, preferably within the next hour or two, if possible? Something's just happened at our office that I'd like—no, that I *need*—the president to comment on. Do you understand, Wesley? Can you do it?"

Wesley's voice sounded very tired on the other end of the line. Surely he knew all about the intensification of press censorship. "No can do, John," he said. Simple as that. "I'm sorry. Of course you can speak with one of my colleagues. I'll see what I can do. Can you call back in an hour?"

An hour and ten minutes later, Bugatti was standing before the control post, four hundred yards in front of the White House. No one got by it without written permission or one of the chips that all White House employees were ordered to have pinned to their chest. The atmosphere bordered on chaos, helped along by a dancing forest of protest signs and raging demonstrators, among which were a sprinkling of well-known actors, authors, and other personalities.

A few months ago this would have looked like a scene out of a science fiction movie. How could it be? American democracy had an ingenious system of checks and balances, specifically to make sure something like this never happened. It was supposed to be foolproof. The attack on the attorney general and the assassination of the chief justice of the Supreme Court had derailed the entire system, and the American way of life appeared to be hurtling towards doomsday. At first it was believed that the White-Headed Eagles were behind the attacks, and all prominent politicians and officials were ordered out of harm's way. But when Moonie Quale denied his militia's involvement, and moments later a bomb threat was phoned in to Congress, the authorities began expanding their investigation, digging deeper. Loose rumors about a conspiracy against the president gained credence, and suddenly many of these same distinguished politicians' and officials' homes were being turned inside out without search warrants. Within a matter of days several members of Congress had been placed under house arrest, accused of having participated in the alleged plans to depose the president and his administration. Everyone thought this wave of paranoia would quickly blow over, but the investigation dragged on, and the politicians remained in detention. This in turn caused a furious reaction from the politicians' constituencies as well as all other political bodies in the country, but nothing helped. The assassinations and bomb threats were facts, the conspiracy rumors were growing, and this was all used to justify the president's next radical move, namely the temporary suspension of Congress. Thus Jansen's authority was absolute. FEMA gave the police and FBI the word, and within hours the streets were filled with uniforms. The procedure followed to the letter a series of presidential decrees that FEMA had worked up years ago but that no one had ever believed would be put into practice on such a scale. While the consequences of Jansen's state of emergency could not yet be compared with the totalitarian regimes of a Pinochet or a Pol Pot, the similarities were growing. Many democratically elected officials feared for their safety and, according to John Bugatti's sources, several had already left the country. When the Democratic national headquarters was bombed and several congressmen and other public servants were murdered, all members of Congress were detained for their own safety.

Most of John's colleagues lost their jobs during the course of the next few days. First the Department of Homeland Security closed down Fox TV, then ABC and CBS. Several national daily newspapers were cut down to a few pages, and one saw well-reputed reporters standing on street corners with their laptops under their arms. They had nowhere to go, they were angry, and many were afraid. What was a person to do in a situation like this? It had happened plenty of times around the world in recent history, but no one seemed ready for it this time, not in the United States. America was so used to practicing free speech that it had become a lifestyle, and now suddenly people were mute. But John also knew plenty of journalists who were presently much more concerned about how they were going to pay off their expensive homes than defending the right to free expression.

John's situation was different. NBC was allowed to stay on the air, and its programming was arranged and approved, thanks to the efforts of Alastair Hopkins. But that still left two questions: Whether there was anything important left to report about under these conditions, and what John should do about it?

John was also fearless. He wasn't long for this world, anyway. If it hadn't been for Danny, he'd have succumbed to AIDS long ago. The treatment helped, but the weariness and the feeling of impotence was working its way deeper and deeper into his body. The lethargy still came and went, but when it came, it was more debilitating than ever. Yes, his condition was irritating and slowly robbing him of his good looks, but he was afraid of nothing, and he now planned to put this to use.

The mob of demonstrators just behind him was forcing its way forward, towards the barrier. Their curses were loud and their sweat was strong. These angry citizens were going to get as close as possible and make themselves heard, no matter what.

He waved his arms to draw the attention of one of the soldiers at the barrier, but the soldier looked straight through him. "Hey! You!" John shouted. "Press Secretary Barefoot is sending someone out here to fetch me. Can't you let me stand inside the barrier until he comes? It's not much fun out here." He opened his jacket, exposing the lining, to show he was unarmed.

The soldier aimed his machine gun at him. "Get away from the barrier!" he commanded, without looking him in the eyes.

"Away? How am I supposed to do that?" he replied as a young man behind him grabbed his arm to avoid being shoved to the ground. It wouldn't be long before the surging crowd got out of control; Bugatti had seen it before. Someone would end up lying there, never to get up again.

"Get back—*now*!" screamed the soldier.

Bugatti stared at the gun barrel and noticed the sweat running down the soldier's face. He forced himself backward with all the strength his weakened body could muster and dialed Wesley's number again on his cell phone. After a long minute's wait, where the tempest around him increased along with cries of panic, he finally heard a woman's voice on the line. "I'm on my way down right now, Mr. Bugatti. We've informed the control post."

Wesley's secretary presented herself as Eleanor. She led him along a path around the side of the White House, saying she was sorry the tumult at the barriers and checkpoints forced them to make a detour. The air was cracking with tension like the moment before the cyanide pellet falls into the bowl of acid.

The lawn over towards Executive Avenue and the fence in front of the Ellipse were swarming with security, but no one checked Bugatti or his companion. They had their attention trained on the mass of humanity that stretched from the White House fence all the way to the other side of the Washington Monument. Bugatti shook his head; there were thousands of people out there. Was the American eagle facing extinction, or was it collecting itself to soar once more, stronger than ever? How was it ever to resurrect itself in this suffocating, poisoned atmosphere?

The secretary led him into the West Wing, followed by two security guards, and there John was greeted by a distraught-looking Wesley. Bugatti was glad he wasn't in his shoes.

Wesley led him past his office, the Roosevelt Room, and Vice President Sunderland's office and into Sunderland's secretary's office next door. He took off his ID chip and motioned for Bugatti to do the same with his guest chip. Then he waved Bugatti in through a narrow door in the back of the room.

They entered a small archive room packed with ring binders, a room Bugatti had never known about during the three previous administrations, where he'd waited for statements from chiefs of staff just on the other side of the wall. Only this time the chief of staff was no longer chief of staff. Against all normal procedure, he'd suddenly gotten to play the role of vice president.

"Who were you thinking I'd speak to, Wesley? And why come here, instead of your off . . . ?" His question was cut off by Barefoot's hand over his mouth.

"The chief of staff's secretary's office is my office now," he said, gently shutting the door.

"Does that mean you're working for Sunderland now, too?" Wesley nodded. Bugatti pursed his lips and gave a low whistle.

"Yes. I've been moved closer to Sunderland and have to do a lot of his secretarial work on top of everything else."

"Jesus Christ! What about Sunderland's old secretary, Margaret? Where's she?"

"She quit."

"You're kidding. But what are we doing in this closet? Has this room always been here?"

"It's my archives. They put in the dividing wall last week when they moved me over here. There's a back door close to the pressroom." He pointed at another narrow door. "It's because here no one can hear us. But we've got to speak softly, okay?"

"Is your office bugged?"

"They all are."

"Then why didn't we meet in town?"

"There are a lot of us who can't go anywhere without being followed by security agents, especially not without our ID chip."

"Meaning . . . ?"

"There's a microphone in the chip. They're listening wherever I go."

"Too fucking much! How about your apartment? Couldn't we meet there?"

Wesley attempted a smile and shook his head. He leaned close to Bugatti.

"John, you're not going to get to speak with the president. It's been days since I've had a private conversation with him, myself. He's not giving interviews anymore, not even to you."

"What's happened? Is he losing his mind? Is that what you're trying to tell me?"

"No."

"It would be understandable after having watched two wives and an unborn son be murdered."

"I don't know if he's going mad or not. I'm not a psychiatrist."

"What about you?"

"What do you mean? Have I gone crazy, too? No, but I'm getting there!" There was sweat on Wesley's forehead. Bugatti had never seen him so disheartened.

"No, I mean, can I interview you? Naturally, I would never use your name, only the usual 'informed sources, close to the president.'"

Wesley shook his head slowly. His expression had changed. It had lost its look of boyish innocence, once and for all. Sometimes fear could cause this, but usually it was due to being disappointed with oneself. Bugatti knew Wesley had always gotten his energy from his straightforwardness and ability to get things done, and all this he'd had to renounce. He was a very unhappy, disillusioned man—that was obvious. He wasn't giving Bugatti an interview because he couldn't. He couldn't because he dared not—it was as simple as that.

"Is there anyone else I can go to?" Bugatti implored. "Is there no one who will say anything? You know how discreet I am. It doesn't have to be that specific. I just want to get a handle on the situation we're in, and where the hell we're headed. I want to be cleared to tell about it somehow—you can understand that. There must be a way, before they shut the media down altogether. Because they *are* going to shut it down, aren't they, Wesley?"

He looked at Bugatti for some time. "Those who are willing or allowed to speak, know nothing, and those who do, won't. Everyone left here is loyal to the president. All of them! Even the secretary of commerce, and you can bet the big business and finance boys haven't been giving him much peace lately."

"The new chief of staff, Burton, what about him?"

"I don't know what's happened, but both Lance Burton and Donald Beglaubter have been completely closed off the past couple of weeks."

"Are they under some kind of pressure?"

"Everyone's under pressure here, but I know what you're driving at. No, I don't know if they're under any specific pressure."

"Secretary of Defense Henderson?"

"He's Jansen's man."

"Vice President Sunderland?"

"Are you kidding?" Wesley shook his head. "They're all one hundred percent loyal. Both the president's staff and the Cabinet do as they're told."

"There's got to be someone who can unseat Jansen, for God's sake. He's violated the Constitution so many times, it's logical to assume there'd be *someone*, isn't it?" Suddenly, Wesley stiffened and clamped his hand over Bugatti's mouth. "John! Shh!" He put his mouth next to Bugatti's ear. "If your mission is to find out if anyone's out to remove Jansen from office, then I'd recommend you get out of this country while you can, understand? No one says the borders are going to remain open. You know too much and you ask too much, so that's my advice to you. Now we're going to go back to my office, put on our chips, and then you're going to ask me silly, trivial questions, okay? But if you're clever, maybe there's a chance you'll be heard by the right people. I don't know precisely where these surveillance tapes circulate, but if the right people hear the right questions, maybe you'll find out something you're looking for. Just be careful in everything you say and do from here on in."

CHAPTER 17

THE LEAVES ON THE BUSHES OUTSIDE WESLEY'S WINDOW WERE ABOUT TO burst into life, and it wouldn't be long before the trees in front of the Eisenhower Executive Office Building would be bright green. This was the time of year when life-affirming signs of springtime were supposed to dispel the dark melancholia of winter, but it wasn't having any effect on him. Sitting in the world's busiest workplace, Wesley felt paralyzed, oppressed, and alone. Far from a new season of hope and renewal, this spring accentuated a feeling of self-hatred and despair that was in danger of engulfing him if he wasn't careful.

Early that morning, one of the White House guards had been attacked with a sharp instrument when he stopped a suspicious person at the appointment gate. He quickly bled to death at the foot of the wrought iron lattice as the assailant was overpowered by soldiers and driven away. From within Thomas Sunderland's office Wesley could faintly hear the ambulance sirens, followed by cries of demonstrators that were quickly silenced by power hoses.

Wesley was told that the attacker had been a journalist from a neoconservative magazine, and the government's reaction was prompt. All the offices that housed *The Washington Times, The Weekly Standard, American Enterprise,* and other neocon publications were immediately closed down.

This, in turn, caused an unexpectedly widespread and violent backlash. Suddenly it was as if everybody who opposed President

Jansen's drastic policies felt threatened, no matter which end of the political spectrum they belonged to. Militias came out of hiding in the wilderness of Bitterroot Range, the Smoky Mountains, the Everglades, and many other places, attacking military installations and police stations simultaneously. Fighting was intense, bloody, destructive, and over with as quickly as it had begun. The chairman of the Joint Chiefs of Staff, General Powers, attempted to play down the insurrection, but the FBI's reports told quite a different story. Hundreds of government troops and police had been killed, with practically no militia losses. These battles revealed the huge difference in morale between the two sides, and even worse, it was estimated that the militias' arsenals had doubled in size thanks to all the weapons and ammunition they'd captured during the fighting. General Powers had a lot to answer for.

This information immediately led to yet another crisis meeting in the Defense Department, and during the next few hours officials from the Department of Homeland Security and FEMA worked up terror scenarios that left both Wesley and the rest of the White House staff thoroughly shaken.

In the middle of all this, his mother had called, her voice shaking as she told him his father could no longer cope with the state of affairs wrought on the country by the government. He'd tongue-lashed her and insulted her for having ever worked for Bruce Jansen. He'd tossed his old Democratic convention badges out the window and, what upset his mother most of all, had pulled his military cadet uniform out of the closet, thrown it on the floor, and pissed on it.

Wesley felt the world closing in on him; he was steadily being suffocated. It wasn't just that the administration was digging deeper and deeper into the unknown, a shaky tunnel that would either collapse at any moment or emerge into a state of total chaos. The worst was the feeling that he'd been trapped by his own vanity and ambition. He'd fought to get this far and wasn't about to give up the status he'd attained. A status that could now be his undoing.

He was preoccupied with these dismal realizations as he left for the Oval Office to have dictated what he was to say at the evening's press conference.

The president looked wretched, and for good reason. He sat behind his desk with dark circles under his eyes, a shadow of the self-confident leader he was supposed to project when speaking to the nation in a couple of hours. He nodded at each of the assembly, one by one, then spoke. "I want to tell you that I received a death threat a half hour ago, one that must be taken seriously. We don't know how, but someone managed to place a written threat in a Secret Service agent's locker." He nodded towards Vice President Sunderland, who held up a copy of the note.

"The original has been sent to technical analysis," Sunderland reported. "So far, we know there are no fingerprints, and it looks like the message was printed out on a White House printer, on official stationery."

The note was passed around. "I'll be damned . . ." mumbled Chief of Communications Donald Beglaubter.

Wesley studied it as well. "The American president is sworn to defend the Constitution," it read.

"Bruce Jansen has not fulfilled his oath and must therefore announce his resignation no later than four A.M. tomorrow, or else his throat will be slit like a pig's within twenty-four hours."

He shook his head. "Okay, this is bad news, of course. There's apparently someone in the White House who has a huge need to express his dissatisfaction, and of course it's a great cause for concern that we don't know who it is. But is this a particularly serious threat? We've seen worse, haven't we?"

Staff chief Burton sat forward on the sofa and looked at Wesley. "Yes, perhaps . . ." he said, and paused. "But the bodyguard whose locker the note was found in was himself found lying in front of the locker with his head half cut off."

Wesley shuddered as he felt the self-loathing inside him turn to fear. Anyone serving the president could have been the victim, but doubtlessly the choice of a highly trained bodyguard had a specific grim, symbolic significance.

Jansen folded his hands over his laptop. "I won't be participating in the press conference this evening. Lance, you and Donald will have to help Wesley put it together. You are to state that there have been encounters with militias, without giving any details of success or failure. Do you understand?"

"Excuse me, Mr. President, but how can we keep something like that secret?" asked Wesley, his eyes fixed on the floor. "For example, we can't stop the pirate radios that are broadcasting all over the country. How many official shortwave transmitters did there used to be, and how many are lying around in attics or basements that still function? Plenty, I'll bet. And what about the Internet, cell phones, and photocopied flyers? What rabbit are we going to pull out of the hat to stop all that?"

Thomas Sunderland looked directly at Wesley. "No, magic tricks may not work here, but we can do something to draw the public's attention elsewhere. You're the communications expert. You're supposed to be good at that sort of thing."

"Right. So maybe now's the time to carpet bomb the militia camps with napalm." Again he regretted his choice of words, especially when he saw the vice president's expression. Maybe it wasn't exactly napalm Sunderland had in mind, but it looked like he'd been considering some kind of massive response. Wesley was sure there'd be plenty of innocent victims. He couldn't bear the thought of it.

President Jansen noted his expression. "Wesley, we're forced to look at the domestic situation now, aren't we? We don't want a civil war on our hands, but we almost have one at the moment, anyway, and it must be put down with the appropriate force." He turned towards Lance Burton. "Yesterday I ordered the Pentagon to immediately call home all American troops stationed abroad. They're shipping out from Europe and the Middle East as we speak."

Wesley felt himself beginning to sweat. He closed his eyes and tried to stay cool. From what Jansen was saying, there'd be a massive "defensive" attack carried out on American soil within twenty-four hours, while at the same time the United States' multitude of interests abroad—after decades of intense cultivation—would be left to fend for themselves. What would the United Nations make of all this? It would doubtlessly be met with rejoicing in the Middle East and probably also in domestic installations housing the military and their families, but how long would the world rejoice when the planet's only superpower disappeared—whether one loved it or hated it—from one day to the next? Okay, the entire US military was returning home—and then what? Would they send an aircraft carrier up the Alabama River to wipe out the militias that had entrenched themselves in Talladega National Forest? Would they use Harpoon missiles to blast the billionaire militia sympathizers' fleet of yachts out of the water down in Tampa and St. Petersburg? Would the marines begin storming city streets, and paratroopers start dropping out of the sky to pacify uppity ranchers in Minnesota? He couldn't conceive any of it. He looked at Donald and Lance, hoping they'd speak up, but they remained silent.

"The staff will receive a list within the next couple of hours stating the executive orders that are to be put into effect," Sunderland said.

"Do you think implementing the executive orders will justify the use of the military in the minds of the public?"

"We have no choice, Wesley, else the situation will get out of control." This time Jansen wasn't looking straight at him. "We have to make the streets as safe as possible for the average, law-abiding citizen."

"What does the UN secretary general have to say? Has he been briefed?" Wesley asked, cautiously. Of course he had to have been notified. Wesley just wanted to hear Jansen say it.

"I'm meeting with our UN ambassador and the secretary general this evening," he replied.

Wesley took a deep breath. "I expect the foreign journalists will have a lot of questions about our calling home the military. Can't your meeting with the secretary general be held before the press conference?"

The vice president broke in. "There won't be any foreign journalists" was all he said.

Chief of Staff Lance Burton gave Wesley a gloomy look. So at least Wesley wasn't the only one who was shocked by this bit of information. He tried to catch Donald Beglaubter's eye, but he was staring into space, expressionless.

Vice President Thomas Sunderland continued. "Naturally, we're in the process of preparing for a flood of protests from foreign diplomats. We don't want them getting their information from their own news media, do we?" There was a slight twitching in the corner of his mouth that Wesley hadn't seen before, a restlessness in this otherwise carefully composed face. Was Sunderland finally beginning to realize that things had gotten out of their control? Was the throne shaking beneath them all?

"In that connection," Sunderland went on, "you should also know that we've put our foreign embassies and consulates under guard, and our diplomats are awaiting further instructions."

Wesley's heart was hammering in his chest, and the skin on his face felt like a tight mask. He prepared himself, then looked directly at Jansen. "Allow me to speak freely for a moment, Mr. President, and then I'll do the job I'm supposed to do."

The vice president was about to protest, but the president nodded to Wesley.

"Aren't we going to cause irreparable damage?" Barefoot continued. "I'm aware that many good things are being done out there and that the intentions are well meant, but everything will fall apart if we fall afoul of the entire country and the rest of the world as well. I'm getting constant phone calls from embassy officials who want to know how safe it is for them to remain here. What do you think they're reporting back to their governments about what's happening in the US? There's no way we can stop them doing it, there are still plenty of means of communication. We can't simply try to isolate ourselves from the rest of the world, can we? Isn't it possible to find a softer, less hasty approach to all this?"

Jansen sat back in his chair with his hands on the armrests, like some benevolent emperor. "There is nothing I'd rather do, Wesley, but the nation is in a state of emergency. There's no longer any middle course. The bombing of the Democratic headquarters, the threats against Congress and myself, the assassinations and the damn militias . . . There's no way back."

Wesley tried to catch Donald Beglaubter's and Lance Burton's glances, but they'd both retreated into decorous shells of obedient civil servants, something Wesley could never do. "Yes, but we risk facing severe punishment later on if we don't apply the brakes here and now. Bestial things are going on out there; we know that. We execute militiamen after snap court-martials that are more like lynchings. I've heard about people being shot down from Alabama to Oregon, and I know they've already executed some of the militia members who are in prison. How do you think this makes people react in the outside world, not to mention average American citizens?"

"There are clear rules for what this state of emergency allows us to do, Wesley," answered Jansen.

"Yes, Mr. President, but tens of thousands of people have gone on strike because the situation has made them lose their jobs, and what do we do? We send out the National Guard against them. All opposition is being crushed so brutally, I'm afraid . . ."

Sunderland broke in bluntly. "That's right, we put down resistance wherever it arises." He looked at his watch, then at President Jansen. "We have most of the strikes in the larger cities under control now, and in a half hour all borders will be closed. I imagine the situation will improve somewhat in the course of tonight, Mr. President, so right now your safety is the highest priority. I am going to order the Secret Service to hold all rooms, chambers, and hallways on the second and third floor under surveillance, starting now. Do you approve, sir?"

Wesley didn't hear Jansen's answer.

Vice President Sunderland nodded to the security guard standing by the door. "Please inform the men outside that the president is leaving the building now."

They walked down to Lance Burton's office and closed the door behind them. Burton sat down at his desk and then, with the help of a remote control, adjusted the lighting and turned on his stereo. Subdued light and quiet classical music calms the soul, as he always used to say, but Wesley didn't expect it to help this time.

"Pinch my arm, I must be having a bad dream," said Wesley quietly.

Donald sat down across from him with his arms crossed and his jaw set. In spite of the anxiety that shone in his eyes, Wesley knew the man would remain clammed up.

"What's happening, Donald? Tell me what's going on."

Donald Beglaubter's mind seemed to be somewhere else. "We just have to decide what you're going to say two hours from now at the press conference. That's what's happening, Wesley, is it not?"

The three men looked at one another. One used to be able to take for granted their being a group that stuck together through thick and thin. Known as "The Triumvirate" and "The Three Musketeers," they knew one another inside and out. They were married in thought, allies in word and pronouncement, the salvage team that could be called upon to write themselves out of any tricky situation. They made the perfect combination: one to untie the Gordian knot, one to bind it together again stronger than ever, and the third to present their results to the public, leaving no shadow of doubt that the problem had been solved. But it wasn't like that now. Burton and Beglaubter were no longer performing their roles, which in turn made it impossible for Wesley to play the court jester with an answer for everything. What had happened to their renowned collaboration?

He drummed his fingers on the glass surface of the coffee table. "Is there one of you to whom I can speak freely?" he asked, looking first at one, then the other. His fingers continued dancing on the tabletop while the stereo played *Ode to Joy*. What could be more ironic?

Chief of Staff Burton spread his arms. "Both of us, naturally! Say whatever you like, Wesley."

He sat for a minute, trying to read Burton's and Beglaubter's facial expressions. Did he detect a glimpse of contact behind Donald's so carefully guarded look?

He stood up, took Lance Burton's remote, and turned up the music. Beethoven knew how to achieve the desired artistic effect; the atmosphere in the room changed in character. Then he removed his ID chip and reached over to do the same with Burton's. If they really were going to talk, it was essential they weren't overheard. But Burton leaned back in his chair, away from Wesley's outstretched arm, and looked at him with defensive animosity, like some threatened, wounded warrior. The reaction surprised Wesley, but he knew Burton would resist if he tried to remove the badge.

So he went back to his seat and sat down.

During the minutes that followed, Lance Burton reiterated the facts and events of the last twenty-four hours, all the time instructing Wesley as to what was allowed and what wasn't. Because, in spite of the fact that the situation everywhere continued to escalate out of control, he had to understand the president's goals remained unchanged. The Washington Decree with its Secure Future program was going to be successfully implemented, whatever the cost. Violence had to be extinguished, even with violence, if need be. Unemployment was going to disappear, no matter what. The media were going to be brought up to a higher moral level; all forms of corruption, organized crime, and drug dealing were going to be wiped out. There would be an election reform to guarantee true democracy. There would be total immigration control and illegal workers would be hunted down and thrown out of the country.

Lance Burton could recite the Washington Decree in his sleep. It was as though he'd been brainwashed by it. If all that he'd just stated didn't happen now, he declared in a convincing voice, it never would. The American liberal tradition had to be put temporarily on hold because that was what the situation demanded. This "fact," plus informing the public about the calling home of American troops to aggressively put down militia insurrections on American soil, were going to be the basic contents of Wesley's press briefing. It was a frightening agenda, definitely not one that he'd ever have expected to hear from the Lance Burton he used to know. He got the impression that everything Burton said was for the benefit of the hidden microphones, but then why didn't he at least give him some kind of sign? A shake of the head or a raised eyebrow?

Wesley could feel his diaphragm contracting. Boy, what he wouldn't do for a nice, fat joint right now. He'd inhale it in one toke.

———————

Back in his office, Wesley's legs were tripping nervously under his desk. He fidgeted with his pen and looked at the clock. He had an hour and a half, within which time whatever pile of crap he planned to say had to be okayed by both Lance Burton and Thomas Sunderland, which probably meant a rewrite or two. How the hell was he ever going to get this done?

He stood up. Maybe he ought to pop into Doggie Rogers's office. Maybe that was all he needed to get his head straight so he could write. He went into the archive, opened the back door to the narrow passageway, and looked to the left and right. The Secret Service guard nodded to him briefly. Then he heard someone in his office and turned to face Donald Beglaubter. His disheveled, thinning hair was a sign that he'd been doing some deep thinking. Wesley closed the door to the passageway. "Let's talk here, in the archive, Donald," he whispered.

He removed their badges and placed them under some old documents. "So, what's happened now?" he asked. Something obviously had.

Baglaubter was calm. "Thomas Sunderland has asked the president if he was considering resigning."

"What?!"

"Lance Burton was there when it happened. He thinks it was meant as an offer to Jansen, not a threat."

"My God! What'd Jansen say?"

"Nothing. He just shook his head."

"Did Sunderland really ask him that? Fucking hell! I'm sure he figures he's the one to take over from Jansen. The Constitution says he can."

"It wasn't discussed, but, yes, I'm sure he does."

"What'd Sunderland do then?"

"He looked satisfied."

This was amazing. What would be next? "What about you, Donald?" Wesley asked. "Are you satisfied, too?"

The White House's acting chief of communications was one of the best problem solvers Wesley had ever met and had been an asset ever since he joined Bruce Jansen's presidential campaign. But now, as he stood there studying his shoes, he was a shadow of his former self, impotent and distracted. "This is the last time you and I discuss things off the record, Wesley," he said, "so listen to what I have to say now and don't ask any questions. I can't answer them anyway." He studied Wesley for a moment. "We all have our reasons for reacting as we do right now. Nothing that's happening has happened by chance. If you think I like the situation and know more than you do, you're mistaken. But I've got my eyes open."

"Yes, but do we see the same things? Don't you think we ought to be discussing what we see?"

"Listen, Wesley, you haven't participated much in all of this until today. I'm sure you've had your reasons; you're not dumb. But none of us can help forming impressions about the others involved in this game, and some of us have long suspected you of playing a double role—you should know that. But since today I'm not so sure, which is why I'm here now. Do you understand?"

So there it was. Wesley couldn't believe his ears. "Me? What are you talking about? I've been protesting what's been going on from the very start!"

"Yes, but not all that much. It's been a kind of charade. Sometimes one makes a point better by staying quiet."

"Just like you, you mean? If I hadn't heard otherwise just now, I'd have gotten the impression you were a proponent of all this." He shook his head. "Tell me, Donald, is someone threatening you?"

"I said not to ask questions."

"What about Lance Burton? What's his position?"

"See? Another question. I honestly can't answer you. All I know is that he's done his own investigating along the way."

Wesley settled for shrugging his shoulders inquiringly so he couldn't be accused of asking a direct question.

Beglaubter looked as if he were considering whether he should say more. Wesley kept quiet; he didn't want to press him this time.

"I've already said too much, but okay, briefly: I don't know what investigations Burton has been making, but it all started when the attorney general's mother was raped. He mentioned several times to me that he thought the attack came a little too conveniently, just like the subsequent attack on Attorney General Lovell and the assassination of the chief justice of the Supreme Court. I think these are the kinds of things he's been investigating, but I'm not sure. Except that no one is above being investigated these days. So if you value your life, you've got to stop saying the kinds of things you said a while ago in Burton's office, and in the Oval Office before that."

Wesley stared deep into his eyes, as though they might reveal some deeper truth, but what he saw was hopelessness and despondency. Wesley knew exactly how it felt.

"I have to go now," said Donald, and replaced his chip. "Jansen and I have a meeting with some people from Internal Revenue." He clapped Wesley on the back, gave him an encouraging smile, and left.

Wesley sat still for a few minutes, trying to digest what Beglaubter had said. Suddenly, there was some shouting outside his door and the sound of people running, and then the shouts got louder.

He put on his badge, opened the door, and could immediately see something was very wrong. All the other office doors were wide open, too, with secretaries standing in some of the doorways, their hands over their faces. All the security guards were gone.

"What's happening?" he yelled, grabbing one of the secretaries.

"Oh, God, there's been an assassination attempt on the president. I think he's alive, but I'm not sure." She'd obviously been crying, but Wesley didn't know how he should feel. Was this good, or bad?

For some unknown reason, President Jansen had chosen to leave the White House via the tunnel to the Treasury Department, and along the way an unidentified man carrying explosives had attacked the entourage. Apparently, one Secret Service or FEMA agent and one other person were dead, and Jansen had been very, very close to being killed, too. Vice President Sunderland had been following a little ways behind and was unharmed, except for the shock that remained etched on his face.

The attack was terrible news for several reasons because if there'd ever been any hope that Jansen would soften up his hard line, it was gone now, for sure. Wesley knew Jansen. Now he'd join the fight with all the means at his disposal. He'd surround himself with bodyguards day and night and have the CIA, FBI, and FEMA deal with any form of resistance. Control would be tightened even more and suspicion and paranoia would flourish, which in turn would result in more disastrous decisions. The prospects were frightening.

After a short consultation with Lance Burton, Wesley canceled the press briefing. The situation was too complicated, too unclear. It might be a long, long time before there was another press conference.

He hunted through his shelves until he found a video that suited the situation. They'd recorded it a week ago, and it depicted a strong president at the top of his form, speaking about alternative sources of fuel to replace disappearing oil reserves, about becoming self-sufficient with energy in a great land with so many resources. About being positive and acting the way Americans were famous for when the going got tough. Wesley had several of these kinds of clips to choose from.

He dispatched the video sequence to the three large remaining networks, and one of them already had it on the air within ten minutes, followed by an ancient Hollywood movie, starring actors now deceased who couldn't protest being used as tranquilizers by the government. Sooner or later he'd have to hunt down a current movie star who still liked Jansen and have him or her interviewed. That is, if such a person were to be found these days.

Afterwards he found Doggie in her office. It was hard to see how she was feeling, but that kind of defense mechanism had become commonplace in the White House.

He sat down across from her and looked at her—this wonderful, intelligent, beautiful woman, the heiress to a huge fortune, who was a thoroughly good person. How had she ever gotten herself caught up in a mess like this?

"He's going to survive, isn't he?" was all she asked. Wesley nodded.

"That's good. He's the only one who can pardon my father."

She wasn't looking at him, and he understood. How else could she preserve—let alone express—such an impossible hope? What else did she have but hope?

"I called Sheriff T. Perkins just now. I'd called him hundreds of time before, but this time I got hold of him. I told him about a lot of realizations I've had regarding my father's case . . . Oh, Wesley, I know things that would postpone his execution, I'm sure of it. Things that could prove his innocence." She looked like she was ready to cry as she said these last words. "T was really listening, too. I just love that man, I just know he's going to try to help me."

Wesley kept looking at her until she looked at him. Her eyes were blue and determined. There, in the smallest and least important office in the White House, sat possibly the only person who still hoped the best for the president. But Wesley couldn't bring himself to tell her this.

All he could do was nod. And take her hand.

CHAPTER 18

THE WORLD FELL APART THE DAY JOHN AND DANNY WERE FOUND TO BE HIV-positive. Not that John was afraid to die—the Bugatti family had always taken a quite humorous attitude towards this particular human frailty. No, it was because an ominous, black cloud had suddenly overshadowed the happy relationship that had been flowering between the two of them.

The world didn't fall apart because it would soon expire, but because it had finally begun to exist. They had been lovers for many years, even though they lived in different cities, with John working in New York and Danny in Washington. Then John had changed his base of operations and moved down to Danny, into his dream house in the right end of Georgetown, between the church and the Pet Gallery. Those were days of innocence, where people's greatest fear was a worldwide computer meltdown as a result of the new millennium. Life was sweet, and the scent of oil paint filled the house as Danny's canvases became increasingly paradisiacal. Then came the sickness.

They both knew why. The temptations of Greenwich Village had always been hard to ignore, and John believed in living life to the fullest.

Now the world had changed completely. John's treatments were still effective enough that he wasn't actually feeling ill, but Danny hadn't been so lucky.

In the beginning, John had fallen for his glossy hair and the spark in his eye, but now the spark had gone out, and even though Danny did his best, he could no longer hide the inevitable. His brushes dried out; the scent disappeared.

John could hear the television running in high gear as he let himself into the house. His heart almost stopped every time he came home to a scene like this, and he had to force himself to place one foot in front of the other to make it to the living room and see if his beloved was still breathing.

He found Danny with his legs up on the coffee table and an empty Martini bottle in his lap. It took a lot of Martini to deaden the awareness of death, but Danny had always had style. He wasn't the type to dislodge his brain with a fifth of whisky, as John would tend to do.

John watched his chest rise and fall with persistent life. "Thank you, my love, for not leaving me," he whispered.

He turned down the TV, leaving the credits of an old Marx Brothers movie to roll silently across the screen. It had been a dramatic day. United, for once, in their opposition to the government, religious organizations from across the sectarian spectrum had held a huge demonstration, their colorful religious garb filling the streets. The police had kept a low profile—they apparently hadn't reached the point of teargassing rabbis, imams, and priests. Most of the electricity in town had been shut down, and the evening air was still ringing with damnations and hymns of protest in God's name.

There were repercussions just as great in other sectors of society. Powerful organizations that traditionally had conflicting interests— like trade unions and big business—were finding common ground. It seemed like anything was possible. Words like *general strike, insurrection,* and *seizure of power* were being whispered in the wings, but the state had big, attentive ears and people were disappearing from their homes in the middle of the night.

Two of John's colleagues hadn't shown up for work that day. He was sure that one of them had gone underground, but that didn't seem to be the case with the other. Miss B, as they called her, had made repeated trips to Somalia and Afghanistan when conditions were at their worst, so it took more to shake her up than the summary execution of militiamen in broad daylight or the sight of uniformed bodies floating down the Potomac. More likely the problem was that her profession had made her too hard-boiled to sense how dangerous the situation could become, to see that she, like the rest of the media, had to conduct herself with extreme caution when dealing with the concept of "the truth." Maybe somewhere else in the world she would have kept quiet; in certain situations she'd learned it was wise to do so. But the other day she'd flipped out at the NBC offices and punched a delegated censor in the face when he demanded that her commentary in a news spot be deleted. She'd been reporting on the military's hunting down of illegal immigrants and how they were being dumped in no-man's-land on the other side of the Mexican border. They had no documents, no identity, and the Mexican authorities didn't want them, either. It was an important and relevant news story, and John was sure that he, too, would have fought for his right to tell how terribly wrong and inhumane this new government policy was. How thousands of banished souls were freezing at night in the open without food, pinned down by American and Mexican soldiers on both sides of the border.

No one had seen Miss B since lunchtime. Some were saying she'd "simply had enough." John feared the worst.

He put his hands to his head and massaged his temples, trying to soothe his mental anguish. Just before he'd left work, a source in the White House had leaked them the news of an assassination attempt on the president, but they were told not to publicize it before they were given permission. That meant one could soon expect countermeasures that were even more extreme, just like what followed previous violent episodes involving the president and his administration.

He poured himself a second solid glass of whisky and looked over wistfully at Danny. His head had fallen on his chest and his spread-out legs were in danger of toppling a variety of pill bottles off the edge of the coffee table. *He'd be so sorry if someone saw him like this,* John thought. He collected the bottles and took them out to the kitchen, then sat down in the dining alcove in the corner of the living room, pulled open a wide drawer under the tabletop, and removed a sheet of paper. He'd divided it into two columns, one for the dramatic episodes that had occurred in the vicinity of the president, and one for what measures the president had subsequently put into effect. The second column gave a clear picture of a country that, from an innocuous announcement of reforms in the social and judicial sector, had steadily developed into a truly ugly police state. John had been on the scene a long time and had witnessed many serious conflicts around the world, so he knew the signs of a democracy's impending collapse when he saw them. The Constitution was no longer really in effect, all opposition was systematically crushed, and the military was loyal to the regime. All borders were to be closed and the country would isolate itself from the rest of the world, as if this hadn't already happened. And finally, there was the classic lie promoted by every dictatorship: the promise of how much better everything would be afterwards.

It wasn't that John couldn't see the positive features of Jansen's agenda. Crime was down as criminals were forced to the surface, the streets were safer, and the suburbs were opened up. They'd begun tearing down condemned buildings in large cities like Detroit, Los Angeles, and Chicago. There were convoys of dump trucks and flatbeds with containers laden with all kinds of big-city debris, and work had been created for everyone. The streets in his own little oasis of Georgetown looked as if they'd been vacuum-cleaned; legions of the unemployed were busy picking up every scrap of litter along roadsides and highways all the way to the Great Falls. Yet on the horizon behind this ultra-tidy landscape one could occasionally spot columns of smoke rising from skirmishes between soldiers and their own landsmen. It was a grotesque sight to behold. Beneath the neat and orderly facade a society was disintegrating.

He sat in the gathering twilight and stared at the sheet of paper, seeing how cause and effect merged into one. Would Jansen have ever gotten the majority of Cabinet members to back his Secure Future program without the support of Attorney General Lovell, and would Lovell have ever supported it if his daughter and poor old mother hadn't been raped? John doubted it. And would the president have gotten away with suspending the parliamentary process without the attempt on the life of the attorney general and the assassination of the chief justice of the Supreme Court? Couldn't the increasing threats against public institutions, the bombing of courthouses and the Democratic headquarters, as well as the murdering of public servants and congressmen, have been a convenient excuse for declaring a national state of emergency?

The more he looked at the sheet of paper, the more he saw a totally different correlation between the two lists. The law of cause and effect had been reversed; a desired effect had created its own cause. The anxiety induced by "The Killer on the Roof" and the murder of some schoolchildren outside Washington had fanned the flames of the eternal national debate about weapon possession and had set the scene for new interpretations of the Second Amendment. Every day minor as well as major incidents were having big repercussions, and they all pointed in the same direction.

President Jansen was steadily approaching his goal of gaining total control over society. John drained his glass in one gulp and reloaded. Why try and stay sober? What difference did it make? There was nothing he could do, anyway. If he began voicing his suspicions—that Jansen and his cohorts had instigated violence, bomb threats, killings, and even the sexual assault of an old lady—he was finished. *Tell the world!* he screamed to himself—silently—as though he could, even if he tried.

It wouldn't be at NBC, that was for sure.

He sat for a moment, studying Danny. Had it been like the old, healthy days, he could have taken his lover by the hand, fled to Paris's Left Bank, and spoken his mind as freely and vehemently as he wanted. He could have gotten a job anywhere—the *Times*, the BBC, ZDF, or *Le Monde*—and Danny would have loved it all. Then they could attend exhibitions in Berlin, the opera in Vienna, or walk together under the colonnades in Bologna. But now it was too late, hundreds of fever attacks and thousands of pills too late. Danny couldn't go anywhere, and John couldn't leave him. He loved this man, who would soon be with him no longer. Why did life have to be like this?

One more glass of whisky, and he began sobbing. He leaned forward and gently took Danny's hand. It was warm, like his own cheeks.

Then, through the thickening alcohol mist, he noticed the news flickering to life on the TV screen. As he slowly turned to focus, he found himself staring straight at President Jansen's face. It had been given a thorough makeup job and filled the whole screen. The president was looking good, as he always did in public.

Bugatti let go of Danny's hand and turned up the sound.

There was no doubt the performance had been prerecorded some time earlier. How else could Jansen sit there, summing up the situation so calmly? Especially when there'd been an attempt on his life only hours before.

John shook his head in an attempt to dispel his inebriation and tried to listen to what was being said. It was a very "personal" speech, directed to a nation of individuals about their "hopes and dreams," as Jansen called it.

Empty words from a forked tongue, thought John.

"There is more that unites us Americans than separates us," said Jansen, his eyes glowing. "There's a great amount of confusion at the moment, but we'll soon find our footing again and proceed towards our common goal. Our troops are being called home from abroad as I speak, to assure the rule of law and the safety of all our citizens. All body bags will be destroyed because there will no longer be any need for them." He held a pregnant pause. "Our soldiers are coming home to help us restore order so that everyone can have the new chance they deserve. In the future, there will be funds to assure basic services and the functioning of society. There will be universal health care, and our courtrooms and prisons will be emptied as we cure the symptoms of criminality. And there will be meaningful jobs for everybody."

John shook his head. This called for yet another whisky.

The camera angle changed so that one could see that the president was sitting in the Cabinet Room, and that he wasn't alone. John had to squint to focus. He'd be damned if they weren't there, all of them: Billy Johnson, Vice President Sunderland, Secretary of Defense Henderson, Lovell, and the rest. Even the national security advisor and the director of the CIA.

Jansen spread out his arms like he was going to give all those present a big hug. "Here, in this historical parlor, sit the people this nation needs. Gifted, brave people, each one with a plan for you—for all of us—to make our dreams reality." He turned back towards the first camera and put on an even more earnest expression. "Unpopular measures will be needed to reach our goal—we know that. We must close our borders to immigration; we must get rid of all weapons. We have to raise our moral standards, and we have to learn how to make do with less."

John shook his head again. Stalin couldn't have said it better. Wesley had done his work much too well. He took another gulp of alcohol and felt like he had to throw up.

"America has been dependent on other countries' raw materials for all too long. Some of my predecessors have gone so far as initiating wars to secure us these resources, and often with catastrophic consequences. But I'm telling you today that we can become self-sufficient. The possibilities abound. Oil deposits have been found in Alaska, huge deposits that will ensure our energy supply for decades to come. And in the meantime we must learn to use less energy and alternative sources of energy. We Americans can do everything—we know that—and we'll show the way for the world again, as we have before."

John was halfway out of his seat and almost fell on his face. His body had suddenly become heavy and ungovernable. One leg shot out instinctively to keep his balance, almost kicking over the coffee table. Then came the dizziness, and he fell across the low table, breaking his whisky glass and landing on the carpet on top of the bottle and a pile of old interior decorator magazines.

This woke Danny up in a combination of confusion and fright.

John waved his hand at the television. "Turn that shit off," he raved, "before I put this bottle through the screen."

Danny had been here before—they both had. John knew this all too well. And even though Danny was so weak he could hardly bend over, he did the same thing every time. No sarcastic comments or disapproving looks. Just a cool washcloth to pat on his lover's forehead, a glass of water to drink, and a small sigh as he set about cleaning up the mess. Danny always made things all right again, soothingly and nonjudgmentally.

John took Danny's free hand and put it to his lips. "I love you, you old bastard. You're the only light in my life."

"Try and concentrate a minute, John." Danny looked distraught behind his smile. "Someone's been looking for you," he said. "That horrid TV host Tom Jumper, together with Miss B. They were here a couple of hours ago, wanting to talk to you. Miss B looked like she was totally out of it." He squeezed John's hand. "What have you got to do with Tom Jumper? The whole country's looking for him. You're not in any trouble, are you, John?"

John sat on the floor, trying to swallow, but his mouth was already like a desert again. He looked about to see if there was a bottle within reach, just a little nip to clear the head. He groped around under a couple of chairs but found nothing other than the fallout from dried-up snacks that had escaped Danny's vacuum cleaner.

So Miss B was on the loose. That, in itself, was good news, but not the fact that she was in the company of Tom Jumper. They made quite an unlikely couple.

"I don't know what they wanted," he said, getting up with difficulty. He looked out the window, where the sky had clouded over and raindrops had begun spattering the back porch.

They came back at night. Suddenly, somehow, they were standing in the backyard in an apocalyptic rain, knocking on the porch door. Danny begged John to stay in bed, whispering about the Pandora's box he'd open by letting them in, but John didn't listen. If *he'd* been standing there in their wet shoes, desperate for help, he'd expect to be let in, sure as hell. There were unwritten laws, especially in his business.

The two refugees stood there, shivering and wet to the bone, looking around as though they expected to be caught in a police searchlight any second. Danny tightened the belt of his robe, beckoned them indoors, and went straight to work as always, helping them out of their wet clothes. There were no protests. "I'll just pop these in the dryer. You can use these in the meantime," he said, laying out two kimonos over the back of a chair.

Miss B was strikingly thinner than John would have expected. She was gracious and vulnerable, and at present she was also a time bomb under the system. John had the greatest respect for her. Next to her stood Tom Jumper in all his pale-skinned, naked glory, staring at him with his TV-trademark brazenness. He had no illusions as to what John thought of him; it was something he was used to. Who could ever love a person who had made a huge fortune by exhibiting and exploiting society's losers for the entertainment of a TV audience? The answer, of course, was the rest of society's losers. But John lacked this curious form of mental and moral degeneracy. To him, Jumper was no less than a disgrace to his profession, with or without an arrest order on his head.

"You've got to help us, John." Miss B wrapped the kimono tight around her gaunt body and took his arm.

"Do your pursuers know you're in Georgetown?" he wanted to know.

"Do you think we'd be standing here if they did?" Tom Jumper was putting on his kimono slowly—typically provocative—but John didn't notice. He'd never been able to stand men who smelled like Jumper, a mixture of sweet sweat and expensive eau de cologne. "No, they don't know where we are. We're not so dumb as to use the net on a cell phone or wireless connections or credit cards. They've got a whole army of security goons these days whose only job is tracing shit like that." He patted his briefcase. "We pay cash."

That briefcase is brim full, thought John. He'd heard what this character made per show. "What are you two doing together?" he finally asked. "Do you know each other?"

Miss B nodded as she rubbed her toes, which were still blue with cold. "Yes, from journalism school. We've been friends a long time."

This was news to John. How many times had he slandered this clown in front of her? A thousand times? Two thousand? "But why are you with him now, Miss B? You know they're looking for him everywhere."

"Me, too, John. They've put a warrant out on me. I spoke with Alastair Hopkins a couple of hours ago and he recommended I hold a very low profile if I valued my freedom."

"It's not just because you punched out that brain-dead censor, is it?"

"The censor? No, John. It's all about the New York sniper. I found out it's not just a madman, like we've been made to believe. I'd been working on the case for a few weeks, until they stopped my investigation."

"I see." He thought immediately of the two-column list he had lying in the drawer. So she'd been starting to suspect some kind of connection, too, had she? If only she had confided in him a little earlier, dammit! "You're not a police reporter, so why'd you concern yourself with that case? Is it something Alastair set you to?"

She shook her head.

"What do you have to support your theory, if anything?"

"You can explain, Tom." She nodded at Jumper.

He took a step forward. "Regardless of what you may think of my show, John, I meet a lot of people that the police would like to have a serious talk with."

Yes, what else was new? Still, his curiosity had been awakened. "So I guess you're going to tell me you've had the killer on your program."

"Listen to what I'm saying. As you may or may not know, I end each of my shows by urging viewers to volunteer for a later show with some kind of particular theme in mind."

Bugatti laughed. "No, I don't think I've ever made it that far."

Miss B took his arm. "John, try and listen. He's okay, you just don't know it." She was right; he sure didn't. On the other hand, he could just make out the contours of a port wine bottle standing on the side table and began considering whether he could stay on his feet that short distance.

Jumper continued. "A few weeks ago we started a theme on our show called 'If your boyfriend was the Killer on the Roof, would you turn him in?'"

Looking longingly at the port bottle, John could suddenly vividly remember exactly why he hated those shows. "Sure, and now it turns out the killer has some greedy, selfish little honey who can't resist the temptation of fame and fortune."

"It wasn't a girlfriend; it was a mother."

"A mother?" John thought of his own mother. If he'd murdered the pope himself, she'd never, ever, have turned him in. On the other hand, he did something far worse the day he proclaimed his homosexuality. He may as well have stabbed her in the heart.

"This is where I come into the picture, John." Miss B lit a cigarette and gave Danny a nod when he pointed at the ashtray. Her hair was still wet, plastered to her neck, just as she often looked in front of the TV cameras when she was off on an assignment. It was a role she was born to play. "Tom called and wanted me to take over after they shut down his show and started chasing him. He felt there was a connection between the warrant for his arrest and the call he received, and I was inclined to agree."

John studied Jumper with new eyes. The notion that his show had been closed down because he had come into the possession of extremely sensitive information—not because the program was a gross sociocultural insult to humanity—bothered the hell out of him. Could it really be possible that this man was a threat to anything other than good taste? Were the pathetic diatribes his assistant held atop his street-corner orange crate merely the authorities' pretense for issuing an arrest warrant for him? Unfortunately it made good sense. He raised his heavy eyelids and gave them both a skeptical look but one tinged with respect.

"Has anyone considered the possibility that this woman, who wanted to turn in her son, was merely out to grab a little attention for herself, put some excitement in her life? Or that she might be one of those crazies who has a habit of taking credit for all kinds of crimes, only this time on behalf of her son?"

Miss B nodded. "Both of these could be possibilities, yes. There's no way we can be sure."

"I'll bet the woman has disappeared in the meantime." John gave a dry laugh.

"No, she died."

"I see. . . ." It wasn't the first time he'd heard stories like this. Plenty of big mouths had been permanently silenced in the course of recent American history. Miss B and Tom Jumper had obviously reached an impasse in their investigation. "Hmm, that's a shame. And I suppose the son has disappeared in the meantime as well?"

"They were both found dead in her living room," Miss B replied. "Food poisoning, apparently. Botulism, more specifically, from some rancid pâté. Very convenient, I'd say. Not something that happens every day in New York."

John tried to shake off the boozy mist that was still clouding his brain. "So then the sniper shootings stopped, or what?" he asked, knowing they hadn't.

Miss B ignored the edge in his voice. "No, but then they could count the son out. Think what a scoop we'd have had, if it had been him. The young man was known for being an excellent marksman. Everyone in his apartment building said so."

"Sure. And it's only reasonable that a mother would suspect her own son." All the alcohol was making him sarcastic now, and John considered whether he should continue on his drinking binge or take the cup of coffee his deathly pale lover was holding out to him.

"Okay, Bugatti, we know you're still skeptical," said Jumper, "but then add the fact that our young man had an employer a few months before his death who could make good use of his shooting talents. Does the address 935 Pennsylvania Avenue mean anything to you?"

John heaved a sigh. Deep inside he'd expected something like this. "FBI headquarters." He turned directly towards Jumper. "Let me get this straight, Tom . . ." This was the first time he'd addressed him by his first name. "You're saying he'd been working for the FBI, was a crack shot, and that his mother claimed he was the killer?"

"Right."

"But he was no longer employed by the FBI at the time of his death, and the shootings continued?"

"That's correct." Jumper nodded and accepted a cup of coffee from Danny.

Now John was more puzzled than skeptical. "So, either the FBI is involved, or the mother was mistaken, or our young man and a couple of his sharpshooting buddies had formed a little New York safari club, meaning there was more than one shooter. Or else it was some other damn scenario altogether."

"Hey, John, c'mon!" Miss B broke in. "You're much too experienced a journalist not to prick up your ears about this. The White House could well be behind the New York shootings. There's no doubt the Killer on the Roof was grist for their mill. It was all Jansen needed to get his big reform plan off the ground—simple as that. We don't know the concrete details, like the order of command and sequence of events, but apparently we know enough that they're doing everything they can to track us down. Do you agree with that at least?"

"I'm all ears, dear, believe me. And you can rest assured I understand very well why you wanted to pursue the story." He'd accepted Danny's cup of coffee, and now he took a gulp. A couple of cups of this potent brew, and he'd be ready for anything.

He made a call to two friends who lived a couple of miles away and were sure to agree to putting up the fugitives for the night and do whatever else was necessary. They were a couple of anarchistic antique dealers who'd sold their boutique long ago, put their millions in the bank, and had begun getting bored. They'd love getting back into the action, even if it were only for a minute.

Jumper shook John's hand. "I have a transmission van waiting for me in Arcola. Put your radio on long wave, and you'll hear from me tomorrow afternoon. I don't know the frequency yet, but I'm sure you'll find it." When he was finished shaking John's hand, he put a scrap of paper in it with an e-mail address.

"How the hell are you going to make it over the river?" John asked. "There are roadblocks at all the bridges."

"I'm going alone. B's going to try to get out of the country and report from abroad; that's all I'm going to tell you. But thanks for your concern. I have a couple of friends in Leesburg who can fetch us tomorrow morning, so don't worry. You and Danny have given us all the help we need."

John's and Danny's friends picked up Jumper and Miss B in a pink-colored camper at two in the morning, just before curfew. No one in the world would suspect them of being anything but what they were: two gay men in a pink velour poof paradise on wheels and a bumper sticker on the back reading VENICE BEACH, HERE WE COME! A safer form of transportation would be hard to find.

When they were gone, John sat down and stared into space, Danny's hand in his. If Miss B and Tom Jumper were onto the scent of what he believed they were, then it was an extremely dangerous situation for both them and himself, not to mention the entire power structure. As soon as Jumper had a microphone in his hand again and a mobile transmitter, all hell would break loose. There would be lives lost before it was over. If only they could be the lives of some of the bastards in the Jansen administration for once.

Danny lay his head on John's shoulder and gave his hand a soft squeeze. This was the sign that he had something serious to say. The more serious, the softer the squeeze.

"Take this to be on the safe side," said Danny, and passed him an envelope as thick as the Sunday *Washington Post*. "There's nine thousand dollars. Don't give me that look, I *am* actually capable of saving money occasionally. So this is for you. You've got to get out of here, John, understand? Go to the airport tonight. Go at five A.M. when the curfew ends and fly to Alaska or Montana. Then you can find a way to cross the border to Canada." He looked him deep in the eyes while John tried to refuse the envelope.

"Yes, John, you have to leave. They're probably not hunting for you yet, but it's surely only a matter of time. You have to expect they'll be shutting down the rest of the TV stations before long, and I wouldn't be able to bear seeing you sitting on your hands, raging about how you can't do anything because I'm holding you back."

John tried to say he didn't feel held back, but Danny stopped him with a stroke of the cheek. So that's how parting felt.

It took John more than three hours to reach Dulles International. Along the way he saw mile after mile of unlit, deserted streets and restaurants and movie theaters with chains across their doors. There

were soldiers everywhere, sitting behind machine guns in their armored vehicles at hundred-yard intervals all the way to the airport,
checking all civilian traffic. The closer they got to the airport, the
longer the lines of cars at the checkpoints. And by the time the terminal finally came into view, he knew he wasn't going to make Flight
6837 to Seattle at 8:00 A.M., which meant he wouldn't catch Flight 883
from Seattle to Anchorage, either. He parked his car between two vans
displaying FEMA logos and wheeled his suitcase into the check-in hall
to join hundreds of tired, anxious fellow passengers. Now he'd have
to improvise and find a new destination.

North Dakota, Montana, Alaska, Idaho—whichever was easiest at
the moment. He chose the shortest line and tried not to think of Danny's face as he stood in the window, waving good-bye. He'd already
convinced himself they'd see each other again. Of course they would—
that was all there was to it. Danny would manage, and they'd be together once more when the time came.

John nodded to a tall man standing in front of him. He looked to
be in his early sixties and was accompanied by a younger and very
beautiful Asian woman, probably his wife. It looked like they'd been
standing there all night. PETER DE BOER was written on his baggage
tag, with an address in Amsterdam. John took a step to the side and
looked at the line of passengers before him. In the cold neon light they
looked more tired and distraught than ever.

He wondered what plane he'd finally end up on.

"Excuse me," said the Dutchman, "are you a US citizen?" John was
still considering what answer to give when the man continued, pointing at a sign a couple of yards away. "If so, you're in the wrong line."

The sign read: FOREIGN CITIZENS ONLY.

John looked around. There were machine-gun-bearing men in uniform at all the counters and exits. No one was speaking to each other.
Practically all that could be heard in the enormous check-in hall was
the muted rumbling of small baggage wheels.

"You have to go over there," said the Dutchman's companion,
pointing at the next counter with its inevitable line of hundreds of
silent people. "I'm not sure how much good it will do, though," she

continued. "They're probably never going to get out of here. If you stand in that line, the only thing you'll accomplish will be that sooner or later you'll be pulled out of line and asked all sorts of questions."

She pointed at a little cluster of official-looking men who'd surrounded a man with an attaché case clutched to his chest. He looked frightened.

The Dutchman put his mouth close to John's ear. "We've been waiting here twenty hours, and that other line hasn't moved an inch the whole time. We'll be lucky to get out of here, too. It looks like they're locking the door to the United States and throwing away the key. I've seen quite a bit in my time, but never anything like this."

CHAPTER 19

PETE BUKOWSKI, THE PRISON GUARD, HAD MADE A MISTAKE. IT WAS A PRETTY big one, but every cloud has a silver lining, they say.

Now it was Friday. He'd had three days off, and for three days his insides had been churning restlessly with apprehension and excitement, so that all he could do was stare into space. Bud Curtis wanted a cell phone, and tonight Pete was going back to death row. Now he had to make the decision of his life and not fuck it up.

To do it, or not to do it—that was the question. No one else could give the answer for him.

The evening before, he'd been silent at the dinner table. Contemplating his wife chewing her food, he saw condemned men before him, consuming their last meal. When she spoke he was lost in a maze of his own thoughts. It made him sad when she placed his hand on her stomach, growing with life. During these past weeks Sussex State Prison had expropriated his whole being, and the mere thought of spending one more day there made him sick.

Afterwards he'd retreated to the veranda to think things through, and Darleen had followed with a cold beer and vigilant gaze. She said she could feel something was on his mind. This he dismissed by saying that, what he was thinking she didn't want to know. And, even though she probably realized this was true, she'd turned on what charm she had and pressed her warm body against his until she'd softened him up. Then the words started pouring out, and strangely enough he felt better when it was over. He'd apparently needed to share his thoughts with someone. In any case, Darleen now knew all about the condemned men's complaints and about how he fastened them to the execution pad and then looked away as they died. About how he passed the hours leaning against the death-row wall. And about how Bud Curtis had offered him a lot of money for a cell phone.

Passing on this last bit of information was Pete's mistake.

The moment Pete's wife realized what this possible wealth could mean, she forgot all about her husband's troubled state of mind and began babbling. There was no end to all the happiness this money could bring. Lots of small things that would enhance her social status and just as many big things that would far exceed what a woman of her class could ever expect from life. She lay wide-awake all night, planning the order in which her needs would be fulfilled. The next day she was so preoccupied, she didn't go to work. Instead she sat in the kitchen reading the real estate ads. There wasn't a new home that wasn't within reach. The girls at the beauty parlor could think what they liked. For sure they'd spend the day gossiping about how Darleen probably hadn't shown up because her husband had beaten her. Most of the women who frequented Lily Johnson's salon were married to prison workers, so they knew what they were talking about. The men who worked at Greensville and Sussex had short fuses, and it was true there'd been times when Pete had wanted to hit her. But even though he'd come close on more than one occasion, and even though Darleen was generally the greatest abomination in his life, it was also just as true that he'd never done it.

Pete had found a little house on the wrong side of the tracks, and his mother had warned him:

"Darleen's not from Waverly; she'll never fit in. You're making the biggest mistake of your life, son."

Pete had asked her to mind her own business.

It was on that occasion Pete learned how right a mother can be.

Darleen was from Claremont, an even smaller town over by James

River, sixteen miles to the east. Here she'd grown up in the mistaken belief that she came from a better place than anyone else in the area, and that Waverly was nothing more than a temporary outpost to park her more than abundant bulk.

Having been instructed in regard to what prejudice can do and how anxiety can make it worse, it's possible he was capable of understanding her to a certain degree. Unlike her hometown, there were black people everywhere in Waverly. For Darleen, a black man meant trouble, and when one had a mind like Darleen's, one was somehow always right. It was true: Claremont suited Darleen better than anywhere else. There, almost everyone was like her: white, lower middle class, overweight, and looking out for themselves. Pete's mother had been right: A girl like her couldn't live in Waverly.

And now Darleen was putting on the pressure. He had to get a cell phone to Bud Curtis, whatever the risk, because now she wanted to be rich fast. She wanted to move back to the river she came from, but this time to the wealthier side. For what could be better for a factory worker's girl from Claremont than to live in a colonial house in Williamsburg, with tourists filing by in admiration? She'd give birth to girls who would wear petticoats and boys who wore three-cornered hats. She would play the Countess of Gloucester and immerse herself in America's most glamorous and patriotic play—a permanent extra among the hundreds of average Americans who each year dressed up in costumes from colonial times and reenacted the War of Independence. So what if the country was in the process of falling apart and no tourists made it all the way down to Virginia? Everything would be back to normal one day. Just as long as they got all that money, everything would be good.

Deep in his soul Pete knew he'd have to find a cell phone if things were going to get better—at home, at least. With that gadget in his hand, he had the chance of not only becoming every bit as rich as Darleen dreamed of but, more important, so rich that he wouldn't have to share Darleen's future with her. He'd already made up his mind. Darleen and the child in her belly would be well provided for, that was certain, but so would he.

He had promised Bud Curtis to get hold of a cell phone within three days, but only if Curtis paid up front. Pete didn't want to be cheated. He'd be powerless if Bud got the phone first. There was just the very banal but obvious problem that Curtis couldn't raise the money without it. So Pete had to give him the phone and take the risk. He threatened revenge if Curtis tried to cheat him. Curtis was made to understand all the things that could go wrong for him. During the execution, for example. Painful things.

So Pete had to get that cell phone. The more he thought about it, the more reasonable it sounded. If their routines at the prison hadn't slackened and the personnel cut back so much, the cell phone would never have had a chance of making it as far as death row. He decided to smuggle it inside his thermos and give it to Bud just before he went off duty. However, thanks to the chaotic state the country was in and all the radical changes that had been implemented, it was practically impossible to get hold of a cell phone that couldn't be traced to its owner. It used to be easy to buy a stolen phone in any drinking joint in the county, but now they all had to be registered at the local police station, and those that weren't were made inactive. So it was no longer an easy task, but Pete managed to pull it off. Bud Curtis's execution was coming up. There were only seventy-two hours left.

Death row had been moved from Mecklenburg Correctional Center to Sussex State Prison just before Pete turned eighteen, and it was here he decided he would work when he finished his military service. He'd be dealing with prisoners who were serving life sentences or were condemned to death, just as his father had. It was a good job that commanded respect, he told himself. It's true that after his father's death, people warned him that life on death row had mortally wounded his father's soul, but Pete knew better. His father had taken his life, not because he had to deal with the condemned men but because he had to take their lives as well, and Pete was having none of it. His dad had worked in Greensville, but Pete would be working at Sussex, where they didn't kill prisoners. They merely stored them until someone else killed them down in Greensville.

And Pete carried out his plan. After six years in the military he applied for the job at Sussex, and with his spotless record, he was hired immediately. It took no time to drive to work, and his job was easy. He took part in the routines, and no one worked too hard. He could have gone on like this for decades if the warden, Bill Pagelow Falso, hadn't succeeded in fulfilling his wish to add a small building to the end of death row. Citizens' rights groups were up in arms when people realized that Sussex suddenly had gotten its own execution chamber, but their protests didn't help.

This didn't sit well with Pete, either, but what was done was done. Unemployment was sky-high in his area, and the house mortgage had to be paid. It was only a little three-room cottage, but it was his and it was going to stay that way. He'd just have to take things as they came. So far, luckily, more experienced guards were being assigned to execution chamber duty.

But then came President Jansen's proclamation of his Safe Future program, and all prisons were gradually emptied, including Sussex. Even prisoners with long sentences were eased back into society with an electronic detector strapped to their legs and the clearly defined task of working with young people in criminal environments. Warden Falso held a meeting with the entire prison staff where he dealt out their new duties. Whatever else one might say about him, Falso was no softie. Without warning, all employees over the age of thirty-five were moved to new jobs outside the prison. Some were to work on the ballistic registration of firearms; others were to act as contact persons for the newly released prisoners. Then there were those who would go from house to house, registering the inhabitants' fingerprints, while others would sit all day in the local schools' gymnasiums and encode all the information that had been gathered. It was a huge amount of work, but few protested. After years of living within Sussex's concrete walls, most of them were ready to say yes to anything.

The younger prison officers weren't as lucky. When they'd finished

letting out the last prisoner and had executed the last of the condemned, there would be use for only very few of them to keep the
prison running. No new jobs had been provided for the rest. Not yet,
at least. Warden Falso made himself clear: Nowhere in his job description did it say he had to provide manpower for that communist pig
Jansen and his perverse ideas.

Pete was chosen to work not only on death row, but also in the execution chamber. He didn't protest. He could handle the job of strapping
down the condemned men, even if his old man couldn't.

He'd said that two weeks ago, and already his soul was being torn
apart.

The first execution wasn't the worst. He performed his duties like
a zombie and remembered nothing afterwards. The second, on the
other hand, was bad. The prisoner had frightened brown eyes and the
wrecked veins and needle scars of a hard-core junkie. Pete could still
feel his lungs almost bursting from that terrifying minute when he
reflexively held his breath.

He'd participated in five executions since the implementation of
President Jansen's reforms, and that was already five times too many.

He tucked the thermos under his arm. He had to get away from
there.

CHAPTER 20

IF ANYONE WAS JUSTIFIED TO COLLAPSE UNDER A CRUSHING WORKLOAD, IT WAS Sheriff T. Perkins. And if there was anyone who hated men in uniforms that stank of day-old sweat, it was his newest police constable, Dody Hall, who turned on the air-conditioning, sat as close as possible to the window in the patrol car, and attempted to screen herself from their body odor with her impressive, fragrant hairdo. T. Perkins rubbed the gray stubble on his chin, looking out the window as the windshield wipers flapped in high gear. He knew what she was thinking, but by now he'd been on duty twice as long as she had, so what did she expect?

"What the hell do we do now?" she asked.

He shrugged his shoulders. It was a good question. On the opposite side of the road a column of trucks was lined up, headlights on, waiting to get through a roadblock the National Guard had set up the week before. Inside the trucks were practically all the goods needed to stock the supermarkets in Mustoe, Vanderpool, and Monterey, but what good did it do, when the soldiers wouldn't let them pass? His phone had been ringing nonstop with anxious calls from supermarket managers, wholesalers serving the region's agricultural sector, and the mayor of Monterey. T wasn't having any particular problems with people getting out of hand, but when it began taking weeks before they could expect the supermarket shelves to be filled—then what?

Any kind of overview of the situation was impossible, and everything was slowly grinding to a halt. Before one knew it, society would be back to bartering. People could no longer be sure they'd get their wages and, after the shootings of workers in Chicago and Miami, they dared not strike.

"Did you hear what I said, T?" came the muted voice at his side.

"Yes, I heard it." He nodded, put the patrol car into reverse, and made a U-turn that almost threw Officer Hall out the passenger door.

"What are you doing?" she barked, shoving him.

"Let's go home and get some sleep. We're not doing any good here."

He turned off his cell phone and slept two hours before his subconscious gnawed its way through the dream barrier. Suddenly he was staring at the wall, wide-awake. Looking out the window, he could see it was still dark. His alarm clock read Friday, March 27, 2009, 4:35 A.M. Too fucking much. How the hell was he supposed to sleep when his whole brain was seething? He knew too many people with too many problems these days. Worst of all was the case of Jim Wahlers, the local undertaker and one of his old friends, who they'd jailed for stockpiling weapons and ammunition for the militias. The FBI had taken him away after being tipped off. They'd moved quickly and with determination, and no matter what names Jim's wife called T, he couldn't tell her where Jim was because he simply didn't know. The sheriff's office had received a fax that he was in solitary confinement and the charges against him were being processed, but how much help was that? T. Perkins doubted very much that she'd be seeing him again.

And there was also the case with Bud Curtis that Doggie Rogers had asked him to help her with. He'd actually already spent almost two weeks on the case—more time than he should have. How was he supposed to spare more time when he didn't have any, and had no new leads or ideas, anyway? He shook his head and clenched his teeth, angry as hell with himself. Why had he said he'd help the girl if he wasn't going to? God, it was hopeless being him.

He pulled a cigarette out of his pack and sat up on the edge of the bed. A couple of quick drags and then back under the covers. That usually helped make things better.

In the meantime he could think about what to say to Doggie when he called her back. She'd contacted him the day before yesterday, and Bud Curtis was to be executed on Monday, in just four days. In other words, he'd already stolen a third of the time she could have been using elsewhere in trying to help her father.

T. Perkins turned on his radio and found WVLS on his FM dial. Never before had he heard so much classical music, now that all local radio stations had been forbidden to broadcast anything that could be taken as being critical of the US government. WVLS took good care of its staff, but the large majority of local radio stations couldn't afford to keep its people these days, which was understandable enough. What sponsors could afford advertising? None that he knew of.

And there, in his sweaty-smelling bedroom with its unusual background music, he stared into the cloud of cigarette smoke and began thinking. Two separate feelings had emerged deep inside him, neither of which had a name or a face. Brooding, instinctive traces of something that had occurred to him before, or would have, had he had the time. And the louder the music grew and the closer the glowing cigarette came to his fingertips, the more he realized that he knew things he couldn't articulate.

This sensation of holding the key to understanding, and then misplacing it, was nothing new. There had been small cases and big ones that had been shelved and sometimes forgotten, but also those where this nagging feeling of knowing something had suddenly blossomed into certainty. Several times he'd been able to supply information on crimes many years after they'd happened, and he'd been able to provide clues in cases as far away as New Orleans, just by digging around in his memory and subconscious until it gave way. That's what was happening now. Two things were sending signals inside him, but his memory was being uncooperative. All he could sense was that Doggie was responsible for one of them, and the other had been there much longer.

He suddenly came to his senses when the cigarette ember reached his fingernail, setting off an evil smell. "What the hell . . . ?!" he yelled, and knew there was no going back to bed now.

After a shower so bracing that it almost lifted him off the bathroom floor, he chucked a couple of bull's-eyes into the kitchen dartboard and called his deputy sheriff, Stanley Kennedy. His boss had been on duty for almost three solid days without a break and was taking the rest of the day off. He'd be back early tomorrow—Saturday—and not a second before. No problem, said the deputy. He'd take over.

T banged down the receiver and stretched as far as the worn-out joint in his shoulder would allow. A plan was slowly taking form inside his brain.

He cast a glance at the living room's far wall where two precise rows of paintings decorated the frayed wallpaper. Most of them were from when his wife was alive—strange pieces of "original" art of the kind that to T's eye resembled the reproductions one could buy via mail order but were reputed to be good investments. The rest he'd inherited from his parents. He was on more solid ground here, with the Virginia landscapes and their immense tobacco fields, and among them a small canvas depicting a young naval cadet in dress uniform beneath a deep blue sky. For T it was the living room's focal point and direction finder. Not that he liked the painting—he didn't—but it helped him collect his thoughts. When he looked at it, he was "home," and he stopped caring about the check forgers in Bethel and the car thieves in Mill Gap. He studied the picture for a moment, feeling a bit sad. Then he rubbed his neck, went over, and took it off its hook. He had use for it.

By now, there was quite a bit of daylight outside. He looked down on the bare trees that separated the road from his land and spotted a vehicle he didn't recognize approaching at high speed.

He placed the painting on the floor and pulled a shirt over his head.

A couple of minutes later, there was a knock on the door. It was two men in prison officer uniforms from Augusta State Prison, down in Craigsville. He knew one of them, or rather he knew the bloodhound that was glowering at the man's feet. They'd used the dog many times to hunt down people on the run.

"All citizens must be registered according to Executive Order 11002, but you haven't responded to our letter, Sheriff Perkins. So you make it necessary for us to come to you, and that'll cost you a fine of three hundred dollars. You ought to know that better than anyone."

Three hundred dollars?! They must be crazy. T. Perkins looked at their badges. The single word INSPECTOR was engraved on them. "Goddammit, man," he protested. "I'm the sheriff in this county! You know damned well I've got plenty to do. I was going to come as soon as I could."

They gave him a cold stare. "It looks like you could now," one said.

"It's five in the morning. What were you expecting?"

"Do you have anyone living here?" asked the other one. "Anyone who isn't registered at this address?"

He shook his head.

"May we come in and check? Not that I need to ask." The officer with the bloodhound released the dog before T. Perkins could answer. While it was sniffing around, the other officer asked him for a blood sample and then sat him down at the kitchen table to fingerprint him.

"There's women's clothes in the closet," shouted the dog handler from the bedroom. "Would you please come in here?"

T. Perkins found him and the dog halfway into the closet. The man backed out, triumphantly clutching a coat hanger with a dress. "Would you please inform us who you have living here?" Now T. Perkins definitely recognized the jerk. He'd always been an asshole.

"No one! That was my wife's dress."

"She's not registered at this address."

"That's probably because she died in 1988."

The man shoved the evidence in T's face. "This dress isn't any goddamn twenty-one years old. I saw one just like it in Walmart last week."

T. Perkins shook his head. "Could be. I don't follow fashion."

When they left, T washed his hands, packed a small bag, placed the little painting behind the driver's seat on the floor of his patrol car, put the siren on the car's roof, and drove all the way to Richmond without being stopped more than a couple of times.

The city was quiet. The commonwealth flag was flying above the administration buildings, and young lovers were cuddling in the cafés just like old times.

He parked the car and walked towards the Supreme Court Building up by the Capitol. Boring his way into Virginia Capitol Police headquarters always felt kind of like running a verbal gauntlet. Smiling faces in blue uniforms greeted him up and down the hallways; he'd probably known almost all of them by name once. But since he wasn't good at pairing faces with names, he nodded politely to all of them with a chummy smile. Here were the hopeful probationers with whom he'd once scraped run-over raccoons off the highways. Here were his old colleagues with whom he'd broken up car-theft rings and busted rapists. Here, too, was his line of access to all the information the country's criminal past had to offer.

And he had a shitload of data to sift through.

As he passed one of his old dart contest archrivals, he fished his ever-present favorite dart out of his coat pocket, aimed at a mini-target on the bulletin board, tossed a bull's-eye, pulled the dart out, and tipped his hat to the man. Then he turned a corner in the direction of Beth Hartley, whose ample body dominated a worn desk littered with stacks of journals. She lifted her eyes and gave him a questioning smile, the same one that had once nearly cost him his marriage in the old days when she worked in his office. She was warm-blooded, always ready for anything, anywhere—the first time being in T's own living room the time she popped by with some information he'd requested. In the end, T. Perkins had had to ask her to transfer to Richmond.

He stared dejectedly at her wedding ring. She'd managed to be taken off the market before he'd become a free man again, dammit. It wasn't the first time this twinge of regret had hit him.

"Yes," he said, "here I am."

She laughed. "What in the world brings you here, honey?"

He could have arrested her just for that tone of voice, rubbing itself up against him like a purring cat. "Oh, I just needed to talk with you, that's all," he replied.

"Okay, toots, that sounds intriguing. Why didn't you call me, then? You know I'm always ready for a bit of you-know-what on the telephone, don't you, little T?"

He leaned towards her desk and wound up peering straight down a dangerously deep cleavage. "I . . . have to speak with you, Beth. The telephone wasn't such a good idea in this case. Can you come outside for a minute? I have something I want to show you."

She fanned her face as though she was having a hot flash. "Well, well, T. What can you show me that I haven't already seen?" She laughed in a way that made the other office girls look up.

"It's something you've seen before. Something you really, really want."

She placed a couple of files on the corner of her desk and turned off her computer. Beth must have been almost sixty by now, but this fact had yet to reach her pituitary gland. There was no doubt that Beth Hartley would continue performing unmentionable, sinful acts with men until she went to her grave. Luring her outdoors wasn't too difficult.

He led her down to where his car was parked on 7th Street and opened the door for her.

She glanced at her watch. "If you were planning to drive me out to some haystack in the countryside, I'm afraid I'll have to disappoint you, honey. We have twenty minutes at the most. I can't be gone longer than that."

T. Perkins sat down in the driver's seat and pulled the painting over from the back seat. "Look. You've always wanted this, Beth, and now you can have it."

It clearly wasn't what she'd been expecting, but this didn't prevent her from staring at the painting with the same kind of desire as if it had been a male stripper or Aladdin's lamp, which—in a way—it was.

T. Perkins was well aware of what he'd brought with him, because it had been a topic of conversation more than once. The painter Edwin Forbes worked for Frank Leslie's *Illustrated Newspaper* during the entire Civil War, and in this case had painted a portrait of a cadet from the Virginia Military Institute who'd partaken in the exceptional battle at New Market. It was said he hadn't done many oil paintings, and this was apparently one that collectors really wanted to get hold of.

T. Perkins didn't know what the painting was worth, and he didn't care. It had hung in his family home for generations, and now it was time for it to move on. Beth had been pestering him for the picture ever since the first time she'd laid eyes on it—and laid him, too, for that matter—and now she was going to get it if she did the right thing.

"Yes, sugar, it's what you think it is. In return, you have to get me all the documents from the Bud Curtis case. Video surveillance tapes, photographs, court records, the stenographer's verbatim report—everything."

His words had the same effect as if he'd pulled an ice-cream cone out of the mouth of a child. She stiffened in a combination of frustration and despair while her eyes remained locked on the picture.

"I don't care how, Beth, just do it." He held the painting in front of her. "I know you can, Beth. You have access to everything. You'll probably have to go through the Investigative Services Unit here in Virginia or use some of our friends in Washington. The case documents are probably gathering dust in the appellate court. I wouldn't be surprised if the Department of Homeland Security had a copy of everything. I want you to siphon off all the data you can find and put it in this." He pulled a flash drive out of his briefcase and laid it in her hand.

Telltale red blotches were beginning to spread across her face.

"T, you're insane," she said, taking a couple of deep breaths. "Totally insane."

"I need it by this evening. Can you do it?"

"Oh, *mon dieu!*" Her mother's origins were not to be mistaken. "How much do you think that painting's worth?"

"How should I know? One hundred thousand, maybe."

She tore her eyes away from the picture while she tried to think. "And you're giving away a hundred thousand for that information? What's the point? You're not even a family relation, are you?"

"The point? The point is, I know someone who's ready to pay whatever it costs. Don't worry, I'll get my money back."

She put her hand to her bosom. Now she was on the verge of hyperventilating. "Oh, *mon dieu!* And here I was expecting we were just going to cuddle a little on the back seat for old times' sake."

He waited in the lounge of the Crowne Plaza for four hours before he saw Beth Hartley enter, wearing an expression that left no doubt that she was anxious to get their meeting over with. He asked her to sit down, but she disregarded him, looking about incessantly.

"Not here where everybody can see us," she whispered, clutching her handbag as though her life depended on it.

He stood up without a word and walked over to the elevator with Beth following behind. He saw that no one else was waiting and pushed the elevator button.

Inside the elevator she immediately reached inside her handbag while she checked the elevator ceiling for signs of video surveillance. She found the little flash drive and dumped it into his jacket pocket. Then she pushed the button for the seventh floor and stood without saying a word until she left the elevator with the painting under her arm. He continued up a couple of floors and, after waiting a half minute, took the elevator on the opposite side of the corridor back down.

T looked for her as he left the lounge, but she wasn't there.

The Virginia Capitol Police was founded back in 1618, but it had never had an employee as quick, efficient, and bright as Beth Hartley. Of this, T had no doubt after he'd been home a couple of hours, sifting through the material she'd given him. There was everything he could ever wish for.

He leaned back in his threadbare easy chair with a cigarette hanging loosely in the corner of his mouth. Bud Curtis had lost his day in court, and this, in all likelihood, had been the correct conclusion. But what if the man had been telling the truth? What then?

There was no doubt that Curtis was as reactionary as they came, but was that a crime? Was there anything wrong with it, if it were all just talk? That's how it usually was with people like him. In T's experience, very few braggarts followed up on their words with deeds.

He nodded to himself. He'd try the simple experiment of forcing himself to believe Bud Curtis's testimony 100 percent. Then it was a case of starting from the beginning and seeing what it led to.

He lit a new cigarette and stared emptily through the cloud of smoke.

During the trial the prosecutor Mortimer Deloitte had claimed that the story of the murder of the president's wife began when Bud Curtis was a young man and had participated in a far-right election campaign. Curtis's defense was that he'd done so solely to win the heart of Doggie's mother, and what was wrong with that? What hormonal young man wouldn't have been capable of doing the same?

Later he'd been successful in the hotel business and after some years had hired a dimwit by the name of O'Neill. Curtis had played with his power over the guy and, yes, he'd gotten him to lick Curtis's spit off the floor during a drunken all-night poker game, among other things. Rather repellent for T's taste, but that's how it was. The defense had argued that it hadn't been Curtis who'd suggested O'Neill unveil the painting, but rather a Secret Service agent who'd given a false name and had managed to disappear without a trace.

Even though Bud Curtis had often bad-mouthed Jansen, everybody who knew Curtis knew he was the argumentative type, and so what? Didn't everyone have some person who was their pet aversion?

And then there was the money transfer from Bud Curtis's account to O'Neill's. When you thought about it, this fatal transaction spoke more in Curtis's favor than against him. The man was a multimillionaire, for Christ's sake, and surely would have given O'Neill an envelope full of cash. On the other hand, this could be precisely why Curtis might have transferred the money so openly. He could have figured that such an obviously clumsy move would make people believe he had nothing to do with it, but the intended effect had boomeranged, anyway.

But this was all speculation. T's impression of Curtis was that he wasn't a man who took unnecessary chances. Therefore something fishy must have been going on. T was convinced that someone else had made that money transfer. Willie—the youngest man in the sheriff's office, with his obsessive affection for Internet technology—could do something like that with his eyes closed. There were plenty of possibilities, especially since identifying the actual sender of an electronic money transfer was impossible.

If one really believed in Curtis, then someone else must have manipulated Toby O'Neill into doing the shooting and had provided him with a weapon at the right moment. And why couldn't that someone be a man with a fictitious name like "Blake Wunderlich"?

Backed up by Curtis's own admission, the prosecutor Mortimer Deloitte had claimed the gun came from Curtis's desk, and then he'd thrown down his trump: The cartridges also bore Curtis's fingerprints. So it didn't do Curtis much good to claim he'd never loaded it.

But, according to the records, these fingerprints were far from perfect. They could have been transferred from somewhere else. T had seen it before, where a fingerprint from a glass, for example, had been photographed, a rubber mold made and then stamped onto the cartridges. This wasn't at all impossible, and someone could also have easily grazed Curtis's skin with these rubber fingerprints so his DNA would be there, too. So it all could have been a setup.

Then there was the whole issue of the glass of water that disappeared, or had never been there. If it were true that Curtis had fetched a glass of water for Mimi Jansen, then this activity would have had to have been recorded somewhere on a surveillance video, but T couldn't see it when he watched the video copies Beth Hartley had provided him. He actually couldn't see much of anything in those throngs of people on the grainy, black-and-white video. That the glass had disappeared in all the confusion was no stranger than so many other aspects of this case.

He frowned. There was still something odd here. A glass tends to break when it hits the floor, and any water in the glass would leave signs of wetness. If Curtis's claim were true, then why didn't the technicians mention broken glass and puddles of water in their report? He shook his head. He had to pursue Bud Curtis's version of events: that there *had* been a glass and there *had* been water. These were just two small details in the midst of all the confusion, and it was certainly not impossible that someone had made this evidence disappear. Why would Curtis lie about such a thing, when he knew the room was under video surveillance? How could anyone have known someone would doctor the video?

The more T. Perkins went over the sequence of events, the more nagging questions emerged. Who gave the shooter the weapon, for example? No one could make a seasoned sheriff believe that the Secret Service agent who'd originally searched and okayed O'Neill, or Ben Kane, who'd searched him immediately prior to the unveiling, couldn't do their job properly. Under all circumstances, the gun's route from Curtis's desk to O'Neill's hand was a series of unanswered questions that the prosecution had done very little to answer.

Perkins returned to reading the case documents. Something else was hard to understand: No one had seen the perpetrator fire the shot. Another thing was, many witnesses had heard O'Neill scream something before he fired, but none of them could say what. T. Perkins simply couldn't understand it. Toby O'Neill may have been pretty dim, but his enunciation wasn't *that* poor. In addition, several of the persons present were highly trained special agents who would have been able to identify a single voice among hundreds on the tape. T. Perkins had once had one of these guys come to his department to help whip a couple of slow-witted new recruits into usable sheriff's deputies. Hadn't the man been able to give a detailed description of another officer who popped in and out of the office in five seconds, wearing twenty-five articles of clothing?

Then why didn't any of these specially trained superagents know who shot O'Neill or what he'd screamed in the seconds before he fired and was subsequently shot himself? Could it be because they'd never been asked? Could it be because he hadn't yelled anything intelligible?

And finally, there was a point the defense had raised, namely, why in the world did Toby O'Neill shoot the man's wife instead of the man himself?

The prosecution's whole theory was built on Bud Curtis having practically hypnotized O'Neill into becoming a killer, and that it was the senator upon whom Curtis's wrath was focused. How could O'Neill not hit his victim at such close range?

T. Perkins looked at the computer screen and beamed up the video recordings for the third time that evening. There were five three-minute files from the surveillance camera in the hallway and two video clips from NBC4, one of them two minutes long, the other, ten. Files one, two, and three showed a slightly impatient O'Neill waiting by the painting, next to a statuelike Secret Service agent in a gray suit. The crude, bashful little man really was acting crude and bashful: picking his nose, scratching his crotch, blowing his nose, and then waiting some more. It was impossible to see if he was concealing a weapon somewhere.

File four showed what much of the case had dealt with: the entourage coming in and stopping at the still-veiled painting, Bud Curtis speaking with Mimi Jansen and then disappearing, and finally the shooting and ensuing confusion.

He studied every individual in the video. They were all there: Bugatti, the soon-to-be president and first lady, Sunderland, Wesley and the rest of the staff, and the black-clad and gray-clad bodyguards. He saw firearms appear in many hands immediately after the first shots. Reminiscent of Lee Harvey Oswald's fate in Dallas, one could clearly read the pain in the assassin's body language as he himself was hit. Still, it wasn't easy to figure out how the man who'd shot O'Neill could pick him out so easily in the crowd, unless he'd had previous knowledge of what was going to happen and who to shoot.

T. Perkins nodded to himself a few times. If he'd been there, he'd have hesitated shooting.

Amongst all those prominent people and amidst all that confusion, how could one be sure of not hitting someone by mistake?

He lit a new cigarette and ran the fourth video file again. The camera angle wasn't good, and the clip wasn't of much use. People were standing packed together, so unfortunately he couldn't see if someone bumped into O'Neill as he fired, which—if it were true—could possibly explain why O'Neill missed his shot.

He clicked on the fifth file, which showed the battleground just as Bud Curtis reentered. There he stood in the doorway as some panic-stricken guests cowered on the floor around him and others charged past him out of the room. T could see no glass of water in his hand, but one hand made a brief movement before both of them flew to his temples in apparent disbelief as he spotted Jansen bent over his wife. One couldn't see Curtis's face from the high camera angle, but his body language clearly communicated shock. Several people were lying on the floor, wounded by ricocheting bullets, and more security was rushing in as others yelled into their lapel microphones for assistance.

It was all very interesting, but, in the end, the videos revealed just as little about what happened as what didn't.

He closed video file five and opened file six. This was NBC4's direct transmission of the flags hanging in the hallway, followed by a minute of unsteady, handheld footage shot over people's heads. One could pick out the moment where O'Neill's arm pulled the tassel of the drape and revealed the painting. Then the photographer focused closely on the painting, as though communicating to the TV viewers his bafflement over the picture's tackiness. Next he panned down to Mimi Jansen's face as she stepped forward. For a moment it appeared as though she were about to laugh, but she managed to maintain her composure. Instead she nodded slowly, but as her eyes traveled up the painting she looked as if she were about to laugh again. T caught himself imitating her grimaces—it was simply impossible not to. Next the camera zoomed out a bit, as though in search of Senator Jansen's face in the crowd, but, with so many people, there wasn't enough room for the cameraman to get a good shot.

At that moment came a cry, presumably from O'Neill as he was shot. It was a thin voice, and even though T reran the sequence several times, it remained unintelligible amidst the muddle of noise and voices around him. Next the cameraman was knocked down as panic-stricken guests made for the exits, and the last sequence showed a blurred picture as the camera fell to the floor and continued running.

T sat for a while, trying to sum up all his impressions, but by now it was late and his brain was overloaded, so it wasn't easy.

He got up, chucked a couple of bull's-eyes into his dartboard, yawned, stretched, sat down again, and opened the last video file.

UNTRANSMITTED RECORDINGS/CAMERAMAN MARVIN GALLEGOS,

NBC4 was its title: ten out-of-focus minutes of footage, taken by the camera lying on its side on the floor.

Yes, he'd have to slog through this one, too.

He was awakened some hours later by his telephone ringing loud enough to rouse the dead. He took the receiver with the same lack of enthusiasm as if he were picking up a decomposed body part.

"Yes?" he said, trying to sound awake. His alarm clock read Saturday, March 28, 2009, 05:27 A.M. Having his sleep interrupted was getting to be a regular occurrence.

He rubbed his eyes. The last frame of Marvin Gallegos's video recording was frozen on the screen before him at a ridiculous angle for any cameraman with respect for himself. The case documents described him being hit by a stray bullet and subsequently dropping his camera, and that all one could see were blurry legs and pant legs dancing back and forth. The prosecutor had called the pictures "surreal" and "impressionistic"—in other words: useless.

But no matter what adjectives Mortimer Deloitte chose to use, the ever-patient, methodical T could think of at least four others that were better suited: naturalistic, realistic, minimalist, and—most important— pluralistic. If one applied these four homespun terms and blended them all together, one got a completely different picture. It was merely a question of finding and precisely identifying the details in the proper context. Thus a new world of possibilities opened, and then it was a matter of asking the right questions. He nodded again, this time at the frozen video image. Yes, through the proper eyes one was able to see the truth.

"Hey, T, are you there? It's me! Dody!" she repeated loudly over the telephone. "You've got to come out here, T. Wake up, now! Leo Mulligan's gone completely crazy!"

He tried opening his eyes wide. It was difficult. The light through his blinds was already heralding the new day. "Leo Mulligan, did you say? You're out at his house? What's going on out there?"

He heard a couple of bangs through the receiver, followed by some muffled sounds. "Fuck!" cried Dody. "Yeah, out at his farm. T, you've gotta come now! Oh, God, I'm afraid Leo's killed the deputy sheriff and the new guy he had with him!" She was gasping for breath. So was T. Perkins.

"What?! You mean Stanley and Willie?"

"Yes, Willie! And Stanley! He shot them. They're lying a few hundred yards into his field. Oh, God, oh, God, T! I'm sure they're dead!"

CHAPTER 21

IT WASN'T THE POLICE WHO CAME TO ROSALIE, BUT ONE OF HIS FRIENDS. HE
stood in the doorway, clutching his baseball cap and wearing a sorrowful expression rarely seen in the neighborhood. A look that instinctively made her hold her breath. He spoke cautiously and slowly
so she wouldn't know all at once. They'd found Frank, he said. He'd
been lying down by the water in Weir Creek Park with glassy eyes
and spotted skin. He'd been dead a while and now they'd collected him.

She called in to work to ask for the day off without saying why, but
was given only two hours. Time that could have been spent in anger
and tears but instead passed in silence, with a blank expression. The
sorrow was there, to be sure, but there was also a sense of relief. Mrs.
Fullbright from upstairs had had visits from the police two times, and
twice she'd been to the morgue to identify her own mutilated flesh
and blood. That was even worse.

It was easier to live with the notion that her Frank had at least died
as a result of his own deeds. Rosalie waited as long as possible before
leaving for work; perhaps she was hoping that James and Dennis
would come rushing through the door. It would have been nice with
a little consolation—a warm hug or some assurance that they'd never
let this happen to them—but they weren't like that. It was probably
too early for them to come home, she told herself. During the day they
held a pretty low profile, but nighttime was another story. This was a
time for flaunting egos in the light of firelit garbage cans, for chilling
with the Rastafarian brothers, for ridiculing the pimps with their gold

chains, for proclaiming that the world had yet to see its greatest rapper, and for dissing the boy bands into extinction. Her sons were so extravagantly full of themselves, she could scream till she was blue in the face and they'd never notice. Coming to her of their own accord and saying they loved her and were sorry they hadn't kept an eye on their brother was simply not their nature.

She gave herself constant pep talks and tried to gain control over her trembling lips and the pile of bills before her. The state of emergency had created serious problems for the accounting department at Mo Goldenbaum's Export-Import, Rosalie's workplace, and if things went on like this, pretty soon Mo would be the only one left in the office. At present the portly man was sweating over his bank credit limit, and Rosalie knew better than anyone how hopeless his fight for survival would be if something didn't happen soon. She looked over at her colleague Henry, who comprised the shipping department, letting her eyes linger on his fleshless face. They'd worked ten feet apart for twenty years and yet she knew almost nothing about him, even in spite of the fact that they were the only two left out of thirty employees. It crossed her mind that Henry might sense the state she was in, look up, and meet her eye. That, if she broke down in tears, he would understand and be able to offer words of deliverance. Or that he'd console her and assure her that Frank had gone to a better place. But Henry was fully occupied by his computer screen, clearly fighting for his existence. What other choice did he have, forty-five years old and never having tried any other work than shuffling containers around between point A and point B? Rosalie understood. These were hard times.

She took a deep breath and fought a moment to get herself under control. Her mother and father had lost half their flock to God, and each time it had added new furrows to their faces. But had she ever seen them complain or give in to adversity or despondency? No, she hadn't. Never had she seen them let themselves go and surrender to their grief. They still had kids left to worry about, kids that had to eat. There was still hope for their remaining children; that was their compass in life. How was her situation any different? Didn't she still have two wonderful boys, as well as a great responsibility? She pursed her lips and looked at the papers lying before her.

The sound of oaths and swear words erupted from her boss's glass cubicle. It wouldn't be long before he'd be pounding his fist into the desk, so hard that the empty Coke cans rattled. Next his face might turn copper red with rage and the glass panes start vibrating with his bellowing. She looked at her watch. He must be listening to some long-wave program. Why did he do it? What was the use? It was always at times like this that he began wailing about wanting to go back to South Africa. Rosalie looked at Henry once more. She knew what effect Mo's outbursts had on him. Every time he yelled, Henry attempted to straighten his skinny posture, but it didn't help. A life of insecurity had made his shoulders go permanently limp.

Mo froze with his hand halfway in the air. It looked as though he'd stopped breathing; the bright red face had turned ashen. For a moment Rosalie was afraid her boss had finally worked himself up to a fatal heart attack. She jumped to her feet at the same time as Henry, expecting to see Mo keel over before she reached his office, but he kept sitting there with his hand in the air, stone-faced.

"What's happened?!" shouted Henry, but Mo waved him away.

"Listen . . ." he said, as the color slowly began returning to his face.

Rosalie plopped down heavily on the worn-out chair reserved for clients, ready to break down. If there was more bad news, she simply wouldn't be able to take it.

"Just listen to what that idiot's saying," said Mo.

It was President Jansen's voice, and it was calm. Some voices are especially well suited to cut through the whistling static of an unused radio frequency, and his was one. Despite the noise and the fading in and out, he seemed intimately close by, his words like an outstretched hand, offered in friendship and solace.

"This morning our most fervent wish was fulfilled," he was saying. "Our competent investigators in New York found the Killer on the Roof at eight A.M., local time, on the outskirts of Fordham University, as he lay in wait for his next victim. After a short exchange of gunfire, he was hit by a bullet identical to those he used himself to spread fear and fatality. According to an FBI spokesman, he expired immediately after being shot, without having given any explanation for his insane, terrorist behavior."

"Gosh, is he dead?" said Henry quietly.

"Fool's luck for Jansen!" snickered Mo Goldenbaum.

"The FBI spokesman has also stated that the investigation's breakthrough came in connection with the fact that census takers in Brooklyn had reached the area around Prospect Park, more precisely Flatbush Avenue. When the census taker came to the perpetrator's apartment, he asked for the man's fingerprints, as the law prescribes. He also noticed how nervous this made the man. The census taker happened to be someone with previous experience in the correctional system, a man trained to notice small signs that signal criminality, and it was precisely this training that aroused his suspicions and led him to recommend the perpetrator's apartment be searched.

"If we hadn't had this alert person doing his job, the citizens of New York would still be unable to go to work or to school without fearing for their lives. Instead, the man's home was searched while he was out, and several pieces of circumstantial evidence were found, indicating that he was the culprit.

"Yesterday's and last night's subsequent close surveillance of the suspect led to the ultimate conclusion of this loathsome drama that's been played out in New York the past couple of months. We thank God that it's finally over. The murder of twenty-seven innocent people brings back memories of many other terrible trials Americans have had to endure in the course of time as the result of madmen with weapons. I feel convinced that these outrages will soon be a thing of the past. During the last month we've confiscated more than a million and a half illegal weapons; laid out end to end, they would reach from Washington to New York. What we're doing is worth it, I tell you. We've already confiscated as much ammunition from ordinary people's homes as was used in warfare throughout the world in 2008, and there's still more. It will be worth it."

Mo Goldenbaum took hold of his desk drawer and pulled it open.

Then he took out a heavy pistol and popped out the magazine. "Phew!" he exhaled. "I just wanted to see if he'd counted my ammunition, too." He laughed so his entire body shook, and Henry gave a thumbs-up sign, relieved. Rosalie couldn't manage to say anything.

"The Department of Homeland Security informs us that a ballistics examination has confirmed that we got the right man. America can now breathe easier."

Rosalie stared into space. She'd heard rumors that there'd been an assassination attempt on the president, but there he was, speaking to the nation. She'd also heard people claim that the Killer on the Roof could not have been working alone, that he had to have had accomplices, but that's not how it sounded now.

So everything should be fine—only it wasn't. Because Frank was dead.

"The American people have been freed of yet another burden," continued President Jansen, as Henry stood up slowly, to emphasize how essential he was. Rosalie didn't follow his example.

"Yet another mentally disturbed person has been neutralized. As a result of the Secure Future program, our country has become a better and safer place in which to live, and we firmly believe that this process will continue. We Americans have a long tradition of creating our own problems, and now it must stop. Just look abroad. See how our support for Saddam Hussein—when we needed him against the Iranian clerics—and our support for Osama bin Laden against the Red Army turned out to be a double-edged sword that was later turned against us with catastrophic consequences. Look what happened when we got ourselves involved in Korea and Vietnam and Somalia. Look at Israel. We lost our sons and made new enemies. Look what we've done to ourselves here, at home. We stick our nose into everything and worry more about foreigners on the other side of the world than we do about ourselves. But that's all ending now. We don't want more problems; we don't want to bury any more sons or daughters. From now on we're letting the world take care of itself while we take care of each other, here, in God's own country. Reforming our way of thinking will pave the way."

At this point the radio transmission was interrupted by a voice that alternated between English and French. Mo Goldenbaum turned down the radio.

"It's a Canadian station; they took it from a television transmission half an hour ago," he explained. Then he turned to his telephone and dialed a number. "Did you see it?" he asked, without introduction. It must be his wife. "Yes, that's right! Now you and the kids can come home again. New York's safe!"

Mo Goldenbaum stretched his huge bulk while the speaker concluded by saying that President Jansen had been forced to postpone a press conference the day before because of an assassination attempt, but the president was unharmed and was now back in Washington.

"Then Tom Jumper was a little quick on the trigger, ha-ha!" Mo laughed so hard that his double chins rippled. "Ten minutes ago, on this very same frequency, he claimed the Killer on the Roof was a concoction of the White House, along with several other recent attacks and murders." He shook his head. "Piss-poor timing, but you've gotta admire the bastard for having guts and managing to elude the FBI so far."

Rosalie rose and walked back to her work desk. A few days ago she would have felt a stone fall from her heart, but now it was too late. The stone could no longer be budged.

The phone rang. Mo Goldenbaum picked it up, then gave a sign through the window that she should take it.

It was the police from the Barkley Avenue precinct. They were very formal, and it was bad news.

They'd arrested James and Dennis as they were in the process of beating up two pushers in broad daylight. One of them was still unconscious but would recover. The boys claimed they were the men who'd sold crack to their now-deceased brother. The police were understanding of their situation, but the law had to take its course. The boys had already been arraigned, and would she be so kind as to come down right away and post their bail. These days they couldn't have people taking up space in jail who hadn't committed a more serious crime. Rosalie sat for so long without answering that the police officer had to ask her again.

"Come up to the station? Now? No, thanks, I don't think so," she finally answered, and gently laid down the receiver. She raised her head and gazed at the unreality of the empty office landscape. Henry nodded at her as though saying everything was okay, no matter what. Only Mo saw the breakdown coming.

She'd practically cried the eyes out of her head; her dark cheeks were striped with salt. Mo and Henry had tried to calm her down, then accepted the futility of their attempt. When you've lost a son, you've got to be allowed to grieve, as Mo said.

She sat at one of the many empty desks at the far end of the open-plan office and tried as well as she could to think. She'd pinched and scraped for five years with nothing to show for it. She had convinced herself that the dream of a tranquil life in the country, down by her sister's, could one day become reality. Now that dream was shattered. The bit of money she'd tucked aside probably wouldn't even cover Frank's funeral, not to mention bail for her two remaining sons. What was she supposed to do? What in the world was she supposed to do? All her life she'd struggled to pay everyone their due, plus have a little left over for a rainy day. What was she supposed to do now, when that wasn't enough?

She looked over at Mo's glass cubicle and saw him shaking his head. Maybe he'd help her. Of course he would, if he could. And Henry, too. But she knew they couldn't, nor could anybody else she knew. In forty-eight years on the planet, she'd experienced plenty of things, but never financial independence, and now this was about to pull her under.

"Can I have permission to go now, Mo?" she asked through the intercom. "I'll work late on Monday instead, okay?"

Clutching her handbag, she shoved her way past the demonstrators in front of the Jansen's Drugstore on East 14th. ONLY TRAITORS SHOP HERE was printed on several of the protest signs. The police didn't try to disperse them; they only held a small passageway open in case anyone felt like tempting fate by going into the store. This had been going on for weeks now. If there was anyone who had suffered financially from the state of emergency, it was the president himself, that was for sure. So much so, that it made sissies of the chorus of moaning shareholders who were watching their own stocks crash.

Emotions were beginning to boil over at the intersection of East 14th Street and Broadway. Here hundreds of the city's citizens had gathered and were literally screaming to the rooftops what they thought should be done with the body of the Killer on the Roof. Despite their bloodthirst and deranged suggestions, their behavior seemed perfectly fitting. New Yorkers were known for their solidarity when it came to feelings—even the darkest kind—and feelings were what this was all about.

Rosalie Lee made her way up to Penn Station. She figured it would take less than three hours to reach Washington with the Acela Express. It would cost every penny she had on her, but only there would she be able to find the solution to her problems. She'd have to borrow money from Doggie, and she knew that a couple of thousand dollars was a sum that Doggie could easily afford.

Rosalie looked at her little wristwatch. It was only 2:00 P.M.; she could be at Doggie's office by six, at the latest.

The cries of the jubilant crowd faded in the background as she stumped past the FEMA vans towards the control post at Penn Station. *When I get to Washington I'll have the guard call her out in front of the White House,* she thought. *I'm sure she's at work today. I know she'll be glad to see me. Yes. I'll borrow two thousand—no, maybe four—and I'll be home before midnight. Then, if I call the duty officer at the Barkley Avenue station, he'll be able to tell me what to do—whether I can just come there and fetch my boys. Maybe they can also tell me what to do with Frank's body.* Keeping her eyes fixed on the soldiers as they searched bags and briefcases at the checkpoint, she attempted momentarily to banish the image of her boy, lying stiff and alone in an ice-cold room.

She tried to concentrate on the soldiers and their hard, vigilant expressions—anything to keep her from screaming.

She headed straight for the train station's closest entrance and held out her bag to the two soldiers who were to lead her through the control post. "Your seat reservation, ma'am, may we see it?" said one of them.

The spell was broken, and thoughts of Frank engulfed her once more. The cold body, the dead stare, but also the soft laugh that long ago had been capable of stopping her bastard of a husband from becoming violent. Seat reservation, they'd said. Back to real life—just like that. She'd seen the roadblocks and knew they meant trouble. She'd also heard some awful stories about things that had been happening, and she'd been able to smell burning tires from the barricade at Brinsmade and Huntington. So how could she let herself be taken so unawares? How had she ever imagined she could take off for Washington and beg Doggie for money, just like that? She, who hadn't even sent Doggie a word of consolation when her father was arrested? What in the world had made her think she was so special?

It was then that she felt a choking grip on her heart. She managed to take a deep breath and raise one arm to her breast while she tried to grab one of the soldiers with the other. They yelled something at her; she didn't hear what, only that she should let go. A couple of passersby tried to steady her as she began toppling over, but they couldn't keep her upright. Nor did Rosalie care any longer. All she could see was her Frank, lying there in Weir Creek Park, dying slowly.

"Ohh, my little boy!" she wailed. "Oh, my beloved son, what have we done to you?"

CHAPTER 22

SHE'D BEEN COMPLETELY CERTAIN THAT T. PERKINS WOULD CONTACT HER. NOW almost two days had gone by and her hopes were beginning to fade. But for a few hours, the period she'd been waiting was exactly the amount of time her father had left to live, and each minute felt like an inevitable tug towards eternity.

Yet Doggie still waited.

Even though it was Saturday, Chief of Staff Lance Burton had called in all the West Wing's personnel. Two days ago there'd been an attempt on Jansen's life, and everyone had to go through a deluge of questioning until every detail and eventuality was laid bare. Yesterday they'd sat in their offices for most of the day, waiting to be called in, but answering the Secret Service's questions to their satisfaction took time. This was a fundamental, serious breach of security, and it was not going to happen again. There was no talk of who had staged the attack, probably because no one knew.

A couple of Ben Kane's men and an interrogation expert from Homeland Security who looked like a fat accountant in a knit sleeveless vest questioned the staff according to rank. First the personnel around the Oval Office, then Burton and Sunderland's staff, then Donald Beglaubter's and Wesley's. Thus did they work their way slowly through all offices and workplaces. It was going to be a long day, and Doggie was way at the end of the list. She absolutely had to get hold of Perkins in the meantime. If they didn't get a stay of execution, it would all be over in sixty hours.

By the time she reached the gatekeeper at 5:55 Saturday morning, she could sense that Jansen was already in the White House. It was something one just knew, as though his presence was nothing less than the White House's heartbeat. Okay, at least he apparently hadn't been seriously injured, because the day before there'd been a surge of rumors to the contrary, including one indicating that the perpetrator who'd thrown the hand grenade had been killed on the spot, together with two other men, possibly security.

A couple of Kane's men were waiting out in the lobby for the personnel and asked them to sit down and wait in their offices until someone came to interview them. Exactly like the day before.

Never before had it been so still in the White House. No one could ignore the deadly atmosphere, and people simply couldn't bring themselves to do any work. It would have to wait until the threat of being accused of something had passed.

Doggie had thoughts of her own on the matter. Now maybe her colleagues were beginning to understand what it was like to be her.

She considered dialing Wesley's extension, then dropped the idea. She didn't want to do him any unintentional harm. Not that anyone was thinking much about their careers these days, but still she knew it wouldn't be good for him to have anything to do with her. So, if she wanted his help in this overmonitored mausoleum, she'd have to be discreet.

She got up from her seat, tucked a protocol file under her arm, and strode resolutely and rapidly past the paralyzed offices in the direction of Wesley's domain. There were a hundred feet at the most from his office to the Oval Office where President Jansen probably was sitting now. She would have to face a barricade of gray and black suits and sets of vigilant eyes, and everyone would regard her as toxic waste. But Doggie hugged the file close to her body and looked straight ahead. When it came down to it, the press secretary's office was the main focus of her sphere of activity, and who could know what important information she might have for Wesley Barefoot? She simply had to appear to have the definitive answer to any and all questions—that was what mattered. That, and Wesley being in his office.

A pair of men with heavy jaws and eyebrows stopped her in front of Wesley's door, pawed her body routinely, opened her file, studied it, and asked why she hadn't stayed in her office as she'd been ordered. Then they looked her straight in the face, noting her defiant lips as she answered. Okay, she'd go back and sit in her office, but in the meantime they'd better let her do her work so that Wesley Barefoot and the president received the material they were waiting for. Then she waited twenty minutes outside his door with the file under her arm, enveloped in vigilant gazes that would have no problem discovering if, against all odds, she'd managed to conceal a deadly weapon in some flap or corner of her diabolical womanliness.

Wesley didn't come out himself; two men left his office, and she was shown in. He was sitting behind his desk, hands wrapped around his morning coffee. He didn't seem himself. He attempted a smile when he saw her, but it didn't work.

"This sure is a heck of a workplace today," she said.

He nodded. "Then you've heard."

"Heard what?"

His head fell a bit. "Then you haven't." He took a deep breath. "Well, you'll be told in a while anyway, so fuck procedure. Donald Beglaubter is dead." His look was almost apologetic as she fumbled after the armrest of his extra chair and sat down.

"Oh, no, say it's not true, Wesley!"

He was studying the top of his desk. "Unfortunately, yes. Donald was killed instantly during the assassination attempt yesterday."

"Oh, God." She felt her neck and chest getting clammy. One of her best friends in recent years was dead and there was Wesley, acting as though he'd only just received the news himself. How could he do this? He was the White House press secretary, for Christ's sake, so if the acting chief of communications were dead, he would have been the first to know. Who else but Wesley could take over Donald's tasks, now that Lance Burton had his hands full as acting chief of staff?

"No, that doesn't make sense," she said slowly. "We were all here all day yesterday, dammit. How can something like that be kept secret for so long? There's something wrong here. You must have known this since yesterday, so why the hell haven't you told me?"

"Believe me, Doggie, I know far from everything." He came over and crouched before her, trying to catch her eye. "I didn't know," he said, but she wasn't ready to look at anyone just now.

"Why'd you come here, Doggie?"

She had to swallow a couple of times before words would come. "Oh, Wesley, I've got to get in to see Jansen. Can't you help me?" She held her head in her hands. "Jansen *must* have my father's execution stayed. It's possible that Dad isn't guilty, Wesley. I'm believing this more and more, but I don't have the time to prove it. T. Perkins is working on it, but we need to have more time." She grabbed his hands. "Wesley, listen: You've got to help me."

He looked at her with sad eyes. It wasn't a good sign.

"I can't, Doggie," he said.

The words had her in a stranglehold; the room felt like a strait-jacket. The clamminess on her chest had turned to drops of sweat. That was some way to have a death sentence flung in your face.

"Try!" she said.

He stood up and leaned against the bookcase with his hands behind his back, trying to get the situation under control. "I have to warn you, Doggie. I don't think it would be wise to bring up your father's case."

He put his hand firmly over his ID badge and motioned for her to do the same. "Don't you know how dangerous it is to be in this building right now?" he whispered. "Donald is dead, and others are dead or missing. There's so much I'd like to understand, that Jansen could probably help me with, but I don't get to be alone with the president anymore. I was with him in the Oval Office yesterday, trying to explain why we had to change course, but he stopped me. He wouldn't hear of it and said that, according to his information, the situation wasn't so bad, that it would soon improve. Then he asked me to leave." Wesley licked his lips. "He asked me to go, and only come back when I was sent for. I've written two speeches for him since then, but we never discussed them at all. It's like he's sealed himself off in that damn office; even Lance Burton practically can't get an audience with him. I think the incident the day before yesterday shocked the hell out of him. He definitely doesn't seem okay." She nodded. Three times had Jansen been a hair's breadth from death, and each time people who meant a lot to him were murdered in his place. Of course he wasn't okay.

She stood up slowly. "I'm going in there," she said, loud enough so that those who were listening in couldn't miss hearing her.

Wesley tried in vain to stop her before she closed the door behind her. The two guards, each with a finger pressed against his earpiece, stopped her in her tracks. "Yes, sir," muttered one of them into his lapel and turned to Doggie. "You are to return to your office. Now!"

Wesley opened his door, wanting to speak to her, but was ordered back into his office like some underling. Everyone was under orders to stay in his or her office until the investigation was finished, they said, himself included. This had to be hard to swallow for a man who'd had such a brilliant career. Even her dear Wesley hadn't the slightest chance of helping her. Unfortunately she was beginning to understand this all too well.

When she made it back to her shoebox of an office, she called the Highland County Sheriff's Office and was told that a serious situation had just come up, but that they'd convey her message. Then she called T. Perkins's cell phone five times and got a voice mail message each time. It was enough to drive a person crazy.

"Please, T!" she begged. "Call me as soon as you can, okay? Call my cell. You have my number."

She ran her hand over her face and suddenly felt ill. The despair and impotence had solidified like a lump of lead in her stomach. If she tried to stand, she'd throw up.

What in the world was she to do? Why had she read so much about how they executed people? It was all so terrible. How could she let them strap her father's body to the gurney and tacitly watch it happen? Watch her diaper-clad father lying there, waiting for the

Pentothal to glide through the tube and thirty seconds later render him unconscious as it reached his brain? See the next poison wave of Pavulon collapse his diaphragm and lungs, and finally, the calcium chloride as it paralyzed his heart and killed him? She momentarily lost her balance and staggered backward against a low set of shelves where she normally stored her half-neglected work cases in tall piles. One pile began to topple, taking the next one with it. Her hand shot out instinctively to inhibit the avalanche and hit the Buddha figurine that had been functioning as a paperweight atop a stack of documents. She took it in her hand to look at it. It felt cold and strange and somehow also fragile, like a relic from the past that could not stand being worshiped or touched.

She looked deep into the figurine's lifeless eyes and called back to mind a busy merchant street in a distant place, from a distant time. A time when Jansen had been close by, where she had been with people who wished her well. Then she hugged the figurine and felt her determination return. If getting through to Jansen was completely impossible, maybe she could go see Thomas Sunderland instead and show him the Buddha. He would doubtlessly despise her for it, but he knew what it meant. Sunderland could let her in to see Jansen if he wanted—he, and no one else. Maybe she could bargain with him, promise to quit her job if he'd arrange an audience with the president. Yes, that's how it had to be. Donald Beglaubter was dead, and no one she liked in this place was persuading her to stay. So why not quit?

She passed several offices with closed doors through which she could just make out fragments of conversation. The interrogations were well under way.

The two security guards in front of Wesley Barefoot's door spotted the little Buddha as she approached the West Wing's inner sanctum and passed a signal to a well-built guard standing before Thomas Sunderland's office. There was a world of difference between the two of them as he towered over her and stuck out his hand. The guard was Ben Kane, a man she hated with a passion, the security guard who had testified against her father. How could they allow him to serve in the White House when his miserable job of searching Toby O'Neill was

the indirect cause of Mimi Jansen being shot? She didn't understand it.

"Let me see that thing," he said, with a special agent's many years'
professional suspiciousness. And, with approximately the same number of years' defiance of authority that her work on the edge of politics
had given her, she answered: "It's a Buddha. It weighs about two
pounds and is made of some shitty, cheap material, so be careful with
pressing it too hard. It's hollow and empty inside and in no way represents a threat to society or the length of your career. It may be ugly,
but it was a present from President Jansen, and now I'm on my way
to him to give it back. Understand, Mr. Kane?"

She'd been hoping he'd step aside so she could continue towards
the last security guard who stood in front of the Oval Office, but
Kane's hand flew so surprisingly fast to the figurine that all she noticed before he grabbed it was the clinking of his gold bracelets.

"Let go!" she shouted, immediately increasing the other guards'
level of preparedness from standby to alert. Some of them reached for
their shoulder holsters, but Doggie didn't care. It was her little souve-
nir, and it symbolized something very important in her life. "Come to
me if you need help" was what Jansen had said at the time. "This
figurine stands for a bond of eternal friendship."

How in the world was she going to make it through to Jansen if she
were attacked by these mountainous testosterone meat loaves?

She made as if to force her way through, but Ben Kane took her
shoulder in a hard grip and shoved her towards the door of Sunderland's office. She could see in his eyes that he was considering how to
handle the situation, and she feared that he'd do her harm. Then she
suddenly slipped backward as the door opened inward and there was
Vice President Sunderland standing in the doorway with a cold expression. He said nothing, merely eyed the security people racing to
the scene, until everyone had settled down. Then he took the little
icon and indicated with a nod of his head that she should follow him
into his office.

Doggie hadn't been in there since Sunderland had been named vice
president. She looked around the room and felt the creases lining up

on her forehead. No matter where one looked, the room bore witness to Sunderland's might and self-exaltation. If she counted closely, she'd be able to find at least twenty framed photos of Thomas Sunderland in the process of shaking the hand of famous Americans. There were also at least ten pictures from his youthful prime where he stood in uniform, gazing out over unknown landscapes. The room was so brightly lit, it could be a movie studio or a third-degree interrogation cell. All the walls were lined with large bulletin boards, studded with press clippings and photographs that reflected how the outside world viewed what was happening in the United States. In spite of her high IQ, Doggie was not equipped with a knowledge of languages that enabled her to evaluate the overall picture, but the headlines in the English-language newspapers like *The Times, The Montreal Gazette,* and *The Australian* left no doubt. The world was appalled by what was happening in the United States.

Sunderland positioned himself before her, blocking her view. "What's going on? Make it quick!" he barked. He seemed harried, as though the foundation of his pillar of stoicism was about to crumble. She'd seen him in many situations before, but only a few times with this ominous glint in his eye that she knew meant one had to be ready for anything.

"I want to go in and give the figurine back to Jansen. He made me a promise once, and he has to fulfill it now."

"The president doesn't have to do anything. He has more important things to think about than your little situation, Dorothy Rogers."

Little situation. She'd counted on all kinds of answers, but not one that was so contemptuous and totally devoid of any empathy or respect. She could have hit him; her insides were shaking. She'd never liked Sunderland. He was a son of a bitch, hard and calculating and cold. Not the worst characteristics for a man with a career like his, only now she truly hated him for it.

"What's . . . What is more important than a person's life?" she asked, her voice trembling.

He leaned back his head. "You're expecting me to let you beg the president to pardon your father, isn't that so?"

"Beg? No, I'm going to ask the president to stay the execution because not to do so would be wrong. Information has come to light that could possibly exonerate my father." There wasn't the slightest reaction in Sunderland's eyes. "Listen here, Sunderland. You want to punish the right man, for God's sake, don't you?"

It was clear he didn't like being addressed so informally—she saw this right away. "What's the evidence?" he asked, his eyes cold as ice.

"There are many factors that don't add up, Mr. Vice President. Just give us a couple of weeks, then we . . ."

"No, I'm sorry, the case is closed as far as we and the courts are concerned."

She could have ripped out his tongue, but instead she prostrated herself again. "I know this is a very undesirable position I'm putting you in, sir, but you are the only one who can give me a few minutes with the president. I'm willing to send in my resignation immediately if only I can be allowed to plead my father's case. Just *one* minute!"

"I'll gladly accept your resignation, but I can't go along with the rest."

She felt her lips tightening. "Then give my figurine back."

But Sunderland held the Buddha close, took a step backward, and leaned against his desk like the class bully flaunting his tyrannical status in the schoolyard. She wasn't getting the figurine back, it was plain as day. He'd given her his contempt, that was all. She couldn't expect anything else.

That was the moment when she had had enough. "Give it to me," she hissed, jumping towards him and grabbing it.

Thomas Sunderland was a bony man, still in possession of an old military man's suppleness and sinewy strength, as she found out when he grabbed her wrist and bent it back, forcing her slowly to her knees. *No, goddammit, no!* she said silently, and lay her weight onto one leg while she hammered the other knee into his groin with all her might. Sunderland's face went expressionless and he fell to the floor, groaning as though he'd just had a vision of the devil himself. He turned his head towards her, his eyes gone mad. She'd just been made public enemy number one, no doubt about it.

"You're not going anywhere," he gasped, as she picked the little Buddha up off the floor. "Do you read me, you cunt?"

It was the disrespect that made her kick him a second time, right there where a man's feelings lie quivering most of his life. There wouldn't be much difference between one kick and two, anyway. Punishment would be severe either way, but it bought her a little time, because for the moment Sunderland had left a state of consciousness.

It felt incorrect and euphoric—all at once.

She strode back to her office, feeling a thousand eyes following her, impaling her. As she collected her things, she could hear shouting from Sunderland's office and heavy footfalls in the corridor. *Smile at them,* she kept telling herself, as she gripped her satchel under her arm and headed for the exit.

It wasn't until she was standing on Pennsylvania Avenue with a mob of demonstrators before her that she realized she'd just slammed the door she had fought half her life to open, a door behind which lurked forces powerful enough to ruin her life. She noticed growing activity in the guardroom behind the wrought iron fence, then looked over her shoulder one last time, ascertaining that the gate guard had identified her and sounded the alarm. She cut across the lanes of the broad street, past the police cars that were on constant duty, and smiled at the officers, making sure they saw her credential badge.

Then she plunged into the mass of demonstrators with their sleepy morning eyes and bitter expressions.

She could hear the shouting of the guards behind her and their shrill whistles as she shoved her way between a cluster of demonstrators standing in front of the equestrian statue at Lafayette Square. Noticing that she'd tossed her official badge on the ground, they looked past her towards the White House where several guards were pouring through the gate. Someone who'd crawled up in a tree yelled that the guards were after her, and the demonstrators automatically closed ranks behind her. No one knew why they were pursuing her, but they'd sensed a compatriot in need, and that was enough for them.

The crowd made way for her like the Red Sea parting for Moses, closing again behind her, yet strangely enough their spontaneous solidarity made her feel even more alone in the world.

She looked up at the buildings that surrounded her. She wasn't sure what to do; where should she head now? At the moment, the number of police and soldiers in Washington was approximately the same as the population of a Scandinavian capital. The odds were grim, but Doggie was determined not to be stopped, and she reached the Hay-Adams Hotel before the police sirens in front of the White House were activated. From there she ran in the chilly morning fog, with her hand to her open collar, through Eye Street and cut diagonally towards the only part of town to which she had no affiliation whatsoever. She maxed out all her credit cards at the first bank ATM she found and hurried on with more than $15,000 buried in her Fendi handbag, the little Buddha lying on top.

She didn't stop until she reached a Hertz rent-a-car on 11th Street. There she stood for a moment, staring blankly at the neon-lit offices until reality finally caught up with her. She couldn't just rent a car, nor would she get far at the airport or Union Station, and going home was out of the question. She simply couldn't go anywhere she used to—not in Washington or Virginia. She was totally alone and completely out in the open. The manhunt had begun, and it was only eight thirty in the morning.

"This is insane!" she chanted again and again to herself, then crossed a parking lot at 11th, heading for smaller streets with less traffic. Ahead of her she saw a couple of police cars on patrol and began walking slower. She loosened the grip on her collar and surveyed how she was dressed. If an even halfway accurate description of her had been sent out, she'd have to find some other clothes, and this wasn't easy in a part of Washington where you didn't run into many clothes shops, especially not one that was open early Saturday morning. She squeezed in between two parked delivery vans and slipped behind them as a patrol car worked its way down the street. After it had passed she stood for a moment, getting her bearings. As far as she could tell, there were only three options. The first was to go back to the White House and say she was sorry, but that, of course, was out of the question.

She had attacked the country's vice president. Even though she hadn't become an expert in court-martial law at Harvard, she knew she risked serious punishment. The second possibility was finding a hotel where the desk clerk wouldn't become overly curious if she paid cash, and lie low for a few days. But how was she to find such a hotel? Not downtown, that was for sure, and Anascostia, south of the river, was a long distance away. Nothing and no one could expect easy passage at the bridges' control posts. She was therefore forced to consider the third dubious option: finding someone at random who had a motor vehicle, who she could persuade to drive her far, far away.

A faint ringing from the depths of her handbag stopped her in her tracks. "Shit!" she swore, yanked her cell phone out through the bundles of dollar bills, and turned it off. Why the hell hadn't she thought of that before? Now they'd doubtlessly tracked her via the phone signal. How efficiently and quickly they could do it, she didn't know, but apparently not so quickly that she was already caught.

She bit her lip. *Could they track her even though it was shut off?* she wondered.

Her body trembled as she tore the battery out and threw it and the phone back in her bag. They weren't getting her *that* easy.

She crossed the street towards a row of parked cars behind which she could hide if more patrol cars came her way.

And with long, striding steps, she headed north.

After she'd been walking fifteen minutes she sensed someone following her. *Don't let it be anyone in a uniform,* she prayed, but didn't turn around until she reached the next stoplight. She was relieved to see it wasn't a cop—at least not in uniform—but just a normal-looking man in his late sixties or thereabouts. Still, it made her uneasy. She tried to distance herself from him by crossing the street to the opposite sidewalk, but he followed her. Maybe she'd expected him to blurt out some kind of nonsense—there were so many weirdos walking the streets—but she wasn't prepared when he reached out and put his hand on her shoulder. She looked into his piercing eyes, considering crying for help, but she didn't dare. *Anything but drawing attention,* she thought, clenching her fists.

"Okay!" she said, confronting him. He was gray-haired and gray-skinned, and the arms of his tweed jacket were too short. "Do we know each other?"

"It was your father who murdered the president's wife. I recognize you from television; you can't deny it!"

She shoved his hand away and looked at him angrily, even though she was filled with all kinds of feeling but anger. She wanted to say to him that it was a case of mistaken identity, that it happened all the time. But she couldn't. Instead she said, "It wasn't my father who killed Mimi Jansen, it was his handyman!"

"Yeah, that's what *you* say."

She pushed him in the chest and went up to the next intersection but saw he was still following her.

Go away! she thought. *What's it all got to do with you? Haul ass, you old fool!*

People in the vicinity began to notice the episode. She surveyed the passing pedestrians' expressions, how they reacted when, in spite of trying to detach himself from her, she still didn't begin running. They were surely telling themselves there had to be some reason; their curiosity had been awakened.

"Why don't you get tired, old man?" she mumbled a few hundred yards farther on, noticing how the neighborhood was changing. She was as far out on the periphery as she had ever been. She had no idea what was in store between here and Adelphi, north of town, but she had to keep going in spite of her chafing shoes and a brutal stitch in her side. She'd passed the cemeteries a while ago where she might have spent the night before continuing on, but it was still broad daylight, and who could have known at the time that this ancient stalker would show up?

Once more he caught up with her, out of breath, as she was turning down a side street. *He must have been a quarterback in college*, she thought, breathing through her teeth.

"I remember you from the trial!" he cried, one step behind her.

"It's your fault everything's going to hell with our country! It's your fault our president has lost his mind, do you realize that?"

She turned suddenly and faced him. "If there's anyone who's lost his mind here, it's you! Why in the world are you running around the streets, carrying on like this, old man? Go home. You'll give yourself a heart attack."

His heavy breathing pumped a rotten odor in her face, but before she could come up with a derisive comment, he hit her hard on the cheekbone so that her head hit the wall behind her and she fell to the sidewalk.

"Don't you call me crazy," he whined, stomping the ground dangerously close to her face.

She pulled herself back against the wall, but the man obviously wasn't finished yet. "Make it stop before we're all slaughtered like dogs, you disgusting cow!" he wailed. He was about to kick her, but a few passersby had begun to gather, calling for him to stop, and then a shadow whizzed past her and pushed the old man away.

"Mind your own business, nigger," the madman hissed, his eyes wide and white spit in the corners of his mouth.

The black man raised a finger. "One more word out of you, you senile, quasi-fascist, albino motherfucker, and I'll take that sad, disgusting, cheap-ass Walmart jacket and shove it in your fucking, miserable excuse for a kissable mouth . . . which mine, on the other hand, happens to be." He pointed at his own mouth, slowly revealing a massive set of white teeth, lips curled back. Some of the bystanders broke out laughing, but the old man didn't hear them. His rage had made him deaf but not dumb.

It took a while before he finished spitting out his gall and finally scuttled off, and by then no one was in doubt as to who she was. "That bitch is named Doggie Rogers—remember her?" he'd said. "They're sticking the needle in her old man on Monday, and I'm looking forward to it!"

After that little speech, no one spoke to her or helped her to her feet. They just stood, craning their necks to get a glimpse of her. She could hear newcomers asking what the old dude had said, and after a few minutes they all left without a word. Only the guy who'd stepped in to help remained.

"That was goddamn fucking unbelievable," he muttered, and stretched out his hand.

She let herself be pulled to her feet. At least no one had mentioned that she was wanted by the authorities. Maybe she was mistaken; maybe she wasn't wanted.

He made a motion to leave, but Doggie didn't let go of his hand. If you couldn't trust someone who'd just helped you like that, who could you trust?

"Do you have a car?" she asked, one side of her head still throbbing.

A brief frown crossed his face, as though he couldn't see what his having a car could possibly have to do with her.

Then he nodded slowly.

She opened her bag discreetly and removed a single bundle of bills; there was no reason for him to see all the cash. "Drive me to New York, and I'll give you this. I can't be sitting behind the wheel myself, I'd be much too exposed. I have to be able to hide myself if necessary. Drive me, and it's yours." She showed him the money.

He stared at it for a long time, as though he was converting the thickness of the bundle into dollar figures. Then he took the money and counted it.

"Hello . . . ?" he finally said. "Girl, there's three thousand dollars here! What's going on?"

She looked at the bundle again. So it was thicker than she'd thought. "I kicked the vice president in the balls. Twice. That means I'm on the run."

He opened his mouth in surprise. This news needed time to circulate in his head—all the way up to his Rastafarian hat and down again—before his face broke into a grin and he emitted a chuckle as deep as an idling Buick LeSabre. "You let him have it right in the nuts? Vice President Sunderland?" He had to catch his breath.

This was the best one he'd heard all day.

He led Doggie around the block and over to one of the most fossilized vehicles she'd ever seen. No matter where one's eye fell on its battered exterior, it was impossible to determine what make—not to mention which model or which year—it was. Parts from at least ten cars had been recruited to carry out this heap's ingenious reconstructions. Doggie's heart sank. How this technical monstrosity was ever supposed to transport itself out on Interstate 95—let alone to New York—was a mystery she didn't feel like trying to solve at the moment.

He saw her skepticism and pulled a key fastened to a canine tooth out of his pocket. "For the three grand you get the car, too, okay?"

Doggie didn't know what to say.

"All right, then just give me twenty-five hundred, and we're even. I'd say it's pretty risky, transporting America's most-wanted ball crusher through ten or so roadblocks."

She sighed. "Do you happen to have a cell phone? I need another SIM card, or else they'll be able to track me." She took her own shiny, hi-tech phone out of her bag and showed it to him.

This brought his charismatic teeth to view once more. "Yeah, baby," he said. "I have a cell phone, but if we're switching SIM cards, I want your phone, too."

Some trade-off! Her phone had cost at least twenty times his.

Wearily she tried to make him aware of the vital importance of getting rid of her SIM card immediately, or at least waiting a month before he used her cell phone. He nodded with his giant grin and handed her a shabby Nokia that doubtlessly had fallen into the local pool hall's latrine more than once. Then he disappeared up the most decrepit front stairs of all the buildings on the block, returning ten minutes later with a plastic bag in each hand.

"A little food for the road and some things you can change into while we're driving." He opened one of the bags and pulled out an XXL Knicks T-shirt. Then he laughed. "Yeah, yeah, don't worry, the rest of the stuff's good enough."

Ollie Boyce Henson—as the Rastafarian was named—obviously had a woman at home who loved bright colors, ruffles, and low necklines. No one in their right mind would ever suspect that this carnival-clad female sitting at Ollie's side, trying to hear herself think to a harsh background of nonstop rap music, was none other than the stylish Harvard grad Doggie Rogers. It didn't take her long to realize that the little cosmetic kit she had with her wasn't exactly compatible with this orgy of colors, and she had to use most of her lipstick to achieve the proper blatant-but-not-quite-cheap effect. One always had to be color coordinated, as her girlfriends at school used to say.

They were stopped several times along the way, but she was never asked for ID. This was partly because she didn't look vaguely like the woman they were after and partly because the volume of the music discouraged any drawn-out inspection. They checked the trunk and the space between the front and back seats, then waved them on with tired expressions. After two weeks of this state of emergency, most of the soldiers carried out their shitty job as though they'd been doing it for decades. They knew they had to do it properly and that they'd be held responsible if they let any suspects slip through, but on the other hand they also knew there was another roadblock thirty miles farther up the highway. Maybe the next set of guards weren't as dead tired; the sheer number of roadblocks made them feel reassured. They waved their rifles slightly to keep traffic moving so the lines of vehicles didn't grow too long, and Ollie and Doggie worked their way steadily northward. The consequences of Jansen's edicts were everywhere to be seen. The FEMA logo had become a common sight, the supermarkets and department stores no longer sported banners announcing sale items, the long-haulers were driving around half-empty, and cars were packed with passengers to save on gas. Orange-clad ex-convicts dotted the roadside with their implements and small pushcarts, tidying up everything in sight, but this couldn't hide a general state of disrepair. Leaky roofs had been temporarily patched up with sheets of plastic, and folks were living in trailers and in their friends' and families' yards, clumped together in order to manage. Construction work had come to a standstill, and soldiers were everywhere. Every single day Doggie's superiors in the White House had proclaimed that they were getting everything under control, that the first wave of intervention and hardship was over. But it was a lie. In truth, the wave was gaining in strength, threatening to unleash a flood that would submerge everything, herself included. It was hard thinking of her father in this situation, but she did.

Constantly.

At first Ollie said nothing. He simply surveyed the sluggish traffic and people being body-searched as he swayed to the music, kept the motor alive, and constantly reached over to stick his hand into his plastic bag, removing one apparently edible item after another. But when she finally asked him to turn off the music before her head exploded, her chauffeur instead began talking nonstop in a way that Doggie found very disturbing. As they passed one town after another, it turned out that nothing was sacred for Ollie Boyce Henson. He laid his own personal rap number on her that encompassed every ho he'd ever serviced, every dude he'd ever whupped, and every little stunt he'd pulled since getting out of reform school. He'd earned himself a bachelor of arts in bullshit, an MA in indiscretion. Ollie Boyce Henson's motormouth represented no less than a danger to the environment.

"You can hang out a couple of days with my cousin; he lives in the Bronx," he said. "Lay a couple of hundred on him, and he'll chuck out the bitch he's got living with him. It's probably not the nicest neighborhood you've ever seen," he added indulgently, "but the way you look, you'll fit right in!" He slapped his thigh and cackled with laughter.

"Thanks, Ollie, but no. I'll figure out what to do," she said, trying to activate her newly acquired cell phone. "How do I get all my telephone numbers from my old cell phone into this one?"

He slammed on the brakes in front of a Burger King and whipped the phone he'd gotten from Doggie out of his pocket. Then he took out the SIM card and snapped it into the phone he'd given Doggie.

"Don't you turn it on!" she warned—too late.

He shook his head. "Just two seconds, then your phone book's saved in the Nokia's memory." She tried to grab it out of his hand, but then it rang, sending a shudder through her entire body.

"Turn it off, turn it off, goddammit! Right away!"

"Whoa!" he exclaimed. "Easy, girl, I'm finished." He waited another second, turned off the phone, and changed the SIM cards back again. It took him half a minute, max, but as far as Doggie was concerned, that was half a minute too long.

"Don't you do that again, Ollie, you hear? Delete my card the next time you turn that thing on, and *don't* use it for a month, else you'll be real sorry. Do you get what I'm saying?"

He tried to put on a frightened expression with a mouth full of potato chips, but it wasn't very reassuring.

She sighed. They were still about seventy miles south of New York, approximately the position where those who were possibly trying to track her now would lose her. She had little choice but to believe this.

She found Rosalie Lee's number and dialed.

The voice at the other end seemed out of breath and listless—not like the Rosalie Doggie used to know. "Oh, Jesus! My God, is that you, Doggie?" Then she heard Rosalie say a quick prayer: "Oh, Jesus, thank you for hearing my prayers. Thank you, Jesus, I love you." Next her voice returned to full strength, although it sounded as if she might break down crying at any moment.

"I'm on my way up to you, Rosalie. Is that okay?"

"On your way up to me?" she almost whispered. "Here in New York? Oh, Jesus, Jesus, I love you!"

"Rosalie . . . ?"

"Oh, yes, Doggie. Come, please do! I tried to get hold of you today, too, yes I did. I called you a couple of hours ago, but we were cut off. Oh, it's one of God's miracles that you're calling now."

So it had been Rosalie who'd called when the cell phone had been lying in her bag. Thank God. Maybe they hadn't been able to track her a little while ago, either. Perhaps there was no one in the world—other than Ollie—who had the slightest idea where she was.

She shook her head. One shouldn't take anything for granted.

"I'm in a really bad situation, Rosalie. I'll tell you more about it, but right now I just want to ask if I can stay with you a couple of days."

The reply was prompt. "You can stay as long as you like," she said. "But, Doggie . . ." Once again she could hear a faint, muttered prayer.

"Doggie . . ." she repeated, "is it possible for you to loan me a couple thousand dollars?"

There were also others for whom life wasn't so easy.

When she was done speaking to Rosalie, Ollie turned his music back on, so high that the license plate and several loose parts of the car began to buzz and rattle.

"Stop!" she screamed.

He gave her a pitying look. "Boy, baby, are you stressed out!"

She wiped the sweat off her forehead with the back of her hand. "Ollie, do you think this contradiction of physics—your car, I mean—can find a radio station that's still on the air?" She pointed at his battered Blaupunkt.

He pressed one of the remaining buttons confidently and raised his finger. "Don't judge a book by the cover, sugar."

Seconds later she discovered that Ollie Boyce Henson's universe contained more facets than she'd dared hope for. Because this crummy little radio not only brought in every little pirate station loud and clear, it did the same with all the police frequencies as well. She frowned as she eavesdropped on one communication after another. The cops were obviously busy as hell. There were still plenty of disobedient citizens who were brave and foolish enough to resist being spot-checked. Plenty who still had weapons hidden away and resisted having their homes searched. Many who'd simply had enough and whose resistance was a reflection of their anxiety and despair. But by now, most of this was just business as usual. What was far worse were the all-points bulletins that were broadcast every five minutes. No matter which frequency she tuned in on, the police, the military, the National Guard—everyone, in democracy's name—was busy trying to apprehend a female White House employee by the name of Dorothy Rogers, aka Doggie. Their description of her was extremely detailed: a white woman with very fair skin, light-brown hair, thirty years old, five foot four with unusually blue eyes, etc., etc. The description of her appearance was so precise and detailed that she slid down in her seat. They'd registered employees at the White House down to their toenails.

Ollie sat beside her, laughing. She felt like punching him. There was absolutely nothing to laugh about. On top of all this, police in patrol cars were urged to switch on their intranet, where they could see video recordings of her leaving the White House, and even in the act of attacking the vice president. Ollie shook his head and laughed even harder. No, in answer to her question, he didn't have a gadget in his car that could beam up that kind of shit.

She listened to them rattle off her habits, her usual haunts, and finally stressed how dangerous she was. They painted a picture not only of a woman whose father had murdered the president's wife, but one who had just this morning attempted to force her way into the Oval Office and murder the president himself.

CHAPTER 23

IT WASN'T HARD TO COUNT THE DAYS; IT WAS HARD NOT TO. IN A COUPLE OF hours they'd be sticking the needle into the guy who'd gassed his wife and her sister, and seventy-two hours later it would be his turn. It was an easy, brutal, bit of math.

Now it was Friday. Bud hadn't seen his lawyers for a couple of days. What was worse, he hadn't seen Pete, the prison guard, either, so all hope was practically gone.

The militiamen in the cells closest to the entrance were screaming back and forth to one another, driving him crazy. "So give them some pills to settle down, goddammit!" he yelled once in a while, but none of the guards reacted. They probably had more radical methods in mind.

Daryl Reid had been raving for hours in the cell to the left about his last meal and how fantastic it was going to be, and Reamur Duke was crying and hovering over his everlasting math puzzles in the cell to the right.

Everything was as usual, except that time was moving faster and faster now.

Bud hadn't seen himself in the mirror for a long time, but he could see it in his hands and feel it way into his soul: He'd aged twenty years during the four months he'd been in prison. *Leave me sitting here a few more months and you won't have to kill me,* he thought. *It'll happen all by itself.* The soul hibernated and the body fell into disrepair—it was unavoidable. Sometimes he caught himself having stared out through the bars for hours at a time, his thoughts full of green fields and the time he'd had a free will, and afterwards he was dead tired. On death row, one quickly lost one's orientation to everything—to the life that once was, to feelings and sensations that dealt with the future, and to details that used to be all-important but had now faded. However, Bud didn't want to let go of himself and was doing his best to remember. He'd be thinking all the beautiful thoughts he possibly could when they strapped him onto the gurney. He would keep his head clear to the end, and then he'd die, liberated in his mind and soul. This was what he worked on every single moment of the day.

By afternoon the militiamen had temporarily ceased their hateful battle cries, so he could hear the clanking of the normal changing-of-the-guard ritual.

"Have you heard, Buddy Boy?" Daryl whispered. "They can't find a doctor for the execution. They have to postpone it till midnight." He laughed, then called down to the prisoner who'd been crying and bitching all morning. "Don't be dumb enough to think you'll get out of it!"

Bud stepped to the bars and pressed his face against them. A little deputation with grave faces was standing before cell number eleven. In their midst the prison director was speaking to the condemned man. But Pete still wasn't there.

Doors opened and closed for the next couple of hours, and the prison priest attempted to calm the poor wretch. This was the corridor to hell.

"Shhh, here we go, Buddy Boy." Daryl chuckled as he ran his knuckles over the bars. "Can't you hear? Pete's coming!"

Bud leaned forward and tried to look down along the cells. A neon light had gone out in the middle of the corridor, leaving it in half darkness. He saw nothing.

"Quit the teasing, Daryl. I hate it."

"Hey, he's coming down here. . . . Yeah, listen! He's coming now!"

There was still some grumbling from the militiamen upstairs, but not much. Then a shadow glided along the floor and stopped.

"It's him, Buddy Boy." Daryl laughed. Suddenly, there he was. Pete seemed calm in the subdued light, but when he stepped closer, the look on his face almost made Bud's heart stop.

Pete turned his head and gave Daryl a cold look in the adjoining cell. "I'm the one who's taking care of you on the last day, Daryl. You know that, don't you? Is there something special I can do for you?"

Daryl gave a hoarse laugh. "No, Pete, I've already ordered everything. Cigarettes, Coke, everything I want to eat. It's been ordered."

"Good, Daryl, then listen: If you tell anyone about *any* of this, I'll piss on your plate of food. Got it?"

There was a frightened outburst from Daryl's cell. "Of course, Pete, of course. Absolutely. You can count on me. I won't say anything. Buddy's one of the cats, you know that."

Pete turned slowly to face Bud. He was so young and fit that it hurt. He would still be able to make love and stretch out under the stars years after Bud had turned to dust. Life still had a million experiences in store for him if he looked out for himself. It was completely unreal to think about.

"Do you have the cell phone?"

Pete patted his thermos. "You put five million in my bank account and you'll get it."

Bud was dripping cold sweat. "I'll do it, Pete, don't worry. But it's late now, and it's Friday besides. I can only do it Monday morning, at the earliest."

Pete shook his head. "I'm loaning you the phone for a half hour to take care of it. Otherwise I'm taking it back, got it? I won't be around by Monday."

Bud looked at the thermos and felt the sweat spreading under his arms. "You said you'd be here the twenty-sixth, but today's the twenty-seventh. That wasn't part of our agreement."

"I'm the one who makes the conditions. They changed my shift. Don't argue with me; just do it. We're coming to get the man in cell eleven in an hour, so you better be ready."

He looked around and unscrewed the top of the thermos. Steam came out when he pulled up the plastic bag. Bud was shaking inside. What if the cell phone hadn't been able to stand the temperature?

Pete unwrapped it, dumped the bag back into the thermos, flipped open the phone, and punched in his code. "I'll wait exactly thirty minutes, Bud—no more!" He eased it through the bars and let it fall into Bud's hand.

Bud didn't know that kind of phone and gave the display a worried look. It was a European or Japanese make and looked simple enough, but his blood froze at the sight of it.

"There's almost no battery left," he ascertained.

Pete shrugged his shoulders. "There's an hour's time left. It's hard as hell to find a cell phone at all these days, so don't bug me about a damn battery charger." He pulled a little piece of paper out of his pocket with his bank account number and the phone's number and passed it to Bud. Then he glanced at his watch and moved on.

Bud closed his eyes and tried to think. By now it was almost Friday midnight. Where the hell on the face of the earth could he find a bank that was open, that would transfer such a large amount on the basis of a phone conversation? It was still night in Europe, in Japan such transactions couldn't be made, and none of his local bank connections were open on Saturday. He couldn't remember his Internet bank code, and he'd never had to memorize his telephone numbers, so he couldn't call his lawyer, his business manager, his accountant, or Doggie, for that matter. On top of that, there was only a half hour until Pete returned, and the battery was almost dead.

"How's it going?" whispered Daryl, but Bud didn't answer. Try as he might, he couldn't even remember how to call information. He rubbed his forehead. *Come on,* Bud admonished himself, *your life's at stake.* The smell of urine grew around him. A piss pot was in use in a neighboring cell.

Come on, Bud, come on . . .

He analyzed the cell phone's display and pushed the menu button. A series of options popped up on the little screen. He pressed the telephone book function and found it empty. Then he tried the stored messages and the phone book, but everything was deleted. He couldn't even call a random person who'd been in contact with the phone's last owner. He could take a picture of his own feet, change the ringtone a dozen ways, and play Deep Abyss or mini golf, but he wasn't able to get hold of one person who could help him find his lawyer's telephone number.

He stuck his hand through the bars and waved for a moment, hoping Pete would see, but nothing happened. No help was to be expected from that quarter.

The man was being careful as hell, which was understandable.

So he punched in Virginia Beach's area code, followed by a totally random number, and hoped it would awaken some poor soul. *Please, let it be a good Christian,* he prayed, and tried to keep from hyperventilating.

After a half minute, there was a woman's voice, tired as a rest home. "Yes?" was all it said. The word felt like the cut of a knife blade.

"This is an emergency," he whispered. "I don't know whom I've called, and I apologize, but my life is in danger and I'm sitting in a dark room and can't see what number I'm dialing." He waited a few seconds that felt like half a lifetime.

"Is there anyone there . . . ?" he whispered.

"Dean, wake up," came from the other end of the line. "There's someone who says it's an emergency. You have to wake up. I don't know what to say to him."

Again there was an eternal, breathless pause. *Help me, please . . .* he thought, over and over again.

"What's this about?" the man asked.

"I'm sitting in a dark room," he whispered. "I've been kidnapped, and they're threatening to kill me if I don't pay a ransom by tonight."

"We can't help you with money; why don't you call the police?"

"The kidnappers are sitting right next to me, so that won't work. I have the money myself, that's no problem, but I need my lawyer's number so he can take care of the transaction. Help me with his phone number and you've saved my life."

"Who's holding you prisoner? Do these people know my number?"

"No, no, I just called your number at random. I'm sitting in the dark. I can't talk anymore. Help me. My lawyer's name is Erland Martin, and his office is in Virginia Beach. He's in the phone book."

"Ernie Martin?"

"No, *Erland.*"

"Erland? Strange name."

"What'd the man say, honey? Did he say 'Erland Martin'?" he heard from the woman in the background.

"Erland, yeah."

"He's the one who got Vivian her divorce. A real dumb bastard, if you ask me. I was in his office on Bendix Road together with her."

The man's voice sounded tired now. "Does your lawyer have his office on Bendix Road?" he asked.

Bud swallowed hard. "Yes, that's him."

"Just a second."

He heard the man sigh and grudgingly get out of bed, open the door, and leave the room—vocalizing his misgivings as he went—and then everything was quiet. Even his wife.

Bud stared woodenly at the cell phone's display. It was hard to see how much battery was left.

Don't beam up the menu, Bud, it'll use too much juice, he instructed himself, as his palms got more and more clammy.

All of a sudden, crying could be heard from Reamur Duke's cell. Reamur quickly recited a couple of number codes, but the crying got louder. That's how Reamur Duke was. In spite of his limited mental capacity he was the most tortured soul on death row.

Bud covered the receiver. "Shhh, Reamur, it's okay," he whispered, but Reamur was not okay. Even though he couldn't comprehend the fact that in four days he'd be lying stiff in a coffin, Reamur understood that his number codes weren't working out and that there no longer was anyone in this world who could give him comfort and help him understand. The cell wasn't what imprisoned Reamur; it was the sum total of not being capable of connecting life's dots. Whatever they were.

"I think the man's crying," the woman whispered on the other end of the line. Bud pressed the receiver tight against his ear.

"Well, I've got the number here. Do you have something to write with?" The man cleared his throat and waited. "No, I suppose you don't." He cleared his throat again. "Anyway, listen, here's the number . . ."

The telephone number started with 757-340, as it should. This was the Virginia Beach area. He knew it by heart, but he didn't recognize the last four digits.

"Is this Martin's private number?"

"I don't know. It was the only one in the phone book," said the man.

"How about looking under 'Erland V. Martin'?"

"V?"

"Yes."

"There are no others with that name. Maybe it's in the yellow pages."

Bud gave a sigh of relief. Of course! The man had looked in the white pages. He should have thought of that himself. This had to be Erland's home number—what could be better? He must be in bed this time of night. "Give me those last four digits again."

Suddenly, Reamur Duke took a deep breath and began chanting new codes so loudly that Bud had a hard time hearing what was being said on the phone.

"What's going on?" asked the man at the other end.

"It's the kidnappers. They're insane. What was the number? I couldn't hear it." The man said it again. Bud thanked him and hung up.

He said the number to himself a couple of times and then punched it in. *Please let this be your private number, Erland,* he prayed, with all his heart.

It was difficult for Erland Martin to conceal his irritation. His private life clearly was not something to be disturbed. Not even by a client who was condemned to death and about to die. But they'd never been such great pals, the two of them, in spite of the fact that Bud had made him a prosperous man and had even named him executor of his estate. It was all just business.

"I can't make a transaction tonight," he said. "Your Internet banking code is at the office, and you're not getting me in there at this time of night."

He asked no questions. Not about how Bud was coping, and definitely not about what else he might be able to do for him. He was cold and calculating, as always, completely devoid of empathy or compassion. Exactly as a top lawyer was supposed to be—when he was on your side, that is. Right now, Bud wasn't sure he was.

"Write down the account number I'm about to give you and transfer the five million dollars immediately."

"How?"

"Take it out of my customers' account."

"That's illegal, Bud, I can't."

"Yes, you can, goddammit. If the client himself asks for it."

"I need to have it in writing."

"Listen, Erland. It won't be long before you won't have to hear from me anymore. But if you don't do this now, my next phone call will assure that you don't cash in on my estate—you get what I'm saying? If you help me, I'll give you a five-hundred-thousand-dollar bonus, but this has got to happen in the next five minutes, understand?"

A sigh came from the other end of the line. If Bud ever got out of this alive—even if he were given one extra week—he'd make life so difficult for Erland V. Martin that he'd really have something to sigh about.

"A man will be calling you in ten minutes, Erland. His name is Pete—that's all you need to know. You confirm to him that you've done as I've told you. Do we understand each other? And one more thing: Give me Doggie's phone number and the number of a certain Sheriff T. Perkins from Highland County."

Pete left the prison twenty minutes before they fetched the man who was next in line to be executed. Pete had suddenly collapsed outside cell number five and vomited all over the floor. Bud didn't know how he'd done it—maybe by sticking a finger down his throat. In any case he succeeded in incurring the wrath of the militiaman in cell five, who damned him to hell and back. But Pete didn't care.

His mission was finished. He'd left the cell phone with Bud, along with precise instructions as to when to expect inspections by the guards and how to hide the phone. In return, Pete had personally been given Erland V. Martin's solemn assurance that his bank account was now bulging with cash.

One of the other guards took over the shift, and Pete was gone. The execution was delayed a little because the doctor had to come all the way from Staunton, and several of the militiamen were screaming their displeasure over the stink of Pete's vomit, but none of the prison officers paid any attention. They were busy preparing the execution.

Peace didn't return to death row for some time. Bud hadn't slept a wink. He'd just lain there, hugging his cell phone and trying to figure out how he could say things in the shortest time possible—and to whom he should say them—before the battery went dead.

A little after six, Saturday morning, when the prisoner's body had been driven away and Pete's replacement was nodding off at his post, he called the Highland County Sheriff's Office.

Bud had rehearsed what he had to say, knowing he had to keep it short. He knew how he'd explain the life of luxury T. Perkins could look forward to if he'd just help him the next couple of days, and he knew exactly what information he wanted to impart that would give Perkins something to work with on Bud's behalf.

He could hear the switchboard lady at the sheriff's office crying when she answered the phone. Someone had just shot and killed two deputies, she sobbed. All she could tell him was that Sheriff Perkins was out at the scene of the shootings.

Bud asked who'd been shot, his voice trembling, trying to sound as upset as possible.

"It was Willie, Willie Riverdale. And Stanley Kennedy," she snuffled.

"God, not Stanley!" His orchestrated outburst was so loud, he was afraid he'd been overheard.

"Oh, no. Did you know him?"

He pressed the receiver to his lips and tried to sound grief-stricken. "Not Stanley! Is Stanley dead?" Then he got to the point: "You've got to give me T. Perkins's cell phone number. Please!"

CHAPTER 24

THREE MEN LAY OUT IN THE MIDDLE OF A FLAT, GRAY-GREEN FALLOW FIELD WHERE corn had once grown. It was early Saturday morning, and T had been late in arriving. His men had been shooting at the house for more than an hour. Two of them were dead, and fifty yards ahead the weather-beaten wooden building was riddled like a sieve. T. Perkins stood by his patrol car a small distance away, looking at his deputy sheriff who lay twisted around with surprised eyes staring into eternity. Leo Mulligan had shot him through the throat—a fatal wound. Behind T stood officers Janusz Kovacs and Dody Hall with grim expressions, ready to fire if the old bastard Mulligan was dumb enough to expose so much as an eyebrow. T told them to stay by the car and ordered Officer Arredondo, who'd managed to sneak up behind a worn-out plow, to start firing when T began running towards the house.

It took a very long second of yelling and shooting from both ahead and behind before T made his way up to a rusty trailer. Ages ago it had been Leo Mulligan's pride and joy; now it served as T. Perkins's cover. He could see everything from here: his dead deputy Stanley Kennedy, lying in the field, Gonzales Arredondo emptying clip after clip from behind the plow, the naked landscape and the flat terrain behind the house, and the department's young mascot, Willie Riverdale, lying halfway up the stairs in a pool of blood.

"I'm thinking Willie's still alive, Dody," he said over his walkie-talkie. "Have you sent for an ambulance?"

He heard a gasp at the other end. It was answer enough. T stared at the perforated house. If Leo Mulligan was still uninjured after a bombardment like that, he must possess some kind of superhuman capacity no one had seen before.

"Arredondo, look over here," he said into the walkie-talkie. "I'm standing behind a pile of iron." The officer nodded. "I can't see if the trailer's drawbar is up or down. Can you?"

"It's pointing straight up in the air," he replied.

"Kovacs!" barked T to the officer back by the patrol car. "Listen: You come up to me while Dody and Arredondo cover you. Everybody got that? I'll keep the walkie-talkie on from now on." He gave a signal, and the inferno of noise and smoke and muzzle fire resumed. Clods of earth sprang into the air in front of Arredondo's plow. Officer Kovacs's face was bathed in sweat as he dove in behind T.

"We're going to push this trailer up to the house, okay?"

"It's gonna be hard, boss. All the tires are flat. This thing's stood here as long as I can remember. I don't think it'll budge."

"Yes, it will. It has to. Willie's still alive. I can see him breathing."

T leaned forward and braced his arms against the tailgate. Then, with one leg back, he gave a shove. The trailer didn't move, but it rocked a bit. "Come on, Kovacs," he grunted.

Rapid shots banged into the front of the trailer the second they shoved it the first inch over the weedy ground. It sounded like a blacksmith pounding iron. T. Perkins hated automatic weapons—he really, really did. The life expectancy of a peace officer was bound to rise if Jansen's ban on firearms turned out to be effective.

"I can't . . ." Kovacs kept groaning as they inched forward. What a whiner. T clenched his teeth and felt his back protesting in every joint, but there was no stopping now. "Dody, do you read me?"

"Yes, I've sent for an ambulance, T. I have. I'm sorry!"

"Now send for Daniel Smith's backhoe digger. Fast! We're going to need some help, or else I'm afraid we'll stay pinned down here in the field."

They kept pushing the trailer forward as well as they could, but got stuck in front of a slight ridge of earth and had to stop. T cursed silently as he looked at Willie staring at them, twenty yards away.

"*Leo!*" he yelled as loud as his tar-lined lungs would possibly allow.

"Leo, come out now! This is T. Perkins speaking! You'll be safe if you come out now. Are you able to come out, Leo? You have to, Leo, because Willie's in very bad shape, and he'll never make it unless you give us a chance to get him out of here. Did you hear that, Willie? We'll stop our shooting for five minutes."

He waited a moment, and when Leo didn't answer he gave Kovacs the sign to start pushing again. Then his cell phone rang. *Shit!* he thought, and considered throwing it as far away as he could. T had been the last one at the station to cave in to the trend and finally buy his own cell phone. It had been an abomination ever since, just like he'd figured.

"Maybe it's the guy with the backhoe digger, boss. You better answer."

T tried to remember the shortest route from Daniel Smith's development firm to Mulligan's house.

"Yes," he said quickly into the phone, and then his jaw dropped. No, it wasn't Daniel Smith, it was the last person in the world he'd expected to hear from: Bud Curtis.

Curtis sounded completely alienated and abject at the other end. He explained he was speaking from an illegal cell phone and there wasn't much time before the battery would run out. *Fine,* thought Perkins as he watched Dody Hall take the phone in the police car and with clear gestures explain she had Daniel Smith on the line and was trying to direct the backhoe digger along the back roads south of town.

But Bud Curtis kept talking, and he made T. Perkins listen. It was a totally schizophrenic experience. Half of him was standing there as chief law enforcer, administering the law of the land with one foot in the lion's mouth and a dead colleague lying before him with birds chirping in the thick creepers on the fence, while the other half was talking to a condemned man from a world where justice and reason had no meaning—a human being before his maker, begging for mercy in the name of innocence. And Perkins believed the man because he'd seen the circumstantial evidence on the videos. He believed Bud Curtis just as he believed the whole horrible situation with Leo Mulligan was a misunderstanding that had gotten completely out of control.

A series of dull blows could be heard from the house that sounded like Leo Mulligan was hammering on the wall from inside. *So apparently, there was still plenty of life in the deranged old brute,* thought T, as the window frames vibrated and one of the panes suddenly fell out. The shattering glass proved too much in the tense atmosphere. The wounded deputy, Willie Riverdale, flinched and tried to move, and a volley of shots erupted from Arredondo's plow, which was immediately returned from the house with a weapon T. Perkins couldn't immediately identify. He'd be damned if he'd get in the way of it, though.

"I have to sign off now, Bud. Put your cell phone on vibrate, and I'll get back to you when the situation out here is under control."

Bud protested, but T assured him that he'd contact him, that he had something to tell him, and that his cell phone had registered Curtis's number. He'd call him back in about an hour's time.

Then he hung up and signaled Kovacs that the break was over.

The tendons in their necks were tight as violin strings, and every fiber of their shoulder muscles strained with overexertion as they resumed nudging the trailer over the bumpy terrain.

"We're not pushing in a straight line," Kovacs gasped.

T peeped around the corner of the trailer and got a glimpse of the old man, less than ten yards away, poised in the empty window frame with blood trickling down his face. If they kept pushing in the same direction, they'd be heading directly alongside the house, forcing Mulligan to change his line of vision so he couldn't avoid seeing the unsuspecting Willie lying on the stairs.

"We're stopping," he whispered to Kovacs. Then he shouted, "Leo, can you hear me?" He was promptly answered with a volley of bullets.

T grabbed the walkie-talkie. "Dody, do you know if Leo Mulligan has a telephone?"

"Sorry, boss, there's none registered at his address. But Arredondo's seen him talking on a cell phone in town."

"Leo," yelled T, "do you have a cell phone in there?" This time there was no shooting.

"Look!" He took his cell phone in his fingertips and waved it cautiously around the corner of the trailer. "Tell me your number, and I'll call you. You need to talk with someone, you really do. Leo, are you listening?"

T heard a shot and felt the projectile practically flay the phone out of his hand. His partner twisted around with a look of confusion as T saw his hand was bleeding. *Shit, that hurts,* he said to himself. He stuck all his fingers in his mouth and felt around with his tongue. They all seemed to be there, except for a little portion of skin on his index finger that had landed in a bush, along with half his new cell phone.

Dody whistled to him and pointed down the gravel road where an extremely tired backhoe digger was chugging towards them with its excavating shovel raised. Leo Mulligan responded with yet another round of well-aimed fire. From where they crouched they could clearly hear the shells clonking against the machine.

"Dody, tell Daniel Smith to drive over here to the trailer," he yelled into his walkie-talkie.

"I'm afraid it's not Daniel," she replied.

"Who is it, then?"

"Jonathan Kennedy!"

"What?!"

"Yeah, it's Stanley's brother."

T. Perkins looked over at his dead deputy sheriff, who was still lying in the field, staring into space. He cursed softly.

"Stop Jonathan and tell him not to do anything on his own initiative—under any circumstances. You hear me, Dody? It won't help his brother if he's killed, too."

"Okay, boss."

He watched as she gave the warning to the backhoe, then watched as it was ignored and the farm machine rumbled past, towards the house. It still had fifty yards to go, but it was already possible to predict what Jonathan Kennedy had in mind. He was going to steer around his dead brother, turn sharply in front of them so he didn't hit Willie on the front stairs, and then ram the house broadside. Jonathan and Stanley had been twins. There was nothing to do about it.

The next few seconds were chaotic, but T would long remember the sound of the house beams splintering like matchsticks. Leo Mulligan fired a couple of rounds straight into the backhoe's tires but couldn't stop the machine's enormous forward inertia. They watched as Jonathan sprang out of the cab and sprinted to the back door. The rifle in his hand was usually employed for hunting foxes on Daniel Smith's farm, and here was a fox that needed flushing out of its lair. They yelled to him, but it was too late. With one jump he was inside the back door. Now all that was left in Jonathan Kennedy's script was the final shoot-out.

Twenty-five minutes later, at about seven thirty, the entire area was thick with people. The ambulance had already left with Willie and Arredondo, who'd had a lump of flesh shot from his shoulder but was in no great danger. Both were doing fine according to the doctor. Thank God they'd been spared the sad chore of informing Willie Riverdale's folks of the death of their son.

They found Leo Mulligan crushed under the chimney that, ironically, was the only masonry in the whole house. Next to him stood his nemesis, Jonathan Kennedy, his face covered in dust and bits of plaster.

"You know what the bastard said just before he died?" asked Kennedy, Dody's handcuffs clanking from his wrists. "He said: 'My son can go to hell. Everything's his fault.'" Dody Hall pulled him away as he proceeded to kick the body. "No, Leo, it's you who can go to hell!" he screamed, as he was led to the patrol car. "Wasn't it you who killed my brother, or was that your son's fault, too?"

T stood for a moment, staring at all the shell holes in the walls. Why had Leo said that about his son? He shook his head. He'd probably never find out. He watched Jonathan Kennedy as Dody and another officer led him away.

He was sure to get a mild sentence.

T worked his way through Mulligan's living room. They'd accused him of stealing seed from a nearby barn. Leo had denied the theft and then turned his shotgun on the officers. A few quick rounds, after which he'd fled inside his house, and the rest was history. As far as T could see, there were no sacks of seed inside the house or in any of the other farm buildings.

He sighed. Leo Mulligan hadn't had an easy life. His wife had flirted with any man who came along, making Leo burn with a jealousy that eventually consumed him, and he murdered her. He'd sat in the state hospital and begged the police to find his son and see that he was well taken care of, and then—when they finally found the kid—he'd had to watch impotently as they let him be adopted. Leo Mulligan had never gotten to see his son again, and after more than thirty years of preventative detention was finally released from the loony bin, only to be accused a few months later of something he apparently hadn't done. And now, there he lay: crushed under the rubble of the chimney he and T's brother-in-law had built with their own hands. What a wasted life.

Aside from the Caterpillar backhoe that now stood in Leo's bedroom and the hundreds of bullet holes that had been provided by Gonzales Arredondo's service revolver and rifle, the living room—despite its layer of dust and debris—was neat and tasteful, as though a woman's touch were still present. The dining room table was covered with a lace tablecloth, and there'd been fresh flowers in the overturned glass vase. Everything was exactly the same as it had been thirty-two years ago when he'd been led away in handcuffs.

T. Perkins looked at the pictures hanging over the hollowed-out easy chair and ran his finger over a pile of copper pots that used to be lined up in a row on an old bureau. The house had apparently just been standing there, waiting to be awakened from its fairy-tale slumber when Leo Mulligan finally got out of the state asylum. Apart from the damage, everything seemed to be just as before.

He studied a framed photograph of the young family standing close together. Leo's wife was strikingly beautiful; was it any wonder that men ran after her, begging for her affection? The boy standing between them was delicate, with a gentle expression. A boy eleven or twelve years old. That is, only a couple of years before the innocent lad saw his father murder his mother and then ran off to begin his career as gigolo for neglected housewives. Looking at this photo, taken on a lovely summer's day, who could imagine all this would take place? T held the picture in front of him and stared into the eyes of the now-deceased homicidal father, the mother—whose eyes' last image was of a baseball bat heading for her skull—and the boy, who now had another name and, hopefully, a better life somewhere. His were lively, boyish eyes with carefree lips that could still break into a smile. How could anything be this boy's fault? What had Leo meant?

The next photo sent chills down his spine. The boy was older here, but the eyes had been crossed out with a felt-tip pen. They were crossed out in the next photograph, too. Leo's son must have been about fifteen at the time, just before his father killed his mother. T shook his head and began rubbing the ink off the frame's dusty glass.

He peered deep into the boy's eyes as they became visible. He noticed his mouth was getting dry. Suddenly it was as if the boy were standing right in front of him. All that was needed to bring the picture up-to-date was to give the skin around these eyes a few wrinkles. T held his breath. *My God,* he thought, *I knew it all along!* This was what had been lurking in his subconscious, pestering him ceaselessly. Why hadn't he been able to bring it to the surface?

He placed the picture frame on the table and took a step back without taking his eyes off those of the boy. There could be no doubt. This adolescent, who'd witnessed his father kill his mother and had fucked women for money, had traveled far since he'd deserted his humble beginnings. Everybody knew him, every man and woman in this suffering nation, and everyone had their own opinion of him.

It was Thomas Sunderland, vice president of the United States, the man at the center of the most forbidding cataclysm an American government had ever unleashed on its citizens.

A few police technicians looked in through the splintered remains of the house's wall, trying to get his attention, but T waved them away and mumbled that they'd have to look after themselves. Then he began searching methodically through every drawer, cupboard, and pile of papers he could find, scarcely knowing what he was looking for. He found relics of bygone days everywhere, relics from a time that a crazy old man had passionately wished would return.

A narrow door at the end of the dining room led him into a small child's bedroom. Its walls were mildewed but still bore witness to a boy having inhabited it many years previously. T looked around. There was a miniature bust of Thomas Jefferson, a kite made of silk paper, and centerfold pictures of David Bowie, Alice Cooper, and a very young Ursula Andress with bare breasts and glistening lips. The bed remained unmade since the last time it was slept in, with *Penthouse* magazines still poorly concealed underneath. The overall impression was scarcely that of a young man the country's vice president would want to be identified with. Still, it was here—amid the cornfields and with a father who'd fought to survive and keep his inner demons under control—that Thomas Sunderland had been molded.

The coats hanging in the hallway were completely shredded by bullet holes. He searched the pockets and kicked the shoes and boots that lay strewn on the floor. On a shelf beneath a shattered mirror lay a sports bag that didn't fit the overall picture of a house long uninhabited. It was red and trendy, so apparently the twenty-first century had made some inroads in Leo Mulligan's existence in spite of everything. T opened it cautiously and saw a white towel upon which was written PROPERTY OF MARION CORRECTIONAL TREATMENT CENTER. They must have thought that letting him have it was the least they could do when they sent him home from the hospital.

T carried the bag in to the dining room table, swept the broken glass and other rubble aside, and emptied it. *No happy memories in here,* he thought, as he made a pile of hospital discharge papers, certificates, medical prescriptions that Mulligan apparently had never had filled, plus all kinds of odds and ends that someone in an institution for the criminally insane might collect over the years. *How little can a person own, and still survive?* he wondered, as he came across some small drawings made by Leo Mulligan's fellow sufferers.

Three of them were signed identically—"With regards from Benno"—but the dates stretched over twenty years. T let his fingers glide lightly over the touchingly naive drawings. He was willing to bet that Benno was still at the institution.

In the bottom of the bag he found a couple of magazines and some tattered, folded-up newspaper clippings. He took the first one and spread it out on the table. He could see no date, but there were several headlines that suggested the early eighties. *Doesn't matter,* he thought, and reached reflexively for a cigarette in his breast pocket. He needed to find one end of this tragic ball of yarn in order to begin unraveling all the unknowns of the case—and this was it. An incipient sense of impending breakthrough began growing inside him, and he stood for a long time with the cigarette in the corner of his mouth before remembering to light it. The caption under a photograph had caught his attention. The large press photo was rather indistinct, thanks to its grainy quality and having been blurred by countless handlings. It depicted two soldiers saluting each other: a high-ranking officer with a mustache and a big smile, facing the camera, and a young soldier whose face was hidden but who obviously was very proud about the situation. If it hadn't been for the caption, T wouldn't have given the picture a second thought and the world would have continued rotating in its uncertain orbit. But there it was: "Former deputy commander in chief of Ramstein Air Base, Lieutenant General Wolfgang Sunderland salutes his son, Captain Thomas Sunderland, for distinction in the battle of Grenada."

T. Perkins took a deep drag on his cigarette. Could there really be a reason to honor anyone for anything that had to do with that act of misguided, macho, military aggression?

He placed the clipping on top of Benno's sketches. The ridiculous invasion of Grenada had taken place in 1983. That is, about eight or nine years before Thomas Sunderland became Bruce Jansen's faithful foot soldier, around the time T met him on the ill-fated trip to China. T let the smoke sieve out through his teeth and took another deep drag. So this was how the path had been cleared for the son of a murderer who grew up in the middle of nowhere to become the most outspoken chief of staff the country had seen for generations. A military man had adopted Leo Mulligan Jr. and had determinedly set about shaping and preparing the young man for the tasks that lay ahead. Outwardly, it looked like a case of the ugly duckling being transformed into a swan, but T wasn't so sure. It was rare that fairy tales and reality were compatible in this wicked world.

He reached into his pocket for the cell phone and swore as he noticed his fingertip was beginning to bleed again, followed by the recollection that his expensive, state-of-the-art cell phone had been blown to bits.

He stopped in mid-movement as the next terrible realization hit him: Without his cell phone, he wouldn't be able to return Bud Curtis's call.

T stepped over a stuffing-sprouting, wrecked chair on his way out of the house and then almost slipped on Willie Riverdale's coagulating blood on the front steps, but he barely noticed. His brain was working at high speed. How was he supposed to call someone back on a destroyed cell phone?

Back at the trailer he found the half of the phone that hadn't been blown away. "Hey," he called to the technicians who were putting Leo Mulligan's weapon arsenal into clear plastic bags. "Do you know how to remove the SIM card from one of these things?"

He held the little electronic mess out to them.

"If there's anything left that works here, it's not the SIM card, chief," said the man who took it.

"Look, there *is* no more SIM card." He pointed at the spot where it once had been.

T stood for a moment, letting cigarette smoke waft in front of his face as he weighed the consequences. Not only did he no longer have Bud Curtis's number, there couldn't be many others who had it, either, and people condemned to die weren't usually listed in the phone book. None of the numbers he had in his head belonged to people who could help him find Curtis's cell phone number, either. But maybe Doggie could—he'd had her phone number in his address book in the glove compartment ever since the trial.

T considered his options and decided to postpone the problem. There was a more urgent matter. He nodded to one of the technicians. "Mind if I borrow your cell phone? Sure would appreciate it."

T hesitated for a moment before punching in the number to police headquarters in Richmond. He asked for Beth Hartley's private number and received a not particularly friendly question in return: Why didn't he ask her himself?

"How on God's earth am I supposed to do that when I don't have her number?" he wanted to know.

"You could ask to be transferred to her desk, for example. She's been here since six this morning, and it doesn't look like she'll be leaving anytime soon."

"On a Saturday?"

"Saturday, Sunday, Monday . . . What the hell's the difference," came the impatient voice. "Don't you wear a uniform yourself?"

After being transferred twice, he finally heard Beth Hartley's fetching voice on the line.

"It's me, Beth . . ." he said. The silence was deafening. "Anything the matter?"

"I'm really busy, T. Didn't you get everything you needed yesterday?"

He suppressed a little chuckle. "My dear Beth, I need your help one more time, and this time it's for something completely different. Would you please give me some information about a certain retired lieutenant general by the name of Wolfgang Sunderland? That's not so difficult, is it?"

"Is that all? It's Saturday, you know? I really should be in my nice, soft bed, getting my beauty sleep." She seemed very, very reserved. Maybe she was afraid of what he might say. He knew the walls had ears, and she wasn't about to jeopardize her newly acquired Edwin Forbes painting because of some careless remark.

"Yeah, yeah, I know, Beth, but I just need his data. When he retired and his last known address."

He could already hear her computer keyboard clattering away in the background. Good old Beth. "The names of his children and stuff like that. Date of birth and death. Any criminal record for him or his family members . . ."

"Why his date of death?" she interrupted. "He's not dead, as far as I can see."

"You mean he's alive?"

"Unless he died yesterday. He's old, but he's alive. And he doesn't live far from you, by the way. He lives in Lexington."

"Lexington, Virginia?"

"Right. Listen, do you want me to fax you his data sheet?"

"No, just give me his address." He looked up and noticed two oil-smudged men in the process of trying to get the backhoe digger out of Leo Mulligan's smashed house. "Hey, just a minute, guys," he shouted. "You better not remove it before we say so. We don't want the ceiling caving in on us, do we?" He shook his head. What air-heads. "Sorry, Beth, but sometimes I wonder what folks have between their ears. Just one more thing: Were there other children than the one son, Thomas?"

"None that were legitimate, in any case." She gave a little laugh—a sign that her old self was returning. Thank God for that.

He switched off the cell phone and stuck it in his inner coat pocket.

"Hey, that's my phone, remember, T?" said the technician, reaching out for it.

T had to shake his head. "Jesus, am I getting senile, or what?" He shook it again and then gave a big smile. "You shouldn't put up with your sheriff running off with your phone, just like that. No way. Here, son, you have my handshake as guarantee that when I come back you'll get a receipt saying I confiscated it. Of course you will."

The first thing he did when he arrived in Lexington around eleven o'clock was make a stop at one of his favorite old haunts, Lexington Restaurant. Here it was possible to order a kind of stew, the various origins of which could be found on the previous week's menu, yet it tasted out of this world and came in such huge portions that the wait-ress had to hold the plate with both hands.

He sat down in a booth by the window facing the parking lot and checked out the counter. It was from the fifties and looked it.

The short-haired waitress already had her ballpoint pen out.

"What brings you this way in these unhappy times, T?" she asked, adjusting her apron over her shabby uniform. There wasn't the man she hadn't flirted with in the course of time, and she wasn't about to stop now, in spite of the date on her birth certificate. "Couldn't live without me a moment longer, could ya', hon?"

"He-he! Who wouldn't drive to the ends of the earth for such a gorgeous sight?" he said, as he tried to remember her name. "Plus your coffee, of course, my sweet. It even beats my own mother's."

She nudged him and giggled. "Aww, go on, T," she replied as she smoothed her uniform over her lovely bosom.

"And some kind of sandwich—I'm starving." He patted his stomach. It was true: He couldn't remember the last time he'd eaten. "By the way, do you happen to know a Wolfgang Sunderland who lives somewhere around here?"

She nodded.

"Do you also know if he's still living in the same house? He's quite an elderly gent, you know."

She nodded again. "He lives a couple of hundred yards towards town, hon. What do you want with that pigheaded old fart?"

"I need to have a little talk with him about his son."

She shook her head emphatically. "May the devil take him!"

"Then you know who he is?"

"Thomas Sunderland, our venerable vice president? Hah! Find me one woman in this end of town between the age of forty and sixty-five who he hasn't been in bed with, and I'll bet she didn't move here till after Thomas moved out."

"That must be quite a few years ago by now," he interjected.

"That's right, little T. He had more hair on his head in those days, but it's not that long ago. Don't remind me, I hate that bastard. He and Jansen are destroying this country. Take a look around. This place used to be packed with guests this time of day, didn't it?"

T nodded towards the two other people sitting in the diner. "Yeah, you've got a point. No risk of my getting claustrophobia here today."

She stretched her back with her hands on her hips. "Yeah, you've always tried being funny, T, but it's no goddamn laughing matter, trying to run a restaurant when there isn't a soul left with money to spend." She kicked open the kitchen door. "But *you* we're gonna keep till one o'clock, hon, because the old tyrant's not finished with his noontime nap before then."

Aside from the rest home, Wolfgang Sunderland's was the most impressive house in the southern end of Lexington's Main Street. T parked his car out front and studied the veranda that was flanked by four enormous columns supporting the balcony two stories above.

One could easily imagine Lieutenant General Sunderland being born and raised and having spent his life in this mansion, apart from when he was off participating in diverse little wars or inspecting US military installations around Europe. One could also easily imagine young Thomas growing up behind these massive walls, infused with the blind faith that no man was his better. It was here he'd had his arrogance and his ruthless commando style instilled, and now everyone was paying for it.

T had been close to both Sunderland and Jansen in China. He'd gotten a relatively clear impression of who Jansen was, behind the facade, but he hadn't had much luck in sussing out Sunderland. It would surely have been easier at the time—or at the trial—if he'd recognized him as Leo Mulligan's son. Sunderland's role had undergone a transformation during Bud Curtis's trial. From being the gray eminence on Jansen's staff he'd turned into a high-profile decision maker. There were so many aspects and incidents in this case in which Sunderland had had a hand. He was the one who'd recruited the Secret Service agents and had approved Curtis's hotel in Virginia Beach, so he had to have played some role in what happened. Whether it was intentional or not was still unclear, so T had to give him the benefit of the doubt for the moment. But he could still clearly remember how Sunderland had sat in the witness box, checking everyone out with sharply attentive, judgmental eyes.

Now the question was whether Sunderland senior would be able to give any useful information about his son.

The old officer still knew how to hold himself erect, but one could see it caused him pain. Needless to say, Wolfgang Sunderland lacked the military poise of his heyday, but he was still an imposing figure. After checking T's identification, he led him into a puritanically austere room whose only decorative elements were the mahogany panels, carved from floor to ceiling. *Cozy as a funeral home,* thought T.

"To what do we owe a visit from a man of the law? Did one of those day-laborer Mexicans down at the Lexington Lodge make a mess of things?" He sat down on the sofa with difficulty and began pouring Wild Turkey into two glasses.

"I've come to ask you a couple of questions about Thomas, General."

"I see . . ." He stopped pouring the bourbon, set the bottle on the table, and struggled to his feet again. Then he extended his hand. "Well, then, I don't believe we have more to talk about today, Sheriff Perkins."

T looked at his rugged paw and remained seated. "I know it's difficult for you, General, but let's have a chat anyway. Better with a bit of frankness between two honorable men than thousands of questions from hoards of federal police, wouldn't you agree?"

"Which means . . . ?"

"Answer my questions and your life goes on as before. Refuse, and you place yourself directly in the line of fire, General. There will be other folks, much less agreeable than myself, who will ask the same questions—again and again. You can bank on it."

Wolfgang Sunderland was born in 1920 and was almost ninety, but if someone had given him a firearm right now, he wouldn't have hesitated emptying the entire magazine into T. Perkins like a nervous, green corporal on patrol behind enemy lines. He was shaking with resentment and had to grab the floor lamp next to the sofa to keep from toppling over. After a moment he regained his composure, made his way back to the sofa, and plopped down again. He emptied one of the whisky glasses and refilled it.

"Your son received honors in Grenada. Was he a brave soldier?"

Wolfgang Sunderland stopped him with an index finger raised in warning. "Call him Thomas or whatever you want, but my son, he's not—you understand?"

"Okay. Was he a courageous soldier?"

The general poured himself yet another bourbon, big enough to fell a horse, sniffed at it, and began laughing as he raised it to his lips. "He was a coward. A disgrace to his family—that's what he was."

"But they gave him a medal, anyway."

He drained his glass and refilled it once more. "I don't feel like answering your question, okay?"

"Then instead maybe you'll tell me what kind of person he is, in your own words."

The old man pursed his lips and looked at him with an expression that was used to being obeyed. "I don't know what authority you have, or why you're here, nor do I care. I assume you know Thomas was adopted."

T nodded.

"He should never have been brought into my home. If it weren't for my barren wife—God be with her—it would never have happened." He took another gulp and held the glass limply between two fingers. "Oh, yes, they gave him the medal, but he didn't deserve it. I ask you: Does an officer deserve a medal for hiding behind his own men while they're being shot to pieces? Not where I come from. But that's my boy! We could already see it when he first joined my men—the way he chased my subordinates' daughters around the family quarters at Ramstein and how fast he ran the other way when faced with the consequences. Do you have any idea of the scandal, when your own son makes your officers' underage daughters pregnant, one after the other?" He shook his head and considered pouring another shot.

"That boy's head was simply screwed together wrong. He duped us all, the little shit. Manipulation was his trademark, believe me. You've never met a young man who was so good at playing people off against each other." He set the glass down heavily and held his head in his wrinkled hands. "He even got his own mother to turn against me. Yes, dammit, I call her his mother because she loved him, God be with her. He turned her against me by telling her lies that no man can stand for. Untruths, understand?" He shook his head again.

T chose to get straight to the point. "Did he accuse you of incest?"

He jerked back in the sofa as though someone had just thrust a bayonet straight at him. "What did you say?!" His face was livid with shock and rage. "What do you think you're doing, coming here in my house and using words like that?"

"I beg your pardon. I'm sorry."

Wolfgang Sunderland tried to focus on the whisky bottle and reached out for it. "The disgusting little prick claimed his father liked to take it up the ass. Do you understand? Can you understand that?!"

"He claimed you were homosexual?"

"Outrageous!" His voice was quaking. "I could have killed him if he hadn't disappeared with his mother."

"She left you then?"

He nodded and half of his next pour missed the glass. "I've been following the little shit's career ever since. Of course he finds himself a Democratic senator to ingratiate himself with. Who the hell else but a fucking Democrat would be dumb enough to invite a poisonous snake into his house?" He gave a bitter laugh. "There are at least ten people left on this street who knew Thomas in the old days. Ask them what they think of him. About all his nasty tricks and pranks." He swept the spilled bourbon off the edge of the coffee table. "You couldn't believe anything if it had to do with him. He was a little brat who never listened to reason and now he's sitting there, laughing at all of us, believe me. 'Vice president.' Hah!" He said it with so much bitterness in his voice that he began shaking again.

"He lived off blackmailing women when he was fifteen, did you know that?" Lieutenant General Sunderland stared at the floor. "The kid only got out of the mess because my wife interceded on his behalf. She was a naive fool for believing him. But the boy had learned his lesson. From then on he curried favor with people so he could misuse them afterwards, you see?"

T nodded. "Yes, I know about that."

"Then maybe you also know he never stopped doing it from then on."

Bill Pagelow Falso, warden of Sussex State Prison in Waverly, Virginia, was a man of principle. T. Perkins hadn't had much to do with him in the beginning, but during the past ten years their paths had crossed so often—and these encounters had been so congenial and professionally fruitful—that they could now look each other in the eye as equals and of the same species. It wasn't that T cared much for Falso's God-fearing philosophy, but he liked his honesty and consistency. There'd been times when T had needed special attention be given to certain inmates who he knew personally, and had paid back the favor by occasionally putting Falso up when he was overcome by the urge to go hunting. Falso loved shooting animals, and T knew everyone who had hunting rights in Highland County. This wasn't a bad system of reciprocity, considering the purpose of T's present mission.

He looked at the road. Skirmishes with militias and forest fires had forced many panic-stricken animals out onto Route 60. The evidence was plentiful in the slippery remains of skunks, possums, and raccoons. He himself had somehow been lucky in never running over any furry creatures in the course of his long odyssey through the Virginia landscape. He tapped the underside of his steering wheel for good luck and looked at his watch. If he kept making good time through the roadblocks down by Macon, Centralia, and Disputanta, he'd be in Waverly well ahead of the day's execution at 6:00 P.M., giving him time for a meeting with Falso.

Off on the horizon lay a smoke screen above Cumberland State Forest. That meant still more trouble with the militias. He made a mental note of how many military vehicles passed him and turned off the road towards Ashby. This was the prelude to yet another bloody showdown.

He popped the glove compartment open and fumbled after his address book, which lay on top of a couple of old darts, behind Dody Hall's secret stash of marshmallows. He took out the little book and one of the darts that he'd equipped with steering feathers and filed down for optimal weight and balance. He could hit a bull's-eye four out of five times with this one, he really could. It was the best dart he'd ever made.

He smiled, looked up Doggie's number, and turned on his walkietalkie. It was at the limit of its range, but it worked. "Hi, Dody, how's it going with Willie Riverdale?"

There was some static, but Dody's voice put him at ease. "He's okay, T. He had a punctured lung, but Willie's a tough young man."

"And Arredondo?"

"He'll be all right. They'll both be back in uniform within the month. You have my personal guarantee, boss."

T wasn't in doubt. Even if she had to change their bandages herself.

"I won't be back before Monday," he said. "You'll have to take care of yourselves. I hereby appoint you my deputy until I return. Okay, Dody?"

If she complained about the temporary promotion, she did so in a very low voice. The question was what the rest of Highland County's sparse population would say to a couple of days under her command.

"Would you put me through to this number?" He gave her Doggie's cell phone number. He'd tell Doggie that he'd done what he could, that he hadn't forgotten her.

"Sorry, boss. There's no connection to the cell phone at the moment. Shall I try again?"

"Call the White House and ask for Dorothy Rogers."

"The White House?"

"Just do it, Dody."

"You're talking about Dorothy Rogers, the one they call Doggie?"

"Yes."

"Boss, there's a warrant out for her. She tried to kill Vice President Sunderland, and she's wanted nationwide. You ought to turn up your police radio a bit."

He frowned, feeling the pressure growing inside his head. "A warrant?"

"Yes. There's a video clip on the net. You can see her kicking him in the balls while he's lying on the floor."

T shook his head. Events were unfolding fast.

"Shall I try her cell phone again, T?"

He looked out over the countryside as the sun slowly moved westward in his rearview mirror.

"No, Dody. No, thanks. I'll get back to you. Have a good watch."

CHAPTER 25

OF ALL THE HOMESPUN LIFE PHILOSOPHIES WESLEY BAREFOOT HAD HEARD IN his relatively short life, one of his mother's assertions—that if one drank two cups of tea for every cup of coffee, then one could basically drink as much coffee as one liked—was the most untrustworthy. Just now, in any case, he was looking with amazement from one almost empty thermos to the other, and then at his hands, which were quivering like the head of a bass drum. If he drank just one more cup of either, he'd short-circuit for sure. So why did he still have this damned unappeasable urge?

It had been a loathsome day, just like the previous ones. Ever since Doggie had left his office in anger, the circumstances surrounding and following her alleged attack on Sunderland had spun out of control. It was being said that she had tried to kill the vice president, and for that reason had vanished. Wesley hoped fervently that the latter part was true. He absentmindedly stirred the remains in the bottom of his coffee cup with his finger while he looked despairingly around his gilded cell. Why the hell hadn't he agreed to intercede for Doggie and her father by getting her an audience with Jansen? What harm could have come from that? The president would merely have turned him down, but at least he would have shown he was willing to do whatever he could for her—because he would, wouldn't he? Or would he? He'd been crazy about her for years, and the possibility of them becoming a couple one day had always titillated the back of his mind. They'd both felt that way—he was sure of it—but he had to admit that her father's trial had gotten in the way. And now he didn't dare try to help her, so why deceive himself? He'd been behaving like a Boy Scout for weeks—no, it was worse than that: He'd been a fellow traveler and a coward, and what had it got him? Now Doggie was gone, and Donald was dead. Lance Burton prowled around like a spider while the rest of the staff had sealed themselves hermetically in their offices, fearful of no longer being able to deliver the goods that were expected of them.

Wesley wished he could do the same—just lock his door and throw away the key. And why not?

He'd been hired to convey tidings of the president's deeds, hopes, and dreams to the rest of the world. Now dream had turned to nightmare: The media was in a stranglehold, his own voice had been stifled, the president had entrenched himself in the Oval Office, and everybody was afraid and alone. If Wesley went out in the hall, his every step would be followed by suspicious eyes and each movement registered and analyzed. If he said something unsolicited, it would be met with mistrust and skepticism; if he laid a friendly hand on someone's shoulder, the person would immediately shy away. No one was in the mood to be accommodating. Wesley felt lost.

He pressed the intercom button. "Eleanor," he said, "would you mind coming in here with a couple of Cokes?"

"You haven't the time; you're supposed to be in Vice President Sunderland's office in two minutes!"

"Now, why is it we're sitting in here?" Wesley asked, looking up at Sunderland's bulletin board with its neatly arranged rows of international newspaper clippings and at least a hundred press photos. There were photographs of Jansen, eyes blazing, and of thousands of deportees sitting in refugee camps along the Mexican border. Shots of ex-convicts wearing diagonal yellow stripes, collecting trash along the highways, and press photos of militia leaders with loaded weapons and hateful expressions. Everything was represented; the world was informed.

At the end of rows of newspaper clippings, there was a half-page feature from Le Figaro with a large picture of President Jansen.

Wesley couldn't understand the text, but he could read the date. So apparently news of the attempt on Jansen's life had found its way abroad.

Nope, there was no need for the White House press service to help disseminate news like that.

"We're sitting in here because the glazier won't be finished with the Oval Office for a couple of more hours," answered Sunderland, without looking up from his desk.

"I see . . ." said Wesley, not knowing what the man was talking about. What was a glass cutter doing in the Oval Office? As far as he knew, the windows were okay.

The president entered, shook hands with Defense Secretary Wayne Henderson and Billy Johnson, Secretary of Homeland Security, then signaled for everyone to sit down. "Well, Lance," he said to his new chief of staff, "do we have the Donald Beglaubter situation under control?"

The choice of words hit Wesley's tortured soul hard—"the Donald Beglaubter situation." Did he speak about what had been done to inform the public—because absolutely nothing had been done—or about sending condolences to Donald's parents and his sister, who worked in the Eisenhower Executive Office Building next door? Did he mention the state funeral at Arlington Cemetery that was to be held on Monday? No. Could it be instead that Jansen meant silencing any speculation as to how things had gone so terribly wrong?

Lance Burton shifted on the sofa next to Wesley and nodded affirmatively.

"Very good . . . And who would like to start? Wayne, what are we saying now? Are we going to capture Moonie Quale by Sunday evening, as you promised us?"

During the past few days it had become easier to see that Defense Secretary Henderson was the government's eldest member. Sometimes lined faces and wrinkled skin speak of a person's courage and the experiences life has sent his or her way, and sometimes they tell more about the consequences of these experiences. Whatever the case, these past weeks had changed Wayne Henderson's skin completely.

"Did I promise that?" Henderson attempted a smile, then realized how ill placed it was. "Yesterday we killed two of the militia coalition's leaders, in any case, and last night we totally wiped out the Missouri Bushwackers. We've uncovered several of the coalition's lines of communication, and we continue working as hard as we can. We've discovered close ties between the militia and rebellious military officers, and I absolutely believe we'll soon have a decisive lead as to Moonie Quale's whereabouts, certainly within the next forty-eight hours, I'd imagine. Until then, we'll have to let things take their course."

"Yes, and we know Quale's been wounded," added Billy Johnson. "Seriously wounded, as a matter of fact. If he goes to a doctor, we've got him, and if he doesn't, matters will take their own course. According to my information, he won't survive a week if his injuries aren't treated."

"Why shouldn't the militias have their own doctors?" asked Wesley, Sunderland's eyes piercing his temples.

"Yes, they do, and we're well aware of this," answered Johnson. "Which is why there isn't a single hospital operation theater in the whole country that FEMA doesn't have under surveillance."

"I was thinking about field hospitals."

Billy Johnson gave a wan smile. "Don't you worry, Barefoot, we'll find them." President Jansen looked at Sunderland. "I understand we're beginning to run out of space in the camps for the internees."

"No, I don't believe so." Thomas Sunderland leaned back and tapped his ballpoint pen on his desk. "Our people are very efficient out there, but shouldn't we take that matter up again later? General Powers's helicopter is expected in half an hour."

Wesley frowned. *Efficient out there*. What was that supposed to mean? It felt as though he'd never sat in a meeting with these men before now. He didn't know them, had no idea what they stood for. Not anymore.

"Okay, we'll get back to that later," said Jansen. "It's true, there are more important things on the agenda, but first, Billy, you have to tell me whether you've found Doggie Rogers."

Wesley was on the edge of his seat. What now?

"No, not yet, but we've tracked her cell phone to somewhere be-tween Philadelphia and Trenton, so we assume she's headed for New York. It was a very brief signal, so we can't be more precise, but that's the lead we're following for now."

"Does she have relatives in New York?"

"No, but several of her old school buddies live there. We're check-ing all possibilities." Wesley noticed how, for a second, Jansen got a faraway look in his eyes, a stark contrast to Sunderland's hard glare. She was still on the loose, but they were on her tail and they'd find her. And here he was, sitting on his hands, letting it happen.

He cleared his throat. "Mr. President, as far as Doggie Rogers is concerned, I believe she tried to get hold of you to ask you to stay her father's execution because new evidence is supposed to have turned up . . ."

Sunderland smacked his pen down on the desk. "I'm well aware you've got your eye on Doggie Rogers!" He glanced over at Lance Bur-ton. "But don't you forget that this same Doggie Rogers assaulted me earlier today, a criminal act that could have ended disastrously. She has nothing new to say about the Bud Curtis case. On the other hand, it's a fact that she was carrying a heavy object under her arm and was on her way to the president's office, so I don't think you should be pleading her case right now, Wesley. It's inappropriate. One's choice of acquaintances can have unfortunate consequences."

"A heavy object? What heavy object?"

"It hasn't been established by our surveillance video, so I can't answer you on that, but while we're on the subject, I would like to know when it was that you spoke with her about this evidence having to do with her father."

Wesley sat for a moment, looking the vice president in the eyes. Should he say that he'd talked with her in his office just before she attacked Sunderland? He'd be surprised if Sunderland didn't already know, but then he must also know their conversation didn't show up on the tape recording. Maybe next, Sunderland would want to know how this could be, and Wesley would be forced to admit he'd put the microphones out of commission. This was a deciding moment. If he confessed, he'd lose his credibility, and what would happen to him then? They talked about camps out there; they talked about surveillance and suspiciousness. There was paranoia everywhere, so what couldn't they do to him if they no longer trusted him? Several congressmen and other prominent persons came to mind who had disappeared recently. Would they ever be found? And would they ever let him leave the room if he finally said things straight out?

"I don't think Doggie is guilty of anything serious, if she's guilty of anything at all." He tried evading the issue.

Billy Johnson's eyes narrowed. "We'll find her, Wesley, and then we'll know. So there's no need to worry. In the kind of war we've got out there at the moment, there's going to be casualties."

"Try to distance yourself, Wesley," said Jansen. Wesley could sense he was irritated, but not to what degree. Still, it was a sign to keep his mouth shut. "We're nearing our goal. Soon America will be the paradise we're all dreaming about, and until then we just have to do our jobs." He turned towards the others. "The British prime minister has contacted us again, gentlemen, and this time he means it. Terry Watts has informed us that, on his way to a state visit to Argentina, he wants to pay us an informal visit—tomorrow—and we propose to comply."

"Tomorrow?! That's what I call fair warning!" said the secretary of defense, the circles under his eyes darkening noticeably. Wesley knew exactly how he was feeling.

"If we accept, we have to make it public this evening, which means you two will be busy." Jansen nodded at Lance Burton and Wesley. "We must assume that Watts basically wants to discuss our domestic situation, but of course that angle is out of the question, so find a plausible approach. And in the meantime, the rest of you see to getting the streets around the White House cleared and security measures optimized."

"Why not hold the meeting at Camp David?" the secretary of defense suggested.

"No, the entire Catoctin Mountain area is too unsecure at the moment," said Billy Johnson.

"Then I propose the meeting be held at the president's country residence in Onancock," said the secretary of defense. Wesley could see his point. How the hell could one hide the present situation in Washington from a foreign delegation on such short notice?

Jansen nodded. "Needless to say, I've already discussed that option with Billy, and he tells me that, even if we close Route 13 up by Pocomoke City, we still won't have the folks down at Willis Wharf under control. Onancock is out of the question."

Billy Johnson didn't look proud of the situation. "I doubt the prime minister will appreciate having rotten fish—and worse—thrown at him."

"Then what about Tangier Island? It's *got* to be safe." It was obvious Secretary of Defense Henderson didn't want any summit meeting being held in his own backyard.

Then Jansen broke in. "We hold the meeting with Terry Watts here in the White House early tomorrow morning, and that's that. You two discuss the security measures with your respective staffs, and see to it that the air space all the way from Dulles Airport is cleared of all traffic except Watts's helicopter." He turned to Lance Burton. "You're in charge of the ceremonies and the state dinner, and you, Thomas . . ."—he laid a piece of paper on Sunderland's desk—"you see to it that this agenda is delivered to the relevant departments. Why not let the State Department get involved and come up with some ideas? What the hell else have they got to do these days?" He gave a short, dry laugh. It wasn't a laugh Wesley had heard before.

"Tomorrow, Watts and I will hold a short and concentrated meeting," Jansen continued, "and after afternoon tea and the official banquet, our helicopter will fly his delegation back to the airport. Everything must be handled adroitly so we give the impression that everything's under control and that we'll soon be able to resume our peaceful trading with the rest of the world. Watts must be able to go directly to the so-called unfettered world press awaiting him in Buenos Aires and—from a totally neutral point of view—tell the media that what is happening in America is the realization of a long-recognized necessity, not the out-of-control revolution the world has made it into." He pointed up at Sunderland's bulletin board. "I think you understand what I'm saying."

They all nodded, except for Wesley.

"Excuse me, Mr. President, but if I'm to write the press release, I must assume that Lance Burton has already been informed as to what it's supposed to say. I mean, guidelines have already been laid down, haven't they?"

Burton laid a hand on Wesley's arm, but he shrugged it off and continued. "So, for me, the question is: Who do we send it to, when most of the media has been shut down during the past week? As I see it, there's pretty much only NBC, *The Wall Street Journal*, *The Washington Post*, the *Herald Tribune*, and *Newsweek* left, and we've severely curtailed their capacity to inform. Has the president considered how we're to make the flow of news function if these few remaining national media sources suddenly go on strike? I mean, it could happen, couldn't it? And if such a situation arises, have we considered letting people from various government departments take over the job? Because if we have, I'm really afraid that we're currying the local and pirate radios' favor, and especially disfavor."

The president looked at him patiently. "By then there won't be any more pirate stations, Wesley."

"Okay. What I'm trying to say is, we can't just settle for sending out press releases stating the official present state of affairs. We'll also have to give the press some stories that aren't completely predictable, stories so their readers won't believe we manipulate everything."

"Like what, for example?"

"Like that this administration has set a time limit on its current methods."

"That's coming, Wesley," the president replied. "The British prime minister's visit is the first step."

"Yes, but, in the future, couldn't we try to nuance our information—admit a mistake now and then—and find other stories that we can cast in a positive light? Small, everyday stories? Otherwise people will understandably lose confidence in the media."

Thomas Sunderland gave one of his hard looks. "If you have some concrete suggestions, Wesley, then write them down and send them to our offices."

The president interrupted his vice president. "I know what you're thinking, Wesley, and you're right. That's an excellent idea. Give the media a little good news every day. Send your suggestions in to Thomas, and he'll choose one."

Wesley nodded. That was something, at least. "Thank you, Mr. President. Tomorrow I think we should run a story on the loosening of state control. That's the kind of thing people want to hear. They don't care about the British prime minister, just as long as they can return to their old way of life. It will make them relax." He took a deep breath. It had been a long time since he'd expressed something meaningful. When one wants something bad enough, one imagines a scenario for achieving it—waiting for the right moment and believing one knows how it will feel afterwards. Herein is to be found the ingredients needed to give a feeling of happiness. And that's how Wesley felt in that brief second where his boss nodded in agreement. But it lasted only the instant that it took to realize he'd capitulated, that he'd finally, definitively signed up as the president's faithful errand boy. "It will make them relax," he'd said. But what was so wonderful about that? Was that what he really wanted? Or was it actually the dream of being able to manipulate the populace that had propelled his career so far?

Jansen nodded. "Good, Wesley. You can write that distribution of foodstuffs will be normalized in the coming week."

"Excuse me, Mr. President," said Billy Johnson. "That's a good idea, but I'm afraid we can't keep a promise like that. The roads are still too unsecured. It could be weeks before we've neutralized the militias. Then of course there will still be the deranged loners to deal with."

"Yes, but at least we will have expressed our good intentions, isn't that correct? If something unexpected happens, it won't be our fault. . . ." He turned to Wesley. "Right?"

He had no idea how to answer.

"That's an excellent idea," said Lance Burton, instead. "But we could also begin by naming the big-brother arrangement for drug addicts and violent criminals. That's a so-called feel-good story, and besides, it holds up."

The president pointed at Wesley and gave him a commanding look. So the resolution was adopted.

"Wesley and I will have a list of next week's sunshine stories ready by this afternoon," Burton bubbled on. Wesley was about to protest, but Burton lay a firm, cautioning hand on his arm.

Jansen smiled. "Good, then! And, as far as Bud Curtis is concerned, the subject has been exhausted. This isn't the proper time for relaxing our system of justice. The vice president has just received a survey confirming that the people feel good about the releasing of prison inmates, but they also go in for the execution of those with death sentences. So we'll be able to say this proves the American people are willing to accept the consequences of a national consensus. Of loving thy neighbor but severely punishing those who overstep certain limits."

Wesley was about to ask how the survey had been made, since the opinion-poll institutes were no longer in operation, but he felt Lance Burton's grip on his arm tighten.

"Here, friends . . ." The president tore some pages out of his yellow notepad and handed them around. "Now I want each of you to write down your honest opinion and give the piece of paper back to me. The question I want you to answer is whether we should continue practicing capital punishment in the United States. Write Y for yes, N for no, and DK for don't know. Here . . . write."

They each wrote down how they felt, folded the paper, and handed it back. Jansen sat for a moment, smiling. "Shall we guess that you've all written DK? Yes, I'll bet you have . . ." He unfolded the yellow sheets of paper, one after the other, and his smile broadened.

"Voilà," he said. "Everybody has written DK except for I believe Thomas, who has written a Y. Is that correct, Thomas?"

The vice president nodded.

"If you—the best and the brightest—can't make up your minds, then we have no reason to assume the American populace feels any different, meaning that we deal out capital punishment, no matter what."

Wesley was chagrined. He would have liked to have written *N*, but he had knowledge of far too many recent nasty crimes. About cannibalism and scenes of prolonged torture, about dismembered children and minds so sick that not even the most intensive psychiatric treatment had any hope of producing a positive effect or sign of atonement. He would have liked to say no, but couldn't, thus making his vote meaningless. Jansen knew exactly what he was doing.

Wesley pulled his arm out of Lance Burton's grip. "Where is it we're headed, then? We execute people by the hundreds every day. If not in the prisons, then out in the forests or along the highways and back roads. How will it all end, if we don't stop one day?"

"How will it end?" Jansen gave him a frown. "I'll tell you how, Wesley: precisely with the fact that we *will* stop. One day people will have had enough."

After the meeting, Wesley joined Chief of Staff Burton in his office. Burton informed his secretary that they wished not to be disturbed, that they had a lot to do and not much time. Then he slammed the door and stood before Wesley, hands at his sides.

"Okay, first we'll discuss things, then we'll write. I suppose you know you're navigating along the very edge of the cliff right now, don't you, Wesley?"

"I am?"

"Well, Jansen and Sunderland *do* need you. No one writes better than you do. What flows from your pen is sheer brilliance—but be careful. You are under surveillance."

"Yes, and you as well. We all are—don't forget it."

Burton sat down and folded his well-worn hands. Hands that had stretched towards heaven in prayers that his father come home safely from Vietnam. Hands that had picked fruit throughout the Midwest to earn enough to feed his small brothers and sisters and tormented mother. Hands that had shook the hand of everyone Wesley admired. "You believe you know something, don't you, Wesley? Something about who rides the high horse and who slogs along behind, in the mud."

"I just know that everything you're saying now is being recorded, and that Sunderland hears all that his people choose to discuss."

"I see! So *that's* what you think you know? Okay, then . . ."

Burton cupped his hands in front of his mouth like a funnel. "Is it really true, what Wesley's saying, Mr. Vice President?" he yelled into thin air. Then he shook his head. "You're so young, kid," he said, poking around in a stack of papers. He pulled forth a light-blue, lined sheet of paper with writing on it and thrust it towards Wesley.

It wasn't hard to recognize Donald Beglaubter's block-letter hand-writing. A hand just as childlike and clumsy as its executor had been mature and gifted.

The paper contained a list of names, more or less in order of rank. All were members of the government or important public officials, and next to each name stood a list of occurrences—not all of which Wesley was familiar with—but each one an instance that gave the same un-pleasant feeling.

It read:

PERSON:	EVENT:
President Bruce Jansen:	Murder of wives Caroll Jansen and Mimi Todd Jansen
Secretary of Defense Wayne Henderson:	Forced to execute fellow soldier during interrogation in Vietnam
Vice President Michael K. Lerner:	???
Chief of Staff/Vice President T. Sunderland:	Lost a platoon of which he was captain in ambush in Grenada
Attorney General Stephen Lovell:	*Mother and daughter raped and seriously injured in attack

Secretary of State Mark Wise:	Daughter-in-law hospitalized in psychiatric ward after witnessing a murder
Chief Supreme Court Justice T. Manning:	*Assassinated
Secretary of Interior Betty Tucker:	Sister murdered
Secretary of Homeland Security Billy Johnson:	Son killed with knife in robbery
Secretary of Agriculture Rod Norton:	Father killed in hunting accident
Secretary of Commerce Jay W. Barket:	*Son's best friend killed in shooting incident
Secretary of Education Lena Cole:	Neighbor killed during break-in
Secretary of Transportation Joseph Barrett:	Best friend killed during military exercise
Acting Chief of Staff Lance Burton:	Sister-in-law paralyzed after shooting attack
Secretary of Labor Alison Ramsey:	???
Acting Chief of Communications D. Beglaubter:	*Nephew in same class as child killed in shooting incident
Press Secretary Wesley Barefoot:	
House Majority Whip Peter Halliwell:	Son killed by gunshot
Senate President Pro Tem Hammond Woodrow:	Involved in accidental shooting as boy
Chairman of the Joint Chiefs of Staff Omar Powers:	Wounded in action; attacked and wounded by Vietnam veteran in Biloxi

Burton's voice brought Wesley's thoughts back into the room. "What do you make of it, Wesley?"

"Wow . . . I don't know what to think. Do you know when Donald wrote it?"

"He gave it to me a day before he was assassinated."

"Why?"

"I'd made a similar list, too. We were going to compare notes." He opened a drawer and laid a sheet of paper next to Donald's. They were surprisingly similar in content.

"The entire Cabinet, and ourselves as well. Jesus!" Wesley almost couldn't believe it. "You have a sister-in-law who was paralyzed after being shot?"

He nodded. "Yes, my youngest brother's wife."

"I don't get it. Most of the persons in charge of running this country have been involved in some kind of terrible episode involving firearms. It's simply unbelievable."

"Yes, but scarcely a coincidence."

"Scarcely a coincidence?" Wesley shook his head. He didn't know *what* it was—coincidence or not. "There's a star next to some of them. What does that mean?"

"That the incident occurred after Jansen became president."

"Oh, right. Of course." He nodded. "What significance does one find here?"

"Whatever significance you like."

Wesley skimmed the list one more time. He, too, had lists in his drawer containing the dates of violent episodes during the past three weeks. Laying all three lists side by side left one with more than mere misgivings—it was enough to make you sick. He wondered for a moment if he shouldn't destroy his own list. On the other hand, could one be certain there was some conscious agenda behind all these dark deeds? Could a person be so cynical as to orchestrate misfortunes such as these, or was there some other cause?

He looked at Burton. "Isn't it possible to imagine that, statistically, practically all families in this country have had experiences like this?"

"No, it isn't."

"But if these aren't coincidences, then this is really terrible. The president has used the criterion that almost all the members of his staff have some violent, negative episode in their past involving firearms."

"Aside from those who have worked for him for many years, yes, that could be the case."

"What about the incidents that have occurred since Jansen took office? There was a shooting at a school, for example. Can anyone in his right mind suggest that these weren't coincidences, either?"

"I don't know. I'm not suggesting anything."

Wesley suddenly froze and looked around like he'd forgotten where he was. God, what had he gotten himself involved in? Here he was, verbalizing the worst accusations imaginable for the surveillance mikes. "Dammit, Lance," he whispered, "you should have stopped me. This room's bugged!"

Lance Burton showed his ivory teeth. "Come here," he said, pulling him into a side chamber that had once functioned mostly as an archive for legal circulars. "Here it is. Anything else you want to know?" He pointed at a stack of black metal boxes.

"I don't get it."

Burton smiled again. "Everything that is said and video-monitored in this place is recorded on these hard disks. Then the information is beamed over to the Department of Homeland Security to be analyzed."

"My God, this makes Nixon's eavesdropping look like amateur night—which it was, kind of." Wesley tried to fathom the ramifications, but it wasn't easy. "Is it you who's in charge of this? I thought it was Sunderland's idea."

"He would have preferred it like that, but I beat him to the punch. Sometimes you've got to be ahead of the game if you want to maintain control and an overall perspective—as you well know."

"But hell, Lance, do you have the vice president bugged as well? I can't imagine him putting up with that."

"So far, the president's, the vice president's, and my office are not under audio surveillance. That was the deal."

"So far? But they wear badges just like the rest of us, don't they?"

"The president's, Sunderland's, mine, and Ben Kane and his people's are merely badges—no microphones."

Wesley raised his eyebrows. "Thanks for the show of confidence!"

Burton looked him in the eye. "This is for real, Wesley. Not one word of this is to get out. You have to promise me that."

Wesley didn't know how he should answer. There were a few too many unknown factors involved here. Lance Burton was capable of seeming ingenuous, but big, brown eyes weren't always to be trusted. To get as far in life as Lance had, one had to cut some corners. But, by and large, he trusted his chief of staff. Burton was a good man, and Wesley was willing to promise him to keep quiet, unless conditions in the future spoke against it. So he nodded. "I promise, Lance. Naturally," he said.

"Good. Then put this on."

He handed Wesley a badge identical to the one he'd been issued.

"Here, wear this one instead. It's just like mine: no mike or perimeter alarm."

It wasn't until then that Wesley noticed his old badge had disappeared. He patted his pockets and looked around on the floor.

"No, you didn't lose it in here. It's lying in the crack between the cushions in Thomas Sunderland's sofa. I knocked it off your jacket at an opportune moment during our meeting before."

Suddenly, Wesley remembered when it had happened. "So that's why you reached out after me. It wasn't only so I'd keep my mouth shut."

"No, not only. We just have to hope the janitorial crew or Sunderland don't find the badge too soon."

"What is it you're trying to achieve?"

"I need proof." He pointed at Donald's paper.

"Then maybe you'd better start listening in on the president."

"Yes, I know, which brings us to the next point. I've ordered the glazier to replace the Oval Office's armored glass windows facing the lawn, but some of the glass panes have bigger ears than others, if you know what I mean."

This sent an icy shudder down Wesley Barefoot's spine. Was this really possible? Could a window pane actually be a bugging device?

"Why are you telling me this, Lance?"

"There's a greater chance that one of us gets out of this unscathed than if I go it alone. That, plus the fact that I trust you, Wesley."

"Will the surveillance done on Jansen and Sunderland be sent to Billy Johnson?"

"No, not at the moment—just all the other tapes."

This wasn't pleasant to contemplate. "You mean, all the bugging of our badges and telephones and all the videos are automatically sent to Homeland Security?"

Burton nodded. "Yes."

Wesley bit his lower lip.

Then Burton pointed at the two black boxes at the bottom of the stack. "Let's concentrate on what's in these two. The top one is connected to the surveillance camera in Sunderland's office—without sound, unfortunately—but the bottom one compensates for that, because it's the one that does the video and sound surveillance on your office, Wesley, and also picks up the signal in your badge. Do you see what I'm saying?"

"So you can spy on the vice president through a combination of the video camera and my badge?" This was getting to be too much. "Is there video surveillance in the Oval Office, too?"

"No, not there." Lance Burton stood up to his full height and opened the cover of a large metal case that hung on the wall above the hard-disk boxes. He threw a couple of switches and activated a monitor that gave an extremely sharp black-and-white picture of what was happening in the vice president's office. "This button here switches between the different cameras," he said, changing from Sunderland's office to Wesley's, to the Roosevelt Room, to down along the hallway. Then he changed back to the meeting that was still going on in Sunderland's office.

Wesley looked at the monitor. The most important politicians in the land were taking a coffee break. If one didn't know better, one might think it was a local Rotary Club meeting: a chat about the world situation over a cup of coffee, and then over to a friendly game of poker. And maybe, in essence, that's all it was.

"Listen . . . !" said Burton, sticking a wire into the box that tapped the sound from Wesley's badge. Apart from a faint buzz and a slightly metallic sound, the signal came through loud and clear, sending another shiver down Wesley's spine. Here sat the president of the United States' chief of staff and press secretary, eavesdropping illegally on the president, the vice president, and the secretaries of Homeland Security and Defense, as they discussed a colossal national crisis. It was the kind of act that gave a long, long prison sentence—if you were lucky. People had been known to simply disappear for less.

He attempted to catch Lance Burton's eye. "Do you think this is ever going to work, Lance? Isn't it much too risky? How can you be positively sure we're not being watched and listened to, even as we speak?" He stared at the closed door into the communications room, expecting Ben Kane's bloodhounds to break it down any second.

Burton shrugged his shoulders. If he'd calculated that risk, he apparently wasn't going to let it bother him. Instead, once more he said, "Listen."

They were stirring their cups of coffee at the moment, sitting across from one another with straight backs and measured movements. No one cleared his throat; nobody spoke evasively or hesitantly. They looked directly at one another as they agreed on how to further tighten the iron grip on their country. How to cripple the outside world's influence on the course of events in the United States and close down foreign satellite transmissions, and how a series of viruses would be released on the Internet to do the job. And how all domestic telecommunication would be curbed and controlled. They did so with the taste of fresh-roasted coffee in their mouths and the feel of fine leather upholstery at their backs. The Department of Homeland Security had already drawn up a timetable, and the Defense Department had taken the appropriate military measures. From what Wesley and Lance could understand, it would all be put into effect in a matter of days. They observed how Thomas Sunderland poured himself a glass of cognac and asked for rapid implementation. They saw how intensely President Jansen was listening to everything and how his face gradually relaxed.

He appeared to be satisfied. This was all about control.

A series of dismal, disquieting thoughts jarred through Wesley's head. It was like hearing a death sentence being pronounced.

"What do we do?" he said, so quietly that it was surprising that Lance Burton heard him.

"Well, Wesley . . . That is what we're going to discuss."

CHAPTER 26

DOGGIE TRIED TO CALL T. PERKINS'S CELL PHONE AS SHE AND OLLIE DROVE through the downtrodden neighborhoods of New Jersey. It was Saturday, about three thirty in the afternoon, and she was getting desperate. What was T up to, since he was so hard to get hold of?

Ollie Boyce Henson was sitting next to her, rocking from side to side, his eyes glued on the female scenery as though these were the first proper ladies he had seen in ages. As though DC had been totally devoid of them.

When they reached the Bronx, she asked him to drop her off a couple of hundred yards from Rosalie's street, convinced that the less he knew about where she was going, the better for both of them. She gave him the $2,500 and asked that he and his car wreck move on.

He raised a fist in acknowledgment and solidarity, the wide grin a clear sign of how pleased he was with the whole deal—as well he should be. For $2,500, he could get whatever he wanted. A few joints from his cousin, a pair of luminous Jordan basketball shoes, and for sure a couple of full-chested, willing honeys who would far surpass those he'd just been drooling over in Jersey. Yes, it was a happy man who boosted the volume on his stereo, floored the gas pedal, and disappeared up the street.

She stood for a moment, feeling a rare pang of envy, thinking that if she had it all to do over again, she'd try to live as simply as Ollie Boyce Henson.

Doggie thought she knew what to expect, but the grimness and poverty that greeted her on Rosalie Lee's street was appalling, even though she'd seen worse conditions where she came from, like filthy trailer parks with filthy kids and corrugated-tin, plastic-sheeted shanty towns that signaled failed lives and impending doom. Still, this type of depressing, graveyard-gray, crumbling, big-city grandeur was more overwhelmingly tangible. It was only a hundred yards from the street corner to Rosalie's doorway, but her anxiety grew every step of the way. Not for fear of being mugged or being paralyzed by despair, but for the unfamiliarity that oozed out of every crack in this concrete quagmire.

She was met by hostile stares as she went. The locals couldn't care less about her gaudy clothes and whether she was a wanted criminal or a TV star, but they *did* care that she was white and obviously unashamed of the fact. They were ready for anything, checking out her vigilant eyes and trying to suss out what she was doing there.

She found a tin plate mounted next to the front door, covered with layers of generations of taped-on names, including Rosalie Lee's. A rancid odor clung to the stairway, and she could feel the building tremble with the presence of so much pent-up humanity. It was like treading into the dragon's cave—fascinating, repellent, and inescapable.

Rosalie's face had never looked so bleak, thought Doggie, as they greeted each other. Her wide mouth and full, bloodred lips and the dimples centered so deliciously in her cheeks—everything was dried out. Doggie received her hugs and words and tears, giving her all the time she needed. No, Rosalie was not doing well.

After listening to an account that was broken by pauses and trembling lips, Doggie gave her friend $5,000 and asked if Rosalie wanted company at the police station, but Rosalie preferred to go alone. Doggie should just make herself at home—whatever was Rosalie's was hers. She started feeling a little better. Now she could bail out her two boys, and she had the money for Frank's coffin.

"Listen, Rosalie, before you go, do you have anything I can dye my hair with?" Doggie asked.

Rosalie gave her a look of mock haughtiness. "Is it so obvious?" she asked, carefully patting her frizzy curls.

Doggie just smiled. "And a pair of scissors?"

As Rosalie's steps faded down the hall, Doggie found her way to the kitchen, where she was greeted by an orgy of light and electricity. Three or four strings of Christmas lights cast drops of color over snuffling spaghetti sauce pots on the stove, a steaming coffee maker, an iron and ironing board that were ready for action, a half-open fridge, a radio with humming jazz music, and a silent, flickering TV the size of a shoebox. All indications of Rosalie's distracted state.

She checked out what was edible in the refrigerator, then went out to the bathroom and took stock of her light brown hairdo that no longer looked like the fortune it had cost a month ago. She heaved a sigh as she picked up the scissors. It was the first time in her life she was cutting her own hair, and the first time it would be so short.

A half hour later she studied the result with a mixture of horror and dismay. Decked out in the clothes of Ollie Boyce Henson's woman, with muddy-black, short hair that looked like it had been attacked by a lawn mower, plus a complexion totally devoid of makeup, any silly adolescent girl's dream that Wesley Barefoot would one day sweep her off her feet seemed light-years away. At most, she might look tasty to some punk reject or heavy metal nerd from Minnesota. Just as she intended.

Pretty upset by the sight in the mirror and feeling longing and loneliness like never before, she made her way back to the kitchen, shut off half the appliances, and turned up the TV.

It read 4 P.M.: SPECIAL WHITE HOUSE PRESS CONFERENCE in the corner of the screen. Her mouth stuffed with food, Doggie watched Wesley loom into the picture, saying that British prime minister Terry Watts would be paying his first visit to the White House in more than four years. Wesley tried to make the world believe that the prime minister and President Jansen were holding a series of cordial discussions whose purpose was to help normalize impressions abroad of the president's current reforms.

Afterwards he cleverly wove in a homey anecdote about how Watts's dog had chewed up half the carpet in the sitting room at 10 Downing Street, but Doggie could see he wasn't enjoying it. His smile sat wrong on his face, and the pores under his sideburns were gradually filling with sweat. She stopped chewing, completely engrossed by the sight of him.

Then he turned to the nearest of the chosen journalists, pursed his lips for a moment, and regained his winning, trademark smile.

"Since the Secure Future campaign began," he said, "more than twenty thousand drug abusers have been let out into society under a kind of big brother arrangement, where they're watched over by ex–drug users who help keep them clean. In a mere matter of weeks it has been possible to achieve what decades of misguided drug abuse policies never could. The system works. Our statistics show that only twelve hundred of the twenty thousand have re-offended and that for each day, the rest are adapting better and better to their new working roles. An infected boil on American society has been punctured."

Next there was a stream of praise for the president's agenda, then a short "documentary" clip that followed the daily life of a drug abuser during his first three weeks under the big brother program. And the results *did* appear miraculous. The pathetic, strung-out, mentally unbalanced, asocial loser they'd plucked out of San Quentin had been transformed into the attentive and engaging man who now stood with his arm around the shoulder of his "big brother" and a broad, confident smile. It was all more than a little hard to believe.

As she swallowed the last of her food, she saw flickering blue lights accompanied by a siren as a patrol car barreled down the street. Anxiously and cautiously she peered out over the kitchen windowsill that was overflowing with a collection of "antique" coffee cans, but saw only a bunch of noisy, posturing kids. One of them looked up at the window and made a suggestive motion with his hips.

She turned around in time to see her own face filling the TV screen—a neat, attractive blonde. A reward had been posted for information that would lead to the apprehension of this "dangerous, mentally deranged" person. Then a police officer held up a Fendi bag just like hers, calling her "an enemy of the United States."

It felt like the sandwich she'd just eaten was about to come back up.

Then a series of photos and descriptions of other wanted persons rolled across the screen, many of whom she knew. There was former vice president Michael K. Lerner and other well-respected politicians who had gone underground, as well as several big-business types and many, many others. The accusations were serious, and if they were caught—which wasn't unlikely with such substantial rewards—their futures looked grim. Just like her own.

She knew most of what they were accused of was false. Not all, but most of it. There she sat, in this moment of reflection, hundreds of miles from the convincing manipulations of the White House, like someone shipwrecked on an island surrounded by sharks. If T. Perkins didn't help her—and she had no way of knowing if he would—there was nothing left to hope for. She felt stranded, isolated, and impotent, far, far away from the sterile cell where her father awaited his fate.

"Time hasn't run out yet, so pull yourself together, girl," Doggie admonished herself, noticing that it was becoming increasingly difficult to think straight. She knew there were many incongruities in her father's case, including the chain of events surrounding the assassination, her father's unshakable plea of innocence, the cocksure attitude of the technical experts, and the jury's anger. The question was: What should she do about it? There was no media to which she could turn in order to win sympathy, for the simple reasons that there were no independent media left, no public authority that wouldn't immediately turn her in, and no lawyer willing to risk their career or possessing the ability to break down the imposing wall of injustice and apathy. Only her friends were left, and there weren't many of them.

She dug Ollie's battered cell phone out of her bag and tried the Highland County Sheriff's Office again.

A switchboard lady of few words asked with whom she was

speaking. She said her name was Doggie. No, unfortunately she couldn't speak to the sheriff due to the fact that he'd taken the next couple of days off, and no, she couldn't reach him on his cell phone since it had recently been put out of commission in the line of duty.

Doggie frowned. So T's cell phone was no longer functioning. No wonder they couldn't communicate.

Then the switchboard lady asked if there was a number Sheriff Perkins could reach her at if he happened to call in, and Doggie was just about to say yes but didn't. If this woman was as empty-minded as she sounded, she would forget the connection between the cell phone and her call within a matter of minutes. Why should she give them another chance to track her?

So she said no, her heart full of doubt.

The two sons came through the door shortly before their mom, showing none of the signs of propriety or humility one might expect from a couple of reprieved sinners whose freedom they owed to the survival instinct of their mother's battle against all odds. Suddenly they were there in the living room, checking her out with gaping eyes and disdainful lips, the one with a backward baseball cap and the other with a tight headscarf and pants so voluminous, they looked like a floor-length denim skirt.

And they didn't take their eyes off Doggie's breasts and her skintight jeans until their mother came blustering into the room.

"Doggie, Doggie, oh, my Lord. This's some bad news, honey." Rosalie Lee threw her handbag on the kitchen table and plopped herself down on a plastic-covered stool, out of breath. "Every police station in New York has your picture hanging on the wall with the country's most wanted! There's a twenty-five-thousand-dollar reward on your head!" She fanned her sweaty face. "Oh, Doggie, that kind of money ain't small change around here, you better believe it. Did anyone see you when you came? Think real hard."

Did anyone see her? "Yeah, they sure did."

Rosalie turned to her boys. "You boys are going to fix this, you hear?

Doggie's just paid your bail, so you make sure they cool it on the street, okay? Go!"

The two boys looked at their mother like she'd just given them a potentially fatal disease. She had to stare them down before they shuffled off.

"What about the guy who drove you here?" Rosalie asked, dabbing her face.

"No, I don't think he'll tell the police. Plus he doesn't know where I am. I had him let me off a ways from here."

"But he knows you're in the Bronx, doesn't he?"

Doggie nodded.

"Listen, baby, I give you two hours at the most before the heat is here. These are new times, Doggie. In the old days, there was a code of honor. The cops lived their lives in Cop-land and we had no business there and folks didn't talk. It's not like that now. We've got to get you out of here, fast as possible. When the boys come back, we'll find you a vehicle. They both drive good enough. A little fast, maybe, that's all. Do you know someone you can visit?" She took a look at Doggie's handbag and dumped the contents on the kitchen table. "You can't be running around with this fancy thing, girl, they know you've got it, so . . ." Her eyes fell on the Buddha figurine that had rolled around before coming to rest between lipsticks, Tampax, and a $7,500-wad of bills.

"Goodness gracious, do you still have that?" Rosalie took the statuette carefully in her big, soft hands and stood completely still, as though the past had put her in a momentary trance.

Doggie no longer had the same fond memories as Rosalie. The only feeling she really had right now was one of thorough exhaustion.

"So where can you go?" was her next question.

These few words suddenly brought the relative importance of the components of Doggie's life into perspective. One spends one's whole life building relationships into a kind of safety net, weaving new ones in all the time, until the mesh is so fine, one can no longer see through it and distinguish—or even clearly remember—one's roots. And now, here she stood, balanced unsteadily on this impenetrable, jiggling net, needing to find a way through to something solid, but too tired to try.

She would so much like to be able to say to Rosalie that, yes, there was someone she knew who she was sure would take her in—that Wesley had a remote cabin where he'd hide her and protect her till the end of time—but a wave of loneliness struck her speechless. "I don't know, Rosalie . . ." she finally said, her voice unsteady. "Only you and my mother come to mind, and my mother's out of the question. That's the first place they'll look."

She felt Rosalie's warm hands on her face, so unexpected yet appropriate. This was as close as she could come to feeling safe. This was her haven. And it was all she had.

Rosalie dried Doggie's cheeks; she knew more than enough about tears. "But tell me: What's this about?" She nodded towards the Buddha.

"I tried to get through to Jansen, but I didn't succeed. It's been a hell of a long time since he's been the man who gave it to me."

"No, it's not Jansen I'm talking about. What about that little note John Bugatti stuck inside it? Have you looked?"

Doggie smiled. "Do you really remember that?"

"I've got one good memory, remember?"

"Then I'm sorry to disappoint you. He didn't put any note inside, Rosalie, he was just being friendly."

The buxom woman sat up straight on her stool. "Oh, yes, he did. He put it in. I saw it, I promise you."

She picked up the figurine and tried to look inside its tiny, open mouth.

"I've done that hundreds of times, Rosalie. You can't see anything because there *isn't* anything."

Rosalie shook her head and stood up. "Never mind, then! You know what? You can go to my sister's. She needn't know ahead of time. She lives in Five Forks, southwest of Richmond. It's a little house, but it's big enough."

Doggie bit the inside of her cheek. South of Richmond—so close to her father. Almost too close. She looked out in the hallway where twenty pair of worn-down Nike footwear were lined up, and suddenly she knew the moment had arrived, the moment where you realize you only have yourself left, and that everything else merely reflects your impotence. The shoes would still be standing there tomorrow and the day after. Their owners would continue living their own lives; it had nothing to do with her. Even if they wanted to help her, she was still trapped in her own situation. She had nowhere to go, her father was about to die, she'd gotten a stranger to drive her to New York, and now another stranger was going to drive her away again.

Altogether, it was painful to think about.

A door slammed and they both looked up. The boys were back.

"How come you're already home?" asked their mother. "You couldn't have given the word to very many."

"Cool it, Mama. We're borrowing J. Firebird's fucking Ford," said the one Doggie judged to be the younger. "It's the kind of wheels you never notice. Let's go."

"What happened, Dennis?"

"The whole street knows that lady's here." The boy turned to Doggie. "You've got a cell phone. Let me have it."

"Why?"

"Hey, lady, you got it off a dude named Ollie, am I right?"

Doggie could feel how her T-shirt was beginning to stick to her skin. "How did you know that?"

"Yo! There's a fucking twenty-five-thousand-dollar reward for turning you in; they just said it on TV."

Rosalie made the sign of the cross while Dennis eyed the stack of bills that were still lying on the table. "Listen. An hour ago every motherfucker on the block knew which direction you came from, and fifty minutes ago they knew where you were dropped off and by who. Dig?"

Doggie looked over at the other silent brother. He nodded in agreement.

Rosalie's eyes narrowed. "How did you know Doggie has that guy Ollie's cell phone? And in God's name, tell me what it means."

"Hey, this here is black man's territory, bongo-bongo land. Can't you hear how they're motivating down on the street? The jungle drums in Throgs Neck do their thing—you know that!" Dennis cocked his head to the side, and his body broke up momentarily in a break-dance. "That-dumb-cocksucker-Ollie, he-was-comin'-on-to-his-cousin, 'bout-his-new-slick-cell-that-cost-a-shitload," he rapped, "and-then-the-nigger-turn-the-damn-thing-on. Need I say more? They track his ass in one minute, flat. Ten fucking pigs, all over him. How long do you think he'll keep his fucking mouth shut down at the station? 'Specially when they wave the twenty-five grand in his sad-ass face."

Doggie ought to have known. She should have given Ollie Boyce Henson an extra five hundred and just got rid of her cell phone.

"Listen, lady, I know what you're thinking: 'Fucking Ollie Boyce Henson,'" crowed Dennis. "But if you'd gone with a cheaper damn cell phone to begin with, this never would've been happening, would it?"

She nodded grudgingly and began collecting her things on the table.

"So what should she do now?" asked Rosalie.

Dennis adjusted his headscarf under his baseball cap and gave his mother a languid look. "First of all, she gives me her fucking cell phone." He turned to Doggie and extended his palm. "You can't use it, anyway. The cops'll track it in no time, maybe they already have. You never know with those pigs. It all depends on if Ollie's already been singing. Here, you get my brother Frank's instead. He doesn't have much use for it anymore. He never really used it anyway; he was too fucking dumb at that shit." He gave his mother an apologetic glance and handed Doggie a phone that at least looked a step up from Ollie's. "The number and PIN code are on the back. Not too fucking bright, but that was our Frank, okay?" He pointed at some numbers scratched into the surface.

"What about my phone numbers in the address book? I don't know them all by heart."

He sighed and pulled the brim of his cap further down his neck. "Okay, lady. I'll punch in a couple of the most important numbers into Frank's phone for you. You only get a minute, then you turn it off. Got it?" He looked at his wrist with an exaggerated gesture, as though he were counting the seconds, even though he wasn't wearing a watch.

She opened Ollie's phone number memory and chose the numbers that were relevant. There weren't many.

When she was done, she lay her hand on top of Rosalie's. "Thanks, Rosalie, I hope this doesn't cause problems for any of you."

"Nonsense. Don't worry about us. I may not be in top form just now, but the brain . . ."—she tapped her curly head—"it's still working okay. Just as soon as you and Dennis have left, I'll send James down to the station so he can report that you came here to have me put you up and that I tried to keep you here, but you took off. We'll say you were heading towards White Plains in a beige Galaxy with black racing stripes. That'll keep them busy, and then James can claim part of the reward. No Ollie Boyce Henson or anybody else is going to put one over Rosalie Lee," she said, patting her chest. "I'll call you early tomorrow morning and tell you how it went."

Dennis handed her Frank's cell phone. He was apparently done coding her numbers in. "And we dump your fucking handbag and those threads you're wearing in a trash can along the way, okay? The first clothes store we hit, you buy something better. And all that shit you've got lying on the table's got to go, too." He took a plastic bag from Jansen's Drugstore and swept pieces of paper, lipsticks, chewing gum, makeup, keys, and everything else into it. Only the Buddha figure was left.

"What about that shit?"

She thought a moment. "I'm keeping it."

Dennis started driving north in J. Firebird's old Ford with Ray Charles playing so loud, the music sounded like the firing of a series of earth-to-air missiles.

He stopped at a clothing store near the zoo and waited a couple of minutes while she equipped herself with the most anonymous, colorless clothes imaginable.

She checked herself out with satisfaction when she was back in the car. Not many people would suspect her of being anything other than some underpaid, small-town librarian.

Then they turned southwest and headed towards Interstate 95.

"You'll be picked up at the George Washington Bridge, okay? It'll cost you a couple grand, but such is life, baby."

"How do I get over the bridge?"

Dennis put on a smile. "It's sorted out."

They turned off the main street just as she could make out the oversized Stars and Stripes blowing in the breeze at the George Washington Bridge's farthest pier and came to a halt in a side street between a van with four flat tires and a truck with a tank trailer. JANSEN'S DRUGSTORES—FRESH MILK FOR ALL HAPPY AMERICANS was written on the shiny, stainless steel sides in huge letters.

She wasn't totally aware of what was going on until Dennis ordered her to give the driver $3,000 and then pushed her up a little steel ladder on one side of the tank.

She bade farewell to Rosalie's youngest son and told him to tell his mother that she hoped she'd have a chance to attend Frank's funeral but couldn't promise anything, and that she'd try and call her the next day if she hadn't been caught by then.

Then they closed the hatch and opened the air valves.

There she'd have to sit in pitch blackness while one of Jansen's Drugstore's drivers made his way down towards Five Forks and Rosalie's unsuspecting sister. In the meantime, her father's time was running out.

CHAPTER 27

SOME HOURS LATER—SHE HAD NO IDEA HOW MANY—DOGGIE WAS FEELING TO-tally whacked and in constant danger of throwing up. Nothing could mask the steel tank's heavy, sour stench of milk gone bad. As the miles were eaten away, the odor became more that of an infant's regurgitation—sweet and sour at the same time and nauseatingly intense. She'd already tried to stand on tiptoes and open the hatch from the inside, but with no success. This, combined with the perpetual pitching and rolling of the steeply curved insides of the tank, made for an exceptionally unbearable experience.

They had waited an hour's time to cross the bridge to New Jersey and had suddenly been directed to the far lane, where they were waved through the control post without being made to stop. *This is the result of my work,* she thought, picturing the piles of material from lobby organizations lying on her desk in the West Wing. If there was something people demanded, it was that milk still be brought out to America's children. And it had been she who had released a directive to that effect with FEMA's stamp of approval on it. "And thank God for that," she whispered, deducing that the dairy truck's high priority was to thank for them being able to speed past mile after mile of idling car motors and honking horns.

They were stopped at roadblocks three more times, and each time she felt a jab of fear of being discovered. Some officious zealot, tire-lessly seeking military promotion by checking out all the most remote possibilities, who would suddenly stick his little head down the tank opening and make the bust of his career among the rotting dairy fumes. But, in spite of her hammering heart and the loud commands shouted at the control posts, it didn't happen.

When her driver finally opened the hatch at a roadside rest place south of Dumfries, the rush of oxygen and glimpse of star-filled sky practically knocked her over, and she had to hold her mouth closed to keep from hyperventilating.

He handed a tiny transistor radio down to her with a strong admonition that she only turn it on while the truck was moving. It was as if he had some reason for wanting her to listen to it. Then he tossed down a sandwich wrapped in tinfoil and asked if she had to go to the toilet. When she didn't answer fast enough, he closed the hatch again.

The darkness and the stench were back.

She turned on the blue display light from Frank Lee's phone to make a flashlight for a moment so she could identify the radio's buttons and dials. Then she turned the radio on and leaned back against the steel container's constant coolness.

No one who had tuned in to American media during the past ten years could fail to recognize the nasal voice immediately as it spewed its agitation out of the tiny speaker. Tom Jumper was a man to whom even the staunchest guardians of good taste had listened, whether they admitted it or not. Both his tongue and mind were so outrageous and agile that his low-brow guests never had a clue as to how they were being pissed on. They just sat there with their overfilled bodies and empty heads, playing his games, while money poured into his bank account by the millions. Doggie hated Jumper and everything he stood for, but here—in the loneliest spot on earth and with the entire country anxious to lay eyes on her—he was her only door to the outside world. The intensity in his voice echoed the good old innocent days, barely four weeks previous. With it came a completely unexpected rush of nostalgia. Then he played an early Emmylou Harris number before unleashing new torrents of words.

"Yo, yo, yo, the hour is twenty-three hundred, Eastern Time, and it's Saturday night—full throttle," he intoned, "and you're listening to Tom Jumper's *Last Bastion*. This is the second day we're broadcasting from our cozy mobile studio, a radio show for all of you who still remember words like *democracy* and *constitutional rights,* not to mention *fresh ground beef, porno flicks,* and *moonlighting.* Happy times! Remember them, friends?"

It gave Doggie a sinking feeling.

Jumper tooted a rubber-bulb bicycle horn and whistled with his fingers. "Hey, that was the jingle for today's good-news story. We've been hearing about the manhunt for Doggie Rogers, the little lady who knocked the vice president's shriveled nuts clear over his left shoulder, and the latest is that little Doggie-dog has dug in her heels and headed for the hills. Take good care of her if you see her out there! I've said it before, and I'll say it again: Anyone who can whup our vice president—and with such style—deserves our deepest respect. Don't let yourselves be tempted by the reward, folks. Forget about playing Judas; help her instead!"

The words took Doggie's breath away. Yes, it seemed like the driver had given her the radio for a reason.

The horn bleated again. "All those who stage a White House walkout like Doggie Rogers are true Americans. Because there are murderers inside there, drowning our nation in blood, and no one in possession of a clear conscience can continue backing them up. Did you believe otherwise? Then it's good that people like Tom Jumper and Miss Doggie Rogers are around to wake you up, America!"

Listening to this was totally unreal. Doggie shook her head.

"Hey, wake up out there," Jumper barked, "it's not even midnight! Open up those ears and listen close, because here comes the day's well-founded shocking allegation, thoroughly researched by my devilishly clever TV-show team. And now I'm gonna say it: New York's Killer on the Roof was a creation of President Jansen and his mob! Whoa! Pardon me? *That* bit of news got you sitting straight up on your fat asses, I can tell! Just remember, Jansen and his disciples are no dummies; they're very crafty. Because, can you honestly say that all these murders in New York and at the school outside Washington, and all the other assassinations and bombings, haven't affected the way you see things? Made you feel a wee bit unsafe?"

Doggie took a deep breath and folded her hands behind her neck.

"Naturally, I'm not speaking to you gun-crazed illiterates who always want to start a ruckus every time a word's used that's more than five letters long—there's no hope for you. No, I mean all the rest of you. Yes, including sweet little Mrs. Jones, sitting in that kitchen." He laughed. "Yes, you, who always makes sure supper's ready on time. Didn't all that have an effect on you? Weren't you thinking: Yes, when there's one insane man shooting down citizens on the streets of New York and another insane man busting into schools and killing schoolkids, I believe the president's right. We've got to ban all that hardware. Weren't you thinking: Hell, yes . . . no, not hell, because you're a nice girl. . . . Yes, by all the angels in heaven, just flush that Colt down the toilet and all the ammunition, too. The president's right, you think, and everyone else thinks. Just look at all the horrible things that are happening everywhere. But listen here: Tom Jumper is telling you we have proof that all those horrible things that are happening are originating in the White House! And the scheme is working! By this I'm not recommending you put that shooter back in the drawer of your nightstand; I just mean the way he's taking them away from us is all wrong. When the White House can hire someone to do in schoolchildren in order to make us hate firearms, things have gone way too far. Do we agree, or what?"

He stopped abruptly and put on more music. The echo of his machine-gun volley of words blended into the intro of an up-tempo country number. He was a master of effect, and Doggie noticed the steel cylinder no longer felt so chilly. At the same time she was really confused. What Tom Jumper had said: Could it really be true, or was this merely the workings of a paranoid madman, high on speculation?

The country music faded, and he continued. "Yo, people, now we're gonna change frequency. Surf a little back and forth on your dial until you hear this music. You all know good ol' Johnny Cash, so just rotate that dial till you find him."

She fumbled after the tuning knob and passed a lot of stations whose previous existence was marked by buzzing static until she heard the dark singing voice.

She could feel how hard her heart was beating. Tom Jumper had just spoken about her, as well as things that would shake up even the most hardened law-and-order lobbyist. What would be next?

"Hey, hey, here we are again, folks. Tom Jumper's *Last Bastion* comin' atcha. Now, where were we? Yo, did you know big business isn't too pleased these days, either? Take the cigarette and ammunition manufacturers, for example. How do you think they've been feeling the past couple of weeks, watching their torrential cash flow evaporate? What do you think the Wall Street wizards and media moguls would prefer to be doing right now? Be standing in the Oval Office with a loaded Umarex Beretta 92FS pointed at the president's pointed little head, or in self-imposed exile, far, far away? Do you have any idea what a dangerous job it is these days, being president of the United States? Hey, I almost feel sorry for the guy. How many people do you think wouldn't mind sticking a rocket up his ass and launching him back to his humble Scandinavian origins? The most hated man in the world! Good ol' Saddam was Father Christmas by comparison. Watch out for the big-money boys, Jansen, that's my advice. They or the mafia or the militias will take you out sooner or later— just wait. Better keep an eye on your so-called faithful backers and lieutenants, too. Maybe they've bought shares in Gun-Ho Sports Cases and are watching their stock fall faster than Enron on a good day." He squeezed his bicycle horn for all it was worth and howled with laughter. Doggie could see his face before her.

"And while we're at it, here's a bit of advice for you, Miss Doggie Rogers: You were last seen with a grossly expensive Fendi bag over your pretty shoulder, so get the hell rid of it! They show it every ten minutes on TV, in case you didn't know."

Another blast on the horn. Doggie hugged her tattered plastic bag, thinking about the thousand-dollar Fendi lying at the bottom of a Bronx garbage can.

"Back to big-time politics, with a big-time scoop. 'Cause, sitting by my side is one of our nation's leading commentators, so let's give him a hand!" He clapped like mad. "We're not naming names, but you know him, believe me. I won't describe him to you either, because he might think I was coming on to him, and he might even like the idea,

ha-ha." More unrestrained laughter. "Well, well, well, my dear anonymous friend. We can reveal that you are a man with a great knowledge of many things. We hear there could be a countercoup against
Jansen in the offing. I say 'countercoup' because wasn't it a coup when
we elected a president who turned out to be Mr. Hyde instead of Dr.
Jekyll? So, Mr. John Doe, Mr. Man-Without-a-Face-or-Name, what do
you have to say about these rumors?"

The voice coming out of the tiny transistor speaker had been intentionally distorted electronically, but not well enough, because it was
practically as easily recognizable and nationally well known as Tom
Jumper's. Doggie had to press her hand to her chest and concentrate
on breathing regularly. It was the voice of her dear friend John Bugatti, perched a mile above the ground on the end of a branch he was
in the process of sawing off. The fall would be fatal if he kept on like
this. Tom Jumper's mudslinging was one thing. Even though it put
him in mortal danger, the loss of this provocateur—if they found
him—would be bearable. But John Bugatti was a different matter.
Here was a man whom everyone took seriously—not least of all in
Washington—and his presence on the program was pure suicide.

"A countercoup, you say. I'm not sure what we ought to call it,
Tom," came Bugatti's toneless, distorted voice. "Is it a countercoup or
just an extreme case of the Constitution's game rules being put into
effect? Something's going on, in any case."

He cleared his throat as usual. *Dammit*, thought Doggie. Couldn't
a pro like him at least turn his head away from the microphone?

"Of course many competent people have already been arrested, but
it will take a whole lot more than that before Jansen's completely unreasonable concoction of presidential decrees are a success. So far,
former vice president Michael K. Lerner—President Jansen's main
rival—is still on the loose. And, just like any other dictatorship, the
resistance of the general public is out there, like the proverbial tip of
the iceberg. Now Jansen has launched his biggest battleship, armed
with all the weapons of totalitarianism, trying to blast his opponents
out of the water. But we all know how it can end, don't we? It could
be the *Titanic* all over again if the government doesn't change course.

That is to say: if Jansen and the rest of his deranged Cabinet don't resign voluntarily."

Jumper tooted his horn. "Now, ladies and gentlemen, that was quite a mouthful from our very special guest. We'd just been talking about Doggie Rogers before you came, Mr. John Doe, and maybe we should take a moment to think about her father, too. After all, according to our impeccable justice system, it was he who brought this whole Armageddon upon us, wasn't it? If it hadn't been for him, people claim, we would never have ended up in the present disastrous situation. But I'm not so sure about that; might it not have happened, anyway? What do you people out there think? In any case, now he's sitting on death row, waiting for that needle. When is execution day, do you happen to know, Mr. No-Name?"

The day after tomorrow, Doggie thought automatically, and shuddered.

"He's to die the day after tomorrow at Sussex State Penitentiary in Waverly, Virginia," echoed Bugatti. Then he added: "And I'm convinced they're murdering an innocent man."

Doggie had to hold her breath. She could sense the dairy tanker was presently moving in slow traffic, and she was afraid she'd scream and someone might hear her. So she froze, paralyzed by her emotions and fear.

"For those of you who have just tuned in, you're visiting Tom Jumper's mobile radio universe, where our studio guest has just dropped a mega-mega-ton bomb into his microphone. Did the man say Bud Curtis was innocent? And upon what do you base this radical supposition, I'd like to ask? I mean, we all know there was a public trial following all the proper judicial procedures. Does this mean we can no longer trust the courts to do their job?" His cackling laughter was its own answer.

Bugatti cleared his throat a couple of times. Doggie really wished he'd stop revealing his identity like this. "Hmm . . . Well, I believe Bud Curtis spoke the truth when he said Mimi Jansen asked him to fetch her a glass of water. And why shouldn't it be true? She'd had a long, strenuous day; she'd just come into a very warm room, straight out of a snowstorm, still wearing an overcoat. And she was just about to give birth, for God's sake. And why wouldn't it be possible for the glass to disappear afterwards? I mean, there were around thirty people present, and it was total chaos."

"Whoa, now. Hold on, Mr. Doe. That still doesn't prove Curtis didn't get his idiot flunky to do the job."

"No, that's right. And still, no one lost any time discrediting everything he said. Curtis was to be made to appear to be a liar, no matter what. That was the simplest course to take. If he could lie about the glass of water, he could lie about anything. Thus the seed of mistrust was planted in the minds of the jury. If, on the other hand, the jury believed he'd actually voluntarily gone to get some water for that poor, pregnant lady, then the issue of his guilt wouldn't have been so cut-and-dried. How could he be so courteous and obliging and murderously calculating at the same time? This is the kind of complex, contradictory psychological profile that a prosecutor hates, and he's not about to let such a trifle spoil his portrayal of a man who's supposed to be guilty as hell." John Bugatti paused to clear his throat. "I also find it very hard to understand that the killer himself was only hit by a single shot. I was there, so . . ." He tried to stop his slip of the tongue but too late. "I mean, I know someone who was present, and many people were hit by ricocheting bullets. So several guns must have been fired, and more than once."

You blew it, John, Doggie said to herself. *Now they really know it's you.*

"And what is that supposed to mean?" asked Jumper. "A security agent doesn't always get his man on the first shot, does he?"

"I wonder. But I *do* know that a remarkable number of people were injured. I think the agents saw several firearms at the moment the assassination took place, and they fired directly at anyone they thought was posing a threat—it wasn't by mistake. They're trained in surveillance and to shoot before they think. And if this theory holds up, then only one of the agents knew who to shoot at, which brings us to the next very disturbing point. Namely, that at the trial, there wasn't *one* of the guests who could testify to having seen the killer's movements at the moment of the crime, nor were there any of them who saw who shot him afterwards."

"Yes, but it was O'Neill who killed Mimi Jansen, wasn't it? He still had the weapon in his hand; we know that for a fact."

"Sure, it was O'Neill who shot Mimi Jansen," replied Bugatti. "No doubt about it. There was just no one who saw him do it. Except for one person—the person who shot O'Neill. And why haven't we ever found out who this person was?"

"Okay, I didn't know that. But there was a ballistics investigation, wasn't there? I mean, the guy who shot the bastard is a damn national hero, so why doesn't he come forward?"

"There was a ballistics study of the bullet that killed Toby O'Neill, yes. But the person who shot O'Neill was never identified, nor do we know what weapon fired the fatal shot. Personally, I believe the man who stopped O'Neill didn't identify himself because he didn't want to be drawn out of the crowd immediately after the incident. If you ask me, it was because he had something on his person that he wanted to keep concealed."

Doggie was overwhelmed. All these words were being said much too late. There she sat in a stinking milk tank, on the FBI's most-wanted list, and unable to do anything but listen.

"Whoa, hold on there," Jumper broke in. "What you're saying is very strange. Why didn't the defense make a bigger deal out of who killed O'Neill?"

"Because that wasn't what the case was about. They overlooked its importance or maybe gave it low priority—I don't know. The subject was never touched upon during the trial."

"I won't want lawyers like that when the time comes, that's for sure. So you're saying the person who shot the perpetrator might have had something to hide? What, for example?"

"Yeah, what do I know . . . ?" Bugatti chose his words carefully. "A spot of gun oil in his pocket from the weapon that killed Mimi Jansen, perhaps. Someone must have given O'Neill the weapon at the last moment. How else could he have gotten it? One would presume he'd been thoroughly searched before they let him in to the reception. Or maybe the person who shot O'Neill had also slipped a water glass into his own pocket—that's also a possibility. But we can only speculate."

Doggie's stomach was in knots, her bladder was full, and her bowels were in turmoil. It was like everything inside her was trying to get out. She gasped for breath. Bugatti had really said a mouthful. For Christ's sake, there must be someone out there who'd heard him, who would take him seriously—a judge, a lawyer, a policeman. She shook her head. Why had Bugatti not said all this sooner?

"This is sure some tasty food for thought you're serving up, Mr. John Doe, I must say. But why did you wait until now to tell us?" Jumper must have read Doggie's mind. "Seems to me you could have made these deductions weeks ago."

Doggie nodded. Yes, John. Why did you wait? Why did *she* wait—and so many others, for that matter? She stamped her foot in frustration, then froze when she heard the steel cylinder's booming echo. But everything outside sounded okay; the truck's motor was in high gear.

She could hear John Bugatti heave a distorted sigh through her little speaker. "Yes, I suppose I could have. But my brain didn't start working in that direction until I realized how many apparently random incidents there had been that might actually fit a pattern—including the Killer on the Roof."

"Then we have to conclude that coordinated criminal acts were committed, possibly orchestrated way up the political ladder."

"Yes, at least some of them."

"Now, dear listeners, during this next musical interlude please meditate on these uppercuts we've just dealt our great American democracy. We're going to play something rather different from Johnny Cash this time, and in the meantime we'll be changing frequencies again, so . . ." Suddenly, there was a loud ringing sound in the studio. "Just a second . . ." he said, then there was noise of tumult and shouting.

"What's happening?" cried Bugatti's distorted voice.

"We've got to get out of here; turn off that switch over there," came Jumper's high-pitched voice in reply.

There was a single *click*, then just low static like on all the other stations.

She sat and stared into the darkness, her insides in revolt. What happened? Had they just caught up with Tom Jumper—and John Bugatti, too? Was this the latest example of gross injustice from her employer's hand?

"Oh, God, I need to find out more; I've got to speak with Bugatti," she whispered, fumbling her way to her plastic bag. She found it and pulled out the little Buddha, then sat still in the pitch blackness, listening to her surroundings.

Just as they were passing what sounded like a big truck, she smashed the figurine on the steel floor with all her might. There was a sharp, lingering echo, but she was sure the noise couldn't be heard from outside.

Then she fished the cell phone out of her pocket and once more turned on the display to use as a flashlight. There were bits of china everywhere, and she preferred not to think about how well the tank would be cleaned before it was filled with milk again. No, she couldn't imagine there being any danger of some child choking on a chunk of her Chinese Buddha. She crawled back and forth, feeling around in the rubble. Years ago in Beijing she'd seen John Bugatti pretend to stuff a piece of paper with a phone number into the statue's mouth; maybe Rosalie was right and he hadn't been pretending? But there was no slip of paper, and that was that.

She lay down on her back, on top of the broken pieces of the Buddha, and prayed they'd reach their destination soon. Too many dark thoughts were circling around in her head, her insides were crying out to be emptied of waste and refilled with new food, and her body was stiff from the tank's incessant vibration and movement. It was torture, of a kind she had never imagined.

What now? she thought, and remembered the time one of her most beloved professors at Harvard had caught her crying after one of his lectures. "Why are you crying?" he'd asked. And when she'd explained between sobs that her head was so filled up that she couldn't think straight, he'd looked at her with the kind of indulgence only shared by equals, and said: "Good Lord, Doggie, this happens to everyone. Your head's swarming, and there isn't space for more. You have to tidy up your mental archive."

At first she hadn't understood what he meant, although she nodded when he asked whether she had other things on her mind besides his class. Then she saw what he was getting at. And now, here she was again, tormented by a headful of unstructured thoughts and a suffering body, and realized the necessity of establishing some order in her bewildered brain. So she staggered to the far end of the cylinder, pulled down her pants, and squatted. There she stayed until she'd excreted all her body had to offer, well aware that the driver would have some extra work when he got back to the depot. *I'll give him another $500,* she decided, and began getting her mind under control, step-by-step. She would spend the night at Rosalie's sister's and deal with tomorrow when the time came. There'd be no more dreaming about the future. Her father would be executed the day after tomorrow, there was no getting around it, but it wasn't her fault. It was horrible, but he wouldn't suffer, that was the important thing. Maybe they would catch her, but there was no way she'd give up without a fight. If they put her in prison, sooner or later she'd be vindicated. There was no room in her mental archive for anxiety. Actually, there was no room for feelings at all—for herself or for anybody else. She pulled up her pants and made her way back to the transistor radio. She switched it on and turned the dial, but could find only static.

"Okay," she said aloud, "that was the archive. Now comes the real work."

She had to picture the scene in her father's Virginia Beach hotel as clearly as possible, so she shut her eyes—even in the darkness—in order to concentrate.

On that fatal evening she had walked towards the passageway to the hotel's conference room, along with all the other VIPs, arm in arm with Bugatti and feeling jubilant. Everything had fallen into place as planned. Bruce Jansen had been elected president, and her father's election night celebration was going spectacularly well, in spite of some kitsch decorations. A double row of senators and their spouses were walking in front of her, and in a matter of weeks she'd actually be fulfilling her dream of working in the White House. Life was good.

"Nice evening, don't you think?" she'd said to Bugatti as they turned a corner from the corridor into the passageway. The sight that greeted her left her—and everyone else—in awe; the entire passage was draped in Stars and Stripes. Then her father had taken over. He'd looked so fantastic in his tuxedo and everything was so perfect that she didn't really hear what he said. Next her father nodded to Toby O'Neill, and she remembered how overwhelmed she had been by a feeling of anticlimax. She could tell John Bugatti had felt it, too. How could her father let that miserable little man perform the unveiling ceremony? He was so wrong and pathetic standing there. Then O'Neill obediently stretched out his arms in his oversized red jacket to let himself be searched by a Secret Service man. For a second she'd wondered at how quickly O'Neill obliged the Secret Service agent, then the events that followed made her forget about it.

She sat on the cold stainless steel, concentrating, and tried to rewind her mental videotape a little. Okay, she had been walking behind the senators and their spouses, all arranged in order of importance. She squeezed her eyes shut even tighter, as though it would help her remember more.

Stephen Lovell had been walking behind her, along with other members of the campaign team, but not Thomas Sunderland. He had placed himself way at the front of the entourage with Ben Kane and two of his security team, directly behind President-Elect Jansen, his wife, and Doggie's father. She'd noticed Sunderland and Kane when the Secret Service agent stepped forward to frisk O'Neill. And suddenly, Ben Kane was standing there, too, not a few yards behind with Sunderland, as he'd been a moment earlier. It wasn't easy placing them correctly at the proper point in time.

In any case, practically everybody had been looking at the huge, repulsive portrait at the moment Toby revealed it, but Doggie had been watching O'Neill. He'd pulled the cord and taken a step back, in the direction of Ben Kane, so they were standing very close. Thomas Sunderland was on tiptoes behind Kane, looking over his shoulder to get a glimpse of the painting.

At least that's what she had thought at the time.

Then the guests had pushed their way closer, and she could no longer see Toby, who was forced against the wall along with the people standing behind him. She'd looked up briefly at the painting, then down at her father. If only he were standing next to O'Neill, she remembered thinking, then he could keep the fool under control, if necessary. But instead she found her father a couple of yards away, listening to something Mimi Jansen was whispering to him, after which he left by a door that Doggie knew led to a small kitchen behind the conference room.

Her stomach began rumbling again. Frowning with concentration, she pressed on her diaphragm until it stopped. She could allow absolutely nothing to interrupt her train of thought right now.

Anyway, according to her father's testimony, he had gone out to the kitchen to fetch Mimi Jansen a glass of water. A glass, according to John Bugatti's theory, that later could have disappeared into Ben Kane's or someone else's pocket. Finding traces of water afterwards was pointless, since half the people in the passageway had thrown themselves to the floor when the first shot rang out, and if Bud Curtis had returned at exactly that moment and dropped the glass in shock over what he saw, then naturally the water would have been absorbed by the clothing of those lying on the floor, and no one would have noticed where the glass ended up in the ensuing panic.

The second after the shot, she'd looked around in confusion and felt Bugatti's pain even before she saw all the blood. The blood seeping through his shirt, the blood spreading beneath Mimi Jansen's body, the blood spattered over the wall behind O'Neill's skinny, twisted corpse. She'd bent over to see where Bugatti had been hit, then looked around desperately and seen Ben Kane's and Sunderland's savage expressions as they reached the dying Mimi Jansen. The area was now a mass of undefined humanity, running and crawling for cover. She'd looked around for her father and found him kneeling next to one of the wounded. His pant legs were wet—with blood, she'd assumed at the time. Now she knew it had been water; she should have realized this much sooner. In her mind's eye she could see Sunderland snarling at the agents who were shielding the president. See him yanking them out of his way, his thin hair flying in all directions, the lining of one jacket pocket inside out and his face going through a series of small explosions.

She heard the whine of the milk tanker's brakes and found herself sliding across the floor of the container. For a moment she thought they'd reached their destination, but the motor resumed its deep rumbling. As she brushed bits of debris from the Buddha off her body, her hand touched something that made her gasp. She grabbed the cell phone and lit the display, already knowing what she would find: a little scrap of paper with a long telephone number in John Bugatti's neat handwriting. A seventeen-year-old number that had probably been changed long ago and, if not, might now have been discovered precisely a half hour too late, judging from the commotion followed by abrupt silence she'd heard on Tom Jumper's radio show.

"Uncle Danny" was written on the paper along with the phone number, precisely as Bugatti had promised. It was a Washington number, of course.

You've got to try it, Doggie, she told herself. *It may still work. Maybe you can leave a message for John; maybe he's okay.*

She punched in the number, heart pounding, and raised the phone slowly to her ear, trying to put off the inevitable tone that meant the number was no longer in service. She held her breath and stared out into darkness as the phone began to ring. Now it was a question of whose number it was and if anyone would answer, considering the time was way past midnight.

Finally, after more than thirty seconds, a tired voice came on the line. "Hello, this is Danny," it said.

Doggie's mouth opened slowly. Oh, God—it was him! It was so unreal, she almost dared not say anything. Why hadn't she believed in Bugatti? Why had she deluded herself all these years, thinking it had merely been a case of an adult momentarily soothing the pain of a child and then forgetting about her? Why hadn't she believed it possible for a person to be faithful all this time?

Shame follows mistrust, she thought, then said hello. "Is this Uncle Danny I'm speaking to?"

His voice sounded weak and far away, yet it was not a voice one

would expect from an older man, like an uncle. "'Uncle Danny' . . . ?"
he repeated. "No one has called me that for at least ten years. With
whom am I speaking?"

She explained who she was and about Bugatti's ancient promise.

"I know" was all he said. "I've heard a lot about you. I wish I could
help, but John has gone underground. I'm hoping he'll call home, but
unfortunately I can't say when."

"You didn't hear him on the radio?" she asked. The vehicle made a
sudden turn, and she had to fight to keep her balance.

"I'm sorry, I didn't hear what you said. There was so much noise
on the line . . ."

"Oh, it was nothing," she quickly replied. Why worry an old man?
"But will you give him a message, if he calls?"

"I'll do my best."

"Tell him I would like to meet him tomorrow afternoon at the Teaism salon on Market Square. I'll be there between one and two. Say it
has to do with Thomas Sunderland."

Uncle Danny sounded worried but said he'd do what he could. What
he said next jerked her back to brutal reality: "Oh, God, just so long as
nothing's happened to him. Maybe he'll never be coming home again."

She understood his concern but hoped fervently she had misun-
derstood the rest. Home, he'd said.

"Excuse me, but what do you mean by 'home again'? Do you live
together?"

He hesitated a moment. "Are you sure you and John know each
other? I mean, you *are* Doggie Rogers, aren't you?"

"Yes. I'm sorry I said that, but at the time John gave me the number, I didn't get the impression you lived together. I thought you were
his uncle."

A slight chuckle confirmed her suspicions. "My dear friend, we
have lived together in my house for ten years now. John and I are lovers, didn't you know?"

"I knew John had a partner, but I didn't know his name. Please
forgive me."

"Does it make a difference?"

"I guess not."

Then she thanked him, said good-bye, and hung up, suddenly realizing she might have made a fatal mistake. She had called Uncle Danny because she needed Bugatti. She truly believed that if there was anyone besides T who could cast doubt on her father's guilt, it was he. John could help stop the madness and gain a stay of execution. Yes, maybe even help to finally exonerate him. She had called Danny in the belief that he was neutral territory. Someone who could not be connected easily with John Bugatti and whose phone wasn't likely to be bugged, a distant family relative who served as a kind of mailbox for a nephew who was constantly on the move. Instead they were a couple who had lived together for years. Having just heard Bugatti's voice on Jumper's program now offered little consolation. The government's well-oiled intelligence machinery had surely had no difficulty identifying Bugatti and had immediately proceeded to tap all the telephone numbers that could have any connection with him—if he hadn't already been captured.

She should have known who "Uncle" Danny was, dammit!

She pounded her fist on the steel floor. This meant they knew her cell phone number as well. In a minute they'd call it so they could cross-scan her exact position. If so, it would all be over in a matter of moments. She could either turn off the phone or wait for it to ring—simple as that. She began counting the seconds.

When she reached two hundred, she exhaled slowly. Okay, she would meet Bugatti tomorrow—*if* he got her message and *if* it were at all possible for him to come. She would explain her theories and listen to his; then they would have to try to get Wesley to somehow slip them into the White House.

It wasn't a brilliant plan, but it was all she'd come up with—and then the phone rang.

CHAPTER 28

SATURDAY AFTERNOON T. PERKINS MET A CONVOY OF MILITARY VEHICLES A FEW miles past the Fort Pickett base that must have been in combat quite recently. He eased off the accelerator and passed it slowly, so he was able to see the dead expression in the soldiers' eyes. There were deep bullet holes in most of the vehicles, and the machine guns' muzzles were black with spent gunpowder. The militiamen down in North Carolina must have lost some of their cockiness.

He turned on the police radio and scanned back and forth, but could pick up only static, even on the police frequencies. But what the hell had he expected? Everything was slowly grinding to a halt. Then he picked the police technician's cell phone off the seat and quickly tried to orient himself on how to use the thing. It was the fourth cell phone he'd had to figure out in one short week, and this was definitely more than a brain assembled over sixty years ago felt like dealing with. When he was a boy, there wasn't even a light switch out in the toilet, so why the hell should he be forced to spend his old age plowing through one electronics manual after the other? It was totally absurd.

He pushed some buttons with his thumb, praying he'd hit Beth Hartley's number.

"I know, I know," he parried when she answered, before her inevitable sigh had a chance to immobilize him. "Just a couple of more completely normal bits of information. I'm sure you can find them in some kind of database. The intranet is still functioning, isn't it . . . ? Hey, Beth, are you there?"

Then the sigh came, anyway. He could clearly imagine the enticing trip it had made, up through Beth's lovely, warm lungs.

"What now, T? Where are you?"

"Don't worry your pretty little head with that. Just give me five minutes, okay?"

"Five minutes?" She gave a scornful laugh. "Okay. Five minutes, then. We're about to have a meeting with the chief. There are problems all over the place, in case you didn't know. Haven't I already told you that once today, by the way?"

"Listen, Beth, this is the information I want, if you can get it: first, the data sheet on a Secret Service agent by the name of Ben Kane. He's head of operations for the White House security force, as far as I know. And I'd like to find out about Thomas Sunderland's military career, if possible. Yes, and by the way, I also want the telephone number of an NBC4 cameraman named Marvin Gallegos. Can you do that for me, do you think?"

"Did you say five minutes? You're completely hopeless, little T." She sighed again and lowered her voice. "Do you have any idea what that painting you gave me is worth?"

"Like I told you, I've heard the sum of one hundred thousand dollars mentioned. Is there something wrong?"

"A hundred thousand dollars? Listen, sweetie, that's very nice, but I think I could get a sack of gold for just the frame, if it were framing *that* picture." She gave a dry chuckle. "Okay, I'll try. Where do I get hold of you? On your cell phone?"

T lit a cigarette—he had to, to keep himself under control. Was the painting really worth so much? No, she must be mistaken. If true, then why in the world had he spent the last thirty years racing around like someone possessed, trying to apprehend all kinds of losers? Why had he and his wife patched up and repaired their pathetic little house, summer after summer? Why hadn't they adopted the children they'd been longing for? It might have taken a couple of hours to have the painting properly appraised. Why the hell hadn't he done it ages ago? He felt his forehead getting sweaty and dried it off with his handkerchief. So much money. Now this case really mattered. "What? My cell phone number?" he said tonelessly, looking at the phone in dismay.

Now, how the hell did one find that out?

He beamed up the cell phone's menu and looked despairingly at the endless number of options.

"Just a sec . . ." he said, and chose the icon that looked like a telephone book. Nothing happened. The damned thing didn't work.

"I think the guy I borrowed this phone from has locked the menu with a PIN code. Can I call you back in ten minutes, Beth?" he asked.

"Let's say a quarter of an hour."

He called Beth back as he turned down the main road to Waverly. She'd been busy.

She hadn't found out much about special agent Ben Kane, but he'd expected as much. Some years of active military duty, and prior to that, all the usual info about high school and a couple of decent, completely normal parents, way out in the sticks—that was all. Even though it had been a few years since Kane had left the Secret Service to start his own security firm, data about current and previous Secret Service employees was inaccessible.

"What about Thomas Sunderland?" he asked.

"Well . . . It kind of looks like his data files have been through more than one filtering process, T. There are bits and pieces here and there that seem out of context, but of course I can't be sure. In any case, when it's information about the country's vice president, there are probably some security procedures involved that I'm not familiar with. Things change fast these days, you know."

"Yes, I know. But isn't there anything about his service in Grenada? He received a medal, I know. They haven't deleted that, for God's sake, have they?"

He heard her fingers on the keyboard in the background. "You're clairvoyant, my love," came the reply. "That's practically all that's mentioned from his early days. There's a little about the military academy but no exam scores. It also says he was custodian at the George C. Marshall Museum in Lexington while he attended high school."

"Get to the point now, Beth," he said. Traffic was moving nicely at the moment, and at this rate he'd be at the turnoff to the state prison in ten minutes. He was damned if he was going to stop to hear about museums in Lexington.

"Okay, okay . . ." She began reading to herself out loud. "'Served with the US Army Rangers . . . rank of captain. . . . Embarked for Grenada from Hunter Army Airfield in Georgia, October 25, 1983. As a result of active participation in this military operation, hospitalized various times with different wounds. . . . No special circumstances upon discharge from hospital. . . . Declared fit for active duty. . . . Decorated February 2, 1984, with a medal for bravery in action. . . . Operation Urgent Fury cost a total of nineteen American lives in Grenada, with one hundred sixteen wounded.'" She cleared her throat and raised her voice. "Look, this is all pretty general information, but it says here that eight men were wounded and one killed under his command, and that he personally got three enlisted men out of the line of fire. There's nothing else about the episode."

"Which battalion was he attached to, can you tell me that?"

"It says the Second Battalion of the Seventy-fifth Rangers."

"Can you also tell me where Ben Kane served?"

She muttered a little to herself as she worked the keyboard. Sometimes he ought to remind himself how much he actually enjoyed hearing a woman's chatter in the background. He stuck out his lower lip. Maybe he could still manage one more ride on love's carousel—and maybe not. How in the world should *he* know, when the first thing he did whenever he got off work was kick off his boots and throw his legs up on the table? Not the best way to pursue life's earthly pleasures.

"How'd you know about that, T?" Beth chuckled. "You *are* clairvoyant, ha-ha! It says here that Ben Kane was a sergeant in the same battalion as Sunderland. It's good for a vice president to have a security officer he can trust, wouldn't you say?"

"Yes, I would." So Kane and Sunderland had been together in Grenada—that damn well figured. And Kane wasn't a Secret Service agent; he was hired directly by the White House. "Beth, just one more thing . . . No, two things: You forgot the information about the NBC4 cameraman, plus I'd like some facts about a murder case."

"Sorry, T, they've come to fetch me now. The meeting's already started. It'll have to wait till Monday. Monday or Tuesday—then I can help you. Okay, honey?"

She hung up abruptly. *Shit!* he thought. This was just what he fucking needed.

He swung off the main road into a much more densely forested
area. Why the hell did they always have to place the country's grim-
mest institutions in the most beautiful surroundings?

He stared at the asphalt and tried to concentrate. A number of
things were clearer now, at least. Like that Sunderland and Kane had
served in the military together, so now he could build his theories
based on that. "Bonds between buddies are thicker than blood and
whisky," as his drunkard of a father used to declare.

He dialed the number of the sheriff's office, hoping that Dody was
still on duty.

The crabby switchboard lady took the phone. He could never remember what her name was. "Hell, T, why don't you use the walkie-
talkie?" she asked with a mouth full of chewing gum. "Oh, you're
too far away, okay . . . No, Dody's gone home. Tell me, did you appoint her to take charge while you cruise around the countryside?
'Cause some of the boys are good and pissed off, in case you didn't
know."

"Yeah, really? Then you tell them that's the way it goes when one's
deputy sheriff goes and gets shot. They ought to be able to understand
that. She was next in the line of command, for God's sake, wasn't she?"

The woman muttered something. She wasn't so bad, but she sure
was stubborn.

"Listen, isn't there anyone in the office?"

The chewing increased in tempo at the other end. "So I'm not anyone, huh?"

"Sure, sure, point taken. But if Dody isn't there, you've got to do
me a favor. Pull Leo Mulligan's file. It's in the green metal cabinet
behind the door. Look under *M*."

"Under *M*. Really, T? I wouldn't have guessed."

He could hear the clattering of her chair and the banging of file
cabinet drawers before she picked up the receiver again. "Okay" was
all she said.

"Try and read me the general description of the psychologist's impression of Leo Mulligan's home life in the period before he bashed his wife's skull in."

"'Try' this and 'try' that. This thing's at least fifty pages long. How do you expect me to find that part?"

He took a deep breath. "*Try* page one, for example. There's a list of the contents, and you look under mental examinations. It's pretty far towards the end."

There was page turning and gum chewing in the background. Then her telephone rang.

"Hey, just let it ring," he barked. She obeyed.

"How far down shall I read, T?"

"Can you find the section called something like 'social' something-or-other 'and mobility'?"

"Yeah, here it is: 'Social Status and Mobility.'" He could just see her, moving her finger over the page, one word at a time. "There's not much here, you know. Just four lines."

"Would you read them, please?"

"Okay, it says . . ." She began a monotone recitation: "'Leo Mulligan grows up with two sisters on the farm on which he was born. . . . Takes over farm and operates it alone until parents' death, after which he marries a grocer's daughter, who—according to several depositions—believes she has married beneath her social status. . . . Wife pushes her son to get ahead in school and ridicules her husband publicly for not having accomplished anything in life. . . . Threatens him with divorce and with showing him "her full potential." . . . That her son "will make it to the top a thousand times further than his father" if only they can get away from him. . . . That one fine day he will experience the truth of her words. Leo Mulligan, who was born to farm life and commonplace values then apparently lost faith in his life's work and the hope that it would be passed on to the next generation, as was the family custom.'" The nameless switchboard operator cleared her throat. If that was four lines, she'd sure taken her time reading them.

"Then there's a section called 'Consequences.' You want to hear that, too?"

"No, no, that's all right. That's plenty for now. But maybe you can find me the address of a cameraman named Marvin Gallegos, from NBC4. You know how, don't you?"

"Aww, Jesus, T. Give me a break." The phone was ringing again in the background. "Can't I take the phone?"

"You just find that address for me."

He studied the countryside outside the patrol car window as he drove, waiting for his last bit of information. There were tall, swaggering trees, completely covered in tangles of parasitic growth. It was like some kind of bewitched forest that beckoned travelers farther and farther into darkness and perdition—not such a bad description, considering his destination. He looked down the next straight stretch of road and thought about all those for whom this was the last image of the outside world. You could call it a kind of via dolorosa. He looked up at the enormous spiderwebs that connected the trees and had hung in precisely the same position, almost like cocoons, for as long as he could remember. In a little while he'd be coming to a marshy area, and then he was almost there.

"Yes, chief, here I am again."

"Okay, great. That sure was quick." He meant it this time.

"If it's the same Marvin Gallegos we're talking about, he'll be hard to get hold of."

T pounded his steering wheel. What now? "What's that supposed to mean? Are you sure it's the right man? Is he a television cameraman?"

"I've got the police report here, T . . . 'Marvin Gallegos, 341 9th Street. Born November 16, 1970. Photographer for *National Geographic*: 1995–2002. Thereafter employed by NBC.' Wanted by the police since the day before yesterday—that is, March twenty-sixth— 'for having distributed video recordings of military encounters with militias.'"

"Why would that be? That's his job, isn't it?"

"Beats me, chief. Maybe he filmed something the authorities didn't want publicized. People being assaulted or tortured, summary executions—what do I know? Our armed forces aren't exactly behaving themselves too well these days."

"He's been reported to the authorities, and . . . ?"

"He's wanted in every state. 'Presumed to have gone underground or left the country.'"

"Yeah, or captured," grunted T, his eyes on the road. Sussex's watchtowers and huge concrete buildings appeared a couple of hundred yards ahead to the right, behind a large, grassy area with a grass-covered rampart.

"Listen," he said, "can you tell me the name of that police technician from Richmond who always keeps a pair of tweezers behind his ear? He's got red hair. He's called Joe of John or something. His name begins with 'Jo,' in any case."

"Don't know him. I never get to meet the weird ones. Why?"

"Because I've got his cell phone and would like to know what his number is."

"Jesus, chief!"

T frowned. "What?"

"I'm sitting in front of a display that's about twenty inches wide. You ordered it yourself. And on it I can see who calls, and from what number—clear as day. This here's a police station, remember, chief?" She read him the number, and T scribbled it down on a scrap of paper with one hand, the other on the wheel and phone held between ear and shoulder. The man's name was Joe Simmons, so he'd been on the right track.

"I have a couple of messages for you, T. Do you want them now?"

"Just a sec. Hang on." One of Sheriff Kitchen's men was standing fifty yards ahead in the middle of the road, motioning for him to stop. He was black, just like 62 percent of the inhabitants of Sussex County, and T knew him well. Behind him and his patrol car, several national organizations against capital punishment were deployed, with earnest-looking demonstrators and the usual protest signs, and along the roadside stood dozens of tents. Their protest had apparently turned into a permanent state of siege.

He nodded to the officer and drove through the multitude of people.

"Okay, you said you had some messages. Anything important?"

"Nothing special, T."

"Thank God!"

"Well, a man named Curtis wanted to get hold of you, but then we were cut off. I don't know, I think his battery ran out. He sounded desperate."

The news was like a slap in the face. *Poor bastard,* thought T.

"And then a woman called for you, too. She sounded like she knew you. A private matter, perhaps?" She gave a short laugh.

"What was her name? Can you remember?"

"Come on, chief! Why should I have to remember anything? They've invented something called the pencil, you know."

"And . . . ?"

She exhaled demonstratively as she paged through her pad of paper. "She said her name was Doggie, but she wouldn't leave a number, poor thing. I wonder why?" A giggle escaped.

T ignored her. "That's nice. But you have that number on your twenty-inch display, right?"

"Just a moment, I have to check . . . Yes, here it is. The phone's registered in the name of one Frank Lee in the Bronx, but it was this 'Doggie' who phoned. No doubt about that."

He scribbled that number down, too, as he turned off the road when he came to the sign at the entrance to Sussex. He'd read that sign so many times before, with its warning against bringing alcohol, poisons, firearms, or ammunition onto the prison grounds. Anyone who did so would be charged with violating Section 18.2-474.1, Code of Virginia. Yes, T knew warnings like these. They were erected all over his territory.

He drove up past the power station and parked his car between two of the white delivery trucks that were always standing in front of the main entrance. He waved up at the closest watchtower, as usual, only this time no one waved back.

What the hell's going on here? he wondered, and looked in through the first perimeter fence. Even here, in the middle of the day, there were no signs of life. Not one single prisoner in his bright-colored jumpsuit poking around among the plants or playing basketball.

All the hallways, from the main guard post to Bill Pagelow Falso's office, were deserted, too.

"Where is everybody?" he asked the only prison employee he ran into. "Isn't it a little early for vacation time?"

"Vacation? Are you kidding, Sheriff? How many of us do you think are left?"

CHAPTER 29

WARDEN FALSO HAD ALWAYS HAD AN ANEMIC SECRETARY WITH A BROAD southern accent and a bosom of more impressive size than the piles of paperwork on her desk. Now the secretarial attraction was gone—along with all the paperwork and everything else in her office—and the gaping file cabinets were as empty as a politician's campaign promise. T continued on to the prison's inner sanctum, Bill Pagelow Falso's windowless office. Here he expected to be greeted by a similar barren sight, but encountered the opposite. Warden Falso looked up at him with heavy eyelids over huge stacks of case files that lay like hopelessly stranded baby whales on his desk. Behind him were three more trolley tables laden with files. Then there was the floor, which served as a wastebasket for discarded papers and the countless Hershey's bar wrappers that did their part in providing a new layer of insulation to Falso's corpulent body.

It was impossible not to notice Falso's distress regarding the state of affairs. The dark circles under his eyes had always been legendary, but now they dominated his face to the point where they paradoxically seemed almost to disappear.

"Mr. T. Perkins himself, I see," came the tired greeting. "How's it goin'?"

T looked around. "How it's going? *You're* asking *me*?"

Falso's bulldog cheeks trembled. "Yeah, this is real life these days. Everything's been stood on its head. Yesterday we released the last prisoners—except those on death row, of course. The rest of the trash is back on the street. Where, in God's name, is it all going to end?"

"I thought the cells would be teeming with militiamen."

"You did, did you? Nay, the military keep them for itself. Just drive up to Quantico Marine Base or Fort A.P. Hill—you'll see what I mean. We only get the ones who are condemned to death—and far from all of them, you can be sure. And thank God for that. Civilian doctors are refusing to come out here anymore. If it weren't for the military doctors, I'd have to stick those needles in the poor idiots myself."

T pointed at the files upon which Falso's beefy arms rested. "If there are no prisoners left, then why all these files?"

"These? With a little luck, a truck will soon be coming to cart all the archives and case files to someplace down in Florida where they're all being stockpiled. So I just have to make sure there isn't something in them we don't want others to read. You understand, don't you?"

T nodded and looked at the papers that had landed on the floor. It looked like plenty of documents weren't going to make the trip to Florida.

As though anyone cared these days.

"I'm going to get to the point, Bill." He took the chair Falso used to cross-examine inmates, pulled it around behind the desk, cleared a space for his laptop, and sat down next to the big man.

"Bud Curtis is still on death row, isn't he?"

"Curtis? Yes, he's meeting God on Monday." Falso didn't seem concerned. In a little less than an hour, at six o'clock, he'd be going down to take charge of the day's execution. Purely routine. Others couldn't stand work like this in the long run, but T was sure Falso could. He believed in himself, and that he was carrying out God's work.

"Listen, Bill. I know you've heard stuff like what I'm about to say in hundreds of cases, but I'm actually convinced that Curtis is innocent." He lay an arm on Falso's shoulder to ward off the man's reaction. "Lend me your ears and eyes for twenty minutes, Bill, and see if you don't agree there's reasonable doubt in this case."

Falso gave T a weary look. "He's already a dead man, T. I can't do anything for a dead man."

"Don't be so sure." He unfolded the laptop and clicked on the folder with the video files. "You've probably seen these video clips before—many times, maybe—but I still want you to hear what I have to say about them, okay?"

"They'll be calling me from down on death row in a moment, just so you know. In fifty minutes I have to start my part of the proceedings for today's execution."

"I'll be as quick as I can." T knew what he was up against. There was no way Falso was going to change his routine.

"This is the sequence where Mimi Jansen is shot." He lit a cigarette and offered one to Falso, who declined. The overflowing ashtray and the man's labored breathing indicated he was reaching his quota. "Check out Thomas Sunderland. See his jacket? Everything's in place." He fast-forwarded.

"Here! This is just a minute later, but now the jacket-pocket lining is inside out, see? His hand's been in and out of his pocket."

Falso shrugged his shoulders.

"And here's another file. This is NBC's cameraman, after he dropped the camera on the floor. The picture's out of focus now, right?"

"Right."

"Good, we agree. But look at this. Everything's out of focus and suddenly there's a little, indistinct spot up here in the corner of the lens. And then, look what happens. The spot stretches slowly downward. Not much, but a little."

"I don't know what you think it's supposed to mean. Where'd you get these files, by the way?" Falso looked at his watch.

T shrugged his shoulders. That was nothing Falso needed to know. "Just wait another minute, Bill. I want to show just one more file, then I'll explain what I think it means. . . . Okay, here you see Bud Curtis talking with Mimi Jansen, right? He's clearly nodding at what she's saying. She's asking for a glass of water, and he's agreeing to get it for her. And now he's leaving to fetch the water; that's what he claimed at the trial, so why not?" T clicked on another file. "And here he comes back in. True enough, there's no glass of water in his hand, even though from the position of his hand it could easily have been there. But look what happens when he reenters: He sees all the people lying on the floor, screaming, and now he looks over to the spot where Mimi Jansen was shot. Look . . . there! There!"

"I still don't know what's happening, T. What am I supposed to see?"

"He gives a start the moment he comes in. He opens his hand a little bit, look!"

"And so . . . ? Come on, T, of course he gives a start. That's not so strange, with people suddenly all over the floor. Listen, I'm on my way to an execution, so this is a kind of awkward moment to plague me with these kinds of details. I know you're good at your job, and I have the greatest respect for you—professionally and as a person—but what is it you're trying to prove?"

"Aw, hell, Bill, you won't be late. That doomed soul won't leave without you."

Falso gave T. Perkins a sharp glance. "You know I don't like it when folks swear, T."

"Sorry, pardon me. Take a good look at this—it's important. I'm convinced it's here that Curtis drops the glass, Bill. Someone's tampered with the video file, I'm sure of it."

"Tampered with it? Why would anyone take the trouble?" He looked doubtful. Doubtful enough to shake a man's convictions. "I tell you, with God as my witness: Your argument's awful shaky, T. It's not like you."

"Dammit, Bill, help me now! Just a couple more clips. Keep your eye on the Secret Service agent and Sunderland and the killer and their relative positions, okay?"

He gave a deep sigh. "I'd really appreciate it if you didn't swear, T. You know how I feel about it." His face turned into a fierce frown. "I'll look at what you brought—though I doubt it'll help Bud Curtis—but only if you watch your language. The Lord hears all! Remember that!"

T sat back in his chair and studied Falso through a cloud of cigarette smoke. "I'm going to tell you what I think happened, Bill. Are you ready now?"

"I'm still here, aren't I?"

"Okay. I can't say why, but our vice president, Thomas Sunderland, is behind this assassination—that's what I think. He wants all this to happen, which is why he's happy to accept Bud Curtis's offer to hold election night at his hotel in Virginia Beach. He finds out that Curtis has said bad things about Jansen and that Curtis has a handyman, Toby O'Neill, who is both easy to manipulate and has an ingrown hatred for Jansen and his wife. Is that plausible—all in all?"

Falso looked at his watch again.

"If you agree that it's plausible so far, then it's not impossible that Sunderland gets a security agent—under a false name—to ask Curtis to have O'Neill unveil the painting. Is it? Next, Sunderland's people lure O'Neill into doing the killing by offering him lots of money. They tell him everything will be okay if he just keeps his mouth shut. You know it from the Bible. They just call him Judas there."

"It's a theory, all right, but it sounds crazy. You can hear that, can't you, T?"

T cast a sidelong glance at the bulging ashtray and ground his cigarette butt into a plate bearing a dry rind of Mrs. Falso's home cooking. "Nevertheless, I think that's what happened. On election evening they have a gun ready that Sunderland's men have stolen from the drawer in Curtis's office. Security had access to all the rooms, so nothing could have been easier. Then they load the weapon with shells already equipped with Curtis's fingerprints that they applied by using some kind of rubber stamp method. After that, the plan was for O'Neill to wait by the painting and shoot Mimi Jansen or the president or both of them. I'm not sure which, and it really doesn't matter now. Then O'Neill was to be immediately dispatched to the next world, too."

T knew Bill Falso hated long explanations. Plus, as prison warden, he'd spent most of his life around people who'd rather lose an arm than tell the truth. His body size had mushroomed in keeping with his growing loathing of other people and all the bullshit he'd heard, and even now T could see how Falso's eyes were darting around the room for something to sink his teeth into while T made his case.

These were extremely bad odds, even for a seasoned sheriff from Highland County.

"I think we should assume that it was Sunderland's men who hacked into Bud Curtis's computer and online bank account and transferred a nice sum of money to O'Neill's account." He was relieved to see that Falso had stopped thinking about food and started listening again. "Slowly, and in all kinds of ways, the masterminds of this plan prepare and plant evidence that can make Curtis the scapegoat. But then several things go wrong that change events and foul up the execution of their conspiracy."

"Yes, mistakes are always one of the aspects of crime," said Falso, and turned his attention to a Hershey's bar on the windowsill.

"Listen, Bill, my theory is that the Secret Service agent who was waiting in the corridor with O'Neill wasn't the guy it originally was supposed to be, that the Secret Service moved in on Jansen's own security people's territory. Yeah, I know I'm on thin ice here . . ."

Falso nodded his agreement as he considered reaching for the Hershey's bar.

"It'd been more logical if O'Neill had had the gun on him from the beginning, and that the Secret Service agent next to him knew the assassination was going to take place. But for some reason it wasn't like that, and here's what I think happened instead:

"The group comes into the corridor. It's likely most of the agents present aren't in on the plot. But Ben Kane is. He's head of Jansen's security corps. That big fellow from the trial with the gold bracelets. He's an old buddy of Sunderland's from their military days, and he's Sunderland's man. Even though it's never been mentioned—let alone proven—*he's* the one who shoots O'Neill. Of course it had always been the plan to have O'Neill shot, just not by Ben Kane, and I'll explain why in a minute."

Falso finally grabbed the candy bar, only to find out it was an empty wrapper. T could imagine how he felt.

"Are you with me, Bill?"

"Yes, I'm with you."

"Okay: They come into the corridor. Kane's walking just in front of Sunderland, and behind them come Jansen and his wife. Here comes a Secret Service agent to search O'Neill for the second time that day. You can see that on the video, but can you see something else, too?"

He clicked on a clip that he'd flagged the night before. "People are very close together here," he continued. "You can see Kane and then Sunderland. And now . . . Now the agent has body-searched O'Neill, with Kane coming up behind them. Take a look at Sunderland's expression while O'Neill's unveiling the painting. Look at Sunderland's face right *there*. See how he looks around and crowds in right behind Kane. He's standing on tiptoes like he's trying to see what's happening over Kane's shoulder. In reality, there was enough room for him to go around Kane, yet he didn't. That's where I think he passes the gun to Kane. And now look how Kane starts forcing his way forward with his right arm concealed behind his back, and the arm stays there until he's behind O'Neill. This is where I believe Kane sticks the weapon in O'Neill's pocket. You can't see it, but I guarantee that's what's happening."

The corners of Falso's mouth turned demonstratively downward. Was it skepticism, or was he still thinking about that Hershey's bar? "That's some theory, I must say. Why in the world wasn't Kane holding the weapon to begin with?" he rumbled.

"Why? That's very simple, Bill. Where would he have kept it?"

"In his jacket or pants pocket—where else?"

"Let me freeze this picture. See his jacket? How would you describe it? It's short, isn't it? It doesn't completely cover his pants pocket, so he couldn't have something that big in his pants pocket without it being partly visible. Now take a look at Kane's jacket pocket. See anything unusual?"

"They're cut at an angle, and there are no flaps. I have a sports jacket like that, too. What does that prove?"

"Now look at Sunderland's jacket. How would you describe it?"

"It's a tweed jacket, a discreet tweed jacket. The pockets have no flaps, either. You see?"

"No, but they're deep and they're open—that's the difference. Ben Kane's jacket pockets are still sewn shut, I promise. Show me ten of Ben Kane's black-suited bodyguards, and I'll show you ten pairs of jacket pockets that are sewn shut so they don't catch on anything at a critical moment. Most of these guys are former elite soldiers. They don't take chances, believe me. And if Kane's pockets aren't sewn, they sure as hell aren't deep enough to hold a weapon of the caliber used to kill Toby O'Neill, anyway."

He excused his profanity and clicked the tape forward again. "Now we come to the shooting—see for yourself. Look how everyone gives a start while they're looking up at the painting. Next we hear some-one scream indistinctly; then we hear the second shot and there's O'Neill—dead. Happens pretty fast, doesn't it? How can it go so fast, Bill, can you tell me that? Who'd be able to identify the perpetrator so quickly in a crowd of panicking people?"

"Someone who was standing right next to him, I presume."

"But none of the security men are standing close enough at that moment. The senators' spouses have all crowded together up by the painting, see? But one of the people in that crowd already knows O'Neill is going to shoot, and that's Ben Kane. And he's ready to kill instantly, with a precise, open shot through all those people. . . . There it is! At the same time, the other agents are each firing at who they think is the culprit. They're shooting to neutralize, not to kill. But some of the bullets ricochet into the crowd—that's what happens in situations like this. One person's hit in the shoulder, another in the arm, a third in the leg, and so on. All those shots are fired by profes-sionals who know what to aim for in a situation like that. None of this sequence of events was dwelt upon very much at the trial, but a lot was made of the fact that Bud Curtis had left the scene and returned only after everything had happened, and that he claimed to have fetched a glass of water that no one could find. Doesn't it seem strange: the court's priorities regarding all the incidents that took place in those moments?"

"Bud Curtis could well have fetched that glass of water, couldn't he? That doesn't disprove his complicity, in my opinion. Why would Curtis lie about something like that?"

"For God's sake, Bill—pardon my language again, I'll try to be careful—but that's what I'm saying! He *wasn't* lying! He *did* have the glass with him! The prosecution just wanted to destroy his credibility with the jury. If he could lie about a little detail like that, what *couldn't* he lie about?"

"I see your point. The only thing you still have to prove is that he had that glass when he came back in. How can you do that?"

T was excited. He was making headway. "You can see now, Bill . . ."

He clicked on a couple of files and hoped it would work. "Look, now I'm connecting the NBC clips together so you can see them in sequence. Both what was shown on TV, and what wasn't—that is, what was recorded on Marvin Gallegos's camera while it was lying on the floor. . . . And now we'll run the entire NBC sequence concurrently with the hotel's surveillance video."

He pointed at the two small pictures on the screen, one on top of the other. "We'll stop the surveillance video exactly when the shooting occurs." T listened intensely to the tape. "Here it comes . . . there!" He pushed PAUSE. "Now we'll run the NBC file to the same spot so they'll be synchronized, then we can rewind and run them together—I hope."

He clicked back and forth a little and could feel how Falso was losing interest. "Just a sec, Bill, I'm not too good at this." He tried again, praying that the gunshots would come at the same time.

One could just make out Gallegos in the background of the surveillance video, standing on tiptoe with his camera. Then the shots came—at the same time on both recordings, luckily—and one could see people throwing themselves to the floor. Then, suddenly, one camera was shooting sideways from the floor while the other showed Bud Curtis entering from the side and giving a little jerk of surprise as the shots fell. T stopped the tapes.

"This is the moment where Bud Curtis drops the glass, if he ever was holding one. We agree on that, don't we? You saw how he gave a start, and now he's standing with his hand open, right?"

Falso folded his hands over his paunch with studied patience. But just one call from death row, and he'd be gone—T knew it. "Yeah, let's say that."

"Okay, look at the picture underneath. The one with the camera lying down. We'll take it frame by frame. One . . . two . . . three . . . and hey! What happened there?"

"It's your gray spot."

"It sure as hell is. Oops, sorry again, Bill. Yes, it is—and why? Because Bud Curtis dropped his glass—there, where he opens his hand on the other video—and he was close enough to Gallegos's camera that a drop of water splashed onto the lens. Just one little drop, but it sure as h . . . heck adds credence to Bud Curtis's testimony."

Bill Pagelow Falso wiped his nose and remained silent. He'd obviously been paying attention. He'd read stacks of trial transcripts in his time and probably knew more about case law than most. Plenty of appeals had crossed his desk, too, and now here was one he couldn't refute on either technical or ethical grounds. The question was whether Falso saw it this way, too.

T leaned in over the desk and lay his hand on Falso's pale arm. "I don't know why Ben Kane wouldn't take responsibility for shooting Toby O'Neill, Bill, I have to admit. Maybe he had something on his person that couldn't stand being discovered. Maybe it was Kane who picked up Curtis's water glass. Then he just stuck it in his pants pocket and got rid of it later."

Falso pulled his arm away. "Then why couldn't he have had the gun in his pants pocket, too?"

T thought a moment. "Maybe he did, now that you mention it!"

"Yes, or else it happened some other way, or yet another way, or none of the above. So maybe you should consider removing Sunderland from the list of suspects, shouldn't you?"

T heaved a sigh. "These last couple of days have been long ones, Bill. I'll get back to you with a decent answer to that question at a later date. But you can't explain away the drop of water, can you?"

Falso shook his head. "No, but if you're right about all this, why don't you go to the state prosecutor?"

"We don't have time. You have no idea how long everything takes these days."

Now it was Falso's turn to give a sigh—one that made his whole huge body expand and recede again. "Yes, you bet I do. If *anyone* does, I do. It really is a mess. But you know the law and you know what my job is, T. So you have to make sure you get this right."

"Then provide me some time. Delay the execution a day or two."

"Nonsense, I can't do that. On what grounds?"

"I don't know. On the grounds of everything I've just told you. Isn't the risk of executing an innocent man grounds enough? Bill, let Curtis fail the medical examination; that'll give us a little time."

Falso gave a dry laugh. "We stopped giving them medical exams a couple of weeks ago. Now we just execute them. Straight from their cell to the execution chamber—end of story. That's the only way we can handle the situation, understand?"

T. Perkins was getting anxious. "How many times have you had to watch, while a doctor punched around in the condemned's arm, looking for a vein he could use?"

"Don't talk about it."

T took a dart out of his breast pocket and jabbed it at the air to demonstrate. "Think of all the times you've had to use the neck because the veins were either no good or infected." He put the dart in his pocket again.

"It doesn't happen that often, but it *does* happen, I'm sorry to say."

"So, say Curtis has a vein infection and has to be treated with antibiotics before the sentence can be carried out. Can't he trade places with the next guy in line? Just one day, please, Bill?"

"I can't, T, you know that."

"Okay, you have a direct line to the governor. The line will be open for the execution this evening. Call him up and tell him there are strong indications that Bud Curtis might be innocent."

"It's not my job to come forth with an allegation like that, and it's not the governor's to listen to it anymore, either, by the way. Now it's the Department of Homeland Security we call."

"I don't give a . . . Sorry, Bill . . . I couldn't care less who you call, just do it! Before they call you up from death row in a second."

"No, T, you're on your own. I don't think the evidence you've shown me is strong enough."

"My God—gosh, Bill! What's wrong with it?"

"What you've indicated yourself. That there isn't a strong enough hypothesis about how the gun made its way to Toby O'Neill, and therefore there's no clear case. I admit the drop on the camera lens is mysterious, but it could be something like spit, sweat—almost anything. People were diving for the floor at that moment."

Falso opened a drawer in his desk and took out a neatly folded handkerchief. It was what he used to dry the condemned's brow as he lay on the pad, being asked if he had any last words. T had seen the ritual performed more than once.

Falso looked at him with his calm, mixed-gray eyes—eyes that, in a couple of minutes, were the last ones a condemned man was ever going to look into. Somehow that gave them a very, very frightening effect. "On the other hand, I find it quite strange that this Ben Kane—if he really was the one who shot O'Neill—didn't take the honor for bringing him down. But if you really are right, and it really was Kane who gave the gun to O'Neill, then I have a possible explanation for why he didn't."

T's hand froze on its way to his packet of cigarettes. "You do?"

"Do security agents wear gloves?"

"No, of course not."

"There you go, then. That was a problem for Ben Kane, if he's the one who passed the gun to O'Neill. Because, as I remember, at the trial there weren't fingerprints mentioned on that weapon other than Bud Curtis's and O'Neill's, were there?"

"Oh . . . no!" T's eyes widened, struck by a bolt of clear-sightedness.

"That might just explain the whole sequence of events," continued Falso. "Sunderland pushed the gun out of his jacket pocket from inside, which is why the lining was hanging out as we saw before. And where was Ben Kane? Right next to Sunderland, ready to take the gun with the flap of his jacket so he could place it in O'Neill's pocket. That way neither of them got their prints on it." He stuck out his lower lip and rubbed his chin. "But I wouldn't be surprised if there were other clues that could tell us about how the gun made its way to O'Neill. A tiny spot of gun oil on Kane's jacket, for example. But this is something a quick-witted wolf like Kane would realize in the middle of everything. Animal instinct. That's probably why he reacted so fast in picking up the glass, too."

T nodded. That could easily be the explanation. Why not?

Falso stood up and grabbed a zippered sweater that he proceeded to put on over his short-sleeved white shirt. T'd seen him do this before, prior to attending to his ritual down on death row. It was probably cold down there.

Warden Falso gave him a look that said the audience was soon over. "If that theory works, both Sunderland's tweed jacket and Kane's were probably destroyed afterwards. Have you happened to check the videos and photographs to see whether they're still wearing these jackets later the same evening? Of course they could have changed into jackets identical with the ones they had on . . ."

T looked at him in amazement. "Jesus . . . uhh . . . Gosh darn it, Bill! That's what happened: one or the other of those scenarios. First you shoot my theories down, then you reinforce them."

"Listen, T: No matter what our deductions lead us to, there are still some game rules. I don't know what's going to become of us in these weird times, but the day of reckoning will come, both for those who followed the rules and those who didn't. Mrs. Falso and I would like to look forward to spending our old age in peace and comfort, so it doesn't make sense for you to ask me to do things that could jeopardize it. I can't just decide whether Bud Curtis should have another chance, all on my own. Not based on speculation of this nature. Come on, old boy, we're just sitting here, playing with possibilities. In reality, everything could have happened completely differently. Remember: Not every lawyer, investigator, technician, judge, witness, and jury member involved with this case has been corrupt, or a dummy. They're my guarantee that I can do the work I do in God's name, with a clear conscience. That's how it's always been, and that's how it's going to stay until I retire soon. You have to understand that."

A crackling voice came over the intercom. Falso nodded. It was time for him to do his share of the work downstairs. They'd removed the prisoner's last-meal tray, and the priest had arrived.

Falso looked at his watch one last time as T frowned. "Come on, Bill. Talk with them at Homeland Security. Time's almost run out. Do it for my sake."

"T, I've heard your case. It's even possible I've given you some useful tips. But I can't go any further with it. You're a sheriff; you know about legal procedure. Use what you know. You've done it before."

"Yeah, but, Bill, we've only got till the day after tomorrow at six P.M."

"Correction. We only have till the day after tomorrow at six A.M. Starting Monday, we're executing two a day, and Bud Curtis has the honor of being the first to try out the new system."

T opened his mouth to protest but realized it was useless. Falso was heading toward the door.

Six in the morning? It was a desperate situation made twelve hours worse. How was he ever going to get to the bottom of this?

Falso looked T. Perkins up and down with a somber expression. "It's time," he said. "I'll have to leave you now."

"Hey, Bill, let me come with you. I want to speak with Bud Curtis— you won't deny me that, will you? Let me speak with Curtis in his cell. Is that a deal?"

CHAPTER 30

T. PERKINS FOUND BUD CURTIS IN THE FAR CORNER OF HIS CELL. HE SAT ON HIS cot facing the steel toilet, staring at the wall. He seemed completely oblivious to the sounds from the cell a few yards away, where they were applying handcuffs for the last time to the man about to be executed. Curtis gave a start when the guard put the key in the lock to let T in, as though he'd miscalculated and it was *he* they were coming to execute. He didn't recognize the sheriff until Perkins stood well inside the cell, and even then the terror and doubt remained engraved in his face.

"I've been allowed to visit you for a moment," said T, looking over his shoulder at the guard who was about to lock the door after himself. He shook his head and patted his revolver. The guard still wasn't convinced that the situation was secure, and threw a set of foot chains over to him.

T nodded, asked Curtis to stretch out his legs, and applied the chains. Bud Curtis's ankles were thin and freckled, and his eyes were full of mistrust, groping for some clue as to what was going on. T tried giving him a smile.

"Put your own cuffs on him, T. Behind the back," said the guard.

T clapped the handcuffs on Curtis, locked them tight to show his good intentions, and sent the prison officer a look that he'd used for years in his reelection campaigns: authoritative, competent, and slightly threatening. It always seemed to have a good effect.

Metallic clanking and some shouting could be heard from cell twelve, sending a shiver of unrest down the row of cells.

"Well, well, well. Sound like today's casket case don't want his life erased," laughed the man in the cell next to Bud Curtis. It was a hollow, nasty laugh, made more macabre by the fact that the man was due to die the following day himself. "He don' fucking wanna, and I don' fucking wanna, either!" he cried, grinning and beating on the bars. His gleeful, defiant scream proclaimed some kind of control of the situation. It sounded like someone who'd already departed this world, and it really got the cellblock going. A chorus of squeals and shrieks emerged from the cells. Howls, cries, bitter invectives, and curse words beyond belief.

Then panic suddenly overcame the condemned man in cell twelve. He tried to release his pain and fear, yelling wildly as he kicked everything in sight, including the guards who were attempting to hold him down. The guard at Curtis's cell door left his bunch of keys dangling in the lock and disappeared down the hall to cell twelve. T and Bud Curtis could hear several prison guards trying to calm the man down, and they heard Falso's voice say, "Just relax, Harrison. It'll all be over soon."

Some consolation.

In the meantime, Curtis's facial expression began to relax a little. "Did you get my message? I mean, the battery ran out," he whispered.

T nodded and held his finger to his lips. He looked at his watch. In five minutes the man Falso called Harrison would be lying on the execution gurney. No dilly-dallying with family farewells. No little room to give one's honey a last hug. The show would begin in five minutes, and that's how long they'd have to wait.

When the deputation with Falso in the lead had made their way down the hall with the condemned man and slammed the door behind them, T backed out of the cell and glanced up and down the hallway. Several arms were waving through the bars, and there was still plenty of shouting and cursing, even though the guards were gone. T eased the bunch of keys out of the lock. This was an unexpected turn of events—a sudden chance. He'd actually only expected to speak with

Curtis, just ask him the few questions he'd been planning to, so he'd feel he was on solid ground when he called the Department of Homeland Security. But now he had the keys in his hand and Falso's words echoing in his head: "Curtis is already a dead man," he'd said. Well, not if he could help it.

He looked at Curtis while he tried to figure out what to do. They had somewhere between twenty minutes and a half hour before the first personnel would come back out of the execution chamber, and by then they should be far, far away. He knew people down in both Sebrell and Courtland. Decent, ordinary folks he could trust, and who trusted him. They'd be able to keep Curtis out of sight for a while. The drive would take twenty minutes at the most—precisely the time he needed. He prayed that by simply nodding and jingling the keys at the video cameras, he'd be able to get Curtis through the hallways and all the locks. The officers watching the monitors in the guardroom would probably wonder why the two men weren't being accompanied by one of the prison personnel, but they'd seen him go down to death row with Falso, so what could there be to worry about?

He placed his mouth close to Curtis's ear. "You just follow me, nice and quiet. They'll think I'm carrying out a federal transfer." He took a firm grip on the man's arm. This really had to look good.

Bud Curtis glanced at him, clenched his teeth, and took a deep breath.

"You take it easy now, Curtis. Don't panic along the way, got it?" Curtis nodded.

"Don't say a word to the other inmates. Look like you're being dragged to the scaffold, understand? Any sign of solidarity from them is the last thing you should expect."

He pulled Curtis out in the corridor and scrutinized the twenty yards up to the first obstacle, a super-secure, armored plate-glass door that functioned partly automatically and partly with a key—a key that he hoped to be able to find on the key ring without too many tries.

"What the fuck, Buddy Boy? What's happening? Boogieman come to get you already?" The black man in the cell next to Curtis's stuck his henna-colored palm through the bars, but Curtis kept his eyes on the floor, like his life was already over. "Hey! Yo! You leavin' Daryl without sayin' good-bye? What about your cigarettes, huh?" he yelled after them, as more prisoners along the hallway began shaking their bars.

It was stress. You couldn't always see it, but they were really wound up and would stay that way until death relaxed them permanently.

Curtis tensed up a little but was completely under control as he turned to his cell neighbor. He had to say something, if the whole cellblock wasn't to flip out again. "Easy, Daryl, easy. I'll be back soon. You'll get your cigarettes, don't worry."

Then Daryl's yellowed teeth broke into one of the biggest smiles T had ever seen—a smile strangely innocent and delighted, and probably the last one to ever cross his face.

Curtis's leg chains jingled and clanked as T pulled him past the cell that had just been vacated, towards the cells where the inmates' orange jumpsuits bore the imprint ENEMY OF THE STATE over the breast pocket. These were the militia prisoners. Their turn was coming soon, too. You could see it in their angry, bitter faces.

"Let's have that Smith and Wesson, Sheriff," one of them hissed. "Then we can really give those cocksucking guards a surprise when they come back."

"Hand that swine over to us," snarled the next. "We'll slit him open from throat to asshole."

T marched Curtis as well as he could past the outstretched arms and tried to get an idea of which key to use before he reached the door. It looked as if at least five of them might work. He took one, but it wouldn't turn in the lock. He tried the next—no luck. As he was fumbling after the third key, he heard someone in cell number one get up and move to the bars.

"T? T. Perkins, is it you?"

He turned and found himself looking straight into the eyes of a skinny, pale little man. A man who he recognized immediately, a man he'd known all his life and who—until all this damned insanity had erupted throughout the nation—had never harmed a fly, as far as he knew. It was Jim Wahlers, who'd been discovered with an arsenal in his basement that could blow the faces off Mount Rushmore. Jim—his old dart partner and Highland County's former undertaker.

"Jim! Goddammit, are you here? What happened?"

"T! Tell my wife I'm in here, will you? No one knows where I am. Not even my lawyer."

T could feel a cold sweat on the palms of his hands. He looked at his old friend's quivering lips and despairing eyes. "Jim, why are you here? It's not because of all those weapons in your basement, is it? What was it you did, Jim?" He stuck the third key in the lock and turned it cautiously. It resisted a bit, but not like the first two.

Jim Wahlers pulled himself together for a moment and grabbed the bars. In a second his face had transformed into a fierce hardness that T had never seen there before. "The bastards say I organized an attack on a military camp, and goddammit, I wish I had!"

Once, Wahlers's hearse had run off the road and the coffin of the widow of an army major down in Clifton Forge had toppled over and opened, flinging her body up against the hearse's rear window. When T and his men arrived, Jim had been standing there, pissing against the window, right where the widow's white, shrunken face was pressed against it. "This is just to let you know that not everyone respects women who spread their legs for pigs in the fucking US Army, you old cow!" he'd hissed, and T had led him away from the hearse so no one would see what he'd done. At the time, T thought shock had made him react with this unusually disrespectful act. But right now, looking deep into Jim Wahlers's eyes behind the bars, this sudden flashback took on a whole other perspective.

He tried to picture the bearded guy with whom he'd motorcycled up to Winchester long ago to play a round of darts against a couple of local braggarts. He laid his hand on the one extended through the bars. "You wish you'd organized that attack, you say? I'm wondering if reality ever entered into the picture with us two. I'm wondering if I ever really knew you, Jim." Then he stepped away from the cell, turned the key, and opened the armored glass door.

"You can go to hell, you fucking pig cop!" bellowed Jim Wahlers, and from the other cells came echoes of agreement, so loud that he could still hear them after he'd slammed the door behind him.

T pulled Curtis close to him and touched the brim of his hat in greeting as he looked up at the next surveillance camera. It was a question of acting completely cool and just hoping the personnel in the death chamber hadn't heard the inmates yelling.

As they made their way down the deserted hallway of the next section, T could see that the leg chains were hindering Curtis in keeping up. It had been a long time since he'd had to move that fast, and his physical strength had obviously deteriorated. Prisoners on death row had a habit of either working out like madmen or just shriveling up.

"Come on, Curtis, just three hallways left, then we're out. You can catch your breath when we're far away from here."

"Why are you doing this, Perkins?" he gasped.

"Why? Because I saw that glass of water in your hand on election night, even though . . . even though it wasn't there, and because I've . . . I've seen new possibilities in your case."

Curtis gave him a strange look. A look that reminded him of Doggie. She'd had that same expression during her father's trial—the look of Medusa, defiantly challenging the course of events and at the same time struggling to maintain her faith in justice. But, besides that, Curtis's face radiated a kind of calm that T had rarely seen. It was hard to imagine what had created this inner harmony. Could it be because there was finally a human being who believed in him? That he no longer was completely alone?

"Watch out here, Bud," T whispered. They turned up the next corridor and headed straight for the guard post that was manned by an overweight young guy, about twenty-five years old. Unfortunately, T had never seen him before.

He pulled his badge out of his back pocket and stepped up to the little window. He gave a hearty "howdy" and laid his badge on the counter. "You can just let us out. Falso'll be sending the papers up here in a little bit. He's busy dispatching a prisoner at the moment." He winked at the guard to let him know he was one of the boys.

The guard peered at the badge with eyes set deep into his fat-laden face. "If the papers are on the way, I think we ought to wait," he replied.

The man wasn't as dumb as he looked.

T pursed his lips and whistled a few bars of a toneless tune. "Could I have a glass of water while I'm waiting, then? Falso's Hershey's bar's still stuck in my teeth. You know how *that* is," he said, in a confidential tone of voice.

The guard looked at them and nodded. He knew they weren't getting out without his pushing the button to unlock the last door. "Wouldn't you rather have a cup of coffee? I was just brewing a pot."

"No, thanks, just water. Aren't you Bambi's son, by the way?" T asked, calmly as he could, while the kid fetched him a glass of water from a sink in the corner. Barney "Bambi" Pellegrino was the fattest prison officer T had ever met at Sussex, so it was an educated guess.

He could feel Curtis's arm quivering next to him and tried not to be affected by the man's nervousness.

"Bambi? Nope, but I knew him. He's the one who died last year with a face full of doughnuts." The guard laughed, opened the window latch, and slid the glass of water over to him.

T took a gulp. It tasted stale, like water that had been standing in a turned-off refrigerator. "He died, did he? Jesus Christ. He was really a nice guy. I can't believe it. But you still remind me of someone I know here at the prison. Maybe it wasn't Bambi I was thinking of . . ."

"Maybe you mean Tammie Cambell down in the canteen. She's my mother."

T had no idea who he was talking about. "God!" he exclaimed, with a sweep of his arm that splashed water all down the front of his uniform. "Tammie!" He brushed the water off and studied the guard for a moment. "Damn, that's right. Now I can see it." He looked at the man's badge.

"Freddie Cambell. So you're little Freddie. Boy, have you grown! What's your mom doing now, Freddie? I suppose she was fired along with all the others. Too bad. Hey, you know what? Can you give me her address? We could probably use a good gal like Tammie up in our canteen."

The man looked at T and rubbed his chin. "Yeah, well, these days she's almost always down at the radio station. W291AJ—you know it? I don't know if they're still on the air. They weren't yesterday, anyway."

"When I get a chance, I'll drive down there and check out the situation. But you're sure we have to wait for Falso? It could still be a while. I've got to deliver this jerk up in Washington, ASAP."

"In Washington?"

"Didn't you hear, Freddie? It was on the NBC news last night. He's to be executed in DC. They're getting their shit together up there."

The guard gave a confused smile behind the glass. "Wow, that's really . . ." Words failed him, so he took another look at T's badge that was still lying on the counter. "Well, I guess you'd better get going, then. It's a long trip."

T could feel how Curtis's arm relaxed immediately.

"Then I'll have time to see your mother on the way back. Thanks for the glass of water . . . and the shower, ha-ha."

The sound of the main door's lock opening was better than any T could remember ever hearing.

"My God," Curtis whispered when they got outside, immediately turning his face towards the sun.

"Now we take it nice and easy. Nice and easy. My car's behind that white van over there." They'd only made ten steps before two things happened that weren't good. The first was that two police officers suddenly came strolling in their direction from the road leading up to the prison. It was the black cop and his partner who'd been keeping their eye on the anti–capital punishment demonstrators. They were heading straight for the prison entrance. *Must be time for their coffee break,* T managed to think, just before something far worse happened. It was Bill Pagelow Falso's voice, screeching over the loudspeaker system.

"Stop, T, else you'll regret this the rest of your life!" boomed the metallic-sounding voice.

Curtis's body jerked involuntarily. The slightly thawing tension changed immediately to panic. His clanking, jingling steps increased in tempo, and his breath came in gasps.

T looked over his shoulder, back at the guard post. There was still only Fat Freddie Cambell in the little room.

"You sure stirred things up down here on death row, do you realize that?" boomed Falso's voice.

"You've really abused my trust in you, T." Then the volume fell. "How far has he got in the parking lot, Cambell?"

Cambell gestured behind the glass as he answered his boss.

"Oh, no . . ." groaned Curtis.

Again the loudspeaker echoed over the parking lot. "You're not taking Curtis off prison ground, T. Not alive—got that? Leave him where he is. And you disappear, you renegade idiot!"

Now the two cops heading towards the entrance were aware that something was wrong and began running towards them. They were young and in good shape. There was about the same distance to them as there was to the patrol car.

"Come on, goddammit, come on, Curtis!" T barked through clenched teeth.

Curtis waddled forward as best he could, heartbreakingly close to a chance to stay alive.

The policemen began yelling at them. Fat Freddie had abandoned his guard post and was heading towards them, too. The indistinct cries of the men on death row could still be heard in the background over the loudspeaker.

That fucking Jim Wahlers . . . thought T. He'd probably been the one who set off the commotion. Who'd ever have imagined his old dart competition partner—with whom he'd once dominated Winchester's dart club with twenty first places in a row—would one day play an instrumental role in T's own demise? Jim Wahlers—fuck him!

Now the white van was just a couple of steps away. Curtis struggled even harder.

"We're gonna make it, Curtis! We'll drive down to the other end of the parking lot and then around, so they won't be able to ram us."

The two police officers fired warning shots in the air while T fumbled in his jacket pocket after his keys. At the same moment Curtis lost his gait as he attempted too-long steps. "Fuck!" he yelled, as the chain pulled his front leg out from under him and he fell helplessly to the ground, face-first.

"I'll have to write a report if you keep this up," wheezed Falso's voice over the loudspeaker. "It's wrong, what you're doing, and God's going to chastise you for it, T! He'll cast you down; you'll regret it!"

T came to a halt. Curtis was lying twisted on the ground five yards behind him, his chained legs flung to the side and his handcuffed wrists bloody and blue with bruises.

"Get out of here, Perkins, before it's too late," Curtis gasped, trying to lift his head. "Tell Doggie I love her. Tell her I didn't do it—then we're quits. Thanks for trying to help me, and get the hell out of here!"

"I'll do everything in my power. Don't give up, Bud—do you hear me?" he shouted, as he threw himself onto the front seat of the patrol car.

He floored the accelerator as he flew around the perimeter of the lot and passed the twenty-five miles per hour sign at the main gate. By then the two cops and Fat Freddie were standing over the still-prostrate figure on the asphalt.

A half hour ago he'd almost convinced the state's most thick-skinned prison warden of Curtis's innocence. Why the hell hadn't he left well enough alone? Then his appeal might already be on its way to the Department of Homeland Security. He could have been in Washington before midnight and presented his case. And what now? If he tried calling Homeland Security, maybe some official would have already heard how he'd instigated an escape attempt by the nation's most infamous condemned prisoner. Maybe, and maybe not. Would his old friend Bill Falso really tip them off? He had no idea.

He shook his head, disgusted with himself. How had he ever imagined that this brainless, spontaneous caper would succeed?

T waved to the new set of officers who were keeping an eye on the demonstrators as his police car sped by them, away from the prison.

Soon the giant, hanging spiderwebs were looming ahead again. "Oh, God, Doggie," he whispered to himself, "what the hell have I done?"

He pulled off the road at a sign that read BIRD REFUGE and grabbed his borrowed cell phone. He looked at his notepad and dialed the number Doggie had called from.

It rang a few times before Frank Lee's voice mail recording informed T that he wasn't around, but the caller could leave a message.

T swore. How could he be sure she'd get his message?

"What the hell," he grunted, and cleared his throat a couple of times. "Doggie, I've just tried to sneak your father out of Sussex, but unfortunately it didn't go so well. Actually, it didn't go well at all. They caught your dad, and I don't think I'm too popular right now, either. But who cares? They can't take my pension." T hated voice mail. He always wound up talking nonsense.

"No, I'm sorry, Doggie. What I wanted to say was that I have important information regarding the case. There are strong indications that Thomas Sunderland had a very dirty hand in orchestrating Mimi Jansen's assassination. We have to meet and find out what can be done. You know everyone in Washington, so you can surely get much further with this information than I ever could, and much faster. Maybe it'll work if we get together and are very, very careful. I don't see any other way right now. What do you think? Let's meet in Washington at noon, tomorrow. I hope that will give you enough time, since I don't know where you are at the moment, do I?"

He stared into space, trying to think of where they could meet. After what he'd done, it sure wouldn't be any police station or public office.

"Let's meet at Barnes and Noble on the corner of 12th and E Street, at noon, tomorrow. I know they're open on Sunday. I guess that's all. Sorry about the long message, but I'm not crazy about sending texts. See you. Good luck."

CHAPTER 31

A COUPLE OF DAYS HAD PASSED, AND BUGATTI HAD MADE NO PROGRESS GETTING out of the United States by airplane. He was surviving but exhausted as hell. Going underground as an overweight, chain-smoking fifty-year-old was one thing; suffering from AIDS on top of this was another. A body so brutally afflicted is in a state of constant suffering. And lack of sleep and vitamins and minerals, plus lack of calm, peace of mind, or anything to look forward to, had drained his poor body almost completely.

Friday had been spent at the airport, waiting and thinking and waiting some more, and on Saturday he had met up with Tom Jumper on his mobile radio show, only to escape capture by the skin of his teeth.

A man couldn't stand much more.

Early that Saturday he'd made the decision to remain in the country. What other choices did he have? He'd just spent twenty-four hours at Dulles Airport, and the lines in front of him hadn't gotten much shorter. For the time being, all departures abroad were allowed only for foreigners and individuals possessing a diplomatic passport. He could have chosen to keep waiting, but, as a lady at the British Airways desk said, prospects weren't good.

So there he'd sat in the check-in hall, head in hands, a well-known journalist at the pinnacle of his career. There wasn't a notable person worth interviewing whom he hadn't interviewed; he considered himself an objective reporter who was good at his job. *Shouldn't let these skills go to waste,* he told himself. *What good does it do, just sitting on your hands in no-man's-land?* He could catch a bus and then another bus, and another, until he reached Canada. It couldn't be totally impossible to get out of this damned country if one tried hard enough. Or else he could stay and fight the good fight. With the United States being run by madmen, he couldn't just carry on with his job like nothing had happened. If he went back to NBC now, he'd have capitulated once and for all.

He hunted around in his pants pocket and found the piece of paper with the e-mail address Tom Jumper had given him two nights ago as he was leaving John and Danny's home. "I have a transmission van in Arcola," he'd said.

This could still be a possibility if he acted fast. He pictured the slim, blond-haired man. They'd make a hell of a couple: NBC's star reporter together with the world's most unscrupulous, sensation-hungry TV host. It was a combination that would make people take notice. But did he dare risk everything? He knew the odds. Jumper was on the run, and the people who were after him were going to catch him sooner or later. And what about himself? What would happen to him? He wasn't crazy about the idea of falling on his sword in the name of professional pride. Was there really no better alternative?

He sat there considering his options as the check-in line refused to budge. Several times he heard the protests of prospective passengers who the security personnel or police had picked out for questioning. One even tried to escape but was caught on the stairs to the parking basement. John could hear the chase's violent conclusion.

How many times had he sat here, peaceful and happy, looking forward to a couple of days in Hawaii or heading up to Quebec, where Danny loved to visit? His present situation seemed totally surrealistic.

Finally he made a decision and headed for the information desk.

"How can I go on the net?" he asked the tired-looking lady.

"There are hot spots throughout this level. Just plug in your computer."

"Yes, I know," John nodded, "but I don't have my laptop with me," he lied, said laptop clenched between his knees. *They're monitoring the*

Internet, Jumper had warned. *They can trace your cell phone and tap your phone. Your credit card can reveal your whereabouts in a matter of seconds.* One couldn't be too careful these days, especially if one was trying to come in contact with Tom Jumper.

The information assistant tried to be helpful. "Then use the Wi-Fi connection on your cell phone. I can show you how, if you haven't tried it before."

"I'm sorry, I know it sounds crazy, but I don't have a cell phone, either."

She gave him a look that left no doubt he'd used up his quota of her attention. "Then you have to go down to one of our business service centers. There's one in both the east and west wing."

The two young women he found in the glass-enclosed service center looked no less tired. "Can you help me?" he asked, trying to adjust his face the way it looked on television. Perhaps one of them would recognize him. "Unfortunately I've had my laptop and my cell phone stolen, and I really need to send an e-mail to NBC. Is that something which can be done from here?"

One lady pointed over at the Internet terminal. "Just swipe your credit card through over there and you're online."

"Well, you see, that's kind of a problem. They stole my credit card, too."

"Then why didn't you send your e-mail from the security booth? You reported the theft, didn't you?"

"Uh, no, because these things were all stolen in town, not out here, and in the meantime something's happened where it's imperative that I contact my office."

The other attendant eyed him closely. "Did you say NBC . . . ? Aren't you the one who's on TV sometimes?"

He cleared his throat. "I suppose I am." He put out his hand. "My name is John Bugatti. I'm a news reporter for NBC."

"Oh, right!" she said. "Now I recognize you. The other day you were reporting on a garden show in front of the Capitol, weren't you? You got in an argument with the lady who'd arranged it, didn't you? You criticized her for . . . What was it now?"

John cringed. "It was about the relative importance of arranging a garden show when the country's in the midst of a crisis."

The young woman's hand flew to her mouth. "Goodness, that's right! And she shoved you, too, didn't she?"

Now the first girl was showing interest, too. "What's happened, since it's so important that you send this e-mail?" She gave a sweet, skeptical little smile, as though the class nerd had just asked her for a date. "Tell us, and I'll let you use my credit card."

"This is simple blackmail." Bugatti laughed weakly, his mind racing to find a ploy.

"We're really not allowed to, you understand."

"Okay, okay, but promise to keep quiet about it, for God's sake." He looked at them sternly until they both nodded. "I saw Tom Jumper getting on a plane a little while ago—disguised as a woman! He was wearing black tights and blue mascara." What harm was there in a little white lie? Jumper was safe for the moment. Hopefully.

Both women stood there with their mouths open. Tom Jumper— wow! One could see they were impressed.

He put his finger to his lips to remind them of their promise and sat down at the computer while one of them swiped her credit card. He wrote in Jumper's e-mail address, plus the words: "Count me in. How do I find you? JB."

It only took half a minute before he received a reply: "This is an automatic answering service. All inquiries can be made by telephone to Gould, Coffey, Morris, & Kaplan," it read.

He took note of the phone number, and one of the young ladies let him use her cell phone while they tried to imagine the phenomenon of Tom Jumper in drag. This was an incredible bit of news that they obviously were going to have a hard time keeping to themselves.

He called the law office. It was a little, efficient firm that specialized in protecting the interests of the entertainment industry's heavyweights. Journalists like him knew these people all too well. If a movie star's cosmetic surgery went wrong, he or she could be sure to receive a calling card from Gould, Coffey, Morris, & Kaplan.

They also got involved if a reporter uncovered some dirt on an actor who didn't meet with the agent's approval. It was a win-win situation for them, no matter what. And the winnings were substantial.

He gave his name to the receptionist and had to wait several minutes before a deep, man's voice identified himself as senior partner Truman Coffey and that he had a personal message for Bugatti.

"How can that be?" asked John.

"Don't ask me. Are you in the vicinity of a fax?"

John got the service center's fax number from one of the girls.

"Please wait by the fax. You'll be receiving confidential information," intoned the lawyer.

Jesus! he thought, when the girl handed him the fax copy a moment later.

"The Pink Box, 12 North Madison St., Middleburg, 2:59 P.M." it read. Not exactly a cornucopia of information.

John could remember he'd been there before, many years ago. He paid an exorbitant amount for the taxi ride with two of Danny's crumpled banknotes and read the sign in front of the miniature stone building. It read: TOURIST INFORMATION CENTER. OPEN WEEKDAYS, 11–3 P.M. WEEKENDS, 11–2 P.M.

The last time he'd visited this pale red building, he'd needed to use the men's room and had been shown the way by an imposingly beautiful eighty-year-old woman with fiery red Lucille Ball lips and a glint in her eye that a few years earlier no man would have been able to forget. She'd spoken about Jacqueline Kennedy as though they'd been close friends, which could have been true, and motioned unsentimentally towards the plot of land next door that housed a wooden pavilion bearing Jackie's memorial plaque.

The pavilion and the plaque were still there, but the old lady was not. He nodded to her replacement and leafed through some tourist brochures as the time approached 2:59.

You better be on time, Tom. They're about to close, he thought, already trying to figure out plan B.

"We're closing in one minute, if there's something I can help you with," said the lady behind the counter. And then the phone rang.

"Yes . . . ? Yes," she answered. "Yes, there is." The woman looked over at John. "Yes. No, I don't know."

Then ask if it's for me, goddammit! he raged silently, considering tearing the phone out of her hand.

"I think it's for you," she finally said, handing him the receiver. "This isn't a public phone booth, you know."

"Yes, it's me," he said, recognizing Jumper's voice.

"Ask her if she has a fax," Jumper said.

He asked and got the same answer about it not being one of their public services, so he laid ten dollars on the counter, saying it had to do with his wife, who was very ill. It worked.

"I'm faxing you the address. Go there immediately" was the last thing Jumper said.

The tourist office had a fax machine, but it was out of paper. John drummed his fingers on the counter while the employee searched in vain for a new roll.

"Then use this," he said, removing Jumper's attorney's fax from his jacket pocket. "Use the back side."

Now he'd been standing at the spot he'd been told to go to for over five hours, and the sky was getting darker and darker. Waiting was starting to become a habit.

"I think you should know it's not so safe out here," this taxi driver had said, as he lit the cigarette butt that had remained unsmoked during the long trip. "There was fighting a couple of miles east of Front Royal the day before yesterday, and there are still militias on the loose. You sure you want to get out here?"

That was one of many questions he'd pondered as he stood there, scouting the undulating planted fields from a niche in the windbreak along the side of the road. He'd read Jumper's fax at least ten times to assure himself that he'd understood it correctly. So here he was, north of Delaplane on Route 17, close to where the railroad line crossed the road, and nothing was happening. Every time an occasional vehicle approached, he grabbed his little suitcase, only to put it down again. A couple of times he thought he saw a patrol car coming and ducked down in the thick brush. He didn't want to have to answer any questions regarding his presence there.

Rain began falling lightly and the wind was starting to blow up from the Shenandoah Valley, and he considered dropping the whole project. "What the hell are you doing out here, Bugatti?" he yelled, up at the threatening clouds. Now it was almost six hours since he was supposed to report for work, and poor Danny must have had his hands full, fending off repeated telephone grillings from Alastair Hopkins. NBC's editor in chief had been a reporter half his life and was a hard man to thwart with lame excuses.

"You don't have any job left anyway, big shot," he sneered at himself. So what was the rush? He had to laugh. Well, a man with AIDS, in the process of giving himself a case of pneumonia, better be in some kind of rush before his body gave up.

"I'm giving you a half hour, Jumper, not a second longer," he told himself. He told himself the same thing an hour later.

Then a massive, white moving van rolled up the road towards him. GULLIVER'S MOVERS, SWIFT & GENTLE GIANTS was written on the cab door. He'd heard of them and at one point had considered using them when Danny was no more; he couldn't stand the thought of living alone in Danny's house. But that was before it had been ascertained that he, too, had AIDS.

He stepped away from the road and was ready to walk back to town, when the truck put on its airbrakes and stopped fifty feet down the road.

A guy opened the passenger door and waved to him. *Sure, why not?* John thought. Jumper obviously wasn't coming anyway, and he couldn't just continue standing there, waiting for pneumonia to finish him off.

The man grabbed his suitcase and asked him to climb into the cab. The driver, big and strong, nodded his consent.

"Okay, let's head south again," the man said into a microphone under his sun visor. The driver backed into a side road and began turning the moving van around.

John was astonished. "Tell me, was it you I was waiting for?" he asked.

The man stuck out his coarse paw. "My name's Phil Kinnead, and that's Pawel. You look wet." Then he turned towards the partition behind them and knocked on it through a thick curtain. "You'll have to step up on the seat to get in there," he said, and pulled the curtain to one side.

A hatch above the back of the seat opened from within, and a head stuck itself out. "We're playing music right now, so come on in." The new man extended his hand and practically pulled him through the hatch into a room of about eight yards square that contained a bed, a little table, a hotplate and refrigerator, as well as a sound mixer that was manned by two guys who presented themselves as friends of Tom Jumper. Above them and stacks of CDs was a glass wall, behind which Tom Jumper sat in a mini-studio, in front of a microphone. He waved through the glass to an accompaniment of country and western music. John hadn't been able to hear a thing outside the van, not even from inside the cab.

"What the hell is this?" he asked the sound engineers. "Did you rent a mobile sound studio from a moving company in Washington?"

They laughed. "This isn't from any moving company. Tom just had their logo copied. No one will suspect us as long as we keep off the main roads."

"But what if you're stopped anyway? Tom will be a sitting duck if they open the back doors." They laughed again. "If they do that, all they'll see is two hundred crates of auditing reports from Virginia's biggest accounting firms, six whole feet into the van from the back doors. It's packed solid with the shit. Believe me, when they see that, they'll let us drive on."

"What are you going to tell them if you get stopped?"

"That the shit's being sent to be destroyed. Incinerated. Depending on where we are, we always know the nearest disposal plant, and that's where we'll say we're going. Simple as that."

John nodded slowly as he removed his wet coat and took his medicine.

"Tom asked us to suggest you take a little nap, so you're fresh for the show later," one of them said.

"We'll wake you up when it's time. When it's the Saturday night show, time waits for no man."

They shook him awake an hour before midnight. Constellations in the sky were gliding rapidly past through a little plexiglass hatch in the roof. They told him he was on in ten minutes and briefed him about what Jumper had in mind to talk about, as well as what he should do if for some reason the show was interrupted. They pointed at a couple of firearms next to the mixer and told him they'd make sure he was safe.

It didn't exactly make him feel more comfortable.

"Where in the world are we?" he asked, rubbing his eyes.

"Beats me. That's the boys in the cab's job, but I figure we're somewhere down around Amisville. We're crisscrossing back and forth. It's just a matter of keeping this buggy moving on the small roads."

"Tom will be calling you John Doe," said the other sound man, "and when we're finished distorting your voice, you won't be able to recognize it yourself, I promise. He's just been talking about Doggie Rogers's escape and the killing of militiamen down by Twin Lakes. You've got to be prepared for him being blunt, no matter what the topic, okay?"

Bugatti knitted his brow and cleared his throat. "Doggie Rogers's escape? What are you talking about?"

"Oh, right, I guess you haven't been able to follow the news. She attacked Sunderland earlier today, and now everyone's out trying to catch her." They both laughed. "They want to bust her for trying to assassinate the VP. Apparently, she kicked him in the balls, which is bad enough, but it's not exactly an assassination attempt!"

"Okay, it's still only a rumor," added the first sound man. "We don't know what she did for sure, but there's going to be plenty of issues to discuss tonight. Later in the program Tom's planning to urge the different units of the army and police to mutiny, so normal law and order can be restored. He's going to try and convince them that they're fighting a hopeless battle for a mentally deranged president, and that they shouldn't fear death. Do you have a problem with that?"

It was hard to say. He had to admit he doubted Bruce Jansen was insane, and he didn't think agitating for mutiny was such a good idea.

"America desperately needs everyone in uniform to wake up," he continued earnestly. "We won't be popular, but people sure as hell will hear what we say."

John took a deep breath. He was having a hard time following all this. Everything was so strange and unreal.

He and Tom Jumper swung well together in front of the microphone, Bugatti had to admit. They began speaking freely from the first moment, which was a relief at a time like this. They discussed Doggie, the Killer on the Roof and their respective conspiracy theories, as well as serious accusations regarding the White House, and began understanding each other with greater and greater clarity.

Bugatti was wishing the same for the listeners.

Then Jumper asked for his version of what happened at the time of the murder of Mimi Jansen in the corridor of the Splendor Hotel.

Does it matter? John asked himself. *Is there still one decent, relevant person who is able to use my viewpoint for anything worthwhile?* But he gave his version of events anyway, including his unfortunate, identity-revealing slip of the tongue.

Afterwards they spoke about Bud Curtis. Tom Jumper called his program the *Last Bastion,* and what could be more fitting when they were on the subject of Curtis? The question was whether what they said would do more harm than good.

After they'd been conversing for half an hour with only a couple of musical interludes, Jumper made a sign to the sound technicians. "Now, dear listeners, during this next musical interlude please meditate on these uppercuts we've just dealt our great American democracy. We're going to play something rather different from Johnny Cash this time, and in the meantime we'll be changing frequencies again, so . . ."

Suddenly a loud ringing in the studio interrupted them. John was completely startled.

"Just a second . . ." said Jumper into the microphone, his eyes on the two sound engineers who were waving their arms on the other side of the glass. Again there was a loud noise, and the men opened the hatch to the truck's cab.

"What's happening?" cried John, watching them pick up the guns from the mixer and release the safety catches. They were in trouble— there was no mistaking it.

"We've got to get out of here!" Jumper yelled to him, pointing at his microphone. "Turn off that switch over there."

Then they flung open the door to the engineering room.

"I'm afraid they've localized us, Tom," one of the engineers shouted. "Phil Kinnead saw some vehicles stopped by the side of the road. Now they're following us."

Jumper opened a drawer underneath the mixer and pulled out a heavy automatic weapon.

"What are you doing?" yelled John. "Are you going to fight back? What if those vehicles are full of soldiers? We'll all be dead before we know it. You know what they do with militiamen they catch after a gun battle, don't you?"

"Shut up, John. Take this and crawl up on the roof through this hatchway. You're just in the way." He handed him a compact little weapon and placed a chair under the plexiglass hatch. "And stay up there till we know how things turn out."

John stared at Jumper, full of wonder. Was this the same man who, just a month ago, could be bothered to spend his time and energy trying to get a woman from Queens to explain why she preferred looking like a whore to wearing a dress that covered her tree-trunk-sized thighs? It was a metamorphosis that could take your breath away.

The driver shouted something to one of the sound engineers while he steered the bus through a sharp curve. "Get up there," ordered the other sound man, shoving John from underneath so he could get through the hatch and up on the roof of the van.

The cold wind hit him right in the face when he was finally all the way up. Headlights from military vehicles were only fifty yards behind them. He lay down flat on his chest, trying to cling to the slippery roof with sweaty hands. Thank God it had at least stopped raining. "Put your foot on the gas!" he yelled into the opening, before they closed it from inside.

Through the distorted plexiglass window he could see them preparing for a fight. Maybe they weren't scared, but he was.

He heard a violent argument erupt inside the van as they approached a fork in the road, with Hume towards the north and Vernon Mills towards the northeast. They were obviously in total disagreement as to which direction to take, though it hardly mattered, since now two more military vehicles were rapidly closing in on them.

"Is this how it's all going to end?" he whispered, thinking about Danny as the van made a sharp turn up Route 688, sending his body sliding sideways. What the hell could he hold on to? Next time they turned like that he'd be flung off the truck. He lifted his head cautiously, spied the plexiglass skylight's frame, grabbed for it, and succeeded in pulling himself back to the middle of the roof. When they wheeled around the next curve he could see that their pursuers from the south had reached the fork before the other vehicles, which looked like personnel carriers. He could also see that there were two armored vehicles of the kind used to bring democracy to Iraq. The shouting inside the van was getting louder; they were apparently urging the driver to coax more power out of the heavily laden vehicle.

John turned his head instinctively, just in time to see streetlamps fly by as they barreled full-speed through the town of Markham. He closed his eyes for the next couple of minutes, praying no cars or pedestrians got in their path. Just as suddenly they were back on a small road, heading in the direction of Sky Meadows State Park. For a moment he thought they'd lost their pursuers, until he heard the first ticking of the armored vehicles' machine guns. He flattened himself even more but could still see the blue-red muzzle fire from the machine guns light up the trees by the roadside. The whole van shuddered as the rear doors were peppered by bullets that spent themselves in the crates of accounting reports. It was a constant smacking noise, like hailstones on a tin roof. He'd heard that same curious, deadly sound half a lifetime ago while covering the drug wars in Colombia, only that time he hadn't been the target.

Shots ripped open the tires on the van's right side just as it reached another thicket of trees, and for a moment John actually considered throwing himself at the tree limbs as they shot past. *Oh, God,* he thought, panicking. *This is it! They're going to see me! These branches are going to knock me off the roof!* Then the truck started swinging wildly, first towards the forest on one side of the road and then a ditch on the other side. The two men in the cab were still shouting at each other as a third man crawled in to them through the partition hatch.

John hugged his weapon and began to pray. Any moment he'd be lying crushed under the huge van, he was sure of it. He could feel every lurch and quiver as the driver fought desperately to keep control, but it was a losing battle. More shots rang out from behind, and tree branches were constantly raking John's back.

"I can't let them notice me, otherwise I'll die right here on the roof," he whispered, and tried to shield his head with his arm. As though that would help.

He felt another great lurch as the front tires finally found traction, and the locked brakes stopped squealing and finally brought the van to a halt. At the same moment he felt his fingernails lose traction as they scraped over the roof's rivets, and peeling paint and his body slid towards the cab until his feet were hanging over the side in midair. The yelling inside the van was replaced by hectic activity that indicated they were getting ready to take up the fight outside the vehicle. They made it out of the cab before their pursuers reached them, but the shots continued, slamming constantly into the back of the truck and past its left side. Before he could try to warn the driver not to exit on the left side, the man jumped out into a hail of bullets. His dead body was blasted ten yards up the road before it hit the ground.

Directly beneath him he saw how two more of the men attempted to run for cover in the dense, pitch-black forest and how a couple of short bursts of fire stopped them in their tracks. Then the pursuing military vehicles finally began screeching to a halt, and he heard hysterical commands surrounding him as soldiers poured out of the personnel carriers. It was a waking nightmare.

His midriff contracted in cramps of fear that sent shivers of pain through his body. He clenched his teeth and could hear the two remaining men in the engineering room screaming beneath him as one of them squeezed himself through the hatchway into the cab, trying to escape. He hoped Tom wasn't one of them. It didn't seem right that a man like him should die like a cornered rat.

Then there was a crash of gunfire from inside the truck. It was a man shooting out through the hatch. *Oh, no! Shit!* This was it. Any second they would fire a shell into the van, and they'd all be incinerated. He tried easing his cramps by inhaling deeply, but nothing helped. If he screamed out his pain and angst, he'd be one dead reporter for sure. Men like him were simply not equipped for situations like this. Maybe one of Associated Press's hotshots who was used to war zones and the closeness of death, but not him.

Why'd you ever do this, John? he tormented himself. *Why didn't you stay in your nice, warm bed in Danny's house? Why didn't you do as your father said, and become a gynecologist?* His masochistic train of thought ended with the sound of three or four short salvos being fired straight in through the cab's windshield to the accompaniment of bursting safety glass.

The man inside had stopped shooting.

"Pull him out through the windshield," yelled one of the officers. "Get him out here on the ground." He heard the ripping of clothing as the body was pulled through the jagged remains of the windshield and over the hood of the cab. "Yep, that's him!" someone yelled, and suddenly John felt his guts relax. They'd gotten Tom Jumper. It was over.

"Is he alive?" someone else asked.

"Are there more in there, asshole?" cried a third soldier, followed by the sound of four or five dull body blows. Each one felt like it had landed on John instead.

"Are there more in there, asshole?!" The shouted question was repeated.

He heard Jumper groan that he was the last one. He groaned once more, and then they shot him without a second thought. Farther behind he could hear the last of the military vehicles arriving, and someone called out that they should take as many live prisoners as they could, not knowing the issue had already been settled. At the same time directly alongside the van, soldiers were muttering about how Jumper's summary execution must not be reported, that he'd died in the heat of battle. That it had been unavoidable.

John noticed once again that he'd forgotten to breathe, and exhaled silently. *Thank you, Tom,* he said to himself, afraid his pounding heart might be audible. *Thank you for saying you were the last one.*

He dragged himself a couple of feet towards the middle of the roof with throbbing fingertips. Behind him the soldiers were discussing what to do with the moving van, eventually deciding it demanded a closer inspection. It was supposed to be the last mobile radio unit with such a powerful transmitter, but one never knew. Perhaps there was a network of transmitters; maybe there were already others who were carrying on Jumper's work.

A couple of the soldiers began rummaging around inside the truck. John's face was ten inches from the plexiglass skylight, but he didn't dare stretch himself forward to look in.

It was at precisely this moment that John remembered his suitcase and laptop, his coat, cell phone, and passport—everything—was all still inside the truck. The adrenaline was pumping so fast, he was afraid the eyes would pop out of his head. Now there was no getting around it: He had to force himself to the skylight to see what was happening. If just one of his possessions caught the attention of a soldier, he was finished. They would realize it had been his distorted voice on the airwaves twenty minutes earlier, they'd check all the bodies and discover that none of them were that of the famous NBC reporter, and then they'd start searching for him until they found him. If they found his passport or driver's license, he'd throw his gun as far into the forest as he could. Then he'd identify himself and surrender, stating his name with as much composure as possible in the hope that it would have a calming effect on his captors. This was his plan of last resort.

He pulled himself forward inch by inch until he could peer down into the sound engineers' room.

No one appeared at first, but then a soldier who had been searching the studio came into view to take a last look around. He had a fat neck and stood with one finger cocked around the trigger of his machine gun.

"There's no one inside here," he yelled out to the others, through the smashed front windshield. John watched the camouflage helmet rotate 360 degrees as the soldier scanned the room one last time— including the ceiling. In a couple of seconds they would be looking straight at each other. John tried to pull back a bit, but the tip of his shirt collar got caught in a rivet that was holding one of the plexiglass hatch's hinges to the roof. In spite of the cold wind, he broke out in a sweat, having no choice but to wait for the soldier's eyes to meet his own. In situations like that, one didn't wait to see if the enemy was willing to surrender; the soldier would tip his machine gun upward, empty it into the ceiling, and that would be that.

John closed his eyes halfway and pictured Danny's tired, beautiful face before him. They'd had a good time together. Better than most.

The soldier's gaze stopped moving across the ceiling. There was no sign of life in the van, and he was gone.

CHAPTER 32

THE SOLDIERS COLLECTED THE BODIES AND LEFT THE MOVING VAN WHERE IT stood. There had been more skirmishes up north along the West Virginia border, and suddenly, after the officers held a meeting under a floodlight from one of their vehicles, everyone was gone. John lay like a corpse on the van's roof until the deep rumbling of the convoy faded completely on the other side of the forest. Then he tried opening the plexiglass hatch, but it was fastened from inside, so he rolled to the edge of the roof and judged that the distance to the ground was about twelve feet. The last time he'd jumped from such a height he'd been a schoolboy and had weighed a quarter of what he did now.

He stuck his gun in his pocket, rotated his body, and slowly, slowly let himself down the side of the van. The roof's steel rivets caught on every fold in his pants and every button on his shirt and poked into his soft body. "Okay, time to let go, old boy," he said, when he was finally hanging over the roof's edge by his fingertips.

The little click his ankle made when he hit the ground was practically inaudible, but it hurt so much that John had to clench his jaw tight to keep from screaming. He was breathing hard and afraid to look at his foot, convinced that it was facing backward. But it wasn't.

Ten minutes later he was sitting in the engineers' room with one of Tom Jumper's colorful neck scarves bound tightly around his swollen ankle, well aware that the sooner he got far away from there, the better.

Stepping around the pool of blood where Jumper had died, he retrieved his suitcase and computer case and left the van. Now the wind outside was ripping through the trees, setting even the heaviest branches in motion. The van's headlights had grown weaker but still lit the road north for a couple of hundred yards. He hitched up the suitcase and tried putting his weight on the damaged ankle. It didn't appear to be broken, but it hurt like hell.

He looked at his watch. It was two o'clock, Sunday morning, in the middle of a curfew that would last another three hours, so he couldn't expect a lift before then—if at all.

He shook his head. Who the hell would be driving through this godforsaken countryside, anyway?

He didn't even know where he was, not to mention where he should be heading. And even if he did, how the hell was he going to manage with this injured foot?

He took a tentative step; it didn't feel good. The suitcase seemed to be filled with lead, and his back and thigh muscles were already bombarding his brain with shooting pains. He'd never been good at pain.

You haven't a choice, he thought. *Hop, stagger, crawl—whatever it takes. Just get away from this goddamn truck.* He looked towards the rolling fields to the south. That direction was out of the question. If a car came, he'd be totally exposed; there'd be nowhere to hide quickly. So he had to head north where there still was some forest to offer cover.

He clenched his teeth and started out, looking over his shoulder constantly. Which was why, after only about twenty small steps, he noticed a blinking blue patrol car light approaching from the south. He immediately ducked into the shrubbery by the side of the road, throwing his suitcase before him, already hearing the police siren. He'd only just hidden himself when the patrol car reached the moving van. He heard the cops get out and begin discussing the situation as his pants sucked up the moldy moisture of the underbrush. Even though the night was pitch-black, he didn't move a muscle because the officers had strong flashlights that they were shining back and forth along the side of the road and into the forest, as well as at the van's shot-up rear end.

Apparently, they were inspecting the big truck's back doors; in any case he could faintly hear their comments about the military's thoroughness and firepower. Their tone of voice was a mixture of envy and disgust.

"We've got to get the technicians up here, Damien. Will you take care of that?" said one of the hushed voices, as it moved alongside the van. "Fingerprints have to be taken, so we're going to have to be careful."

Shit. They were already bringing technicians out. That meant the area would be crawling with cops. John tried to distribute his weight better in the underbrush; he was going to be there a long time. The question was whether it would be better being caught by the police than by the military. It was a tough call.

The policeman walked around to the front of the van and shined his flashlight on the pool of blood left on the ground where the van's driver had landed. It was less than thirty feet from where John was crouching, swallowing his pain like a wounded animal. The officer gave a low whistle as he poked the asphalt and tried to reconstruct the scene in his mind. He didn't seem the type who would show much mercy if John were discovered.

"They're asking if we want anything from town," the other cop called, from down by the patrol car.

"Not here," came the reply.

"Hey, here comes a motorcycle from the direction of Linden. Should I stop it?" yelled the other cop.

"No, I'll stop it up here. You can cover me," he yelled back.

A half minute later John could hear the motorcycle's motor and then see a cone of light flickering through the treetops. The motor decelerated, and the machine rolled to a halt by the cab of the van, where the policeman had his gun trained on its driver.

"I've got a pass," shouted the motorcyclist. "I'm a doctor. I'm on my way to Rockville, up in Maryland, where I live. I work at Bethesda Naval Hospital."

He raised his hands in the air as the officer approached. Then the cop frisked him with one hand, the other hand holding the gun pointed at his head, before asking to see the man's pass. He wasn't taking any chances. There'd been too many stories lately about police-men who hadn't been careful enough.

"Everything's all right here," he reported to his partner.

"What's been going on here?" asked the motorcyclist, when his pass had been returned.

"We stopped a pirate radio station half an hour ago."

"I see . . . Looks like it was pretty violent."

"Yes, it was."

"Anyone killed?"

"I'm not at liberty to say. Would you please move on."

He walked the motorcycle forward a bit. "Can't I just take a pee, now that I'm here?" the driver asked.

"Just as long as you leave right after."

He let the motor idle, dismounted, and took five steps straight to-wards John. "Finally," he said, unzipping his leather pants.

John pulled back an inch, his eyes on the heavy motorcycle boots and the studs that went halfway up the pant legs. "Here comes . . ." the driver sighed, as his stream of urine began soaking the ground around John.

"Ahhh . . ." came the standard sound of satisfaction, then it stopped abruptly.

John hadn't moved a muscle or made a sound the whole time, but it wasn't enough. "What the hell . . . ?" the man said softly, and took a step backward. He looked over at the cop, who was halfway through the hatch between the cab and the sound room. John kept holding his breath. Maybe the guy had only noticed his suitcase. As though that wouldn't be bad enough.

"What are you doing here?" he whispered, but John didn't answer.

"Were you in the van?" he asked, slowly crouching down. John remained silent.

"Are you injured?"

Finally John exhaled. "Yes, slightly. Nothing serious," he whispered.

"Listen! In ten seconds I'm going to walk the bike over here, then you get on, okay? Can you manage that?"

"I don't know. There's something the matter with one of my feet."

"Ten seconds, okay? Before that cop crawls back out of the truck again." He strode back to his treasure of a bike and gave it a little throttle while John reached back for his suitcase and stood up. How was he ever going to stay perched on the back of a motorcycle with a suitcase and a laptop and a useless foot? It had been a hundred years since he'd been on a motorcycle, and even then he hadn't been very good at it.

The driver rolled his machine towards him. He looked to be about John's age, with a long, shaggy gray mustache. He had wrinkles in his face that even the largest helmet couldn't conceal.

The guy looked at his suitcase with disapproval. "Leave it here," he whispered.

"I can't. They can trace me with that," he whispered back, and before he knew it, the man had positioned it on the gas tank between his arms.

"C'mon," he whispered, and pulled an extra helmet out of one of his saddlebags.

John clenched his teeth again and supported himself on his bad foot while he swung his good one over the back of the motorcycle.

"Put this helmet on. Then we can talk while we're driving."

John stuck the laptop between himself and the driver and put on his helmet. There was a little microphone by the mouth hole, just like motorcycle cops had.

"Hold on tight." The command came through a speaker inside the helmet. Before he could answer, the other police officer reached the cab of the van.

"Hey, what's going on here?" he shouted as the motorcycle revved up. John managed to look back in time to see both cops drawing their weapons before his head was slung back by the accelerating motorcycle.

"I think they're going to shoot," yelled John, as loud as he could.

"So let them, but don't scream so loud or you'll make me deaf."

John heard the crack of shots as they reached the first turn in the road.

"Oh, thank God, thank God," he whispered, as he realized he hadn't been hit.

He explained to his savior what had happened as they roared through the night landscape. Not in detail, but most of it.

"Bloody hell! Did they really get Tom Jumper?" the driver asked. "Is there anyone who knows you were on his radio program?"

"I wouldn't be surprised."

"You are in deep shit, Mr. Bugatti, but I guess that's nothing new for you. Where are you headed now?"

"I don't know. I can't figure out what to do. You said you were on your way to Rockville, that you were a doctor."

"That's what I said, yes."

"It's not true?"

"What do *you* think?"

"But you have a pass."

"Yes, for myself, but not for you, so we can't stop anymore."

"I assume you're aware that every police and military unit in Virginia is already on the lookout for us."

"Yes, that's not too hard to figure out. But there's not much army out tonight; FEMA's ordered most of them to Washington because of the British prime minister's visit." Then he gave the throttle another twist. John had never driven so fast in his life. "Do you have someone you can stay with?" he asked.

"Maybe, and maybe not. But I know a lot of people around Washington and New York."

"You're not going to New York. That party's over for you." He laid the motorcycle into a curve. John had to close his eyes. "Hey, you don't have to hold on to me so tight. Nothing's going to happen." He laughed and John loosened his grip. "Who do you know in Washington? Can't you call them and have them meet you somewhere?"

"I don't think I'd ask anyone to do that."

"Well, I'll get the both of us over the Potomac at White's Ferry. They're waiting for me down there. Then we'll see what we can do. Is there anyone you want to call?"

"I can't."

"Why not?"

"It's not a good idea for me to use my cell phone. I've been told they can track it."

"Then why don't you use mine?" the driver asked, while the wind flattened John's cheeks back to his ears. You can just speak into the microphone. I'll connect you. What's the number?"

In the old days John would be consumed by jealousy if Danny took too long answering the phone, but now he just got anxious.

And it didn't sound like Danny was doing well at all when he finally took the phone. "My God, John, where are you?" he asked, having trouble breathing, and coughing a little. "No, you better not tell me. Maybe it's best I don't know." He coughed again; it hurt John to hear it. "Are you okay, John? Tell me."

"Yes, no matter what you may hear, I'm okay, Danny. Understand? Don't believe what other people tell you."

"You make me afraid when you talk like that, John. What might people say?"

"Nothing, Danny. I just want you to know I'm okay."

"I have a message to you from Doggie Rogers." Bugatti could hear his driver grunt in surprise.

"Who's with you, John? Is someone listening to us?"

"Yes, but don't worry. It's okay. It's a friend."

Danny sighed on the other end of the line, but not like after the hundreds of times John had lied before. This time it was almost as though Danny was hoping he was out having a good time. At least that's how he sounded.

Out having a good time? He had a hard time remembering what it was like.

"He's seeing to my transportation, Danny, that's all. We're on a motorcycle right now, and he's listening in."

"Okay. Then take good care of my friend, you there. Please?" he said.

"Don't worry, I will," answered the biker.

"Doggie Rogers called?" said John. "When was that?"

"It wasn't that long ago. A couple of hours, I think. What time is it now?"

"Around two thirty."

"Yes, that sounds about right. She said you should try to meet her in Washington tomorrow. I couldn't bring myself to tell her you were far, far away. Because you are, aren't you?"

"Just tell me where she wanted me to meet her, Danny."

"At Market Square. At a tea salon called Teaism. Between one and two in the afternoon. God, you're not around here, are you, John? Should I meet you there, too?"

"No, Danny, I'm not near Washington. You just look after yourself. I'll call again as soon as I have a chance."

He tapped the driver on the back to let him know he was finished talking. The conversation hadn't been very uplifting, to say the least. Danny sounded in worse shape than ever. And then the message from Doggie, that they should meet in the lion's den. Two of the most wanted fugitives in the United States.

How was he ever going to make it to Market Square?

They were heading north via small, crooked side roads. John asked several times what the purpose of the driver's trip was and what he actually did for a living, but each time was told that, just like Danny, the less he knew, the better.

It wasn't a very satisfactory answer for a journalist like John.

Out on Route 15, just north of Leesburg, they discovered they were being followed and gave the motorcycle more gas. It was a relatively anonymous pickup with a set of fog lights and other flashy extras, but from the speed at which it was traveling, there was no doubt it was following them. It had popped up from an even smaller side road, as though it had been waiting for them.

"Hold on tight!" yelled John's driver, and he wasn't kidding. They swung out into the middle of the road, and the motor revved up to a high-pitched, skull-splitting whine. John tried to get a glimpse of the speedometer, but his view was blocked by a set of shoulders as wide as John was tall. The landscape was a blur; they must have been doing at least 120 miles per hour.

Then there was a ringing inside the helmet, and the guy connected his phone.

"We're right behind you, Sean," a voice said. "I guess you noticed."

Okay, it was someone he knew—a friend. The question was, what kind of friend?

"So what's going on?" John's rescuer—apparently named Sean— asked. "Why are you showing up now?" John couldn't have put the question better himself.

"We've been waiting for you for a quarter of an hour. There's a bunch of patrol cars heading straight for us from the north. They've localized you."

"How many vehicles?"

"Three."

"How close together are they?"

"Close."

"Okay, good. And what do you guys recommend?"

"Maintain your speed. When you meet them—and you will, before you reach the shortcut to the ferry—brake hard and make for the side of the road. We have a vehicle coming at them from behind, so don't worry—we'll take care of them. Just drive off on the side of the road as soon as the first patrol car spots you."

Sean laughed. "Sounds like this is going to be heavy."

"We've fixed situations worse than this, you know that."

They broke phone contact. Sean remained still as a statue for a few moments as they barreled over the asphalt.

"I'm assuming we're in the same boat here, right?" he finally said.

"Of course," John answered. He dared not answer otherwise. It all sounded worrying in the extreme, but what could he do now, rocketing across Virginia on the back of a motorcycle?

"Good. When we go our separate ways, forget you ever heard my name. Forget all of this, okay? *I* know who *you* are, Bugatti, and I heard you tonight on Jumper's program. That was good work you did, no doubt about it. You have to be in Washington tomorrow, and I'll see to it that you make it. Then you forget all about this."

"Are you going to Washington yourself?"

"Let's call it that."

"And you know a way to get over on the cable boat at White's Ferry, even at four o'clock Sunday morning?"

"That's right."

"Something tells me you're connected with the militia coalition. Am I right?"

"Hey, dude, give it a rest. Hate to tell you, John, but now I'm going to have to dump your suitcase. In a little while we're *really* going to have to hold on. You get rid of your laptop, too, understand? Now! Else this can all end in a real fucking mess."

John saw his suitcase flick by his head like a shadow, about to bust into pieces and spray its contents all over the road. John sighed and launched his laptop towards a similar fate. The little sucker had cost him over $1,100 out of his own pocket.

"What do you have to do in Washington?" John kept up, cautiously, but he got no response.

"Hey, now I can see blue lights flashing ahead of us!" Sean punched a series of numbered buttons on his control panel to contact the pickup that was following them at a distance of fifty yards. "Do you see them?" he asked.

"Roger," a voice replied. "Take care of yourself. Big brother's got the 'swatter.'"

"Fine. See you in Cairo, the sixth of October."

"There's a lot of wind in here. . . . What'd you say?"

"See you in Cairo, the sixth of October!" Sean yelled again.

"Yeah, that's right," said a crackling voice in response.

What the hell are they talking about? John wondered, and noticed the bike braking slightly.

"Ten seconds!" Sean yelled into his microphone, and John instinctively squeezed his body closer to the driver's. Strangely enough, he no longer felt afraid. Maybe he'd stopped feeling altogether.

He heard the police car sirens just before the motorcycle began to spin out. As the brakes locked, the back wheel started churning sideways across the asphalt in a cloud of burnt rubber. For a moment they were still propelled forward, but practically sideways, so he could see three patrol cars positioned abreast, four hundred feet ahead, heading straight for them. But then the bike straightened out, wobbling a couple of times before Sean slammed on the brakes a second time. Just as John was certain they'd both be heading over the bike's front forks, he released the brakes again and banked the motorcycle into a sharp turn, careening towards the shoulder of the road.

John could see lights off in the distance, maybe from farms where the morning milking had already begun. He could remember what it was like from all the times he was at his uncle's when he was a boy. They'd gotten up much too early. Not a life for him, he thought in the seconds he reckoned would be his last, but then the bike straightened up and came to a halt.

The next second the souped-up pickup shot past them. He heard it braking and the men shooting from inside at the same time. But it wasn't the usual heavy gunfire, it was more like explosions, and the same sounds erupted from the other vehicle that was pursuing the patrol cars from behind. All three police cars lit up as they were hit and then, at the same moment as Sean started gunning the throttle again, they exploded simultaneously in a merciless sea of flames.

The pickup stopped diagonally across the road, less than thirty yards from the inferno. Two men jumped out and sprayed the police cars with machine-gun fire as Sean popped the clutch. In less than ten seconds he cut around the burning vehicles and past his accomplices. John could see figures inside the cars, desperately trying to kick the windows out until they were consumed by the flames.

It was cold-blooded murder.

They didn't speak until White's Ferry Road made a sharp turn down along the river and the beautiful view engulfed them in a playful, early-morning embrace that hinted at springtime.

"They're already coming after us over there, see?" he said, pointing out over the calm waters.

It was true. The rope ferry was heading towards them from the Maryland shore, over by the east side of the Potomac.

He'd taken that ferry once, long ago. It had been a day in autumn with the foliage flaming in all the colors of an artist's palette. Nothing on earth could have been more beautiful.

CHAPTER 33

THE COMMOTION ON DEATH ROW ALL STARTED WHEN THEY RECAPTURED BUD and threw him back in his cell. A few of the inmates wailed out their frustration over the fact that an otherwise completely improbable escape attempt had been thwarted, but most of them joined in the disturbance because they had no other way to express their fundamental hatred for everything and everyone—probably themselves in particular. The entire unit was transformed into an inferno of cell thrashing, pissing on the walls, and barrages of curses.

The prison guards responded quickly. They hauled fire hoses down to the cells of the prisoners who had reacted most violently, and each massive shot of water through the bars was followed by a splat as the inmate was smacked against the wall. Cell by cell the tumult gradually began to subside.

Daryl kept heckling Bud about the cigarettes he believed were owed him, until Curtis retreated to the far corner of his cell. The pain in his soul had become unbearable.

Now all hope was gone. All that was left was his meager apportionment of time, and the pain; the rest of life's options were spent. T. Perkins had yelled to him not to give up. But he had, nonetheless.

Death row woke up the next morning after a few hours' calm. Some of the militiamen up by the unit's entrance began shouting slogans, and others joined in with songs proclaiming Moonie Quale the country's next president, who would preside over an era where everything was put back to "normal," where Americans could once again hold their heads high. Some complained loudly that it was all because of Bud Curtis, that it was even his fault that life on death row was intolerable. Their exertions earned them another dousing with the fire hoses, after which Bud could sense how their silent hatred permeated his cell, right down to the steel cot upon which he would be sitting the last twenty-three hours before they finally took his miserable life.

Death row was fully manned, and more than one guard let himself be affected by the inmates' rotten mood and whacked the bars of Curtis's cell with his nightstick as he went by.

"We just might take you first, you miserable cocksucker," they snarled at him.

As punishment for their disobedience the day before, they weren't fed until three o'clock that afternoon, about the same time as Daryl Reid received his much-publicized last meal. The priest had already been in to see him before proceeding to give the rest of the prisoners his blessing. It was Sunday, in spite of everything.

Daryl himself was one of the few inmates who appeared to be completely unaffected by the few hours in which he had to live, expressing his noisy satisfaction with each item on the menu. No one could avoid hearing in detail how much better his food was than the crap being served to the others. Yes, Daryl was determined to make it through the day without breaking down.

For his own part, Bud wasn't sure it would be so easy when his time came.

He had worked hard all his life. A whole lot of people had found employment thanks to his diligence and great visions. And he'd never really crossed anyone when it came to doing business. He'd given everyone a fair shake. It wasn't unreasonable for him to imagine that, besides gaining people's respect for his efforts, he could also win their love. That his ex-wife, his daughter, and his many employees would forgive him his eccentricities and think of him and remember him with affection. Now, with his life almost over, he couldn't see any indication that he'd succeeded. Not even with his precious Doggie. He knew she had respect for him and was capable of forgiving him his peculiarities, but she'd never expressed it. Maybe it was simply a fact of life that human beings offered more tenderness and encouragement to their progeny than their progenitor.

Bud's thoughts drifted back through the years, to the time when his father used to come home late every evening from the tobacco field with deep cracks in his worn-out hands. Had he ever told his father how thankful he was that he never drank up his wages like the other day laborers, that he appreciated the fact that there was food on the table every day? No, he never had. Nor had he ever hugged his mother as she had hugged him. He had moved on without thinking twice, as though life with his parents were something one had to endure and get over with. And now, here he was, without a hand to hold and no one to tell him his life hadn't been worthless.

Where was Doggie right now? Didn't she want to come to him? Didn't his lawyers, either? Or any of his family or old friends? If so, they had better hurry, because after Daryl was executed it meant no more visits for Bud. He knew the procedures. Nothing that could upset the condemned just before they were executed—that was Warden Falso's policy. A policy that was surely based on experience.

He tried to read a little from the Bible that lay open on his cot. Finding consolation wasn't easy. What kind of consolation could make him forgive and forget the injustice committed against him? Make him forget the leather straps and the lethal needle?

Perhaps he would go to heaven, but it was hard to say for a man who never in his life had thought in these kinds of terms.

Daryl was looking good as they handcuffed him in the hallway in front of Bud's cell. He'd consumed all the food that had been laid before him, and the two jumbo bottles of Coke had sent him running to his steel toilet four or five times. Now there he was, wearing a spotless white T-shirt, smiling contentedly with his belly full. He smoothed back his thinning, gray, frizzy hair and looked like he was about to take an enjoyable stroll in the countryside or visit old friends. Maybe he really saw it like this—that death was a good thing. And maybe it was. Not only for Daryl, who'd spent the past ten years of his life in this wretched place, but for Bud as well.

"See ya tomorrow, Buddy Boy," he said, and winked. "I don't know if they allow smoking in heaven, so I better give you these back."

He tried to hand him what was left of the cigarettes Bud had given him the day before, but Bud shook his head. "Give them to one of the others, Daryl. May God be with you."

Two prison guards led him away, one hand under each arm. It was the last time Bud would have to watch a scene like this. It was all for the best.

"Take care of yourself," he heard Daryl say to each inmate as he passed. His was the only voice to be heard.

They slammed the door separating the execution unit from the rest of death row, apparently a signal for the militia members to continue venting their hatred. They kicked and shook the bars of their cells and smashed their fists into the steel bed frames and toilets, screaming about how America was being eaten alive by worms in Washington and that Bud Curtis deserved being offed immediately.

Bud barely even heard them. He'd given up caring. They could trash the whole prison and yell their lungs out for all he cared. In fact, he wished they would.

Falso's voice rang out over the speaker system a few times, warning them to shut up, or else. Presumably they were disturbing Falso's death ritual on the other side of the steel door. But what did it matter if Daryl received a little vocal accompaniment on his way to meet his maker? Was it upsetting the military chaplain as he said the last rites? Maybe the screaming made it impossible for Falso to hear himself pronounce the death sentence.

Finally, Bud put his hands over his ears. He hated them, one and all.

"Bastards!" he heard himself yell. "You're all a bunch of bastards! Goddamn murderers and bastards—that's what you are! I'm the only one here who doesn't have blood on his hands. You disgust me—all of you. You should never have been born. You were all a goddamn, fucking, horrible mistake!" He took a deep breath to achieve higher volume. "That goes for you fucking pig cops, too! Do you hear me, you fucking murderers, or are you too busy taking care of Daryl?"

By now one of the militiamen had hammered his toilet loose, and a small stream of water was making its way out of his cell and down the hallway. Another had succeeded in ripping out his sink and had begun smashing it against the bars of his cell, screaming: "Come here, Curtis, let's wash your filthy mouth out with soap. Let me ram this down your throat, then we won't have to listen to you anymore!"

Bud almost laughed; everything was so grotesque. "Beautiful, you idiots," he said quietly. "Wreck everything, then you can wallow in your own shit until they come to take you away." He noticed how reacting loosened him up, so he started screaming again as loud as he could. "Go ahead, fuck up your beds so they're uncomfortable as hell the rest of your days!" He shrieked with laughter, and the more they carried on, the more he laughed.

Then they heard the unit's main door being unlocked, and two officers rushed in and ran the length of the hallway, appraising the situation. They looked ready to panic. Bud recognized one of them as the portly Freddie Cambell from the guard post the day before. It was the first time Bud had ever seen him on death row. Freddie looked around in confusion, shouted something to his partner, ran down to the door to the death chamber, and began banging on it.

A minute later more guards arrived to cool the inmates down with the fire hoses. Bud was hit right in the face and could feel the skin practically being blasted off. The stream of water pinned him to the back wall for the ten seconds it was trained on him, then he fell to the floor, hitting his head on the edge of his bed frame and almost passing out.

After three minutes of total chaos, there was only the sound of dripping, trickling water. Falso was back, taking stock of his men's work, but Curtis couldn't quite hear what he was saying.

It was something about enough being enough, and they had no other choice.

Then they entered his cell and beat him about the head and shoulders until he began drifting into unconsciousness again—where nothing mattered or hurt anymore and his soul could find peace.

A half hour later they revived him with a bucket of water. And it began all over again.

CHAPTER 34

IT WAS AFTER TWO O'CLOCK SUNDAY MORNING. THE CURFEW HAD JUST BEGUN by the time the milk truck stopped in front of Josefine Maddox's yard in southern Virginia. Doggie was totally exhausted in both body and soul.

"Do you have a cell phone?" she asked the driver when he let her out of the milk container. Solid ground and the sudden fresh air made her dizzy.

"No, we're not allowed to make private calls during working hours."

"How about a CB radio?"

"You think that's a jumbo jet cockpit I've got up there?"

"But I have a problem," she told the driver.

He gave her a weary look. He'd been on the job more than twenty hours; what did he care if she had problems? Hadn't he done all that he could?

"I have to meet a man in Washington at noon."

"What? You're fucking kidding!" He looked seriously annoyed. "What kind of shit is this? Why'd we drive all the way down here, then?"

"That transistor radio you gave me, remember? You heard the same program as I did, right? So you know what's happened. Didn't you want me to hear what they were saying about me and my father?"

He stared at her blankly.

"My dad's innocent. I've got to go to Washington and speak with the president."

"Tell me, wasn't it Washington you escaped from yesterday? Why do you want to go back now? You expect them to have the red carpet and champagne ready?" Then he smiled for once. She hadn't heard him this talkative.

"A lot has happened since yesterday. I still have friends in Washington; they'll give me a hand." She took a deep breath. "Listen, we know President Jansen had nothing to do with his wife's death, right? If what Bugatti said on Tom Jumper's program is correct, then it's someone high up in the government who's behind it, and the president has a right to know, don't you think?"

"It's curfew. We have to wait till five before we can go."

"Then you'll drive me up there?"

"It's on my way, isn't it? But it'll cost you."

"Of course, what else? Is fifteen hundred dollars enough?"

"Two thou," he said matter-of-factly. A man of principle.

"Okay, that's a deal. But there's one other thing. . . ." She handed him the $2,000 and added $1,500, then told him how she'd relieved herself in the tank, and about the pieces of plaster all over its stainless steel floor. She'd expected him to be pissed off, naturally enough, but she wasn't ready for his explosion of rage. After all, she had told him voluntarily and was willing to pay him extra. But the skin of his dark face became noticeably lighter, and he went into a kind of spontaneous war dance of fury. She'd never heard such an uninterrupted string of curses and oaths in her life. If there was one thing for sure, he yelled, it was that he had to report for work in New York the next evening, and the milk container had to be as sterile as an operating theater during a heart transplant. What had she been thinking, filthy whore, shitting on the floor of his tank?

She didn't answer, just stuck another hundred-dollar bill in his breast pocket and left him fuming in front of his dairy truck. Then she suggested that, if he asked nicely, he'd probably be able to borrow a broom, a rag, and a wet mop from Rosalie Lee's sister.

Rosalie's sister's place was set back from the road, the paint peeling off its walls as though it hadn't been kept up for decades. It looked dismal and destitute in the pale moonlight. Half the shutters lay on the ground, the front porch railing had collapsed, and there were piles of trash and discarded junk everywhere. Things that had cost blood, sweat, and tears at the time were now rotting and rusting away, negating a life of toil and modest dreams.

She knocked on the door several times and waited. *Maybe she's not here anymore,* she thought, and cupped her hands around her mouth. "Mrs. Maddox!" she shouted, up towards the second-floor windows. "I've been sent here by your sister. Please, won't you open the door?"

It took another five minutes before the shape of a little, worn-out woman appeared behind the screen door. "I have a knife," came a slow, rusty voice.

Doggie pressed her face against the screen. "I'm not going to do anything to you, Mrs. Maddox, okay? Rosalie sent me down here. Maybe I can stay and sleep a few hours. I can pay you."

She wanted to see the money, she said, and Doggie waved two hundred-dollar bills. She didn't say hello as she opened the door.

"Thank you, Mrs. Maddox," said Doggie, handing her the money.

Josefine Maddox didn't look at all like Rosalie. She was small and wiry, and her face was completely expressionless. A grubby kimono hung from her bony shoulders, and her tattered slippers were two sizes too big. Still, there was something imposing and dynamic about the woman. Her life had doubtlessly had more than its share of trials, but her deportment showed that not only had she dealt with them, but she still hadn't given up the fight.

Her eyes narrowed. "What have you done?" she asked, sticking the money into the pocket of her kimono.

"I attacked the vice president."

"Did he die?" she asked.

"No, he's just fine. It was nothing, really."

"You can stay here till it gets light, then you have to leave."

Doggie nodded.

"It's not safe here," Josefine continued. "The militias have been inside my house two times. They're camped in the forest behind here."

"Did they do anything to you?"

"The militias? Goodness no! It's the soldiers you've got to watch out for. Yesterday they cut the phone lines. They probably expect the militias will be back, which they likely will." She pricked up her ears. "Listen, they're shooting again. It's closer than yesterday."

Doggie held her breath but heard nothing. This Mrs. Maddox must have had the hearing of a Doberman.

"The soldiers asked me to clear out, but where the hell to? I don't know anyone lives around here no more, and I ain't going back to New York, neither. It's the city of Satan. Worse than Sodom and Gomorrah, as far as I'm concerned, and always has been, amen! So I'm staying, I am. Sure as Jesus is my Lord and savior."

There was a knock on the door. It was the driver.

He gave Doggie a cold look and handed her some money. "Here's two thousand. I'm keeping the sixteen hundred. You're going to have to find someone else to drive for you. You're not coming with me."

She tried to give back the money. "But how can I find someone else to help me? Listen, I'm really sorry about what I did. I'm sorry, I'm sorry, I'm sorry, but I just couldn't hold myself any longer. You know how many hours I had to sit there."

"Find someone else," he repeated, and turned towards Josefine to ask to borrow some implements to clean out his milk container.

"How much do you want, then?" Doggie pleaded, rummaging around in her plastic bag for more banknotes.

"I don't want your fucking money. I'm *not* driving you!" He turned on his heel and disappeared into the milk tank with a mop and broom.

Doggie Rogers sat in the kitchen, staring at a cup of weak tea, trying to figure out how to tackle the situation. "I wonder, do you know anyone who can drive me to Washington when the curfew's over?"

Josefine shook her head.

"You said they cut the telephone lines. Does that mean you have no phone connection at all? No cell phone?"

The way the old lady laughed was answer enough.

Doggie bit her lip. The people who were after her knew she had

Frank Lee's cell phone, of that she was certain. Two hours ago she'd called Uncle Danny, believing his phone was safe, only to find out he was John Bugatti's lover. Doggie didn't know how the government's state-of-emergency surveillance system functioned—it wasn't something they advertised in the White House—but she was sure they kept a close eye or ear on powerful journalists like Bugatti. Which meant they knew she wanted to meet him that afternoon at the teahouse in Washington. Which also meant they knew she was presently somewhere in Virginia. Why else would her cell phone have rung just after her conversation with Uncle Danny? Rosalie wouldn't have called her in the middle of the night, and she was the only one who knew the number. Or was she? Doggie doubted it could have been one of Frank's friends. His brother Dennis had said he never used his cell phone, so why would someone suddenly call him?

No, the only possibility was that the phone was tapped, she was convinced. The phone call had been in order to track her whereabouts. The only question was:

Had they succeeded?

She tried to relax her shoulders. *Take it easy,* she admonished herself. How could they know where she was now? At best, they only knew she was somewhere in Virginia, and Virginia was a pretty big place to have to find somebody.

She sat and thought a little more. If whoever had called her had been working for the government, they must have known whose phone she was using and sooner or later would be showing up at Rosalie's door to force the truth out of her. On the other hand, Rosalie's eldest son, James, had voluntarily gone to the police station to tell the cops she'd been in their home, and they had no way of knowing that in the meantime little-brother Dennis had driven her to the milk truck by the Washington Bridge. James would never have told them.

No, of course he wouldn't, but sooner or later her pursuers would put two and two together. So there she was, with no way of moving on and no way to warn Bugatti via Uncle Danny. If she used the cell phone one more time, they'd be able to trace her exact location, but if she did nothing, she'd be sending John Bugatti straight into a trap.

And in the meantime, her father was awaiting his death not far from Josefine Maddox's house. She could do nothing to save either of them. Nothing whatsoever.

"May I call you Josefine?" she asked cautiously, trying to catch the skinny woman's attention, but the old lady was staring off into the forest and didn't answer.

"Josefine, you have to help me. Don't you think you can find someone who'll drive me to Washington? I'll pay. You, as well. If it's not enough, I can make sure you get the rest later. She stuck her hand into the plastic bag to find what remained of her cash.

"No, I don't know anyone . . ." whispered Rosalie's sister. "Be quiet now . . ."

Doggie could hear it, too: new rounds of fire from deep within the forest.

"They're not close by," said Doggie.

"Shhh! Listen!"

But she could hear nothing.

Josefine picked up the same big knife with which she had greeted Doggie.

"What's happening?" whispered Doggie. "I can't hear anything."

She followed a couple of steps behind Josefine into the dark living room with its lingering odor of old man and cigar.

"They came in this way last time," she whispered, pointing towards the moonlit patio. "And I think they're trying again."

Doggie's eyes moved across the edge of the forest and along the black earth up to the house. Maybe there was a chance she could force her driver to take her to Washington if she threatened to report him to the police. Would he take such a threat seriously? Perhaps he would; she suspected life had given him enough to tend to already.

Josefine stopped suddenly. "Get out of here!" she spat into the darkness.

Doggie didn't see the shadow until it began trying to force open the patio door. "Let me in," called a deep voice, "or I'll break the door down, and you *know* I will!"

"I have guests. You can't come in today."

"I'll count to three. One . . ."

At this point Josefine began invoking Jesus and all the apostles. "Why me?" she implored. "Haven't I always minded my own business?"

"Two . . ."

Then she stepped to the door and unlocked it.

"What's that vehicle parked in your front yard?" asked the voice.

"Just take it and clear out," said Josefine. She turned on the light, and the living room revealed itself in all its repulsiveness. Every surface—every corner—was a deep, dark brown from her deceased husband's tobacco habit, as were the curtains and furniture.

The militia soldier stepped through the doorway and examined Doggie. "Are you the one who came with the milk truck?"

What he lacked in height he made up for in breadth. Weeks in the forest had left their mark all over his clothes and face. His hair was disheveled and his skin bore witness to the days and nights of living close to the earth and far from a bath. There was an emblem sewed on the shoulder of his military shirt consisting of a couple of Gothic letters, a spread-winged eagle, and a pair of crossed weapons. While Doggie didn't recognize the emblem, it resembled those of the other militias. There had never been much emphasis on originality in those circles.

"The milk tanker's run out of gas. It's just by chance I got stuck here."

The man's eyes lit up with suspicion as he turned to Josefine. "You've got a pickup parked over behind the shed."

"So you finally saw it. Go ahead, take it. We bought it thirty years ago, and even then it was a bad deal. If you can get it to run, more power to you. My husband sure couldn't. But first you've got to find a way to pump up the tires. They're as flat as a sow's ass." She cackled and put down the knife.

"Is there diesel in the tank?"

"Probably."

Doggie shook her head. Now he was going to siphon off the diesel for the milk truck. But then he'd have to confront the outraged driver, who definitely wouldn't give up his truck without a fight.

"Where are you driving to?" she asked, avoiding his eyes.

"None of your business, little lady."

"Okay, you don't know who I am, do you?" Her raised eyebrow emphasized the scorn in her voice. "I'm Doggie Rogers, the one who assaulted the vice president. Don't you follow the news? Everyone in the country's looking for me. I'm in deeper shit than you are, so I think you ought to tell me where you're going."

He looked skeptical. "Doggie Rogers? Prove it."

She went out to the kitchen and fished her White House ID out of her bag. "The hair's a little different, but look at the eyes. Are you convinced now?" she asked.

He studied the photo for a moment, then grabbed the plastic bag out of her hand. "What else you got in there?" She tried to grab it back, but he shoved her away.

"Well, hello there," he said, removing a bundle of banknotes. "Thirty-seven hundred dollars," he counted. "Not bad! This money is hereby confiscated by the Pulaski Militia. Would you like a receipt?" He gave a grunt that was as close as he could come to a laugh. What the hell, he could make any noise he wanted with the little automatic he had stuck in his belt. Fucking jerk.

It occurred to Doggie that, if he came from Pulaski, this wasn't really his home turf. "Are you going to Pulaski?" she asked.

He didn't answer. Instead he dumped out the contents of her plastic bag, including her cell phone.

"Bingo!" he cried. "This is almost even better."

"Don't you turn that on," she hissed.

He raised a finger, warning her not to come closer.

"If you do, this place will be swamped with cops and soldiers within twenty minutes. Do you understand me? Aside from Michael K. Lerner, Moonie Quale, Tom Jumper, and John Bugatti, I'm the most wanted person in the US, believe me. You're not using that phone, got it?"

He raised his head slowly, revealing the full scope of his defiant jaw. If she could have, she would have punched it free of his ugly face.

"I see the PIN code's been scratched on the backside." He grunt-laughed again. "Bravo, lady. Thanks a lot."

Doggie lunged at him and tried to grab the phone—then kick it—out of his hand, but without success. When he got tired of her fulminations he swung a heavy fist into her chest that sent her flying backward into a musty easy chair. There she sat, gasping for breath, as he turned on the phone and dialed a number.

He nodded as he stared into space. "Benson here. I'm coming to Cairo. . . . Yeah, opportunity knocked. I'll be there in four or five hours. . . . Yeah, around eight or nine. Is the 'swatter' in position?" He nodded again. "Do we have the manpower? Fantastic! It's gonna be like a lightning bolt, for God's sake! Listen, I've got Doggie Rogers with me here. . . . Yes, her. . . . Yeah, I've got her under control. She's got a White House ID, so maybe . . . Right. Precisely. I'll bring her with me." He folded the phone together and stuck it in his pocket.

"Turn it all the way off!" she hissed again. It was the only way the words would come out.

"Sorry. My cell phone battery ran out last week, and I'll kill you before I'll let you turn it off. Just try me."

"You bastard! Don't say I didn't warn you!"

He took Josefine by the jaw and pressed her thin face even thinner. "Go to bed, woman. We're leaving now."

Then he pushed her over and dragged Doggie out of the chair. "Get your coat on," he ordered. Out in the bitter cold he headed for the shed behind which stood the pickup. As they passed the dairy truck, complaints and curses could be heard from within the milk container. The driver was still performing his dirty task.

"What the hell? Is there someone in there?" said the man, giving her a shake as he took the gun out of his belt for the first time. "Get up into the cab. I'll kill you if you so much as stick one toe out, you understand?"

She obeyed and could hear him mounting the stainless steel cylinder. Then he yelled down through the hole in the top, and there were muffled sounds inside the container, accompanied by indistinct shouting. Then suddenly they were both standing in front of the truck. Her driver was even more livid than before, if that were possible, but it did him little good.

Two hours later they were heading north. The militiaman was sitting opposite her inside the container in the near-darkness, rolling himself a cigarette. He was unshaven and scruffy and, with his weapon in his belt, could have been one of Che Guevara's guerrilla warriors. The hatch above them was open, so they could see the last fading stars in the early morning sky; there was no way her captor was going to let himself be locked inside. Up in the cab the driver had undergone a transformation and had become mild as a lamb. The miracle came as a result of having to give up his gun and his wallet. Not because he'd suddenly been rendered both defenseless and penniless—which was bad enough—but because the militiaman had found his home address and informed him that his family would pay the consequences if he didn't drive where he was told. Just a simple phone call, he said, tapping Doggie's cell phone, and it was all over for his wife and two over-fed daughters. He'd hate to have to do it, he said, because he had two daughters himself. But that's how it was.

This had had the desired effect, and now the driver was back behind the wheel, hamstrung and grumbling softly, as the milk truck tore through the landscape. The faster the better, if he were to reach New York by nightfall.

We'll never make it, thought Doggie. *They will have localized us long before.*

The militiaman took a couple of drags on his cigarette and checked the contents of the driver's wallet one more time, emptying it, item for item. Then he took the money he'd gotten off Doggie and placed it in the wallet alongside the money that she had given the driver. Next he reached inside his breast pocket and took out two sheets of lined, folded-up paper. He unfolded them and studied them for a moment with obvious satisfaction, folded them up again, and stuck them in the wallet. He looked pretty proud of himself as he put the wallet back into the pocket of his camouflage jacket.

"Where are we going?" she asked for the fifth time.

"To Cairo, I told you."

"Yeah, that much I understand. But is it Cairo in Georgia or West Virginia, or where? There are Cairos in every other state in the country, so which one?"

The guy didn't answer, he just spat on the floor. More cleaning work for the driver.

"I have to be in Washington by noon. My father's life depends on it, understand?"

"What can you do about it there?"

Doggie noticed his attentive expression. He wasn't as dumb as he looked. Yes, what could she do in Washington? She couldn't very well say she was going to pay the president a visit. She'd better not say much, in fact. She bit her upper lip. Damn that cold floor—here she was again! And she was in more danger than ever.

"What are your daughters' names?" she asked. Surefire way to soften a person up, she figured.

He looked at her contemptuously. "What's your boyfriend's name?" he mimicked. "Then I can send him a postcard telling him where the garbage can is that's got your head in it because you couldn't keep your mouth shut with shit like that."

She looked at the floor. "What are you going to use my ID card for? You'll never get into the White House with it, if that's what you think."

"Names and pictures can be changed if necessary. And it may become necessary, so shut up. Or maybe we'll send *you* in."

Then the cell phone rang and the man took it out of his pocket.

Doggie froze. "Don't answer it," she whispered. "Right now they know approximately where we are, but not exactly. You'll be helping them trap us. Turn it off! Now!"

He looked at the display panel. "Yeah, it's Benson here. . . ." He shook his head and looked at her. "We were cut off. Maybe the signal's too weak." He looked around at the curved steel walls as though they may have had to do with the phone going dead.

"Turn it off now," she repeated.

"Hey . . ." He was looking at the display again. "Someone's left a message on your voice mail."

"How do you know?"

"Don't you know your own telephone? You can see it there." He pointed at an icon on the display.

"Turn that thing off," she said once again, feeling her forehead getting clammy. Who could have left her a message?

"Okay, it's a guy who calls himself 'T.' Funny name. He sounds pretty old. Hope it's not your boyfriend." He laughed.

So the bitchy switchboard lady in the Highland County Sheriff's Office *had* given T her number after all.

She leaned towards him quickly, trying to grab the phone. "Give it to me," she commanded.

"He says he has important information. That Thomas Sunderland is involved in the matter. Does he mean our vice president?"

She dried her forehead and nodded, waiting until he'd listened to the rest of the message.

"May I hear it, too?"

"Oh, getting brave now, are we? A minute ago, you wanted me to turn it off, didn't you?"

"I'm sorry. Let me hear the message for myself—please!" Then she would take the cell phone and smash it to bits.

He pushed a button and handed her the phone.

She waved her hand impatiently as she listened. *Hurry up, T,* she beseeched him silently, *get a move on before they find us.*

But T couldn't hurry up because he had so much to tell. And the longer she listened to the message, the uneasier she became.

T had gotten some important information regarding the case, yes. Thomas Sunderland was involved, and T wanted to meet her in Washington at twelve noon, at Barnes & Noble on the corner of 12th and E Streets.

He had given her a ray of hope, but at the same time she was choked with panic. There she was, sitting across from an armed militia fanatic, pinned down on her way to God knows where, and had two fateful, closely timed meetings in Washington in a few hours. Luckily, the two meeting places were as close together as could be, but suddenly she realized each of them was positioned more or less along a side of the block that housed the Hoover Building—FBI headquarters. What the hell had she and T been thinking?

She shook her head. In T's case, it could be that he did not yet know she was the focus of a nationwide manhunt. But how could he not? He was a police officer, for Christ's sake. Was there something fishy about this meeting? Could it be a trap? No, dammit, she wasn't going to start mistrusting *him*! After all, she, herself, had chosen a place that was just as dumb and potentially fatal.

Then she raised her arm to fling the cell phone against the floor.

Maybe the guy had foreseen it; maybe his fight for survival out there in the forest had sharpened his senses and instinct. In any case, the next thing she knew was the sensation of excruciating pain in her underarm and wrist. She never saw the rigid side of his hand coming, she just felt the blow as her arm was sucked in close to her body in a reflex. Then he plucked the cell phone out of her numb hand and shoved her over backward.

"Turn it off," she pleaded, and then it rang again.

He looked irresolute for a moment before he answered. "Benson here. Is it you, Eric?"

Doggie shook her head. In five minutes the guardians of law and order would be descending on them, stopping them at a roadblock if they didn't prefer blasting them off the road from a helicopter.

"Turn the thing off, you asshole!" she screamed, as loud as she could.

He frowned, asked again if it was Eric, and clapped the phone together. This time he turned it off.

"It's your fault," she said, trying to get some feeling back in her arm. "You should have listened to me."

"They asked if it was your voice; they could hear yelling in the background."

"I'll bet," she said. But the thought of it gave her the shivers.

"They know we're heading north, they said."

"Are we?"

"Shut the fuck up. I ought to hog-tie you and throw you out with this cell phone stuck in your little pink panties."

"Then why don't you?"

His face was indistinct, but the glow from his cigarette was pulsing more rapidly.

"What's a swatter? You mentioned it on the phone before."

"Shut the fuck up, I said."

"Oh, is it something bad? I thought it was some kind of dildo. Weren't you speaking with your wife?"

"You be quiet, Doggie Rogers, or I'll strangle you."

She sat for a while, studying the open hatch in the roof of the container. An Olympic gymnast would probably be able to spring up, crawl out, and close the hatch before this idiot knew what had happened.

Then she heard the sound of sirens in the distance. So the chase was on. The police, the National Guard, the military, or agents from the FBI or FEMA—it didn't matter. Right now they were all her enemies.

"What'll you do if we're stopped, and I begin to scream?"

"You won't."

"Don't bet on it."

"It's hard to scream with your throat slit, wouldn't you say?" He tossed his cigarette on the floor.

"Why are you bringing me with you, anyway?"

He gave a big smile for the first time. "There's a reward for turning you in, and it's big. I don't know whether it's dead or alive, but it makes no difference to me."

She looked up at the hole in the roof again. In theory she could get her elbows up over the edge of the opening if she just jumped a foot and a half. She tensed her thigh muscles. If he pulled a knife, she'd give it a try.

"Okay, I promise to keep quiet if you tell me where we're going," she said, as calmly as she could. "I'll know when we get there, so why not tell me now?"

He shot a wad of snot across the steel floor. "Washington, okay?

Now, no more questions." Washington! Then there was still hope. "Okay . . ." she said, looking at his muddy boots, thinking they'd stand out in squeaky-clean DC. "So what's happening in Washington?"

"What was it I just told you?"

"Okay, I'll keep quiet."

The sun rose at exactly six o'clock, and the sound of police sirens blended with the noise of other vehicle motors. Several times it sounded like they were passing cars that were stopped. She could hear shouts and commands from outside, and the milk truck slowed down. After making a couple of quick turns the sounds disappeared again. They drove a few minutes more before the driver aired out his brakes a couple of times and came to a halt.

"What the hell's he doing?" The militiaman who called himself Benson assumed a squatting position, ready to jump up.

"Maybe we've come to a roadblock," she whispered. "Keep quiet."

They sat still for a moment until the driver's head popped into view in the hatch opening.

"I have to close this," he said. "There's a long line of cars ahead of us, so there must be a roadblock. I'm not going to let them see a dairy truck with New York plates and its hatch open."

The militiaman took out his gun and stood up. "You're not closing it, got it?" Doggie looked up at the driver.

"We've been lucky so far," he said. "There haven't been very many soldiers and cops, but it's not going to stay that way."

"What's going on?" she asked.

The driver looked up as a car drove by. Then he said, "One of the pirate radio stations was saying that all military and police units have been called to Washington. The British prime minister is paying a visit to the president in a couple of hours, and they're not taking any chances. But we're approaching a roadblock now, so we have to close the hatch again."

He took hold of the hatch lid and tipped it a little.

"Hey, are you deaf, or what?" Benson had his little automatic pointed at him. "I make that call, and it's all over for your family. You follow me?"

The driver froze, the stainless steel reflecting the sun's rays up on his face, or else they'd stopped on a hilltop.

He looked like he was preparing his words to sound as convincing as possible. "I promise to open it again," he said. "I promise."

"Fuck you, you sad-ass, black ghoul!"

The dark face above them seemed to change character. It was as though a cloud had blocked the sun, removing all the face's worry lines, as though all his anguished doubts had left him. "So you're saying you haven't called anyone about my family yet?"

"No, but I will if you keep this up. Get back in the cab and keep driving." The muzzle of Benson's gun was now touching the driver's forehead.

"Okay, okay. If that's how it's gotta be, then that's how it's gotta be," he said, retreating from the opening.

If he doesn't shut the hatch again, we're caught within a quarter of an hour, Doggie thought in the millisecond before a black arm appeared and there was the infernal noise of three shots fired in rapid succession that made the entire container vibrate. She didn't see Benson go down, just felt the warm blood spray her face. Then the hatch was banged shut.

So the driver had had another weapon and decided to take the consequences. But now his family was safe.

They were approaching a roadblock, and there she sat, with a perforated body next to her. And the darkness was blacker than ever.

CHAPTER 35

WESLEY WAS IN A VERY DESPERATE SITUATION. INSANITY RULED NO MATTER where he looked, and there was absolutely no one who could deny being deeply affected by it. Old friends had become bitter enemies, and former enemies had unexpectedly begun agreeing on everything. All kinds of militias had come together as one, and in the meantime people dared not speak their minds in that fortress of freedom, the Lily-White House.

One began hearing rumors of desertion in the military and plans of a countercoup. Officers had already been executed, but many had also escaped. The chairman of the Joint Chiefs of Staff, General Powers, had already had to explain himself many times in the Crisis Room and assure the National Security Council of his loyalty.

No, there was no longer anything that was sacred. Not the laws of the land, universal codes of ethics and morals, nor the Ten Commandments. All norms and customs were there to be ignored or desecrated, and Wesley planned to put a stop to it.

Lance Burton had become his one remaining ally in the White House since Donald Beglaubter had been murdered and Doggie had disappeared. But Lance was getting on in years, and it was getting easier and easier to see the toll his job was taking on him. He'd worked at least sixteen hours a day the previous week, and even this Sunday they'd been ordered to work from early morning. Lance had complained about a slight pain in his chest, but there he sat in his office as always, trying to stay on top of the most urgent matters as well as attempting to keep a lid on all the secrets in his closetful of electronics.

They had only spoken together once since they'd sworn to each other that, when the time came, at least one of them would step forward and tell about their surveillance of Jansen and Sunderland's offices. But when was that? Wesley certainly didn't know. Their pact was making him uneasy.

Tomorrow—Monday—when the glazier was finished with the windows, they could begin bugging the Oval Office. Then, Burton had said, they could see what came out of it. The possibilities weren't pleasant to think about.

He was sitting with his head buried in his notes for the positive speech of the day when his secretary came in. Her eyes looked swollen, which wasn't normal for a woman whose basic training in life had consisted mainly of looking fabulous, regardless of the circumstances. Her mother ran the information department of *Beauty Parlor,* a weekly magazine with beauty tips for every kind of woman imaginable, yet here she stood, a living betrayal of all she'd been taught.

"What's going on, Eleanor?" he asked.

She said nothing; she simply couldn't get the words out.

"Just sit down, okay?" He pointed to his easy chair, but she remained standing.

"Take your time, Eleanor. Just let it come." He tried to find something in his desk drawer to console her with—a clean handkerchief, a Kleenex—but found nothing.

"I'm okay," she said and dried her eyes. This clearly was not the case, but it was the right signal to send.

"Come on, just say it, Eleanor. I'm sure it's something we can fix."

Sometimes the wrong comment at the right time can give results. The result in this case was a torrent of tears that at best would massacre her mascara, at worst was the beginning of a nervous breakdown that would leave him with an even more impossible workload. He stood up and held her, coaxing her to verbalize her problem.

He looked into her troubled eyes. "We all have our problems these days, Eleanor," he said. "What's yours?"

She gave him a look that would get the immediate attention of any man. "We were woken up this morning by some men knocking on our door. They accused my husband of aiding families of interned politicians, and then they took him with them. He didn't even have time to put his coat on. . . ." She started to sob, and he could barely hear what she said. "Right in front of our children," she added. Then she pressed her lips together, got herself under control, and gave vent to her anger. "What that man really needs is to get laid!"

"I'm sorry, Eleanor. Who? Your husband?"

"Oh, come on, Wesley." Her eyes were full of scorn. "Some of the girls have been trying to figure out how they can get next to Jansen. The only thing he needs is to have his brains fucked out. Thoroughly! Clear all that creepy stuff out of his mind. He's suffering from some kind of mental block. At least that's the conclusion most of us have reached, me included."

Wesley looked at his otherwise chaste secretary and shook his head. Yes, she must be close to a breakdown, but who could blame her? "Okay, Eleanor. If only it were that simple." He turned away from her. "Where is your husband now? Do you know?"

He could hear she was struggling to hold back the tears again. "He's up on Nebraska Avenue."

"Homeland Security?"

"Yes."

He looked at his watch. It was five minutes to eleven. "I'll see what I can do," he said. "There's a meeting in the Oval Office in twenty minutes. Secretary Johnson from Homeland Security will be there."

They were sitting with cups of steaming coffee, but no one touched them. There were only two hours until Terry Watts, the British prime minister, was due to land on the White House lawn, and Secretary Billy Johnson from Homeland Security, Secretary of Defense Wayne Henderson, and Secretary of State Mark Wise all were worried that security was not optimal.

"There are a hell of a lot of things that can go wrong," said

Johnson. "We're not sure what the White-Headed Eagles and the other militia groups are up to. We just know there has been a great increase in their activity the last twenty hours. At least ten of their leaders have been observed away from their normal preserves, and one of Moonie Quale's sergeant at arms was pinned down yesterday, twelve miles outside of Washington."

"And then we got him to talk?" Sunderland broke in. He seemed more concerned than usual.

"No, unfortunately. Some shots were exchanged, and he managed to blow his brains out."

"Shit," said Sunderland and sank back in his seat.

"Yes, but we know from different sources that something's brewing," Johnson continued, "something that we suspect is going to happen today. My people are insisting that we close the bridges over the river and shut down all traffic from 12th to 18th Streets to the west, and from Independence Avenue to K Street, south to north. They say it's the only way we can guarantee full control of the situation. We can start implementing it now."

"Hear, hear," said the secretary of defense.

"But how do we know Terry Watts will believe our illusion of everything being normal? If the PM sees the Ellipse completely empty of people when his helicopter lands, won't he sense something's wrong?" asked the secretary of state.

"We can station military personnel in civilian clothes throughout the area," Chairman of the Joint Chiefs of Staff Omar Powers contributed. "We have at least two thousand men we can have in position within the hour. That's time enough."

President Jansen looked at all of them calmly from behind his desk. "A plan like that is out of the question. An hour and a half ago a thirty-man team from the British special forces, SAS, landed down by the National Mall. Billy Johnson's men from FEMA are to work with them the next fifteen hours, which means that the British will be able to detect and register any of our military in civilian clothes. We can't do anything that radical without being found out. I agree completely with an enlarged security zone, but otherwise we must stick to normal security procedures for a visit from a head of state."

"I'm sorry, Mr. President, but we *have to* install plainclothes soldiers. Don't worry, we can do it so the SAS won't get suspicious." Billy Johnson shifted his large body in his seat. "You see, during the past couple of days we've come to realize that a large portion of the capital that's keeping the militias going is coming from big business. We've succeeded in pinpointing unusually large transactions. The folks in heavy industry—not least the weapons industry—have plenty of cash to throw around, as we well know. Terry Watts's visit is a unique opportunity for these finance men to see to it that the situation in this country is revealed to the rest of the world, once and for all. I'm not sitting here saying we can expect an armed attack or an assassination attempt; there are so many other possibilities. Flyers or powerful loudspeakers, for example. And even though we have pretty good control of the organized demonstrations, we can't totally prevent a sudden big disturbance in the crowds over at the Lincoln Memorial or Franklin Square from resulting in the use of tear gas or water cannons. I'm afraid anything's possible. We cannot guarantee full control unless we close the area off completely and have plenty of personnel in the vicinity."

Jansen thought a moment and nodded. It was obvious that the realization that things had to be this way wasn't sitting well with him. Wesley knew how pragmatic he could be, given the chance.

"Can we trust your people, Billy?" Jansen asked. "You have a lot of personnel under your command."

Which was exactly what Wesley was thinking.

"There's been some purging these last few days. Everything's under control, yes."

"And you, Omar? Do you also have control of your troops?"

"Completely, sir. We're using only elite units here. All good people, be sure of it."

"I don't want to end up like Anwar Sadat, you understand."

"No, of course not." General Powers raised his arms and spread out his hands, as Wesley had seen so many times before when he spoke to his troops—in Iraq, in Sudan, in Israel. "You can have total confidence in my men and women, Mr. President—which Anwar Sadat unfortunately couldn't. This here is the United States of America."

Wesley glanced over at Lance Burton, who he was sure was having more or less the same thoughts on the matter as he was, as far as Powers's last declaration was concerned. He sensed approaching catastrophe, which made it quite difficult to deal with the fact that in twenty minutes he'd be standing on the pressroom podium, improvising over the theme of the British prime minister's state visit, then switch to a totally irrelevant exposé of the unusually large number of gallstone operations there had been around the country over the past few days. That was the day's good-news story, carefully chosen by Thomas Sunderland, but—incredibly enough—suggested by Wesley himself. So while he was enlightening the population as to how many tons of gallstones had been removed during the past twenty-four hours, Billy Johnson and Omar Powers's troops would be putting a tight lid on Washington, coming down hard on the slightest signs of irregularity in a scenario that left nothing to chance. That included emptying the metro of all homeless persons and other undesirables, laying an iron ring around all the approach roads, hassling innocent citizens, getting them off the streets, interning them—"disappearing" them. All this, when he could be—should be—standing before the live news cameras, warning people to stay indoors and look out for themselves and their loved ones. That anyone who came anywhere near the Capitol or the White House couldn't count on returning home safely. The staging of this glorious state visit was not going to come off without violent repercussions—that's what he ought to be saying. But he knew he wouldn't.

"Fine. That's fine, Omar," said the president. "It's not that I'm worried about standing forth today." He looked over at Sunderland. "By the way, what is the status of 'Dot com,' Thomas? How far are we?"

Sunderland stole a glance at Wesley. "I'm not sure this is the proper forum, Mr. President. Can we wait with that one?"

Jansen followed Sunderland's eyes and fixed his on Wesley. Bruce Jansen seemed composed, practically serene, as though nothing in this world could shake his belief that everything he did was for the common good. "What we're referring to, Wesley, is that we are now ready to . . ."—he wiggled two fingers of each hand to make quotation marks—". . . 'regulate' the Internet. Naturally, you can't make this public, but of course you should know about it. I believe Vice President Sunderland agrees with me on this."

Wesley could see the disapproval radiating from Thomas Sunderland. Of course Sunderland knew Wesley was a vigorous opponent of closing down the Internet, and that he'd fight it tooth and nail.

"We can't. We can't close down the Internet," said Wesley. "It will make life hell for hundreds of millions of people. The financial sector will break down completely, and it's in bad enough shape as it is. In these modern times you simply cannot sabotage the Internet; the consequences would be incalculable. The whole world would turn against us."

"Stop, Wesley. We're not talking about putting satellites out of commission, okay? However, I can see from Sunderland that we better move on to the next item on the agenda." The president's expression left no doubt that the subject was closed. "But for your information, we *can* do this and we will, after Prime Minister Watts's visit is over. It's essential, if we're to maintain control of the situation. It's merely a question of where we'll start and how long it will continue." He caught Sunderland's eye.

"Yes, Thomas?"

"The prime minister will be arriving soon. We ought to run through our plan one more time."

"Yes, let's. You'll be told more later, Wesley. But you should know our first objective is merely to infect specific websites with a fatal virus. You can probably figure out which ones I have in mind."

"Yes," he said quietly. There wasn't much else he could say. It was all downhill from here, not the first time in history those in power had attempted to suppress the opposition's right to express itself.

No, Hitler and Stalin had not lived in vain. Of course he could do without the extremist websites—the Ku Klux Klan, Hells Angels, Moral Minority, the White-Headed Eagles, and the child porn, bomb recipe, and satanic cult freaks. For his sake they could all be banished to a desert island and wind each other up to their heart's content. But what about the opposition with a legitimate bone to pick? The righteous indignation of the common man or the masses who were not clever enough to formulate themselves? Should they also be trampled underfoot?

Jansen clapped his hands one time. "Good. Let us take the security procedures first, then we'll run through the entire agenda, step-by-step. Would you be so kind as to keep notes, Lance?"

More than one member of the White House security team had noticed Eleanor Poppins's physical attributes and were happy to let her wait for Wesley outside the Oval Office. She'd fixed her makeup and, in spite of the dark circles under her eyes, had brought herself up to par in terms of authoritativeness and charm. There were many who would have given their right arm for a few minutes' private audience with Wesley's secretary, but at the moment Wesley wasn't one of them.

She greeted him nervously. "What did Billy Johnson say, Wesley? Did you ask him?"

He looked at her, wishing she would just disappear. Who the hell had he thought he was, giving her false hopes? There was no way he could have brought up a subject as insignificant as the detainment of Eleanor Poppins's husband when the president and all the others had much bigger fish to fry. No, he hadn't done what he'd promised, and he wasn't very pleased with himself.

"Not really, Eleanor," he answered.

"'Not really'? What does that mean?"

"I'm just telling you he didn't say anything definite. He wasn't familiar with the case."

"But you mentioned it."

"Yeah, yeah, but it didn't lead to much. He didn't know anything about it, Eleanor." She followed him into his office.

"But you said he should help, didn't you?"

"Yes, Eleanor, I did." He looked at his watch. He felt sorry for her, but there weren't many minutes left before he had to be in the pressroom. Enough was enough. Couldn't she see his hands were tied, that what she was asking of him was a waste of time? That he already had more than enough nasty problems to deal with?

A faint ringing could be heard from the secretary's switchboard.

"I'm expecting an important phone call, Eleanor," he said, both relieved and apologetic, and signaled that she should go transfer the call
in to him. "We'll discuss your husband's predicament later, okay?"

The way she closed the door after her expressed—better than words
ever could—how much stature he'd lost in her eyes. Wesley drove the
self-contempt out of his mind and picked up the phone on the first ring.
If it weren't because he simply wanted to get rid of Eleanor, he'd never
have taken the call.

"Wesley Barefoot," he said curtly, signaling that he was a very
busy man.

"I'll say it fast. You don't say anything."

Wesley sat up straight in his chair, amazed. It was Doggie. His
mind began flying in ten different directions.

Don't say her name, he told himself, *just listen. But please let me
know you're okay!* Maybe it was safe to talk and maybe it wasn't—only
Lance Burton knew the answer to that. Or were there others listening
in? Were there other surveillance systems he didn't know about? Did
they register all phone calls as a matter of course? Certainly. If they
were lucky, she was calling from a number that wouldn't arouse suspicion. He knew she would try to be careful. If he didn't say anything
in particular, nothing in particular would be registered. Not that he
didn't wish he could. He had an overwhelming desire to say something so she knew he wanted to do the right thing, for them and the
rest of mankind, but he dared not move his lips.

"I'm okay," she said. It was certainly the voice of composure, but
she obviously wasn't all alone. He could hear street noises in the background, like there was traffic nearby and the streets were wet. She
could be anywhere. He looked out his window. It was raining.

"I'm meeting T soon. You might hear from me again—I think you
will. We're going to try and get in."

Get in? Hopefully, she didn't mean the White House. He shook his
head. Of course she did.

"Are you in Washington?" he asked, regretting it immediately.

"I just want to tell you to watch out today. Everywhere you go. I
have a feeling."

He wanted to ask why, and whether *she* was "watching out." What was he supposed to do? But the phone conversation was over. He imagined she smiled as she said good-bye and hung up.

He sat, staring out the window for a minute or two. It had begun raining hard.

Then his door opened; Eleanor was standing in the doorway. Her eyes were calculating, taking in any and every detail that might enhance the chances of her getting her husband back.

She saw how he attempted to avoid her gaze, supporting her suspicions as to whom the caller was. Finally he looked at her. "Were you listening in, Eleanor?" he asked.

She nodded very slowly. These were grounds for dismissal, but she didn't care. Wesley represented her only chance to have her husband freed; this was what mattered most. "I think you'd better speak with Billy Johnson again, Wesley. Later today, preferably. Aside from that, it's time you went down to the pressroom."

CHAPTER 36

IT HAD GONE JUST AS ROSALIE AND HER BOYS HAD PREDICTED. OLLIE BOYCE Henson had sung to the police the moment he heard about the reward for Doggie Rogers, and the manhunt was under way.

And while the dairy truck was making its way south with the country's most-wanted woman in its stainless steel container, Rosalie's eldest son, James Lee Jr., turned up at the police station and told the story about how Doggie Rogers had tried to have them put her up and how he, his brother, and his mother had tried unsuccessfully to keep her there while they contacted the authorities.

The police officers naturally wanted to know how a diminutive woman could outmaneuver such a big, strong boy like him, but James had anticipated the question. She had already escaped the FBI, Secret Service, the military, and the CIA, he said, so how could they expect three regular people to do any better? Without a doubt Doggie Rogers was a cunning bitch who knew what to do, and when. Out the back door, down the fire escape, and she was gone in a beige-colored Galaxy. They had yelled out the window for someone to follow her, but she'd shaken off her pursuers somewhere near White Plains. He had witnesses, he said. The license plate had been beat up and illegible, but otherwise the car had been in fucking good shape, with plenty of chrome and black racing stripes on the hood, so it should be easy to recognize.

He ended his statement by demanding the reward if his information led to her apprehension. It was their problem that they'd already promised it to Ollie Boyce Henson.

The alibi should have put them in the clear, but that night Rosalie couldn't sleep. She was too discouraged in heart and mind.

A couple of days ago, there had been three healthy boys sleeping in the bedroom next to hers, and now there were only two. Suddenly it was as if the coldness of the empty bed was spreading through the apartment, demolishing any fragile dreams of a bright future. The fear of losing another child dominated everything, including her grief, and the shame she felt over not grieving enough made sleep impossible.

She lay in bed all night, praying to Jesus and wishing she could cry, but her head was too full of dark thoughts.

Early the next morning she was awakened by her neighbor Annabelle Morrison. Bubbling with excitement, she told Rosalie what had been happening during the night. It had all begun with a pirate radio's claim that soldiers had successfully traced Tom Jumper's mobile transmitter and had subsequently killed him on a rural Virginia road, north of Front Royal. The incident had ignited massive spontaneous protests nationwide; even big Hollywood stars with plenty to lose had vented their outrage. A couple of hours later the same pirate station began listing the Jansen's drugstores all over the country that had been plundered, starting in Des Moines and eventually reaching the Jansen's Drugstore at Dewey and Randall, right down the street. Now, apparently, all the locals were headed for the store on Harding Avenue. It was a case of first come, first served, her neighbor said.

Rosalie asked Annabelle to calm down a little, that she, Rosalie, had been brought up to respect the law, as Annabelle Morrison well knew. Besides, Dennis and James were still sleeping, and she didn't want the boys overhearing them and getting bright ideas. Then anything might happen.

When Annabelle finally headed off for the store on Harding Avenue with a pile of empty plastic bags under her arm, Rosalie turned on her CD player to hear a little Sonny Rollins in an attempt to offset the growing commotion of sirens and yelling outside. This usually had a calming effect on her boys as well but not this time. After two minutes they were standing before her with their sideways baseball caps, looking much too alert for that time of morning. They had sharp instincts when it came to easy money.

They left the apartment without saying a word, and Rosalie was alone in the kitchen like so many times before. She felt like a hostage with a hood over her head, like a prisoner in solitary confinement who had never been sentenced. Time disappeared, leaving nothing good in its wake and offering little hope for the future.

She folded her hands and attempted to digest all her neighbor had told her. Had this been the United States' "Crystal Night"? Was this the beginning of the end, with only suffering, death, and destruction to look forward to?

She prayed to Jesus and tried to find peace of mind. But every time she heard tumult on the street she had to start over.

Thus she sat for two hours until the neighborhood once again grew quiet, but her boys had yet to return. Did that mean they hadn't taken part in the plundering—or that they had?

"Dear Jesus in heaven, please don't let them be in trouble," she prayed, battling a sense of dread. How could she go on living if another of her boys were killed? She put her hand to her breast and stood up, once again feeling about to pass out.

By now it was stark daylight, and even though there were dark clouds building to the south, one couldn't have asked for a more beautiful spring morning. Birds were chattering, perched on the roof gutters high above. It had been years since she'd noticed them; among the many sounds one heard in her neighborhood, this was rarely one of them. She went to the window to see if she could identify any of them, at the same time noticing two white men climbing out of their car and heading for her apartment building. They looked like undertakers in their black suits. They would be ringing her doorbell in a minute, she was sure of it—stand in her doorway with grave expressions and give her bad news. Nothing happened by the book these days. It was no longer the older, veteran cops who came at times like this. It could be any kind of representative of the law.

She opened the door on the first ring and nodded curtly to the two G-men, but she simply couldn't bring herself to look them in the eyes. Let them speak their piece, emit their odor of masculine vitality, and lead her by the arm to her easy chair, but not expect any eye contact. Sight was the only one of the senses that was selective, and she aimed to make use of that special feature.

"Say it," she said calmly, her eyes fastened on the doormat Dennis had won ten years ago in a bingo game at the YMCA over by Castle Hill. "Is it both of them? Are they badly hurt? Just say it."

"Mrs. Lee, we have a search warrant here . . ." The slighter man stuck a piece of paper in front of her face. It held no meaning for her.

She swallowed the lump that had been growing in her throat.

"Ma'am, you had a wanted person in your apartment yesterday. Doggie Rogers," said the other one.

She nodded. Was that all, or was there more? "Yes, that's true. We reported it down at the station a long time ago." Rosalie looked at the smaller man's neck, scrawny and white as chalk. Was it about to produce words that would make her break down in tears? "She disappeared suddenly down our fire escape, you know. . . ." Rosalie summoned her courage and raised her eyes to theirs. "Then you didn't come here because of my sons?"

"James and Dennis? Yes, as a matter of fact we'd very much like to speak with them, too," said the bigger one.

"I see." She exhaled the breath she'd been holding. So they knew nothing. But that still didn't mean the danger had passed. "Well, they aren't home right now," she stated.

They thrust the photocopy of a search warrant in her hand with the Federal Emergency Management Agency's stamp on it and went to work. They were thorough, and after ten minutes returned and laid two joints before her on the coffee table. She needn't worry, they said, just as long as they didn't find anything worse than that.

"If you do, it's my son Frank," she quickly assured them. "I suppose you know. He died from an overdose yesterday," she said, thinking they were sure to take the joints with them and smoke them themselves. One heard stories like this all the time.

While they were in the process of sniffing her laundry, turning over mattresses, and poking around everywhere in the kitchen, Rosalie sat herself down by the window and scanned the street. More than any-thing she was wishing she'd spy her boys down there so her pulse could return to normal. When she did, she'd use sign language to make them disappear again. She wasn't worried about what James might say if they questioned him, but one never knew with Dennis. That boy had always had problems keeping his mouth shut at strategic moments—something he'd inherited from his father.

The soldiers must have stopped the protesting and plundering, be-cause the neighborhood was settling down again. She saw only one of her neighbors struggling up the front stairs with a stack of stolen goods in his embrace—that was all. Fine, just as long as her own boys showed up soon.

"What's this?" asked one of the detectives, placing a photo album in front of her. He pointed at a photograph taken in Beijing Airport many years ago. It was a considerably more streamlined Rosalie, standing next to Senator Jansen and smiling.

"Yes, that's me and the president in China," she said. "If you keep looking you'll come to pictures of me and the vice president and a couple with Doggie Rogers as quite a young girl."

They asked what the occasion was in Beijing with the president, and in the course of answering she forgot to keep her eye on the street. Suddenly there were sounds of footsteps on the stairs and a key in the lock, and there they stood: James and Dennis with armfuls of stuff from Jansen's Drugstore.

A couple of seconds passed before they let it all cascade to the floor in realization of the situation they'd walked into. A situation that was emphasized by the drawn weapon of one of the cops.

"It looks like you two have some explaining to do," he said, waving his gun in the direction of the wall so his partner could frisk them.

"Yo, man, these's purchased goods, fair and square," popped out of Dennis. "Lotta bargains down on the street today, and that ain't no shit."

Rosalie watched in horror as the little detective with the skinny neck stuck his gun all the way into Dennis's ear and cocked it. "What-ever you two say from now on can and will be used against you. You're to open your mouths only in answer to a question, and I would strongly advise you to speak the truth. You're busted if we're in a moment's doubt—got it?"

Dennis nodded. Thank God for that.

"Where'd you get the goods?" the cop asked, and returned his weapon to its holster.

"We bought them off some mother down on the street who'd boosted them from the drugstore down on Castle Hill."

That went over like a lead balloon.

"Okay, take the other one out in the kitchen and question him, Jeff," said the bigger one. "Then we'll compare notes and see what happens."

The detective called Jeff gave James a rough shove. He was at least a foot shorter than Rosalie's son, with a neck thinner than James's arm, but he was also the one bearing a firearm.

"Hey, man, take it easy, take it easy!" James exclaimed. "We don't have to go through all this hassle. It's my baby brother, dig? Don't mind him, he don't know what he's saying half the time. We were down at Castle Hill about thirty minutes. The shit was lyin' everywhere, swear to God. We just scored things other folks had stolen and left behind, and that's the truth, take it or leave it."

That one was a little better, a little more plausible. One had to take that into consideration.

"How did Doggie Rogers contact you before she showed up?" asked Detective Jeff.

"Contact us? She didn't, dickhead, she just showed up!" Dennis was so busy playing smart-ass, he realized too late—again—what words were coming out of his mouth. By then the bigger detective was in the process of hammering the butt of his gun into the nape of Dennis's neck. Rosalie sank into her chair and watched helplessly as her youngest son's body sank lifelessly to the floor and flopped halfway under a chest of drawers.

"It's time to cut the crap, see?" Knocking criminal suspects unconscious seemed to be standard procedure for this lawman. "We know Rogers contacted you ahead of time on Ollie Boyce Henson's cell phone. The call's been registered, okay?"

Still shaken, Rosalie nodded uncertainly while James stood silently, slouched against the wall, arms hanging at his sides.

"Where is Ollie Boyce Henson's cell phone?" Jeff asked.

Rosalie could feel the tears start to come. She couldn't take any more. All these accusations, all these interrogations, all these threats and violence taken out on her sons. "I suppose she's taken it with her" was all she said.

James stood up a little straighter. "We never saw her cell phone, and she didn't stay long, okay?" he added.

"Then what's this?" Jeff held up a clear plastic bag with Ollie's cell phone. "It was in the garbage can out in the kitchen."

Rosalie couldn't believe her eyes. No one should be allowed to be so stupid! How could she and the boys have overlooked something like that?! They could have gotten rid of it along with Doggie's clothes. Or thrown it far out into the Hudson River, or so many other things.

"We've never seen it before," said James, nice and easy, pulling one leg up under him against the wall. "Guess she just tossed it there."

"Why would she have wanted to do that?"

"Fucked if I know. Must have known it could be traced, what else?"

"Traced? How? How could she know we'd find the guy who'd given it to her?"

"Look, we told everything down at the police station already. Also that she wasn't your average bitch. She was cunning. That's what I said, word for word. Check it out in your report," said her eldest son, acting offended.

Take it easy, you, pleaded Rosalie's eyes, but James ignored her.

"We found this, too." Jeff showed her the empty hair-dying package.

"That's right, I put a little color in my hair this morning," she said, her heart in her mouth. At least they hadn't found Doggie's hair clippings. She must have flushed them down the toilet. Praise the Lord for that.

He studied her hair intently and finally seemed convinced. She exhaled again, imperceptibly.

"Okay, we'll give you one last chance now," said the other detective.

"Since the time James contacted the police last night we've been tapping all the telephone numbers registered at this address—four in all. A cell phone in your name," he pointed at James, "a land-line in your mother's name, a cell phone belonging to little brother here—who seems to be waking up now, by the way . . ." He nudged Dennis with the tip of his shoe. "And last of all, a cell phone that was registered in the name of your deceased brother."

Detective Jeff took over. "If we'd had the time to check it out, we probably would have turned up some pretty juicy stuff about this little family and its acquaintances. But for the moment what interests us is that someone made a call on your dead brother's phone—Frank, I believe his name was. But how can that be? He couldn't very well have made the call himself, I mean, being dead and all, could he?"

Rosalie went back to studying the floor.

"How the fuck should I know what Frank was doing just before he died?" said James. "He could have sold his cell phone for a fix. It was shooting dope that killed him, as you fucking well know."

The other detective who was standing in the kitchen doorway stuck his hand in his jacket pocket and yet another plastic bag appeared. Rosalie didn't know what it was, but James didn't look pleased at the discovery.

"This gun, was it Frank's, too?"

Looking at the smooth, gray object, Rosalie was close to tears again. Could they really have been so dumb as to let all this evidence lie around the apartment? What would be next?

"Yeah," said James, keeping his attitude in place. "I don't know how many times we warned that boy. Couldn't make him understand. He had his own thing."

"Then I sincerely hope it's his fingerprints we find on it. I assume you're willing to let us dust it, since you're so sure it was Frank's."

"I'm not willing to do a fucking thing. I've done what I was supposed to."

The detective called Jeff went and stood in James's face. Despite their height difference, he looked him in the eyes with the kind of self-confidence that came not only from having a weapon and an armed partner, but also signaled that he'd handled guys much bigger and badder than James in his time.

Unfortunately, James overlooked his body language.

"You're the eldest, aren't you?" asked Jeff.

James didn't answer. He didn't have to. He knew they knew he was.

"Good, then I'm holding you responsible if we find it necessary to take your mother along to the station because you refuse to tell us everything you know."

James was looking less and less pleased. Just as long as he didn't overreact for her sake.

Jeff turned to Rosalie. "We'll let it rest with the firearm for now. The point is, we already know most of the story, so all we're looking for now is your confirmation of some details."

It wasn't a question, but Rosalie nodded anyway.

"At two A.M. last night we localized Doggie Rogers somewhere down in Virginia, with the help of your deceased son's cell phone. Have you anything to add, Mrs. Lee?"

She shook her head. How could she have been so naive as to believe they'd get out of this easily? That she could appease men like these?

"She had just been speaking to a man in Georgetown. A Danny Hargraves. Do you know him, Mrs. Lee?"

"Danny Hargraves? No, I don't."

"Okay, you don't, you say . . ." He picked up the photo album from the China trip and began paging through it. "Then I think you ought to take a closer look at this picture here." He pointed at a shot of the Beijing hotel's lobby, where Doggie, Rosalie, and John Bugatti were standing, pointing at the floormat in front of the elevator. Suddenly, Rosalie remembered how it had tickled them to see this mat that resembled a huge baby's bib with the day of the week printed on it, and how it was changed each day. They'd had some fun times there before tragedy struck. It was all so sad to think about now.

"You know John Bugatti here, but you don't know Danny Hargraves?"

"No. And I didn't know he had any connection with John Bugatti. I was never with John in private, and it's seventeen years since I saw him."

"John Bugatti is wanted by the authorities, did you know that?" She made the sign of the cross. "Oh, no. What's he done?"

"Then maybe you don't know Doggie Rogers is meeting him in Washington today, either? She never mentioned that to you?"

"By the Holy Father—no!" What in the world did they suspect her of having to do with all this?

She shook her head and looked at her son who was still stretched out on the floor. How was it all going to end?

She noticed Dennis's body moving slightly. It looked like he was stretching one arm, inch by inch, farther under the chest of drawers.

Oh, my God, she thought, *what's he up to? What's he got lying under there—some weapon? Was he suddenly going to turn a gun on these detectives?* She wouldn't put it past him. How could she have failed so miserably in driving this pigheaded, macho behavior out of her children? Did they really take so much after their father?

Then she saw James flattening himself more and more against the wall. He'd also noticed Dennis and was having a hard time staying nonchalant.

"Hey, man, listen," he said, getting both FBI men's attention. "My mom went to China once and Doggie Rogers was there, too, okay? She had our address, that's all."

Rosalie nudged Dennis cautiously, but he kept on. She was sure this was going to end badly. In a moment, there would be shooting and someone was going to wind up dead. So she kicked him in the side— still with no effect. Now his arm was completely outstretched under the dresser.

"But you must know this man, Mrs. Lee," Jeff continued, pointing at a picture of a tired T. Perkins standing before a giant portrait of Chairman Mao in Tiananmen Square.

"Yes, he was one of the contest winners, too. There were three of us. He was a very nice man." She kicked Dennis so hard this time with the point of her shoe that he gave a start. It couldn't be long before the investigators noticed him.

The other detective nodded. "T. Perkins sent a message to Doggie Rogers's cell phone last night. Do you know where Sheriff Perkins got her number?"

"No. . . ." In a second she was going to have to stomp on Dennis's rib cage. "No, I do not. From Doggie Rogers herself, I imagine." Her heart was beating like it was just before the time she collapsed in front of Penn Station.

"There are several aspects of this we don't understand." It was Jeff's turn again. "It looks like we're going to have to take all of you in."

Something was going to happen now, she was sure of it. So she swung her foot back and kicked her son so hard that his body buckled and he let out a howl.

"Stand up, boy!" she commanded. "Now, you two tell these men what you know, you hear?" Dennis looked up at her. He was furious now, and he was the type who didn't know how to gear down once he got going. Both his mother and teachers at school knew all about it.

"You boys tell them how you wanted Doggie Rogers to leave immediately when you found out the authorities were looking for her. That at one point you knocked her down and then she escaped while you were trying to get her to the police station. And that it was me who let her get away. I had no idea she'd done something bad. Was it that serious? Just let us know how we can help; we'll do everything we can. I'm very close friends with the president, and I wish him only the best."

She looked at them earnestly as she bent over to Dennis and stretched out her hand. "Come on, Dennis. Get up and tell them everything. Don't worry 'bout me, I'll be all right. I mean, I didn't know she'd broken the law."

He took her hand grudgingly and looked up at his big brother. James had been in trouble more than once in his life but had always managed to get out of it. He could tell that now there was a chance to do it again, so he gave his younger brother a stern look and shook his head.

She saw the two FBI men looking at each other out of the corners of their eyes. They'd for sure heard excuses like hers ever since they'd joined the Bureau.

"Hold on," said Jeff, as his cell phone rang. He listened for a long time, then answered with a simple "Yeah." With his poker face in place it was impossible to tell if it was good news or bad.

He hung up and looked straight at Rosalie. "That was one of my colleagues in Richmond. They've just been to your sister Josefine's home, questioning her."

Her shoulders went limp. Dear Jesus—that, too?

"You see? We know everything. Your sister was a pretty tough customer, says my colleague, but in the end she told them everything."

"She knew nothing, I promise you!" She looked at Dennis, who was rubbing his side. "The boys don't have anything to do with this, either. It's like I said: It was me who sent Doggie down to my sister's. Doggie asked for my help; I had no idea what she'd done. I still don't— won't you please tell me what it was? But my sister, she didn't know a thing. Honest!"

"Your sister's telephone has been out of order the last twenty-four hours. The militia cut the lines. We know she didn't know that Doggie Rogers was coming. We also know more or less how Miss Rogers got down there, and we know her cell phone was on once more this morning. There were signs of a struggle in Mrs. Maddox's house, and she claimed it had been the militiamen. Doggie Rogers has disappeared and so has the militia. Do you know if Miss Rogers had anything to do with them, Mrs. Lee?"

"She didn't, I'm sure of it. She never would. She wasn't like that, far as I know."

They weren't impressed. "We must ask that you and your sons don't leave town," said Jeff. "We'll be calling you in to give a deposition at a later point."

"What about Doggie Rogers? Have you arrested her?"

"We can't give you that information."

Rosalie looked at them and nodded. She could see the satisfaction in their eyes. No, they hadn't caught her yet, or they'd have said it, but it wouldn't be long.

All she wanted them to do now was leave. Then she would call Doggie and warn her. She didn't care if they found out. What could they do to her?

The two men packed some of their discoveries into their briefcases and went out into the hall. Then one of them turned around and said, "Mrs. Lee, if T. Perkins or John Bugatti call, drag the conversation out, understand? If we can tell you're trying to help us, we'll ignore your and your sons' offenses. Do you know what I'm saying?"

She nodded.

"And Mrs. Lee, one last thing: You can forget about calling Doggie Rogers when we leave. Her phone was turned off hours ago."

Finally they'd gone, and Rosalie had to make sure. She went over to the chest of drawers, got down on her knees with a little grunt, and peered underneath. Yes, it was just as she had expected.

A little revolver lay against the wall, wedged behind the bureau's left rear leg.

CHAPTER 37

THE DRIVER LET DOGGIE OFF ON A SIDE STREET JUST BEFORE THE PEDESTRIAN bridge over to Theodore Roosevelt Island, towards Washington City. It was only a little before ten, Sunday morning, yet it was dark as evening, and rain was pelting down.

"You have enough time to walk the rest of the way," said the milk truck driver, and handed her a blue poncho.

"I can't take you downtown because of the roadblocks, but it's just over the footbridge and straight out Constitution Ave. I suppose you know the way."

Yes, he could bet she did.

She put on the poncho and pulled its hood over her head. "What about the dead guy inside the tank? What'll you do with him? Aren't you afraid about what could happen?"

"Afraid?" He gave a faint smile. "We'll see. I'll probably get rid of him somewhere along the way." He opened his wallet, the one he'd retrieved from the body. "Here. This is yours." He gave her $1,700 and kept the rest, just as they'd agreed.

Doggie put the money in her back pocket.

"And these—they're not mine, either." He took the militiaman's two drawings out of his wallet and handed them to her.

She looked at them for a moment and then folded them so they wouldn't get soaking wet. They were slightly blurred cross-section drawings of a column with some curves in front. She couldn't tell what they were, offhand.

"They're not mine," she said, but put them in the plastic bag anyway.

"Take care of yourself, lady" were his last words before the milk truck again began rumbling northward, spraying water from its rear tires.

"Just over the footbridge and straight out Constitution Avenue." *Just,* the driver had said. He hadn't had the vaguest idea. Problems began arising already at the pedestrian bridge. There were poncho-clad soldiers every hundred yards, checking people as they passed, crouching in the pounding rain. Some people were stopped, had a flashlight shined in their face, and were body-searched. Everyone had to show what they had in their bags, but they weren't interested in Doggie's plastic bag. There was a battered cell phone and a couple of wet drawings and all the odds and ends of ladies' accessories she'd had in her Fendi bag.

"They can't be interested in someone who looks like me," she reasoned, praying she wouldn't have to face the glare of the flashlight. She'd noticed the sheets of plastic-coated MOST WANTED photos some of the soldiers were holding and saw them again a little farther on, fastened to the bridge's railing. There were many pictures, some small and some large. There was Michael K. Lerner, the journalist Miss B, Moonie Quale, a few other militia leaders—and herself. Being represented in this gallery didn't exactly cheer her up.

"Halt!" she heard a soldier yell from the end of the bridge. He was looking straight at her, pointing his flashlight at her face. "Step forward!" he ordered and pushed the flashlight switch. It clicked but wouldn't go on. He shook it and clicked it on and off a few times while she felt her knees begin to wobble. There was no getting away.

"Fucking piece of shit," snarled the soldier, knocking the flashlight against the palm of his hand. He tried turning it on again. Still no luck.

He squinted into her face as rain sloshed off his hood. Then he said, "Move on," and stuffed the flashlight under his poncho. The other soldiers glanced at her briefly and also waved her on.

Apparently, they took her for some kind of bag lady. True enough, she wasn't a particularly lovely sight to behold. Her coal-black, spiky hair had given up the fight and was plastered to her head; the remains of her makeup were less than tidy. She hadn't had a bath in a very long time, and the trip down to Five Forks and back to Washington had left its messy imprint on her grayish horror costume. She wasn't easy to recognize.

The level of police activity was much higher when she got across the bridge. The National Guard was lined up along the road all the way from the Watergate to the Lincoln Memorial. She heard a couple of passersby saying it was impossible to walk through the park for all the undercover agents and policemen.

Dammit, she thought. There was only one way, then: along the path that followed the river, all the way to K or L Street. She'd have to see how best to get from there to 8th Street. She had to move.

She made it to the Washington, DC, post office around eleven o'clock and found something as rare as a pay phone in working order. She looked at the layer of mud that had become a permanent feature of her pant legs, shook her head, and dialed Wesley's direct number. This, of course, was a really stupid idea, but hearing his voice would give her the moral support she needed right now. She couldn't say directly that she was going to try making it into the White House, but he'd understand what she meant. He was a clever guy.

Their conversation was short. It felt good to hear his voice, just as she'd hoped. Now she was expecting he'd take the proper precautions.

The smile on her lips died as she replaced the receiver and looked around. She'd been met by a disquieting sight every time she looked south. All the streets leading to the university and the White House were swarming with black uniforms, and everyone headed that way was stopped and asked for identification. Most were turned back.

So they'd sealed off the area surrounding the White House. Of course. The British delegation mustn't be allowed to see the people's discontent. The helicopter with the prime minister and his entourage would land on the White House lawn in front of the Oval Office. He would remain in the Oval Office until the helicopter came and fetched him again. It was that simple.

With such massive control around Pennsylvania Avenue, she was forced to make a detour north to the Metro Center, around Chinatown, and then down to Barnes & Noble. She picked up her pace a bit, her feet squishing as though there was oatmeal inside her shoes. She gasped for breath like a chain smoker as first her raincoat and then the rest of her clothes also got soaked through. It wasn't so strange that people were staring at her, the way she looked. Who'd be dumb enough to go out in this kind of weather, dressed as she was, and without an umbrella? Who else besides some poor wretch who didn't know better? *Poor girl,* eyes were saying as she rushed by. Strangely empty eyes.

The city wasn't itself anymore.

As she approached Barnes & Noble from F Street, things seemed completely normal. Too normal, actually, and this made her nervous. Soldiers were lined up with bulletproof vests and full combat uniforms just one block farther on but not here. There weren't even policemen patrolling. A few customers went in and out of the bookstore fifty yards down the street, but that was it.

She stole a glance at the upstairs windows of the neighboring buildings and tried to spot an alert face, but there was nothing unusual to see there, either.

They're waiting for us in the bookstore—of course they are. Don't try and fool yourself, Doggie Rogers, you're too smart for that, she thought to herself, and hugged the wall of the building to escape the waterfall from the overflowing roof gutter. There were twenty minutes until her meeting with T. If this was going to work, she'd have to catch him before he reached the shop.

Where will he park? she asked herself. *Over on Tenth?* Maybe she just ought to stay where she was. If he showed up on the other side of the corner entrance, she'd bolt towards him, even though the chances of getting away were slim. But she was hoping for—and counting on—his coming from the north end. He probably would. It was much easier to find a parking place up there.

At ten minutes to twelve she sat down on the sidewalk against the wall of the building, paying no attention to the flood beneath her.

That's what a real bag lady does, she thought, because that's what she was. A shopping cart would probably have helped the overall effect, but attitude was what was most important. She laid her chin on her knees. That way she could glance up and down the street, only moving her eyes.

"Come on, T," she whispered, while she tried to relax her body.

Not ten minutes went by before she saw a poorly camouflaged FBI agent approaching her from down on the corner. His black raincoat was still almost dry, but the brim of his hat was saturated from the rain. *So, up pops the G-man,* she thought. *I wonder if he was given the sign by someone up in one of those windows.* She looked up again, but saw no one, and stuck her hand in the plastic bag as she followed his progress out of the corner of her eye. She trawled the bottom with her hand until she found her eyeliner in a corner. Then she broke off the point of the eyeliner on the surface of the sidewalk and crumbled it between her fingers. The FBI guy was approaching fast.

With her head hidden between her knees, she put her hand to her face and smeared the black stuff around her eyes, humming as she did so. He was only ten yards from her and already addressing her when she leaned back her head and let the streaming rain do the rest. It stung, but she could tell it was working. No makeup could stay put for long under those conditions.

He nudged her with his foot. "May I see some identification." It wasn't a question.

She looked up at him, wide-eyed. "Hey, beautiful. Did you say you'd like to see my cunt?" She tried to sound a little drunk and laughed hollowly, while her heart was hammering with fear. Then she cast her eyes down at the cascading water and kept humming.

"You can't sit here," he said, and pushed once more with his shoe.

"Hey, man, maybe you wanna take me to the hotel?" she drawled. "Okay by me. I'll do it wherever you say." She looked at him yieldingly, with her mouth agape. "I'll fuck you like you've never been fucked before. Shit, do you look good! Give me a hand here, okay?"

He shook his head and leaned his head towards his lapel microphone. "What should I do with her?" he asked. "You have to come with me," he said, when he'd gotten the answer in his earpiece. "You can't sit here."

"Why not? Where am I supposed to go?"

"You have to get off the street."

He dragged her past the first window of the bookshop, down towards the corner. Like many Barnes & Noble facades, the windows reached from street level to second floor. In a few minutes T would be wandering around in there, looking for her. If she didn't do something, his search would be in vain.

She tried to pull her arm away, but the FBI agent's grip was firm and determined. He had to get her away from the street, and fast. Those were his orders.

Just five yards from the corner she caught sight of T, on his way down the bookstore's escalator, wearing what was for him an unusually anonymous jacket. Even the cowboy boots had yielded to a normal pair with laces. He looked pale, like a man who hadn't slept for several days, but in T's case, you couldn't judge the book by the cover. She observed how his tired eyes were shooting a hundred snapshots around the room. It was a professional at work.

"I'm goin' in here," she yelled into the man's ear.

"No, you're not. You're going and sit in the van around the corner."

"I've gotta take a piss. They always let me. I used to work here, get it? So let go of me, jerk, I'm goin' in."

He tried to ignore her while she pulled in the other direction. If he were going to get her to come, he was going to have to fight for it.

"Listen: I've gotta go in here. I gotta piss. Otherwise I'll fucking piss in your goddamn fucking van, okay? I don't give a shit what you say." The grip on her arm tightened.

"Hey, you fucking bum, you're not gonna use force on a lady, are you?" She let herself flop down on the sidewalk. "I just have to take a piss, okay? Let me go in, and then I'll disappear from the 'hood, okay? Otherwise we can just pick up where we left off when I come out. Okay?"

He let her slide all the way to the ground. "What now?" he said into his lapel, then nodded his head a couple of times. "Yeah, we still have the guy under surveillance. He's looking for her. Yes. All right."

He looked down at her. "So get out of the area when you're done, understand?" She was no longer his focus of interest. She was nothing.

She nodded. Did she understand? Absolutely.

She felt dozens of pairs of eyes watching her as she approached the escalator. It was hard to tell whether this was caused by her bizarre appearance or because the ears that went with the eyes had been listening in on her and the FBI agent. Probably both. In any case, there were a lot of earpieces being worn in that bookshop—that was for sure.

Halfway up the escalator she spied T looking around in the science book department. At one point it appeared as though he were looking straight at her, and she lifted her hand slightly from the rail's rubber belt. But then his gaze continued on, out the windows. *Shit, he didn't recognize me,* she thought. Just so long as he was patient. In any case, she couldn't make contact now. "We still have the guy under surveillance," they'd said.

On the second floor she hurried straight past the racks of DVDs to the restrooms. She hadn't been faking—she had to go. If she'd been dragged to the police van she'd probably have carried out her threat.

Inside the ladies' room she bumped into a woman who was drying her hands in front of the mirror. An elegant, feminine woman, like so many of the customers in Barnes & Noble—that is, if one ignored the FBI identification card tucked into the waist of her slacks.

There were agents everywhere.

Doggie glanced at herself in the mirror as she shuffled by. It wasn't so strange they couldn't recognize her—she could hardly recognize herself. What a messy, pathetic sight. Like a rat backed into a corner— that's how she looked. And that's exactly what she was.

She sat down in one of the stalls. The next ten minutes would show whether her venture was going to succeed. Ten crucial, unnerving minutes. If they arrested her she'd have a lot to answer for. She'd probably survive, one way or another, but for her father it would be all over. Therefore she had no choice but to go on. She had to make it into the White House. That was her next hurdle.

And as she sat there obeying nature's call, she realized how she'd do it. It was so simple. But she absolutely had to get out of the store with T. Otherwise it wouldn't work.

She dabbed her face with toilet paper, trying not to wipe off the eyeliner.

"Yes, she's still in the toilet" came the hushed voice of the woman on the other side of the door.

"Yes, I'll keep an eye on her. . . . No, otherwise nothing. . . . Yes, I'm ready."

Like hell you are, thought Doggie. Then she pulled her soaked pants back on and took a hundred-dollar bill out of the plastic bag.

She stepped past the woman without looking at her and left the restroom, leaving a wet trail all the way to the café in the back, where she asked for a cup of tea at the counter. The waitress did a double take before her eyes came to rest on the large banknote that was being thrust towards her.

"Give me that sandwich there, too," Doggie said, pointing.

She took a couple of swallows of tea and didn't feel anyone watching her. After a couple of bites of the sandwich she passed the children's book department and chose a book on her way back down the escalator, constantly on the lookout for the sheriff of Highland County.

But T was nowhere to be seen, and she felt the panic rising as she looked at her watch. It wasn't even ten past twelve. He couldn't have left the store already, for God's sake.

She tried to look around calmly in all directions as she headed for the counter to pay, but he simply wasn't there.

Then she picked up a book from the new arrivals table and pretended to look at it while the personnel watched to see if she'd do any damage. She knew one of the clerks would soon show her the door if she wasn't careful.

Just behind her an agent was scouting the room, and in front of her one was looking out the window. The woman from the restroom was now positioned at the top of the escalator, watching the entrance. They were on full alert, and here she stood like a scarecrow, visible to everyone in the world, and no one suspected anything. She was the swan who'd turned into an ugly duckling.

Please, T, come out, come out, wherever you are, she pleaded silently and put the book down again. Then she headed towards a corner where an older couple stood, speaking softly and paging through a huge book. They shrank away when they caught sight of her.

If I go outside to look for him, they won't let me in again, she thought. But what if he'd really left?

She walked around the escalator and to the back of the store. A couple of agentlike types were hanging around, but they, too, moved away when she approached.

Then she gave up and headed for the entrance. T was gone. This was the worst thing that could happen.

It was raining harder than ever outside. The FBI agent had run for cover, and the gutters were like rivers. She had to be down at Market Square in three-quarters of an hour to meet Bugatti, but the walk itself would take only a few minutes if she headed straight for the square. By walking past the Metro Center parking lot and up around the Franklin Square neighborhood, she could use up extra time and still arrive early enough to try and stop Bugatti from entering the tea house. Maybe she'd get lucky and spot T along the way. She hoped so very, very much.

She glanced over her shoulder to see if anyone was following her, but the street was deserted. She sped up her pace, looking down side streets as she passed, but there was no T.

Her mind was racing. T had disappeared from Barnes & Noble. The agent had said they'd been keeping him under surveillance; maybe they thought he could lead them to her. Perhaps it wasn't such a good idea to find T, but one thing was for sure: Getting into the White House wouldn't be easy without him. Maybe Bugatti would be able to help instead, but right now she just didn't know.

She looked behind her one more time. A man was walking, bent over, on the opposite side of the street, fifty yards behind her. It was hard to see him clearly because her vision was blurred by the rain, but Doggie wasn't taking any chances. She began walking slightly faster and was horrified to notice that there was now another man following along a little ways behind the first one. By the time she reached the courthouse she was considering dropping the meeting with Bugatti— but how? It was her responsibility to warn him.

She'd felt uneasy ever since she'd set her foot on the pedestrian bridge over the Potomac, but now she was really afraid. The man behind her was like a fog that could envelop her at any moment. Or another man could suddenly appear in front of her. They said that most concentration camp prisoners became passive the longer they were in captivity, and that the daily suffering blunted speculations about the probability of their own death. She knew this was one of nature's quirks, where the destitute and doomed found a kind of peace of mind in resigning themselves to their fate. But before that point was a limited time span where fear took over, where one had survived long enough to imagine one had found a way out—only to realize one had been mistaken.

This was precisely Doggie's state of mind as she cut across Indiana Avenue with the two men on her heels.

Why don't you just give up? The obvious question was growing in her consciousness. *Market Square is just down at the end of Indiana Avenue, but so is FBI headquarters. These men are on their home turf. They're playing cat and mouse and are just waiting to see your next move before they pounce,* Doggie thought.

"Pull yourself together," she said out loud. She had to warn Bugatti if she could. Then she'd see what happened afterwards.

That was the moment where she began thinking maybe it all wasn't worth it. When she reached Market Square again she'd be almost back where she started, a few hundred yards from Barnes & Noble. If she showed up at the spot where they most likely already knew John Bugatti would be waiting for her, it probably wouldn't be so difficult to put two and two together. Pressing her luck was a bad idea—she could sense it. No, one shouldn't tempt the same opponent two times in a row.

So she stopped and turned around.

The first man was only twenty yards away now. He'd catch up with her if she didn't start running. The last downpour had soaked him to the skin, and he didn't seem to be enjoying it. Then he raised his head and looked right at her.

It was T.

She was about to shout with joy when she saw him nod behind him.

"Follow me very closely," he muttered as he passed her. His breathing sounded like a faulty ventilation system.

She followed three steps behind him, down towards Market Square, crossing the map of the world that was engraved into the square's granite surface. Then she looked up 8th Street towards Teaism, the tearoom. There didn't seem to be any sign of Bugatti. She looked at her watch. It was still too early.

They turned down Pennsylvania Avenue towards the Capitol with the other man trailing along behind and then turned up 6th Street. She turned around again. The guy was gone, so she caught up with T.

He didn't look at her. Instead he pulled a pack of cigarettes out of his coat pocket and tried to light one in the downpour. He was unsuccessful.

"I've got to meet John Bugatti down by Market Square now," she hissed. "What do I do?"

"Don't do it. We'll have the whole police force after us. You've got to figure we're being watched all the time. Just come with me."

"But the guy who was following us is gone."

"They're never gone."

"Was he after us?"

"What do you think? He and his buddies have been on my tail ever since I left Barnes & Noble."

"I just saw him. Where is he now?"

"He's standing, watching us a little farther up, but we're going to ditch him, along with all the others. Come on, but keep your distance."

Something came over T when they made it up to the grassy areas between the law courts. A hop and a jump and they were on the other side of the courthouse. He scanned the area as he walked and then bolted across the street. "Follow close—get it? Don't think. Just do as I say!"

She nodded. Exhaustion was setting in. How the hell could that bony man hold such a pace?

"Are you ready?" he asked, before racing up H Street like he was determined to win a marathon. Then he hauled her in between two parked cars, shoved something into the trunk's lock, turned it, opened the trunk, pushed her in, and slid in after her, after which he pulled the trunk closed.

Suddenly her whole universe consisted of a tiny crack of light, the rain hammering on the trunk, and T's wheezing breathing. Then she felt how badly she was positioned and how sharp T's bones were. It was uncomfortable as hell. She must have made some little sound, because T shushed her, and then she heard the hurried steps of people on the street. First one pair of feet, then several. Some men were calling to each other, but it was impossible to hear what they were saying.

They lay like that for a while, until they could hear the voices growing fainter.

"I can't lie like this much longer, T," she whispered. "I'm getting impaled on your knee."

"We're staying here ten minutes more, at least. They're still around."

"I can't hear anything."

He tried pulling his knee in closer to his body. A few minutes later they could hear more steps and voices, then all was quiet.

"Two more minutes," he said. "They think we've escaped by car. They just heard one take off down H Street."

"Did you hear them say that? I didn't!" He kept waiting.

Suddenly he shoved the trunk open. They were back in the downpour. "Good old Buick," he said, patting it once they were out again.

"We've got to get back. Hurry up," he ordered, pulling her towards the courthouse.

"That one," he cried, when they'd reached the courthouse square. He pointed at a shabby police car. So this was where he'd parked.

Pretty smart, she thought, as he opened the door and shoved her into the back seat. She looked through the steamed-up windows at the silhouettes of twenty or so patrol cars like his that were parked in the parking lot. Good camouflage.

They crouched down in the seats so they weren't as easy to spot from outside, and T handed her an old, stiff rag to dry herself off.

"Thank God it was *you* following me, T. But what happened, actually? When did you spot me?"

T ran his fingers through his hair and found an almost empty but dry pack of cigarettes in the glove compartment. "I saw you from the first floor of Barnes & Noble while that Fed was dragging you up the street."

"How'd you recognize me?"

"I didn't. Not until you raised your hand when you were going up the escalator."

She put her hand to her breast. "You saw that! But . . . where'd you go?"

"I disappeared out onto the street. You're wanted by the police, you know."

"Yeah, I'll say. I've been running for my life the past twenty-four hours."

"Yes, I'm sorry, but I only found out last night when I parked here. Apparently, they had a bulletin out for you over the police radio all day yesterday. Tell me exactly what the hell has happened."

It took a cigarette's time to fill him in briefly.

"Okay. I strongly warn against driving in the vicinity of the White House, Doggie. For several reasons."

"What I'm afraid of is that I'll have to, anyway, T. But first I've got to get hold of Bugatti. You have a cell phone?"

Police sirens could be heard in different directions as he handed her the phone.

She removed Bugatti's slip of paper from the little Buddha statue and punched in Danny's number.

"Hello?" There was a voice immediately.

"It's me," she said, and the person hung up.

"Short conversation," said T, and lit another cigarette.

She looked at the floor of the car and kicked one of the many empty beer and soft drink cans.

"Yeah, sorry about the mess," he said quietly. "I was sitting here all night, trying to think."

She nodded. She couldn't care less about the trash in T's patrol car.

"Bugatti's boyfriend was trying to warn me, I'm sure of it," she said. "Maybe his line is tapped. Maybe they're already there."

"I'd believe the latter, if I were you."

"Oh, God, T, what are we going to do? They may be arresting Bugatti as we speak."

"There's nothing you can do. . . . Just listen!"

She heard the sirens echoing off the monumental courthouse walls. No, there was nothing they could do.

"Doggie, I wanted to warn you, because this is much bigger and more dangerous than you may think." He related the events of the previous day. She broke in when he came to the account of Sunderland's childhood and his talk with Sunderland's adoptive father.

"So you suspect Sunderland is behind all this," she said slowly.

"Absolutely."

"John Bugatti and I do, too."

"Listen to an old hand, Doggie. Nothing has happened by chance here: the charges against your father, the assassination of Mimi Jansen, the assassination attempt on the president, all the horrible events that have been happening around the country, the unjust measures used against members of government and the Cabinet, the choice of 'trustworthy' people around the president. Sunderland's behind all of it. It's becoming clearer and clearer to me."

"I have some theories about the murder itself."

"So do I, but let that rest a moment, or else we'll lose time."

"You're thinking about my father?"

T took a deep drag on his cigarette. "No. Yes, him, too, of course, but first we've got to ask some questions of ourselves and others, before we know what our next move should be."

"What questions? There are plenty of them."

"What I'm wondering is: Why?" He stubbed his cigarette out in an overflowing ashtray.

"Why what? Why Sunderland's doing this?"

He nodded.

"He wants to be president."

"I think so, too," T agreed, "and with all the skeletons in his closet, this is the only way he can do it. And it'll work, too, if we don't stop him. You realize that, don't you?"

"How will it work?"

"Lyndon B. Johnson became president, and so did Gerald Ford."

"But Jansen has neither died nor resigned."

"Not yet—no. But everything inside me says it's going to happen today. Look at this town. It's crackling with tension. There are thousands of armed plainclothesmen down on the Ellipse. Sunderland needs to have it happen before the entire country falls apart."

"So you think Jansen will be murdered today and that Sunderland expects to be installed in his place." She took a deep breath. "Jesus, T! Everyone thinks Sunderland's completely loyal to Jansen. How will he avoid being brought to account for Jansen's deeds afterwards? How's he going to get someone to pick him as Jansen's successor? It won't be easy for him."

"Listen, Doggie. Sunderland will call off the state of emergency immediately. He'll claim he was trying to stop the president the whole time. That he's just received highly incriminating evidence that the president misused his power to provoke the state of emergency. That Jansen was sick in the head. That the sniper killings in New York, the school shootings—everything—was instigated by him."

"He won't get very far. It'll all be disproved."

"He's prepared for that, believe me. He'll find people to back up his claims. Important people."

"Not anyone in the White House."

"Yes, I think so, though they may not know it yet themselves."

Even though she was still dripping wet and the temperature in the car was near freezing, she began sweating. "Yes, you're right. He'll blame Jansen for everything, except the murder of his own wife. That's why my father must die. Then everything will be taken care of."

"Yes. Your father was useful to Sunderland. And now Sunderland will make sure that no one can claim he tampered with your father's trial after he's become president."

"What do you mean?"

"Mortimer Deloitte, the prosecutor, has disappeared. I'm sure he was on Sunderland's payroll. There were too many loose ends in that case. Like who shot Toby O'Neill, for example. Deloitte's failure to investigate that was no procedural mistake. He did it on purpose."

"My God! But they'll find Deloitte, won't they?"

"Not alive, if you ask me."

"T, we have to make it to the White House. We've got to speak to Jansen."

"That won't happen. We'll never get in. The British prime minister is arriving in a little while. They're on full alert. They'll arrest you immediately if you try it."

"Listen, T, what the hell else are we going to do, huh? There's hardly any time left. Do you want us to lodge a complaint with the Human Rights Commission in the Hague first?" She raised her hand to ward off his reply. He obviously didn't know what to say, anyway. "You're getting me into the White House—end of story. Say that you've captured me and now you're bringing me in. Try to picture it: You've got a sheriff's uniform on under that silly coat, don't you? Why shouldn't they believe you? We'll call Wesley and tell him what's happening. Come on, let's do it now."

"I heard this morning that Marvin Gallegos was tracked down and shot by the authorities."

"Okay, I know I've heard that name before, but I can't remember who he was. Is it important for us?"

"He was John Bugatti's cameraman. The one who dropped his camera during the assassination and let it keep running."

She nodded. Now she remembered him. He hadn't had much to say on the witness stand. "Yes, but there was nothing on that film that was usable."

"Yes, there was. I think it proved that your father went out for a glass of water and dropped it when he returned, just as he claimed. The tape's been manipulated."

"How do you know that?"

"I've seen the film clips. You can see where they did it."

Shivers ran down her back. "What you're saying is, Gallegos was killed just to be on the safe side. So he couldn't help analyze the tapes if it became relevant at a later date."

"By then they would have edited the tapes left and right, and he would have been able to see it. He would have been a dangerous witness. They're saying he was working with the militias, and it was in this connection that he was shot."

"And you think they'll do something similar with you and me if we get near the White House."

"Something along those lines. Absolutely."

"What about Bugatti?"

T put out his second cigarette. "There's nothing we can do, Doggie. I'm really sorry to say it, but that's the way it is. He's going to have to try and take care of himself."

She put her head in her hands. Ice-cold, hair-raising shivers began wracking her body again. "You say you think they'll carry out the assassination today?"

"It stands to reason."

"Then we have to go over there. For the sake of my father and the whole country. If you won't help me, T, I'll do it alone. I mean it!"

"Do you, really?" T shook his head, put his hand in his coat pocket, and pulled out his car keys. He fumbled with the cigarette pack and shook out the last one.

"Then we're going to do it in style," he said, and turned the key in the ignition. Suddenly one more voice joined the chorus of police sirens.

CHAPTER 38

THE NIGHT HAD BEEN MERCIFUL. IF IT HADN'T BEEN FOR A CHANCE MOTOR-
cyclist named Sean, John Bugatti would have been lying next to Tom
Jumper in the Front Royal morgue, or wherever it was they'd taken
him—he was sure of it.

Besides hanging on for dear life, he'd been weighing his options as
they'd rocketed through the Virginia woods. Perhaps it was best if he
just completely disappeared, starting with random, abandoned hide-
outs to sleep in by day and heading south by night. If there was anyone who knew the dangers out there, he did, thus giving him a greater
chance to avoid them. And if he could walk fifteen miles each night—
which wasn't that unreasonable—and could keep up his supply of
medicine, he could be in Miami in a couple of months. In Miami he
knew a lot of exile Cubans, including ones who could slip him into
their old homeland. He'd always liked Cuba.

But then he came to his senses, remembering how his illness was
slowly debilitating him and realizing how hard it was to ignore his
conscience.

John and Sean reached Brickyard Road, close to Great Falls, by the
time the sun had been working its way into the sky for a half hour's
time. They pulled up alongside three light military vehicles and were
received by eight well-appointed men in army officers' uniforms. They
immediately saluted Bugatti's rescuer as though he were their superior. Judging by the tiredness in their faces, they'd been waiting for

some time, and Sean didn't plan to keep them waiting much longer. As far as John could tell by their quiet conversation, they had to meet two other groups in "Cairo," and the sixth of October was mentioned again. Today was the twenty-ninth of March, so the date must have had another meaning—but what?

While Sean changed into uniform his men were questioning him about John's identity and what he was doing there. His presence clearly made them uneasy until Sean told them about their escape and how John had nearly lost his life while appearing on Tom Jumper's pirate radio show. Then some of them recognized him, and a couple even nodded. They had heard the program and also knew Jumper was dead.

"Where are you going?" one asked John, and he told him.

"That tea salon is next to the FBI building—have you thought about that?" said another. "You're wanted, so do you think it's wise?"

"We can give him this, can't we?" This time it was a soldier holding a transparent package he had just taken out of his vehicle. "It doesn't fit any of us, anyway."

"What is it?" John asked, turning to Sean and suddenly seeing another man standing there: different hairstyle, false mustache, and a look of authority in his eye that could make his men cast themselves willingly into the jaws of death.

"Wait here, Bugatti," said the transformed Sean. "In two hours you'll be picked up and driven into town, all right? And remember: You've never seen me. Follow the driver's instructions; we'll brief him before he picks you up." He turned towards his men. "How many are we still missing?"

"Ronnie Benson and Shooter," one of them answered.

Sean nodded. "Okay, Shooter's gone straight to the rendezvous, and Ronnie will have to take care of himself. We can manage without him." He gave John a slap on the back in parting and climbed onto the front seat of the first vehicle.

One of the soldiers gave John a Budweiser and a bologna sandwich, and the unit drove off.

Inside the clear plastic bag he found a gray-green officer's uniform from Marlow White. It was obviously new, with brass buttons, black bands on the arms, and stripes down the legs, plus a variety of medals. He had no idea what they stood for; he could be a general in the medical marines or a choirboy on a submarine for all he knew. John had never been in the military, though he'd had lovers who were. No, there was nothing sexier than a man in uniform—and now he was one, too.

He emptied his pockets and laid the contents—a handkerchief, the cell phone that he hadn't dared to use, and the cash he'd been given by Danny—on a mossy tree stump by the edge of the road, along with his folded-up civilian clothes. Then he put on the uniform and tried to imagine how he looked. He was sure he didn't cut as sharp a profile as the boys he used to chase.

He put the money in his pocket and considered tossing his cell phone way into the underbrush, but instead put it in the inner pocket of his uniform, sat down on his old clothes, and began massaging his tender ankle. Thank God the swelling was starting to go down. The jump off of the radio transmission van could have been much worse. He rotated his ankle gingerly and tried to think.

They had mentioned that date—the sixth of October—a date he was certain symbolized something else. Somewhere in an abandoned corner of his memory he knew what, too. It just lay there, waiting to burst into his consciousness.

He was picked up by a jeep, and he and the driver bumped along forest roads and byways for over three hours without either of them saying a word.

At one point the driver passed him an ID card, and John took it with apprehension.

It read: "Tony Clark, major, 54 years, medical corps," along with some other information. Was he really supposed to show this if it was demanded of him? He didn't resemble this Major Clark in the slightest. They must be kidding.

Just as he was about to raise a protest, the silent driver pointed at a little box sitting on the seat. John opened it, revealing contents that would thrill any variety artist who needed to make several fast character changes. He sighed and adjusted the rearview mirror. The wig had better fit, and the mustache not fall off.

He was finally let off at Staunton Park, and from there he made for downtown Washington on foot while the sky became more and more overcast and occasional raindrops pelted his shoulders. Several soldiers saluted him along the way, and he returned the gesture.

He'd gotten as far as the Canadian embassy and had yet to be asked to identify himself. If only he could continue on like this and no one suddenly had use for his medical expertise—which was not unthinkable. There was a nasty mood in the air, a sense of impending violence. Someone could easily get hurt, and it wasn't hard to associate this regime with the kind that maintained its authority through the barrel of a gun. There were military vehicles everywhere. Occasional rolls of barbed wire blocked the streets, and crack soldiers with automatic weapons were turning pedestrians back where they came from, while those who were allowed to proceed picked up their pace, worry painted on their faces. Otherwise the scene was strangely quiet, like a battlefield moments before dawn where troops in their trenches are waiting for the whistle to go over the top.

It had begun raining like hell by the time he reached Market Square, and his mustache threatened to come undone more than once. A look at his watch confirmed he was at least an hour and a half early. *I can wait for Doggie inside the tearoom,* he thought, the wet uniform plastered to his body. Still limping slightly from his fall, he entered the red building that housed the Teaism salon and nodded amiably to the manager, a guy of Mexican origin they called Roberto. John had always liked this place.

"Give me an oysterburger and a single trunk oolong tea," he said, and sat himself on a stool by the window. From there he could see over to the Residences where Wesley lived. Could that be why she'd chosen this spot to meet? Was Wesley going to be participating, too?

He took a couple of bites of food and looked around the appealing little restaurant. Two young Latino types sporting black baseball caps and the traces of mustaches stood behind the teakwood counter, joking good-naturedly. They were obviously brothers. He devoured the sight of their broad shoulders and reflexively sat up straight and thrust out his chest.

Besides himself and the personnel, there were only three customers, tight-lipped white men in their forties in light-blue shirts, sitting at the same table, each with a cup in front of him. *They don't look like tea drinkers,* he thought, and looked out the window again, this time over at the Atlantic café across the street. He could just make out some indistinct shapes staring out of the rain-spattered windows. From what he could see, they looked exactly like the men sitting a few feet away from him. Then his gaze panned up the street to the entrance to the underground parking lot in the Lansburg Building. CLEARANCE: 6 FT. 8 IN. was written above it, and under the sign a dark-blue van blocked the entrance and exit lanes. They won't stay there forever, he decided, and let his eyes skim the menu. It had been a couple of years since he'd been here, and the prices were pretty much unchanged. *Good place,* he thought, looking up again in time to see a man get out of the dark-blue van. He was in his forties, once again in a light-blue shirt, this time under a gray suit that was quickly turning black in the rain.

John turned his head slowly towards the three men with teacups. None had moved an inch since he came. Then slowly, slowly, he looked across the street. The blurred shapes of the men in the Atlantic café hadn't moved, either.

That was when the thought struck him. He pushed back his plate, dabbed his lips with his napkin, stood up, and nonchalantly walked past the three men and down the steel staircase to the restrooms. They didn't watch him go. They didn't do anything.

He ignored the little pond with Koi carp at the foot of the stairs as he headed straight for the men's room.

Something's wrong, he thought, staring unseeingly at the bottom of the massive sink. *What would happen if I tried to call Danny?* He shook his head to try to banish the idea.

But what else to do? he reasoned. *There are all those men up there, for God's sake, just waiting. And they have plenty of time.* He looked in the mirror and could confirm that the mustache was in place. He wasn't easy to recognize, thank God. Small details like his new hairdo and restyled eyebrows definitely helped.

I have to get away from here, but I've got to warn Doggie first. It's either me or her they're waiting for. He considered his options and felt an icy shiver in his stomach. But how the hell to warn her? He didn't have her cell phone number, and he had no idea where she was. So he had no choice but to call Danny and hear whether she had given a counterorder. And if not, things were going to be bad. The boys upstairs weren't waiting for nothing.

He turned on the phone and dialed the number. *This has got to be quick,* he told himself. Just time enough for Danny to give him a message, if there was one, and then get out of the tearoom.

The phone was answered almost immediately.

"Hey, Danny Boy," he said, but Danny didn't answer.

"Is it you? Is something the matter?" He could hear Danny was there. When you've lain in the same bed for years, your partner's breathing pattern becomes imprinted on your brain. It was Danny, but still it wasn't.

"No, it's okay, I was just sleeping," Danny's voice said. It sounded natural enough, but the red warning lights were flashing in John's head. He hung up. If Danny had been sleeping, it would have taken him ages and a day to pick up the phone.

"Oh, Danny, no!" he whispered, and sat down heavily on the toilet seat. "What has happened to you?" He stared at the cell phone's display and considered calling again.

Then he let his hands fall in his lap and found himself praying instead.

He stood between the steel masts before the US Navy Memorial at Market Square and let his eyes pan all the way around the wet, glistening street. There were hundreds of uniforms to be seen, but none of them looked at him. They just paced around, eyes front, as though they were programmed to move only from point A to point B. Maybe it was because of the rain; maybe they were just making their way up Pennsylvania Avenue towards the White House for some reason or other.

Then he punched in the number of his editor in chief. John felt safe calling Alastair Hopkins—he was sly and experienced. He'd know if his phone was being tapped, and he'd know how to tackle the situation.

John looked at the statue on the square. A sailor stood in the rain, waiting on the pier with his duffel bag. Somehow he felt an affinity with him. What awaited the two of them out there?

He heard a click on the line. "This is Alastair Hopkins's telephone. With whom am I speaking?"

Oh, hell, it was Hopkins's secretary, Deirdre Boyd. His heart sank. She was an unendearing creature who could put a serious fright into the most hardened lawyers. The epitome of a superior being, an impudent, high-class spinster, and to top it off she was a Scot with a capital S, from her unmanageable shortish hair down to her brown walking shoes. Miserly about everything: a smile or a positive word. Even information was hard to get out of her, although that was the purpose of her job. She would under no circumstances transfer his call directly into Hopkins's office. Not a journalist who had deserted his workplace and was wanted by the authorities, besides.

Before he knew what he was doing, he said, "This is Sunderland," in a high voice. "Give me Hopkins."

"Sunderland?" she asked. She knew exactly who Sunderland was. "We're not hiring. Try somewhere else."

Dumb bitch. Never afraid of anything.

"*Thomas* Sunderland, your vice president." He pulled his collar up around his ears. Why the hell had he used that name, instead of someone Deirdre had a little bit of respect for—whoever that could be, besides her boss.

"If it's Editor in Chief Hopkins you wish to speak to, I suggest you look out your window. I assume you're in the White House. He's standing on the lawn with the other bleating sheep, waiting for Prime Minister Watts to arrive. Good-bye!"

So Prime Minister Watts was on his way to Washington! That was why there were so many soldiers and police. President Jansen was having his first official state visit. Pretty brave of him, considering the circumstances.

"Just hold on, now," said John in a cold voice. "So Hopkins is out there. Good, I'll find him, but while I have you, I need you to answer a question for me."

"My job description doesn't include functioning as a search engine."

"You may not have a job much longer, period. I want you to find out what a 'swatter' could be, besides a flyswatter."

"Is it because you're too embarrassed to ask your own people? Is it something you ought to know yourself?"

"Look it up."

He could picture her: snug sweater, flat chest, lips pursed. No assignment good enough. But her keyboard was working in the background.

"Well, well," she said. "It would seem there are also electric fly-swatters. Was that what you wanted?"

He could have killed her. "No, that's not it. Try again."

"Any model in particular?"

"What do you mean?"

"There are many different ones. You're probably thinking about the 9M17P."

He almost bit his tongue. "Oh, right. Umm . . . Can you describe it?"

"The dimensions are only given metrically. It's eleven hundred sixty millimeters long and weighs thirty-one and a half kilograms. Its range is between five hundred and twenty-five hundred meters, and it has a velocity of one hundred fifty to one hundred seventy meters per second. Penetration strength is five hundred millimeters, and chances of a direct hit with model C are ninety percent. Satisfied?"

It was a totally surreal and horrific experience, hearing these words from this woman's mouth, standing in a public square on Pennsylvania Avenue.

"A missile, in other words."

"Well, it doesn't sound like a Barbie doll. Is there more I can do for you, Mr. Vice President? Shall I send you a copy of the United States Constitution and underline the part about freedom of expression?" He had to admire her defiant courage.

"Yes, there is something else, now that you mention it. Please look up 'the sixth of October' on Wikipedia, and see what it says."

"It was my grandfather's birthday, along with Carole Lombard's—how about that?"

"Excuse me, but would you be so kind as to give me your name?"

"Naturally. I'm not ashamed. Deirdre Boyd. Did you wish to invite me out? Because in that case I regret to tell you that my integrity forbids me to accept."

No, there could be no doubt. Vice president or not, Sunderland was not her cup of tea. If only he had said he was someone else.

"Mrs. Boyd . . ." he said, raising his voice.

"Miss!"

"Miss Boyd, please pull yourself together. I'm speaking to your boss in five minutes. Don't let my impression of an obstinate, cheeky employee be a lasting one."

It must have been the term *cheeky* that did it. This was not the kind of predicate a Vassar girl appreciated having attached to her name.

"Okay. This is the last favor. I'm a busy person!" she snapped, but he could hear her working at the keyboard again.

"Yes," she said after a half minute. "It's the date in 2000 when Slobodan Milošević resigned. Is that it?"

"No, I don't think so."

"The sixth of October is also 'Germany-USA Day.'"

"What else is there?"

"There are three pages of listings here. It would help if you could be more specific."

"'Cairo,' then. See if there's a sixth of October that has anything to do with Cairo."

This time only five seconds passed. "It's an Egyptian national holiday celebrating the victories of the October War. I thought they lost that one. . . . Ohh, here it says that President Sadat was assassinated that day in 1981."

John stiffened. He'd known it all along. Her words reached his brain at the same time as his own realization.

He hung up immediately and looked through the mist towards the White House. He'd been racing through Virginia all night on the back of the motorcycle of a coup leader, and it looked very much like he and his eight officer-conspirators were in Washington at this very moment. "Big brother has the swatter," they'd said. He suspected that meant it was already in position, and when it was time, they'd fire the missile in cold blood, and the country would be minus a president. Egypt's President Sadat's trusted protectors had led the treachery that had him killed. Murdered in broad daylight by members of his own corps of bodyguards during a military parade. Even the best-protected person has his Achilles' heel.

At that moment his cell phone rang. He looked at it for ten seconds and then raised it to his ear.

"Yes . . . ?" he said, listening intently, but he heard nothing. He'd been localized.

He turned the thing off and threw it in the nearest trash can.

Making it to the White House turned out to be a drawn-out undertaking. Normally it would take fifteen or twenty minutes, but this time it took an hour, partly because his ankle was hurting again and partly because of the constant stopping of people by the security forces. Not to mention the masses of soldiers who were making their way up Pennsylvania Avenue, who John tried to keep pace with. Even though the atmosphere was hectic and the camouflage-clad men's patience was at the breaking point, he figured there was less chance of him being stopped if he stayed with them. It was the other ones who made him nervous, the ones in civilian clothes, motionless except for their eyes. Those were the ones he didn't want questioning him. They never saluted or paid attention to his medals. They observed his body language and how his tiniest face muscles behaved. If he were stopped by them, it was all over.

He reached the West Wing control post at a quarter past one, at the same moment as a helicopter swung into view above Lafayette Square and headed over the myriad of White House chimneys.

Jesus Christ, he thought, his heart pounding. *Now it's happening.* In a way, he couldn't have asked for a better moment.

"Let me through!" he called to some soldiers in ponchos. "It's an emergency!" They were unimpressed and ordered him to turn back if he didn't want problems.

The whupping sound of the rotary blades sliced through the air and faded behind the building.

"Ninety percent accuracy," the Scottish banshee had told him.

"Let me through!" he screamed, this time to the guard behind the fence. "You better listen to me or you'll regret it. I have proof that someone's about to assassinate the president!"

The word *assassinate* got the guard to reach for his telephone, some of the soldiers to freeze, and two plainclothes agents to crowd in on him from either side with drawn weapons. He saw how ready they were to use them—one false move, and he'd be dead. So he raised his hands slowly in the air. "Let me speak to Wesley Barefoot immediately," he said.

One of the plainclothesmen began talking into his lapel mike, but it wasn't Barefoot he'd called.

He had been sitting in a little office for ten minutes. They'd considered handcuffing him, but for the moment the security agents were content to keep him covered with their weapons. A lot of muttering had gone on into lapel microphones, and security people were being positioned at strategic points inside the White House. Some suspected he had been sent in as a diversionary maneuver. They were taking nothing for granted.

The next security agent who came in was one he'd seen many times before. The man with the glittering, gold bracelets, the one he had suggested—before an open mike on Tom Jumper's radio program— could be implicated in the murder of Mimi Jansen. Here was the man whom John had the least desire to see in the whole world right now: Ben Kane, Sunderland's shadow.

"You searched him?" Kane asked.

The other security agents nodded.

"And . . . ?"

"No weapon. False mustache and wig. Eyeliner on his eyebrows."

"Identity?"

"Tony Clark, fifty-four years old. Officer in the medical corps. Reported as fallen in a skirmish in the Catoctin Mountains. Ostensibly an officer who deserted and joined the militia."

John saw Kane's smile and was powerless to keep his hands still on the chair's armrest. He stared helplessly at his fidgeting fingers. The fight was lost.

Ben Kane squatted in front of him. "Mr. Tony Clark . . . I see. . . . Seems to me you look exactly like a certain Mr. John Bugatti, who, until only a few days ago, was one of our nation's very best reporters but ended up a pathetic, pathological liar on the run. Doesn't that fit your CV a little better? Or do you really prefer to be a dead officer in the medical corps? Because that can be arranged if you insist."

"Let me speak to the president" was all he said. What else *could* he say?

"You can go; I'll take care of this," said Kane to his men. That sounded very ominous. His men were leaving when another security officer stuck his head in the door.

"Sunderland wants you down in Burton's office. Now!" was all he said.

Kane stood up and gave John a deadly look. "You remain seated. Don't worry, we'll get to the bottom of this. And you," he said, addressing two of his subordinates, "you don't go anywhere. And you two stand guard outside the door. And keep a damn good eye on him!"

He left the office door open, and as soon as he had disappeared across the lobby in the direction of the chief of staff's office, Bugatti began a verbal bombardment of the two men left in the room.

"Don't you realize it's him, not me, who must be stopped? Don't you know what he's capable of? I'll tell you."

He began talking as fast as he could, telling about the killing of the president's wife and the shooting of Toby O'Neill. About the rebel soldiers in the forest who were preparing to fire an antitank missile at the nation's commander in chief. About time running out and about this Tower of Babel that was on the verge of falling.

His torrent of words fell on deaf ears. The two men couldn't care less. They'd been ordered to guard him, not listen to him.

There was some commotion at the entrance to the lobby, and a few seconds later a little delegation filed past his door towards the Roosevelt Room. John could hear they were British diplomats—they always stood out in the crowd. They looked in at him as they went by, but all they saw was a man in an officer's uniform, sitting on a chair.

Shall I try and get their attention? he thought for a second, and then he spotted Wesley, gesticulating energetically as he spoke to the diplomat he was walking beside.

"Wesley!" he cried, as loud as he could, but was clobbered on the back of the neck as he was about to yell again. It didn't knock him unconscious—it didn't even hurt much—but suddenly he didn't have any control over his muscles. He couldn't cry out, and his legs wouldn't obey him when he tried to stand up. He fought with the armrest, but there was no longer any coordination between any parts of his body.

He was dumbfounded. He tried to form words, but none would come out. All that was left was his brain telling him that everything had stopped just as salvation was in sight.

"John?" He heard a voice over by the door. He tried turning his head, but his body still wouldn't obey.

In spite of the security guards' protests, they towed him over to Wesley's office. "You know where he is, so don't worry," Wesley reasoned, and, with his position in mind, they were forced to obey. Kane would be returning in a couple of minutes, and until then there was no way they were moving an inch from Press Secretary Wesley Barefoot's office door.

Wesley gave John some water to drink and said he was sorry that unfortunately his secretary was on sick leave. That she had broken down after they'd come and arrested her husband, and if she'd been there, he might have been able to offer him something stronger to drink.

John shook his head. It didn't matter.

Then he cleared his throat a couple of times, and in a quiet, guarded voice told Wesley what he'd been through and what he knew.

CHAPTER 39

"I HAVE TO GET IN TO SEE PRESIDENT JANSEN AS SOON AS POSSIBLE," SAID Wesley to the Secret Service agents stationed in front of the Oval Office.

"I'm sorry, Mr. Barefoot," said one of them. These men were trained in refusing people; it didn't matter whom. "We've been given specific orders that the president's meeting with the prime minister not be interrupted—under any circumstances. Even the telephones and intercom are shut off."

"Okay, I understand, but I've just received information whose only interpretation can be that there's about to be an attempt on the president's life."

"Yes, we know about these rumors. They're being dealt with."

Wesley was taken aback. "It's a missile attack we're talking about that apparently can happen at any time."

"We're aware of it. You don't have to worry, Mr. Barefoot, they're working on it."

He stepped back from the Oval Office door. He had other things to tell the president besides warning him about the assassination attempt. Like new information concerning the murder of Jansen's wife that meant the president should be extra watchful around his closest, most trusted advisors. That there was reason to believe Bud Curtis was innocent. That John Bugatti was presently sitting in his office and had plenty to tell at the risk of his own life. That his secretary couldn't work as long as her husband was being detained. That President Jansen had to do something about all of this for the best of the country and his own survival. But Wesley was being denied the opportunity—at least for now.

He glanced over towards Lance Burton's office. They had barely spoken since Burton had revealed his surveillance center to him the day before. The implication was that it was better this way—Wesley would take care of his job, and Burton would see to the rest. The point was that Burton wouldn't place Wesley in unnecessary danger, and if Burton were removed, Wesley would take over the surveillance. If Burton were gone—God forbid—Wesley would replace him anyway. Who else was qualified?

He looked at the closed doors in the corridor around the Oval Office.

They were all so very powerful, the men who sat behind these doors. But perhaps it was behind his own door that the most powerful man of all was sitting. John Bugatti was possibly the most important witness and defender of truth to be found in the whole country just now. It was he who still had eyes that could see and an intellect that hadn't fallen victim to self-deception. And it was also he who Wesley was powerless to protect. It was a desperate situation.

He made up his mind and stepped over to Lance Burton's office. The chief of staff was simply going to have to leave his preserve. If he didn't demand entry to all these doors and convene the people behind them, nothing was going to happen. Burton had to do this, otherwise there would be consequences too awful to contemplate. And according to Bugatti, there wasn't much time.

Wesley had expected to be greeted by Burton's secretary's usual mechanical, tight smile, but her seat was empty and the door to Burton's office open. This was very unusual.

He could hear hushed voices from within the office, so he approached cautiously and knocked on the doorframe.

The sight that greeted him was just as unexpected as it was unwelcome. Lance Burton was sitting behind his desk, hands folded, looking at him as if he were a stranger. Vice President Sunderland was standing by the window with his back to them, and Ben Kane was standing next to Burton, in front of the open door to the little surveillance room, his hand on Burton's shoulder. None of them spoke, nor was it necessary, because then the voices he'd heard from outside resumed from the door opening behind Kane. They came from the speakers inside the surveillance room.

And what they were listening to was seriously compromising for Lance Burton, for it was nothing less than the British prime minister's voice that filled the office. It was easy to hear that Burton's built-in window microphones in the Oval Office were already functioning optimally; it was as though they were in the same room.

Then Sunderland turned around, his face white with rage. But his hand was well under control as he turned off the listening-in mode. "Kane, go in and stop the video machines," he said, waiting a moment before he looked at Wesley.

"You know anything about this?"

"No," he said, without looking at Burton.

"I hope not, for your sake. But we'll find that out later. . . . So you have absolutely no knowledge of this equipment, you say?"

"No—and I'm deeply shocked and outraged." He said this looking straight at Burton, who let his eyes fall, making it easier for Wesley to betray him. That was Lance in a nutshell.

"But you knew about the audio monitoring?"

"Yes, former vice president Lerner was so kind as to inform us about it, remember? But I didn't know the equipment was in here, and definitely not that it was used to eavesdrop on the Oval Office. Has the president approved of this?"

Sunderland didn't answer. Instead his attention focused on Ben Kane, who had just reappeared from behind the door. They nodded to each other—the surveillance gear had been shut off. Kane went over and whispered something in Sunderland's ear. Wesley could imagine what.

"Is John Bugatti in your office?" Sunderland asked.

"Yes."

"You know he's wanted, don't you?"

"Yes."

"That he's spreading rumors about me."

"No, I didn't know that. What rumors?" Wesley studied Sunderland's eyes. They were like a weasel's—vicious and unpredictable.

Sunderland didn't answer. Instead he nodded to Kane, who immediately heaved Burton out of his seat.

"We'll get back to this later, Wesley. And, Kane, you take the chief of staff over to the Situation Room and make sure he's well guarded, understand? And get back here as fast as you can." Chief of Staff Burton's face revealed nothing as he was led out of the room. His bearing was dignified, like a serene, resigned condemned man on his way to the scaffold. Wesley knew he had nothing to fear; Burton would keep his mouth shut to the end.

"You stay in this room. Got it, Wesley?" said Sunderland.

Then he called a couple of Secret Service agents over from across the hall. "Barefoot is to be kept in Burton's office until further orders, understand?"

After which he closed the door and left Wesley alone with his dark thoughts about the responsibility he had inherited from Burton.

A much too large responsibility. Once upon a time he'd told his mother that he was going to try to get to work for Jansen, just as she had, and she had stroked his cheek as though he had already vanished from her life and off the planet. She'd known what was to come: He would somehow be swallowed up—either by the void or the exuberance—and that's what happened.

Right now he was just wishing his mother had never let him go. Life had held so many other possibilities then.

He opened the door to the surveillance cubbyhole and found the main switch, after which he turned on each individual apparatus until the room was dotted with little red lights. Now he'd have to find out if it all worked.

He proceeded to open the metal box above the equipment and turned on the monitor. A grayish picture flickered on the screen, and the show was under way. He took the selector knob and changed from one camera to another. First the camera in the empty lobby and then to the ones that followed Sunderland into the Roosevelt Room. From there he checked out the guards outside the chief of staff's door and then the two security men standing before his own door, watching over Bugatti. Then he saw Bugatti himself, pacing back and forth in Wesley's office. It was clear that his restlessness was propelled more by frustration than fear. Wesley moved on to the Roosevelt Room, where Sunderland was receiving the British delegation. The hearty mood lasted a little while, but gradually the delegates' expressions turned more and more serious, and then to shock.

Wesley found the volume control and turned it up just as Sunderland held up an inauspicious notebook.

"It's all here," Wesley heard him say. "Every time I've become aware of another of the president's injustices, I've written it down in this notebook. You can see what he's been doing to this country, day by day. It's all here. I would ask you to deliver this to Prime Minister Watts the moment you leave the White House, and that the contents be made public, but that my name be kept out of it for the time being. It's impossible to say how long it will take to have the president removed from office, but until then our lives are at stake. He's ordered so many killings already—what's one more to him? And I could easily be the next victim."

Wesley had to find a stool and sit down.

The leader of the delegation nodded gravely, accepted the notebook, and passed it immediately to a subordinate who dropped it into his briefcase. Sunderland had planned this well.

"At the same time I would like to appeal to the international community to begin investigating ways in which it can help. It could be a matter for the United Nations, but that means of recourse may already be cut off, at least as long as foreign diplomats aren't allowed much freedom of movement these days. Or so I've been told."

"Don't worry, we'll find a way," one of the diplomats answered.

"This evening I will tender my resignation. Perhaps now is also the time to inform you that I plan to seek political asylum in the British embassy. Do you agree to that?"

"Yes, naturally," answered the delegation leader. "But it's hard to say whether the rules of diplomacy will be upheld, given the current situation."

"I have to take the chance." Vice President Sunderland shook hands with the British diplomat. "Now I will give you gentlemen the opportunity to discuss the situation among yourselves. And I hope you'll have a chance to glance through my diary. Some of it is gruesome reading, but I felt it was best that way. Of course I have other kinds of material evidence when the time comes, hopefully. But now I must return to my other duties. I will be seeing you in the State Dining Room at three thirty."

He shook hands with the rest of the delegation and walked out of the room.

Wesley patted the video machine. *Gotcha now,* he thought, before doubt set in. He still didn't know anything for sure. Maybe Sunderland's version really could be true, and Jansen was behind it all. Even with time running out, it was hard to eliminate either possibility with the evidence at hand.

Fucking load of shit, he thought.

Then he switched through the surveillance cameras to find Sunderland and see where he was headed.

On the third try he found himself looking inside his own office, with Bugatti over by the door connecting Wesley's and Sunderland's offices. A door that hadn't been opened since Wesley had taken over Sunderland's secretary's room.

I'm afraid it's locked, my friend, he said silently, as Bugatti reached out his hand and turned the knob. Which was why he froze when the door swung open.

Wesley flew out of the control room and over to the intercom on Lance Burton's desk. "Don't do it, John!" he cried. "Go out through my archive room instead, then down to the pressroom! The press conference is being held on the lawn, so stay in the pressroom. Find somewhere to hide—you know the place. And *stay* there, understand?"

He punched the intercom button a couple of times. It was completely dead.

He raced back to the monitor to see that his office was now empty. Then he switched to the camera in the corridor to the pressroom, but Bugatti wasn't there, either.

"Goddammit, John, you dumb bastard!" he muttered, and moved to the camera in Sunderland's office. There he was, the idiot, rummaging through all the drawers in the vice president's desk. He clicked to the camera in the hallway between the Roosevelt Room and Sunderland's office, just as Sunderland was approaching his office door.

Wesley's heart was pumping so wildly, it made his temples throb. Sunderland had just come in the door of his office and discovered Bugatti, who immediately froze, half-crouched over a desk drawer.

He could see they were exchanging words, but there was no sound.

"Goddammit!" he swore, trying to find the wire that caught the signal from Wesley's ID badge, still wedged between the cushions in the sofa. He finally found it and plugged it in.

The scene being enacted before him on the monitor progressed in a horribly simple and methodical fashion. It laid bare not only the extent of Sunderland's villainy, but also the definitive end of a fine and honorable journalist's attempt to survive to tell the biggest story of his life and maybe even save his country.

Sunderland wasn't wasting time. In keeping with an old military man's custom for dealing with completely incalculable situations, he walked calmly over to a cabinet in the corner and removed an old service pistol, like he'd done on a couple of very rare jovial occasions when he wanted to show off living proof of his manhood. He flipped off the safety, aimed the gun slowly at Bugatti's body, and squeezed the trigger.

The loud report of the gunshot temporarily blew out the microphone in Wesley's chip in the sofa, but he could see gun smoke rising in the air and a beloved friend being pitched backward against the wall and gliding to the floor behind the desk, leaving the stain from his mortal wound behind him.

Then the sound came back.

"Help! Help!" Sunderland was shouting, as he calmly laid the gun on his desk. "Get in here and help me!"

Wesley couldn't take any more. The last thing he saw before he sank to the floor with his head in his hands was the door flying open and two bodyguards, weapons extended, approaching the vice president's desk.

CHAPTER 40

THOMAS SUNDERLAND HAD HAD HIS WINGS CLIPPED AS A BOY. HE WAS SMACKED around regularly until the day in his sixteenth year when his father beat his mother's vivacious face in with a baseball bat.

His name had been Junior at the time—Leo Mulligan Jr., to be precise—and it was not a name he'd been proud of.

And Junior had packed up and took off down the farmhouse road before the authorities could manage to make him a guardian of the state.

Junior Mulligan wanted to go where the action was. He wanted to try everything America had to offer, and it was no new dream of his, either. He'd always heard that "this is a country where a man can get what he wants."

The third time a motorist stopped to give him a lift during his escape, it was a woman whose ripe curves longed for caressing. This chance meeting taught Junior that no person is unapproachable as long as one is able to determine the outcome.

Then came a period of months where neglected suburban housewives instructed Junior in how he could stretch them tight as a bow in bed while the husband was at work. And in return he taught these women how best they could express their appreciation in the form of larger-denomination dollar bills. If they didn't do it of their own accord, he threatened them. Twenty bucks for him to keep his mouth shut—it was worth it. Husbands' reactions in cases like this were known for being pretty straightforward in this neck of the woods.

In this way, there was always enough money for a room, plus a little extra, with evenings off. Long speculative evenings where he read and dreamed and planned out his life. Basically, Junior wanted to be the country's leader, where no one stood over him and no one could ever again try raising a hand against him without knowing the consequences.

That was his plan.

When the police caught up with him in Gilbert's Corner, his father had already been institutionalized indefinitely at Marion Correctional Treatment Center, so the court case about who would take custody of him was not unproblematic. There was an uncle in Ohio who wanted him, but the uncle's chances weren't helped when he happened to mention how great it would be, having an extra hand in the tobacco fields. To make sure this wouldn't happen, Junior employed his newly acquired talents of manipulation, picking out from among the court spectators a faded woman in her early forties who'd been eyeing him with a look that begged being taken advantage of, this time not so much in bed as in winning pity and compassion.

Mrs. Sunderland, as the woman was named, soon talked her husband and the judge into adopting little Leo. Junior had made a good choice; he'd avoided further criminal charges and at the same time planted himself in a solid, traditional family with stock holdings that were soaring in value. Thus his next springboard towards the summit was in place. This, in fact, was already more like a seven-league jump towards his goal.

There was much debate in the home on Main Street in Lexington as to the new son's name. Junior wanted very much to be named Thomas, as in Thomas Jefferson—the greatest of all presidents.

He was handed his new name certificate in a brown envelope on an ordinary Wednesday afternoon, and thus was Leo Mulligan Jr. definitively history, while Thomas Sunderland—the land's future vice president—became a budding reality.

Young Thomas's adoptive father, Colonel Wolfgang Sunderland, was immune to feelings, and at first their quarrels were drawn out and one-sided, but then they moved to a military base in Germany, and one day the situation was reversed. It happened the morning Thomas discovered his father in bed with a black man, enlisted as an aide-de-camp, who performed his officer's servant duties with greater zeal than regulations prescribed. Commander Sunderland had hereby lost the war on the home front, and a fervent hatred between father and son became formalized and intensified.

From that day on, Thomas could pretty much do as he pleased.

The first to suffer at Ramstein Air Base were the officers' daughters. These Thomas bedded one after another, and the ones he occasionally made pregnant he handed over to a shady abortionist. Next to suffer was the Sunderlands's laboriously built—but sizable—family fortune.

One could say Thomas's discovery that morning on the base made his own personal declaration of independence a reality. From now on, it was merely a matter of planning. Nothing stood in his way.

At least so he believed, until he had Sergeant Kane under his command in the invasion of Grenada.

For Captain Thomas Sunderland, this mission to the warm climate of the Caribbean came as a refreshing break from tedious army-base life. He was young and ambitious and suddenly saw the chance for a chestful of medals. He had his battalion under control, and the men were in good spirits as they waded onto Grenada's beach. No one could know that Sunderland and his troops were soon to run into a Cuban tank crew that lacked the appropriate awe at the sight of uniformed Americans with rolled-up sleeves, nor would anyone expect it would take only one round from the tank to pulverize the battalion.

One dead and three seriously injured soldiers lay next to him when Thomas regained consciousness in a crater the size of a suburban swimming pool, and his men on the flanks were being shot at by snipers. He tried once to get his men's attention, but their fear and confusion was contagious, so he curled up, knees to his chest and hands over his ears.

It was left to the burly Sergeant Kane to pull the three wounded men out of the shell hole and bring them out of harm's way, a good hundred yards back. And, being the cold-blooded devil he was, he then stormed back to the crater to see how his captain was doing, staying there until reinforcements subdued the snipers an hour later.

"Well done, Kane," said Thomas when it was all over, and clapped him on the back. "I can use a man like you when I become president one day."

Kane winked at him and laughed. "I'll be looking forward to it, sir," he said.

Thomas looked up at the bright blue sky above them. "Yes, I can understand your laugh, Kane. But somehow, what happened today has brought me a step closer to the White House."

Kane's smile tightened. "Okay, Captain, I can hear you have great goals, but what did you mean by this bringing you a step closer to the White House?"

Sunderland looked at his young sergeant for a moment. He had never told anyone what he was about to say, but now was the time, he could feel it. So he told Kane about his dreams and his plan, and Kane understood—Thomas could tell that ahead of time. And yes, Kane admitted, it was probably true that participating in active war duty was very helpful. A patriotic temperament and demonstrated bravery were said to be keywords to winning votes.

"Just think of Eisenhower and Kennedy," Kane said. "You're fortunate. You have the proper background, a fucking rich family, and no skeletons in the closet. That's just what it takes to become president. It's something I'm lacking, in any case."

That was the moment when the awful truth dawned on Thomas: He could never become president. People like Kane knew only part of his background. In reality he was the son of a murderer and had lived off having sex with married women and blackmailing them. If he hadn't been underage at the time of his apprehension and the judge hadn't been a softie, he would also have had a police record.

No, Junior Mulligan was not made of the stuff of presidents, and one fine day the truth would surely be known. When the opposition became tough enough—not now or five years from now, but in the final phase where the throne was in reach—the truth would come out. That's what better men than he had been forced to realize in the course of history. Perhaps Thomas Sunderland could become president one day, but not Leo Mulligan Jr. That wouldn't be compatible with the American Dream.

This, too, he told his young sergeant in the bottom of the shell crater. Kane fished around in his breast pocket after a little plastic bag. "Nope, it doesn't look like you'll ever become president," he said, adding, "unless you sneak in the back door."

"The back door? What do you mean?"

His subordinate thought a moment as he rolled a joint. "Yes, like the vice presidents. You know, Lyndon B. Johnson, Theodore Roosevelt, Andrew Johnson, and . . . What the hell was the name of the one who succeeded Garfield? Right, Chester Arthur. Or what about Gerald Ford, for that matter?" He grinned. "They all wound up becoming president without being elected."

Sunderland shook his head, trying to get it all straight in his mind. First he would have to become vice president, surviving all the checks and investigations that entailed, and then the president would have to be gotten rid of. It wasn't a very tenable plan.

"But why do you want to be president?" Kane asked. "There are plenty of other ways to gain a hell of a lot of power. No, you become one of the president's advisors, and you'll see who really pulls the strings."

It was with these words that a new craving was fostered in Thomas's brain. Ben Kane had cut the Gordian knot. If Thomas couldn't achieve his dream of becoming president, at least he could come close. All he had to do was ingratiate himself with a strong candidate and make himself absolutely indispensable. It was that simple.

He smiled; the project was under way.

"Good, Kane," he said. "Then I think we should begin by reporting that it was me—and not you—who brought the wounded to safety under fire. I promise you won't regret it—trust me. The medal will eventually help both of us."

So they began planning together. Kane had no major demands. He came from a lower-middle-class family, where dreams were something one had at night after a good slew of spareribs. Yes, he'd help out. And when Sunderland swore an oath that he would fight just as hard for Ben Kane's career as his own, and that Kane would be well rewarded economically when the time came, the pact was a reality.

On this they shook hands.

The years that followed were mainly spent studying politics and economics and finding the right presidential candidate to hook up with.

And Thomas found his man when Bruce Jansen won the governorship of Virginia. Not because Thomas was a Democrat—if anything, he was more the opposite—but because he clearly sensed that this candidate was best at catching the fancy of female voters and making his opponents break out in a sweat. Yes, he had found the right man, no doubt about it.

Then Thomas found himself a rather younger woman who looked good standing at his side—cool, subdued, and from a suitable family. She looked after her affairs, he after his, and they basically lived separate lives, as they both preferred. He still had his flings, only now he was very careful.

It all went by the book: two children at boarding school, nothing to worry about, nothing to get in his way.

Jansen got the most loyal and indispensable worker one could wish for when he hired Thomas Sunderland, and he soon became heavily dependent on his campaign manager and strategic sparring partner.

Then, as fate would have it, Jansen's first wife was murdered on a trip to China. Caroll Jansen was a disgusting bitch and considered by many to be a pain in the ass, so it wasn't the murder itself that made an impression on Thomas, but rather what it did to Senator Jansen. If it hadn't been for Thomas and a couple of other key staff members to whom Jansen could entrust the most vital decision-making, Thomas was convinced the senator would have stopped his political career right there. Jansen was engulfed by depression, corroded by doubt—a troubling development to be sure but also exciting in terms of the doors it opened.

"If they had been married several years or if Senator Jansen had been older," Jansen's doctor stated some months later, "I'm afraid the grief would have driven him mad."

And Thomas's dream became more intense, more real. Could it be he was already in possession of the key to the Oval Office? Jansen wasn't invincible. Perhaps the presidency wasn't that unthinkable after all, and maybe he could help matters along when the time came. It could just be that Ben Kane's comment—about aiming for the vice presidency and then getting the president out of the picture—wasn't so crazy. Sure, he could become president—why not? Just not by being elected. He would have himself appointed—*that* was the solution, and then his true past wouldn't matter. The first step was to become chief of staff, then work to have the vice president deposed at some point and afterwards make sure it was he who was asked to fill the vacancy. And finally he would find a way to eliminate the president himself. This was how he could achieve his goal, thanks to the murder of Jansen's wife. It would be a long and difficult road, but it could be done.

It definitely could.

Sunderland commenced to learn how to work with all kinds of people. Within the Democratic Party he built a reputation as a problem solver and someone to be trusted. A machine that never broke down. Even leading Republicans stated that, as long as Sunderland was a member of Jansen's staff, there would always be someone to reason with. He was offered the chance to be a candidate in several constituencies, but said no every time, which ironically gained him respect as a modest soul who wasn't trying to feather his own nest.

As Jansen's right-hand man he was given the opportunity of attending congressional hearings, lobbying, and sending flowers to the wives of important figures on their birthdays. The most important members of the Senate curried his favor; powerful men found him cooperative and offered him high positions.

But Thomas declined. As far as he was concerned, there was no one in the country who was as obvious presidential material as Jansen, so why not stay where he was?

If only they knew his real agenda and how much he despised them all. That Junior Mulligan was alive and well behind Thomas Sunderland's polished facade, that he dug up all the dirt on his colleagues he possibly could, and that if he respected anyone, it was himself.

Because it wasn't Junior Mulligan's plan to remain a lackey the rest of his life—on the contrary. The plan was to make the others *his* lackeys, come what may.

In the meantime Ben Kane remained in the army, honing his talents as a martial artist. First he learned how to kill people quickly and silently, then he learned to master forgetting his deeds, and eventually he qualified for the elite Secret Service squad—the agents who looked after those who allegedly looked after everyone else.

He resigned from the Secret Service after ten years of loyal service and established his own security firm. For a few years he gained experience by providing protection for greedy, unscrupulous executives who did business in Iraq, Liberia, and Colombia. There were usually casualties on both sides, but the money was good. Kane was a pro, and Thomas could clearly see how useful he could be.

Some years later, when Thomas suggested to Jansen that they had use for a private security corps to supplement the Secret Service, the senator was skeptical at first. But Thomas was insistent, and when Jansen finally met Kane, the matter was quickly settled. Jansen liked the idea of controlling his own bodyguards and paying for them himself.

Yes, Kane, the country boy, was definitely talented, and so was Thomas.

Thomas cleared the next-to-last hurdle on his agenda a couple of years after Jansen lost his first wife in China. He introduced the senator to

the intelligent and pretty Mimi Todd, and Jansen found her irresistible. Thus had Sunderland supplied his presidential candidate with a
wife; now he just had to see to it that Jansen lost her, too.

Kane and Thomas had planned it well. They had chosen election
night as the best time to have Mimi Jansen murdered, they'd found
the perfect setting, and everything had been worked out to the smallest detail. They had even found the world's best string-puller in Bud
Curtis. The situation could hardly have been more advantageous when
Curtis offered to have Jansen hold election night at one of his hotels,
especially when it turned out that Curtis had someone like Toby
O'Neill working for him.

O'Neill was the ideal scapegoat, the perfect Lee Harvey Oswald. A
dim-witted, rabid little man, not bright enough to say no when they
offered him the money they later withdrew from Curtis's account. It
apparently never occurred to him how he'd never have an opportunity to use the money. Another good reason for choosing him.

So Toby O'Neill was to murder Mimi Jansen, but unlike the aftermath of the assassination of President Kennedy, this time, there was
to be left no chance of speculation about a conspiracy or a motive. The
man behind the killing—that is, Curtis—had to be conspicuous,
found guilty of hatching the assassination plot, and severely punished. They had even found a pliant, pretentious state attorney to assure that the case proceeded according to plan and that they had
successfully covered their tracks. Then that would be that.

Still, things almost went badly wrong before they even began.

Until now Jansen's security had pretty much been in the hands of
Ben Kane's private agents, but in the days before election night the
Secret Service began taking its job very seriously. Everything and
everyone in the hotel was checked and double-checked, first by Kane's
men and then by the gray-clad Secret Service. If Thomas—and therefore also Jansen—hadn't insisted they stay, the Secret Service would
have asked Kane's men to disappear altogether. But now the problem
was that the allocation of duties was no longer in Kane's hands. A
situation that Kane meant to have rectified when Jansen was finally
installed in the Oval Office.

According to their original plan, Kane himself was to inspect the hotel passageway before Toby O'Neill was in position. The gun with the fake fingerprints was supposed to have been lying behind the American flag, then picked up and used by O'Neill. Not easy to carry off but workable. That is, until the Secret Service took over, checking everything in the passageway and everywhere else a mere hour and a half before Jansen's helicopter was due to land.

How were they supposed to conceal the fucking weapon now, with these gray bloodhounds and their X-ray vision? Kane knew it was simply impossible.

That was why Ben Kane, for once worried and uncertain, suddenly approached Thomas and signaled their need to talk in private.

"I can't have that thing on me, Thomas," Kane said. "Those gray bastards will smell a rat if I try. They've got eyes in the back of their heads. You're going to have to take it with you and give it to Toby. You've been cleared, no one will suspect you, and you won't be frisked. Can you do it, Thomas? Otherwise we'll have to call it all off."

For a moment Sunderland saw his bold, grand agenda in ruins. How was he supposed to deliver the gun to the shooter without leaving fingerprints? How was he ever going to do it with so many people vying for his attention? It wasn't that he was afraid to do it; it just couldn't be done.

"It won't work, Ben." He shook his head. "I'm too much the center of attention, and I can't suddenly be wearing gloves. It just won't work," he said.

Ben Kane nodded. He could see it was true.

So they discussed alternatives until they came up with a solution. Again, not ideal, but feasible. Then they rehearsed how to do it for a half hour until they could carry it out with their eyes closed.

Once they got to the passageway they would proceed as close to the wall as possible. Thomas would have Bud Curtis's revolver in his jacket pocket, with Ben Kane walking directly in front of him. Then putting his hand inside his jacket, he would come up alongside Kane after O'Neill had been searched by the Secret Service for the final time and work the gun out of his pocket from behind the pocket lining inside the jacket. At that moment Kane would take the gun with a corner of his own jacket, make his way up to Toby O'Neill, and slip it into the man's garish red jacket pocket. By that point the crowd's attention would be focused on the imminent unveiling of the painting, so that part of the procedure would scarcely be the most difficult as long as Kane made sure he positioned himself properly.

So that was how it had to be, if it had to be here and now.

They called O'Neill over and made him understand the plan had been changed a bit, which didn't seem to bother Toby at all. He was to let himself be body-searched as many times as the Secret Service wanted, and after that, things would be simple. When he could feel that Kane had put the gun in his pocket, he was to wait a couple of seconds, remove the weapon, and fire it straight at Jansen's wife.

What could be easier? They could see O'Neill tremble with anticipation at the mere thought. Sick in the head or not, he was their man—perfect for doing the job and then being done in himself.

Or so they thought.

The agreement, of course, was that he should kill only Mimi Jansen—no more, no less. So Kane passed Toby the revolver, and he shot his victim, but then the idiot decided to shoot again.

"The bastard dies and that's the way it's gotta be!" snarled O'Neill and turned the gun on Jansen, throwing Sunderland into instant panic. Which was why Kane took out his own weapon and killed O'Neill on the spot, contrary to the original plan, which was that he'd let one of his own men or one of the Secret Service agents finish the job. The problem was that only Kane and Thomas were close enough at the time to hear what the imbecile said, so there was no choice. Kane had to shoot him because he couldn't be sure the other agents would react in time. And the ensuing confusion and panic proved Kane right. Yes, he was a professional. If Jansen had been assassinated, Vice President Michael K. Lerner would have automatically become president, and Thomas would be out of the picture. All would have been lost.

In the end, however, the result was the same. Jansen was alive, and Toby O'Neill was dead.

From the moment he shot O'Neill, Kane had no choice but to begin improvising. First he plucked Curtis's glass off the floor and shoved it in his own pocket. Next he disappeared for a few minutes to get rid of the glass, his weapon, and his jacket with the oil traces from Curtis's gun inside the pocket. No one could tell Kane had changed jackets since he had several identical ones. And the agreement with chief prosecutor Mortimer Deloitte was to not deal with the question of who killed Toby O'Neill unless it was demanded by the defense.

And they'd been very careful in making sure there were no such demands from that quarter. Thanks to Kane, palms were greased all around. Many incriminating clues were made to disappear, like the water glass and its image on cameraman Marvin Gallegos's video, as well as any way of determining the nonexistence of the imaginary FBI agent Blake Wunderlich. Then fabricated evidence and false charges succeeded in convicting Curtis of masterminding the atrocity, and the stage was set for the unleashing of the Washington Decree in all its terrible glory. In the ensuing chaos it was also easy to facilitate the disappearance of key individuals who might have helped expose the trial as a monstrous miscarriage of justice and possibly even uncover the true culprits. There was no way Sunderland and Kane were going to let the truth sabotage Jansen's presidency and their futures.

By now Jansen had been president for a couple of weeks, and every-thing was going according to plan. The next stage involved destabiliz-ing Jansen psychologically and forcing Vice President Lerner to quit. Lerner was an extremely competent and influential politician whose will did not bend easily and whom Sunderland saw as a wild card, a potential threat.

The next step was getting rid of the president, and in this respect Jansen himself was a big help. One could begin to see how he was beginning to change even before he was sworn into office, and Thomas followed this development closely and with great pleasure. He observed how Jansen withdrew more and more into himself and didn't sleep for days at a time. How he became easily irritated, was given to angry outbursts, and sowed confusion among his staff and in his Cabinet. How he sat, staring into space before his computer screen, seemingly grappling with a mental block. An unstable man with a murky soul, it would be like pushing a button when the time came, for Jansen was obviously consumed by grief and defenseless—this was Thomas's honest analysis.

So the shock effect was infinitely greater for him than anybody else the day—two weeks after the election—when Jansen presented his law-and-order scheme. Thomas had gone home that evening thoroughly shaken and spent most of the night in his lonely double bed reading the proposal over and over again. He analyzed it from every angle until he gradually began seeing how he could turn this pending cataclysm to his advantage.

He realized he'd been wrong. Jansen had risen above his grief, and no matter how much he had suffered, he was by no means disabled or unable to perform the duties his office demanded. On the contrary, President Jansen was merely doing what many who held his position before him should have done.

Thomas got out of bed that night in early February, poured himself a glass of whisky, and threw his legs up on his living room coffee table. The curtain was going up on a cruel and wonderful piece of theater. Upon closer examination, the possibilities actually looked better than before. Heads would roll, but heads were something there was plenty of.

He turned on the TV and ascertained with satisfaction that a news bulletin about a shooting that afternoon at a school outside Washington was being repeated endlessly on all channels. It turned out that one of the victims was the son of House Majority Whip Peter Halliwell, and that two of the three others came from wealthy families. What could be better? This was news that was sure to send appalled citizens out on the streets to demonstrate.

The Washington school shooting alternated with a news flash about the Killer on the Roof in New York, another scenario with all the right ingredients. It was almost like Thomas had written the script himself. Shots from crime scenes that zoomed in on spent cartridge casings with patches of blood on the sidewalk and short interviews with local inhabitants scanning the rooftops with frightened eyes. Panic was spreading, and people were saying it had all better end soon before the whole city was infected.

As he watched, a smile began spreading across his face. *This is good for Jansen, and it's even better for me,* he thought. One was almost tempted to believe it had all been staged in the White House, even by Jansen himself. He emptied his glass and shook his head. No, this wasn't something the president could have concocted, even in his darkest moment. He began to laugh. Jansen couldn't have instigated this, but his chief of staff could have—easily—if it hadn't happened on its own.

He poured himself another highball and thought the situation through again.

Jansen hadn't asked for Thomas's advice when he chose his Cabinet members, as one might otherwise have expected, considering he was the White House's incoming chief of staff and a longtime, trusted associate. Naturally, Thomas had been more than a little incensed at the time, but now he understood things better.

Jansen had had a plan, he could see that now.

Thomas had particularly disagreed with Jansen's choice of Billy Johnson. Shouldn't the president be more concerned about the fact that Johnson had spent time in a psychiatric ward after the killing of his son, Sunderland had asked at the time. Was this really the kind of man one wanted to have running the Department of Homeland Security?

Yet Jansen had been insistent—he remembered this very clearly. What had Thomas been thinking that day? Why was it only dawning on him now, what a good choice Billy Johnson had been?

Yes, it was because Billy Johnson had lost a son, a tragedy that had affected him deeply, just as personal tragedy had affected Jansen. And Johnson hated firearms with a passion, just like Jansen. It was that simple. These were the kinds of people Jansen wanted working for him.

Thomas set down his whisky glass and called Kane. It didn't take too much orientation from Sunderland before Kane, too, began seeing the possibilities. After discussing what their next move should be, Thomas asked him to check out all the Cabinet members' backgrounds. He wanted to know how many more of them had close relatives who had been victims of shootings or other violent acts.

The answer he received shortly before dawn started his pulse racing with excitement. Kane's investigation revealed that over half the families of the president's staff and Cabinet had suffered violent episodes similar to Johnson's. And if it were up to Thomas, the number of apparently random acts of violence would continue to increase, not least of all ones affecting Cabinet members. Then Thomas would do all he could to make Jansen's draconian proposals reality, which in turn would intensify the situation immensely. The country needed to experience an unprecedented wave of violence to justify Jansen's unleashing of the executive decrees, and Congress would have no choice but to acquiesce. There would be assassinations, bombings, kidnappings, and other acts of terror until the country was declared in a state of national emergency, which would castrate Congress and transfer power to the Federal Emergency Management Agency. In the midst of all this, the vice president was sure to resign in protest, and then there would be no one with the authority to oppose the president appointing his chief of staff to the job.

In the meantime all Sunderland had to do was covertly maintain good relationships with the opposition and all the politicians who had abandoned Jansen. Because when the day came for Jansen to die—and that day wouldn't be so far off—Thomas would need plenty of allies. This meant making sure the opposition was kept informed of his robust efforts to stop the madness.

Then, with the president out of the picture, he would be the obvious choice to succeed him. Who else?

The day after Jansen put forth his law-and-order proposal, Kane was already busy changing the mind of one of its less enthusiastic supporters, Attorney General Lovell. It had been no problem paying a couple of hoodlums to assault his mother and daughter; they even threw in raping Lovell's mother at no extra charge. Nor had it been a problem for Kane to definitively eliminate the perpetrators the same night. Then they had the attorney general in the palm of their hand— or so Sunderland thought.

But rumors were being whispered in the White House corridors that Attorney General Lovell and the chief justice of the Supreme Court were going to demand a congressional debate over the new law proposals. So once again, there was a situation for Ben Kane to take care of.

Chief Justice Manning's body was practically torn in two when the limousine carrying him and the attorney general was blown up on its way to Capitol Hill. Lovell was luckier, but the attempt on his life put an end to any qualms he had about Jansen's "antiviolence" campaign and transformed him into a wholehearted Jansen supporter.

Unfortunately, occasional small, improvised adjustments and corrections like these were unavoidable at times like this.

The Killer on the Roof—who was found dead in his apartment after neighbors had begun noticing a funny smell—was a similar case.

The apartment's inhabitants turned out to be an old lady and her son, a previous FBI employee who had been taking out his revenge over being kicked out of the Bureau by personally reducing the population of New York, one by one. After eating a pâté infected with botulism, the mother and son had died a slow, stealthy death. A journalist from NBC, known as Miss B and renowned for her controversial and critical journalism, became interested in the case after a tip from Tom Jumper. However, since her phone was being tapped, Miss B unwittingly put Thomas and Kane on the trail of the sniper as well.

Thus Kane and his men were the first to reach the malodorous apartment and secretly confiscate the high-powered rifle that had killed so many of New York's citizens.

Then Kane hired a hit man to carry on with the job, using the same weapon as the original "Killer." The more panic, the more sympathy for Jansen's agenda, said Kane. Thomas agreed. Kane could stop the new "Killer" when he'd served his purpose.

Which is what he did.

The contract killer lived in Brooklyn's Prospect Park, and the inventive Kane arranged for census takers in a new, nationwide census to canvass precisely that neighborhood, seeing to it that the killer would arouse the suspicion of the census taker who knocked on his door. Kane was also behind the subsequent search of the culprit's apartment and having him shadowed, and was responsible for putting the police on his trail and finally gunning him down.

Later, Tom Jumper insinuated that the White House had been involved in the killings, but that didn't matter much, as long as Thomas wasn't left with the responsibility for them or the bomb threats Kane had instigated against Congress and other places.

But these were matters he and Kane could work out.

In the meantime the whole country slowed down with impotence and confusion, encouraging the militias to crawl out of their holes and perform hitherto unseen acts of violent insurrection. The White-Headed Eagles' bombing of the Democratic headquarters, for example. It was a beauty, and Thomas couldn't have engineered it better himself. He was on a roll.

The worst hitch in Thomas's master plan was that President Jansen had begun barricading himself in the Oval Office. His doctor pronounced it a kind of paranoia, but it was far more likely that Jansen was very aware of how vulnerable he was. The deaths of a couple of congressmen was the handwriting on the wall. Jansen knew he, too, might well be on somebody's hit list, but he had no way of knowing that "somebody" was his own vice president.

It was at about this point that the president asked Lance Burton to beef up surveillance in the White House. A wise decision, except if you asked Thomas Sunderland.

Thomas then proceeded to wait for an opportunity to kill Jansen, and his first chance came a couple of weeks later as the result of two unrelated events.

The first had to do with a minor incident where a Secret Service agent overheard a conversation between Sunderland and Kane. Kane felt uncomfortable about what the agent might have heard, so he slit the agent's throat and left a note in his locker, threatening the president with the same fate. A dramatic and effective little number that made the proper impression. Thomas was quite satisfied.

Then there was Donald Beglaubter, who appeared to be in agreement with Jansen's decrees, but then began investigating the blowing up of the limousine with Chief Supreme Court Justice Manning and Attorney General Lovell. Beglaubter was a clever man—possibly the best brain in the White House—and Thomas was convinced there was a good chance that his investigation would eventually turn something up. Beglaubter had to go, preferably along with Jansen.

So Kane tossed a hand grenade at the president as he and Donald Beglaubter were walking through the tunnel to the Treasury Department. He'd hidden in a little niche for two hours, waiting for the right moment, but succeeded in only half his mission. Beglaubter lost his head, but the king kept his.

In the ensuing confusion, Kane rejoined the other bodyguards, and the following investigation predictably led nowhere. Kane, the master manipulator, turned the situation to his own advantage, accusing the Secret Service of cowardice and dereliction of duty and recommending it be relieved of most of its duties in the West Wing.

Jansen followed his advice. After all, a Secret Service agent had been blamed for not having searched Toby O'Neill properly on election night. Thus Kane and his men had attained the elbow room they needed.

After this failed assassination attempt, the president totally entrenched himself in his office and was completely unapproachable. Plans for the next try would have to wait.

But not for long. The British prime minister had succeeded in luring Jansen into the open, and now Kane and Sunderland saw their new chance during the joint press conference.

There was a series of unexpected events earlier in the day, but nothing that altered their plan. After John Bugatti's surprise appearance in the White House, his body was dumped unceremoniously in the West Wing basement; his boyfriend already lay strangled in their bed in Georgetown. Then Thomas successfully passed his "diary" to the British delegation. His pitch had worked; he had their total support. Both Lance Burton and Wesley were under close guard. Burton would soon meet his maker, while Wesley's fate had not yet been decided. And the evening before, a rebel group of army officers had received their final instructions via one of Kane's contacts. All the hardware was in place, and these men knew how to use it. Only their leader, "Sean," was aware that their mission was being financed by a handful of captains of industry, and only a couple of these knew exactly what their investment was being used for and that ultimately Kane was working for Thomas. Always with an eye on his future, Thomas knew he had to ingratiate himself with the big finance boys, and this was a sure way to do it.

Now two heads of state were to die. The pillars of the White House would wobble, the two mightiest western nations would reel, and the world would have its eyes opened. And by the time the dust had settled, Thomas would be president, busy reestablishing conditions as they were before Jansen took office. The entire Cabinet and all top officials would be fired. The dumbest of them would be prosecuted for treason, and the brightest would appear to have committed suicide, starting with Lance Burton and Billy Johnson.

He would call off the state of emergency and make peace with the militias, the right-wingers, the lobbyists, the Senate, and the House of Representatives. The only thing he was worried about was what former vice president Michael K. Lerner might do. How would he try to stop Sunderland if he reappeared on the political scene? How many votes could he win? He'd disappeared completely since quitting his job in protest. Apparently, Jansen wasn't interested in his scalp, but Thomas was. He'd ordered Kane and his men to find him and neutralize him as quickly as possible.

The United States of America was to have a cynical gigolo and son of a wife killer as its next president whether it wanted him or not.

Thomas looked at his watch. He was expected for tea in the State Dining Room at 3:30 P.M., after the press conference on the terrace outside the diplomats' reception hall. It would be an exceptional press conference, not least of all because it would be the first one in his career Thomas wouldn't be attending. He studied the rain pelting his window until Kane came in the door.

"What about the rain?" Sunderland asked.

"No problem. It's letting up now," answered Kane.

"You got Burton out of the way?"

"You bet. Two men are guarding him as though their lives depend on it—which they do."

"And Barefoot. What's your take on him?"

"He didn't have anything to do with Burton's little surveillance scheme."

"According to who?" asked Sunderland. "Burton?"

"Burton's been through a pretty robust interrogation. He has too weak a character to make a convincing liar. He would have betrayed Barefoot long ago."

"Fine, then we keep Wesley. He could be a witness for us. We'll have to work on him when this is all over." He banged his hand on his desk. "Now sit down a moment, Kane. We've got a big day ahead of us."

Kane usually preferred standing, but he set his two-hundred-and-twenty-pound bulk down on Sunderland's sofa.

"You say Burton's been through quite an interrogation," Thomas continued. "No marks on the body, I hope."

"No, none of importance."

"He's going to have to disappear."

"Yes, we know that."

"What have you told the FBI about Bugatti?" asked Thomas.

"Just what we agreed. That Bugatti forced his way into your office and threatened you. That you had no way of knowing he was unarmed and shot him. Case closed."

"Are you completely certain we're prepared for our retaliation against the Cairo group? There cannot be a single one of them left who can tell about my role here, Ben."

"It's a hundred percent under control. We're going to gas them while they're still in the monument."

Thomas nodded. "Be thorough."

"Yes, sir."

"No survivors—got it?"

"Yes, sir."

"And you have an updated list of all the renegade officers around the country?"

"Yes, and at the moment it's being forwarded to FEMA."

"They're to be gotten rid of all at once—and fast—before the confusion dies down, understand?"

"Yes. The directive we're sending FEMA states that over half of these men are extremely dangerous and that no means should be spared to stop them."

"And Moonie Quale?"

Kane sat forward eagerly on the sofa. "He still thinks we're giving him amnesty."

"Where is he now?"

"Up in Seattle, still suffering from his injuries."

"It's a good thing we kept him alive," said Sunderland, and laughed. "Think of the useful information he's given us. Ironic, isn't it, that for the past two weeks we've had in custody the man whom the enemy sees as their leader? That's hysterical." He gave his lieutenant a conspiratorial wink. "That was good thinking, Kane. And you say now he's in the safe house in Seattle?"

"Yes." Ben Kane looked pretty pleased with himself. Everything was progressing on schedule.

"Bomb the house flat."

"Orders have already been given."

"Moonie Quale's death will be my first victorious act as president, do you realize that? Without him, most of the militias will throw down their weapons." He smiled. "And your men—what about them?"

"I'm keeping two. They're okay."

"And the others?"

"I'm putting them in the line of fire. They'll be standing behind the president. They won't have a chance, and it'll look completely natural."

"Very wise, Kane, very wise! And Bud Curtis? You had his execution moved up to six o'clock tomorrow morning?"

"Yes, but we're implementing another plan because it's looking very much like a certain Sheriff T. Perkins may be able to prove Curtis was innocent."

"T. Perkins . . . ?" Thomas could remember the man from the trip to China and how he'd hoped the sheriff would be eliminated from the quiz show in the first round. This was the guy who had brought him in to the courthouse in Monterey in his youth, when he was on the run. Just imagine if Perkins had recognized him in China? He shook his head. What the hell was it with all these people from that trip popping up in his life again to cause him so many problems? Fucking Doggie Rogers, whom he still had to deal with, Bugatti, who was taken care of, to a lesser extent Wesley Barefoot, and now this skinny sheriff who never said a word. "Sheriff Perkins is a dead man," he decided. "I hope we agree on that."

"Sure, but there were plenty of people who heard Jumper and Bugatti's radio program that night, so there could well be others who will try and demand an investigation into Curtis's trial."

"Yeah, Tom Jumper—go figure! That ridiculous, worthless white trash turned out to be the only one with any balls. Amazing." He smiled, remembering the pictures he'd seen of Jumper inside the transmission van. There hadn't been much left to recognize. "Have you prepared a statement refuting the claims he and Bugatti made on that program?"

"Yes, long ago."

"Okay, as to the Bud Curtis matter, we'll go over to plan B. When are the militias planning to storm the prison?"

"In twenty minutes."

"And we let the militia prisoners go free?"

"For the moment, yes."

"And Bud Curtis?"

Kane drew his thumb across his throat.

CHAPTER 41

DOGGIE AND T ARRIVED AT THE WHITE HOUSE THE SAME MOMENT A HELICOPTER
came plowing its way noisily over the uniform-clad mass of humanity
and turned south.

Doggie clutched her midriff, her stomach tied in knots.

T took a deep drag off his cigarette and pointed at a line of patrol
cars and white vans bearing discreet FEMA emblems, parked in front
of concrete barriers. He backed his own sheriff's car in between two
of them, turned off his blue, blinking lights, and turned to her.

"You leave this to me now, Doggie," he said, stubbing out his butt
in the ashtray. "Don't say a word, no matter what, do you understand?
Give me a look if there's something that bothers you, and just remember that it's me who makes the decisions."

Doggie nodded. Wild horses wouldn't get her to open her mouth.

"Lean forward," he said next and clapped his handcuffs around her
wrists. "Now you offer a little resistance as you get out of the car, and
I'll pull you the rest of the way out, okay?"

"Yes, just so long as you don't start beating the shit out of me." She
smiled.

He didn't smile back. "If that will save our asses in this imbecilic
caper, I'll do that, too."

Then he yanked her out of the car and shoved her along before him
in the lessening drizzle, through the concrete barriers and up to the
guard post. She felt like an outcast on her way to a public stoning.

Everyone was staring at her, including the soldiers, but no one tried to stop them, not even the undercover agents. Things didn't start getting intense until they reached the control post with its concentration of decorated uniforms.

Here they pointed small, nasty automatics at them and demanded positive ID, looking as though they were hoping the identification wouldn't be satisfactory so they could shoot them on the spot if they made a false move. T made some grumbling noises before he showed them his badge and raised his arms in the air to be searched, and Doggie followed his example. The soldiers groped professionally all over their bodies, hands stopping occasionally to make sure what they were feeling wasn't a concealed weapon. They weren't being rude, but the dangerous intimacy of the situation made Doggie feel sick.

Then the soldiers retreated a step.

"This is Doggie Rogers. You know who she is," said T matter-of-factly. "She is to be brought directly to the Secret Service, so call them now, okay? She has important information they have to get out of her."

The soldier in charge, who stood on the other side of the wrought iron fence, nodded to the guard in the control booth whom Doggie used to greet every morning. A gate was opened and a photograph of Doggie passed on to the commanding officer. He held up the picture next to Doggie's face to determine whether they were the same person.

"It *is* her, believe me," said T.

"Not the woman she once was," the soldier ascertained, shaking his head.

Doggie looked at T, feeling her heart pumping heavily. Open season had been declared, and there was no way to defend herself, nowhere to hide. And here she was, her existence totally dependent on the taciturn, bony man who was standing next to her, dying for a cigarette.

T squinted his eyes in concentration, trying to decipher the telecommunication that was taking place behind the armored glass. Then the guard nodded a couple of times and reported to the officer outside, using a sign language that might as well have been the green light for their immediate disposal.

Instead a small pack of men in black suits began making haste straight for them along the White House paths. Their leader waved the iron gate open, and they were propelled into the lion's den.

Three minutes later they were sitting in Ben Kane's office—a small, windowless chamber that Doggie had never set foot in.

The atmosphere in the White House was hectic, perhaps with a tinge of panic. People she had never seen before were half running up and down the corridors. Clusters of security agents were constantly regrouping, and the ones keeping them company all had vacant expressions as they listened intently to what was coming through their earpieces.

One of Kane's men sat down across from T and asked him where he had caught Doggie and who his White House contact was. He was less than pleased when T merely shrugged his shoulders and pulled out a cigarette.

"Smoking is prohibited in the White House," barked the guard standing by the door. He was one Doggie recognized as spending almost an hour each day chain-smoking under John F. Kennedy's magnolia tree.

Then the first guy repeated his question, and when T answered by asking for a cup of coffee, he gave up. It was clear there were plenty more important jobs they could be—and would prefer to be—doing instead of dicking around with some ornery hick sheriff.

So they asked him to open the handcuffs and lock her arms behind her chair, which T did without hesitation.

"Kane will have to deal with this himself," said Kane's lieutenant to the others.

"There's no way Ben Kane is going to interview me," she said, shifting to make her arms and wrists a bit less uncomfortable. "Send for Wesley Barefoot or Lance Burton. They're the only ones I speak to, besides the president!"

The men surrounding her were pretty much the same ones as Sunderland had presented a year ago in the governor's office in Richmond.

Their job was to provide security and peace of mind, but that was of little consolation in the present situation. Their whispering together in the corner gave her the creeps.

She checked T out. He hadn't so much as raised an eyebrow the whole time. *What the hell's going on inside your head, T?* she wondered. They'd agreed their goal was to get hold of Wesley, and, failing that, find another way to get through to the president. So why was he sitting there, sleepy-eyed, asking for coffee?

"They're saying Kane is busy with Lance Burton," reported the chain-smoker with his hand to his earpiece. "Hartmond's coming instead."

"Why him? He's Secret Service," said another of Kane's men.

"Don't worry, Jones is coming, too," replied the first.

This was enough for T. Standing up, he said, "You guys have a nice wait. I haven't had a bite to eat all day, so I'm going down to the canteen." He raised his hand to ward off their protests. "You can find me there if you need me. Then I'm heading home. Highland County Sheriff's Office—that's where you can send the reward."

He swaggered out of the room like a cowboy without a horse. In another situation this show of bravado might have seemed comical. How was this eccentric country cop ever going to find his way around in this labyrinth? He probably couldn't even find the men's room.

He turned towards her on his way out and shook his head almost imperceptibly as though he could sense what she was thinking. It wasn't a signal not to worry—not by any means. It was just a reminder not to say a word, no matter what they did to try and make her talk.

As Doggie waited for her interrogators, the handcuffs were beginning to make her hands go numb. *This is how my father was sitting the last time I saw him,* she thought. It almost made her cry. A few more hours and his handcuffs would be replaced with leather straps on the execution gurney.

She leaned forward so eagle eye couldn't see the emotion welling up inside her. *Oh, God* . . . her heart began pleading. But no, she had to pull herself together and concentrate on the situation at hand.

Then the two men arrived and asked the others to leave.

Both were to be feared, in spite of their diametrically opposite appearances. One was thin, dark, and silent—a man Ben Kane had hired just after the attempt on Jansen's life in the White House tunnel—and the other was a flabby, pale, older man who reminded her of the librarian in Chesapeake when she was a child.

They were the same men who questioned the West Wing personnel after the assassination attempt, and rumor had it that they hated each other, since Jones was on Ben Kane's payroll and Hartmond worked for the Secret Service. But both of them had the habit of going straight for their victim's jugular—showing no mercy and offering no promises of leniency if they talked. Their job was to extract information, even if that meant using unconventional methods.

"You are charged with attempting to kill the vice president. Do you know what the consequences could be, Miss Rogers?"

She shut herself off and studied the wall behind Kane's desk instead, where at least twenty framed photographs were on display of Kane with some of the people he'd been a bodyguard for. Many were prominent names, and several had their arm around the shoulder of a grinning Kane. They were like certificates of merit hanging on the wall of a doctor or a psychologist—they were his profession's stamp of approval.

"You won't achieve anything by remaining silent, Doggie Rogers. We're pretty persistent, as you well know," said Hartmond, who had crammed himself into the seat opposite her.

"Who do you work for, Miss Rogers? You're going to have to tell us if you're to have hope of receiving any form of leniency from the court."

But it was like he wasn't even there. Wasn't that how T had told her to behave?

Hartmond tilted his head. "Miss Rogers, your father is to be executed a few hours from now. Speak to me, and I'll see what I can do. Maybe there's still hope for him if you talk now."

Then she focused her eyes on him.

"I said maybe, Miss Rogers. Let me hear what you can give me." He was already looking self-confident, the dumb bastard. "Who paid you?"

She took a deep breath. "Do something for my father? How do you mean?"

"I could take that phone there and call Homeland Security, for example. They're the ones in charge of appeals and stays of execution these days."

"Then take the phone," she said immediately. T wouldn't be pleased, but what else could she do? Hartmond leaned forward in anticipation. He already thought he had her backed up to the edge of the cliff.

She checked out Jones from the corner of her eye. He didn't seem to be following the interrogation; someone was apparently talking to him through his earpiece.

"Kane's on his way to the Situation Room with Lance Burton," said Jones, removing his hand from his earpiece. "The chief of staff has been arrested."

A shiver went through her body. Lance Burton—arrested? What would be next?

Hartmond's eyes bore down on Doggie. "Hello? Miss Rogers? If you wish to save your father's life, then answer my question."

She caught an unconscious flickering of his eyes. Behind his fixed expression she could see his mind was somewhere else. It was circling around his next question like a hungry buzzard, but his eyes betrayed a heat-seeking missile that hadn't a chance of hitting its target. Call Homeland Security? That was the last thing he'd do, she could tell. Her father wasn't even an issue.

She sat on the edge of her chair, and he smiled at her indulgently. To him, her reaction was a sign of confidentiality. He'd delivered a couple of his lines, and she was already prepared to sing. His partner watched as a smile grew on his lips, then saw it vanish as she reared back her head and spat in his face. There was no masking his surprise and confusion. Now he really looked like the public librarian who didn't know how to handle a roomful of unruly kids.

She sat back again, studying him as he dried off his face with a calmness that clearly signaled the opposite, especially as far as her own fate was concerned. It felt good in the moment, but that was all. *She* was the one handcuffed to the chair.

"We'll get what we want out of you, Miss Rogers, don't worry. If you want to do yourself a favor, then talk to me. Some of my colleagues don't possess my sense of humor." This time his smile didn't work at all.

Now she knew the two agents would trade roles. She could see in Hartmond's eyes that he would yield to Jones's more straightforward approach. Something was about to happen; she just didn't know what. Would Jones grab her head and twist it until her neck cracked? Maybe he would force water down her throat with a funnel until she was about to suffocate. She was scared now, in any case.

Jones stood up and walked around behind her. He had beautiful, ice-cold eyes, but it was his hands she was watching. What were they about to do? They hovered over her body like a bird of prey searching for the most vulnerable spot on its victim's body, then swooped down to gently caress her pulsing carotid artery.

He lowered his face until it was level with hers. "We're here to find answers, Miss Rogers, so I'm asking you: Who do you work for?" He stroked her neck as he spoke.

"I don't work for anybody. I'm a White House employee. Let me speak to Wesley Barefoot."

"Is he involved in this, Miss Rogers?"

She could feel the panic rising. "What's this all about? I haven't done anything, and Wesley Barefoot has nothing at all to do with any of this. Have you gone totally paranoid?"

He increased the pressure on her artery. A tiny squeeze, but it started all her warning lights flashing.

"Why did you want to kill the vice president?" he asked, relieving the pressure again.

Doggie looked over at Hartmond with pleading eyes. "Help me," she entreated. "Make that phone call, and I'll tell you everything. Just get them to grant my father a stay of execution."

But Hartmond ignored her. One didn't easily forget being spat on.

"You're not going to just sit there and let Jones strangle me, are you?" she tried. "You're not like Kane's men."

Jones pressed a little more, barely noticeably, but suddenly the two men seemed far away and the room began darkening. The next moment he relaxed the pressure, blood circulation returned to her brain, and her senses returned to normal.

"Why did you want to kill the vice president?" Jones repeated. "Who paid you?"

Please, T, get back here. Make them stop, Doggie prayed silently, and then she noticed that Jones's hands were no longer hovering about her neck.

She looked up at them and detected a sudden, instinctive alertness in their expressions, like a rodent raising its head even before the scent of danger reaches its nostrils. They turned instantly towards the door, before she heard the muffled sound of a gunshot.

Commotion erupted immediately in the hallway. Figures and footsteps raced past the half-open door, and the two men's bodies tensed.

"Did that shot come from the Oval Office?" asked Hartmond, trying to remain calm.

"If you have anything to do with this, you're dead meat," Jones snarled to Doggie. "Where'd that damn sheriff go?" he demanded, striking her straight in the mouth. "Are the two of you part of this?"

Doggie sucked on her lip; the blood tasted warm and sweet. She was beginning to lose her grip.

"No!" she shouted back. "Not at all! We haven't done a thing, can't you understand?"

Jones put his hand up to his earpiece. "It's the vice president! They say he's calling for help!" He gave her one savage look and shot out the door.

Her heart was hammering wildly. Had T done something crazy? Was he all right?

"I have nothing to do with this," she said again, looking at Hartmond imploringly.

Then the man picked up the telephone and began dialing. Was he actually going to help her now?

"Yes, call them," she urged. "Make them stay the execution, and I'll tell you everything."

He raised his hand to quiet her. "We have a crisis situation over here," he said into the phone. "There's been a shot fired inside the vice president's office. . . . No, I don't know what happened. I'm here interrogating Doggie Rogers. . . . No, I'm not getting anything out of her. . . . No, it's doubtful. . . . Yes, Jones went over there. . . . Yes, I'll let you know."

He hung up and gave her a fierce look, similar to Jones's. "You stay put if you're really interested in saving your father. You still may have a chance when I get back."

Then he, too, was gone.

Just before he slammed the door she got a glimpse of the lobby's high ceiling. She remembered the first time she'd stood there, taken in by the White House's impressive grandeur. A memory from another lifetime altogether. If, on that first day—in the midst of all that splendor—she'd had a premonition of her present desperate situation, she would have turned around and walked out the door.

She squeezed her eyes shut. No tears would come, but her numb, fettered hands were shaking. She filled her lungs with air and concentrated on thinking rationally.

If she could hop the chair over to Kane's desk, maybe she could lean over and use her chin to press Wesley's number on the intercom. Just maybe.

She laid her weight cautiously forward and began her attempt. If she fell, she was finished. She straightened her legs and succeeded in hopping a quarter of a step forward. She tried again.

This time her foot caught under an electric cord. Doggie pitched forward and banged her forehead on the edge of the desk. The room began rotating, and she hit her head again on something as she fell to the floor.

She landed halfway under Kane's desk with her legs under her and the tendons in her wrists about to snap. The pain was indescribable but she dared not make a sound. Instead she prayed.

Oh, God, why are you letting this happen? What have I ever done to you? Help me, please help me.

She kicked with her legs and tried to wriggle into a better position, but it was hopeless. So she prayed some more.

Then she heard someone come in. Twisting herself around, she could see it was T. Perkins.

He closed the door after him. "Hey, Doggie, what are you doing? Are you okay?" he asked, pulling her into an upright position. "There was a shot fired over in the West Wing." For once he sounded definitely agitated. "Sounded like a high caliber. It's time for us to move—now or never."

She could smell his aftershave as he bent over her and unlocked the handcuffs. It was the best smell in the world.

"Where do we go, Doggie?" he asked. "You're the one who knows her way around here."

"Have you seen Wesley?" she asked instead, massaging her wrists.

"I've seen nothing but gray security agents and black security agents, plus some pretty serious-looking British ones," Perkins said. "Prime Minister Watts brought plenty of protection; they're stationed all over the place."

"Who was shot? Do you know?"

"No, but don't worry about that now. We've got to get out of here."

But suddenly fear froze her on the spot. Her hand flew to her mouth. What if something had happened to Wesley?

"Come on, Doggie, let's go!"

Yes, Doggie, come on! her insides screamed. *Come on, think! Do something!*

Her eyes flew around the office and came to rest on a suit hanging behind the door. It was definitely on the big side, but T would blend in better if he had it on.

"Here," she said, thrusting it towards him. "Take this with you!"

Next she rummaged feverishly through several of Kane's desk drawers until she found what she was looking for: two ID badges with the built-in microphones. They lay all the way at the back of a drawer, under stacks of black-and-white portrait photos of people she didn't recognize but immediately felt sorry for.

She opened the door cautiously and checked in both directions. The lobby was full of people, all of whom were looking towards the section of the building that housed the Oval Office and the vice president's office.

So she pulled T out into the hallway and steered him in the opposite direction, towards her own office. Not that it would be a very good destination at the moment—it was sure to be the first place they'd look for her. No, it was because it was the section farthest away from the fray, with the smallest offices for employees with the lowest status.

Doggie cast a quick glance into her old office. Her desk appeared untouched, although one of her piles of journals had spilled over onto the floor. *Looks like those cases will have to wait,* she thought, with some satisfaction. But what difference did it make? What difference had her job *ever* made, for that matter?

"Here, T," she said, opening the door across the hall. It was the office in which two of the wing's worst magpies exchanged beauty tips and mindless gossip every day while they practiced walking in their new too-high heels. The stench of cheap "exclusive" perfume was still very present, Doggie noticed.

"These hens deal only with market conditions, so they don't work on Sundays," she said quietly. "Lock the door, T, and I'll try to see if I can get hold of Wesley."

She dialed his in-house number and waited. *Take it easy,* she told herself when there was no answer. *There could be any number of reasons. Try again in a couple of minutes.*

"Look at this," said T, removing a pleated, canary-yellow dress from a closet behind the door. Just the kind of little number one of these bimbos would wear to festivities at the White House. Doggie knew the type. These women were prepared to strike if, one evening, they were lucky enough to be seated next to an eligible career diplomat of the proper vintage, from the right continent.

"You're not getting me into that, T," she said.

"And you really expect me to climb into this circus tent?" T retorted, holding up Kane's Armani suit. "Try looking at yourself," he said, nudging her over towards a full-length mirror inside the closet door. The cheap threads she'd bought that distant morning in the Bronx looked worse than a worn-out, two-piece burlap coal sack. Every crease and wrinkle was caked with an indeterminable substance, her fake black hair hung in greasy clumps, and her complexion was reminiscent of the surface of a neglected toilet.

She emptied her pockets of the rest of her cash and the militiaman's two drawings. Then she ordered T to turn his back as she removed her ratty blouse and pants and stuck her head into a little sink in the corner of the office and went to work.

After the third washing the water in the sink was still gray, so she took a towel and tried to rub the rest of the filth out of her hair and off her face. When she was finished she looked at herself again in the mirror, amazed. If there ever was anyone with rosy cheeks, it was she. She looked like a farm girl, straight out of a Douglas Sirk movie.

Last of all she pulled the dress on over her head and combed her hair.

"Wouldn't you say this was overdoing it a bit, for a Sunday afternoon?" she asked, turning towards T. His eyes appraised her approvingly, then himself, less approvingly. Was he really going to have to wade around inside this Armani suit? It was a sure attention-getter.

"Overdoing it? No, it's better—much better. But what are we going to do about me?"

She quickly hitched up his jacket and bunched the trousers at the back, under his tightened belt.

"Okay," she said, "that's better. But you're just going to have to live with that huge jacket."

He found it helped if he stuck out his chest. Then he, too, emptied his coat pockets—sheriff's badge, lighter, wallet and change, car keys, and his faithful talisman, the dart—dumping everything into the Armani jacket pockets. It made him look weightier, but not enough, so he took his classic western-style revolver and stuck it in his belt. This did little to enhance the overall impression.

"Leave that thing, T," she recommended.

He looked at her as though she'd shot his horse.

"If you pull it out around here, they'll shoot you dead, so just leave it behind." He put on a pained expression and stuck the gun under a stack of papers.

"Now we put these on," said Doggie and handed him an ID badge. "We won't get far without them."

He took the thing, turning it over and over in his hand before pinning it so high on his lapel that no one could avoid noticing it.

"This is a test," she said, putting on her own. "To all of you listening in, this is Doggie Rogers speaking. My father is innocent, and that's why I'm here. The charge they've made against me of trying to kill the vice president is total nonsense. The only thing I killed was Sunderland's self-respect, which, of course, is probably worse than murder. But the son of a bitch deserved it. He's the one who was behind the killing of Mimi Jansen and the chief justice of the Supreme Court, among others. Sunderland isn't the man he pretends to be, just so you know. Did all of you hear that?" A smile flashed across her face. Maybe not the smartest thing to do, but it felt good.

"I'll try getting hold of Wesley again," she said, but gave up after his phone rang ten times. This time she was really worried. "What now, T?"

"While I was waiting for a chance to get you out of Kane's office I overheard someone saying there was to be a press conference outside, in front of the diplomatic reception room at three twenty. That's very soon. Do you know where it is?"

She looked at him. A press conference out on the terrace? "That's very unusual." She shook her head. "Thomas Sunderland always used to be against outdoor press conferences. 'The weather can be unpredictable, and so can the security.' I've heard him say it himself."

"And so . . . ?"

"So we always hold them indoors, even though Jansen hates it. The last time one was held outside was in Richmond during his election campaign."

T's jaw dropped for a moment. "But this time he's letting it happen. . . . Isn't that strange?"

She instinctively remembered the two drawings she'd emptied out of her pocket that were lying on the desk. She picked them up.

Suddenly both of them could see what the sketches meant. And it wasn't good at all.

CHAPTER 42

WESLEY NO LONGER KNEW WHO HE WAS OR WHERE HE WAS HEADED. UNTIL A couple of weeks ago everything in his life had been organized according to a formula that he'd always believed would lead him to the top, step-by-step. Now a matter of mere minutes in front of the monitor in Lance Burton's surveillance room had shown his years of effort to have been to no avail. He had witnessed Sunderland murdering Bugatti, and suddenly the future had lost any structure or meaning. Now there was only one thing left that was certain: If he survived the present catastrophe, his striving-to-reach-the-top days were definitively over.

There had to be other ways to make a living.

He watched the screen as Kane's men carried John Bugatti's body out of Sunderland's office. Then he forced himself to switch to the camera in the corridor to see his old friend for the last time as he disappeared down the hall.

All the people in the hallway just stood and watched—American security, the expressionless British special agents, the diplomats who happened to be passing by.

He clicked to the camera outside the Oval Office, the door to which was still hermetically sealed, and then on to the camera in the reception room where small groups from the British delegation were standing, talking in hushed voices.

Then he switched back to Sunderland's office to see Ben Kane's back towering over the vice president's desk.

Wesley turned up the sound from the ID badge that was still

stuck in the sofa. The sound was slightly muffled, but he could hear everything.

"Barefoot. What's your take on him?"

"He didn't have anything to do with Burton's little surveillance scheme."

"According to who? Burton?"

"Burton's been through a pretty robust interrogation. He has too weak a character to make a convincing liar. He would have betrayed Wesley Barefoot long ago."

"Good. Then we keep Wesley. He'll be good to have on our side when this is all over. Now sit down a moment, Kane. We've got a big day ahead of us."

At this point Kane sat down on the sofa, his huge body ending any chance of hearing the little microphone.

At least these two sadists don't suspect me, Wesley thought, without feeling any sense of relief. He could still see John Bugatti's lifeless body before him, and he couldn't stop wondering what they'd been putting Lance Burton through.

He tried fruitlessly to glean some meaning from watching the two men gesticulating on the screen. Then, after about a minute, Kane shifted his body, and some of the sound returned.

"He still thinks we're giving him amnesty," Kane was saying.

Wesley sat up straight. Who were they talking about now? Was it an exiled politician?

"Where is he now?" asked Sunderland.

"Up in Seattle, still suffering from his injuries."

"It's a good thing we kept him alive," Sunderland said, and laughed. "Think of the useful information he's given us. Ironic, isn't it, that for the past two weeks we've had in custody the man whom the enemy sees as their leader?"

Jesus Christ! They were talking about Moonie Quale! What the hell was the connection here? Wesley leaned over to make sure the video's hard disk was recording everything.

Please, someone out there—see this! he prayed, hoping some decent person over in Homeland Security happened to be watching and listening, so that there might be a chance of this shocking information making its way to the outside world.

"That was good thinking, Kane. And you say now he's in the safe house in Seattle?" Kane shifted back on the sofa, and the sound was gone again.

Wesley viewed the silent horror movie on the monitor while he turned over recent events in his mind. What did it matter that he couldn't hear what they were saying now? Hadn't he already heard enough? He had just been witness to nothing less than an admission of high treason. If he had anything to say about it, these digitalized video files would be Sunderland's personal and political epitaph. But how was he going to get away from here? Would it be possible to get a message to the president that he'd been confined to Burton's office? Maybe the men at the guard post. At least they weren't Kane's men, as far as he knew.

He left the little room, went over to Burton's desk, pressed a few buttons on the intercom, confirming that it was still dead. It was the same with the telephone. What the hell was he going to do? His cell phone was lying on the desk in his own office, and there were no cameras in Burton's office to which he could cry out for help. Nor did the badge Burton had given him have a microphone.

He parted the curtains and looked out the window towards Pennsylvania Avenue. The rain had lessened but not the presence of Kane's black devils.

He stepped back from the window and closed the curtain. This was the height of irony. Here he sat, trapped with knowledge that could topple the world's greatest democracy and unable to do a damned thing about it.

He pricked up his ears. What was that sound out in the corridor? He sprang back to the surveillance room to check the hall monitor.

It was just as he thought: President Jansen and his prominent guest had just emerged from the Oval Office.

Wesley looked at the grainy image of Prime Minister Watts as he crossed the corridor to confer with members of his delegation. He seemed completely worn-out, and his expression was very grave.

A couple of yards farther on, Jansen was holding a discussion with Ben Kane. Maybe Thomas Sunderland's faithful servant was in the process of giving the president his own special version of the shooting of John Bugatti.

Then Sunderland appeared in the corner of the picture. His gestures were surely meant to imply that everything was under control now.

Bastard, thought Wesley, and he turned his attention back to the prime minister. Suddenly, Watts's expression changed dramatically— for the worse. This must be the moment his diplomats were relaying the information they'd been given by Sunderland, telling the prime minister that the president of the United States had lost his mind, had committed countless horrific acts, and was responsible for throwing the entire nation into chaos.

So Wesley wasn't surprised to see Watts wave a couple of his bodyguards closer to him, then maintain a few steps' distance behind Jansen as they headed for the White House lawn.

"What the hell is Jansen going to think when he sees I'm not waiting for him on the podium?" mumbled Wesley to himself, as he tried to find a screen with a camera trained on the area outside the diplomatic reception hall. Unsuccessful, he instead tried to find a camera that was monitoring either Kane or Sunderland. Again, no luck. "Hell!" he swore, and began clicking feverishly between the cameras inside all the other offices. Not even the US embassy in Saigon at the ignominious conclusion of the Vietnam War could have been more deserted.

He shook his head. Was this really the world's stronghold of freedom?

Then he tried a setting on the control board next to which was written OFFICE 15. It was the next-to-last of the monitored offices, and he expected it to be empty like all the rest.

He stiffened at what he saw, unable to believe his eyes, his head no longer able to absorb more shocking input. He stuck his face right up to the screen. By God, it was true! There was his old traveling companion from China, Sheriff T. Perkins, applying a badge to the lapel of a comically oversized Armani jacket draped around his body. And wasn't that Doggie, in a pleated yellow dress, looking more pale and haggard than he'd ever seen her?

Under different circumstances this might have been a joyous moment. Instead it was a new source of anxiety.

How'd they get into the building? he wondered. Even in his wildest fantasy he'd never imagined Doggie would actually act on the short telephone message she'd given him. And now, there she was. What did she think she was doing? Did she really believe she'd be able to force her way through this morass of madmen to deliver a plea to the president for her father's life? What on earth were they up to?

Now he had to get out of here, no matter what, and maybe this was the moment. There were only two of Kane's men guarding him; almost all the rest of the security agents were keeping an eye on the president, prime minister, and their entourage. From the monitor he could see that, besides the two guards, there were some British diplomats still standing outside the door as well.

He clenched his teeth. *In a second I'm going out that door, straight into the midst of these Englishmen, and then strolling with them down the hallway,* he told himself. Kane's men wouldn't try to stop him in a situation like that, and if they did, he would start shouting out all that he'd just heard and witnessed, even if it cost him his life.

He looked through the door opening into Burton's office and heard a very faint click, like the unclasping of a lady's intimate undergarment, only it didn't give at all the same kind of enjoyable associations. He turned the monitor sound all the way down and felt his measured breathing disintegrate into uncontrolled hyperventilation. He rose and stepped quickly into the office, directly into the scrutinizing gaze of Ben Kane.

"I've come to convey the vice president's apologies," Kane said, looking over Wesley's shoulder. Was he expecting others to pop out of the surveillance room, or what?

He continued. "It was the vice president's duty to act resolutely, you understand, but now we're convinced you didn't have anything to do with Burton's eavesdropping on the president's office."

He's been told to say that, the piece of shit, thought Wesley. If only Kane knew what *he* knew. One day this security goon was going to pay for the waking nightmare he'd helped create! But the words that emerged from Wesley's mouth were: "That's all right, I understand completely."

Kane motioned towards the door. "The press conference is beginning in a couple of minutes. President Jansen is expecting you to introduce him and the prime minister."

He was led through the Cabinet conference room, where all the double doors had been thrown open wide and sheaves of light were pouring in through the windows. For a moment the scene looked so grand and righteous. Never before had he seen his workplace illuminated so beautifully; never had the sweet scent from the freshly mowed White House lawn been stronger.

When he got outside he looked up at the sky. The blue hole in the clouds seemed to be getting larger.

His eyes panned the scene. It was almost quiet. Most of the people assembled outside were closing their umbrellas. FEMA agents were deployed around the periphery of the lawn, vigilant and ready, and a forest of microphones rose in lonely majesty from the podium. Ten yards back on the glistening lawn a long row of photographers and cameramen stood with their equipment, prepared for action. And next to them waited the usual mob of journalists, capable of killing for the chance to ask the first question.

Jansen and Prime Minister Watts were standing just outside the White House, and behind them were positioned the bodyguards, eyes darting incessantly in all directions from behind their Ray-Bans.

Most of the Cabinet sat next to the door on a row of upholstered chairs. Less-important guests from the British embassy and the State Department were sitting on the side of the podium where Wesley was positioned, and behind them was a row of empty folding chairs, soon to be occupied by lower-ranking members of the British delegation who were still standing in the corridors, grappling with how to tackle the new, suddenly ominous situation.

Wesley had to think clearly. The most important thing right now was to have a quick word with Jansen before he had to orient the press regarding the state visit. It was essential that Jansen knew what the British delegation had been told about him, and by whom. Right now could be his only chance. Later might be much too late.

He scouted the area reserved for Cabinet members, looking for Sunderland, but his seat was vacant. How the hell could that be? He was always where the action was.

A nasty thought struck him as he realized that Doggie and T. Perkins were presently situated in an office a mere fifty yards away.

Had Sunderland gotten wind of their presence? God forbid.

"I just want to have a couple of words with the president," he said casually to Kane. He turned to head for the podium, but Kane's hard grip on his arm stopped him in his tracks. A quick, professional move that went unnoticed by the guests and media.

"Don't you think it can wait?" Kane said indulgently, trying to make it sound like a question while his eyes betrayed a carrion hawk that had just gotten wind of rotting flesh.

There could be little doubt that Kane had put two and two together when he caught Wesley stepping out of Burton's surveillance room. And now Kane could sense that Wesley was about to relay what he knew to the president.

He attempted to alleviate Kane's suspicion with a wide smile. "The president may have a last-minute statement he wants me to make. This is normal procedure, so what's the problem?"

But Kane's expression didn't change, and his grip tightened. "Normal procedure? But you know that's not true, Mr. Barefoot."

Wesley had to control himself. *Let fucking go if you don't want me to start screaming all your dirty, treasonous deeds to the whole world*, he thought—but said nothing.

"You just go up there and introduce the president and Watts, okay?" It was like Kane was speaking to a child.

Wesley stared at the restless fingers of Kane's right hand. Was he about to reach for his automatic and shoot the White House press secretary in front of all these people? Did Kane sense so clearly what Wesley would say when he went up to the microphone? Wesley was convinced he did. Kane was standing motionlessly, waiting to make his next move. But how did Kane imagine he'd ever get away with shooting him?

Wesley nodded. "Yes, of course it can wait. I'll introduce them now."

In the second when Ben Kane released his grip, Wesley was ready to bolt the short distance over to the president. But a second later a paralyzing blow to his throat stopped him in his tracks. He heard utterances of surprise from people behind him as Kane grabbed him to support him, waving people away as though it was a simple case of dizziness. Wesley was stunned, able to neither move nor speak, but Kane's assurances made the guests relax again.

It was all over in a matter of seconds.

Then he got Wesley over to an empty seat in the back row near the rostrum and waved over one of his men to ask him to give the president a message.

"Wesley Barefoot has suffered a dizzy spell," he said, adding that there seemed to be something contagious going around since Lance Burton had apparently been struck by the same bug. Therefore the president was going to have to make the introduction himself.

Kane leaned down over Wesley as soon as the man was gone. "Just so you know: I just don't trust you, Barefoot," he whispered. "Sunderland is determined to keep you; he'll need a witness from the White House staff he can trust when this is all over, but it won't work, if you ask me. You know and see too much, and you talk with too many people. You're going to be a problem, I can feel it. What the hell was it you were doing in Burton's surveillance room? Can you answer me that?"

Wesley attempted to straighten his shoulders to allow his lungs to give him a better chance to breathe. His tongue lay immobilized in his mouth, blocking that source of oxygen. He was just capable of moving his head slightly to follow his surroundings with his eyes but was incapable of reacting.

Kane lay a hand on his shoulder and let it slowly glide towards his neck. "No, Barefoot," he repeated, "I don't trust you at all. I can see it in your eyes, you're not on our side. I can almost smell it."

He could feel Kane's fingers edging towards his carotid artery. Then came the slightly increasing pressure. He stared at his numb legs that sprawled before him on the wet grass and his useless hands lying in his lap, palms up. As he was concentrating on trying to move one of his fingers, an icy wave spread out from his shoulders as Kane continued squeezing.

He's going to do it. He's going to kill me in front of all these people and cameras, Wesley convinced himself. Afterwards, Kane's hand on Wesley's neck would be explained as an act of caring, that he'd been taking Wesley's pulse because he was worried about the press secretary's condition. He would be admonished for not having called a doctor immediately but would respond that he had no idea it was so serious, that death had struck so unexpectedly.

In the meantime Wesley's lungs were again beginning to function. He turned his eyes to the empty rostrum, thinking that what used to be his altar was going to become his tombstone. It was nothing dramatic, just a sorrowful, solitary feeling of not having achieved what life had to offer.

Then some of the British delegation showed up and sat down on the chairs in front of him, noticing neither him nor Kane. They were all looking at the empty lectern and whispering to one another. Then a couple of female delegates arrived who were not quite as discreet.

"What do you think Watts is going to say to all this?" one of them asked. Wesley tried to kick the woman's chair leg, but his foot barely moved.

"Watts? Hah! He'll keep the facade in place, my dear, you can rest assured," the other one whispered back.

The pressure of Kane's hand on his neck stole his power of concentration. He was beginning to feel a sensation like approaching sleep. It was not unpleasant, more a feeling of relief.

He looked out at the Washington Monument in the distance. Majestic clouds swirled above the obelisk, leaving more and more ice-blue sky. The buds on the cherry trees were already threatening to blossom.

It was an immensely lovely day to die.

He managed to notice a shadow moving across the lawn as his head fell to his chest and everything became grayer. When the silhouette came to a halt next to him, he could somehow sense that it hadn't stopped by chance. Then he could feel a new hand on his shoulder, moving slowly towards Kane's tightening fingers and finally grabbing them and pulling them away from his neck.

He could feel a struggle of hands on his shoulders and then how Kane took a hard grip on the hand of the stranger.

Even though Wesley couldn't see Kane, he could sense he was not in control of the situation. He thought he heard Kane's voice, and then his eyelids began feeling less heavy and his blood resumed its job of pumping oxygen to his brain. He took a huge gulp of air and felt the prickly return of feeling to his legs and arms. Then he tipped his head up, and there stood Doggie in her pleated dress, caught in the grip of Kane's viselike paw.

Kane stuck his head between Wesley and Doggie's. "I'll kill him if there's so much as a peep out of you, Doggie Rogers," he hissed. "What the hell are you doing here, anyway? Don't you value your life more than that?" He raised his head again and prepared for an opportune moment to neutralize the two of them.

What's he going to do? Wesley wondered. *What excuse is he going to invent this time?* With his body beginning to function again, he turned his head farther so he could see the row of Cabinet members.

On the far side of the VIP tribunal one of Billy Johnson's bodyguards was whispering to his boss. At first the secretary of the Department of Homeland Security's expression remained calm, then it changed dramatically. He nodded curtly to his bodyguard, and then they both began scrutinizing the horizon in all directions. Wesley tried to follow their gaze; something serious must be happening out there. Then he turned his head away from Johnson and spied Sheriff T. Perkins over in the direction of the south entrance to the Oval Office, standing behind two of Kane's men. At just that moment their eyes met, and T lifted his hand slightly in recognition, but Wesley was unable to reciprocate.

Then the assembly stood up. Many began clapping, but far from everyone, including the diplomats sitting in front of Wesley.

Wesley tried standing up, too, but his body was not yet ready to obey. Then Doggie suddenly gave Kane a shove and managed to drop a sheet of paper in Wesley's lap without being noticed. Wesley stared at the paper, trying to focus. It seemed to be some kind of technical drawing, but he didn't know of what. It looked like a cross section, along with a series of numbers and a couple of curves emerging from the cross section. At the top of the page were written the words *assassination attempt?, ballistic trajectory?,* and *Monument?* in smudged lipstick. It was Doggie's handwriting. He raised his eyes to the Washington Monument once more.

His hands began to quiver, then his whole body. He couldn't tell whether it was his blood circulation returning or the realization of impending disaster.

Wesley could feel Kane's rage through the one hand he still had positioned behind his neck. In reality, Kane knew he should be figuring how to get out of there, but first he had to see to it that Wesley and Doggie didn't wreck the plan.

Wesley's mouth was getting drier as his anxiety grew; the danger was imminent. They were planning a gruesome attack from the top of the monument, and Kane knew all about it. No wonder Thomas Sunderland hadn't shown up for the press conference!

Then a wave of warmth wakened his body parts. Maybe his temperature was returning to normal. He tried to speak but couldn't. He stamped his feet hard on the grass; it felt like they could bear his weight.

"Ladies and gentlemen . . ." It was the voice of Secretary of the Interior Betty Tucker. In her tight dress, she didn't have to do much to get the crowd's attention. "The President of the United States of America, Bruce Jansen."

"We've got a situation here." Wesley could hear Kane muttering into his lapel microphone.

"You bastard!" Suddenly the words escaped Wesley's mouth. So his power of speech was returning, too.

He could sense Doggie's agitation; she had heard Kane's message as well. He glanced up at her. Her face was white as a sheet. From fear, perhaps, but not helplessness. He knew her; in a second he was afraid she would overreact.

He shook his head at her, but she merely smiled back. It was a horrible, unreal feeling, her standing there, so vibrant and alive. *Don't let it happen!* he pleaded silently. Behind the president he could see the black-clad agents' attention focused on Kane as they listened to him through their earpieces. In three seconds they'd storm over and forcibly remove him and Doggie. Without the eyes of the world watching, they would find an isolated spot to liquidate them, then invent a suitable story. And in the meantime Kane would escape. A simple, classic plan.

He tilted forward in his seat to try and judge whether his legs could support him.

"Good afternoon, ladies and gentlemen!" came the president's voice from the podium. "It's wonderful to see all of you assembled for this happy occasion." He waved to a couple of reporters.

"Prime Minister Watts has come to pay us a visit, and the bonds between our two nations have once again proven their strength and durability."

As Jansen continued reading the speech Wesley had written the night before, Doggie squeezed his shoulder cautiously with her free hand. It was a signal. She was about to tear herself free of Kane and charge towards the rostrum, and Wesley would have to fill the role of bodyguard as well as he could. First he'd try the same kind of karate chop to Kane's neck as Kane had dealt him, and it would have to be quick, before Kane had a chance to go for his weapon. He'd have to improvise; then whatever happened would happen. Just so long as Doggie didn't suffer as a consequence.

But just as Doggie was literally swinging into action she was struck by Kane's blow to her neck, just like the one he'd administered to Wesley.

Before Doggie had sunk to the ground, Wesley was up and running towards the podium, causing both Homeland Security agents and Kane's men to draw their weapons.

"Get away from here!" screamed Wesley, as he felt a shot from Kane's gun hammer into his buttock. "Stop them, Mr. President!" he yelled, as he fell to the ground and rolled over a few times, propelled both by his momentum and the incredible pain. For a moment the president looked down at him, then gave a sign to the security men to hold their fire. But it didn't stop Kane from shooting again. This time Wesley didn't know where he'd been hit, but the impact propelled him three more feet along the slippery grass. Now he could hear cries and commotion from the assembled guests behind him while the TV cameras zoomed in on his writhing, bloody body.

Then he could hear gasps from the audience and pulled himself up on his elbows to face his assailant, who was about to administer the coup de grâce. Kane had his gun aimed perfectly, hand steady, but his eyes were blank. Suddenly his other hand reached for his neck, where a dart was embedded in his jugular vein, creating a little spray of blood like a punctured garden hose.

By now several bodyguards had thrown themselves at the president and prime minister and shoved them off the podium. In the meantime, Ben Kane had flopped to the ground, and Secret Service agents had overmanned Sheriff Perkins, the dart champion.

"Watch out, get away from here! It's a conspiracy! They're about to fire a missile from the Washington Monument!" Wesley managed to yell before a roar erupted from the top of the obelisk. He didn't see what happened next, heard only a whoosh of air, desperate screams, and finally the deafening explosion as the missile blew up the entrance to the White House reception hall, transforming its mighty pillars to rubble.

CHAPTER 43

THE FOLLOWING MINUTES WERE LIKE ARMAGEDDON. THERE WERE BODY PARTS powdered white by the thick cloud of plaster dust. Feverish hands lifting chunks of rubble off of victims and screams of pain and despair filling the air.

The corpses of the bodyguards lying on top of the president were dragged aside, and Jansen and Prime Minister Watts were brought to the Cabinet Room. They lay the president on the conference table and other, less-important persons—like Wesley—on the floor, while the dead were left lying where they fell. The Diplomatic Reception Room was completely pulverized and still burning, while reporters, cameramen, and photographers on the lawn in front of the hall struggled to get their wounded colleagues down to the southern entrance of the park. Cameras and all sorts of electronic equipment lay strewn everywhere like beer cans after a rock concert. Behind it all rose a chorus of sirens.

Wesley looked up gratefully at a British security agent who was putting his finger deep into a hole in one of Wesley's arteries that had been ripped open along with a section of his chest.

He could feel all too clearly the projectile that was lodged in his hip socket, but not Kane's other shot that had passed through his upper arm and taken a chunk of chest muscle with it. "Why can't I feel anything in my chest?" he asked.

"You will shortly, I'm afraid," the man answered, with an upper-class British accent that almost made Wesley smile.

He looked over towards Jansen. The president was lying on the table, a doctor on either side. All Wesley could see of him was a sock, hanging half off a foot. The doctors were conferring in hushed voices; evidently their provisional attempts to stop his wounds from bleeding had been successful.

Prime Minister Watts was sitting on a chair with a wet towel over his face, apparently temporarily deafened by the explosion. He was in deep shock but had definitely gotten off easier than his bodyguards.

"Can you see a black-haired woman in a yellow dress anywhere?" Wesley asked his attendant.

He shook his head.

"Not outside, either?"

"No, I'm afraid."

"What happened outside, over there on the right where I had been sitting?" he asked, almost not wanting to hear the answer.

The Englishman hesitated a moment. "A lot of them ended up under a column that fell over," he answered, and pressed his finger harder into the hole in Wesley's chest. Wesley was beginning to feel the blood loss. His fingers and toes were turning cold. But if Doggie were dead, what difference did it make?

A large man came into the room to orient himself as to the president's condition. Help would be there soon, he reported, but regretted that the emergency vehicles had been delayed by all the roadblocks. The fire, however, was already under control—FEMA's state of readiness had functioned well, he said. Then the man turned towards Wesley and squatted down in front of him. It was Billy Johnson. He laid a hand on Wesley's cheek and looked at him with steady, sorrowful eyes.

"How's it going, Wesley?"

Wesley nodded silently.

"Thank you for what you did. . . ." Johnson tried to say more, but the words stuck in his throat.

Wesley grabbed his shirt sleeve. "Have you seen Doggie, Billy?" he whispered. "She was sitting over where I was sitting. Do you know anything?"

The Homeland Security secretary turned his head away without answering.

Wesley closed his eyes and tried to conjure up her face before him. How had things come to this? Why hadn't he made her his long ago, and never let go? Why hadn't they gotten out while they could?

He was starting to feel the wound in his chest; it didn't hurt—it just felt wrong. He shut his eyes tighter and tried to sense her smell, hear her voice.

"I'm here, Wesley," said her voice, and Wesley opened his eyes a crack and smiled at the picture of her face before it began fading away.

"Here! I'm here!" He felt a light hand on his chest.

"Here—feel it." This time she put her face down to his and kissed him gently. "I'm okay," she said.

He opened his eyes as well he could. There she was, sitting before him. Was it true? He couldn't believe it. Then he fumbled for her hand.

"My God, Wesley, you're ice-cold!" she whispered. "How much blood has he lost?" she asked the Englishman. He said nothing.

Wesley tried to fix his eyes on her. It wasn't easy because the light was changing all the time, but yes, it was she. There she sat with her weird hair, smiling at him, even though she'd been wounded herself. A cut ran from her cheekbone to her chin, and her hair was completely gray with dust. But there she was, looking him in the eyes and smiling—the most beautiful woman in the world.

"You're fantastic, Wesley, simply fantastic," she said, rubbing his hand to warm it up. He closed his eyes for a moment and was filled by a kind of ethereal peace.

Then one of the black-clad security guards approached them. "You come with me, Miss Rogers," he said, grabbing her arm.

"Leave her be," Wesley ordered, opening his eyes again, but the guard pulled her to her feet.

"Did you hear what Barefoot told you?" came a weak voice. Wesley looked up and could see the president's foot move a bit as he spoke. This got the guard to stop. After a moment he loosened his grip and left.

The question was when he would be back. Perhaps he was one of those who still obeyed Sunderland's every whim. Maybe it wasn't over yet.

"Doggie, listen!" whispered Wesley. "The last twenty minutes up to the explosion have been videotaped. You have to get to Lance Burton's office and see what's on that tape, understand? The black box on top stores all the video recordings. Push the PLAY button and send the signal out over the intranet through my server. Do you think you can figure that out?"

She nodded.

"And watch out for Sunderland, if he's around."

She nodded again.

He looked at the Englishman who was still helping stem the bleeding. "Are you armed?" Wesley asked. The man nodded. "Then you go with her and watch out for her, okay?"

The man nodded again, took Wesley's hand, and pressed it deep into the chest wound. It felt warm and sticky and much too soft—a totally surrealistic sensation.

"Press!" he said. "Help is on the way. Don't worry, you're going to make it." Then he and Doggie disappeared.

"Is it you, Wesley?" came the president's voice from the table.

"Yes, Mr. President," he whispered.

"Did he answer?"

"Yes, Mr. President," said one of the doctors. "He said 'yes.'"

God, please keep an eye on her, Wesley prayed to himself. Maybe Sunderland's men had got there first and deleted the files, and all was lost. Without evidence, that bastard Sunderland would have his way.

Wesley tried to concentrate on his wound, pushing harder on it. Now he couldn't feel his fingers anymore; his whole hand was numb.

Then he heard Thomas Sunderland's voice in the corridor. It sounded appalled, compassionate, paternal, and at a loss—all at once. "Where is he?" he called out, as he came through the door and rushed to the conference table. Wesley could see his shoes under the table. They were the only ones in the entire room that had maintained their polish.

"How is he doing?" he asked with concern. "Tell me straight." The two doctors didn't answer.

"I'm okay, Thomas," came Jansen's weak reply. "And you?"

Sunderland tried to produce a sigh of relief. "Oh, thank God! I'm also okay, Mr. President. I wasn't that close when it happened."

You bet your ass you weren't, thought Wesley, and tried to say it out loud. But he was so weak, no words would come out. Soon he wouldn't be able to keep pressing on his wound, either.

"We have to get the president out of here. To a secure hospital." Sunderland sounded concerned. "We don't know the cause or the extent of the situation, and maybe it's not over yet. We have to move the president. Can he be moved?"

Mendacious cocksucker! yelled Wesley in his head.

"We're waiting for the ambulance," said one of the doctors.

"When it arrives, I'm coming along," Sunderland stated. "I've seen to it that they're ready to receive him. How about Prime Minister Watts?"

Did Sunderland say he'd seen to it that they were ready? *Who* was ready? It didn't sound reassuring.

Again, Wesley tried to say something, but his strength was gone— except for his heart, which was beating hard to compensate for the loss of blood. It hurt almost more than the injuries themselves.

"Where is Watts?" Sunderland repeated.

Prime Minister Watts lifted his hand so Sunderland could see where he was sitting.

"Oh, thank God. There you are, Mr. Prime Minister."

Sunderland stepped over Wesley without noticing him; he was already maneuvering his guns into position. A whole other diplomatic agenda had begun. It was time to line up one's allies for the showdown. "And your people, Mr. Prime Minister? Have the losses been great?"

Watts let the towel fall from his forehead and spread his arms out, expressing better than words that he had no grasp of what had happened. Sunderland nodded sympathetically. Then he saw Wesley. His eyes were cold, but the words were fittingly civilized.

"And here we have the hero of the day. Excellent work, Wesley Barefoot. How is Mr. Barefoot's condition?" he inquired, turning to the doctors.

"He'll make it if we stop the bleeding," said one.

"See to it he is brought to the same place as the president."

Yeah, and that'll be the end of us, thought Wesley.

Then Sunderland walked around slowly, seeing to the rest of the wounded, assuming a convincing protective-father-of-the-country air. A good moment to score cheap points, and he knew it. Like all true politicians he'd learned that the cheap points often wound up counting for more than hard-earned ones.

Wesley managed to wag a foot at the prime minister, but Watts had replaced the wet towel over his dust- and smoke-injured eyes. The wailing of several ambulances was beginning to grow in the background, as was the sound of an approaching helicopter.

Then Wesley lifted his leg as high as it would go and let it drop hard to the floor. Prime Minister Watts removed the towel again and looked down at Wesley with badly bloodshot eyes. Wesley whispered something, but Watts didn't hear it.

The PM squeezed his eyes shut. *His vision was probably impaired,* thought Wesley, so he raised and dropped his leg once more. That was it. Now his energy was gone; he couldn't even feel his heart beating any longer.

So that was that; soon it would all be over. The thought didn't even grieve him.

He smiled to Watts and was about to close his eyes and surrender to the fatigue when the prime minister got up. Slowly it became apparent how lucky he'd been—unlike his two dead bodyguards. Aside from his inflamed eyes and one shredded pant leg, he had not suffered one obvious injury.

Still, he approached Wesley with unsteady steps, hunched forward. And his mouth was open, even though it hadn't uttered a word since the attack.

He bent over as far as he could and put his ear up to Wesley's mouth.

"It's Sunderland who's behind all of it," Wesley barely got out.

Watts pulled his head back and looked at him, perplexed. Then he turned his head around and put the other ear up to Wesley's mouth. Apparently, he'd gone deaf in the one ear.

"It's Sunderland's work—all of it," Wesley whispered again. It seemed like the prime minister was holding his breath, the better to catch what was being said with what was left of his hearing. Then he turned his face towards Wesley.

"I hear you," he said, and put his ear back to Wesley's mouth.

"Turn on the television. There's a TV screen behind that panel there." Wesley nodded towards the far wall. "The remote control's on the tea table."

Watts stood up slowly, almost bent double. He was unable to stand up straight. Then he went over to the tea table and turned on the television.

Usually the monitor in the Cabinet Room was reserved for video recordings of a governmental-administrative nature or the ones that were used in the Situation Room. Otherwise it was tuned in to NBC.

Which it was now.

By craning his neck as far as it would go, Wesley could just see the screen.

It was an appalling scene with lots of people running aimlessly around. Smoke from the fire obscured the Ellipse and allowed only glimpses of what was going on. There was a great number of soldiers in bulletproof vests surrounding the Washington Monument; something was about to happen.

Wesley began hearing what followed outside the second before the TV screen showed soldiers beginning their counterattack on the terrorists up in the monument, eight hundred yards away. Several tear gas grenades were launched at the panorama windows at the top of the obelisk, and return gunfire from within the monument could also be heard. Except for the anti-terror corps, the surrounding area had been completely cleared. The commentator, who was standing three hundred feet away, sounded like he was the one being fired at while his cameraman panned through the smoke around the White House, then zoomed in on the massacre taking place inside the colossal American monument.

Next it zoomed in on the damage done to the front of the presidential residence. The row of bodies before the sea of flames and the battling firemen was growing constantly. A real-life soundtrack was provided a second ahead of the silent pictures on the screen by the actual tumult and screaming Wesley was hearing outside the Cabinet Room. It was a heartbreaking moment, and if he could, he would have cried. If only he could have prevented it all from happening. But now the hungry TV camera lenses really had something to chew on; it was like a prime-time show, disastrously out of control.

"Can't we turn that off?" Sunderland cried out, when he noticed the British PM standing with the remote control.

Then the picture on the screen changed. It was the head of NBC himself, Alastair Hopkins, looking straight at America from under his bushy eyebrows. He began speaking the words Wesley had been hoping to hear for weeks: "We have a history-making news flash from our direct line to the White House pressroom, where a moment ago we received evidence that high-placed public servants—in whom the American voters have placed their utter confidence—have possibly been responsible for a series of treasonous and tragic events leading up to, and including, today's attack on the White House."

Wesley lowered his head again, looked under the conference table, and watched Sunderland's shoes as they strode towards Prime Minister Watts, taking no heed of the wounded lying on the floor. Sunderland's dark agenda for reaching the pinnacle of power had turned into a frantic fight for his life as people in the room blocked his path, and the scene on the TV changed once more.

The clip that was now being shown meant the end of the road for Thomas Sunderland. Wesley ought to know because he had taped it himself. It was Sunderland's conversation with Ben Kane. So Doggie *had* succeeded in coupling the video machines to the intranet! Thank God for that. The picture quality wasn't good, but there was no mistaking the leading actors.

A sense of indescribable relief and deliverance swept over Wesley. Now he could begin to believe this nightmare would have an end.

"You got Burton out of the way?" came Sunderland's voice from the television screen.

Wesley could see President Jansen's foot twitching on the table end above him. The room was silent apart from the sound from the TV and

Sunderland's heavy breathing. Then, on cue, all the feet under the table turned in the direction of Sunderland's, like a colony of spiders that had simultaneously spotted a fly caught in its web. In the meantime the damning video clip continued flickering mercilessly, inescapably over the screen.

"It's been manipulated!" screamed Sunderland. "Turn that shit off; none of it's true, goddammit!" But no one was listening. All ears were concentrating on hearing about what Kane and Sunderland had done with Chief of Staff Lance Burton. Then Sunderland's feet suddenly disappeared upward, and footsteps bounded across the conference table.

Sunderland jumped straight from the table out through the double doors, into the smoking inferno of the corridor.

"Stop that man!" yelled Prime Minister Watts at the top of his voice. This caused the firemen outside to turn around instinctively, in time to see a desperate Sunderland, unable to decide in which direction to run. Then one of them trained his fire hose on the vice president, knocking his feet out from under him and shooting him across the terrace like tumbleweed in a prairie storm. But when the firefighter turned his hose back on the flames, Sunderland was on his feet again. Then he disappeared from Wesley's field of vision.

"What's he doing?" came the president's weak voice from above him.

"As far as I can see, he's trying to get the gun out of his bodyguard's hand," answered one of the doctors.

"Trying?"

"Yes, the guard's body is lying crushed under a column, and the vice president can't get to the hand with the gun."

"Bring Sunderland in here; don't let him get away," whispered Jansen weakly.

Wesley no longer had the strength to keep his hand pressed on his chest wound. His heart wasn't beating so hard now. It felt good, almost liberating.

Then indistinct shouting was heard outside.

"I think they got him," said one of the doctors. "The guards down at Executive Avenue spotted him."

"Tell them to make sure he doesn't escape," whispered Jansen.

Try as he might, Wesley was losing his powers of concentration, and the sounds in the room and on the TV merged into one.

"Have they got him?" asked the president.

"No, but it seems he's coming back here voluntarily," said a doctor.

Suddenly a dripping-wet silhouette stood in the opening of the veranda door, thinning hair plastered to its head and jaw jutting defiantly. A totally debased human being.

For a moment the vice president stared down at Wesley with an insane look in his eyes that shone with a combination of confusion and contempt. Wesley gave a sunny smile in return.

This apparently was more than Sunderland could take. Stepping over to the oaken chair from which he'd dispatched many official duties, he gripped it so hard his knuckles turned white. Then he took a couple of deep breaths and suddenly raised the chair over his head, ready to smash in the skull of his defenseless commander in chief.

In spite of his failing heart, it gave Wesley a start. Then came the dry, popping sound of two quick shots, and Sunderland froze with the chair in midair, his spine splintered in two.

Wesley heard the chair and then the vice president crash to the floor around him, with Ben Kane still on the TV monitor, explaining to Sunderland how the militias were just about to storm the prison in Waverly and slaughter Bud Curtis.

Then he heard no more.

CHAPTER 44

DOGGIE STOOD FOR A LONG TIME, WATCHING THE AMBULANCES WORK THEIR WAY towards the southwest exit. She had a hard time relaxing, even though the doctors had assured her Wesley would survive and was in good hands. She'd done all she could to persuade the doctors to let her come along, but they refused. He was already getting blood transfusions, and the operating table was ready—that's what counted, they told her.

Then a Secret Service agent approached and said she'd have to come along and answer some questions.

She tore her eyes away from the red, flashing ambulance lights and followed the agent to the West Wing, still a flickering inferno, with rubble and battling firemen. The firefighters were silent. What was there to say?

The agent showed her into Lance Burton's reception room and asked her to wait until they were finished with their present interviewee. Would she like a cup of coffee in the meantime, he asked.

She shook her head. She was happy just to sit down. It was exactly 4:00 P.M., Sunday, and it looked like she had succeeded in her mission.

"Are you *sure* word's been given to the prison to put off my father's execution?" she asked the agent. The man nodded briefly, just as he had the first two times she'd asked.

She stretched out in Lance Burton's secretary's chair and closed her eyes. She was totally burnt out. They'd have to awaken her when they were ready.

She awoke with a start when Billy Johnson placed a hand on her shoulder.

"It's your turn now, Doggie Rogers," he said.

She looked up at him, unfocused. "How long have I been sitting here?" she asked.

"You've slept for three hours. It's seven o'clock in the evening. Sorry you've had to wait so long."

There were many people assembled in Burton's chamber that she recognized but hadn't seen in several weeks. This included the Senate's president pro tem, Hammond Woodrow, the Speaker of the House of Representatives, the minority leader, the acting Chief Supreme Court Justice, Homeland Security Chief Johnson, and finally Chairman of the Joint Chiefs of Staff Omar Powers. Their heads turned in her direction as though she were an oracle, about to reveal the future.

The first words out of her mouth were: "My father is innocent. The killing of Mimi Jansen was Sunderland's work. I can't prove it right now, but the evidence is there. Will someone please assure me that his execution will be stopped and his case reviewed? You have to promise me before I can start answering questions."

She looked at them, one by one, and saw with horror how they avoided her eyes. Finally, Billy Johnson spoke. "I'm sorry, Miss Rogers, but it's too late."

Her body reacted before her brain, in the form of a cold sweat and something that felt like a blow to the stomach. She was ready to throw up, and a security cop rushed over to her.

No, no, no—she wasn't having it; it couldn't be! The words had never been said; her ears must be playing tricks on her. How could a man in Johnson's position say it was too late? How could he feed her such a rotten lie?

She wanted to scream but couldn't.

"I regret it with all my heart, Doggie," Johnson concluded softly, and folded his hands.

She tried to collect herself; the battle wasn't lost yet. She just had to ask the right questions in the proper fashion. "How do you know it's too late? It's not until tomorrow."

He looked at her sadly. "It's not that, Doggie. Something else awful has happened, I'm afraid." He nodded to General Powers, who took over.

"My condolences, Miss Rogers, but your father was killed at about the same time as the attack on the White House."

She stared at him. What was it he'd said?

"Yes, I'm afraid it's true. The militias stormed the prison this afternoon to free their compatriots, and at the same time all the other inmates were liquidated—pardon the expression. We suspect they didn't want any witnesses."

The militias, he'd said. No, she wasn't about to accept that. What could they have had against her father? These men were lying; it was just a nasty, psychological tactic to destabilize her before they hit her with their damned questions.

"The militias blew open the doors to the prison with hand grenades, then they forced their way to death row and freed their men," the general continued. "We found your father's body in his cell. He'd been shot, like all the rest of the prisoners. My deepest, deepest regrets, Miss Rogers."

This was when her tears started rolling. His deepest regrets, he'd said.

Johnson laid a hand on her shoulder. It felt like an electric shock going through her body. "Here," he said, handing her a handkerchief.

She dried her eyes as he explained they'd gotten their information from the local police, and that their own technicians were on the way. Apparently, there were still several unanswered questions, including what had become of the prison warden and one of his men. They were expected to be hiding out in a nearby marsh and could likely shed more light on the situation when they were found.

As though more light could bring her father back.

When she had drunk a little tea and could once again look them in the eye, she accepted Johnson's thanks for the resourcefulness she'd shown earlier by shouting her accusations against Thomas Sunderland into the badge microphone.

She nodded. "So you heard that," she said quietly.

Johnson confirmed that the machinations of the Department of

Homeland Security had been regrettably slow. Otherwise they could surely have minimized the deadly extent of the attack, he admitted sadly, adding that she also deserved praise for having saved Wesley Barefoot's life and for having gotten hold of the terrorists' technical sketches. Both acts had been instrumental in saving the life of the president. Furthermore, there were strong indications that Barefoot was one of the few men who hadn't abandoned his honor to let himself be corrupted by Sunderland's pathological agenda or Jansen's systematic abuse of his office.

"Where did you get those drawings, by the way?" Johnson asked.

She looked at him blankly. Did he mention men of honor? What about himself? Was he just passing the buck; had he nothing at all to answer for?

Johnson repeated the question.

She looked straight at him. "The drawings? It's a long story, and not particularly important. And besides, there are plenty of other people to thank. Where is Sheriff T. Perkins, for example? Nothing's happened to him, I hope."

"He's being questioned in one of the other offices."

"He's not going to be charged for throwing that dart, is he?"

"I rather believe he'll be recommended for a medal, Miss Rogers," said Johnson. That was good.

"And Wesley? How is he doing?"

"He lost quite a bit of blood and is hopefully lying on the operating table as we speak. Luckily, none of his injuries were life threatening. He's trying to get the doctors to let him come over here tonight, but I doubt they will."

She thought about her father and tried not to cry; she'd have plenty of time for that. Right now, there were other things to concentrate on. Like Wesley's well-being. And that this nightmare didn't continue.

"And Lance Burton?" she asked.

"He's hospitalized at Bethesda and is doing all right. But unfortunately we found the body of John Bugatti about an hour ago, down in the basement. Wesley Barefoot gave us a brief report on the way to the hospital. That's how we knew where to find Bugatti."

"John's dead. . . ." she said softly, seeing him before her as he waited for her in vain in the tea salon. It was she who had gotten him to come to Washington; it was her fault. Lips pressed together, she told herself she'd have to be careful now if she didn't want to break down altogether.

"We saw how he was killed on the video." Billy Johnson shook his head. "Yes, John Bugatti also played a major roll in unraveling this mess. We have a lot to thank him for, especially knowing how ill he was."

She looked at her feet. "Was he ill? I didn't know." She shook her head. "And his boyfriend, Uncle Danny. Does anyone know anything about him?"

"Yes, I'm sorry to say the police found him dead at home when they came to deliver the message about John Bugatti's death. He'd apparently been strangled."

This was too much to bear. She hit her knee with her fist again and again until General Powers stopped her. She didn't want to have any more to do with it. She wanted out.

"I have to go home and get some sleep," she said, rising to her feet. "I can't take any more. Will someone please have me brought home?"

Here the Senate's president pro tem Woodrow straightened up in his chair. "Miss Rogers! At this moment the country is without a leader, and the vice president is dead. Time is of the essence here. The Constitution demands that we find a solution quickly, as I'm sure you're aware. You must assist us in our work. There are plenty of others who are being interviewed regarding the present situation, and we will surely be wanting to speak to you again. By tomorrow we must decide under which conditions we can continue governing this land and have some idea who is to be held accountable for what has happened. You'll be brought home, Miss Rogers, but it will have to wait. I hope you understand."

Billy Johnson tried to straighten up in his chair as well, but with less success. "We have to use the time on these hearings that they require, Doggie," he said. "I know it's rough on you, but right now congressmen are already holding meetings, gossip is rife, and we have to inform these people about what is going on. The guilty must be found out, and the rest of us will have to try to redeem ourselves. We must take responsibility, we must take our punishment, but first we have to do our best to grasp all the aspects of what has befallen us. Don't you agree?"

It was nighttime and lights were burning all over the White House. It was as though a clear message was being sent that a new page was being turned in American history.

Doggie had cried. She had answered questions, she had dozed a little, answered new questions from new people, and had cried some more. Many tears were to fall, but that's how it was to grieve alone. What did it matter that people she didn't even know came up and hugged her? It was *she* whose father lay in his own blood in a cell where he never should have been.

Her crazy, clever, loving father was dead. Not even her mother would despair over his loss. So it was all up to her.

Outside Doggie's little sphere the Senate was about to gather. The House Speaker had returned to ask more questions, this time in the company of former vice president Michael K. Lerner, who'd been hiding out in a hunting cabin near Knoxville with two former Senate colleagues. And there were questions enough. About Sunderland and Ben Kane and his men—who were either dead or under arrest—and about Wesley's and her relationship.

But most of their queries dealt with the president—his mental condition and what she knew about it. She had a strong feeling they had already made up their minds: The president couldn't be held responsible for Sunderland's criminal acts but was still guilty of grossly abusing his office.

Which was true enough. Thousands of people had lost their lives, fortunes had evaporated, and "American values" and the judicial foundation of the country had been trashed. She could tell from the eyes of her questioners that they weren't interested in reinstating the judicial and constitutional apparatus exactly as it was before. It was more about respecting the individual citizen's set of values. They wanted to find their way back to the middle of the American road, they said. It was just a question of whether they could.

Finally, Doggie could sense their urgency in having the nation's highest positions filled as quickly as possible. She could tell the two men sitting across from her considered themselves prime candidates.

Just before they let her go they informed her there would be a Senate hearing, and she was very welcome to participate.

She nodded with a weary smile, knowing that being "welcome" meant she was expected to attend. Last of all they reminded her about the funeral tomorrow at Arlington Cemetery of a person whom they called "one of this conflict's great heroes."

It rang hollow when they said it, but yes, Doggie nodded, she'd be there. Donald Beglaubter *was* "one of this conflict's great heroes." Did they think he'd already been forgotten?

They'd said she would be driven home but hadn't arranged for a chauffeur. Empty promises already seemed typical of these two men. So she went to her office and found some extra outerwear. She thought a moment about her Fendi bag and that she missed it. *You must be crazy,* she told herself.

When she made it down to the control post, the same guard was sitting there who hadn't recognized her the day before. Now he did. "There's been a call for you, Miss Rogers. You are to go back, through the building, and down to the fountain. A Mr. T. Perkins is waiting for you."

The glow of the fire had finally died out, and the floodlights that had been illuminating the area were soon to be switched off. The throngs of people had dispersed, leaving only filthy, exhausted firefighters and rescue personnel—plus, of course, the ever-present FEMA agents and the reporters. She saw T standing by the fountain, in the process of lighting a cigarette. He appeared thinner than ever as he looked over and noticed her. Approaching him, his eyes held so much sympathy that she broke into tears before reaching his embrace.

"I've arranged for transportation down to the prison," he told her quietly when she'd settled down and nodded towards a helicopter standing on the lawn with its slowly whooshing rotor blade. "Shall we take this? It's your decision, Doggie."

"Do I get to see my father?" she whispered.

"That's the whole idea, girl."

She looked at the chopper. She'd wanted to do something like this all her life. To ascend from precisely this spot in a helicopter with the American bald eagle on its side. To see the White House disappear under her feet and glide over the Washington Monument, the Mall, and the winding Potomac. She had imagined gravity releasing her as she pondered the weighty words of great Americans. Instead all she was feeling was spite and a defiled soul. Living out this dream was going to be a rude awakening. Washington was a shadow of itself, and so was she.

An officer led her to the aircraft and showed her to her seat. A nurse who was standing behind the pilot nodded to her. What was *she* doing there? Were they afraid she would fall completely apart at the sight of her father?

She could understand if they were.

"That's where you sit," said the officer, pointing to an empty seat.

A bulky plaid blanket had been thrown onto the seat next to her. She sat down and pulled the blanket towards her to wrap around herself and get some rest. Then came the shock, for under the blanket, there lay Wesley, dozing. He was pale, and the sight of his strong arms with rolled-up sleeves made her want to touch him. But then she noticed the needle in the crook of his arm and the tubing leading to a plastic bag hooked onto the wall of the helicopter.

She looked at the nurse.

"He's okay," the woman said. "He's tired, of course, but he demanded to be brought along." She smiled. "We tried to make him change his mind, but you can imagine how much luck we had."

"What about his injuries?"

"He'll be all right; we're taking good care of him."

She looked over at T, who was nodding his agreement. She couldn't have asked for two better escorts on this dreadful journey.

She placed her hand cautiously on Wesley's arm. It was nice and warm now, thank God.

He gave a little shiver, then his eyes opened, and he looked at her so tenderly, she was ready to cry again.

"I'm so, so sorry, Doggie," he said weakly. His eyes were lusterless, and for the first time she noticed the contours of all the bandaging under his loose clothing.

Then she put her head next to his, feeling his breath on her cheek.

CHAPTER 45

THEY LANDED ON SUSSEX STATE PRISON'S ENORMOUS PARKING LOT WITH
the white aura of the morning sun rising behind the depths of the
forest. Dew was still glistening on the flowers behind the silver-gray
fence.

Wesley squeezed Doggie's hand and told her things were going to
be okay. Nobody hoped he was right more than she.

They stepped out onto the asphalt and were greeted by a little
deputation that was standing before a row of official-looking vehicles,
including those of the local police and FBI.

A man rolled a wheelchair out to the helicopter in spite of Wesley's
protests. Those were the conditions, the nurse said, if he hoped to
come inside.

"We're not finished with our investigation," said a man in a police
uniform, stepping forward. He shook their hands. "There are still
plenty of fingerprints that need registering, but if you just follow Sergeant Laurel here, you should be able to get into death row by now.
We've been instructed by Secretary Billy Johnson and former vice
president Lerner to help you with whatever you need. I can see I
needn't emphasize that you mustn't touch anything since you've
brought a professional along." He greeted T. Perkins like an old friend,
which he probably was.

Doggie looked over at the flat cement blocks where human beings
were kept out of sight the rest of their lives. Her father had lost his life
somewhere inside this hideous, infamous monument to "justice."
Once, as a teenager—lost in Victorian romanticism—she had asked

where he would die, given the choice. She'd hoped he would say the
Taj Mahal or atop Mount Ararat, and she had cried when he said he
would like to die in his mother's arms. She remembered how his answer had made death so real for her.

Now death had come, with no arms to hold him.

They were led down a long hallway where Doggie had never been
before. Behind her, Wesley was still going on about being able to walk
by himself as T pushed him along. In the meantime Sergeant Laurel
tried to explain in as mild terms as possible all the bloodstains they
encountered along the way.

Doggie had tried to imagine Sussex's death row many times, but
she wasn't prepared for what she saw. None of them were.

The corpses had been removed everywhere else, but not here. Even
though it was cool in the cellblocks, the stink of dead bodies was already pervasive. There were remains of blood everywhere on the floor
and walls.

"Oh, no," she exclaimed, and grabbed Wesley's hand behind her.

"Yes, I'm sorry," said the sergeant. "Obviously no one told you how
far we'd gotten in the cleanup. This is the last area that hasn't been
reached yet. I'm afraid we're lacking manpower these days."

T mumbled something to himself and shook his head. Apparently,
even *he* wasn't used to sights like this. He gave her a somber look. "Are
you sure, Doggie? You don't have to come in."

She just nodded, and T walked over to a group of white-clad technicians. They had bloody plastic bags on their feet and blood far up
their arms. Walking around, taking pictures of corpses from every
angle—it was all the same to them. Her father was just another entry
in their journal.

Her chest felt tight. How was she supposed to be able to go and look
into the cells? What was she supposed to see? And how could they
just let people lie like that for so long?

"Hey, T, you owe me a cell phone," called out one of the technicians, who then stuck out his hand. T rummaged around in his pocket,

pulled out the cell phone, and gave it to the man. This little, everyday exchange seemed grotesquely out of place in the midst of such a hellish scene.

A new wave of paralyzing despair washed over Doggie, and for a moment she had to stop and lean against the bars of the first cell.

"Your father's down here, Miss Rogers," said the police sergeant, fifteen feet farther along the corridor.

She let go of the bars hesitantly, got a quick hug from Wesley, and strode past a row of empty cells with wide-open doors.

"There's nothing to see at this end. There were militiamen in these first seven or eight cells, and the rest of them were vacant, down to number fourteen, where your father was."

"Vacant?"

"Yes, vacant. These ones had already been executed," he said. "Space had to be made for new condemned men; the tempo of executions had been speeded up, you know. Excuse me for saying it, but your father was to be the first one executed under the new two-executions-per-day quota." He looked at his watch. "In fact he was scheduled to be executed five minutes ago."

Now he had said that loathsome word five times in a row. One more time and she'd scream to high heaven. She fought to control her trembling lower lip and forced herself to keep walking.

T. Perkins was already standing in front of her father's cell and raised a cautioning hand as she approached. "I don't know if you ought to see this, Doggie," he said.

But she clasped his hand tight and made herself take the last couple of steps. Her father was lying squeezed up under the sink against the far wall. A solitary, little, crumpled orange-red bundle with one stuck-out arm that had left a bloody trail on the wall. An indeterminable organic red-and-gray mass lay spread out on the bed next to him. She heard herself sob and felt Wesley take her other hand.

"Oh, God, T, we came so close," she sobbed. "We were so damned, damned close!" Sheriff Perkins remained silent. For once words failed him.

"I'm sorry you had to see your father like this," the cop interjected.

"We haven't touched him yet; the technicians have just finished going through all the cells, and next it's the police pathologists' turn."

"But I assume we can go in now," said T. The officer nodded.

"Are you sure you want to come in, Doggie?" asked T.

She watched him enter the cell, as prudently and respectfully as he possibly could. It was clear he was on familiar ground. He stepped over the pool of blood, squatted down, and carefully took hold of the orange jumpsuit. "I'm going to turn him over," he informed her. "It won't be a pretty sight. He's been shot in the head."

She felt Wesley's hand tighten.

Then T shook his head, and Doggie suddenly felt she was about to faint.

"I can't look at him, T. I can't."

"You don't have to, actually. It's not him, Doggie. It's not your father."

Still she took a deep breath and looked directly at the corpse's face. It was an appalling sight: a quarter of the skull was gone along with one eye, and the nose was an unrecognizable, bloody pulp. Stunned as she was, she smiled briefly.

"No, it . . . It's not him," she stuttered in amazement.

"I don't understand this!" exclaimed the police officer. "It says ENEMY OF THE STATE on the front of his jumpsuit, so he must be one of the militia." He looked around. "Someone must have made a mistake with this inmate list. It says here Bud Curtis was supposed to be in cell number fourteen."

T bent over and picked up a bloody metal object from under the sink. It was a cell phone. He looked at the display. "The battery's dead," he said. "Now I can see that phone wasn't of much help to your father. Come, Doggie, we'll have to look in the other cells."

"I can't do it, T," she said, feeling hope fade.

He nodded. "Okay, I'll take care of it, then."

She followed slowly behind T, together with Wesley, and glanced into the adjoining cell where a lifeless black face peered back at her, looking innocent as a child's.

Then there were four cells with white inmates, none of whom could have been older than fifty. Then two more cells—one black man, one white, both in their twenties.

Doggie's breathing came heavier and heavier, and she gripped Wesley's hand tight as she watched T inspect one pen after another.

Finally he reported that there was only one white man in the six remaining cells, and he definitely wasn't her father.

He swung the last cell door shut and turned to the police sergeant. "Do you think there's anyone present now who had guard duty here at the time of the attack?" he asked.

"Here? No, there's only one guard in here," the man replied, pointing at the body lying at the end of the corridor, "and he was on afternoon duty."

T's eyes flashed with annoyance. "No, no. I don't mean in here, I mean a *live* one, someone who's somewhere in this prison at the present time who was on duty here the night before last."

"Just a minute."

He made inquiries over his walkie-talkie. "Someone's on the way down. He's one of the reserves we've had to call in. He just arrived for his shift. He had no idea what had happened."

Five minutes later a very distraught prison officer appeared. Totally disheveled and with cuts on his knuckles, he had been drinking and partying ever since his last shift, and now his pickled brain was struggling to fathom the sight that greeted him.

"I . . . I . . . I . . ." he stammered as he stared at the body of the prison guard, lying at the door to the death chamber. "I got off around six o'clock yesterday morning. We . . . We were always changing the work schedule around. God, it could just as well have been my shift. Wow . . . This is enough to really make you t . . . twisted." He tried to smile, but seeing how inappropriate it was, he quickly took off his cap and looked apologetically at the body of his dead colleague. "He . . . That was Lassie," he said, mostly to himself. "That's what we called him." He pointed at the guard's thick, golden-red hair by way of explanation. "Wh . . . Why haven't they taken him away yet?"

"Where is Bud Curtis?" asked T sharply.

The man waved his hand towards cell fourteen. "O . . . Over there, I assume."

"Come," said T. They entered the cell and went over to the body. "Well?"

"That . . . That's not Curtis."

"No, I'm fucking well aware of that! But why is he here, and where is Curtis? Was Curtis in this cell while you were on duty?"

"Hell, yes," said the guard, and slipped into a more collegial tone of voice. "Look." He showed T his battered knuckles. "I was in here myself, teaching him a little discipline, know what I mean? Hell, yes."

Doggie felt like teaching him a little discipline herself.

"Why?" T demanded.

"Because . . . Falso said we should."

T turned to Doggie. "There's something here that is a hundred percent wrong," he said. "I know Falso in and out. He's not like that."

"But . . . But he *did*. And him . . ." He pointed at the dead man in the cell. "He's the one from cell seven. He was a late arrival. He cut the heads off some . . . some soldiers up in . . . in Richmond," he said.

"And he was from one of the militias?" asked T. The guy nodded.

"Were there any transports?"

"Trans . . . ports?"

"For Christ's sake, you feebleminded bum. *Yes, transports!* Were there condemned men transported to other prisons yesterday?"

He shrugged his shoulders. "M . . . Maybe later. I left at six in the morning, you know."

"Have there been any the past few days?"

He shook his head.

Doggie heard Wesley in the wheelchair behind her. "Are there other places where they carry out executions?" he asked the officer, but T answered instead.

"They do in Greensville Correctional Center, down by Jarrett. I know the number." He dictated it to Wesley, who punched it into his cell phone, then handed the phone to T.

Doggie could sense T's gravity. It was almost six thirty, a half hour since her father was to have been executed. *Was to have been.* Thinking of it that way still allowed her to cling to hope.

"Give me Gordon Hinkley," said T to the person who answered the phone, then he put his hand over the receiver. "The warden isn't there; he's sick," he whispered. A moment passed, then he put his question to the warden's deputy.

"You received a transfer yesterday, you say?" He nodded, then his face darkened. Again, Doggie felt ready to faint.

"Hmm . . . uh-huh . . . okay."

"Say something, T!" she shouted. "Is it him?"

T frowned. "It happened at six A.M., you say. . . . Are you certain . . . ? No, you can't check the name when you don't know where the prisoner's been transferred from, for God's sake. You get them all the time, don't you?"

Doggie wanted to cover her ears but couldn't.

"You say you don't know where the journal is? You son of a bitch, I'm standing here in Waverly with people from the White House, waiting to pick up a prisoner, and now I want a plain answer, or else you can take your employment contract and stick it where the sun never shines, got it? Yes, that means *up your ass*! How dim can a person be? Now get going!"

He leaned over and stroked Doggie's hair. "We're waiting. . . . Take courage, girl."

She held her breath.

"A Steven Stoklosa, you say. Are you sure?" She raised her head.

"Good! And there are no more scheduled? Okay. Listen: You're not to execute more inmates until you receive new directives, do you understand. . . . ? On who's authority? The attorney general and Michael K. Lerner! That's right, the one who was vice president before Sunderland. And on top of that, you can add the chairmen of all the fucking committees you can think of—got it? You do? Good! And one more thing: Are they executing people other places apart from your prison and Sussex? Yes, here in Virginia, fool. . . . Thank you." He hung up and dried the sweat off his brow.

"Well, we still don't know where your father is, Doggie."

"Have Warden Falso and that prison officer been found?" Wesley asked the police sergeant.

"No. We presumed they'd gone into hiding or had been shot by the militias in a marsh near here, but we haven't found any bodies down there. All we can do is fear for their lives. Maybe the militias took them hostage."

Wesley looked at Doggie and shook his head. "We don't know a thing, Doggie. We don't know where they are, and we don't know if your father's with them."

"Do you have any idea where they could be?" T asked the tipsy guard.

"No. . . . No idea. Falso's . . . not the type who . . . who does something like that."

"Do what?"

"Cut and run. . . . Just haul ass." He pointed at the dead officer. "Can't . . . Can't we move him. I . . . I know his son."

"Come on," said the police sergeant, "I'll give you a hand. We'll move him over to the canteen with the others."

"What a crock of shit," said alcohol-breath.

They lifted the body up and began carrying it off. It was a pitiful procession, but still, it demanded respect. They bowed their heads.

Then Wesley grabbed T by the arm. "T! Do you think anyone has checked behind that door the body was lying in front of?"

T looked at Wesley quizzically, but Doggie understood immediately and sprang for the door at the end of the cells.

She flung it open.

It was much warmer inside than on death row. She was greeted by a strong, acrid, sweetish smell. It came from a corpse that was lying against the wall.

T came rushing up. "Let me by, Doggie," he said, and edged into the room.

She put her hand to her mouth to try to keep from vomiting as she looked around at a condemned man's last occupancy—the witness room, the holding cell, and the execution chamber.

So this was what it was like, this unholy place. The last stop before oblivion.

She looked down at the body. It was a man in a police uniform, probably the missing officer. He was lying in a completely sterile room with two rows of seats facing the execution chamber, a closed-off room with glass walls that were mostly covered by curtains.

"My God," T exclaimed. "It's Freddie Cambell. I knew the man."

He had been shot in the middle of the chest. There was a big hole, but almost no blood. He was quite young and overweight, and took up almost all the little space there was between the rows of seats and the death chamber.

"He'd been blocking the door into the execution chamber," T muttered. "I think you ought to look away now, Doggie. I'm not sure what's coming next."

She looked at him for a split second before she realized what was going on.

"*No!*" she cried, as she tore open the curtains. Six feet on the other side of the glass lay her father on the gurney, bathed in sharp light, his head turned the other way. Every detail in this hi-tech burial chamber was as sterile as an operating theater—and much too peaceful. The tension made her movements jerky, and she began to sweat. She was unable to move.

"Where the hell's the needle and the straps?" T swore. "He's not strapped down. Help me get this meat loaf away from the door." Then he began tugging at the corpse. "This chamber is a hundred percent airtight and soundproofed; your father will suffocate in there. We've got to move this body. *Now!*"

"Oh, God, T, he's lying so still," wailed Doggie. "Do you think . . . ?" She bent over, grabbed one of Freddie Cambell's legs, and pulled until they succeeded in moving him away enough so they could wrench open the door.

Doggie was hit by a wave of disgusting, dry, musty air as she forced her way through the door and saw the next body on the floor, a portly white man with a black wristwatch, wearing a short-sleeved shirt.

"It's Warden Falso," she heard T groan, as fresh air filled the chamber. But Doggie wasn't concerned about Falso or anyone else at the moment. She threw herself at her father's body and touched his face. The skin was dry as parchment. Then she turned his head towards her and stared into his lifeless, battered face. *Oh, God,* she thought, and felt for the pulse in his neck. Feeling none, she tried again.

She pressed harder and suddenly felt a tiny quiver. Then he slowly opened his eyes and stared at her with absolutely no sign of recognition.

The miracle had happened.

It took a lot of energy to breathe life back into Warden Falso, but half an hour later, both men were sitting in the warden's office, looking sickly pale and deeply grateful.

"Aside from keeping us from being suffocated in there, I'd have been a dead man by now anyway, if it hadn't been for you, T. Do you realize that?" Falso said gravely. "If it hadn't been for that darn Curtis case, I'd have been sitting in my office yesterday morning when the militias attacked." He looked at T intently. "Your visit the day before yesterday and your whole fight to get Curtis's case reopened had made quite an impression, but I wasn't a hundred percent certain."

He turned to Doggie. "I regret having to tell you this, but I had my men beat up your father. They beat him until he couldn't scream his innocence anymore—that's when I finally believed him." He laid a hand on Curtis's leg. "I'm sorry, Bud," he said, "but I had no other choice. I had to make sure—and fast."

"But what if he'd confessed?" Doggie was having a hard time suppressing her anger. "People do that under torture. You ought to know that."

Warden Falso looked at her somberly. "If he'd confessed? Then I'm afraid there would be no one left for you to get mad at."

"Tell us what happened yesterday, Bill," said T, and lit a new cigarette on the stub of the last one.

"Well, when Bud regained consciousness after our . . . treatment yesterday afternoon, I went down to tell him I'd decided to stay preparations for his execution. By this point I thought he was innocent."

Doggie looked at her father. He nodded slowly, then said, "Yes, Falso had just come into my cell when we heard the militias blow up the main doors; then came all the shooting."

Falso shook his head. "I didn't get what was happening right away, but then I could hear them shouting that the moment of reckoning had come. They were screaming like wild beasts, and I knew the odds were bad."

He heaved a deep sigh, took a box of Hershey's bars out of his drawer, and took one after offering them around. No one else felt like eating. "You could hear the explosion each time they blew open a new door, and they were advancing fast."

Her father nodded. He was clearly marked by the hell he had been through. "They yelled that they were coming for me," he said.

"There was a guy in cell number seven," Falso continued. "He was a militiaman, too, but from another organization they weren't connected to. . . . He was sleeping. . . ." He fastened his eyes on the carpet. What he was about to say was apparently something he wasn't proud of. "So I knocked him unconscious and pulled him into your father's cell."

"The militias must have known you'd gone down to death row," said T.

"Yes, but not the ones who blasted their way down there. On the other hand they knew which cell was your father's. They called him 'the initiator of the new state of affairs,' meaning he had to bear the responsibility for all the country's woes, for which he had to pay with his life. So one of them emptied his automatic through the bars of your father's cell and killed the other guy, believing they'd settled the score with your father."

"But they forgot you."

Falso shrugged. "Apparently. They had enough work on their hands, polishing off the other prisoners and getting out of there."

"Why'd they have to do that?"

"That's how they were. The other inmates weren't their kind."

T was already working on rolling a new cigarette. "Those two officers that were shot—were they present on death row when the militias broke into Sussex?"

"No, just me and Curtis. The other two fled down there, thinking they'd escape the attack. They didn't succeed, unfortunately."

"And in the meantime the two of you went and hid in the execution chamber?" asked T.

"Yes. Then Freddie Cambell had the same idea, but he didn't make it."

Now Doggie's father's eyes were on the floor as well. "We could sense through the soundproofing where he was lying, bleeding to death on the other side of the door. We tried to open the door to push him out of the way, but he was too heavy."

"And the other guard out in the corridor? He must have been killed later than Cambell." T took a drag on his new cigarette.

Falso scratched his forehead. "Lassie? It's hard to say, but I'm afraid they played with him a little before they finished him off. I just know Lassie had plenty of enemies among the inmates. Plus he was the one with the keys."

T stuck out his lower lip. "And no one knew you and Curtis were in the death chamber?"

"In all likelihood, no. It all happened so darned fast. From the time they blew up the entrance till they were gone again took all of about three or four minutes, as far as I can tell."

"And they shot the militiaman in number fourteen, you say?"

"Yes, along with all the others. The technicians say they weren't choosy. They just fired into the cells, one after another. It was a straightforward liquidation."

Doggie squeezed her father's hand. It was only days ago that he had pleaded his innocence before her, hands cuffed behind him, and she'd turned her back on him. She had let him down that day. How was she ever going to expiate her guilt? How was he ever going to ignore it?

She looked at his battered face and felt full of shame.

For a moment he looked directly at her, as though he were speaking to her with his eyes. He seemed to be telling her that he understood but just couldn't express it. That he could forgive, but didn't find it necessary.

Then he gave a smile, barely noticeable, and turned towards Barefoot.

Wesley was sitting motionless in his wheelchair. He was very pale and sweaty, and a little blood was seeping through his bandages and shirt. He was staring silently at Doggie, probably not even aware that she was looking back. She'd never seen anyone looking at her like that before.

She was just about to say something to him when her father squeezed her hand. "Well, children, when's the wedding?" he said, so quietly that everyone heard it. She had never considered that question, had never even considered considering it.

Her father looked at her through swollen eyes. She couldn't see the smile lines for all the swelling, but she could hear it in his voice.

"In any case I insist the celebration be held at the Splendor Hotel in Virginia Beach." He managed a short laugh. "Things can't go wrong *every* time, for Christ's sake."

EPILOGUE

THE COMPANY PLANE LANDED AT KRALENDIJK'S AIRPORT ON THE ISLAND OF Bonaire in fantastically fine weather. Siesta time was over, and small vans buzzed around the narrow streets. The air was full of Caribbean rhythms, hurried feet, and the scent of sage and sea.

One of the flight attendants accompanied T. Perkins, Rosalie Lee, Doggie, and Wesley into town in a minibus.

"I'm sorry," she said, when she saw Rosalie's eyes light up as they drove along a row of colorful boutiques, full of every knickknack imaginable. "We don't have time to stop because the boat's already waiting down by Oranje Pan. It's a bit of a trip out to the island, and night falls suddenly at these latitudes."

No one had told them they had one more island to go. In reality, they hadn't been told much at all. Only that they were the first visitors to be allowed, their destination was somewhere in the Dutch Antilles, they should bring enough clothes for a few days, and that they must under no condition tell anyone about their trip.

Wesley shook his head and looked out the minibus's dusty windows and through a palm grove, until he saw the bright azure sea on the horizon. It was somewhere out there they were heading.

If they'd been wanting to find a place to keep Bruce Jansen out of the limelight, this was it.

Less than an hour later they were seated in the Jansen concern's giant, ancient motorboat with its brand-new logo on the bow, gazing back at the rapidly receding coastline.

Wesley passed the time listening to the boat's local crew members chattering away in Papiamento. The Caribbean's blue sky seemed to be lying right on top of the glassy waves. He let one hand trail in the water; he wouldn't mind sitting like this forever.

He looked at Doggie's sun-bleached hair and smiled. They'd both had their doubts, but now he was glad they'd decided to come. God knows they could use a change of scenery.

The media was up and running again a mere two hours after the attack on the White House. The first story started on the Internet, and soon everybody knew that a house had been blown up in Seattle and Moonie Quale's body had been found lying in the rubble.

The militias' situation was already demoralizing enough, and with the death of Moonie Quale the most poorly organized units began surrendering their weapons. A ceasefire was declared after another night of pitched battles with the most rabid groups, then a general amnesty, and hundreds of thousands of citizens turned in their firearms—even Wesley's father.

Almost everywhere society was beginning to function again. A tangible sense of relief washed over the land, almost like after the passing of a massive, destructive storm.

Congress convened precisely twenty-four hours after the attack and immediately suspended Jansen's appointment to the vice presidency of the deceased Thomas Sunderland, then reinstated the former vice president Michael K. Lerner in his position of successor to the throne. The members agreed it was best for the country if all speculation was set aside as to whether Lerner had actually resigned or been fired by Jansen. Who else except Lerner had made the right pronouncements at the right time? Yes, Lerner was in the clear, and how many others could say the same?

Later the same day Jansen was formally removed from office, and Lerner was sworn in as president.

In the meantime Wesley had been flown back from the prison in Waverly to the hospital in Washington, where he was recuperating until the political sequel began to unfold.

"What do you think Jansen's going to be like?" Doggie asked Wesley, playing with his hand in the foamy water alongside the boat.

"Who knows? Maybe he'll just be himself. In Bermuda shorts."

She peered at him over her sunglasses and stuck out her tongue. They'd done a lot of speculating: How does a person look who has been banished for life from the country of which he's happened to be president?

"I have a feeling he's okay. Otherwise he wouldn't have invited us, would he?" interjected Rosalie. She'd rolled up the pant legs of her white ducks and was trailing her feet in the water. It was like out of a vacation advertisement.

"Time will tell," droned T in the background, waving smoke out of his face.

There was an unswerving, severe consistency in the results of the congressional hearings. Of all the Cabinet and inner-circle officials of the former government only two were spared; the rest were sacked with no pension. Several of them could expect to face criminal charges. Someone had to take the fall, and the knowledge of that alone had its effect. Most tragic was the suicide of Secretary of the Interior Betty Tucker and Billy Johnson's fatal heart attack after he'd been formally indicted. The newspapers wrote that in Johnson's case the thunderbolt of justice had missed its mark, and the Homeland Security boss would surely have been acquitted. With that, Wesley was in total agreement. Who besides Billy Johnson had done so much to repair the damage?

Wesley and Doggie were star witnesses from day one, but when it came to Jansen's indictment, they had to disqualify themselves. How were they supposed to differentiate between the acts perpetrated by

Jansen, and those of Sunderland, when they had no concrete knowledge or evidence? How could anyone else, for that matter?

There was an attempt to coerce Chief of Staff Lance Burton and a couple of other officials close to the president into testifying that Jansen had intentionally led the nation into disaster, but all these aides refused. And the only thing one could conclude with certainty from all the testimony was that President Jansen had been wretchedly advised from day one by Sunderland, and that in any case he was so strongly affected by the murder of his wife and unborn child that one had to conclude he had been unfit for office the entire length of his presidency.

So, what to do with a United States president like him? Should one man, who'd reaped so much misery, go free? No, he shouldn't—almost everyone agreed on that—and a movement demanding harsh punishment spread across the country like wildfire. For a few days it seemed the nation's hard-earned return to peace was already about to disintegrate, but then President Lerner stepped in and granted Jansen amnesty on the grounds of having an unsound mind.

This caused an immediate outcry in Congress. Some were suddenly convinced that Lerner's decision could only be because the new president was basically a believer in Jansen's reforms, while others said the hunting cabin Lerner had hid out in belonged to Jansen's Drugstore. But Lerner struck back; the amnesty was by no means without conditions. Jansen was to leave the country—go into exile—and never return to politics. That succeeded in ending dissent.

President Lerner's position was definitely not weakened by that ruling, either. But there were still those who wondered.

"Isn't it fantastic?" Doggie prodded T. Perkins with her bare toes. "Whaddaya say, T?"

T let go of the railing and turned towards them. "Well . . ." he eventually answered, "sure is blue as hell, in any case."

Wesley laughed and had to hold his chest. His musculature had a habit of complaining when he sat upright for long periods of time.

"Are you okay, baby?" Doggie asked.

Wesley nodded. He couldn't be more okay. Here they sat, under the life-affirming feather-light sky. They were alive. Doggie had said yes to sharing her life with him. So what could the past do, other than glide into the background?

He looked devotedly at his fellow passengers. At Rosalie who sat there, fighting to keep her flower-bedecked sun hat in place, and at T, who was actually showing the beginnings of a tan. The group had shrunk since the trip to China many years ago. Each had lost a part of him- or herself, but here they sat.

"Penny for your thoughts, Wesley," said Rosalie.

"I'm thinking about us. And being here. And John Bugatti. And all of us who were in China together."

Rosalie nodded. "I think it's all gonna work out. There's still plenty of shit to deal with, but at the same time it's really something, what a big effect some of these reforms have had. Do you know what I mean?"

Wesley nodded.

"Am I right, T?" she said, nudging him so the ashes fell down his chest.

T. Perkins nodded, and Rosalie laughed. "I'm just glad my sons have found work. My employer, Mo Goldenbaum, got them some good jobs down at the harbor. They didn't dare refuse. It could have been a whole lot worse," she said, revealing almost all her teeth in a generous smile. "Now they're even paying rent at home—can you believe it?" She slapped her thigh and laughed even harder. "So you can't say nothing's happened in this country of ours, can y'all?"

That's right, thought Wesley. A lot had happened in just these last five weeks. President Lerner had performed well—surprisingly well. There were many—those who previously considered him a bureaucratic, dull-witted, southern Democrat—who now saw themselves proven wrong.

Lerner had set the stage for reconciliation. Investigations and hearings had not gone on endlessly, the judicial purge had been handled soberly, and—aside from the radical fringe—Congress could work together in spite of its differences. It's true that many were incensed upon hearing that Jansen's life in exile was to be spent on a tropical island owned by the Jansen concern, but otherwise the new president enjoyed everybody's respect. Some even went so far as to say he was a born statesman.

"No, Rosalie, that's right," Wesley finally replied. "A lot of good things *have* happened."

It was a new America that had risen from the ashes—that's how it appeared to Wesley. Bruce Jansen had put forth a vision that had gone wrong along the way, but his successor understood what needed to be done to try and preserve its best aspects in a difficult time. Of course Lerner met resistance, but he had many good cards to play. There was plenty of work, and the economy surged ahead. Families were reunited, like Wesley's secretary, Eleanor, and her husband. The judicial system was transforming for the better, and there was talk of eventually closing prisons if the lack of business continued.

And the latest positive development was that both chambers of Congress were talking seriously about reforming the electoral system and creating a responsible body of laws regarding weapon possession. There was plenty of disagreement and debate, but this was American democracy at work, and at a very opportune moment, too, with the nation largely disarmed and its citizens liberated from the paranoia of feeling the need to defend themselves with guns.

He didn't like to use expressions like "system change," but that's how it looked to Wesley. One felt it clearly, walking around the streets: People felt safe. Life seemed to have a purpose. The TV news's horror stories became fewer and fewer, US soldiers had come home, and the world was looking on in wonder.

He looked out over the sea, hair blowing in the wind. He and Doggie had been together for more than two months, and they'd begun making plans. Things would be different now. Much different. Bud Curtis didn't want to work anymore. It was time to enjoy life, he said. It would please him greatly if Wesley and Doggie took over the hotel chain, and he asked them to think about it.

Wesley looked over at her bare midriff and imagined how the soft skin would feel to the touch.

"This is beautiful," declared Rosalie.

"Yeah," Doggie agreed.

The island's palm trees could now be seen clearly, and then the house, perched on a hilltop. Perhaps not as big as they'd expected, but still it sparkled like a diamond in the hot sun, seemingly its own source of light.

And then there were all the security agents, waiting at the pier.

"I think President Jansen is just about ready to receive you. He's been looking very forward to this," said the head servant, leading them through a series of chambers that exhibited a riot of lush colors. There were jade-colored, Japanese lacquered chests and Persian wall tapestries in blue and gold, not to mention all the sweet-scented flowers. And there was the eternal, quiet roar of the sea—a sound to soothe the soul.

They could clearly hear his voice behind a massive camphorwood double door, covered in symbolic carvings.

Rosalie smiled, and Doggie squeezed Wesley's hand. It felt like a portentous moment.

"He sounds pretty good, doesn't he?" Rosalie whispered. "Not exactly like an exile in disgrace, in any case."

They heard Jansen's voice approaching. "Welcome, welcome," he said, throwing the doors wide open. A fantastic, sunlit room revealed itself behind him, with panorama windows facing the cliffs, white marble floors, and floor-to-ceiling ebony curtains. "Welcome to my exile," he said, surprisingly low-key. "My own Saint Helena." He was suntanned and well rested, but the ardor in his eyes was gone. There were only traces of scars left on his face, and his teeth had been repaired, but the scars on his soul were beyond the reach of even the cleverest plastic surgeon.

He embraced T. Perkins and Rosalie Lee and thanked them sincerely for coming. "I've certainly been looking forward to this. I don't get that many visitors, as you can imagine," he said, smiling quietly.

When Doggie stepped forward and put out her hand, he stood still for a moment to compose himself. Then he drew her to him. Wesley couldn't hear what he whispered in her ear, but she gave several small nods. Begging forgiveness wasn't something that came easily for Jansen. He released her and dried his cheek, eyes on the floor. Slowly his eyes moved up the length of Wesley's body, until they met those of his former press chief.

"My dear Wesley . . ." he began, then embraced him silently. When he could speak again, he said, "I'm so sorry, Wesley. Are you all right? Is your arm okay? Can you lift it again?"

Wesley nodded. "Yes, I'm almost good as new."

The world's once most powerful man eyed Wesley, looking as though he might launch into an all-encompassing testimonial. Then he sighed and his eyes returned to the floor. "I regret what happened, Wesley," he said quietly. "It all just got out of hand."

Then he turned around, took Rosalie's arm, and led her over to a glass cupola at the far end of the room in which a lemon tree was blooming, and where one could see through the plexiglass floor straight into the lush undergrowth below.

Rosalie gave a nervous little laugh, feeling a bit dizzy as she peered down, and took a step back.

"Here comes Abrecita," said Jansen, as a golden-brown, slim, probably fortyish woman entered the room. He took the glasses off the tray she was carrying and handed them around. He was obviously receptive to her enchanting eyes and smile, though he tried to avoid showing it.

Wesley looked at Doggie. She'd noticed it, too.

"Cheers, my dear friends," he said. "No matter what life may have had in store for me, it was you—my old travel companions from China—to whom I owe my life today. When you reconstruct the story, nothing seems to have happened by chance. Seventeen years ago I had an idea for a quiz show, and now I've come full circle. A lot of unforeseen circumstances arose from that idea, but one of the few good ones was your finding each other—and my finding you. I want to thank you for that." He raised his glass. "Thank you, Rosalie, thank you, Sheriff T, thank you, Doggie, and thank you, Wesley." Lowering his head once more, he added, "And thanks to John Bugatti and Donald Beglaubter, too. They gave their lives for their convictions and the struggle for justice, and no one can regret what happened more than I." He looked up again. "I'm deeply thankful for being alive today," he declared, raising his glass to each of them in turn.

"I hope you have some nice days here," he continued. "You decide yourselves how long you want to stay. My old company has placed a plane at your disposal whenever you want to leave. In the meantime the island is all yours. And I hope you can put up with my bodyguards— I have to, in any case."

He tried smiling, but this time it didn't work. "I work a couple of hours every day," he said, "but I'm sure we'll find time for some good moments together."

Wesley looked over at Jansen's desk; it aroused peculiar memories.

"Yes, Wesley. They let me take it with me. Maybe President Lerner didn't feel right, keeping it." Still no smile. Then his servant came in to announce it was the period of the day when phone lines were open.

"You must excuse me," he said. "I have some phone calls this time of day that can't be postponed. But it'll only take about a half an hour, so just enjoy yourselves. I'm sure Abrecita won't mind showing you around."

The terrace was completely enchanting in the reddish glow of the setting sun, like the hanging gardens of Babylon, surrounded by bougainvillea, citrus, and bay trees and a profusion of hand-painted crocks containing all sorts of flowers.

Rosalie put her hand to her breast and swayed a little.

"Yes, you should probably stand back from the railing; it's a long way down," cautioned Abrecita, taking Rosalie's arm.

Doggie stood still and took in the scenery. "God, is this marvelous," she said.

"Thank you. We look after it ourselves," said Abrecita, removing a few dead leaves from a hibiscus in full red and white flower.

Wesley nodded. The human survival instinct was really incredible.

He filled his lungs with air and sea fog that was beginning to rise off the water, thinking back to a string of terrible consequences of Jansen's term in office: the closing of borders, deportation of "undesirables," the summary execution of militia members, the strangling of the free press. But there was also the disappearance of private weapon arsenals and of the long lines of unemployed. And now here Wesley was, in this earthly paradise.

The question was, whether it was also a paradise for Jansen. "You can look for truth and happiness your whole life, but there's no guarantee you'll find it," as Wesley's father used to say.

Yes, the circle had been completed, as Jansen said, and here they were, together again.

You can't master fate, Wesley said to himself. *Fate has a mind of its own.*

His eye fell on a gorgeous, neon-green butterfly, and he began following its progress from flower to flower around the house.

Then he heard Jansen's voice, coming from behind a curtain-covered doorway.

He must be discussing the drugstore business, he thought. *What else does he have to spend his time on?* He took a step closer—what harm could it do?

Jansen had set his telephone on speakerphone, and Wesley thought he recognized the voice at the end of the line. He stepped behind a citrus tree to follow the conversation more discreetly and try and get a glimpse inside.

Jansen's workroom seemed by no means pretentious. No carpets, no easy chair—just a lot of bookshelves and bulletin boards. He imagined it to be quite a small room, a little oasis within his island oasis where he could get further away from it all. As melancholy and reserved as Jansen had seemed, he probably needed a refuge like this.

Wesley took a step closer to have a better look inside when the billowing curtains allowed. He'd expected to see Jansen sitting quietly at his desk, not with his feet up on it, gesturing and smiling. Nor had he expected the office to be so large. It was déjà vu, like turning the clock twelve months back to the long meetings and briefings on the campaign trail. This was Jansen in his natural element. Wesley was surprised to see that he appeared to be enjoying himself enormously.

Then the wind lifted the curtain for a moment, but it was long enough; the sight he saw spoke for itself.

One of the walls gave uncomfortable associations. It was covered with clippings of all the current major news stories from around the world and the United States; many lines of text were underlined in red.

Photographs of world leaders were complemented by handwritten comments. There were maps, satellite pictures, and photocopied documents. It was like Thomas Sunderland's office when he took over the vice presidency.

Wesley felt his breathing getting deeper. The closer he got to the door, the more the sound of the sea receded, and Jansen's voice grew clearer.

"And last of all, Michael," Jansen was saying, "I definitely don't think you should discuss the Afghani pipeline with the Russian president. Just string him along; he won't dare act on his own. In the meantime you can round up the steel producers in the eastern states. Let them come with an option; they're well-softened up by now, I can assure you. Just stick to our plan—take it nice and easy. I mean it: Don't push things, Michael. You can put Congress into the picture when the time comes. And if it becomes a question of new legislation, make sure you—and only you—dictate the wording. Do you understand?"

Wesley was breathing so hard by now, he had to take a step back from the door and seek the support of the citrus tree.

"Yes!" came the answer over the telephone speaker. It was clearly the voice of Michael K. Lerner, the forty-fifth president of the United States. "Don't worry, I'll go nice and easy, just as we agreed. Thank you very, very much for your advice. I'll call you tomorrow at the same time, as usual," concluded Lerner. "Good-bye, Mr. President."

"Good-bye, Michael. You know where you can find me."

AFTERWORD

THE FEDERAL EMERGENCY MANAGEMENT AGENCY (FEMA) WAS CREATED DURING
the Nixon administration and led an existence largely unnoticed
by the public for years.

FEMA was primarily devised to deal with the effects of a nuclear war
but was also meant to be useful in the event of a natural catastrophe.

Enormous sums have been earmarked for FEMA over the years, on
top of its official congressionally approved budget. One can imagine that
the more money FEMA was given in the absence of a natural catastrophe
or atomic war, the harder it became for the agency to defend its budget.

But of course the agency found a way to use its funding anyway.
Giant underground facilities were built and personnel trained to take
over the functions and duties of publicly elected officials in prepara-
tion for the day natural or man-made disaster finally struck.

In the end it appears that an entire, nonelected governing system
was established, with what could be described as a shadow Cabinet
and shadow president.

Had the American public known more at the time about the actual
scope of FEMA's power, activities, and its enormous budget—
swallowing funds that could have been put to more obviously sensible
use—it is not unlikely that serious protest would have arisen.

But then came the eleventh of September 2001, and FEMA suddenly had a means of legitimizing its existence. On top of natural and
nuclear catastrophe, there was now the threat of terrorism in all shapes
and forms.

In all likelihood this is why FEMA has been able to maintain its
funding, and there is evidence to suggest that in recent years FEMA
has mostly been preoccupied with a series of preventative measures in
the event of a massive terrorist threat. One of these measures is said
to be the construction of hundreds of internment camps, capable of
containing millions of detainees. It is a measure that has never at any
point been discussed or debated publicly, and therefore the question

of when use of these camps would become necessary—and whom would be imprisoned in them—has never been answered.

Nor may one forget the existence of presidential decrees, capable of bestowing even farther-reaching authority upon FEMA, so that in the event of the "great catastrophe," Congress would be rendered powerless, and the president and FEMA would have unlimited, unchecked authority.

It is, among other things, this movement from democracy to autocracy that I have tried to deal with in *The Washington Decree*.

Judging from the Federal Emergency Management Agency's wretched handling of Hurricane Katrina in 2005, one is tempted to believe that the priority of dealing with natural catastrophes has been seriously downgraded by the agency. In its obsession to unearth and fight terror threats everywhere, FEMA has forgotten one of its basic reasons for existing.

Therefore the helicopters arrived too late in Louisiana, (poor) people weren't evacuated in time, and the government ignored urgent warnings that New Orleans's levees would never withstand a natural catastrophe of this kind. One wonders if FEMA's response would have been more efficient had Hurricane Katrina been a terrorist attack.

The federal government's reflexive denial of any blame in the matter meant that FEMA's director, Michael Brown, had to go. An obvious scapegoat, he had been given the wrong portfolio to deal with the job at hand. FEMA's fortune in funds and the government's efforts had long been focused elsewhere.

In order to be able to understand the likelihood of an apparently democratic and bureaucratic society like the United States being subjected to cataclysms of the kind that occur in *The Washington Decree*, it is necessary to know certain specific terminology that is used throughout the novel, the most important of which is explained in the pages that follow. I have also included a list of the executive orders employed in the event of a national emergency.

—Jussi Adler-Olsen

ACKNOWLEDGMENTS

THANKS TO MY WIFE, HANNE ADLER-OLSEN, FOR INSPIRATION AND MANY GOOD observations. Without her, the pleasure of writing would not have been present.

Thanks also to Henning Kure, Jesper Helbo, Tomas Stender, Eddie Kiran, Elsebeth Wæhrens, Rasmus Dahlberg, and Søren Schou for their insightful commentary. Thanks to Gitte and Peter Q. Rannes and the Danish Writers and Translators Center in Hald for providing essential peace and quiet to complete this book.

Thanks to Kjeld Skjærbæk, who patiently accompanied me to Virginia to interview weapon dealers and museum personnel, as well as the man on the street and many others.

Thanks to Henrik Rehr and Jeannie Kim, who tuned us into everyday life in the United States. Thanks to Patricia White for introducing me to New York street language, and thanks for the friendly reception at the Lynchburg Museum and by the local weapon dealers and pawnbrokers in Front Royal.

A big thank-you to my American translator, Steve Schein, and Carl Pedersen, Center for the Study of the Americas, for refining my knowledge.

APPENDIX

THE NATIONAL SECURITY COUNCIL

Federal agency created by the National Security Act of 1947, whose purpose is to advise the president about national, international, and military affairs related to national security. The president is chairman of the NSC. The other members are the vice president, the secretary of the interior, and the secretary of defense. Advisors include the chief of staff, the director of the CIA, and others who the president may choose, with Senate approval. The NSC staff is headed by the national security advisor, who is considered an important guide for the president.

FEMA: FEDERAL EMERGENCY MANAGEMENT AGENCY

Federal agency originally created by executive order during the Nixon presidency for the purpose of dealing with the catastrophic situations that could arise in the event of a nuclear attack on the United States. Since then, the agency has been made responsible for coordinating all other kinds of preparedness in the event of a national emergency. All of Nixon's successors have added new decrees to refine and strengthen the agency, to the point where it is the most powerful organ in the United States today—even compared with the executive branch and Congress. It has the authority to suspend laws, resettle entire sections of the population, arrest and detain citizens without a warrant, and imprison them without a trial. The agency may confiscate and take control of property, food depots, transportation networks, and may even suspend the US Constitution. A group of officials are employed by FEMA whose primary task is to be ready to overtake the duties normally performed by members of Congress—indeed, the duties of all government officials, including the president himself. Thus, a shadow government under FEMA is permanently available in the event of a catastrophe that requires the replacement of elected politicians.

The legal basis for FEMA is established without congressional ratification; executive orders need merely be published in the Federal Registry to become valid. Congress has absolutely no influence regarding FEMA's duties, budget, strategy, or development.

FEMA's budget is enormous, but since the agency was created, only about 6 percent has been spent on matters directly related to national emergencies. The rest has been used on the hiring and training of a huge personnel apparatus, the building up of an unbelievably refined infrastructure, plus the construction of giant subterranean complexes to protect important federal government officials in the event of a national emergency, whether the cause be domestic or foreign. Executive Order 12656 appoints the National Security Council as FEMA's steering body, enabling an incumbent government to increase all forms of intelligence gathering on—and surveillance of—American citizens, impose drastic limits on their movement within the country, and segregate massive groups of civilians. Accordingly, the National Guard is given the authority to close all the country's borders and take over control of airports and harbors.

Listed below are a few of the executive orders that are at the Federal Emergency Management Agency's disposal, where the US Constitution and Bill of Rights can be instantly overridden by a mere presidential signature:

Executive Order 10990
Allows the government to take over all modes of transportation and control of highways and seaports.

Executive Order 10995
Allows the government to seize and control the communication media, including radio, television, newspapers, telephones, the Internet, and much more. This executive order suspends the First Amendment.

Executive Order 10997
Allows the government to take over all electrical power, gas, petroleum, fuels, and minerals.

Executive Order 10998
Allows the government to seize all means of transportation—including personal cars, trucks, or vehicles of any kind—and gives it total control over all highways, seaports, and waterways.

Executive Order 10999

Allows the government to take over all food resources and farms. All private, unsupervised stockpiling and hoarding is forbidden.

Executive Order 11000

Allows the government to mobilize civilians into work brigades under government supervision.

Executive Order 11001

Allows the government to take over all health, education, and welfare functions.

Executive Order 11002

Authorizes the postmaster general to carry out a national registration of all persons.

Executive Order 11003

Allows the government to take over all airports and aircraft, including commercial aircraft.

Executive Order 11004

Allows the Housing and Finance Authority to relocate communities, build new housing with public funds, designate areas to be abandoned, and establish new locations for populations.

Executive Order 11005

Allows the government to take over railroads, inland waterways, and public storage facilities.

Executive Order 11049

Authorizes federal departments and agencies to manage emergency preparedness, consolidating twenty-one operative executive orders issued over a fifteen-year period.

Executive Order 11051

Specifies the responsibility of the Office of Emergency Planning and gives authorization to put all executive orders into effect in times of increased international tension and economic or financial crisis.

Executive Order 11310

Authorizes the Department of Justice to enforce executive orders, to implement industrial support, to establish judicial and legislative liaisons, to control all aliens, to operate penal and correctional institutions, and to advise and assist the president.

Executive Order 11490

Gives the president control over all US citizens, businesses, and churches.

Executive Order 11921

Allows the Federal Emergency Preparedness Agency to develop plans to establish control over the mechanisms of production and distribution, energy sources, wages, salaries, credit, and the flow of money in any undefined national emergency. It also provides that a state of emergency declared by the president may not be reviewed by Congress for six months.

Executive Order 12565

Deals with the definition of "a state of emergency," the government takeover of all municipal judicial functions, the enforcement of price control, the banning of entering or leaving the country, the control of all travel within the country, the expansion of compulsory military service, and much more.

Executive Order 12919

Instructs public servants in how to be prepared to take over control of practically all aspects of the national economy in the event of a state of emergency.

Executive Order 13010

Instructs FEMA in how to take control of all state institutions in the event of a state of emergency.

With these executive orders and others, FEMA is given unlimited authority in all crisis situations, including a military state of emergency.

A military state of emergency can be declared as a result of natural catastrophes, stock market crises, computer crashes (like the predicted Y2K crisis at the change of the millennium), power outages, riots, and biological weapon attacks—in short, anything that can lead to the breakdown of society and the forces of law and order.

All US citizens are liable to arrest and imprisonment without charge in the event of a military state of emergency. Freedom of speech and the right of assembly may be suspended and censorship of the media implemented.

The right to own and bear weapons may also be suspended. The military and National Guard will be empowered to search private homes and businesses, and confiscate weapons and hoarded foodstuffs, without a warrant.

FEMA has far-reaching authority in every aspect of society, but this is nothing new. Already in 1983 General Frank Salzedo, the chief of FEMA's civil preparedness department, declared that, as he saw it, FEMA's role was "a brand new bulwark against the assassination of civil and state leaders and the sabotage of, and attacks on, civil and military institutions, as well as the influence of political dissent on opinion—in the United States or globally—in times of crisis."

JUSSI ADLER-OLSEN

"Adler-Olsen merges story lines . . . with ingenious aplomb, effortlessly mixing hilarities with horrors."
—*Publishers Weekly* (starred review)

For a complete list of titles,
please visit prh.com/JussiAdlerOlsen